MW01170754

SHIRTALOON

HE WHO FIGHTS
WITH
MONSTERS

BOOK TWELVE

aethonbooks.com

HE WHO FIGHTS WITH MONSTERS ELEVEN
©2025 SHIRTALOON

Aethon Books
www.aethonbooks.com

Print and eBook design and formatting by Kevin G. Summers. Cover art by Harry Bui.

Published by Aethon Books LLC.

Aethon Books is not responsible for websites (or their content) that are not owned by the publisher.

ALSO IN SERIES

Want to discuss our books with other readers and even the authors?

JOIN THE AETHON DISCORD!

Calling all LitRPG fans: be the first to discover groundbreaking new releases, access incredible deals, and participate in thrilling giveaways by subscribing to our exclusive LitRPG Newsletter.

https://aethonbooks.com/litrpg-newsletter/

AUTHOR'S NOTE

At the rear of the book, and as an attached file for the audiobook, are a series of appendices. They deal with the mechanical aspects of the system that would by intrusive in the chapters themselves, particularly in the audiobook version. I think we all remember certain chapters of the earlier books in the series.

The appendices consist of Jason's character sheet, shortened summaries of his abilities at gold rank, and a list of his increasingly absurd boons and afflictions. Note that not every ability is directly demonstrated in the book, but are included for the sake of completion.

o

DON'T TELL HUMPHREY

What I did on your holidays, by Velitraxistaasch, age 22 and 3/4 (home schooled).

Dear Jason,

This is stupid. Why do I have to do this dumb exercise, like I'm a child? I'm a small business owner! Please don't tell ~~Da~~ Humphrey about that, Uncle Jason. You know he'll just start trying to take over, thinking I can't do it, when I definitely can. I've made almost no flour silos explode! Set fire to one farmer, and suddenly, I'm the irresponsible one. He got healed!

I agreed to do this stupid thing before Humphrey stopped to ask why I was ordering industrial quantities of flour. Honestly, I do not understand how he hasn't figured out that I run a bakery. Maybe if he and Sophie weren't going off to their room several times a day, he wouldn't be so distracted. What are they even doing in there? They use a privacy screen, so I can't tell, and Auntie Farrah refused to help me disable it so we could peek.

Anyway, now Humphrey is making me do this, so you know all the things that happened while you're away fighting a space bird and the guy who makes universes. Who sucks, but you know that. Humphrey thought you should hear about all the stuff we did, and we did have lots of fun adventures. Not like when you're around, though. All the crazy stuff happens when you're here.

Remember when we were in that transformation zone, before you left? Good guys and bad guys all scattered around, trying to find each other. We got to fight all different kinds of monsters. That was so fun. Everyone was trying to take over places so they could be king of the pocket universe or something. I just liked having cool fights and seeing weird stuff happen. Mostly. When people started giving up their territory to you and then had to poop for three days, that was gross.

Of course, you ended up being king or whatever. We had to fight all those people with wings, but some of them went to live in your soul? Then we had to fight a giant tree, and that went to live in your soul too, and now it's a whole forest? You're weird, Uncle Jason, and that's coming from a dragon that can turn into anyone, which makes me the most handsome boy. Because I can turn into whoever is the most handsome, and then become even more handsome, with a moustache.

I haven't even talked about all the crazy stuff you did either. You made a rabbit man who controlled lightning towers, and now I'm not the youngest, finally. Doesn't stop Humphrey from treating me like I'm still a kid. Nik has been off learning to be an adventurer at the same place where ~~Da~~ Humphrey grew up. That was where we met and you guessed that I was a dragon because of my inescapably regal bearing.

Oh, and we had to fight those priests and their undead army again. What kind of idiot worships things that died already? If you can't worship it while it's still alive, move on, stupid! You and Uncle Gary had to fight the leftover bits of their dumb dead god.

Ugh, now I'm sad. Uncle Gary was amazing when he drank from that god's weird cup and was all big and gold and on fire. But now he's gone. It's been a lot of years, but I still miss him. He was the best at scratching behind my ears when I'm a puppy. Don't tell Humphrey. But the stupid cup made him get sick and die. You won't catch me drinking things out of strange cups. Unless it smells really good, obviously. A lot of things good for dunking biscuits come in cups.

When that was all done, you went and made a city out of clouds, except deep underground. Which makes no sense, by the way. Clouds go in the sky, Uncle Jason. Get your act together. And then you went off and left us all behind. Again. Didn't Humphrey get done telling you off about that, right before you did it again? Anyway, you've been gone for so long now, doing more weird stuff without us. But we've been doing fun things too, so nyah.

Your friend Zara has joined Team Biscuit (best name ever) and has been blowing things up with big storms. No one makes her write stupid things when she does it, and she doesn't even own a bakery. She's supposedly not a princess anymore, but she keeps telling people that so much that it definitely seems like she's still a princess.

We had lots of fun adventures, but not the things that make kings and gods cranky, like when you're around. Everyone split up when they started to get close to gold rank, and they're waiting for you to come together again. They had to go off and learn about themselves or some nonsense. Why does everyone think it's so hard? Sophie ran out on Humphrey, so he could figure out that dragons aren't just lizards that sit on piles of gold. Which is stupid, so I told him off and he figured it out, because I'm great.

Apparently, Rufus' family runs a school, and Lindy went to teach there. She talks a lot, but lets me steal biscuits, sometimes, so I think she's a good teacher. She and Stella have been going into their room a lot, like Humphrey and Sophie. What are all these people doing? Neil said that I would figure it out when I wanted to have an egg, which makes no sense. I have eggs for breakfast every day.

Clive started up some place where people supposedly do magic things but mostly write things on bits of paper. I don't know why, because I'm doing it now and I do not see the appeal. Luckily, some other boring magic people tried doing things to Clive, so Lindy, Stella and me got to have some sneaky fun. If we're going to go out and blow things up, why is it that I get in trouble for doing it on my own? And it was more or less an accident anyway. I definitely didn't hear about flour being explosive and wanted to see for myself.

Last I heard, Nik was running around with Uncle Neil. The Adventure Society seems super-excited about sending Nik places, rather than putting him with a team. Neil is making sure they don't take advantage, and not moping about some girl he knew years ago, apparently. I think Nik really wants to see you again, because you kind of created him and then ran off, which was mean of you, Uncle Jason. You should be nicer to him.

Everyone is getting super-strong now. We're waiting for you to come back before gathering together again, but we're not the only ones. People got really worked up about something you apparently did and now we're all waiting for you to come back.

I don't know what 'the System' is, but lots of people want to talk to you about it. You should come hide in my bakery so I can ~~steal all your recipes~~ give you this letter Humphrey is making me write.

Your pal,

Stash

1

WHY HE HASN'T

JASON ASANO THOUGHT HE WOULD NEVER ENDURE PAIN AS comprehensive as the Builder's attack on his soul. The Cosmic Throne proved him to be profoundly mistaken. His true body was now an entire universe, and only an avatar had sat on the throne. Even so, the agony was mind-blanking. He awoke, face down on the throne room's grimy floor, having tumbled off the throne and down the stairs of the dais.

"Is it done?" he managed to croak out.

"It is done," Raythe said.

Jason rolled onto his back with a groan, then pushed himself to a sitting position. He looked around and saw that all the great astral beings were gone. Only Raythe remained, the prime avatar of the great astral being who governed time itself. Her master was gone, no longer possessing her body. The only other people in the room were Jason's familiars and the avatar of the tree city.

"How long was I out?" he asked.

"That is complicated," Raythe said. "We are at the boundary of reality and unreality, where time is subjective at best and arguably doesn't exist at all."

"Okay, that's the long answer. Is there a short one?"

"Approximately seven hours, if we leave this place soon," Shade said as the familiar emerged from Jason shadow.

"Which I highly recommend," Raythe said. "The time here is synchronised with your universe while this castle is still connected to it, which it will only be for a short amount of subjective time. It would be best if you don't arrive back in your universe a year from now. Or a year before now. You don't have to rush out the door, but don't tarry longer than you need to recover."

"Yeah, I don't think I'll be doing any rushing," Jason said. "The great astral beings didn't gather dust, though, did they?"

"When it was done, it was done," Raythe said. "There was no purpose in lingering."

"They didn't draw anything on my face before they left, did they?"

"No."

Jason groaned again as he got unsteadily to his feet.

"That shook my soul like it was a snow globe. Did it have any impact on my domains? More importantly, the people in them?"

"No. It was your mortal aspect that was inadequate to endure the task. Your transcendent aspect is a universe and can soak up a few spiritual tremors."

"That's good."

He winced as he rubbed his temples with the heels of his hand.

"I don't suppose you know a good hangover cure."

"For the backlash of setting the new status quo for the cosmos while still mortal? I'm afraid you'll need to ride that one out, Jason Asano."

"How badly did I mess it up?"

"The great astral beings are satisfied. That is as much as any could ask from you, and more than we expected."

"*All* of them are satisfied? Or a motion-passing plurality, with the rest looking to hunt me down for revenge?"

"The nameless are unhappy, as they would be with anything short of complete cosmic anarchy. They will not seek you out, however. The others are satisfied."

"Even the World-Phoenix?"

"It would seem that the restoration of the throne set a new status quo based on things as they were at the moment of restoration. The World-Phoenix in its current state is now its new baseline."

"Winners all around, then. Now, what did I get wrong?"

"Wrong is not the right word. There were changes, and not all from you. After sundering the throne, the great astral beings placed strictures on the cosmic order, to maintain stability. They are now releasing those strictures."

"Any of them I need to know about right now?"

"Not from what they have done."

"So, there's something I did that I need to know about."

"You will be able to sense it once your soul recovers from the shock. The throne could never be restored to what it was. Part of you was imprinted upon it. An echo of you, spread across the cosmos."

"Did I just make Airwolf real in every universe?"

"No. You made your interface available to everyone with essences or the potential to get them."

"Huh. Is that with all the special features?"

"Not as a default. It allows for people to view their own information and nothing more, but that has already started to change. Species gift evolutions and even essence abilities are expanding the base effects, just as yours did."

"How did the cosmos spring this on people? Just windows popping up in front of them?"

"Yes."

"Did everyone freak out?"

"Surprise was a common reaction, yes."

"How many people died?"

"The interface, or the System, as it's calling itself, appeared to wait for a moment of safety before revealing itself to individuals."

"So, no traffic accidents because a window popped up in people's faces?"

"I won't say there weren't mishaps, but most of the deaths came from reactions to the System, not the System itself. Religious furore, superstition. Mass killings to keep the new power from teaching things to oppressed members of society."

Jason hung his head.

"I got people killed, then."

"You may have reshaped the cosmos, Asano, but do not consider yourself so grand as to own tribalism, greed and prejudice. People are responsible for their own actions, and ignorance will take any excuse it can get. I shouldn't need to tell you that."

"I suppose not."

The cathedralesque throne room was beginning to crumble. The lights that made up the ceiling were starting to dim and the brickwork of the walls was breaking apart. It was little more than pebbles and falling dust, but Jason could feel the integrity of the reality around him coming apart.

"Okay," he said. "This place is coming apart at the seams. It's time to hobble for our lives."

Miles Cotezee, a senior Adventure Society official, hurried through the Vitesse campus of the Magic Research Association. The always busy grounds were even more so than normal in the wake of what had just happened. Fortunately, Vitesse had not fallen into chaos. It took more than an illusionary window that told you your essence advancement to upset the cart. In a major adventuring city, it was just the latest oddity in a world full of bizarre events. If anything, it was refreshing that the new magic thing wasn't actively trying to kill them.

The nature of this new 'System' was not completely alien to members of the major organisations in Vitesse and around the world. No small amount of analysis had been dedicated to Jason Asano's abilities, and the System was swiftly linked to him. As such, the Adventure Society had deployed Miles to seek out Clive Standish.

Miles had worked with Clive, Belinda and Sophie when the three of them were tracing a portal magic network the Builder cult had used. That was at a time when Asano was believed dead and their team was scattered in various pursuits.

Standish had been silver rank when Miles worked with him, and was best known as a team member of Danielle Geller's son. Things were very different now. From revealing the impending messenger invasion to building a rival to the Magic Society, Standish was well and truly famous in his own right.

In just a handful of years since its inception, the Magical Research Association had exploded into prominence. While the Magic Society leveraged its research and secrets for political power, the MRA gave open access to records and research libraries. Many of the most prominent academics continued to side with the Magic Society for the greater personal gain. The MRA was, instead, a bastion for young, bold and innovative researchers.

The openness of the research association plundered patronage that once would have gone to the Magic Society. Compared to the society hoarding their knowledge for political gain, organisations funded the MRA knowing the results would be freely available. Government authorities, the Adventure Society and a variety of churches, especially that of

Knowledge, all contributed. More than just funding, they were a shield against the Magic Society as it tried to crush its upstart rival.

The future of the MRA looked bright, despite the Magic Society's best efforts. They were already closely associated with the new sky communication network, and there were rumours of a transportation network being quietly researched. This was the result of years of study into the same network Clive had been tracking years earlier.

Miles and Clive had remained friendly over the years, making him the natural person to send when the Adventure Society wanted something from Clive and his association. The MRA campus was swarming with people in the wake of what had happened, but Miles was a known factor. He entered the administration building and managed to fight his way to Clive's office through only a minimum of bureaucratic run-around.

Miles counted nine people gathered in the spacious outer office. This included Clive's assistant, Jeff, at his desk. Miles recognised a few upper-echelon members of the association, plus members of various other societies, associations and institutes. They were standing in silence with uncomfortable expressions on their faces. Miles realised why when moans of pleasure emanated through the closed door of the inner office.

"Oh, yeah. That's the stuff," Clive's voice came through the door. "I've been waiting for this for so long. Knowing I could do this and having it denied to me was torturous. It's like something that's been pent up for years has started gushing out of me."

Miles moved up to Jeff.

"Who is he in there with?"

"I have no idea, Mr Cotezee," Jeff said. "No one came through this way, so they must have portalled in. His wife, maybe?"

"Have you ever seen her?" Miles said. "The Adventure Society has been trying to identify her for years."

"No, I've just heard his friends talking about her, and he doesn't like it when they do."

Jeff leaned in closer.

"I don't think the marriage is in the best shape," he said in a conspiratorial whisper. "They don't seem to spend a lot of time together, and I've heard she's quite... free with her affections."

An excited noise came from the inner office.

"Oh, wow! I didn't think so much would come out just from rubbing the shaft!"

Miles and Jeff shared a look until Clive's door burst open and he emerged holding a magical staff. Sparks were streaming out from a metal cup set into the end.

"Jeff! Get someone from the Item Catalogue Department over here. They wildly miscategorised what this thing does. And see if you can find out where my party members are. I think we'll be getting together soon."

Clive finally seemed to notice all the people, panning his gaze over them unhappily.

"Yes, this was Jason," he told them. "No, I don't know how. Yes, I have guesses; no, I won't tell you what they are. Now, all of you go away."

"Archchancellor Standish, I need to talk to about— AARGH!"

The woman who spoke was sucked through a hole that appeared in the ceiling in a rush of air. Miles saw her hurtling skyward before the hole closed again. Clive swept back into his office and slammed the door as most of the others scrambled to leave. Only Miles and Jeff remained, looking up at the ceiling.

"She was silver rank," Miles observed. "She'll be fine, right?"

"The archchancellor has the landing zone fenced off so no one gets landed on. I can't believe he had all this installed and hasn't gotten around to an automated privacy screen."

Anna Tilden was in the home office of her New York apartment, looking out over Central Park. She was listening to her assistant, Michael Aram, as he summarised a report.

"…confirmed to be non-synchronous. That suggests there is an intelligence behind this 'System,' and that this intelligence is either benevolent or sees some benefit in minimising casualties from the event."

"But there were casualties."

"Most are related to reactions to the event, rather than the event itself. The death toll is surprisingly low, with stress-induced heart attacks being the main culprit."

"Small mercies. No bonus points for guessing who the intelligence behind this is. Have you formally confirmed it?"

"We've reached out to multiple contacts who have experienced Jason Asano's interface. The formatting of the interface matches their recall exactly. It's him, ma'am."

Anna ran her hands over her tired face.

"Remore was right," she said. "If anything, he was understating it. When Asano comes back—and we have to assume he will now—this world is going to change. I want the transcripts of every word Remore is known to have uttered since arriving on this planet, along with the latest analysis on Boris Ketland and the Taika Williams debrief files."

"Yes, ma'am. And, if I may say, the world already has changed."

"I suppose so. Everyone on Earth who's hit puberty just got a taste of magic."

"It's more fundamental than that, ma'am. This System will change the way whole sections of societies operate. As an example, the ability to accurately assess one's own condition will change the face of medicine. A number of online diagnostic websites and alternative health organisations are assembling a class action suit against the Asano clan."

"It hasn't even been a day."

"No, ma'am."

"Who do they even intend to serve? The Asano clan have been buried under vampire territory for half a decade. We don't know if they're alive or dead."

"I believe they intend to serve the Japanese Asano clan, residing in Asano Village in Australia."

"I thought they and Jason had some kind of feud."

"Yes, ma'am."

"Speaking of vampires, do we know if this affected them?"

"Not confirmed, ma'am, although early reports suggest no. It seems that the vampires are learning that something happened to the humans from their feeding stock."

"They're people, Aram. Not feeding stock."

"Sorry, ma'am."

"What do you think will happen with the vampires when Asano returns?"

"Analysts have produced a number of potential scenarios, ma'am, but they are all wildly speculative due to lack of information. They're basically saying it's anyone's guess."

"Then what's your guess? You've met him."

"Ma'am, I once watched a bronze-rank Jason Asano fight a silver-ranker to a no-score draw. That was two ranks ago, minimum, and before he changed how the world works. If I were a vampire living on top of the land Asano gave his family, I'd be looking into the viability of colonising Mars."

"But Asano's power hasn't reclaimed his former territory?"

"Not as of the last report I saw, ma'am. That came in around two hours ago."

"Alright. Go get me those materials."

"Yes, ma'am."

He turned to leave, but stopped at the door and turned around.

"Ma'am, if Asano has the power to do this to everyone in the world, why can't he restore his domains?"

"I suspect that he can. That leads me to the question of why he hasn't."

2

IF WE CAN'T CHANGE FOR THE BETTER

JASON SLOWLY RECOVERED AS HE HOBBLED ALONG THE PATH OF LIGHT that stretched through an empty void, from the crumbling castle they just left to a doorway back into Jason's private universe. The pathway was growing unstable, with sections blurring, dimming or breaking off entirely and drifting into the dark. Raythe still kept company with Jason, his familiars and Arbour, the tree who now lived in his soul.

"Why did you stay when the others left?" Jason asked Raythe.

"To check on you. Dawn will want to know how you are doing. And to remind you that you and I still have business, beyond that of the Cosmic Throne."

"What kind of business?"

"That can wait. You've been kept from friends and family long enough, and have plenty to deal with in the aftermath of what just happened. You need to form a prime avatar and restore the bridge between worlds. That may seem like a small thing after restoring the Cosmic Throne, but—"

"No," Jason said. "It's not small."

Raythe smiled and nodded. "You shall see me again when it is done. Not too soon, as you have earned your rest."

Jason looked around as they drew closer to the end of the path. It terminated in a doorway, floating in the void.

"How are you getting out of here?" he asked. "You can't just float around the astral, right? I know it's borderline for you, but you're still a mortal. Just."

"This space belongs to the throne, and once this path is gone, the avatars of doom will resume their ancient charge. I have a vessel I left at the gateway to your universe."

"It has a gate? My head is still an angry beehive, so I don't have a proper sense of things, yet."

"Yes, it has gateways, although you are the impassable gatekeeper. Your soul is a universe now. An actual pocket of reality in the astral, so it can be visited. But your universe is also a soul, so it cannot be penetrated without your allowance. Your astral kingdom will never have the vastness of a universe seeded by the Builder, but for all their grandeur, ordinary universes have their time. They die. Yours never will."

"Yeah," Jason said. "I still haven't gotten my head around true immortality. Maybe I should do something that will help me comprehend the vastness of eternity."

"Such as?"

"Well, I could binge-watch one of those soaps that's been running since the sixties. If that doesn't feel like eternity, I don't know what would."

"You want to watch soap?" Raythe asked.

"Lady Raythe," Shade interjected. "Mr Asano is immortal now. I believe that his deeds today will be the start of his life as a cosmic figure of note."

"Agreed."

"Allow me to share some wisdom in advance that, with time, will doubtlessly spread across the cosmos: when Mr Asano says things you do not understand, do not ask questions."

"Wouldn't that mean you sometimes miss information which is important to know?"

"That price, Lady Raythe, is entirely worth paying."

They reached the end of the path and entered the doorway in space. The pathway collapsed behind them and a heavy iron door slid across the doorway. They were standing on a catwalk over the magma pit in Jason's private fortress.

"I guess it's time to go and see what my universe is like," he said. "If nothing else, we need to find the exit where our guest parked her car."

"It is not a car," Raythe said. "And surely you have recovered enough by now that you can take in the scope of your realm at a thought. It is your true self, after all. You are using that avatar to restrain your mind because you aren't used to thinking like a transcendent. That body you're in is not you any more than a breath expelled from your mouth is."

"Yeah, I could let my mind go all transcendent," Jason said. "I've done it before — with mixed results. But where's the sense of exploration in that?"

They took an elevating platform into the upper chambers of the fortress. The architecture was classically villainous, all massive hallways of dark metal and bright crimson, with sharp corners and stark decor.

"The layout appears to have changed," Shade said. "Perhaps you should take Lady Raythe's advice, lest we wander around lost."

"What did I just say about a sense of exploration, Shade? The fortress can't have changed that much."

"Mr Asano, that sign has directions to an airlock."

"What?"

Jason and the others were standing on one level of a multi-storey observation lounge, looking through a massive curved window that spanned every level. Through the window, they could see an Earth-like planet.

"The shape of this window is rather akin to that of an enormous eye," Shade observed.

"Is it?" Jason asked innocently.

"Mr Asano, are we in an evil space station in the shape of your head?"

"I have no idea what you're talking about."

"It is, indeed," Raythe said. "My dimensional vessel is at a docking port. It seems that Asano chose a space station as the first port of call to those who approach his universe through astral travel."

"I wasn't really choosing," Jason said. "This all just kind of happened."

"Mr Asano, we will need to find a shuttle bay, or a teleportation room or whatever means you have to go to and from this place and the planet. Again, I ask you to allow yourself the knowledge of your new realm's geography."

"And deny myself the joy of discovery?"

"I am sorry, Mr Asano, but yes. The longer you wander around aimlessly, the longer until you start reuniting with your loved ones."

Jason looked over at Shade and sighed.

"Yeah," he conceded.

Jason stopped letting his consciousness focus into a single avatar and the avatar faded into nothingness. For the first time, Jason allowed himself to be actively conscious of his new nature as a living universe. It was miniscule, as universes went. Just a single planetary system. The sun at its heart blazed not just with heat and light, but with magic.

The most habitable planet was like Earth, in the solar system's goldilocks zone. Teeming with life, it was pristine, wild and untamed. The only developed area was Arbour, the tree city where the handful of people residing on the planet were located.

The space station above the planet was the seat of Jason's power and the reliquary for his astral king relics. It also served as an orbital station and point of entry for dimensional visitors.

An avatar reappeared next to Raythe.

"I'll show you the way to your vessel," Jason said.

Clive marched back out of his office. His assistant and Miles Cotezee were sharing tea and scones.

Jeff tapped a folder on his table.

"This is what I have so far on the locations of your team members, Archchancellor. I'm still waiting on several more. Don't expect anything on Asano, Remore and Williams, of course. If they return to this world, I imagine you will know before any source I have."

"Thank you," Clive said. "Why hasn't anyone from cataloguing arrived yet?"

"I believe there was some question of who to send."

"Why not just send Mickel?"

"Security Director Warnock found out that he was a spy for the Magic Society, Archchancellor. You threw him through the ceiling."

"That was him?"

"Yes, Archchancellor."

"Why can't they decide who to send instead?"

"They're afraid of being thrown through the ceiling, Archchancellor."

"Are they spies too?"

"Not that I am aware, Archchancellor. I believe they are concerned about Herbert Norris."

"Who?"

"The former Vice-Dean of Alchemy. You tossed him through the ceiling for, and I quote, 'asking inane questions.'"

"Oh, him. He *was* asking inane questions."

"Some might suggest that was an overreaction, Archchancellor."

"Would they now?"

"Actually, no, Archchancellor. They're afraid of getting thrown through the ceiling."

Clive made grumbling sounds and took a device off his head. It was a metal headband with four vertical protrusions spaced evenly around it. He placed it on Jeff's desk, next to the tea tray, and then opened a small portal. He took a document from the portal and sat it next to the headband.

"Take this device down to the procurements office and have them replicate another ten. The designs for it are in the folder. Then send the original back here and the rest to the cataloguing department. I want every single item we have re-examined."

"What is it?" Miles asked, picking up the headband.

"It's a device for analysing items using a person's own aura and magic senses," Clive said. "Devices like this are nothing new, but the problem was always interpreting the results objectively. I made this years ago, trying to replicate Jason Asano's ability, but I could never replicate his interface. Now we don't need to, and it works perfectly."

Jeff took the device from Miles, grabbed the folder and headed off. Clive took his seat and grabbed a jam and cream scone.

"I imagine that the Adventure Society has a lot of questions," Clive said to Miles.

"Everyone has a lot of questions, Clive. I was instructed to ask a slew of pointed and forceful questions while being very polite and not making you angry in any way."

Clive chuckled.

"That reminds me of my Magic Society official days. Trust me, Miles, you want to be on top of the organisational pyramid. Mid-level bureaucracy is no way to live."

"Unfortunately, the Adventure Society makes you earn your promotions. Maybe I should have joined the Magic Society and bribed my way to the top."

Clive picked up the folder with the information on his team members and started flicking through the reports.

"I don't think anyone is getting their answers, Miles. Not until Jason comes back."

"Can you at least tell me when you expect that to be? If I don't give my bosses something, they'll just send me right back here."

"I can't be certain when he'll be back," Clive said. "If everything went as planned, Jason is a universe now."

"I'm sorry, did you just say that Asano is a universe?"

"That won't be news," Clive said. "After more than a decade of dealing with messengers, the society knows what an astral king is. The question is how quickly Jason can assemble a new body. He needs a prime avatar to go wandering around outside, and they are, apparently, hard to make."

"So, you don't know how long it will take."

"No, I don't. Jason has a plan, though."

"You say that like it's a bad thing."

"Jason's plans have a way of going really, really bad for someone. Mostly that someone is whoever he's up against, but not always."

"And who is it that he's up against?"

Yumi Asano walked into her office to find an avatar of her grandson sitting in her chair.

"G'day, Grandmother."

Magic left Yumi looking no older than Jason, despite the decades in age difference.

"Jason, do have any idea of the chaos you've caused?"

"You know, that's the same question you ask me every time I visit."

"That's because you only ever visit after you've tipped over the biggest applecart you can find."

"I also came by on your birthday."

"You did," Yumi conceded. "But most of the time, you aren't sending these avatars here for social visits. You could have warned us about this System business."

"No, Grandmother, I couldn't. Otherwise, I would have. I just repaired one of the key mechanisms of the entire cosmos, and I had no idea how that would go. Was anyone hurt?"

"Was anyone... you can't just skip past 'I repaired the cosmos,' Grandson."

Yumi staggered as the room pulsed, like a heartbeat. For a fleeting instant, she felt a power so vast, it was like catching a glimpse of the universe and seeing how small she was within it.

"You will find, Grandmother, as will the Earth, that on this planet, I can do anything I please. Now, was anyone hurt when the System came into being?"

Yumi looked at Jason warily, not answering. He looked like her grandson, but there was something inside him that was very alien. She couldn't help but wonder if any of the boy she knew was still in there.

"It is still me, Grandmother. We all change with time, magic or not. If we can't change for the better, we should at least change in ways that allow us to meet our responsibilities."

"And what do you see as your responsibilities, Jason?"

"This family. This clan. The people who ended up in this place because of their connection to me. The troubles they've faced; being trapped here. A lot of people have been caught in my wake. I can't give them back the lives they had, but I can at least make sure they aren't trapped in this astral space. Or stuck in my domains, worried about being grabbed and leveraged by the wider world."

Yumi nodded.

"I'm glad you understand. People are worried, Jason. Less than fifteen years ago, no one knew magic existed. Now we live in an age of wonders and horrors. This magical realm is lovely, but we've been trapped here for years. There are children in here who have never seen the world outside. Teenagers who have lived their whole lives inside your domains. How will you fix that? Or even get back to it? If you can do anything you want, why haven't you restored the domains and kicked out all the vampires?"

"I'll get to that. How many people were hurt when the System first appeared?"

"Isn't this place a part of you? Can't you just tell?"

"Things were hazy for me at that time the System appeared."

"We suffered little. A few scrapes and bruises. Taika's mother fell off her scooter, but she wasn't hurt. She's bronze rank and was wearing enchanted riding gear."

"That's good."

"Now, why are there still vampires sitting over our heads?"

"I need to make what's called a prime avatar. Avatars like this one can't leave my territory, but a prime avatar can. I won't go into the specifics, but basically, I have cosmic power and mortal power. The prime avatar is tied to my mortal power, which is much lower than my cosmic aspect. Accumulating the power to create such an avatar would take twenty-seven years at my current strength."

"What does that have to do with vampires?"

"The most powerful vampires on Earth got that way by consuming blood infused with power stolen from reality cores."

"I am aware."

"The power of those cores is the kind I need to make an avatar. And, while I didn't use it much, I've always had the ability to strip it right out of the vampires. That's what I'm going to do."

"They aren't going to enjoy that, are they?"

"No, Grandmother. They are not."

"Good."

3
WE'RE ALL STUCK IN A HOLE

NIGEL THORNTON HADN'T BEEN THE FIRST PERSON ON EARTH TO HIT GOLD rank, or even the first to do it without cores. The US had non-core training programs long before Farrah Hurin arrived, so that title went to some unnamed yank. Nigel's claim to fame was being the first outside of the US to hit the milestone core-free.

The rest of his team were core-users, and still only silver rank. There were only so many places on Earth that spawned gold-rank monsters, and the cores taken from them were arguably the most precious commodity on Earth. They certainly didn't find their way into the hands of a squad of mercenaries.

Nigel's team was the same nine-person unit it had been almost two decades earlier. Back then, magic was still a secret and they were part of the Network's secret paramilitary wing. His team had stayed together when the Network fractured, surviving through years of upheavals. From the reveal of magic to the vampire war, they had weathered countless storms.

When the Network schismed into different factions, Nigel and his team had gotten out. Sickened by the infighting and the actions of the Australian government, they had decided to go it alone. The world had no shortage of work for people with a specific set of skills, and a gold-ranker for hire was a rare commodity.

Although they had done jobs for a variety of employers, they were most frequently contracted by United Nations official Anna Tilden. They had worked for her in their Network days and now they were her first call for black bag operations. That included their current assignment. The team was embedded in France, deep inside vampire territory. It was a region they knew well, having been hired to extract people from vampire blood farms many times. They had been there for almost two months, watching the former Asano clan land for changes.

The first priority when embedded in hostile territory was to avoid being discovered. Fortunately for the team, vampires were prone to murdering one another. If the occasional one stumbled onto the team and went missing, its absence didn't alert the rest. The vampires weren't wary towards humans in the area, as the only value it held was symbolic. Without the protection of the domain aura, the former Asano territory held no strategic or tactical value. That lack of importance was not lost on certain members of the team.

"I don't know what we're still doing here," Orange complained. "Sitting in a building every day, watching the edge of a city? We can't see a damn thing from the outside, and if we tried going in, we'd be lunch inside of an hour."

"We're here because we're being paid to be here," Darcy told him.

They were in an underground room that Woolzy had made with magic, sealing the hard-packed earthen walls until they felt like smooth porcelain. One concealed entrance above them led to a section of woodland not too far from Saint Étienne. The room was loaded up with camping gear, but there was no getting around that they were nine people living in a hole in the ground. Even if three were always off on observation duty, it was starting to feel—and smell—like living in an old fried chicken box.

"You're both right," Higgy said. "Yes, this is the job, and we're being paid well. But he's not wrong to wonder what all this is in aid of, or how much longer we'll be out here."

"It's obvious we're waiting for something," Digit said. "Something big enough that we don't need to get close to see it."

"Then let them watch on bloody satellites," Orange said. "Why does the UN need us out here on the quiet? I thought the UN's job was to ask people to stop violating human rights, and then get sad when they say no."

"Anna knows something," Digit said. "She knows something is going to happen, and she wants an eyes-on report the moment it does."

The others all turned to look at Nigel, sitting silently.

"Yep," he said, and left it at that.

"Honestly, the why of all this isn't even the problem," Orange said. "My question is why are we spending our lives living in holes in the ground? We've been doing this long enough that I'm richer than mud cake. Between the nine of us, we have family connections in every Network faction. This work has brought us contacts across the whole damn planet. Why are we crating ourselves in a dirt box instead of sitting on a beach?"

"I find that hard to argue with," Higgy said. "If we've got enough money to live like kings…"

He nodded at Darcy.

"…and one queen, then why are we living in caves and digging bunkers out in the woods?"

Of the six in the bunker, five again turned to look at their leader.

"You want to retire?" Nigel asked them.

"Don't you?" Higgy asked.

"As a matter of fact," Nigel said, "I do. Maybe not completely, though. Semi-retire. Live the high life, but if the right job comes along—"

"Or the right payday," Darcy cut in.

"Or the right payday," Nigel conceded. "Then, maybe we saddle up again. If that's what we want to do, then that's what we'll do. Together, like always. You're right, Orange; we have accumulated a lot of wealth. And the connections we've built up are probably worth more than the money. But how much is enough? Where is safe? The United States and China are fairly safe for most people, but we aren't most people. What happens when someone in charge wants something from us that we don't want to give?"

"Thorny," Higgy said to Nigel, "let's not pretend like you can't write your own ticket. You hit gold rank outside of any of the big groups and they all want to recruit you."

"Or kill you before someone else does," Orange added.

"They won't try," Nigel said. "No one has managed to kill a gold-ranker yet, even with other gold-rankers. As far as I'm aware, the only ones to die followed Jason Asano into the sealed transformation zone in Slovakia. One didn't come out again and another one did, then turned into a monster."

"Which one was that?" Orange asked.

"Vietnamese guy," Darcy said. "Worked for the Chinese. Followed Asano into a transformation zone and turned into a tentacle monster when he came out. Every major magical faction had people there, and they still barely managed to kill it."

"There was Jack Gerling too," Higgy said.

"I thought he went to work for the vampires," Darcy said.

"No, he's right," Nigel said. "I forgot about him because he's still around. He died in the transformation zone here in France. The vampire queen brought him back as some kind of blood clone slave."

"I guess the moral is to avoid following Jason Asano into big magic domes," Orange said. "Makes me think about those astral proto-spaces we went into with him. We might have been lucky to get out without turning into wombat snakes or something."

"Wombat snakes?" Nigel asked.

"We have officially veered too far off topic," Higgy said. "Thorny, I can tell you've got some kind of retirement plan in mind. But for some reason, you haven't told us yet."

"Yeah," Nigel admitted. "I have a plan. And no, I haven't told any of you yet."

"Why not?" Darcy asked.

"It's too unreliable. Too many unknown factors. On a basic level, the plan is simple: we find a safe place to land. Somewhere the people in charge will value us without trying to bend us over."

"And where do you expect to find that?" Orange asked. "Some little island in the Pacific with white beaches and blue water? That's big enough to import beer, but too small for the Network to set up shop? We all get bungalows and clean up any monsters that turn up?"

"That actually sounds pretty good," Higgy said.

"It does," Nigel said. "Maybe that's what we'll do."

"But you have something else in mind, don't you?" Digit asked. "Something more ambitious, meaning a huge pain in the arse for us."

"I do," Nigel said.

"Out with it, then," Orange said.

"It's going to sound like a terrible idea if I say it now," Nigel said.

"Say it anyway," Darcy told him. "We're all stuck in a hole, Nige. It's not like you can run off."

Nigel sighed.

"Fine," he said. "I want to join the Asano clan."

"Are you out of your frigging gourd?" Orange asked. "The whole reason we're here is that the Asano clan vanished. Everything they had now belongs to the biggest, nastiest pack of ravening vampires on the face of the Earth. Jason Asano hasn't been seen in a squillion bloody years. His magic town probably lost its power because he cacked it and his family's most likely dead too. And we're here for what? To check if all these dead pricks are going to magically reappear?"

"In fairness," Woolzy said, "if they're going to reappear, then magically is how it's going to happen."

"You weren't wrong about it being an unreliable plan," Darcy told Nigel. "Why is that where you're putting your hopes? What do you know that we don't? Is that why Anna sent us here, watching this place after years without change? She thinks the Asanos are coming back?"

Nigel rubbed his chin thoughtfully for a moment.

"Yes," he said. "She thinks they're coming back."

"Why?" Orange asked. "The vampires have been sitting on the holes the Asano clan vanished into for years. We don't know if those astral spaces are even still there. Or if the vampires figured out how to crack them open and ate everyone inside. Or if the clan all starved to death in there."

"They didn't starve to death," Higgy said. "Thorny and I went into one once, playing bodyguard for Anna. They had full-blown farms in there, growing magic food like you've never seen."

"What very few people know," Nigel said, "is that right before we were sent out here, the Asano clan reached out."

"How?" Higgy asked.

"Rufus Remore. He left the place the Asano clan are hiding and made his way through vampire territory, completely unnoticed."

"Well, damn," Digit said. "We don't get any closer than the edge of the old clan territory, and that magic door the Asanos keep locked is right in the middle of it."

"But he's alive," Darcy said. "And the rest of them too?"

"Yes," Nigel said. "And they're getting ready to make a move. Remore reached out to certain people. Anna Tilden and Boris Ketland, for sure. I don't know who else, if anyone. For all I know, telling you just doubled the number of people who know about it."

"So, the Asano clan is coming back?" Higgy asked. "Properly back? Magic domain, the whole lot?"

"Remore certainly thinks so."

"Let's assume he's right," Higgy said. "The Asano clan comes back out and reclaims their territory. Who is to say they keep it? They lost it once before."

"According to Remore, it was some kind of ruse by Jason Asano," Nigel said. "A 'fool your friends to fool your enemies' scenario."

"He's alive too, then?" Darcy asked. "Is he coming back as well?"

"Yes. And supposedly with a dozen gold-rankers as strong as Remore himself. And you've seen that guy fight."

"I haven't," Orange said. "There's just a flash of light and then every prick's dead. I wouldn't cross that bloke for quids."

Orange emphasised his words with expressive arm gestures, which were not appreciated in the confines of their little bunker.

"Okay," Higgy said. "Let's say all that's true. Asano and his clan come back, stronger than ever and rock solid. What makes you think that the clan is a good place for us to land, and that they'll even take us?"

"They'll take us because they know us," Nigel said. "They know who we are, what we've done, and what we haven't."

"Sure," Orange said. "That's why they take us. Why should we take them?"

"Because they're loyal," Nigel said. "The one thing they've consistently done is take care of their own. Not just themselves, but everyone who has helped them or gotten caught up in their mess. They took them in and shielded them. The only ones who they cut ties with was the Network, who screwed Asano time and again. And I'll remind you that we cut ties with them too. I'm not saying the Asano clan is perfect, or that I like every choice they've made. But their leadership has demonstrated some actual integrity. There's a lot less of that going around than I'd like."

"You say this based on what?" Orange asked. "Rumours and second-hand stories? A few visits to clan territory when we were operating out of the military bases they hosted? That's without even thinking about Jason Asano himself. What changes when he shows up? That guy was a lit fuse when he sodded off."

"I did tell you this was unreliable," Nigel said. "That's why I didn't say anything until you all pushed. I want more information before we do a single bloody thing. It's why we're here. I want to see what the Asano clan does when they're under the gun and not ready to put on a show for visitors. I don't want to make any promises to you all that I can't keep."

He checked his watch. "It's time to relieve the others. Orange, Darce; you come with me."

The most dangerous time for Nigel and his team was when they were swapping out observers. This happened three times per day; twice during daylight and once at night, when the vampires were more active. Fortunately, Farrah Hurin had given them proper aura training, which they had been practising for well over a decade. They weren't sloppy at all with their aura control, and vampires were better at manipulating auras than detecting them.

The major threat was a gold-rank vampire in the wrong place when the team made a move. The city had several, so even if Nigel could take on one, more would be on them before the fight was done. Accordingly, the team were always diligent. Each time they swapped out people at their observation post, they moved slowly and carefully.

The observation post itself was on the outskirts of Saint Étienne, still in ruins from the original vampire occupation. Just outside of the area claimed by Jason Asano, it was a section of city not replaced with a replica made from Asano's weird magic clouds. Best of all, the vampires ignored it in favour of the luxurious cloud buildings of the city proper.

The post itself was on the third floor of a mostly collapsed building. With the area around it surrounded by overgrown rubble, it was easy to approach from their bunker in the woods without needing to move into the open. As most of the other buildings had been toppled entirely, the sight-lines from the upper floor were good.

The area had been largely reclaimed by nature in the years since Jason turned a transformation zone into a domain under his control. Grass grew up through shattered streets while bushes, vines and moss grew over the rubble. Only a handful of buildings were even partially standing, and they too were covered in the encroaching green.

Nigel, Orange and Darcy picked their way carefully through the overgrown ruins. The sky was clear, giving them enough moonlight to see. That also made them more visible to the vampires, or anything else roaming about. The magic level had been reduced since the clan domain went away, but even a silent kill on a bronze-rank monster could be a problem. The senses of a vampire were sharp already, but especially so when it came to smelling blood.

They reached the right building without incident and slipped inside, joining Cobbo, Jonno and Green. What remained of the third floor was set up as their observation post. The handful of intact rooms offered views in multiple directions, including the Asano territory. They couldn't see deep into the city, but it was enough that any major events wouldn't be missed.

The biggest problem was that the roof was not intact and none of the windows had any glass, making rainy days bad and windy, rainy days completely miserable.

The inside of the room was etched with sigils that would mask their presence, from their auras to their body heat. Woolzy had learned them from Farrah back in their Network days and was now an old hand at them. Even a gold-ranker would have to pay direct attention to the building to sense them. Despite requests from the team, Nigel had not allowed any rain-shielding magic.

Nigel didn't ask if anything had changed. They had been in place for months, and if anything happened, the others would have mentioned it immediately. The trio being replaced got up to leave and their replacements prepared to settle in. It was a bright night, with a clear sky and a gibbous moon, so they noticed immediately when the change came.

The silver moonlight spilling through the window was suddenly replaced with blue and orange.

4

A SILENT CITY

WHEN THE LIGHT COMING THROUGH THE WINDOW TURNED FROM MOON silver to orange and blue, Nigel and his team moved to look outside. The moon was still there, but its luminance was being outshone by a massive, nebulous eye, floating over the city like an alien invader. Colour spread out from it, more like fire crawling across the sky than simple light. The orange danced like fire and the blue swam like water, painting the city below.

They had barely caught sight of it when the eye's aura hit them like a bomb. It had not just spiritual but physical force behind it, sending all but the gold-rank Nigel stumbling back.

"That's not even the full force of it," Nigel said. "We're on the periphery. It's much stronger inside the boundaries of the old clan."

"That wasn't the full strength?" Darcy asked, wary of moving back to the window. "What is that?"

"It's him. Asano. You've felt his aura before."

"I've never felt anything like that," Orange said.

"It's changed," Nigel said, "but I recognise the core aspects. But this is something we've never seen from him. Get back to the others and move to fallback position three."

"Three?" Orange asked.

"Whatever is happening here," Nigel said, "it just changed the colour of the sky. I want you all as far from this as you can possibly be."

"We don't want you anywhere near this either," Darcy said.

Nigel turned to look at her.

"Whatever it is we've been waiting for, Darce, it's happening now. I'm the only gold-ranker among us. I'm the only one with a real shot of getting in there, taking a closer look and getting out."

"You're going in there?" Orange asked. "You don't have to do that just for a job."

"I know. But. Whatever's going on out there, it's big. Getting ahead of the information curve will give us a better chance of navigating whatever comes next. I'll learn what I can and then get out. If I don't join you within three hours of reaching the fallout position, use one of our exfil plans; don't tell me which one. We'll regroup in Casablanca."

Nigel didn't wait for further argument, leaping through a window that hadn't held glass in years.

As Nigel moved through the streets of what had once been Saint Étienne, the replica nature of the city started to reveal itself. What looked and felt like stone and metal warped like clay, the colour fading as sections of building and street turned into cloud substance. Nigel cautiously touched some of it and found it thick and sticky, like glue.

The city's horrific denizens were taking to the streets, and the vampires weren't the greatest number. Many were ghouls; vampiric victims warped into mindless, withered servants. They were erupting from doorways and bursting up from cellars, driven to a frenzy by the aura. Vampires came out after them, trying and often failing to assert control.

Nigel watched from hiding as the vampires themselves seemed to have trouble reining in their own mania. Wide-eyed and twitchy, some even joined the ghouls, scrambling up walls like animals or leaping right onto the rooftops. From there, vampires and ghouls alike started shrieking at the eye in the sky.

Nigel had seen similar behaviour before. When vampires lost control of their predatory instincts, they became savage beasts, with no thoughts beyond killing and feeding. He also knew that these were the weaker vampires, far more aggressive, but mercifully less powerful.

Nigel watched out for the frenzied ones, but it was the stronger vampires he kept an eye on. They maintained control of themselves but looked unsettled, casting worried looks at the sky. Some tried to re-establish command over the ghouls and even their fellow vampires. Others moved up to the rooftops for a better look at the eye. More than a few started running, although there was no consensus on direction. From what Nigel could see, they chose to either head for the centre of the city or to flee it entirely.

Nigel followed those heading deeper in, spending more time hiding than moving. In his hand was a gold-rank pistol with a magical silencer; a rare gift from a powerful and grateful client. He used it to put down a couple of vampires, both slower-moving bronze-rankers that caught him between hiding spots. He dropped them in an instant and moved on without bothering to hide the bodies.

The gun made no sound at all and the smell of blood was already in the air. As the aura-induced madness intensified, ghouls were attacking their masters and the vampires were feeding on each other. Those trying to get them under control gave up and started running with the others.

The aura driving their behaviour was tyrannical, angry and hungry, as if the aura itself had become vampiric. Nigel was relieved that, while terrifying, it did not affect him as it did the vampires. It was a cyclone of power that moved around him as if he were in the eye of the storm. He could sense that the aura was gold-ranked, but also that some other power lay beyond it. He'd never sensed anything beyond gold rank before, and that was rare enough. Whatever lay behind this aura, it was clearly not of Earth.

Nigel felt the moment the aura shifted. He wasn't sure how, exactly, as it still wasn't affecting him, but the vampires reacted immediately. The vampires and ghouls on the rooftops had been screaming rage at the eye in the sky, but now those screams turned to fear. They joined the vampires that had retained sense enough to run and started fleeing, either across the rooves or leaping down to the street.

The chaos made it harder to stay hidden. Nigel ducked down a stairwell and into a cellar. The ghouls that had once been inside had ripped apart the door on their way out. He had not been in there long when a gold-rank vampire entered in a blur of movement.

Nigel froze. He was confident of fighting one vampire in isolation, but the fight would inevitably bring more down on him. He watched as the vampire panned its gaze over the cellar while sniffing the air. Its eyes passed over him as if he weren't there and, after a moment, it left. After it did, mist appeared around Nigel's body and a voice came from nowhere.

"You can move safely now. They will neither see nor sense you, so long as they don't touch you."

"Jason?"

"Can't really talk, Nigel; I'm in the middle of a thing. G'day, though."

Nigel made his way back outside, the mist shroud moving with him. The streets were teeming with ghouls and vampires. There were even some blood servants; humans who had been fed on vampire blood. They were stronger and faster than normal people, but enslaved by the blood's addictive properties.

The rooftops and even the walls had ghouls and vampires running along them, clawed hands and feet digging into tile and brick. The buildings continued to devolve into thick cloud substance, sometimes forcing ghouls to yank themselves out. The buildings warped and undulated as Nigel watched, disgorging vampires right through the walls.

He was careful to avoid all of it, but it was hard when the city itself was changing around him. A balcony he was hiding on might collapse, or the street turn to cloudy glue under his feet. Fortunately, the city's monstrous denizens were having as much trouble or more, and things only got worse for them. Nigel heard Jason's voice again, but not as a nearby whisper. This time, it crashed from the sky like thunder.

"BLEED FOR ME."

Nigel recognised the incantation from Jason's bloodletting spell, but the results were more extreme than what he had seen in the past. The effect on the ghouls was familiar, if exaggerated, as they bled from every hole in their bodies. The vampiric servants fell to the ground, in flailing seizures. As for the vampires, mist rose from their bodies like steam, but darker. Nigel would have guessed it was red, but it was hard to tell in the eerie light. The smell was much easier to identify as the coppery tang of blood filled the air.

There had already been a scent of blood carried on the breeze, but it quickly grew thick and heavy. Haze filled the streets as blood mist poured off the vampires, creating a sanguine humidity.

Even the vampires that had maintained their senses were now turning to madness. Nigel leapt to a balcony and ducked down to avoid the tide of ghouls dotted with vampires. Nigel and his team had known there were ghouls in the city, which was normal for any vampire enclave, but the number of the emaciated creatures was startling. It looked like the vampires had been using the city to build a new army of them, probably using spent humans from the blood farms.

Jason's voice spoke again, once more crashing from the sky.

"YOUR BLOOD IS NOT YOURS TO KEEP, BUT MINE ON WHICH TO FEAST."

The moment the thunderous incantation was completed, the blood haze filling the streets started to clear. It rose into the sky, splitting into streamers that converged on the giant eye. When they reached it, they were drawn in and devoured. As the eye absorbed more and more blood, it shifted from blue and orange to purple and red. The light coming from it changed with them until the city looked painted in blood and shadow.

On the streets, the fleeing ghouls and vampires were suddenly stopped in their tracks as a forest of bizarre shadow arms erupted from every dark crevice and cranny. The arms were void black and utterly inhuman; something between tentacles and the twisted branches of a dead tree. Each limb ended in fingers with too many knuckles, tapering to wicked points. As they dug into flesh, the vampires and their ghoul creations squealed like tortured pigs.

Grasping, twisted limbs wrapped around bodies and snatched at heads, sharp fingers jabbing into mouths and digging into eyes. More than just on the street, many were left hanging from walls, caught climbing or mid-jump. They now hung like insects in a web and, like a spider's prey, they were being drained.

The vampires used a variety of powers to try and escape. Nigel saw one turn into a weasel and try to slip away, only to be skewered by sharp fingers and pinned to a wall. Similar fates met all those who shape-shifted into various animals. Those who turned into smoke and mist fared far worse. While they did escape the arms, a surge of aura surrounded them. Their smoke and mist forms turned dark, thickening into more of the blood mist and vanishing into the haze.

As the blood evacuated their bodies, the vampires withered, their bodies emaciated and limp. Once the last gasps of blood mist sputtered from their bodies, they were barely distinguishable from the ghouls. The younger vampires fell apart into congealed gobbets, splashing onto the street. The older ones crumbled to dust and were carried away on the breeze.

Only the vampires were shedding the blood mist. From the ghouls, blood spattered to the ground, thick and dead. Nigel noticed that some of the vampires weren't shedding mist. These were mostly weaker ones, bronze rank and a few scant silvers. They were still trapped, but their blood spilled from their bodies and onto the ground.

Nigel made his way through the nightmare landscape, barely bothering to hide now. The freakish arms avoided him, and everything else was either dead or dying. He leapt onto a rooftop and saw only a handful of the blood mist streams still rising from the streets. He guessed that these were the gold-rank vampires, apparently failing to escape the fate of their lessers.

Nigel watched from a roof as the last of the blood haze rose from the city and was drunk up by the eye. There were no more howls of rage or fear or agony. Only whimpers remained; a city of ghouls clinging to the last vestiges of their perverse existence, a scant few of their masters doing the same. Jason's voice rang out one more time, booming across a conquered city.

"MINE IS THE JUDGEMENT, AND THE JUDGEMENT IS DEATH."

All the blood collected in the eye erupted at once, up from the eye into a cloud that spread over the entire city. Blood rain fell, but each droplet was transformed before it ever reached the ground. Dark blood drops became shimmering motes of gold, silver and blue light. When they struck the mist shrouding Nigel, or hit the tiled rooftops, they vanished without effect. The ghouls and vampires did not get off so easily.

Where the rain touched the vampires and ghouls still trapped in shadowy limbs, their flesh exploded. The blood servants that hadn't already died in seizures didn't explode when touched by the shining raindrops. Only their blood did, turning each into a gruesome and extremely deceased mess.

The process of killing off anything that had survived the blood draining was accompanied by fresh howls of intense agony. Nigel looked up at the eye, once more blue and orange. By the time the shining rain stopped falling, there were no more howls and no more whimpers.

Nigel was the only thing alive in a silent city.

5

THE FUNDAMENTAL THINGS

NIGEL LOOKED UP, WATCHING THE NIGHT SKY CLOSE OVER THE NEBULOUS eye. The blue and orange light painting the city disappeared with it, allowing the moonlight to once more have primacy. The macabre remnants of the city were illuminated in silver. The buildings were warped, like plastic models melted under a hot lamp. Some sections had broken down entirely, leaking cloud material that sparkled in the moonlight.

Pools of blood and streaks of gore shone black under the silver light. They had no smell to them, as if everything that made the congealing fluids blood had been leached out of them. The sanguine aroma that had drenched the air was no longer carried on the fresh night breeze.

"You've been diligent in your training, I see."

Nigel spun around upon hearing Jason's voice. His aura senses hadn't registered the man's approach and still didn't recognise his presence. To his supernatural perception, Jason Asano and the world around him were one and the same. Jason was standing on the roof in a floral shirt, tan shorts and sandals. He slouched casually, hands in his pockets. While moonlight washed the colour out of everything else, it lit him up like he was standing centre stage.

"Nigel? You okay, mate? You look a bit shell-shocked."

Nigel continued to stare at him.

"You're going to ask that after what you just did?"

"Yeah, fair enough."

"Are you back?" Nigel asked. "Or are you some kind of illusion?"

"Not exactly. This body is an avatar. A physical projection from another universe, like an interdimensional phone call."

"But you are still alive."

"Was that even a question? The answer is more complicated than you'd think, I'll admit. I guess it depends on how you define alive."

"Are you undead?"

"No. I guess I'm… I don't know. Geographical?"

"What does that even mean?"

"Let's put that aside for now. For practical purposes, I'm alive. You thought I was dead, though? I'd have thought the System would have put that idea to bed."

"One of the prevailing theories is that the System is what's left of the magic that once inhabited this place. That the domains fell because you died and their power seeped into the planet, and once it permeated the entire Earth, the System happened."

"People actually think that?"

"The impossible isn't what it used to be, Asano."

"I suppose not."

Nigel looked at the man, an utterly incongruous figure in the dark and blood-soaked city.

"You seem relaxed for a man that just turned a city into a grave."

"I'm trying to be a better man than the one who left this world. But I don't have it in me to mourn the ones who had it coming. Not anymore."

"Who decides who has it coming? I won't argue about killing vampires, but I just saw a power the Earth has never seen. What is to stop you from deciding anyone you don't like has it coming? Where's the line?"

"Wherever I decide it is."

"Why do you get to make that judgement?"

"Who do you think should decide where I use my power, Nigel? Some faction leader? A president or a prime minister? A parliament or a congress? The United Nations?"

"I don't know, but you just wiped out a city. That's a dangerous power to leave unaccountable to anyone."

Jason tilted his head, peering at Nigel. He realised that Jason was reading the emotions in his aura.

"You're asking me this because you're afraid of yourself, aren't you? Of the power you have as a gold-ranker," Jason said.

"Yes," Nigel admitted.

"Who do you work for now, Nigel? Who do you answer to?"

"Myself. My conscience. My team and I are private contractors. This job is for Anna Tilden, but my team and I aren't attached to any group. We answer to each other, choosing which jobs to take and which to refuse. My team are the ones who hold me to account."

Jason smiled.

"Mine too. I didn't have them on Earth, which is probably how I went so astray. If not for Farrah, I'd have lost myself completely, I think."

"Sometimes I question myself. The power I have at this rank is right out of a comic book. I could knock down a building with my bare hands. Throw a train like a javelin. My team are my brothers and sisters, but they don't have this much power. It scares me sometimes."

Jason nodded.

"I understand. Maybe more than anyone. You're a gold-ranker with no affiliation? You got out when the Network fell apart?"

"Yeah."

"But you were silver, then, and no one much cared, right? Until you hit gold rank, and suddenly, everyone wants a piece of you, and they aren't scrupulous about how to get it."

"No, they're not."

"Sucks, doesn't it?"

"Yes."

"Well, I didn't handle it very well, so I might not have the best advice. For what it's worth, though, I think you're on the right track. Listen to the people you trust. Let them show you when you're heading off the rails."

"I need more than that. Sooner or later, someone is going to decide they don't like a gold-rank free agent and start looking for levers."

"Your family. Your team's families."

"Yeah. A lot of the team come from old Network families, so they have protection enough for now. But if people with real power come along..."

"You don't trust the Network factions to not sell them out."

"No. I don't."

Nigel walked to the edge of the rooftop and looked out over the city.

"I've been looking for a place we can all belong," he said. "Where our families can be safe and the people in charge won't use us for things we don't want to do."

"Are you asking to join the Asano clan?"

"I don't know. Maybe. I don't know if they'd have us, and I'd want to know more before we agree to be a part of it. But I saw you, during your time here. What loyalty and betrayal meant to you."

Jason nodded.

"When you have so much power that you can solve most of the old problems," he said, "you realise that it's the fundamental things that really matter."

"Yes."

"Well, I'm not going to say you can be in or out. I'll leave that to my grandmother. But I think it might be a good fit, so I'll have a word with her."

"There's a few things I'd like to know, Asano."

"I'm guessing there's more than a few, but go on."

"I understand you wanted to clear the city of vampires, but why do it this way? To show the rest of the world what happens when they cross you? Letting me see so I can go back and tell everyone how dangerous you are?"

Jason shook his head.

"Nah, mate. The people who make the decisions in this world don't scare, no matter how real the threat. I learned that the last time I was here. Once I'm back, they'll take their shots and pay the price for trying. I don't like it, but there's nothing I can do to stop it. Not without becoming just like them."

"Like them how?"

"Letting innocent people pay the price for what I want."

Jason gestured at himself.

"This, the gawking tourist outfit, is aspirational. Casual. Fun. A little dorky. It's who I want to be. But this…"

He spread his arms out to indicate the city around them.

"This is who I am. When I have to be. This wasn't a show, Nigel. This was a practical necessity. I left all these cloud buildings intact in the hope that the vampires would move in. I wasn't taking their blood, but the remnants of reality core energy, from when they were infusing the power of those cores into blood."

"And that's why some weren't drained," Nigel realised. "They were the younger ones, who had never fed on reality core blood."

"Yes."

"How powerful are you? Are you at the rank after gold?"

"That's complicated. Technically, I'm both gold rank and a rank that's beyond diamond. In this place, my domain, I'm extremely powerful. I don't like the term 'holy ground,' but that's essentially what we're talking about. I'm not a god, but I do certain things the way that gods do. When I come to Earth, it will be in a mortal vessel. Gold rank, like you. It will have power like what you saw here, but scaled back. An extension of myself, a more developed version of this avatar. Killing it won't hurt me, just cost me time to make a new one."

"Did the same thing happen in Slovakia as happened here?"

"Yes. But the vampires there kept their blood farm within the domain, so I was able to rescue those people. Here, the blood farm is off site, outside the reach of my power. This avatar can't go beyond the boundary of my domain, so I can't intercede there myself. You know the blood farms they used, don't you?"

"Yeah," Nigel said. "We've been here for months, scouted it all out. We just didn't have the numbers to rescue the people, or a way to extract them if we did. After your domains went down, mainland Europe fell entirely to the vampires."

"The clan can offer you numbers and safety. Is the rest of your team nearby?"

"Yeah. If I move fast, I can reach them before they evacuate the region."

"Then please go and bring them back. In the meantime, I will clean the city."

"It's quite a mess."

A nearby patch of blood smeared across the roof burst into ghostly white flame.

"That won't be a problem," Jason said.

Sophie swung her leg in a horizontal kick that hit nothing. A wind blade shot out, widening as it passed over the plain. The horizontal wave of razor-sharp air passed over the grass, shimmering like a heat haze and humming like an engine. In its path was a massive horde of stonehide lizards, the crashing sound of their feet overpowering the sound of the wind blade.

It was a large herd, far too many to come from a normal manifestation. They were left over from the monster surge, four years previous, and hidden in an uninhabited mountain range. Sophie's contract was firstly to eliminate them before they caused havoc on the trading routes of the flat-lands. Once that was done, she needed to investigate what had driven them down from the mountains. They'd been up there for years without bothering anyone, and the Adventure Society wanted to know what had changed.

As the wind blade struck the stampeding herd, secondary wind blades erupted from the struck monsters. Those in turn triggered more and more secondary blades, bouncing back and forth between the monsters until the massive herd became a meat grinder of rent armour and spraying blood.

Sophie stood and watched, listening as the countless cracks of new wind blades rang like a thunderstorm. The gem in her wristband blinked, indicating someone was contacting her sky talk tablet. She pulled it out of a dimensional pouch and accepted the call. Clive's face appeared on the tablet.

"It's time?" she asked.

"It's time. The portal to Jason's soul realm has opened up again. Finish whatever business you're on and make your way to Yaresh."

Sophie ended the call, put the tablet away and turned back to the horde of monsters. Despite the power of her gold-rank wind blade, stonehide lizards were tough, even for silver-rank monsters. They were all savagely lacerated, but had yet to fall. The only ones that had died so far were those trampled in the frenzied stampede. By the time the magic of her attack was expended and the blade storm came to an end, the stonehide lizards were rushing all the harder. Bellowing in rage, they hurled themselves across the plain in Sophie's direction.

She watched their approach, took out a sandwich and bit into it. From the sky, a sound started at a high pitch, growing deeper as the source descended at breakneck speed. Humphrey landed in the middle of the herd like a bomb. The shockwave of his abrupt arrival flung the monsters away from his impact point. The force of the wave ripped bodies apart in the air, splitting them along lines broken in their armour by wind blades.

Pieces of monster flew more than a kilometre away, several chunks avoiding Sophie as she manipulated the air to deflect them. A massive cloud of dust followed, again moving around Sophie thanks to her wind control.

Visibility died as the cloud surrounded her. A figure came striding out, tall and broad-shouldered. Dust had caked onto his armour, muting its colourful rainbow scales. He pulled his helmet off with a grin.

"Took you long enough," she told him. "I was starting think that Nik would rank up before—"

She dropped her sandwich as he pulled her into a passionate kiss. A moustachioed dog dashed out of the dust cloud like a cheetah, snatching the sandwich before it hit the ground.

"...whatever business you're on and make your way to Yaresh," Clive said. The image on his tablet of Sophie nodded and the call ended.

"Would it kill you to say goodbye like a normal person?" he muttered, and shoved the tablet into his storage space. He went to the outer office.

"Jeff, how are preparations for my trip away?"

"Vice Chancellor Grantham reported that she was read up on everything and ready to stand in during your absence. She did request a meeting to go over any last details, and update you on the portal network project."

"That's fine. Set something up."

"She suggested a dinner meeting."

"That's fine. Tonight would be best, if she can accommodate it. I want to leave tomorrow."

"I'm sure she will, Archchancellor. And, if I might suggest, sir, do dress up nicely."

"Why?" Clive asked. "I've got too much to do to go fancying myself up just to eat and go over administrative details."

Jeff watched as Clive stalked back into his office, closing the door behind him. Jeff shook his head sadly.

"That poor, poor woman," he muttered.

6
YOU DON'T WANT GLORY

JASON AND HIS THREE FAMILIARS STOOD IN A DOORWAY THAT OPENED ONTO a blank void, serving as a private dock to the deep astral. Any cosmic visitors had to approach Jason's astral kingdom from elsewhere, as this was for his use alone. It had once led to the Cosmic Throne, but Jason had relinquished that link.

As they watched, a nebulous orange and blue eye opened in the dark. Motes of light poured from it in a torrent, dancing sparks of blue, silver and gold. They swam through the void like a school of luminescent deep-sea fish, lighting up the dark. Despite the appearance, they were not living things but shards of the fundamental substance that made up physical reality. First stolen from Earth's transformation zones, then consumed by vampires, Jason had subsequently sieved it from their bodies and taken it for himself.

"It is insufficient to complete your prime avatar," Shade observed.

"Yeah," Jason agreed in a dissatisfied tone. "I don't like my options for getting the rest of what I need either. Having Rufus raid the factions on Earth for any reality core stockpiles would make things very hard for Grandmother, diplomatically. The messengers are made of the stuff I need, but they're all indoctrinated slaves. Killing them in a war is one thing, but I'm not going to have the team round them up and drag them into my domain for me to consume."

"There are more vampires on Earth," Colin said. "The clan has strong people now. They could grab vampires for you to eat."

"They could," Jason mused. "There's an argument that they're victims as well, but they're too far gone for any chance at redemption. But I don't want the clan doing something that predatory. I know I'm not great leader material, but I am responsible for them. Part of leadership is about setting a culture, and I want them to be better than me."

"You can't protect them from never dirtying their hands," Colin said.

"No," Jason agreed, "but I can keep them to doing it only if they have to. I don't absolutely need this from them, so I'm not going to send them off to kidnap things that think and feel, just so I can squeeze the life out of said kidnapped things and consume it."

"I agree that would be best avoided," Shade said.

"I have a suggestion," Gordon said. The sweet tones of his voice emitted from all twelve of the spheres he had at gold rank, making him sound like a choir of angels. It masked what Jason knew to be the familiar's nervousness at speaking. He was new to being understood by everyone.

"Please, share," Jason encouraged.

"You gave something to the goddess of Death once, as part of a bargain."

Jason's eyes went wide. "That's brilliant, Gordon."

Gordon's orbs dimmed bashfully.

"What am I missing?" Colin asked. He was in his blood clone form, looking like Jason but sculpted from wet, blood-red clay.

"I made a bargain with Death," Jason said. "To swear off resurrection, for myself or anyone else at my hands."

"I remember," Colin said. "Really stupid choice. I can't believe you gave away power like that."

"We needed a miracle," Jason said, "and we got one. I don't bring it up to relitigate that decision, though. The point is that I had the power to resurrect at the time. I'd drained enough reality material from messengers to build myself a new body if I died. I gave it up to the goddess when I made the deal, but now that I won't use it to come back to life, she may be willing to return it."

"Do you think that likely?" Shade asked.

"I don't know," Jason said. "I probably got in her good graces by shutting Undeath down so hard. Can't hurt to ask."

Fiorella liked portal duty. A nice quiet room where nothing ever happened, and the best part: the chair reclined. For someone who enjoyed napping, it was the most coveted posting in the militia for the city of Rexion.

She had only been a girl when the old city fell, and had grown up in Rexion. She'd been in the crowd, sitting on her father's shoulders when they had the big ceremony to name their new home. Her memories of those days were the hazy recollections of a child. Fear and hopelessness as the Builder cult, the messengers and then the undead came underground, one after the other. Abandoning their home. Hiding in some strange place her mother said was inside a man's soul—that part still didn't make sense to her—and finally arriving in their new home.

People had been scared. They had gone through so much; lost so much. Seen people and experienced events that were powerful, confusing and bizarre. It was hard to tell saviours from enemies, especially when one became the other. It had been one thing after the next, and when they arrived in the city, what no one expected was peace and safety. For some, it took years to accept. Some never did, ever wary of some unspecified cataclysm.

The city was no less strange than anything else they had been through. So empty, with how few brighthearts were left. The buildings that turned into fog, reshaped themselves and turned into different buildings. It still happened occasionally, but it was all the time when Fiorella was still a child.

More people from the surface arrived, but these were neither foes nor saviours. They came not for war but for trade. The new growing chambers produced so much food, and the people on the surface were apparently very hungry. She heard stories of them facing their own messengers, who destroyed their surface growing chambers, called farms. They needed food and had much to offer in return. Most valuable was what the Church of Fertility could provide: children. In only a few years, the streets had been teeming with them, too many to raise as anything but a community.

The portal chamber had always been there, ever since the beginning. There were all kinds of stories about it. That it led to the place they had all sheltered in after fleeing the old city. That it was the inside of a person's soul. Fiorella's memories of being inside were patchy, just a few images and emotions. Mostly fear and loss.

The portal was only ever used occasionally, by Council Leader Lorenn or visitors from the surface. Then, a few years ago, it closed. When that happened, the militia started putting on extra people. There was talk of some invisible protection having gone away. While many didn't believe it, Fiorella did. Her aura senses were a little stronger than those of most brighthearts and she had felt the change. Something that had always been there, without her ever noticing, was suddenly gone.

That had been Fiorella's impetus for joining the militia, but the results were not what she expected. For one thing, she turned out to have little talent for combat. She was trained to draw out her elemental powers, but she was never any good with them in the combat drills. She found her niche in the militia's logistics and administration divisions, cycling through a variety of duties in both.

No new threat ever came. Council Leader Lorenn had been diligent in safeguarding the city without the vanished aura and its mysterious, unspecified protection. Through years of negotiation, the surface entrances to Rexion were now administered by the city, alongside some organisation from the surface. Fiorella had been assigned up there a couple of times, finding the open sky unsettling, but also fascinating.

Although she was no slacker, Fiorella's favourite duty remained watching the portal chamber. It was a room that looked to be made of sand-coloured brick and no decorations. At one end, by the door, was a desk with a very comfortable chair. At the other was the portal itself: a white stone archway. It was closed by the time Fiorella signed on, but she had a memory of it from childhood. Swirling colours of blue, silver and gold. Pretty, but unnerving.

Now, Fiorella's work roster left her periodically assigned to watch that very portal. It stayed closed, nothing ever happening. Napping wasn't strictly allowed, but more than one superior officer had quietly mentioned that alternating good naps with good books was an acceptable way to pass the time. The large reclining chair behind the desk was not as comfortable as it was by accident.

Fiorella hadn't been on duty when the portal had opened again a little over a week ago. There had been a big hubbub at first, a group of combat militia replacing the one administrator in watching the portal. That hadn't lasted long. Council Leader Lorenn had gone into the portal with a few of the city's elite veterans, returning quickly and removing the troops on her return. The role of watching the portal fell once more to administration and Fiorella was placed back on the roster.

It had been exciting for the first couple of days, despite the inactivity. She'd been briefed on all the people who might come out, and the ones who would inevitably visit from the surface. A device was set up in the corner so the sky network tablets would work through the portal. It looked like a lamp.

After being assigned, she sat behind the desk, imagining all the exciting things she might witness. The people who were likely to come through in either direction were apparently all famous up on the surface. Some of the names in that briefing list she'd heard in stories told by the older militia members. Stories she'd always thought were fanciful, but now she would get to see these people and judge for herself.

Two days into staring at the portal while almost nothing happened, the novelty had worn off. No one had arrived to go in, and one person had come out. When a priest of the Healer named Carlos Quilido emerged, she was bursting with questions. After one look at his stormy face, her questions died on her lips. He shoved a bundle of letters into her hands and went back without a word. If not for the briefings, she wouldn't have even known his name.

The only real difference after the portal opened was the silver, blue and gold light filling the once-empty arch. The colours weren't especially bright, but they did swirl around a lot, making it harder to nap. Not impossible, however, and Fiorella was roused from sleep by a gentle knocking on the table.

"Denny?" she asked blearily. "Is it shift change?"

"I have no idea. And my friends call me Jason."

Her eyes swam into focus as she sat up and looked at the man casually half-sitting on the table. He was a human, with a human face. It had hair on it. She wondered what a human was doing there.

Her sleepy brain finally caught up with what was happening and she almost fell bolting out of her chair.

"You're him," she said. "You are him, right? Sorry, Mr Asano, sir. That is you, right?"

She hoped the whimpering sound was only happening inside her head. This was the person they had talked about first and last in the briefing. The one who, should he emerge from the portal, meant she had to send a message to her superior and the Council Leader's office. It was supposedly his soul on the other side of the portal that people could somehow live inside of.

"Um, I need to go tell people you're here, sir. If that's alright."

"I'll make you a deal," he said. "You call me Jason instead of sir, and you can do whatever you like."

"Uh, yes, sir. Jason. Sorry."

He let out a chuckle. It was a friendly, comforting sound. With everything that had been said about him, she was expecting some intimidating patrician figure. Instead, he looked like any human she'd see at the shaft market where most of the surface people shopped.

"Sir... sorry again. Jason. Is it true that your soul is on the other side of that portal?"

"That's complicated, as you might imagine. But yes. How old are you? Early twenties? Old enough to have lived through all the trouble. You would have been a little girl when you and your people took shelter in there. I don't imagine you remember much, or clearly."

"No, sir."

He smiled and shook his head.

"What's your name?"

"Fiorella, sir."

"It's probably time you go tell someone I'm here, Fiorella."

Her eyes went wide. "Yes, sir!"

After she bolted out of the room, Shade emerged from Jason's shadow.

"Why did you ask her name when you already knew it?" the familiar asked.

"I don't want to rub it in their faces that this place is my domain. This is their home. And it creeps people out when they know you can be—and probably are—watching them at every moment."

"I don't understand why people have a problem with that."

"That's because watching people from the shadows is kind of your thing."

***

Council Leader Lorenn's office was modest. She was seated not behind her desk but on one of a pair of couches, with Jason sat opposite.

"Again, Council Leader, I'd like to express my apologies for withdrawing the protection of my aura without warning, but I was always watching. I saw your efforts to protect your people, both militarily and diplomatically. You are a good leader."

"I understand your reasons, Mr Asano. I might have had trouble believing them, had we not been through that transformation zone together. And while your aura may have gone, the infrastructure never showed the slightest indication of failure."

"Fortunately, I didn't have to take things that far for my ruse to work. Even if my identity had been eliminated, my power would have remained."

Lorenn nodded.

"I won't pretend to understand the nature of the battles you fight, Mr Asano. What I will do is apologise, in turn."

"For what?"

"After the transformation zone, I was tired. Afraid to hope and quick to doubt."

"That's nothing to apologise for, Council Leader. My tribulations are meagre things compared to what you and your people suffered, yet I handled them with not a scrap of your grace and equanimity. That you came out of that anything more than a quivering wreck is a triumph. You have nothing but my admiration."

"Thank you, although you had little time to see past the façade. We all have our scars."

Jason's shoulders loosened up, slumping a little.

"Don't we just."

"My point, Mr Asano, is that you were off and away before I even began to grapple with what you had left us. This place is a wonder. People I have met from the surface say that cloud vehicles such as yours are rare and precious things. An entire city of such construction is unheard of, even amongst the marvels of the surface world."

"The surface world has no shortage of wonders."

"I don't doubt it, but this city stands amongst the best of them. The requests to come and study it have proven that."

"Have you accepted any of those requests?"

"No. This is our city, but your power. I would not do so without your consent."

Jason nodded.

"There is a person who I have somewhat accidentally dodged for most of two decades now. They are a diamond-ranker and created my cloud flask. I think letting them study this place would be fair compensation, so long as they don't interfere with your people. Emir Bahadir will have their contact details."

"Very well. But you keep deflecting from my topic, Mr Asano. After the transformation zone, I was bone weary. For so long, I had been putting one foot in front of the other, waiting for the next disaster. Always on watch for the next problem. Once I finally accepted that we have found safety, I looked back and realised just how much we owe you. It's obvious, but I was too caught up to see it until you were gone. You are the saviour of the brighthearts."

"Many people were a part of this. Including you."

"Not everyone carried my people in their soul, or fought a god."

"If you need someone to build a statue of, Council Leader, then choose Gareth Xandier. He fought that god too, and it'll look better anyway."

"We did."

"Oh."

"Mr Asano, you sheltered us when we were lost. Not just kept our people safe but welcomed them into your very soul. Then you reclaimed our home and rebuilt it out of miracles. The ground we walk and the homes we live in are expressions of your power. This is the kind of story myths are made of."

Jason leaned back into the couch and sighed.

"Then let it fade," he said. "Myths are just old stories. Let me be that. If you're going to talk about what happened here, don't make it about me. That doesn't help anyone. Talk about the people who came from the surface to help. That's useful. Something that can build bridges. Let me be a footnote."

"Why shy away from fame? From what I can tell, you aren't short of it on the surface."

"Maybe a while back. In certain places. But there are always new stories. New heroes. It's been time enough that I can be just some guy. As much as any gold-ranker can be. If I do something a little special, that's expected of gold-rankers. I won't stand out like before."

"I'm not sure that anyone but you believes that."

"Call it a hope."

"You don't want glory?"

"I've had glory. It's an empty thing. The time it cost me with my friends and my family are among my greatest regrets."

"I feel like you deserve more."

"Fame isn't a prize, Council Leader. It's a price. Surely you know that."

Lorenn nodded contemplatively. "Yes, I suppose I do. But surely there is something we can do for you."

"Open a good sandwich shop."

7

THE POWER LOOMING OVER
US ALL

Lorenn and Jason were on opposite couches in the former's office. The setting was casual, but their discussion had the potential to shape the brightheart city for generations.

"I respect that you have done what you can to give us autonomy," Lorenn said, "but there are some issues that can only be resolved by you."

"Religious issues?"

"Yes. You are, of course, aware of much of the political situation in the city. Many diplomatic and religious issues are settled outside of your domain, however. In one of the surface shafts, a town has been dug into the sides. It was placed just beyond the area of control because it was first excavated when the transformation zone was active."

"People waited there for the zone to drop. I remember."

"Since that time, it has been massively expanded. We call it Outer Rexion now. The statue of your friend is there. The population is mostly transitory. Merchants and diplomats from the surface. Most of the churches regularly cycle through their assigned clergy, as few enjoy spending so much time underground. Only those worshipping gods such as Earth, Stone and Deep seem to like it very much."

"But their inability to situate temples in the city proper is causing issues?"

"Yes. The priests tell me that you hold dominion and the gods cannot encroach upon it with their power."

"That's correct."

Lorenn gave Jason an uneasy look.

"It's true, then. You have the power to refuse the gods?"

"It's not as contentious as you make it sound. It's true that I was mistrustful of gods when I first came to this world, but they're like anyone else. You have good ones and bad ones. I know that isn't news to you. Undeath is a complete prick, obviously, but some of the others have been kind and friendly to me."

He scowled.

"And a little thirsty," he grumblingly added.

"Thirsty? Gods drink?"

Jason let out a chuckle.

"Never mind. Tell me about the ramifications of the temples being excluded. I'm assuming there has been some resentment?"

"There has. Not from the clergy, to my surprise. Their gods have apparently explained things to them and they've been quite understanding. The resentment comes from two sides, each presenting their own challenges."

"One being external, I assume? People asking that if you're refusing access to the gods, what are you hiding? Are the dark gods taking root here, far from the light?"

"Exactly. Even if the church officials and our diplomatic contacts understand, some people will believe what they want, regardless of the truth. Anger is easy to stoke, and those who would undermine our autonomy to exploit us are not shy about doing so."

"That's not unique. I come from a whole other universe and the same thing happens."

"What do you do about it there?"

"Mostly give rich people everything they want and then claim that we didn't."

"How does that help?"

"It doesn't."

"Aren't you rich?"

"Extremely."

"So, you haven't really done anything about it, then."

He leaned forward on the couch and shook his head.

"Don't tempt me. I have this incredible urge to go back to my world and fix all the problems. I have wealth and power enough to reshape my home planet's entire civilisation."

"Then, why don't you?"

"I've been watching you for years, and you're a good leader. I am not. I have more power than any one person should, but not the knowledge, experience and wisdom to use it well. If I start instituting simple solutions to complex problems, I'll do more harm than good. But I can't just do nothing with it either. When I act, it has to be with caution. I need to rely on those with the knowledge and experience I lack. People like you. Even then, I'm going to stumble, and I won't be the one suffering from the consequences of my missteps."

He sighed.

"I don't know why you even asked me that. I'm not saying anything you don't know. You're a capable and experienced leader, where I'm just some guy who stumbled into vast cosmic power."

"That is exactly why. I lead my people, but you are the power looming over us all. Our autonomy exists only so long as you allow it. You saved my people and built our home, but you could equally bring it all down on top of us."

Jason frowned.

"I understand," he told her. "I don't like this power dynamic either. I preferred it when I could swan around, making jokes that no one understood but me. Now, I have to be careful with every word."

Lorenn nodded. "Such is the nature of leadership and the danger of power. I will confess to not liking the fate of my people being in the hands of an outsider. I find it easier to think of you as a god."

"I'm not a god."

"For practical purposes, you are. You have unassailable power. A domain upon which even gods cannot trespass. Gods that treat you more like one of them than one of us. When I think of you as a divine authority, rather than a person, your role in our lives suddenly makes sense. But, as you say, you are not a god. It comforts me that you understand your power over us is not to be used lightly."

"It doesn't comfort me. I feel like a child who ate a spirit coin and could wreck anything they touch with their carelessness. I can only try to avoid inflicting too much damage while I learn about how to use my power—and how to not use it. If you are willing, I'm hoping that you and I could speak on this topic from time to time. I could learn a lot about leadership from you."

"I am open to that."

"Thank you. Now, speaking of leadership, let's get back to specifics. I imagine there is some resentment amongst your own people at the exclusion of temples from the main city."

"Yes. We did have priests and temples in the old city. They fell defending it, shielding the rest of us as we evacuated. We honour those memories. Many would like to join those churches, but the temples are in the part of the city built for outsiders. It is an obstacle for many, and excluding the Church of Fertility is especially contentious. We were brought to the brink of extinction, and they are vital to rebuilding our population. Many consider it disrespectful to keep them at a distance."

Jason nodded.

"Now that the other claims on my spiritual attention have been completed, I can make some changes here. If I withdraw my dominion over certain parts of the city, the gods can claim them and temples may be built. Decide which temples you want built and where, and I'll make it possible."

"We'll need to negotiate with the churches."

"It's your city, so I shall leave that in your hands. Let me know when you've made your decisions."

"And if you don't like my decisions?"

"It's your city," Jason said again. "It will take more than me disagreeing with you to intervene. I'm not saying I wouldn't step in, but that would be an extreme measure. Anything that drastic is likely as repugnant to you as to me, like wanting to build a temple of Undeath."

Lorenn scowled.

"Repugnant indeed. I would like some measure of where you see the line, however. There is no escaping the fact that you are the ultimate authority here."

Jason nodded, staying silent for a moment as he thought about it.

"Here's an example," he said. "I detest slavery. That's far from a unique position when even the meagrest scrap of empathy or decency will get you there. It's a core value from the society I was raised in, and one that didn't waver for me when so many others did. Many societies on the surface use an indenture system that is little more than slavery with a coat of paint. Rife with corruption and abuse and absent of consequence. The usual exploitation of the powerless. If your ruling council wanted to institute that system here, I would argue against it, repeatedly and loudly. I would not, however, stop you. It is not for me to tell your people how to conduct themselves. To a point."

"At what point would you intervene, then?"

"If you implemented that system, it could easily devolve to a point that I can no longer tolerate the abuses. I could see myself stepping in, even knowing that doing so would have unintentional knock-on effects. If I judged that my intervention was worth the damage it would cause, I would act. But that would be a last resort, after failing to convince your leadership to shift course on their own."

Lorenn leaned back into the couch.

"I can't say I like the fact that you can come in and just change things, consequences be damned. But your reluctance to do so is more than I would expect for someone in your position."

Jason nodded. "Power and ideals are a volatile mix. I've managed to temper the latter as I've acquired the former. Hopefully to the stage where I'm not a complete disaster. I can't promise that I won't make mistakes, though. If anything, I can almost promise I will."

"I think that we are discussing worst-case scenarios here," Lorenn said. "You and I seem to share more values than we conflict upon. I don't think that we can progress any further on that at this time, so let's table that discussion and move back to practical concerns."

"Certainly. Please continue."

"There is a matter that is less urgent than temple locations, and perhaps affects you more than me."

"Oh?"

"There are priests staying in Outer Rexion."

"I would expect as much, given the temples there."

"It would be more correct to say that these are former priests. They are not here for the temples, but for you. They have been petitioning for residency in the main city. Thus far, we have refused them."

"They're here for me?"

"They came here because our city is a manifestation of your power. That isn't something we tell people, but more than enough know for it to not be called a secret."

"What is their interest in my... wait. How much do you know about these people?"

"That they claim you saved them. That they have spent two decades researching you, because you spent most of that time dead or in other dimensions."

Jason groaned and ran a hand over his face.

"I think I know who they are," he said.

"What is their interest in you?"

"Centuries ago, there was a conflict. A cult to one of the great astral beings had a schism. A faction broke away, more interested in power and politics than the ideals they claimed to still follow. Common in the history of my planet, but we don't have gods stepping in to intervene."

"Are these people from that cult?"

"No. This splinter group overstepped and ended up being hunted down by a bunch of churches. A lot of people from those churches were trapped and held in stasis for centuries. I released them around twenty years ago now, but many didn't have anyone to go back to. Some had descendants, and others went back to their churches. But some gave up on their faith after their ordeal, or weren't accepted back. Purity rejected all of them, probably because the real Purity had been replaced during their entrapment. You heard about the events surrounding the god of Purity?"

"I did."

"My guess would be that these people are former priests, looking for something to follow. I'm mysterious enough that they don't realise how bad an idea it is to pick me."

"So, they're priests of you?"

"No!"

"If I understand it correctly, this city is a temple to you."

"No— I mean, kind of, yeah. But no."

"Well, I'm going to leave them to you regardless."

"Oh, thank you. I can't wait to deal with that."

"I can have them brought to the city immediately."

"No. I'll go to them, once I have an avatar that can leave my domains. And there's one more thing we need to discuss."

"Oh?"

"The old city had an astral space. The new one does as well, but I have kept it sealed."

"Why?"

"When I formed the city, the interior of the astral space was, for some reason, outside of my control. Or, more precisely, it was too delicate. It was in an embryonic state, not reaching completion until much later. I didn't understand why until I realised it was waiting for me to complete the transformation of my realm."

"Embryonic?"

"Yes."

"Suggesting something was gestating in there. Waiting to be born."

"Yes."

"Something you aren't happy to tell me about."

"It's going to be complicated for you politically, should word get out. But this is your home and you deserve to know, so I'm going to show you."

Jason floated through the air so high, he was practically orbital. Lorenn was beside him and they were both shrouded in an orb of invisible mist. The planet below was utterly unlike Earth, equal parts beautiful and apocalyptic. Elemental forces so vast, they could be seen from space clashed upon the surface. Hurricanes crashed into supervolcanoes. Earthquakes carved canyons so massive that they became seas as tidal waves filled them. It was gorgeous, wild destruction.

"I don't even know how to understand what I'm looking at," Lorenn said. "The sheer scale of it. I lived my life in a cave system even low-rankers could travel through in a day."

"This the largest astral space I've seen. And I can see how planets might be an alarming concept to someone who had never been on the surface of one."

"Why don't things fall off the bottom?"

"Oh, I'm not getting into that. My friends will be arriving soon. Ask Travis Noble."

"The astral space in our city wasn't this large. Not even a fraction of this."

"That's one of the reasons it took so long to resolve itself. The other is the bit you aren't going to like."

"And what is that?"

The invisible sphere shot around the planet, chasing the sun. A shape crested the horizon as they moved, resolving itself into an impossibly tall tree, kilometres high.

"That is like the tree in the transformation zone," Lorenn said.

"Yes. And more will grow here, in time. This is a messenger-birthing planet, and the messengers that it births here are of the elemental type. It has been producing them for a few years now."

Lorenn wheeled on Jason.

"Elemental messengers?"

"I understand your concern," Jason said, then shook his head. "No, of course I don't understand. But I comprehend why you and your people would feel only hatred for them. The end of your civilisation began with elemental messengers. You naturally and obviously don't want them in your city, so I sealed this place away."

"You should destroy them."

"They're children, Council Leader. And they aren't the ones that destroyed your city. They aren't corrupted and mindless. I'm only showing you this place because the aperture to this realm is in your city. I don't see a reason for your people to ever interact with it, but I'm not foolish enough to assume it will never happen. I wanted you to know so you weren't blindsided should its existence ever become public."

Lorenn stared out at the planet below and the towering tree.

"I will need time to come to terms with this, Asano."

"Of course. I'll take you home."

8

THE TOPIC OF PANTS

THERE WERE TWO SHAFTS LEADING INTO THE BRIGHTHEART CITY. ONE HAD been dug upwards by elemental messengers, and that had become the main shaft. The other had been dug down by regular messengers. It was now heavily fortified, even though the messengers on the surface were gone.

In that second shaft, Jason's avatar floated in the air, at the very edge of his domain. There was a brightheart fortress on the spot and Jason was hovering in front of a wall that sealed the entire shaft. A woman appeared in front of him, just outside his area of control. She had plain, stark features, pale skin and dark hair. She wore a simple grey dress with a faded blue flower pattern.

"You want something from me," Death said.

"I do."

"Is a temple of my church in brightheart territory conditional on getting what you want?"

"No. This is one thing and that is another. Your miracle helped save them. It put to rest their fallen who had been perverted into macabre creations. If they want to worship you for that, or even simply be grateful, I won't get in the way. To do so because you refused to give back something I already traded away would be petty."

Death nodded.

"Such would be unbecoming at our level. I will return what was taken, Jason Asano, now that it cannot be used for its original purpose."

She held out her hand and a sphere appeared over it, shimmering blue, silver and gold. Jason reached out to touch it and it vanished.

"Thank you," he said.

"Thank you for stymieing Undeath. The greatest opportunity to enact his purpose in centuries was quashed because of you."

"It took a lot more than me to stop him, and he accomplished far more than I would like."

"We share this view. But we must accept that we did all we could, and celebrate that it was more than what was likely. In immortality, there are no absolutes in victory or defeat, especially over time. People live and die. Civilisations rise and fall. There will be a time when even this planet will be gone, and we gods with it, yet you will remain. You are so very young for an immortal, and some things only time can teach. But you will learn them, whether you like it or not."

"I suppose I will. Thank you, Death."

"Thank you, Jason Asano."

The pair vanished, and the brighthearts watching from inside the fortress allowed themselves to breathe again.

The creation of the prime avatar was a surprisingly unspectacular affair. The reality material taken back from Death was added to the swarm of lights in Jason's void and they coalesced into a male, human body, floating naked and hairless in the dark. Jason stood at the doorway to the void in a basic avatar, alongside his familiars.

"You should make some tweaks," Colin suggested, pointing up and down at the body. "You could change that part."

"You just pointed at the whole thing," Jason said.

"I know where I was pointing."

"You do realise you look exactly like it?"

"Yeah, but I make this look good. It's about how you inhabit the body. Gravitas. You wouldn't understand."

Jason gave his familiar a flat look.

"Don't feel bad," Colin said. "I just happen to have a primal hunger that the ladies respond to."

"Are you getting interested in women?"

"Ick, no. Wait, do I get to eat them?"

"No!"

"Then definitely not."

"Please don't go around eating women."

"You're saying that I can eat men?"

"Absolutely not."

"Okay."

"Okay?"

"I said okay," Colin insisted while Jason stared at him with suspicion.

"Colin."

"Yes?"

"You can't eat gender fluid and non-binary people either."

"Oh, come on. It's like you don't want me to eat anyone."

"You can eat monsters."

"What about people who attack us? You want me to not help in fights until I make sure they aren't on the list of things I'm not allowed to eat?"

"Look, if it comes to a fight, you can... nibble."

"Nibble?"

"Yeah. Nibble."

"So, I can eat bits of people?"

"Bad people. In a fight."

"That sounds like a double standard."

"It's about context. It's like how, in everyday life, I don't get to stab people. But in a fight, I'm allowed to stab people. So, when we get in a fight with people, that's when you're allowed to, you know... eat them a little bit."

"So, if I start a fight, I *can* eat people?"

"No starting fights. And if a fight does happen, you can only eat them *a little bit*. No fully eating people."

"Not ever?"

"Maybe if they're already dead. And they really sucked. Or it's really important you rebuild your biomass immediately."

"This is all too complicated," Colin said. "It sounds like you're making it up as you go along."

"That would be accurate, yes," Jason acknowledged.

"See, this is the problem," Colin said. "The ladies like me because I'm definitive in my actions. If I want something, I eat it."

"Please stop saying 'the ladies.'"

"One of us should," Colin said, pointing to the avatar floating in the void. "You clearly need some help, physically. Maybe reduce the chin a little."

"The chin did reduce a little."

"And there's that much left? How many rank-ups will it take before you have a normal person's face?"

"You have the same face!"

"You need to grow back that beard. Do you still have some of Jory's hair growth cream?"

"Look, I just took the template for my body and adjusted for normal gold-rank changes. It will work better as a seat for my consciousness if I don't go messing around with it. And it's more an ointment than a cream."

"Mr Asano," Shade interjected. "Could I, perchance, make a request?"

"Of course," Jason said. "What do you need?"

"For this conversation to end before all two hundred and eleven of my bodies decide to destroy themselves rather than continue listening to it."

Jason looked at Shade from under raised eyebrows.

"It might be time to get started, yeah."

Jason's basic avatar vanished. The prime avatar floated out of the void and through the doorway. As its feet touched the catwalk, it opened its eyes. Jason's consciousness settled into it, turning it from a thing into a person.

Jason felt the spiritual noise fade away as he inhabited his new avatar. For years, he'd been dealing with an awareness of every action of every person in every domain he possessed. Louder were the countless people across the cosmos connected to the System. His perception of them was sealed away, lest it destroy his mind at his current level of power, but it was a cosmos worth of muted mumbles.

His perception of his domains and the System were still accessible, should he have need of them, but they weren't pressing in on him. The prime avatar was like a quiet room in a busy house; the noise couldn't get in until he stepped outside. For the first time in a long time, Jason felt like a relatively normal person.

He held out his hands and stared at them as he flexed his fingers. When he rubbed his hands together, he smiled at the sensation.

"A real body," he said. "It's still an avatar, I know, but it doesn't feel like one."

"Fingers aren't all that," Colin said. "I went without fingers for years, and I turned out fine. Can we go eat something now?"

Jason chuckled.

"Sure, buddy. Let's go get some lunch."

"Can it be people?"

"No! We just talked about this."

"Can we be flexible? How about if I eat a crappy person?"

"What did I just say about eating people, Colin?"

"Wash them first?"

"I'm pretty sure I said don't."

"Then can we go have a fight? You said I can eat people when we're fighting."

"Mr Asano," Shade said. "Perhaps before we engage with the topic of lunch, you should engage with the topic of pants."

A spherical cloud plunged through the upper atmosphere, dropping from a space station shaped like Jason's head. Flames ignited around the cloud from the friction of their rapid passage, but the cloud was unaffected. Inside the cloud, it was cool and stable. Jason, in his new avatar body, relaxed and enjoyed the ride.

"I need to deal with the things inside my realm first," Jason told Shade. He was reclining in a cloud chair while Shade stood primly beside it. Colin and Gordon were eagerly watching the dancing orange light that filtered through the wall of the sphere.

"I would have thought you would rush outside your domain," Shade told Jason.

"I want to, and that's why I haven't. I've been in here so long that, once I leave, I'll keep finding excuses to not come back. Carlos has gone pretty stir-crazy as it is, and I should prioritise his work in any case. It can help a lot of people. Maybe even some of the vampires on Earth."

"I counsel keeping your expectations measured, Mr Asano. Even if he is successful, in developing a treatment for vampirism, it will only work on lesser vampires. Those who have had the curse forcibly inflicted upon them. That is not common on Earth. The vampires there have always been cautious when propagating their own kind. They make ghouls and blood servants rather than lesser vampires."

"I know," Jason said softly. "It's just that so many have died, or been bled out in those horrifying farms. It makes me wonder if I should have stayed and fought."

"No, Mr Asano. I can confidently say that if you had stayed, you and the vampires would have ultimately entered a race to see who could inflict the worst atrocities on the other. I have no doubt you would have won against the vampires, but it would have been the Earth that lost. Be it you or the vampire queen, the world would be ruled by a monster."

"Yeah," Jason agreed. "I guess leaving was best."

"And humanity must be allowed to resolve its own challenges."

"Do you ever get sick of being right, Shade?"

"I have made my own mistakes, Mr Asano. You just don't notice with the frequency and magnitude of your own."

Colin utterly failed to smother a laugh while Gordon's giggle was the sound of a trickling stream. Jason shook his head at the abject betrayal of his familiars.

As their descent continued, Jason pulled up his character sheet, a screen floating in front of him. Looking over his abilities, he smiled at the effects of using great astral beings to grind levels. His abilities ranged from the third to fifth level of gold rank, and for the first time, his perception power wasn't the highest, if only by a slim margin.

That position was now held by his cloak power. It was integral to the way he fought, even the way he moved. It had become a part of him, to the point of feeling exposed without it. But while he had no shame in his chuuni ways, spending all his time in a cloak made of darkness was too edgelord, even for him.

The cloak was also the opposite of incognito. Now that Jason could disguise his magic eyes as normal ones, many activities would be a lot easier. Something as simple as going into a bakery and buying a pie would be less hassle if his nebulous eyes were hidden. A void cloak that was blown by dimensional winds would undermine that significantly.

The biggest change was that he had left the identity of an outworlder behind. Originally, his character screen had listed his race as a formerly human outworlder. It now said 'nature' instead of 'race,' calling him a 'prime avatar of an astral nexus.' He wasn't sure if dropping the term 'race' meant he was now beyond mortal classification, or if the system had gotten more politically correct.

Was it an internal change, based on his nature or changing sensibilities, or something more external? Social change was slow in Pallimustus, but rapid in many parts of Earth, especially the ones Jason dealt with. Was the System reacting to changing values? He decided to put the question to Shade.

"The System is clearly tied to you, Mr Asano, but also to the cosmos at large now. As such, I am not sure anyone other than you could determine the truth. If I were to forward a hypothesis, it would be that 'race' is a term you took from games on Earth and cannot adequately represent the breadth of individuals it now needs to. As such, it has taken the broad term 'nature' to represent the nature of people across the cosmos."

"That makes sense. I've still got the six powers that used to be racial gifts. They seem a bit OP, if I'm being entirely honest."

"Mr Asano, your transcendence, incomplete as it is, has taken the form of an astral nexus. While this is not something I am aware of from experience, it seems clear that what you are a nexus of is astral kings, great astral beings, and gods. The three supreme entities of the cosmos. You may be lacking in capabilities compared to each—often significantly so—but your power reflects aspects of all three. As your prime avatar is a direct embodiment of that power, were you expecting any less?"

"That's fair, I guess."

"And you should not underestimate the abilities of others. What may seem unassuming at first may prove more powerful than you realise. Look at the abilities of Mr Standish. His gifts focus on knowledge and magic. Not overtly powerful, but in playing to his strengths, they led him down a certain path. Imagine if he had more generic abilities that did not make full use of his astounding mind. If he used special attacks instead of spells, like most humans, would he be a middle-of-the-road adventurer that no one had ever heard of, or a Magic Society official in a backwater branch? What of the knowledge he used to stop the Builder from initiating his invasion years early? Would he have spent the years of your absence devising a method to repair the link between two universes? You change worlds, Mr Asano, but so does he. Without him, you would have failed many times, and it was his inherent abilities and their evolutions that set him down that path. Just as yours do for you."

"That's definitely true. My abilities almost seem disappointing when you put it that way."

"I am disappointed in the one that allows me to turn my shadow bodies into transport. Now that it allows Colin and Gordon to alter a vehicle I create, I just know they're going add…"

The shadow creature shuddered.

"…*colours*."

9

BUTCHERY

JASON DIDN'T NEED TO FLY AROUND IN A SPHERE OR HAVE SHADE TURN into a vehicle to get around his realm. But after years of being what amounted to a disembodied spirit in landscapes that were more metaphor than reality, he was enjoying the feeling of limitation. And, as he had alerted Carlos of his approach, the priest had the chance to prepare for an event he'd been working towards for more than fifteen years.

Carlos had been conducting his research inside Jason's soul realm because here the fundamental rules of reality could be altered. Pain, damage, even death itself could be suspended. He had been using that cheat to advance his research in ways that would otherwise be illegal, unethical and lethal. But, while Jason's avatars had been helping, making those changes at his direction, there was only so much his avatars could do without Jason's direct intervention. But now, with Jason's return, the next big step could be taken.

Now that Jason was no longer distracted, he could give his full attention and focus to Carlos and his work. He let Shade glide him over the streets of Arbour as a black skimmer. The roads were collections of rocks set out in wide pathways, less surface to drive on than navigation aids for the winding routes through the tree city.

The current residents were all high-rankers who could provide their own—usually flying—transportation. For the future, large constructs of living wood were scattered throughout the city. Shaped like buses, but on legs instead of wheels, they would provide a public transportation system, not only able to navigate the roads but also climb the larger trees of the very vertical city. While inactive, as they were now, they could sink their root-legs into the ground to absorb nutrients, or climb high into the trees for more sunlight.

Shade's black skimmer was free of colour. Allowing Colin and Gordon to influence the vehicle would add defensive properties, but in Jason's astral kingdom, the greatest threat was something they could not guard against: a cranky shadow familiar.

The vehicle slowed to a stop at a large stone building, set on the ground between a trio of massive trees. A group came out to greet Jason, comprised of Carlos, Cassin Amouz and one of Jason's avatars.

Cassin Amouz had arrived within hours of Carlos giving a letter to the desk attendant in Rexion, stationed outside the portal to Jason's kingdom. A portal courier saw that the letter reached Rimaros with haste and another portal brought Cassin to Yaresh. His gold-rank speed allowed him to reach the shaft and descend with swiftness, now that it was largely safe.

Cassin was heavily invested in Carlos' research, both literally and figuratively. He had poured the considerable wealth of his family into it, in hope of saving his son. Gibson Amouz had been held in magical stasis for years, and even then might have passed away without Jason's realm turning off death itself. He had been caught midway through an elaborate corruption ritual by the inaptly named Order of Redeeming Light.

Saving Gibson was Cassin's goal, but for Carlos, it was a first step. What they learned in doing so would hopefully lead to purging other dreadful afflictions, beyond even the most powerful essence abilities. Cassin had provided every resource necessary for Carlos to save Gibson, and pledged to support his research perpetually if successful.

The avatar melted in an instant and flowed through the air as a liquid of red, black, blue and orange. Jason extended a hand and it was absorbed into his body. Absorbed with it was the knowledge and memories the avatar had acquired in more than a decade as Carlos' assistant. Jason blinked a few times as he processed everything the avatar had seen, done and learned working for Carlos.

"You've been at this for a long time, Carlos, and I see from my avatar that you wasted none of it. I'm guessing you'd be happy to not stand on ceremony and just get to it?"

Relief showed in Carlos' entire body as nervous tension left it. Rather than respond, the Healer priest turned and went inside, waving at Jason to follow. What came after was lengthy and complicated. The interior of the building had a hospital's sterility, nothing like the earthy scents and warm colours of the autumnal city outside. The operating theatre was filled with specialised tools, many developed by Carlos in the preceding years. Dominating the room was a tank where Gibson Amouz floated, upright and unconscious.

The original research assistants were long gone, replaced with a slew of compliant avatars. They didn't even have Jason's appearance, the way the one he absorbed had, let alone any of his personality. These were simple dark figures, like bland copies of Shade, but each bore a single nebulous eye on their heads. Carlos liked them because they were precise, tireless and silent.

The process of saving Gibson had more in common with surgical procedures of Earth than traditional Pallimustus ritual healing. Carlos had developed a method of causing all the tainted magic in Gibson to physically manifest, then cut it right out and off of his body.

It was grim, visceral work; Carlos, Jason and the avatars were painted in blood and gore. A gold-ranker might have survived the process, but only Jason eliminating the concept of death and pain allowed Gibson to make it through. Finally, the corrupting magic was excised and Carlos used more traditional magic to restore the boy's savaged body.

Cassin Amouz watched the entire process, hour after hour, with unflinching resolution. When all was done, Carlos ran every test he could to determine Gibson's condition. Declaring there was nothing left but to wait for Gibson to awaken, Carlos led Jason out, leaving Cassin with his son in a recovery room.

Carlos and Jason staggered, exhausted, into crystal wash showers. They had burned through and recovered astounding amounts of mana over seven hours of intense ritual magic and painstaking pseudo-surgery. Elaborate sigils carved into flesh with painstaking precision. Mana carefully channelled through devices designed and built by Carlos himself in his research.

They stumbled out of the building in fresh clothes and fell onto a wooden bench in front of the stone building. They took in the evening air, cool, fresh and earthy. Even Jason's prime avatar was strained by a sequence of interlocking rituals more intense and extended than anything he had done before. He did recover much faster than Carlos, however, drawing on the power of his kingdom.

"This is just the beginning," Carlos declared with weary satisfaction.

"I hope you learn a lot from this," Jason told him.

"I believe I will," Carlos said. "I had every measuring tool that could even potentially be useful in there, and a few I invented myself. But there is a long way to go. The next step is refining the procedure. This crude butchery that relies on the local god to alter reality is an unsustainable approach."

"I'm not a god, Carlos."

"You suppressed the very concept of death."

"At most, I'll accept god-adjacent."

Carlos turned to look at Jason. "You haven't noticed, have you?"

"Noticed what?"

"How long have you been wearing that special avatar of yours?"

"Well, that took about seven hours, so, eight or nine hours."

"I've worked with your avatars for a long time now, Jason. They are a bland lot, for the most part, but I've become familiar with the linguistic quirks they've inherited from you. The way your translation power handles turning your language into mine. This new avatar isn't speaking my language."

"It's not?" Jason said, listening to his own voice. He'd become so used to his mouth using myriad languages, it had become background noise. When he concentrated now, what he heard was English.

"You're speaking a language that my mind says is mine, but isn't. I have enough control over my perception to recognise that it's not my mind understanding you, but my soul. This is how gods sound."

"That's not good. I can mask my eyes now, so it's easier to buy pies, but now you're telling me voice is all weird?"

"It's not that it sounds different. If anything, you sound more natural than ever. I suspect that people are going to hear their own language from you, whatever language you use."

"Like when gods speak to people."

"Exactly. It's like there's a power infused into your words. Not aura, exactly, but something similar. I'm not sure how to describe—"

"Authority," Jason interjected. "I suspect the word you're looking for is authority."

"Yes," Carlos said, nodding. "That's the word."

Jason shook his head.

"That might be a problem," he said. "I'll have to see what I can do about suppressing it, but it's one more thing on the list at this stage. Training never stops, does it?"

"Not if you're doing it right," Carlos said with a chuckle. The apparent success of his procedure after so many years of build-up had transformed the tense man into a languid puddle.

"What now for you?" Jason asked. "Refining the procedure, obviously, but what's the next practical step?"

"Assessing young Gibson. Getting as much information as I can from him. I need to monitor his recovery closely and make sure it's complete. As for the procedure, I have two goals. One is removing the reliance on you, and the other is having the procedure work on the fully converted, not just someone halfway through the process of corruption."

"How long until you're confident of working on someone fully affected by the Order of Redeeming Light's ritual?"

"You're thinking of Miss Wexler's mother?"

"All of them. While those we know matter to us, we have to keep sight of the wider implications. The greater good we can accomplish."

"I am glad you're not short-sighted in this. While my goal is to escape reliance on your soul realm, it remains a valuable asset in the short term."

"You should know that I will be taking my astral kingdom away in a little while. I'll be returning to my homeworld for a time, and I will need my prime avatar to open doorways to it."

"That wasn't an issue before."

"The rules are different now. Very different. The portals I established before were to a hazy half-reality. This place is only a pocket universe, but it is a universe, complete and whole."

"That is unfortunate."

"Possibly not. Much of what we did today was reminiscent of how medicine works on Earth, where I come from. I don't imagine there will be a lot of direct crossover, but there might be a lot for you to learn there."

"You would take me?"

"I intend to take a lot of people. Seeing an entire other universe is a rare opportunity, perhaps especcially so for you. My world has an entirely different medical paradigm, not to mention a very large number of vampires. Your ultimate goal is a cure for vampirism, is it not?"

"Lesser vampirism, yes. Those who have accepted it into their souls are beyond any intervention."

"I have some things to settle here, before I set out. But you can work on the other victims here while we travel. How long will it take for you to consider using this process on those fully affected by the Order of Redeeming Light's influence?"

"I can do it soon, if they're willing to accept a butcher job like this one. I want to use those procedures to make the process less aggressive."

"And therefore survivable outside my kingdom."

"Precisely. How long that takes depends on how much we get from today's results. We need to see how Gibson progresses over the next few weeks. I've been preparing for this for a long time, and I won't squander this opportunity by rushing things now."

"Let's try and get the Redeeming Light victims sorted out first, then. I have some things to do before I head for Earth, so you'll have time to assess Gibson and decide if you want to join me. I genuinely think there are things for you to learn there and you've been working for so long, with so much focus. You could stand to clear your head."

Carlos stood up and paced a little, running a hand through his hair.

"Arabelle keeps telling me the same thing," he said.

"And she's right. But I recognise how important this work is. I want you to know how much I admire what you're doing, and why you're doing it. I've saved quite a lot of lives as an adventurer, but I'm famously the guy with the evil powers. I have one cleansing power, and even that kills my enemies. The only solutions I have to offer come in the form of violence and horror. You're doing something that will help people heal from some of the worst things that can be done to a person."

"I'm a priest of the Healer. It's my duty."

"Duty will take you far, Carlos, but this is well past that. I know you've been through some things. I don't know what they are, but I'm sure they're a part of what has made you so driven. That doesn't change the fact that you are doing something amazing here. Something good."

"Good enough that you'd put a temple of the Healer in the brightheart city? Even before the portal shut, I wasn't going to church very often. It was too far away for me to leave the work that long."

"Actually, Carlos, that's already in the works. If it's been a while, you might want to go say g'day to your god, though. He might think you've ghosted him."

"My god does not think I've abandoned him."

"I don't know, mate. Someone doesn't hear from you in a while, they start to worry. Get insecure. Did something happen to Carlos? Is he alright? Has he been hanging out with other gods? I knew I saw him looking at the temple of Lust, and he says he wasn't, but I know what—"

"With all due respect, Mr Asano, please go away."

"Fair enough."

JUST SOME GUY

As he walked the short distance between Carlos' research centre and the portal leading out of the astral kingdom, Jason contemplated what Carlos had said about how he sounded when he spoke. He drew up his character sheet and looked over the 'inherent gifts' his prime avatar possessed, replacing his old outworlder abilities.

Inherent Gifts

- [Prime Avatar]
- [Numen]
- [System Administrator]
- [Sacred Phoenix]
- [Relics of the King]
- [Palanquin]

It would take time to fully explore these new abilities, but they were easy enough to categorise. He'd lost very little, with most of his old capabilities consolidated into his new ones, with extra powers on top. It was certainly enough to make up for the first of his new abilities doing almost nothing, from a practical perspective.

Prime Avatar was little more than the ability to have a prime avatar, offering neither combat nor utility powers. It was possibly his most important ability long term, however. The prime avatar would allow him to advance the aspect of his power that was still mortal and ultimately achieve full transcendence.

The Sacred Phoenix ability combined powers previously gained from the World-Phoenix and the Death goddess. Palanquin was the closest to one of his old abilities, allowing Shade to take on travel forms and his other familiars to modify them.

The three remaining gifts each seemed related to a different kind of transcendent entity. System Administrator, unsurprisingly, represented Jason's relation to the System now affecting essence-users across the cosmos. His role in that was akin to that of a great astral being, but most of his control was sealed away until he reached full transcendence. Until then, he would have to settle for his prime avatar having a suite of System-related abilities.

Relics of the King allowed him to tap into his soul forge, astral throne and astral gate. His prime avatar couldn't draw on them as powerfully as his previous mortal body could, but it would suffer little to no backlash for doing so. He would no longer be wrecking himself for months after using them.

The last inherent gift, Numen, was an overtly divine power, and the one Jason focused on.

> **[Numen]:** Your transcendent power has aspects of divinity that are imbued into the avatar that is the mortal embodiment of your will and power. Your avatar can express that power in ways that reflect your hegemonic and defiant nature. Traits and abilities your avatar inherits include: establishing spiritual domains; Akashic Speech; stripping and transforming remnant magic from magic entities you have killed or destroyed; being immune to rank suppression as well as detection, tracking and assessment magic; negating aura-related abilities by fully suppressing the aura of the ability's user.

Shade emerged from Jason's shadow to float alongside him as he walked, looking at the system window holding Jason's attention.

"Priest Quilido is right, Mr Asano. That your power is partially divine in nature is not a question but a fact."

Jason focused on the Akashic Speech aspect of the ability.

Help: [Akashic Speech]

Akashic Speech taps into the fundamental interconnectedness of all things in the cosmos to communicate in a way that is intrinsically understood by all things capable of communication. Despite the term 'speech,' this ability impacts all forms of communication, and is perceived by all entities in the form most natural to them. Full use of this ability is only capable by transcendent entities. Mortal limitations limit the effectiveness of this capability.

"Mortal limitations limit the effectiveness of this capability," Jason read. "Limit it by how much, do you think?"

"I imagine that any entity capable of something you would recognise as language would be covered, Mr Asano. Even extreme cases, such as communicating through telepathy, scent or colour coding, so long as the mentality behind it at least vaguely operates as a language. I suspect only that which is wholly alien to you, not just in method but in mentality, will fall outside of that ability."

"So, it's basically a new version of my old translation power, bundled up with some of my other abilities and given a god polish. Collecting up my old abilities and giving me more seems a bit cheaty, even if the Prime Avatar ability is a dud, power-wise."

"We have discussed this already, Mr Asano. Even simple powers can have formidable results."

"I know. How much do you think that adding some god sprinkles to my powers will stand out? Do you think I can suppress it?"

"I think it will largely go unnoticed, Mr Asano. Your voice and your aura will be the most evident, so the effects on those will be what you need to suppress. I am afraid, however, that anyone sufficiently powerful or attentive will notice, unless you completely retract your aura and don't speak. As the former is not practical, and the latter isn't possible, I'm afraid that anonymity will be difficult. On the positive side, that's not much of a change."

"What is that supposed to mean?"

"Mr Asano, the Adventure Society crafted an entire new identity for you and you immediately revealed it to almost everyone you met."

"There were extenuating circumstances."

"Such as not being bothered to try very hard?"

"I didn't say they were good circumstances, just extenuating ones. Look, I'll probably be able to suppress the god taint to a degree, right?"

"Taint, Mr Asano?"

"I can't let myself treat being a bit goddy as a good thing. Next thing you know, I'll have eighteen wives and a gun stockpile in my wilderness compound. Rick Geller probably thinks I already do."

"I will refrain from dignifying that. As for the question of suppression, the aura aspect will be easier to mask. You are well trained in that regard. Hiding the way you speak will be harder. Although people will hear your words in their native language, it is possible for those with strong control over their perception to recognise that you are actually using the old language."

"The old language?"

"It has many names. The divine tongue. The words of creation. You have been using it for years. The name of your sword is engraved on its blade in that language. Your Mark of Sin ability burns the ideograph for 'sin' into people in that language. I suspect using that language is a key aspect of the ability."

"You didn't think to mention that I was talking in some ancient god language?"

"I had assumed it was an aspect of your previous translation power. That ability allowed you speak in the languages of those around you, and you have been speaking primarily to great astral beings. It also happens to be my native language."

"I suppose your dad is a great astral being. This speech power is going to make it hard to be a face in the crowd, even if people do hear it as if I'm talking in their native tongue."

"Yes. With your old power, you were actually speaking the languages, so you could only use one at a time. Now everyone will hear you in their own language. If people notice that different members of a group are perceiving the same words in different languages, that will certainly stand out. The only solution I can see, Mr Asano, would be to start learning languages and not use the Akashic Speech. I think, however, it may be time to embrace that you are not, as you said, 'a face in the crowd.' I suspect that more of your nature will be evident once you leave your own realm, suppressed aura or not."

"Why do you say that?"

"Your prime avatar is something akin to a hole in the universe. A channel between this realm, which is your true self, and that body. An ambassador, if you will, of a place without limits. Here, in your astral kingdom, your avatar belongs. Once it enters a normal universe, it will be a living expression of infinite and alien power. A gate to something beyond mortal constraint. To most, it might seem like the normal presence of a high-ranker. And I imagine you will be able to mask your presence through aura manipulation, as before. But to anyone paying attention, there will always be indicators."

Jason sighed.

"I liked being just some guy. And I know that I haven't really been that in a long time, but it's about more than just what I am or what I'm caught up in."

He tapped his forehead.

"Up here, I've always been some guy, caught up in crazy cosmic forces. I know that, at this point, I am the crazy cosmic forces, but I don't want to let go of that part of myself. It feels like that sense of being an ordinary bloke is all that's keeping me grounded to what I was. If I let that go, however much of a fiction it is now, I don't know what I'll become."

"As someone who has lived for an extremely long time, Mr Asano, I have some bad news: change is inevitable. You will not be the man you are now in a million years. In a billion. The key is to not think in millions of years. That is how great astral beings think, and they need mortals to do their short-term thinking for them. Your ability to inhabit a moment is your strength. It's why the World-Phoenix sent Dawn to you. It's how you won the battle for the Cosmic Throne. Trust yourself, Mr Asano, and those of us who stand beside you."

"Thank you, Shade."

"Of course, Mr Asano. It is best that we had this talk now, before you take your prime avatar outside."

Jason looked ahead to the portal they had almost reached, standing in a clearing.

"This is going to be a whole thing, isn't it?"

"You may be forgetting, Mr Asano, but it always is."

The crowd of people was skittish, ragged and malnourished. They looked around, hunched and twitchy as if expecting an attack. Nigel watched, frowning at their condition as Asano clan members led them off, accompanied by the rest of Nigel's team. Nigel himself walked in another direction, alongside Rufus.

"Every time we liberate one of those damn blood farms," Nigel said, "the condition we find people in still gets to me."

"Thank you for helping us with this one," Rufus said.

The Asano clan had inherited what remained of the military infrastructure left behind when the bases in their territory were abandoned. Much of it had been destroyed during the vampires' tenure, but what remained included a number of intact or salvageable vehicles. The blood farm victims had been brought to the clan in military trucks and would be housed in military dormitories for the immediacy. The dorms were cloud constructs, so more luxurious than they seemed at a glance.

Nigel's team and the clan members moved the blood farm victims while Nigel and Rufus headed for a more modest vehicle that would return them to the city.

"How many farms were left running while the Asanos were hiding in their magic hole?" Nigel asked bitterly.

"It was an unfortunate necessity," Rufus said.

"Necessary for what? What is worth all the suffering we could have stopped?"

"A battle on a scale you and I could never fully comprehend. Stakes that span not just this universe but countless others, on a time scale of trillions of years. If you want more details, ask Jason when you see him next."

"He always used to talk about saving the world. I was never clear on what from, and now you're saying he's moved on to saving the universe?"

"This world almost broke apart like a biscuit in a cup of coffee. He stopped that from happening. Barely. As for his latest battle, again, ask him yourself. He'll explain or not."

They reached an open-top military Jeep that looked like it was from the eighties.

"They weren't using vehicles like this at the military bases," Nigel pointed out.

"This one was created by the domain," Rufus said. "It's made of clouds."

Nigel looked it over warily as he climbed into the passenger seat. Despite looking like old, cracked leather, it felt impossibly plush. Rufus smiled at his startled expression and started up the vehicle. The military base was set away from the city proper, but not too far. It would only be a short drive through the countryside.

"You sound critical for someone who says he's looking to join our clan," Rufus observed.

"I'm not looking to join anything until I know what I'm leading my people into," Nigel said. "The good and the bad. Then we can decide if we want in, and they can decide if they want us."

"I can respect that," Rufus said. "I can tell you a little about how the clan works, if you want to hear it."

"I'd appreciate that."

"The first thing you should know is that we don't work with traditional money. The coin of the realm here is either spirit coins or, more commonly, clan contribution points. You can exchange either for regular money at the clan exchange, along with most other luxuries."

"Luxuries? What about the basics? You've been isolated for years."

"We're self-sustaining for the basics. The astral spaces provide plenty of food and water. We have some sizeable farms in there now. As for infrastructure, the land itself provides. Every clan member gets a home, and it's all made of clouds. It adapts to your needs. You can even just ask it and it'll change."

"Tell me more about those clan contribution points."

"Everyone gets what they need in terms of food, lodging and other basic needs. Free public transport, free healing. Simple clothes. No one has to wonder where they'll sleep that night, or where their next meal is coming from. But it's all basic. The fundamentals of living a life. Anything more requires contribution points. A nicer home. Nicer clothes. A jet ski. Going out to a restaurant."

"And how do you get these points? Fighting monsters?"

"If you like. And you're qualified. But points are easy to earn. Maybe you're the one who makes those nicer clothes, or works in that restaurant. Training, too. We have a school for ritual magic. A training centre for those who do want to fight monsters. All the essence-users have to go through a basic program there. Children accrue points for their families by attending school. Enough that they can afford essences when they're old enough to use them."

"You sell essences for these points?"

"We do. Jason left us a significant supply, and we collect more in the astral spaces."

"How expensive are they?"

"The costs for the common ones we collect ourselves are minimal. The high-rarity ones that Jason left behind, that don't manifest in the territories here, are the most expensive."

"How many of the clan members are essence-users?"

"Almost all. Basic essences are inexpensive enough, and there are many excellent yet affordable combinations. A few people hold out, saving up for more expensive essences. Some don't like the idea of changing themselves with magic and avoid essences altogether, but they are very much a minority."

"Health, long life and no longer needing the bathroom are strong motivators."

"Indeed they are. Still, some refuse, whatever you tell them. Especially now that the combinations are becoming less reliable."

Nigel paused his questions as the car reached the outer limits of the city proper. He couldn't help but think back to blood raining from the sky as the streets filled with screams of inhuman torment. He shook his head, throwing off the memories.

"Less reliable?" he asked.

"The previously fixed essence combinations are starting to add variety to the confluence essences they produce. The same combinations no longer get the same result every time. It's been escalating here for a while. Haven't people noticed in the wider world yet?"

"Maybe. My connections aren't what they were."

"But you do have them. Someone sent you here."

"Anna Tilden. You know her, right?"

"We've met."

"I need to settle up with her. We came here for a job, and it's only right we finish it before we look at joining your clan. Assuming you'll have us."

"That's up to the Matriarch. And it's not my clan, as such. I'm more of an honorary member. Formally joining would complicate things with my family back home. Our position is complicated."

"Does an honorary member get contribution points?"

"Yes, if services are rendered. Your participation in the blood farm liberation will earn you and your team some as well. If you don't end up joining the clan, I would suggest exchanging them for spirit coins or Earth currency."

"You can trade points for money?"

"Yes."

"Not all of my members are completely sold on my plan of joining the clan, but I think you just turned a couple of them around."

11

ON A WHIM

Jason stood in front of the portal. He took a long breath and let it out slowly.

"Here we go."

He stepped through and emerged in the portal room of Rexion, which had changed quickly in his absence. Previously empty but for one desk staffed by a bored attendant, it was now a combination greeting room and administrative centre. A path ran through the room from the portal to the door, with a half dozen staff now stationed to either side.

In the middle of the room was Marla. The leader of the brightheart military was an arresting visage, with hair and eyes glowing like molten steel. She was no delicate beauty, however, but had a powerful warrior's physique. As the others in the room gawped at Jason, her eyes only widened a little before she schooled her expression back to neutrality.

"You've got quite the presence, Mr Asano. Did you eat that mountain shaped like your head?"

Jason chuckled as a smile teased at Marla's lips. He'd never seen her make a joke before, and for good reason. In the time they'd known each other, they had been fighting for the survival of what was left of her people, in the ashes of their home. Seeing the lightness she had now made him smile. It was a good reminder that the struggles they went through had been worth it.

"I didn't eat it," he said. "Not exactly. What warrants a reception from someone as important as yourself?"

"No offence, Mr Asano, but when you show up, it usually leads to things that our administrative staff need to pass up the line."

"Fair enough. But I have no business with Rexion today, other than finally moving beyond its borders. When your ruling council is done negotiating with the churches, I'll come along and deal with it. Just ask when you're ready."

"Ask who? Will you be leaving a representative? Lorenn thought that might be a good idea."

"Unnecessary. You don't need to ask anyone; you just have to ask. I'll know."

"That's a little disconcerting."

"Give it some thought," Jason told her. "Then you'll realise it's a lot disconcerting."

He looked around at the staff, who were still staring at him like he had three heads. If it was this bad in his domain, it would be worse once he left it, so he concentrated on retracting his presence. It was similar to doing so with his aura, both being expressions of his soul's power. He saw the result in the faces around him as they became less slack-jawed and pulled themselves together.

"Better?" he asked.

"Better," Marla confirmed.

"This may be more of a problem than I anticipated. Before I'm out and about for the day, I could use somewhere quiet to practise keeping it under wraps."

"I can arrange that. Fiorella?"

After getting no response, she turned to look at one of the staff.

"*Fiorella?*"

"Yes, Commander!" the young woman said, shooting up from her chair. She shook her head and blinked rapidly while standing at military attention.

"See Mr Asano to Ambassador Suite Seven. I believe that one is empty."

Fiorella watched Asano float, cross-legged, in the middle of the room. It had been a well-appointed luxury suite when they arrived, but dissolved into cloud-stuff the moment they entered. It turned into a plain white room, empty but for a luxurious armchair for Fiorella. Asano had said nothing and immediately floated up to meditate in the middle of the room. She had waited and watched as his arresting presence slowly diminished.

When he'd first emerged from the portal, it was like a bomb went off. The world wasn't literally bending around him, but it had felt like it was. He stood out like someone standing in front of a painted background instead of a real one. It was almost dizzying to look at, and distracting enough that she embarrassed herself in front of the commander.

She had led Asano to the main diplomatic building, where visiting dignitaries were housed and could hold meetings. As they walked, she was building up the courage to ask a question when he spoke first.

"It's good to see you again," Asano told her. "Sorry if I was a little more startling, this time."

"You're always startling," she said, immediately closing her eyes in a blushing wince.

He let out a good-natured chuckle.

"Why are you so different?" she asked.

"When I'm out and about like this, I'm using avatars. Puppet bodies. This one holds more of my power than the others, and it tends to leak. I need to practise keeping it under control."

She sat and watched him do exactly that for several hours. When he roused, the room swirled and returned to its original state of well-furnished luxury. He grabbed fruit from a bowl on a side table and fell into a chair, looking casual and relaxed. She felt just the opposite, her whole body tense as a tightly clenched fist.

He chatted companionably, asking her questions about the city, the militia and her life living in both. She barely remembered her answers, her mind filled with his alien eyes that seemed to look right through her. He seemed genuinely interested, which surprised her.

By the time he was done, he seemed much as he had in their previous encounter: imposing and powerful, but no more so than any other high-ranker. There was still something there, though, that seemed a little off. Something about the way he spoke, like it was reaching into her mind without passing through her ears first. Looking at him, really looking, there was something about him she couldn't place. If she wasn't staring right at him, she doubted she would notice. Then she realised she was staring right at him, in complete silence. He laughed as she felt her face burn with embarrassment.

"How is it?" he asked. "Do you think I can walk around without attracting too much attention?"

"I don't think so, Mr Asano."

"I told you to call me Jason."

"People tell me a lot of things, Mr Asano. I'm not always the best at following orders."

He laughed again, something she was finding he did a lot. It was a little unnerving, like watching a war golem fold laundry.

"Thank you, Fiorella. I think I'm just about ready to get out and about. Thank you for keeping me company."

He stood up and she did the same.

"I can escort you to—"

"I know the way. It was nice seeing you again."

He walked through the wall like it was an illusion. Fiorella walked over and ran her hand over it, finding it completely solid.

Whether visiting or leaving, moving in or out of Rexion was for high-ranking individuals. A massive shaft was the way into and out of the brightheart city, and there were neither elevators nor stairs. It was wide enough that many flying vehicles could move up and down at once, and a handful belonged to the Rexion Transport Authority. Those mostly gathered dust, however. Anyone who could not arrange their own passage was strongly advised to stay where they were.

Traffic in and out of the city went through a transport authority customs station in the cavernous tunnel leading to the shaft. Jason tested his ability to blend in by joining the queue for exit inspection. The people around him were mostly silver, but he spotted a few golds and some bold bronze-rankers. He got a few odd looks, especially from the other golds, but gold-rankers always paid attention to one another. To his satisfaction, there was nothing more to it than that.

The transport authority staff were silver-rank brighthearts. Anything less, and the high-rankers moving through customs would start pushing around their weight. From what Jason saw, the gold-rankers comported themselves with decorum, not deigning to make an issue of their power.

On the surface, gold-rankers would normally get their own priority access for something like this, if they were subject to it at all. The transit station was still inside Jason's domain, however. Stories still made the rounds about what happened to troublemakers in the early days, and now rumours did much of their work for them.

Reaching the front of his line without incident, Jason encountered an attendant in a security booth of magically reinforced glass. The attendant had silver hair and eyes, like Sophie, denoting a metal-aspect brightheart. She looked slightly bored but alert.

"Documentation, please."

"I'm sorry, but I don't have any."

Her boredom was instantly replaced with professional wariness.

"What happened to it?" she asked.

"I never got any."

"How did you get into the city without paperwork?"

"I, uh, built it."

"You built your paperwork?"

"No, I built the city."

"Who do you think you are, Jason Asano?"

"Yes."

She sighed. "Sir, please step out of the line and join that queue where they establish your—"

"Bernice," Jason said. "Look at me. Really look."

She did, with a look of suspicion.

"How do you know my name?"

"I know more than your name, Bernice. I've known you for most of your life. When you snuck off to swim in the kelp fields in the water chambers. I knew you when Giram asked you to marry him. When you cried alone upon finding out you weren't pregnant, then cried with your husband when you finally were. He's bit of a blubberer, that husband of yours."

"I don't know what game you're—"

"Look at me, Bernice."

"You are not going to—"

Look at me.

Bernice's eyes went wide and Jason gave her an apologetic smile.

"Sorry to be forceful," he said. "I probably should have just skipped the line, but I wanted to check something. Were you warned I might be coming?"

She gave a jerking, nervous nod.

"We were all talking about it, but we didn't think…"

Jason chuckled.

"Not everyone thought I was real."

"No."

Jason held out his thumb and forefinger and created a gold spirit coin between them. He imprinted his aura on it and tossed it to Bernice, who almost dropped it.

"Now," Jason told her, "you have something to show Herk next time he runs his mouth in the break room."

Bernice stared at the coin sitting in her hand, as if unsure it was real.

"Can I go, then?" Jason asked. "I don't want to hold up the line."

Bernice shook her head, as if waking up from a trance. She looked at the line behind Jason, who didn't seem to have noticed her borderline-religious experience.

"Uh, no," she said.

"What?"

"I mean, a magic coin is great and all, but if I start letting people through with something like that, I'm going to get fired. If you don't have papers, you need to join that queue back there and get new ones."

Jason turned and looked at the slow-moving queue.

"Seriously?"

She shrugged apologetically.

"Unless you want to force your way past," she said. "If you're really who you say you are, that shouldn't be hard."

Jason let out a groan.

"It was nice meeting you, Bernice."

He left the line and trudged over to the other queue. He could have easily circumvented the whole process, either with magic or by calling in a high-ranking bureaucrat. That would only cause problems for Bernice, however. He chided himself on getting other people caught up in things he did on a whim.

———

"And what did she do?" Marla asked as Fiorella gave her report.

"She made him go get his papers because he didn't have any."

"How did she do that?"

"By telling him to, so far as I can tell."

"And he did it?"

"It would seem so, Commander. He didn't jump the queue either. Waited more than half an hour."

"Anyone other than…" Marla picked up the personnel file on her desk and looked it over again. "…Bernice notice anything about him?"

"No, Commander. From what I was able to tell, he stood out no more than any other gold-ranker."

"He adapts fast," Marla mused.

"Isn't that a good thing?" Fiorella asked. "Isn't that why we're all in this city instead of the ruins of the one that used to stand here?"

"Yes," Marla said. "But there's danger in someone with the power of a god and the thinking of mortal."

"Does he really have the power of a god?"

"In this city, he does."

She once more glanced over the file in her hands.

"Get me some more information on this Bernice. If she can handle Asano, I think she might be wasted where she is. Let's look into getting her a promotion."

The difficulties in navigating the shaft reinforced that this was not a place for low-rankers. There was no illumination attached to the shaft itself, although the heavy traffic was a stream of lights moving up and down. Jason reflected that it looked like a busy highway at night. Most of the traffic was made up of flying trade barges, but there was no shortage of multi-person skimmers and personal transport devices, all shedding light of various colours. Some people, like Jason himself, simply flew without visible aid.

Jason wanted to pause as he reached the threshold of his domain's power, but it would have held up traffic. As such, his first departure from his domain in years was an unceremonious thing. His power was harder to hide once he left, drawing a few nearby gazes, but he quickly got it under control. He wasn't the only one to demonstrate an unsettled aura passing in or out of his domain, so he didn't stand out too much.

It was just outside of his domain that Jason found the border town that had built up at the outskirts of Rexion, dug into the walls of the shaft. It was managed by the brighthearts but had a mostly transient population of surface dwellers. It had begun as a small outpost, founded back in the transformation zone months. Now, years later, it was a massive town circling the shaft.

Nothing was left of the original uncut walls. The natural stone had been carved out, leaving something like a subterranean Las Vegas ringed around the shaft. Magical signs and decorations washed everything in a mishmash of cyberpunk neon. A few establishments ran right up to the edge with massive viewing windows, but most of the space near the shaft was taken up by entertainment and shopping plazas. A few tunnels led deeper into the town, away from prime shaft-side areas too expensive for warehousing.

The landing platforms were differentiated by usage. Large ones led to access tunnels that could accommodate the trade barges. Smaller ones fed visitors into the plazas lined with taverns, shops and gambling halls. Jason overheard someone call the area The Ring.

Jason grinned as he floated towards a landing platform for individual travellers. In his domains, he saw everything. He didn't consciously process it, but if he wanted to watch something that happened in some corner of Rexion seven years ago, the memory danced up from the back of his mind. But this place was outside of his domain, offering all new experiences to explore.

As he walked through the plaza with people bustling around him, he extended his senses through the town. He was gentle and delicate, to the point that most gold-rankers wouldn't notice, and various places in the town were shielded against such perception. Not enough to stop a gold-ranker, but enough that it would be rude and obvious if he pushed through to take a peek. He sensed a familiar aura, even though it was now gold rank instead of silver, and he headed in that direction.

MANDATORY TEAM ACTIVITY

THE SUBTERRANEAN BORDER TOWN OF OUTER REXION WAS A RING OF lights in the dark. Accommodation anywhere but the back tunnels was expensive by most standards, but gold-rank adventurers had standards all of their own. Zara Nareen entered her suite and immediately spotted something different from when she left it. Someone had been in her room, despite explicit instructions to the contrary.

It was a multi-room suite, the primary room centred on two chairs and a couch set around a low table. There was something new on the table, but she didn't concentrate on that for the moment. Distracting her could easily be the plan, setting her up for an attack from behind. Instead, she pushed her magical perception out hard, in clear disregard of propriety.

She sensed no one else in the suite. She felt the agitation of those in the nearby rooms, but they were suppressing their anger. Social norms were all well and good, but no one wanted to bang on the gold-ranker's door and tell them to stop making a magical racket.

Zara took slow steps forward, looking around. If she couldn't sense anyone, either no one was there or the person there was very dangerous. She moved to the coffee table for a closer look at what had been left on it: a plate of red and white baked squares. Her shoulders slumped as the tension left her body. She smiled at a memory from half her lifetime ago.

"All these years and you're still barging in uninvited."

"I think 'barge' is a little harsh," Jason said as he stepped out of a corner shadow that should not have been able to hide a person. He shrugged off his cloak and it dissolved into nothing.

Zara shook her head, picked up one of the baked confectionaries and delicately bit off a corner. Then she elegantly lowered herself into an armchair as Jason dropped himself into the other like a sack of potatoes.

"I'm a little surprised you're the first one here," Jason told her. "I'm also a little surprised you're still turning your hair and eyes copper."

A contrite expression crossed his face.

"I had no right to tell you what to do with your body, even if my anger was justified. I'm sorry for that."

"We both made some bad choices back then. And you would have had to make fewer of them if I hadn't dragged you into my mess."

"Those are old stories, and these are new times," Jason said. "Perhaps it's time to let all that go. And it does look good on you, although I suspect most things do."

"Are you flirting with me, Jason?"

"No, I just have eyes. Why are you still wearing a different colour?"

"The sapphire hair is iconic to the royal family. I'm still adopted into House Nareen, and it makes things easier."

"Still publicly on the outs with the royal family?"

"No. Politics is more changeable than the sea and there has been plenty of time for that to blow over. But I like being part of my mother's family, and staying there keeps me out of the worst of it. Especially since my brother became the new Storm King. And my father has become softer since retirement. I was spending time with him in Rimaros when I was sent word you were back. That's why I'm the first one here."

They sat back in their armchairs, looking one another over. Neither of them had aged in the fifteen years since they had last met. Zara knew that ranking up had changed little about her appearance, but Jason was a different story. His face had already changed a lot at silver rank, but his strange, nebulous eyes always drew the attention. Now he had the same eyes he had when they met at iron rank; dark, challenging and playful.

"Have your eyes changed back, or are they a disguise, like mine?"

"Just a disguise. How effective it will be, I'm not sure. I'm having trouble containing myself."

"You always did."

He flashed that infuriating impish grin. He was more handsome than when they'd met, yet still somewhat plain by gold-rank standards. His chin was still somehow too prominent after ranking up no less than four times. It left his face oddly out of balance, yet it suited him perfectly. He always had a way of leaving her off balance as well.

More profound than the physical changes was the way his mental state affected his physicality. Back then, he'd been twitchy, wild and energetic, as if he were hopped up on something. Like a rabbit, jumping on the spot, unsure whether to play or dash away.

Now he was still. Certain. He looked at the world as if, whatever he decided, it was the world that would have to answer. Not many people recognised that look. Most never met a diamond-ranker, let alone enough to know that they all had it. Zara was one of the few who did.

"Where did you get the ingredients?" she asked.

"The ingredients?"

"For the gem berry milk nut squares. We're so far underground that the rock around us would be molten if not for the natural array," she said. "The bronze-rankers here have to wear specialised magic items just to survive."

"I'm aware."

"And you've been down here for what? A decade and a half?"

"About that, yeah."

"So, where did you get gem berries and milk nuts to make this slice?"

She took another bite, then spoke with her mouth full, in distinctly unladylike fashion.

"It tastes exactly the same!"

"That's because it's the same batch," he told her.

She swallowed it all in a gulp, not carefully chewing as she had before.

"You fed me twenty-year-old baked goods?"

He reached for the plate. "If you don't want it..."

Jason's hand was slapped away by a concentrated burst of compressed air that didn't disturb anything else in the room. He leaned back, his grin somehow becoming even more smug.

"That was some precise wind control."

"I did do a little practise on the way to gold rank, you know. I hate to break it to you, but time moves on while you're off having cosmic adventures. The rest of us are living lives."

She barely caught the flash of sadness before he reached out for the plate again. He took a slice and stuffed half of it in his mouth, waggling his eyebrows at her. But the mask had slipped a little, and didn't quite fit anymore.

"It must be strange for you," she said. "You go off and do these amazing things. Walking between worlds. But then you come back and everything has changed on you. Missing the lives of friends. Some girl you met once that used your name, landing you in the middle of a political tangle you neither asked for nor deserved."

"Why did you?" he asked. "I never cared to ask, back then, but why me? Like you said, we only ever met a few times. I'll grant you, that first time, it was memorable, but I was no one back then."

"Do you really want me to answer that?"

"Should I?"

"No. I complicated things for you the last time you came back. I hope I've managed to learn better in all this time."

She sighed and set her half-eaten slice down on the plate before leaning back and staring at Jason.

"You know I've been working with the team in your absence."

"No you haven't."

Her eyebrows rose.

"You haven't been working with the team, Zara; you've been in it. You've spent more time working with them than I have, even with them scattering since reaching gold rank. You're as much a part of the group as I am. Maybe even more so."

Zara took a long breath and let it out slowly as she stared at Jason.

"It took me a long time to feel like I belonged," she said. "Once I did, I felt an insecurity that maybe it was just in my head. That you would come back and kick me out. I asked to join you once before, and I know the circumstances were different, but I remember how angry you were. The way you looked at me."

"I wasn't angry at you, Zara. I was just angry."

"It felt like you were angry at me."

"Yeah, well, maybe a bit."

"I don't think I ever let go of that fear, not entirely. The way things ended with my last team…"

"Do you mind if I ask about them?"

"Rosa retired. She works for the Adventure Society now. Orin is still adventuring. Hit gold rank not that long ago. He's in a team with Kasper Irios and his friends. He's—"

"The friend you invoked my name for so he didn't get stuck marrying you."

"Yes. Not my finest hour. It turns out my father was already working to… it doesn't matter. Kasper is an adventurer now, and Orin is the only one on his team to hit gold so far."

"Amos Pensinata's influence?"

"I don't know. No one's really seen him since the transformation zone. He was around for a little while, settling the affairs of Orin's team. Then he just kind of vanished. Some people say he retired, others that he's working on getting to diamond rank. He clearly wants to be left alone, so I never dug deeper."

She sighed.

"I still think about my old team a lot. I wasn't with them for all that long, but it felt like I was building a place to belong. They were a Rimaros team who trained the same way I did. We thought the same, tactically and strategically. It was different with your team."

"*Our* team."

"Our team. Thank you. They were still figuring things out when Sophie recruited me. Losing you, Taika and Rufus all at once left massive gaps in their tactical options. I felt like a stranger trying to fill three holes when I didn't fit in any of them. They didn't seem worried because the way they work is so adaptable, but that's not the way we train in Rimaros. For a long time, I thought I'd made a mistake."

"But not now."

"No. When Sophie pulled me in, I felt bereft of purpose. She told me there are worse things you can dedicate a life to than helping people. It's strange how you can dismiss an idea for seeming so simple and obvious. I'd convinced myself that I had to find something complicated and unexpected to set me on my life path. It's why I went chasing you."

"Just that?"

"I'll ask again: do you really want me to answer that?"

"No," he said. "Not today. Do you know when the others will get here?"

"Should be in the next few days. Travis will be soon, as he's still working out of Rimaros. He's been doing cloud flask research with House de Varco and that diamond-ranker who hates you. The others are farther away, mostly Vitesse. Last I heard, Neil was in the Mirror Kingdom with Nik."

Zara was startled at the smile that lit up Jason's face.

"How's my little rabbit guy doing? He must have found a team by now, right?"

"Actually, he's been working with the Adventure Society. They shop him out for expeditions that could use a communications and coordination specialist. He's in very high demand, from what I've heard."

"That diamond-ranker is going to come here, aren't they?"

"I suspect so. They didn't like you dodging them for fifteen years."

"Are you using non-binary pronouns or did this diamond-ranker split themselves into multiple people with magic?"

"Pronouns. High-ranking shape-shifters often switch around their gender. Travis introduced the concept of chosen pronouns and it's catching on amongst gold- and diamond-rankers. Apparently. I don't talk to that many diamond-rankers."

"See, this is favouritism. Knowledge wouldn't let me go around disseminating ideas from Earth."

A new voice answered. "Only ones you didn't understand for yourself. You introduced several concepts related to cooking that I did not impede at all."

Zara looked around the room and saw nothing, though she sensed a barely discernible divine aura. She looked to Jason, whose attempt at looking cranky was plainly undercut with amusement.

"Oh, look at this," he complained to the room. "I'm out of my domain five minutes and already you're eavesdropping."

"Are you saying you never used your omniscience within your domain?" Knowledge asked.

"Yeah, well… shut up."

After some disembodied laughter, the divine aura vanished. Zara stared as he shook his head in amusement, as if nothing out of the ordinary had happened.

"Does that happen often?" she asked.

"You mean gods having a chat?"

"Yes."

"I dunno. How much is often? I'm in the club now, so I imagine it'll keep happening."

"The club?"

"My membership is a bit odd. I'm not a god, obviously, but I'm not entirely… not a god either."

"You're a demigod?"

"It's more complicated than that. You want to see?"

"See what?"

He didn't move. He stayed sitting where he was, eyes locked on her. His dark eyes gave way to the orange and blue ones, but there was no other visible change. At the same time, she felt the change, and she instinctively pushed back in her chair. Like a god's aura, it was vast and connected to some distant force. It was as if he had become an unstable portal to some place of incomprehensible power.

And as suddenly as the sensation appeared, it vanished.

"What are you?" she asked breathlessly.

"Complicated. I'll save the big explanations for when we're all together. I'll probably need Clive's help explaining certain parts anyway."

"Things are going to get strange, aren't they?"

"Strange how?" Jason asked with unconvincing innocence.

"You know the Magic Society and Adventure Society are going to be all over you about this System thing."

"I'm more worried about Clive, to be honest. How excited was he when it happened?"

"It's probably best you don't know."

"That bad, huh?"

"I'm sure he won't make a big deal of it," Zara lied.

"I'd run off to the other universe without him, but I'll need him to set that up."

"The other universe. Where you're from."

"Yeah. I'll be heading over there in not too long. You're coming, right?"

"Can I?"

"Honestly, it's probably not up to you. I'm guessing Hump will make it a mandatory team activity."

13
TRY NOT TO BRING DOWN CIVILISATION

Outer Rexion had many temples, but they weren't clustered together, as was the norm. With the town itself circling a massive shaft, the temple district likewise took the form of a ring. Positioned just behind the shaft-side plazas and entertainment districts, the houses of the holy were conveniently located for post-sin repentance.

What the locals called the Worship Ring was a wide boulevard. The cavernous ceiling accommodated the often exotic architecture of the temples, lining both sides of the broad street. Around each temple were annexes, stalls and shop fronts. Ritual supplies, holy books and iconography were all available, along with more specific products.

In defiance of geology and physics, underground rivers fed the growth chambers that produced all the food and water for Rexion. Accordingly, there was a small temple to the god of rivers in Outer Rexion, abutted by the world's least successful fishing supply shop.

Jason walked around the Worship Ring, down the wide and busy boulevard. He immediately recognised how much prime real estate had been allocated to the churches. He suspected the brighthearts had been generous when expanding the original outpost, since no temples could be built in Rexion proper.

The original brightheart city had its own temples and priesthoods, devoted to the same gods the surface dwellers worshipped. Those temples were long buried and the clergy long dead. The domains of the gods had been overrun by the Undeath priesthood, following the spiritual rules of holy war. It was something Jason understood; an instinctive knowledge that came from possessing domains himself.

Domains were, ordinarily, inviolable. A god could not move in on another god's territory, but their followers could. The first step was for the mortal servants of one god to conquer the territory around the spiritual domain of another. With sufficiently thorough control of the area around the domain, they could then invade it to claim for their own god.

Just as Undeath had claimed the site of the old city, so too did Jason in resolving the transformation zone. The priests were eradicated, along with the god's power, embodied in the avatar. When Jason conquered the transformation zone, there was no one and nothing left to contest the ground.

As he made his way around the Worship Ring, he brushed against the domains of the various gods. It was a strange and complicated sensation, something between a handshake, a warning and a dating profile. He stopped in front of the temple of Hero, where a sculpture stood in the middle of the boulevard. An edifice of bronze, silver and gold, with a lot of dark iron, people had to navigate around it to continue along their way.

The sculpture depicted a leonid figure. Fierce and menacing, it radiated power. The golden mane shone faintly with light and the dark armour glowed where the plates met. Jason could feel heat radiating from it. He wasn't sure how long he stood staring as the street traffic flowed past. He was stirred from his reverie by a voice right beside him.

"He wasn't like that. Angry and violent. He could be, yes, but only when he had to. So often are we only remembered for that which we didn't want to do in the first place."

Jason turned to see a man who looked to be in his mid-forties, but his silver rank meant that the real number would be much higher.

"You met him?" Jason asked.

"I once had the privilege. Quite a few years ago, now, on the other side of the world. But I have researched him quite extensively."

"Vitesse?"

"Greenstone," the man said with a smile. "You're him, aren't you?"

Jason took a closer look at the man. He wore simple-coloured robes, like a priest of one of the more humble gods. Similar to those of the Healer, but without markings and a light sandy colour, rather than brown.

"You're one of them, aren't you?" Jason asked. "The former priests."

"We like to think of ourselves as seekers of purpose. But yes, Lord Asano. I am."

"Don't call me Lord."

"But that is what you—"

"I know what I am."

"Then what should we call you?"

"My name is Jason. If you insist on being formal, Mr Asano will do."

"Many of us are here, waiting for your return. We keep watch on this sculpture, knowing that you would come. We have been waiting for so long. For your guidance. And our purpose."

"Everyone seeks purpose. I'm not your messiah."

"Aren't you? We have studied your ways. Your nature. Your companions. You walk with gods and travel beyond reality. What was once yours alone you have gifted to every essence-user. If you are not a god walking amongst us, you are akin to one. Do you even realise how your voice resonates in my mind like a song of the heavens?"

Jason muffled a groan.

"If you want someone to worship, look around. There are literally temples in every direction. There's a reason I don't have one."

"But you do. Rexion is your temple."

"No, it isn't. It's a home for a people who were almost wiped out. It belongs to them."

"But your power—"

"Is irrelevant. You want me to be a god? If I hear about any of you proclaiming Rexion to be a temple or otherwise causing trouble for the brighthearts, then you will see my wrath."

"Please do not be angry, Lo—"

"You're not going to listen, are you? It's been almost twenty years. Even if you had nothing left when I set you free, that's enough time to build a life all over again. To find a purpose, or to make one for yourselves. I know a lot of you have. But the others like you, you've spent it waiting for me to set you on some ill-defined path. And it's not even me you're waiting for. If you've been at it this long, you've built up some idea of me and convinced yourselves it will solve all your problems. That no one else can. I've seen where that leads, on the world I come from. But I'll never be the person you're imagining. No one can be."

Jason threw out his arms, gesturing at the temples around them.

"That guidance you're looking for? That purpose? That is what gods do. If none of them can fill the hole inside you, I certainly can't."

"Gods have failed us. You walk on the ground, yet possess their divinity. Not distant and heartless. You know what it is to struggle with the rest of us."

"That doesn't make me responsible for you. I'm the guy that saved you a long time ago. I will accept your gratitude, but you're wasting the time you've gotten back. I'm not your path. You have to find your own."

"We venerate you."

"Don't."

Jason shook his head. He'd used his aura as a privacy shield, but he could sense the people watching them from a distance. More like this man. Their emotions were singular and driven. Obsessive. None of his words had put so much as a dent in the feelings of the man in front of him. He was hanging on Jason's every word yet hearing none of them.

He looked up at the sculpture of Gary, angry more than anything at being interrupted. There was no point wasting any more words on the man, so he didn't, instead vanishing into the sculpture's shadow. He emerged somewhere he really didn't want to be, but needed to.

The temple was one of the more unusual ones, a tower shaped like an arm jutting up from the ground. Clenched in the hand at the top was a head glaring imperiously down on those passing. Jason glared back up at it.

"Really?" he asked.

"It's religion," Dominion said, appearing next to Jason. "Showmanship is part of the deal."

None of the passers-by seemed to notice the god.

"I didn't handle that situation very well," Jason said.

"There isn't a good way to deal with that kind. Unless you want to kill them all."

"No."

"Then, sooner or later, there's going to be a cult."

"I think…" Jason trailed off, then let out a sigh. "I think I'm going to need some guidance. I'm not ready for what the power I have now will mean to people."

"Yeah, you're going to mess some things up. That's nothing new, but the scale you'll be doing it on is. You could do some real damage now."

"Yeah," Jason agreed, his voice resigned. "I was hoping you had some advice."

"Have you considered giant banners with your face on them?"

"That's your advice?"

"This is how you ask for it? You know you're terrible at praying, right? Rocking up to a temple and glaring at it like it owes you money."

"That's… not entirely unfair," Jason conceded.

He turned to look at Dominion standing beside him.

"Do you actually rule anything?" Jason asked.

"My clergy knows damn well to follow orders."

"But that's it, right?"

"I am not a ruler, Jason. Kings and emperors rule. Caliphs and prime ministers and greater district regional distribution managers. They rule; I am the very concept of ruling. I am not a hegemon but hegemony itself."

Jason thought on Dominion's words while looking up at the menacing temple visage.

"Showmanship is part of the deal," he said. "I was once told that you are the one that decides who rules and who serves. But that wasn't right, was it?"

"No. There is no divine right of kings. Mortals choose and I try to help them not make a *complete* mess of things."

"That former priest was right, wasn't he? I'm not just some guy. I can't be anymore."

"Not when they know who you are. But you don't have to let them. I wander around all the time and no one has a clue."

"I don't suppose you have some tips on hiding all that power? I can do it well enough when I concentrate, but it's like trying to hold in a poo. The moment things get exciting, it's going to pop out, whether I like it or not."

"I can help you with that."

Dominion casually held out a fist-sized orb. Inside, sparks of blue, silver and gold danced around one another. Jason reached out to accept it.

Item: [Projection Command: Presence] (transcendent rank, legendary)
The authority to control the presence of an expression of transcendent power. (consumable, magic core).

- Effect: Gain control over the presence of your transcendent power, denying mortals the power to perceive it.
- Uses remaining: 1/1

"Thank you," Jason said as he absorbed it into his inventory for later.

"You realise it's only a stop-gap measure. A way to hide yourself while you get a handle on interacting with the mortal world. You will need to get that under control if you don't want to be a god of chaos."

"Still not a god."

"Is there really a difference?"

"Well, someday this planet will die and you gods with it."

Dominion let out a wincing chuckle.

"That's a horrible thing to say."

"Sorry."

"Also, I know you're new to operating on a god level, but we tend to avoid the word 'poo.' It doesn't convey the dignity we're going for."

"I'll keep that in mind."

"Why did you really come here, Jason? You didn't need me to tell you that there's nothing you can do about your would-be followers. The Adventure Society is watching them, as are several churches, including mine. Even you aren't oblivious enough to not have guessed that."

"What do you mean, even me?"

"I said what I said. Why did you come to see me, Jason?"

Jason grimaced, not answering immediately.

"On Pallimustus, I'm not an outlier. This prime avatar is just gold rank. If I try going rampant, there are forces that will spank me for it. I've gotten away with a lot by being too important to someone or other to just get snuffed out, but I'm immortal now. It's easy enough to kill my avatar and give me a quarter-century time out."

"Ah. Your concern is the realm of your birth. The relative power you will have there."

"Yes. I don't know if there's anyone on Earth stronger than I am now. Boris, probably. Maybe Rufus. But that only makes it worse. It'll be me and all my friends. We could probably conquer the world for a Sunday Fun Day. Just the possibility of that is going to get people making drastic choices."

"Yes. Enough personal power makes you a political power, whether you like it or not. Every high-ranker has to learn that lesson, but you're not practising with wooden swords, are you?"

"No. And it's going to be so much worse on Earth. Here, the cultures have adapted to individuals with so much power. Over there, power has always been collective. There have always been those who concentrated that power, but there were limits. They always needed people to make it work."

"As I see it, you have two choices. Conquer your world or stand apart from it. Above it. Like a god. You have to rule them, or make them realise that you are so far above them that you have no interest in their little games. Anything in between and it will be chaos."

"No half measures."

"No half measures," Dominion agreed. "When you act—however you act—it must be definitive. Beyond challenge. And when you refrain from acting, you must be beyond question."

"How can I be beyond question? There will always be those who doubt and disagree."

"When I say beyond question, I do not mean a question of morals or values but of power. Make them see that they are nothing before you. That when you choose action, they cannot stop you. That when you choose inaction, they cannot compel you. Whether you are their ruler or their god, to see you, they must always look up."

"Might makes right."

"Yes. You don't like it, I know, but it is the reality. Civilisation is built on not just ideals, but the power to enforce them. And there are always hands in which that power disproportionately rests. The moment you arrive on Earth, those hands will be yours. So, try not to bring down civilisation."

"Thanks."

Dominion grinned. "You didn't come to me for easy answers."

"It would have been nice, though."

"Wouldn't it just. Speaking of power, though, there's some knowledge that Knowledge might not want you to know."

"And what's that?"

"She can peek into the head of your prime avatar, but not your true self. The living universe."

"My consciousness is seated in the prime avatar. Isn't that the same thing?"

"No. You can keep things from your avatar, if you don't want them disseminated amongst the gods. Knowledge can be such a gossip."

"By which you mean the goddess of Knowledge likes to spread knowledge."

"It was more fun the way I said it."

Jason gave Dominion a curious look.

"No one has ever said that to me before. Can you teach me to hide things from my avatar?"

"Someone is already lined up for that. For now, just enjoy yourself. Your friends are about to start arriving."

14

WE HAVE FOREVER

Trading with Rexion—even Outer Rexion—came with many complications. Both natural and magical environmental conditions outright killed people unless they were brighthearts or at least silver rank. The effects of the natural array inside Rexion were not as severe as when the array was rendered unstable by the messengers, twenty years earlier. What remained was still enough to cause problems for the weak and ill-prepared.

The ambient magic interfered with many forms of elemental magic and was hostile to extremely high-rankers. Diamond-rankers and many at the peak of gold found themselves suffering headaches and vertigo. It wasn't enough to impede their formidable prowess, but it was highly unpleasant. There were also monsters. Most had learned to avoid the shaft, but some were freshly spawned and didn't know better. Others were just too stupid to care. As a result, those heading up or down the shaft needed protection, or the power to protect themselves.

Because of the difficulties involved, neither guards nor manual labour could be found cheaply. Many turned to repurposed labour constructs, widely available after the reconstruction of Yaresh. While most merchants wanted them, the initial outlay was high. They were also expensive to repair, and not designed for combat. As a result, silver-rankers filled the gaps.

Many silver-rankers were craftspeople looking to fund their work, or noble scions cut off from the family purse. For those unwilling to adventure, or sign contracts that would tie them up as noble family guards for years, there were limited opportunities to make money. While working the shaft didn't pay as well as adventuring, all it took was a desire for money and a willingness to suffer some indignity.

That indignity often proved the sticking point that made silver-rank labour a problem. Used to running a workshop or being served by others, fighting and hauling goods was something they felt was below them. For some, this work became a valuable lesson in humility. In others, it brought their sense of entitlement to the fore. Needing to prove they were more than just thugs and labourers, the silver-rankers started throwing their weight around.

The brighthearts controlled Outer Rexion and the town at the top of the shaft, but the Adventure Society managed traffic moving up and down. The high-level society officials, up on the surface, considered this an excellent opportunity to track who came and went. The people actually doing the work considered the Office of Shaft Traffic Control one of the worst assignments available.

Being a shaft traffic controller was a complex, frustrating and occasionally dangerous job. Frustrated, entitled silver-rankers always thought that their business was the most important, and they were the worst done by. When things inevitably went wrong, they grew volatile. The Adventure Society maintained a security force, but they were sometimes slow to act. It didn't help that the security force itself was a punishment duty for recalcitrant adventurers.

The society was at least wise enough to not put malcontent adventurers in charge of anything. A cadre of society officials held the positions of authority, charged with keeping the security force itself in line. These were not coveted roles.

Miguel Ladiv had once foolishly imagined that a cushy job in the Adventure Society would be his for the taking. After all, his uncle was deputy director of the Adventure Society branch in Rimaros. He had seemed so welcoming, too, when Miguel said he wanted to follow him into society. Unfortunately, Uncle Vidal's enthusiasm for nepotism proved to be of the 'chance to prove yourself' variety. Before he knew what had happened, Miguel found himself deep underground, in charge of a cycling array of malcontent adventurers.

"Adventurers have to deal with monsters," Vidal had told him. "Adventure Society officials have to deal with adventurers, which is

106 | SHIRTALOON & TRAVIS DEVERELL

worse. I'm not going to lie to you; this job will be awful. You may get beaten up and you'll definitely want to quit. But if you do the job, and do it well, you'll be setting yourself up for big things. For one thing, you're going to show the people that matter that you're not taking the easy way."

"Okay, Uncle, hear me out: what if we try doing things the easy way so they think I'm innovative and willing to do the unexpected?"

"The easy way is *always* expected, Miguel. Now, the other thing this job will do is let you run into some big names. A lot of important officials, diplomats and adventurers come through here."

"You want me to suck up to famous adventurers?"

"No, that will just backfire on you. But people like that pay attention to what's going on around them. They wouldn't have lived that long if they didn't. If they see you doing your job well now, they'll remember that down the line. Getting into the top levels of the Adventure Society is a game of politics. Someday, a big adventurer who knows your face, and remembers that you're diligent and capable, will open doors that all the hard work in the world will not."

His uncle had been right, of course: Miguel had definitely wanted to quit. He'd wanted an easy life, and this was anything but. To his surprise, he never quite did. He wasn't heir to the family title, like his uncle, but he still had his pride. For five years now, he'd been wrangling idiot adventurers to keep order over idiot non-adventurers. He was astounded there hadn't been some kind of blood bath between entitled merchant guards and his idiot adventurers.

He'd also seen some of those big names his uncle had mentioned. Members of famous teams like Moon's Edge and Biscuit. Even the Yaresh diamond-rankers, Allayeth and Charist, although that was rare. The natural array made diamond-rankers uncomfortable, though, so he saw visitors that prestigious seldomly.

Today was scheduled to be one of those rare days. The famous treasure hunter, Emir Bahadir, was going to arrive. With him would be the inventor of the sky link communication tablets, along with a diamond-ranker Miguel had never heard of. They would be arriving down the shaft, as portals were extremely unreliable this close to Rexion proper. Even so, there was a small portal arrival area, tucked behind Miguel's office.

Miguel's security office was right on the edge of the shaft, abutting the largest of the Outer Rexion's landing platforms. It was a curved quarter-dome of glass, opaque from the outside but allowing him to watch the shaft traffic from within. He knew the VIPs were arriving when he saw a large cloud vessel moving down.

Cloud constructs were popular vehicles, but were notoriously unstable in the depths. They were also small, for personal use. Scaling the size up sent the price soaring, making other designs more viable. This vehicle was an oversized cloud carriage, able to hold a dozen or more in comfort. That made it too pricy for any but the larger noble houses, merchant barons or high-ranking adventurers.

Miguel had some paperwork with the details of the visitors on it. He grabbed the folder and headed outside, meandering across the landing platform. A half-dozen bureaucrats from the Office of Shaft Traffic Control rushed past him, scrambling to meet the visitors.

The cloud carriage reached the platform and was waved into position by the landing guide's signal flags. The vehicle was much too large for the four people who emerged. As they disembarked, the vehicle dissolved and was drawn into a locket around the neck of one of the four passengers.

Miguel was certain that person was the diamond-ranker who went by Cloudweaver. It was unclear if he should address them as Cloudweaver or *the* Cloudweaver. Taking on such names had been common amongst high-rankers for a long time. The non-gendered pronouns the paperwork warned him to use were new, but likewise a high-rank trend. It was unusual, but he had encountered them before in the course of his job.

Despite their rank, Cloudweaver was visibly unremarkable. They looked like a woman to Miguel, albeit with short hair and a face that was boyish, but delicate and pretty. He couldn't sense an aura, but there was something about their presence that stood out. It was as if they were painted in vibrant colours while everyone else was washed out.

Of the two men, the taller was the most striking of the group. Impeccably dressed, handsome and black as midnight, he had rainbow beads woven into his hair. He was emitting a polite amount of aura, advertising his gold rank That was clearly the treasure hunter. The woman next to him, also gold rank, was his wife. Her hair was long, dark and straight, and so shiny, it reflected the colourful lights of the nearby plaza. She panned over everything with a sharp gaze, Miguel flushing as she paused on him for a moment.

The last member of the group had pale skin and a slightly nervous look about him. At silver, he was the lowest rank of the group and didn't look comfortable in his long coat, shifting as if unused to wearing it. His neck craned as he looked around like a country boy on his first trip to the city.

The Adventure Society officials were attempting to greet the group, with mixed success. Emir Bahadir and—Miguel checked his paperwork—Travis Noble were chatting with each other, ignoring the officials. The diamond-ranker looked angry and annoyed as they rubbed at their temples.

Technically, Miguel's job was to stop these people from causing problems, just like he was everyone else. Anyone who thought that was remotely possible was an idiot. His real job was to stop anyone stupid enough to try and cause them trouble. Failing that, it was to scrape what was left of the troublemakers off the wall, then try to identify them for his report.

The long-haired woman, Constance Bahadir, was the one dealing with the officials, and certainly seemed more professional than her companions. Miguel was introduced and spoke with her long enough to offer a security detail. She declined.

Cloudweaver ran out of patience with the meet and greet. The air thrummed as aura erupted out of them and washed over the town. Miguel managed to swallow a groan at how much work that was going to cost him as the whole town was disrupted.

"He's not here," they growled. "We came all the way down this hole full of headache-inducing magic and he's not even here?"

"He's probably doing something dimensional," Emir said. "He's always up to things like that. Let's go find somewhere to sit down and get a drink."

"I would suggest the bar called the Speckled Egg," Miguel offered. "It's pricy, but close, and the walls are enchanted to filter the natural array out of the ambient magic. Many of our more powerful visitors find it more accommodating to their needs."

Emir looked Miguel over for a second, then gave a small nod. Miguel pointed back at the plaza and gave Emir simple directions. The four visitors left, some of the officials attempting to talk their way into accompanying them. A couple flashed dark looks at Miguel, which he ignored.

Miguel headed back for his office when he saw a line of dark energy, dancing like fire, appear on the ground in the portal area. From it rose an obsidian arch, containing a sheet of the same shadowy power. Portals weren't impossible to open in Outer Rexion, but they were difficult.

Usually, only portal specialists made the attempt, and he waited to see who emerged. To his surprise, it was his uncle.

"Miguel? Perfect. Good news, nephew; I'm getting you off this job."

"Why?" Miguel asked, having trusted his uncle's good news too many times before.

"Because I've gotten you a new one, obviously. You are going to be the Adventure Society liaison with Jason Asano."

"Isn't that the job you've been constantly complaining about since I was little?"

"No, I don't think so."

"I'm quite certain it is. Remember Aunt Maria's birthday when you accidentally drank the gold-rank wine? You wouldn't stop talking about it while the Healer priestess was removing the poison."

"That doesn't sound familiar. You're probably thinking of something else."

Miguel was about to respond when a second person emerged from the portal. His aura was silver rank, projected just enough to be polite, yet his presence stood out like the Cloudweaver's.

"Your uncle loved the job," the man said. "We hardly ever used him as bait when trawling for sea monsters."

Miguel immediately understood two things. This man had to be Jason Asano, and he was not a silver-ranker, whatever his aura claimed.

"It's an honour to meet you, sir," he said. "However, with respect, I feel that being your liaison with the Adventure Society is not a position that would have a positive outcome."

"And why do you say that?" Asano asked.

"I've heard of you, sir."

Jason laughed and slapped a hand on Vidal's shoulder.

"You were right, he'll do just fine. I have a long-overdue meeting with a diamond-ranker, but get him set up."

Asano stepped into Vidal's shadow and fell into it, as if it was a hole in the ground. Miguel stared at the spot for a long time.

"Uncle?"

"Yes, Miguel?"

"Do you remember when I took this job and you told me I could quit if I wanted to?"

"I do."

"I'm going to do that now."

"No, you're not."

"Yes, I am. I'm doing it now. I quit."

"Sorry, boy. You should have tried that before people realised you were competent. Now, follow me through this portal. I have a lot to explain."

Jason and the Cloudweaver were opposite one another in a booth at the Speckled Egg. The bar was large and clean, but cultivated a dingy atmosphere with dim lighting and décor heavy on dark wood and leather. Constance, Travis and Emir were sharing a round table next to the booth. Travis was already onto his third massive glass of some extremely blue beverage.

"What did you do to my cloud flask?" the Cloudweaver demanded.

Jason grinned at the question. They had sat in seething silence through his reunion with Travis, Constance and Emir. He could feel them heating up like a kettle and finally sat down to talk before they boiled over.

"I turned it into *my* cloud flask," he said. "Leaving control access in a soul-bound item is always going to be unreliable. You had to know that. I pulled it into my soul instead of leaving it on the outside, and all your influence got pushed out."

"How did you do that?"

"This is starting to feel like an interrogation, and I'm not sure you're holding the moral high ground here. You're the one who left shady back door access in my cloud flask."

"Shady Back Door Access," Travis echoed, his words slightly slurred. "Name of your sex tape."

"Uh, that's great, mate," Jason said. "But maybe go over to the bar before the diamond-ranker murders you with their eyes."

Travis looked at the Cloudweaver, visibly gulped and hurried off. He hurried back, grabbed his half-finished drink and hurried away again.

"If I choose to make this an interrogation," the Cloudweaver continued, "then that is what it shall be."

"It will be a short one, then," Jason rebutted. "I have neither interest nor obligation in putting up with you playing strict nanny."

The diamond-ranker's presence pressed in on Jason with such precision that no one else in the bar so much as glanced over. Jason opened his avatar up to his true self, fending off their power. A crack appeared in the wall next to them and they both backed off.

"That's pretty good," Jason said. "You're on the road to cultivating a transcendent aspect. I haven't really looked into how ranking up through diamond works yet. But don't wave your stick at me, mate. Mine's bigger."

"If I used aura instead of presence, I could make that puppet you're wearing bleed out its ears and die."

"Sure, but that doesn't get you what you want. You're too smart to not know that. You're poking me to see what happens. I'm guessing the diamond-rank community is curious and wants you to feel me out."

The anger in the Cloudweaver's face vanished and they sat back with a smile.

"Yes," they said. "When you came to this world for a second time, you were unstable. Prone to lashing out and making angry decisions. That was containable when you were just some silver-ranker. Now you're gold rank and something far more on top. We need to know if we should put you down while we still can."

"I understand," Jason said. "Wondering whether my power makes me too dangerous is kind of my thing."

"Are you?"

"Probably, but you missed your window. I'm fully immortal now; no more conditional resurrections. You can't stop me from coming back because I don't have to. As you said, you can break the puppet, but I just have to build a new one."

He smiled.

"They call diamond-rankers immortal, but we know you're not. Not really. You can make them stay down, with enough effort. It doesn't even take that much, really. Not with the right powers."

"Is that a threat?"

"I have forever and can't be stopped. You came here to see what happens if you and your friends decide to string me up. Now you know."

"We already knew. It was suggested that we point out that your friends are not as immortal as you are, and you've sworn off resurrections for everyone, not just yourself."

"It was suggested, was it?"

"It was."

"And how was that suggestion received?"

"Some of us are very old, Asano. Old enough to have seen the world burn and history end. Magic helped civilisation rise up much earlier here than on your world. Earlier than most on this planet even realise. When diamond-rankers go to war, only they survive. We want to avoid that just as much as you."

"I'm not a diamond-ranker."

"No. On the mortal plane, you are below us, but in the realm to which we aspire, we are below you. Our hope is that we can guide one another in the areas we each lack."

"I've got too much going on to even think about a diamond-rank transcendent study group."

"Of course you do. You're young, but we have forever. I've waited almost two decades to just hear about what you've done with your cloud flask. I would appreciate it if we could finally get to it now, though. If more of your friends arrive, I get the feeling it'll be another two decades at least."

15

LIKE AN ADVENTURER

RICK GELLER AND HIS TEAM ARRIVED JUST AS A BROTHEL FIRE SENT A group of scantily clad women stumbling onto the street and right into Jason. Dustin Kettering, from Rick's team, went inside and used his ice powers to extinguish the blaze.

"Are you setting these up?" Rick asked Jason incredulously.

"I'm genuinely not," Jason assured him. "Were you cursed by the god of lust or something?"

"No," Rick said, then gave his wife Hannah a side glance. She gave him an admonishing slap on the shoulder.

As Jason's friends arrived in ones and twos, the reunions were everything he'd been hoping for: hugs and jibes and promises of countless stories. More than just his team, many of his friends from across the planet had gathered. Danielle Geller and her husband, Keith. The Remore family, minus Rufus. Jory Tillman and Gilbert Bertinelli both arrived with Clive.

Neil and Nik were portalled in from the Mirror Kingdom by the Mirror King's own portal specialist, courtesy of Team Shining Scabbard. They were led by Sigrid Freyn, a famously capable leader and healer Neil had been training with. Their teams had formed a friendship years earlier, going through the Reaper trials and training together at iron rank. Not having seen Jason since his first supposed death, Sigrid's now-husband, Prince Valdis, insisted on bringing the whole team along.

"Dad will miss Sigrid more than me," Valdis assured Jason on their arrival. "With how horny and immortal he is, the kingdom's thick with princes and princesses. He'll take a good adventurer over any of his kids."

"Then perhaps you should focus on being a good adventurer, instead of a mediocre prince," Sigrid pointed out. "Also, that is a gross misrepresentation of your father and your king. Be more respectful."

"This is why he likes her better," Valdis confided.

For all the joy of old friends coming together, Jason couldn't help but feel an undercurrent of melancholy. This wasn't the first reunion after events had dragged him away from his friends for years. This time, he had missed more in their lives than before, and it would take time to learn who his friends were now.

Belinda was so much more centred than when he had left. She no longer skirted around the edges of the group like an uncertain outsider, instead standing comfortably amongst the others. Estella, next to her, was much more a part of the group now. Their awkwardness with Jory was noticeable, but also something they'd clearly come to terms with. Just reading body language showed Jason the years-long stories he'd not been around for.

Humphrey had talked with him about his propensity for leaving the team for years at a time. They understood that Jason did not want to leave alone but, however justified, his extended absences came with consequences.

Once everyone had arrived, they gathered around a banquet table in an outrageously expensive shaft-side restaurant. Sitting next to Jason, Humphrey leaned in close.

"Are you alright, Jason?"

"Yep. Why do you ask?"

"Your face is kind of switching back and forth between happy and angry."

"Happy means I'm thinking about being back here with everyone."

"And what does angry mean you're thinking about?"

"What happens to the next prick that tries to make me leave again."

"And that," Sophie said, "was when he challenged Humphrey to a duel for my hand in marriage."

"I would like to point out," Humphrey said, "that it would have been easier to de-escalate the situation if you hadn't been cheering him on."

"But then he might not have fought you!"

"I didn't want him to fight me!"

"Oh, so you want one of those submissive wives that only do what *you* want?"

"What? No, that's not what I… hey, don't you Jason me. I have Jason for that now."

She grinned and leaned in for a kiss, leaving his expression cranky but appeased.

"I assume you won, and Sophie doesn't have to marry some random guy, right?" Nik asked. He was seated on the other side of Jason from Humphrey.

"I certainly hope not," Danielle said. "I'm not willing to give Sophie up as a daughter-in-law at this stage, and killing her new paramour wouldn't be good for my reputation."

"I could do it," Keith said.

"Of course you could, dear," Danielle said, patting him on the shoulder.

"No," Jason said.

"I didn't even say anything yet," Clive complained.

"And you don't need to."

"That's just prejudicial," Clive said.

"So, that's not a notebook you have hidden under the banquet table?"

"Uh… no."

Late into the evening, the group had left the restaurant and taken over the lounge area of a nearby bar. Jason and Neil were sat together on a couch, a table full of empty glasses in front of them.

"So," Jason said, slurring his words only a little, "you just told her it was for the best and immediately skipped town?"

"Yeah," Neil said, likewise slightly wobbly. "I just kind of dropped it on her and left. I knew if I stayed, I'd make some kind of stupid decision."

"It doesn't matter how fast you run when you make the stupid choice first. You seriously didn't go for a discussion before ending things? You just decided for both of you and did a runner?"

"I did discuss it."

"With Cassandra? You said you blindsided her and bolted."

"With Nik."

"Well, I think I've spotted where you went wrong there, mate: Nik is a different person. Also, how old was he back then?"

"Um, five, maybe."

"Yeah, that was a great idea. And this was what? Ten years ago?"

"About that. Do you think I messed up?"

"Well, you dumped her, basically shouted why at her while bolting out the door and then ghosted her for a decade. I'm going to say, yeah, you messed up."

Neil let out a groan and Jason put a commiserating arm around his slumped shoulders.

"Don't worry about it, mate. We can fix this."

Neil perked up, eyes full of drunken hope.

"You really think so?"

"No, she's probably found someone much better. But we can try."

Neil slumped back and let out another groan.

"So, that's the plan," Jason summarised. "Head to Estercost to see how many people from Earth we can round up. Then we head to Rimaros, fix up the link between worlds and then ride it to the other universe. Anyone interested in seeing an alternate reality is welcome to come along."

"You think it will be that simple?" Danielle Geller asked.

"Yes," Jason said. "But simple is not the same thing as easy, as Clive is happy to explain."

Zara's suite was large, but still crowded with all of Jason friends packed in.

"Actually, I don't have time for that," Clive said. "Jason, you and I need to sit down and—"

"No time! We have to plan sightseeing stops along the trip. Definitely Greenstone. I'd love to see this world's version of Australia, but I'm told everyone would die."

"Jason," Clive said through gritted teeth, "we really have to—"

"We can't just go making elaborate plans," Humphrey pointed out.

"We tried that fifteen years ago and we only got from Rimaros to Yaresh. I think we should keep our plans more flexible."

"Okay, you all need to stop—"

"Good thinking, Hump. Keep our options open, that's sound tactical thinking."

"Jason, you need to take this—"

"Don't call me Hump."

"Did someone use silence magic on me? This is not—"

"Good meeting, everyone. Give it some thought and we'll regroup in Yaresh."

"Jason," Clive warned, "don't you dare—"

A portal opened up, then closed again after Jason ducked through. The rest of the group filtered out, leaving Clive, Belinda, Estella and Zara.

"I forgot," Clive said, shaking his head. "It's been too long, and I forgot."

Belinda gave Clive an awkward pat on the back.

"I don't mean to interrupt," Zara said, "but I need to go check out of the room."

Marcus Xenoria was a massive leonid who liked to wander around with a huge axe slung casually over his shoulder. On meeting him, many wondered how that was helpful when his job primarily involved politics and bureaucracy. By the end of that meeting, they'd usually figured it out. As a high-level agent of the Adventure Society's continental council, Marcus was a troubleshooter and enforcer. On hearing of Jason's return, he had once again been dispatched to Yaresh.

Technically, Asano had already made contact with the Adventure Society, although that didn't really count. He'd portalled directly into the —portal shielded—Rimaros branch office, abducting the deputy-director. The higher-ups had not been mollified when Ladiv announced that his nephew would be the society's contact point for Asano.

Miguel Ladiv was now standing next to Marcus at the Adventure Society campus teleport platform in Yaresh. The boy looked like nervous sweat would make his new suit slip right off his body.

Asano emerged from the portal wearing a suit in the Rimaros summer style. It was more than a decade out of date, but he managed to make it look classic rather than dated. He managed this through a combination of excellent design, swagger, and enough confidence to knock out a wall.

He stopped, his eyes glancing over Miguel before fixing on Marcus. They were not the eyes Marcus remembered, instead being dark and human. Behind Jason, the group emerging from the portal was eclectic even by Marcus' standards. First came Jason's shadow familiar, who was also a little different. There were flecks of glowing white in his dark form, marking out eyes and what was possibly the outline of some kind of formalwear.

Next came the most alien of the familiars, the avatar of doom. It had more orbs floating around it than before, but was otherwise the same at a glance. It was followed by what looked like Asano again, but with red orbs for eyes. He didn't carry himself quite the same, looking more like a boy trying to imitate his older brother.

Marcus recognised Jason's familiars, but wasn't expecting the last figure to emerge. It looked like a wood carving of Asano brought to life, complete with a coarse hessian version of his cloak. He joined the others in flanking Asano.

"A little high rank for a new familiar, aren't you, Asano?" Marcus asked by way of greeting.

"Not a familiar," Jason told him. "This is Arbour, one of my Voices of the Will."

"That's a phrase you might want to be careful about throwing around. We've been fighting the messengers a long time now."

"Noted."

"I'm here because the Adventure Society is very eager for a debrief."

"Just the Adventure Society?"

"We made sure the others will leave you alone. For a while, at least, and no promises if we don't get some answers out of you to pass along."

Jason smiled sadly.

"There's a lot of answers I want as well," he said, then slowly turned on the spot while looking around.

The Adventure Society campus was one of the few places left standing after the Battle of Yaresh, but he could see the reconstructed city all around. Most of the city was built into living trees, as was normal for an elf city. He could see one section of the city instead made from towers of glass, rising through the trees in the distance.

"Whoever they put me in a room with needs to understand that they get answers when I get mine."

"They'll understand. We're getting used to getting caught in the wake of your chaos. You didn't see the political tangle as the churches of Liberty and Knowledge fought over those Builder cultists you ripped the star seeds out of. I'm assuming that was one of your questions."

"It was," Jason told him. "Sorry if I'm a little contentious. I was half expecting to find a gaggle of society officials waiting for me."

"Oh, I imagine they'll find you soon enough. But for now, I'm here to give you something we've been remiss with in the past."

"And what's that?"

"You've spent your entire career dealing with things beyond the purview of normal adventurers. Well beyond. And every time you do, there's been someone waiting to give you grief when they should be throwing you a parade."

He held out his hand and Jason shook it. The size difference was like a child shaking hands with a big furry mascot.

"Thank you, Jason Asano, for saving us from whatever gods-bedamned cosmic nonsense was coming for us this time. And thank you for doing it like an adventurer."

16

PEOPLE THINK YOU'RE BLOWING UP CITIES

SHORTLY AFTER VISITING YARESH, JASON AND SOPHIE HAD PARTICIPATED in a fighting arena. The venue, like most of the city, had been wiped out during the messenger invasion. As part of the reconstruction, the old arena was replaced with a massive mirage chamber. The domed building, constructed from hexagonal segments of stained glass, was a landmark that curved high over the trees.

Mirage chambers created false environments where people could be projected into as illusionary doubles of themselves. Because these illusion bodies were made using soul projection, the real body could experience everything their replicas did. This meant that pain was real, but the only actual harm they faced was psychological. The doubles could be injured or even die without the real body suffering the same.

Smaller mirage chambers were used for training purposes, such as the one at the Geller family training centre in Greenstone. Massive arena venues, like the new one in Yaresh, were designed for public spectacle. These were magical colosseums where the dead gladiators respawned at the end, ready to fight another day. The gladiators here were also not slaves. Dedicated mirage fighters were akin to athletic stars on Earth, earning wealth and fame for their skills.

Despite the existence of such celebrities, however, the biggest spectacles came from the inclusion of famous adventurers on the drawcard. Whether against one another or the local professionals, adventurer participation always pulled in crowds. This was amply demonstrated by the full seating around the arena, despite the short notice of the current event.

The Duke of Yaresh was in the largest of the VIP boxes. The size of a ballroom, it had one glass wall that looked out onto the arena, and could also serve as a projection screen when powers and the environment obscured the action. It wasn't the fighting that the duke was here for, however. Inside the room right now was arguably the most prestigious gathering the city had ever seen. With Yaresh attempting to re-establish itself as a regional power, social gathering like this would help mark it as a place of influence and power.

That Yaresh had not just one but two resident diamond-rankers was an incredible boon. Lord Charist was the more social of the two, but it was the more reclusive Lady Allayeth who graced the room with her presence today. Around her was the team she had raised up herself, Moon's Edge, now famous in their own right. Compared to some of the others present, however, they were practically anonymous.

The duke had—in private—laughed like a madman as internationally famous adventurers descended on his city, one after another. Team Biscuit had been on the rise for years, much of their early reputation built right here in Yaresh. Not only were they known for their success in the field, but the team also boasted many impressive members.

Gellers were always noticeable, of course, especially the son of Danielle Geller. They also counted the Archchancellor of the Magic Research Association in their number. He was famous as much for the Magic Society's hatred of him as the success of his fledgeling organisation. Then there was a former holder of the Hurricane Princess title. Zara Nareen wasn't *technically* a princess at the moment, but anyone who thought she was genuinely ostracised from the Storm Kingdom's royal family was a political buffoon.

In the cavalcade of famous adventurers descending upon Yaresh, Team Biscuit was only the beginning. Team Blood and Gold had a husband-and-wife duo from the Remore family, plus the vaunted treasure hunter, Emir Bahadir. Team Shining Scabbard was a well-known group who apparently knew Team Biscuit from years earlier. They also had royalty in the group, although that was less impressive with the Mirror Kingdom's surplus of princes and princesses. That said, the duke admired the administrative prowess of Prince Valdis in assembling the arena event in less than two days.

There were others as well. Danielle Geller was talking with the enormous Adventure Society official, who mercifully hadn't brought his axe this time. There were also some local luminaries, although they seemed less impressive in this company. Notable in their absence were certain members of Yaresh high society known for letting their petty pride create diplomatic issues. The duke was pleasantly surprised at not only their absence, but their failure to come to his door, complaining at their exclusion. If he got nothing else from the night, he intended to learn how Prince Valdis had managed that minor miracle.

The duke moderated himself while circulating amongst the visitors. As valuable as these connections were, he was cognisant of this being a genuine social event. These were actual friends, reuniting after a long time apart, not a calculated political exchange. The inclusion of select locals demonstrated the political dexterity of the Mirror Kingdom prince.

The duke was diligent in his attention to all the attendees, not just those who were famous adventurers. This proved wise when the fashion designer turned out to be one of those octuplet sets that every major city seemed to have one of. The duke was careful not to offend any gods, let alone one as important as Fertility, and it reminded him to be wary of dragons lurking around Jason Asano.

The person this gathering had been arranged for was the one the duke knew the least about. He had heard a great deal, but little of it seemed reliable. The stories surrounding Asano were contradictory, nonsensical and often straight-up unbelievable. Even so, he was unable to dismiss them out of hand. Too many had been confirmed by people whose judgement he trusted.

Asano himself was standing in front of the glass, watching the matches below. The duke was patient, and perhaps a little trepidatious, given what he wanted to discuss. More than just taking a measure of the man, the duke needed to know if Asano's return heralded the same chaos as it had in the past.

The duke moved to stand next to Asano when the stocky elf he was speaking with headed for the buffet table. Asano greeted him somewhat standoffishly, not taking his eyes from the match below. The duke followed his gaze to see Prince Valdis once again in a fight. An enthusiastic and repeat participant, his sword master specialty excelled against other essence-users.

The prince was fast, elusive and made powerful hit-and-run strikes in a skirmisher combat style. It had proven effective in duels against even the prestigious adventurers gathered around, and made a grand spectacle for the citizens of Yaresh watching. Its biggest weakness was against evasion-type protection specialists, as a dark-skinned woman with silver hair was demonstrating.

The duel came to an end, the prince taking his rare loss in stride as he played up to the crowd. The illusionary arena of sand and stone vanished, revealing the very full stands arrayed around the mirage chamber. The duke stood beside Asano, watching the prince walk off as the next challenger came out.

"That is her husband, yes?" the duke said.

"They haven't married yet. Soon, I expect."

"Who do you think will win?"

"She will. Humphrey is well-trained, but he's a monster fighter at heart. He was trained to work in a team, fighting hordes and giants, not people. He's good at it, don't get me wrong, but Sophie is something special. She learned to fight in a cage, where losing meant waking up in a ditch, or chained to a bed. That breeds a determination to win that's hard to match."

The duke found himself a little confused. Some of his advisors had warned that being in Asano's presence was intimidating, but he found it not the case at all. Asano radiated nothing more than a polite amount of aura that revealed his rank.

"You have a remarkable and loyal group of friends, to come running from across the world."

"I do," he agreed warmly. "I simply wish I didn't find myself removed from them for so long. Or so often."

The duke steeled his resolve. He'd been told that blunt honesty was the best approach with Asano, but that seemed dangerous.

"I hope you will forgive my rudeness, Mr Asano, but will you be staying in Yaresh long?"

"No. Worried I'll cause trouble?"

"Cause might be the wrong word, and I certainly want to make no accusations. That being said, Adventure Society branch directors have standing orders to go on low alert should you arrive in their area. That order was reissued when they got word of your return."

"That seems a little excessive."

"Perhaps so, Mr Asano. But when you went to Rimaros, the Builder almost dropped another city on it out of the sky. There's a new island there now. Here in Yaresh, the messengers tore the city down to the foundations."

"The Builder attacked everywhere, as did the messengers. We only came to Yaresh because you were already fighting the messengers here."

"But you cannot deny that both forces seem more interested in you than other adventurers. And from here, you went to the brightheart city, which, to my understanding, you entirely wiped from reality."

"I built a new one."

"And a very nice one it is, but I believe most people are happy with the cities they already have."

"Well, the brighthearts weren't. Theirs was an undead wasteland."

"So I understand. But the fact stands, Mr Asano, that cities have a habit of requiring significant rebuilding after you've passed through."

"I do want to claim extenuating circumstances," Asano acknowledged, his tone weary but amused. "But there's only so many times every city you visit can blow up before people think you're blowing up cities."

Relief flooded through the duke. He saw a small smile cross Asano's lips and realised the man was probably reading his emotions. It was rude, but also a little impressive. It was hard to do so unnoticed on someone of the same rank, even if the duke got to gold rank through monster cores.

"You've been to Rexion?" Asano asked.

"Many times. I was not being obsequious when I said it was a very nice place. The relationship with Rexion was critical to feeding my people in the early days of the reconstruction. We're still in the process of restoring the wider region, even now. Remnants of the apocalypse beasts unleashed by the messengers took years to fully root out. Even now, we can never be entirely certain we got them all."

The duke shook his head before continuing.

"Whole towns were depopulated, and trying to get people to move in and restart the farms was difficult. There was a lot of reluctance, and understandably so. Whole towns full of people who died under extremes of misery and violence? Seeing family members transformed into monsters and puppets? Quite aside from the trauma people need to confront, those are conditions for spawning some of the nastier kinds of undead."

"I saw something similar in the original brightheart city."

"No Undeath priests here, thankfully. There were some regular necromancers, but the Adventure Society dealt with them quite aggressively."

"It sounds like you've had your work cut out for you."

"Indeed. Before the messengers, there were always those looking to snake my position. Sniping politicians and backstabbing noble houses.

Now they've spent a decade praying for my good health. No one wants to be duke when it means rebuilding the whole damn duchy from nothing."

"And now that you're seeing results, you don't want the city-destroying guy to tear it all down again."

"I do not mean to accuse or offend, Mr Asano, nor am I asking you to leave. But yes, I fear what your presence means for us. When fate places someone at the centre of events, it is those around them who tend to suffer."

"Something I have sadly come to learn. I understand, Duke, and sympathise with your position."

"Thank you. I won't pretend to understand the events you find yourself at the centre of. I am simply asking if your return signals a threat to Yaresh of which I am unaware."

"Not that I'm aware of, Duke. But it's the one you don't know about that gets you, isn't it?"

"Yes," the duke agreed. "Yes, it is."

Jason watched the duke move on to other conversations as Farrah took his place. Humphrey had lost, as predicted, but had made it harder on Sophie than expected.

"You've been dodging me," Jason said, keeping his gaze fixed on the arena. "Odd behaviour for a reunion."

"Yeah," Farrah conceded, more subdued than he was used to.

"Something to do with you still being silver rank?"

"Yeah."

Jason's team had all reached gold. Rick Geller's was getting there, with Rick and his sister Phoebe both having done so recently. The rest of their team were in the upper reaches of silver.

"We need to have a decent talk about things," Farrah said. "And I suppose I have a choice to make."

"Yes," Jason said softly.

"I felt it, you know? The moment you became… whatever you are now. The System showed up for everyone, but I *felt* it."

"I know. Have you talked about it with anyone?"

She shook her head.

"Did you know?" she asked. "When we formed that bond. When we strengthened it. Did you know?"

"No. Neither of us knew, back then."

"Dawn didn't tell you something?"

"I don't think even she knew. There are things she told me that she was absolutely wrong about. What's happening with me—with us—is probably not unique, but it's rare. Even by cosmic standards. We're making up the rules as we go."

He turned to look around the room behind them, their conversation kept private by his aura.

"We can have this out properly when we're alone," he said.

She nodded. "It is good having you back, Jason."

She walked away, and Rick Geller moved to join Jason in her place. They watched his sister walk out to meet Sophie in the arena.

"You and me in a mirage chamber again," Rick said.

"Don't remind me," Jason responded.

"You say that as if you weren't the one who had his whole team stomped by someone who didn't know magic even existed a year earlier."

"By running around like a fool and cackling like a witch. Surely, it's been long enough that those recordings are all gone."

"Are you kidding? It's required training material at the family training centre. I didn't hear the end of it when I spent a year instructing in Greenstone."

Jason waved over a server, grabbing glasses of wine for himself and Rick. Then he held up his glass.

"To Jonah."

Rick's eyes softened and he clinked his glass to Jason's.

"To Jonah," he echoed, then drained the glass.

Jonah had been a member of Rick's team until the ill-fated expedition from Greenstone that had killed many adventurers, including Farrah. Jonah had been captured and implanted with a star seed by the Builder cult, and died in the process of having it extracted. He had been part of the group that fought Jason all those years ago, in the Geller mirage chamber.

Rick nodded to Jason and then moved on. The next person to circulate Jason's way was Clive, holding a notebook. He was shoved out of the way by an excited Prince Valdis.

"Jason! When are you going to get out there? Everyone wants to see how you got to gold rank when you spent the last fifteen years sitting in a magic box meditating or whatever."

"That's not really how it worked."

"Then show us!"

"Sorry about him," Sigrid said, also moving past an increasingly cranky Clive.

"I'm not sure that me going down there is a good idea," Jason said. "Mirage chambers are soul projection devices. I don't know how they'll interact with my avatar, which is also a soul projection device."

"You're just scared of how badly I'll beat you, aren't you?"

"You got me, Valdis. I'm just scared."

"Or harder to provoke than a nine-year-old," Sigrid muttered.

Clive, watching the exchange, turned to the room.

"Hey, everyone!" he announced. "Who wants to see Jason Asano in a proper gold-rank fight?"

Jason gave Clive a flat look as the room filled with cheers.

17

WE NEED TO PUT A STOP TO IT

JASON WALKED WITH CLIVE AND VALDIS DOWN A TUNNEL TOWARDS THE mirage chamber's participant lobby. The passage was cavernous, their footsteps echoing on the blue tiles. Glow stones set into the walls, ceiling and even the floor let off a teal light with a shimmer effect that made the hallway feel like it was underwater.

"This reminds me of the underwater subway back in Greenstone," Clive said.

"Don't change the subject," Jason said. "This is not a good idea."

"It's a great idea," Valdis said. "I can tell because it was mine."

"We have no idea how my avatar will interact with the mirage chamber's soul projector."

"I know," Clive said. "Maybe if someone took five minutes to answer a few questions, we'd have a better idea of what is going to happen."

"Five minutes? I know a lady who can more or less stop time, and even she couldn't get through your questions in five minutes. And if I did give you some time, are you suggesting we'd get around to 'how does your prime avatar affect mirage chambers?' in the first five minutes?"

"We might have," Clive said unconvincingly. "Anyway, it should produce some interesting interactions. I wonder if they'll let me set up some testing equipment in their control chamber."

Jason turned to Valdis. "Clive was the one who peer pressured me into this. I should be fighting him."

"Proposal rejected," Valdis said. "You couldn't duel worth a damn at iron rank, so I want to see what you've got now. I heard about your duel in Rimaros. They said you dropped your opponent by looking at him, and a gold-ranker had to step in so you didn't kill him."

"Yeah," Jason said with a sigh. "I'm pretty sure that's why the diamond-rankers wanted to check I wasn't a violent madman now."

"Which diamond-rankers?" Clive asked.

"Um, all of them, I think?"

"That would explain why my father was asking about you," Valdis said. "I think he loaned me his portal specialist so he can interrogate me about you later."

"Forget that guy," Jason said. "Just bunk off to another universe with me."

"Deal," Valdis said, then looked slightly shifty. "If the wife says yes."

The Yaresh mirage chamber was a lot larger and more involved than the one Jason had used back in Greenstone. There was a nest of control and service rooms, access shafts and mana conduit tunnels, and they were just the magical aspects. Like a sports arena on Earth, most of the attendees would be normal-rankers, which meant the necessity of toilets. Lots and lots of toilets. He had grown used to their absence, spending most of his time around high-rankers, so it was jarring to see so much plumbing infrastructure.

Valdis led them to a central participants lobby. This was a waiting area for fighters, and quite like the VIP room upstairs, with a lounge area, bar and huge viewing screen. Some of Jason's friends were down here, already fought or waiting to go. The local fighters watched them all like hawks, especially Valdis.

Jason and Valdis circulated for a while, waiting for their turn. The walls in the lobby were artfully painted metal panels, and Clive was intercepted trying to discreetly remove one in the corner. Jason left that behind as attendants led him and Valdis down different tunnels towards the projection booths.

"I just don't think we should jump right in without some kind of testing first," Jason explained to the attendant.

"It will be just fine, Mr Asano. We've had Lord Charist himself use this mirage chamber. You're not saying you've got more power running through you than he does, are you?"

"Actually, that's a complex question with no definitive answer, which is kind of the whole point of…"

Jason stopped trying when the attendant closed the door in his face, leaving him alone in the booth. There was no more to it than walls painted dark green, a flat couch and a dim glow stone in the ceiling.

"He's right," Jason told himself. "If it can handle a diamond-ranker, one gold-rank flesh puppet isn't going to blow the whole thing up."

He lay down on the couch, expecting everything to go black and his consciousness shift to an illusionary double. Instead, he felt the magic of it settle over him and bounce off. It seemed that Dominion's gift to help Jason contain his presence didn't leave enough for the chamber to latch on to.

He relaxed his control, letting out enough for the chamber's magic to get a read on him. He hadn't done this in a long time and was now able to sense the magic going to work. It also wasn't powerful enough to knock him out. Instead, it split his attention in multiple places, much like when he went 'overseer god mode' in his soul realm. He put his hands behind his head, lay back and let his attention focus on the replica now standing in the main chamber.

In the mirage chamber's core power distribution node, several artificers were supervising and maintaining the flow of power. The mirage chamber was more than just a spectacle for the populace; it also served as a regulation hub for the city's magical infrastructure. The need to rebuild the entire city had been a chance to recreate it as a unified, efficient and integrated system.

One of the artificers, Munsen, was both new to his position and disgruntled to be in it. At fifteen years old, he was an apprentice artificer. He should have been learning to build sky ships or magic cannons for the walls. Instead, he was stuck in a humid room with a pair of old men.

Munsen blamed his parents, mostly for calling him Munsen. Yes, he understood that an adventurer saved them while his mother was pregnant, but Munsen was no name for an elf. It was a name for someone stuck in a room watching magical readings not change.

Then one did.

Munsen immediately sat bolt upright. His eyes scanned over the panel in front of him, made up of tightly packed crystals. He watched lights trace their way through crystals in complex patterns. His eyebrows rose as he deciphered the light sequences, for while Munsen was a complainer, he was not a slacker. He might be new to the job, but he *knew* the job.

"Bob?" Munsen said, turning to look at the chief supervisor. Names really did curse people into this job.

"I've told you to call me Roberto or Chief Supervisor," Bob said.

"Alright, *Chief Supervisor*," Munsen said. "What does it mean when the mana flow conduit is showing on the board as teal?"

"Teal?"

"Yeah, teal. Blue-green. This one here."

He pointed and the other two crowded around Munsen's chair to see. Bob was in charge, but Munsen had quickly learned that it was Aeoliandor who understood how it all worked. How he'd wound up here despite having a proper elf name, Munsen had no idea.

"Look," Munsen said, pointing. "There's an ongoing power surge in projector booth seven."

"We need to close that booth before someone uses it," Bob said. "That much power would kill a gold-ranker."

"Clearly not," Aeoliandor countered. "It's marked as active, with a gold-ranker in there right now. But we should get them out, yes."

Bob wandered towards his office and the communication tablet he had in there. The remaining two continued to watch the board.

"Some kind of accumulator misalignment?" Munsen suggested. "Feeding in too much power?"

"No, look," Aeoliandor said. "It's not feeding *into* the booth. It's coming out. An overflow, slowly spreading through the whole system and imprinting on all the mana."

"Imprinting it with what?"

"I'm not sure, but we need to put a stop to it. Trigger the emergency shutdown."

"I can't."

"Why not?"

"Bob had the system removed. He said there shouldn't be a way to black out the whole city just sitting around."

Aeoliandor glared in the direction of Bob's office.

"It wasn't just sitting arou... damn it, Bob. Munny, you remember the procedure I showed you for manual shutdown?"

"Yeah, but doesn't that take a while?"

"Yes, Munsen, it does. That's why we had an emergency shutdown system."

The illusionary double of Valdis arrived in the arena first. That wasn't a surprise, as he was well used to the process and Jason had still been complaining the last Valdis had seen him. The prince hoped it really was just grumbling. He didn't want to miss this opportunity.

Valdis had always loved pitting himself against well-known warriors. Winning or losing didn't matter. It was about pushing himself that little bit harder. Stretching his limits a little further. Jason Asano was a rare treat: a specialty Valdis had never faced before. Affliction skirmisher was a rare power set, and a very different beast to a normal affliction specialist. As for what kind of opponent he would make, Valdis couldn't wait to see.

The randomly selected battleground was disappointingly the same sandy arena he had faced Sophie Wexler in. It was popular as it made it easy for the crowds to see the action, but it advantaged some power sets over others. For Valdis, it was excellent, but it should be the opposite for Asano. His understanding was that Jason's style favoured complex environments.

Finally, Asano appeared in the opposite alcove. He was still wearing the suit from the party, quickly put together by his tailor friend. Asano looked at him and started walking out. Valdis did the same. Dark mist shrouded Asano for a moment, and he looked very different when he emerged from the haze. He now wore dark red robes, mostly obscured by a cloak unlike anything Valdis had ever seen. He knew Asano had the Cloak of Night ability, and that the look grew more individual to the user as it ranked up. This was the first time he'd seen it look like a portal into some distant, starry void.

Asano's human eyes were gone, replaced with twin nebulas glowing from within the dark hood. He was also not walking, instead gliding over the ground, his feet fully obscured by the cloak wrapped around him. Valdis grinned as they moved closer and drew his longsword.

"Very intimidating," he said. "Too bad about the arena, though. I would have liked to face you in a jungle or something. This open space is perfect for me, so maybe we do best two out of three."

"That's why you'll lose," Jason said. His voice was different, lacking the usual playfulness. Valdis hoped that he had more to offer than just theatrics.

"You think I'll lose because I have the advantage?" Valdis asked.

"You'll lose because you look at the world and think you're the one that needs to change."

Valdis laughed with delight.

"That's the spirit! Ready to go?"

"Proceed."

With no more warning than that, Valdis vanished. He appeared behind Jason, his sword already cutting a horizontal path at Jason's neck. He abandoned the strike when he realised that shadow arms were stabbing out of Jason's cloak like a porcupine's quills, each holding a sinister black and red dagger. Valdis withdrew as Jason slowly turned, letting out a murderer's chuckle as the arms retracted back into his cloak.

"I hope that was just a test," Jason said. "If you're going to be that predictable, this isn't going to take long."

Valdis loved this kind of fight. Hit and run, trading barbs along with blades.

"You think you're disappointed?" he shot back. "What happened to that talk about changing the world?"

"As you wish."

Jason turned his head to the right, then panned it around. Everything that fell into his sight was plunged into darkness as the illusionary sun was blotted out. Not a complete absence of light but a deep twilight where countless shadows careened through the gloom.

Fortunately, it could only impede Valdis so far. The dancing shadows were real, but no more than blurs in the dark to his vision. His Mind's Eye ability compensated at close range, allowing him to perfectly sense the space around him. At greater distances, he could feel the auras moving around that had to be Asano's shadow familiar.

Less fortunate was the fact that every shadow was duplicating Asano's aura. There had to be well over a hundred of them, maybe two hundred. It was good that this was a new, high-end arena that allowed summoned familiars to be called upon. Older and smaller venues lacked the feature. This suited Valdis just fine, as he wanted to face Asano's full capability. Asano's real body could be any of the auras Valdis picked up, or none of them at all. Making his aura vanish was another trick on the list Valdis was familiar with.

"Nice trick," Valdis called into the dark. "What ability are you using to blot out the light?"

"Midnight Eyes," Jason's voice came from all around in a chorus. "Perception ability. Lets me suppress light sources as far as I can see, to the limits of my aura."

"So, if I can suppress your aura, I can turn it off?"

The only response was sinister laughter coming from every direction. Valdis was long past the point of being shaken by theatrics, but there was an unsettling glee to it that felt genuinely unhinged.

Valdis grinned as a jolt of excitement ran through him. His normal duelling strategy was to keep the enemy on the back foot, interspersing quick exchanges with banter, at least in the early stage. The idea was to make the opponent fall into his pace and feel like they were being played with. Controlled. Asano turning the tactic back on him dispelled any lingering disappointment about the arena selection.

Asano was clearly in no rush either. On the top of the threat list from Asano, at least to Valdis, were his deceptively simple spells. Valdis excelled at deflecting magic projectiles and avoiding area spells, but Asano used little to none of either. His spells had minimal immediate effect, but they unfailingly landed. Without powerful resistances, a fully enclosed barrier or a few other niche protections, there was no evading them.

Jason might not be a traditional affliction specialist, but afflictions were still his bread and butter. If he wasn't jumping at the first chance to apply them, it meant that he was toying with Valdis. Rather than be offended, he was excited. If Asano was this confident, he would surely make this an epic clash.

"Have you had enough time to adjust to the dark?" the chorus asked. "Are you ready to start for real now?"

"It sounds like you're looking down on me."

"I would never do that," Asano said, this time only one voice. Valdis focused his attention that way and saw a lighter patch within the gloom. He suddenly could sense which of the auras was real, and saw Asano standing on the spot, casually eating a sandwich.

Valdis almost took the bait. He felt the mana surge inside him to launch an attack, but his instincts pulled him back.

"You won't get me that easily."

"No?" Jason asked. He reached out and plucked from the air a half coconut with a straw and a little umbrella.

"No," Valdis said, but he gave Jason a flat look. "Laying it on a bit thick, aren't you?"

"Are you kidding? I just picked up fresh ingredients for the first time in years. You feel free to run around in the dark while I eat this and we can talk after you lose."

It was almost enough to make Valdis lunge at Asano, but he held back from the obvious trap yet again. He took a breath, clearing his mind from Asano's provocation. Then he swung his sword.

At gold rank, Seeker Blade fired off a storm of curved force blades that sought out every enemy he could perceive. It was one of his favourites, a precious area attack when he had been limited in that area for so long. One of the blades shot out after Asano and his sandwich, but the real targets were all the other auras in range.

Valdis felt the closer shadow bodies get mowed down, too close to avoid the blades. It was a good start, but most of the other bodies were startlingly effective at avoiding the attack. They could shadow jump freely in the gloom, but teleporting wasn't enough to avoid the blades. They would simply turn and hunt you down again.

The trick with teleporting was to do so at the very last moment. The blades would explode upon striking the target, so pinpoint timing was required. It also required an understanding of the ability, but it was both common and famous, so it was no surprise that Asano's familiar was prepared. The shadow familiar's precision was uncanny, almost none of the bodies falling after the initial burst. In total, he estimated having felled around a fifth of them.

As for the blade that went for Asano himself, he ignored it and kept eating his sandwich. Four blue and orange orbs appeared around him, one turning into a shield that absorbed the strike.

As the shield turned back to an orb, Valdis saw Jason dip the sandwich into the hood and it came out with another bite missing. As Asano looked back, Valdis couldn't see his expression under the hood, yet he was certain it was a grin. The half-finished snack and beverage vanished into dimensional storage and Jason casually brushed off his hand. Then he looked up at Valdis and spoke.

"Bleed for me."

18
A LUNATIC'S NIGHTMARE

THE MIRAGE CHAMBER IN YARESH WAS ONE OF THE NEWEST IN THE WORLD and featured the latest design innovations. Seating was arranged by rank, not because of privilege but because the projections in each section were tailored to different perceptual speeds. When gold-rank fighters were just a blur to lower-rank spectators, it required a curated experience of replays and slow motion for them to enjoy the experience.

Jason had seen some of this from the VIP section, finding it startlingly similar to sports coverage on Earth. There were even commentators. That audio hadn't been piped into the VIP room; it had been playing quietly in the participants' lounge.

The projections not only slowed things down but allowed the audience to see through things they normally couldn't, like the darkness Jason had plunged the arena into. While it looked impressive to the naked eye, it wasn't conducive to keeping track of the action.

From the stands, it looked like the arena was filled with shifting shadows, dancing like a fire that absorbed light instead of shedding it. Just enough of the arena's illusionary sunlight filtered through to create a perpetual murk. Occasional flashes of purple and orange lit up the dark for fleeting moments, revealing glimpses of disturbing silhouettes.

Inside the darkness lurked dark and alien figures. They had a multitude of arms like the branches of barren winter trees. The limbs jutted up from trunks that were vaguely human-shaped, before twisting down like the legs of a spider. Clasped in the pointed fingers at the end of each arm were vicious daggers. Ornate workings of glossy red and black, they would not have looked out of place on a sacrificial altar.

The core bodies of the monstrosities were only the size of a person, but they crowded the arena, leaving no space to hide. What had once been an empty ring of sand was now a bizarre garden of horrors, stolen from a lunatic's nightmare and hidden in the unnatural dark.

In the middle of this was the flashing form of Prince Valdis. Like a fabled hero, he dashed through the nightmare creatures, fending off daggers with his gleaming sword. Too fast for almost anyone to follow, only the projections showed his struggles in any comprehensible way.

Valdis was a gold-ranker, and he hadn't gotten there by ever letting himself take the easy way. He'd fought monsters and cultists. Hunted down necromancers and soul engineers. This was not his first time dancing through the madness of some wizard who turned the world around him into a weapon.

Valdis was as orthodox an adventurer as Jason was bizarre. His essences were common; his ability list full of famous, yet basic, powers. It was not hard to research what Valdis was capable of, compared to the bizarre show Jason was putting on. Even so, most adventurers found Valdis extremely hard to beat. His abilities were simple and predictable, but they were common as dirt for a reason.

Surprise was all well and good, but surprise worked once. Speed, efficiency and versatility worked every time. Valdis was a sword master first, and everything else second. Everything he did was either to advance his training or eliminate an obstacle to that training. If he hadn't found someone he loved in his team, he wouldn't have married because it would have been too much of a time sink.

The result of all this was that Valdis was not intimidated by the terrifying display Jason was putting on. Yes, it was a field of nightmares, but Valdis had slain nightmares before. His mind was razor-focused on what to avoid, opportunities to strike, and ameliorating mistakes already made.

It was interesting that he was fighting the very origin of the System to which everyone now had access. It had told him about the mistake he had made in attempting to cut down all of Asano's familiars. Not only had most of them survived, but it had acquainted Valdis with one of Jason's more annoying abilities.

- You have sinned.
- You have suffered 210 instances of [Sin] for attacking [System Administrator] and his allies within his aura. This cannot be resisted, circumventing ability [Sword Soul].

The message read as if the afflictions were retaliation for attacking the originator of the System, but that was just how the System referred to Asano. This was a function of Jason's aura ability, afflicting any who came after his allies. Even the normally potent affliction-absorbing power Valdis possessed was unable to stop it, although the affliction alone did little. The issue was how it interacted with Jason's other abilities to reduce resistances and increase necrotic damage.

It wasn't hard to get information on Jason's core abilities. They were much less common than those of Valdis, but Jason had been around long enough, and was famous enough, that many of his powers had been tracked and catalogued. The Sin affliction only increased any subsequent necrotic damage, but did not deal any itself. It meant that Valdis needed to avoid follow-up attacks, but avoiding hits was what he did.

Jason's familiars were almost unrecognisable with twisted tree-branch arms sprouting from them. Unlike trees, however, they were extremely mobile. Valdis was constantly on the move as they shadow-jumped through the gloom, in relentless pursuit. It took more than raw speed to evade them, even with the speed Valdis had at his command. Fortunately, he had no shortage of evasion abilities.

Even amongst orthodox sword-masters like Valdis, each adventurer's power set had its own nuances. Valdis' specialty was force projections. Blade projections helped him attack at range or increase his damage up close, but his real signature was afterimages.

He had a slate of evasion powers that left behind images that, at low rank, had been illusions that made useful distractions. At gold rank, they did so much more. Many of his afterimage abilities now produced full force constructs. Some were dangerous and explosive, a threat to anyone trying to hunt him down. Others were hardy, long-lasting and could even fight on their own.

The crowd was eating the battle up and the commentators played up the dark wizard and shining hero narrative.

"Keep an eye on those replays, folks. At any given moment, our valiant prince seems on the cusp of being taken down, only to escape the clutches of sinister sorcery yet again! And remember, this blink-and-you'll-miss-it action is being brought to you by Barrington's Barrels, the best coopers in Upper Fisker! If you're buying a barrel, you'd best be buying a Barrington's Barrels barrel. Gods bedamned, who writes this crap?"

"Ted, they can still hear you. Putting your hand over the pickup doesn't stop the sound projector."

"What? Oh, sorry, folks, there was a little magical issue with the announcement system there…"

Valdis dashed through the arena, barely a blur as his gleaming swords deflected the rain of daggers stabbing at him from every direction. His raw speed, incredible as it was, wasn't up to the task of fending off the forest of blades alone. His abilities left behind afterimages that would fight back and slow down the pursuing familiars, or even explode and wipe one or two of them out.

The afterimages were key to buying Valdis enough breathing room to devise a counterattack. He was still in a constant state of flight, but he was at least free enough to consider how to turn the tables. The critical point would be identifying where Jason himself was amongst all the shadows and dagger-wielding tentacle arms.

While Valdis was working to give himself space, Jason wasn't idle, sending out an array of spells. All of the familiars echoed his chanting, so Valdis couldn't trace him by sound. It was also impossible to track his location by aura, when every familiar possessed a perfect replica of it. What Valdis suspected Jason didn't know was that he was already sneaking an extra trick from his sleeve.

The advantage of having such a well-known power set was that people didn't expect to be surprised by it. But, as Valdis had learned, that expectation could kill. While the gist of his power set was a surprise to no one, few people outside his own team knew every quirk and nuance. That was especially true as he ranked up, not just from fresh aspects to the abilities but synergies that people weren't expecting.

Valdis couldn't see through darkness with his perception ability, but it did give him perfect awareness of his surroundings within a short distance. It was the cornerstone of his uncanny ability to dodge and deflect attacks, and perfect for someone needing to track a storm of daggers jabbing in from every angle. What was much less known was that it gave him the same ability to sense the space around each of his long-term afterimages. While it seemed like he was being chased around the arena at random, he was, in fact, building a network of perception nodes.

While this was happening, Jason continued his attack. Spells were flung in Valdis' direction, and even he couldn't dodge every attack from the forest of arms. The cuts from the daggers weren't a threat by themselves, but the afflictions they delivered were a different story.

- You have been struck by special attack [Punish] wielded by [Hand of the Reaper].
- You have been dealt necrotic damage. Damage increased by all instances of [Sin].
- You have suffered instances of [Sin], [Wages of Sin], [Thief of Spirit], [Creeping Death], [Rigor Mortis] and [Weakness of the Flesh].
- Your resistances are reduced by the aura [Hegemony].
- You have failed to resist.
- Ability [Sword Soul] has absorbed the afflictions, negating them.
- Capacity of [Sword Soul] has been diminished.
- You have been struck by [Ruin, the Blade of Tribulation].
- You have suffered instances of [Ruination of the Blood], [Ruination of the Flesh] and [Ruination of the Spirit].
- Your resistances are reduced by the aura [Hegemony].
- You have failed to resist.
- Ability [Sword Soul] has absorbed the afflictions, negating them.
- Capacity of [Sword Soul] has been diminished.

Sword Soul was an extremely powerful defensive ability. Not only did it absorb almost any affliction, but passively buffed his other abilities for any unused capacity. It gave Valdis breathing room against someone like Jason, but he'd never experienced its capacity draining so far or so fast. Many essence-users and monsters had a few afflictions, but the rapid depletion of his Sword Soul capacity was more terrifying than all of Asano's theatrics.

There were some afflictions that Sword Soul wouldn't absorb, however. More Sin stacks piled up as the afterimages fought off Jason's familiars. It also didn't stop wounding effects, like Jason's famous bleed attacks.

- You have been struck by special attack [Leech Bite] wielded by [Hand of the Reaper].
- You have suffered [Bleeding]. [Sword Soul] cannot absorb wounding effects.
- As you have an existing [Bleeding] effect, you have been drained of health and stamina.
- You have suffered instances of [Leech Toxin], [Tainted Meridians], [Thief of Life], [Creeping Death], [Rigor Mortis] and [Weakness of the Flesh].
- Your resistances are reduced by the aura [Hegemony].
- You have failed to resist.
- Ability [Sword Soul] has absorbed the afflictions, negating them.
- Capacity of [Sword Soul] has been diminished.
- You have been struck by [Ruin, the Blade of Tribulation].
- You have suffered instances of [Ruination of the Blood], [Ruination of the Flesh] and [Ruination of the Spirit].
- Your resistances are reduced by the aura [Hegemony].
- You have failed to resist.
- Ability [Sword Soul] has absorbed the afflictions, negating them.
- Capacity of [Sword Soul] has been diminished.

The bleeding and necrotic damage were stacking up, with all the Sin stacks Valdis had taken, but he was gold rank. It would take more than that to slow him down, let alone put him in real danger. The true threat was his Sword Soul running out, at which point afflictions would start landing on him like bricks from the sky. He needed to hunt Jason down before his Sword Soul was expended, but Asano was making himself hard to find.

Jason was almost indistinguishable from his familiars, wrapped in a cloak he turned black and sprouting the same nest of arms. In the gloom, there was no telling the difference, visually. This was where the experience Valdis had built up came into play. As the son of the Mirror King, Valdis was more experienced than most with people using illusions and mirror duplicates to hide themselves.

Using essence abilities was the key to being a good adventurer. Going beyond them was the key to being a great one. Valdis had spent years learning the hard way how to spot the potential tells that differentiated a magician from their clones, duplicates and illusions.

Some made a mistake with disguising their aura, while others left small visible flaws in their disguise that a keen eye could spot. The real experts didn't make such mistakes, however. The secret to teasing out their real location was in watching behaviour, and that was the case for Asano. His aura control was perfect and the gloom covered minor visual inconsistencies. But Asano and his familiars were not the same entity. Even disguised as his familiar, there were subtle differences in the way he moved.

It shouldn't have mattered. Even with perception powers, Asano was so hard to make out that anyone busy dodging daggers in the dark wouldn't notice. What Valdis had learned from hard-earned experience was that the things that shouldn't matter were often the keys to victory. His network of afterimages wasn't just fending off shadow familiars but also letting him watch them.

One of his afterimage variants lasted a long time, making his search for Asano possible. They were turning red, which he'd never seen before, but whatever Asano was doing, it didn't seem to work. The afterimages were immune to most afflictions and weren't being destroyed, and that was what mattered. They let him keep an eye out, and let him spot one of the creepy arm trees moving a little differently than the others. Without hesitation, he pounced.

Part of being an orthodox human essence-user was being very focused on special attacks. Valdis had a smorgasbord of such abilities, for killing things in every situation. Some specialised in cutting down spectral monsters, others in cracking armour or breaching magical barriers. For Jason, he appeared out of nowhere and unleashed his attack for *absolutely killing the damn thing right now.*

Cross Slash was one of the most common attacks in the world. Easily obtained through the sword essence, it allowed for multiple, near-instantaneous strikes. At low ranks, it was a solid workhorse of a move, useful for dropping weaker creatures in a single hit. As things grew much tougher at silver rank, it became a mana efficient means to pile-on damage. At gold rank, however, it became a different beast entirely.

At gold rank, a mana-intensive, long cooldown variant became available. It could inflict countless strikes so swiftly that it bent time itself to do so. It became such a trump card that Valdis had lost his fight with Sophie Wexler when he was gobsmacked at how she'd countered it. She had accelerated time herself, perfectly blocking each strike with raw skill, then punched him in his astonished face.

That was not something Jason could do. Valdis' sword passed right through Jason's body before he had a chance to react. Through his neck and through his head. Through his limbs so many times, they were not just cut off but cut to pieces, all in a single instant. It was so fast that Asano was still standing when he started to fall apart.

19

WHEN PEOPLE SEE MY POWERS

LIFE FORCE WAS AN ODD THING. THE MORE JASON ROSE IN RANK, THE more his body became an arbitrarily shaped collection of blood, flesh and bone. The very concept of life force was increasingly divorced from the condition of his body, becoming more like abstract health points from a game.

The way life force manifested at high levels differed from person to person. For most, they seemed impervious to damage when their life force was high. Their health points were reduced with minimal, if any, injury to show for it. For others, including Jason, it worked differently. Like a vampire, his body seemed almost too vulnerable for its rank, yet instantaneously healed outrageous and seemingly lethal injuries.

Valdis was well-versed in the variations of life force. For all the damage he had unloaded on Jason, he knew there was no one-shotting a gold-ranker. The moment his attack landed, he dashed back to avoid dagger-wielding shadow arms. Staying on the move, he unleashed another of his big-ticket attacks, Blade Wave Barrage. As the name suggested, it sent a storm of razor-sharp force waves in Jason's direction.

By the time they arrived, Jason's segmented body had already made itself whole. Strands of blood had reached out, grabbed the chunks of his body and yanked themselves back together as if nothing had happened.

Jason pulled his cloak around himself, appearing as if he were a portal to a starry void. Valdis believed it was nothing but more theatrics until his blade waves shot through the portal and sailed off into the void.

"Wait, *what*?"

In the participants lobby, Emir and Constance were lounging by a projection screen watching the fight and listening to the commentary. He had a beverage in a long-stemmed glass, while she was empty-handed, keeping her mind on her own upcoming fight. Although she had reached gold rank, she had always been a better administrator than fighter. She was nervous about fighting in front of such a large crowd. Emir didn't care, as he had been a fighter enough to have long ago learned how to take the losses.

He chuckled when Valdis' attack vanished through Jason, who was apparently now the living portal he looked like.

"I was waiting for that," he said, saluting the projection screen with his glass before sipping from it.

"What was that?" Constance asked.

"That cloak ability of his," Emir said. "Most people think that the gold-rank ability just turns you insubstantial, and it does, but that's more of a secondary effect. What it really does is become an aperture to a dimensional space. I know a guy who likes baiting charge attacks into it. Living things kind of pop back into normal reality, but it messes them up quite badly."

"That sounds strong."

"Very. It's a fantastic ability, but timing and judgement is everything. The mana consumption is apparently heinous, so you have to pick your moments carefully. I've never known anyone who could sustain it for more than a few seconds at a time."

The commentator was likewise astounded by the turn of events.

"What did we just see? Have my eyes gone wonky? Judging by the roar of the crowd I can hear all the way from my booth, I'm going to say no! Our dark sorcerer just turned into *a hole in the universe* that sucked away our hero's attacks! We thought the prince had finally caught the villain by the ankle, but he's once again on the back foot!"

"What exactly is the point of this man?" Constance asked. "We can see what's happening without him explaining things."

"It's about excitement," Emir said. "There's nothing wrong with a little showmanship. Jason understands that very well."

"A little too well," Constance pointed out. "And I don't think this commentator is very good. I think he's meant to be contextualising the curated events being slowed down and displayed, but he's mostly just yelling."

"WOO!" the commentator yelled. "Distracted by whatever we just saw, Prince Valdis is once more fleeing the creepy dagger trees. The crowd is going absolutely wild! It feels like the roof could blast right off the arena. Ted, what did I tell you about coming into the booth while I'm..."

There was some mumbling through which only a few words could be made out.

"...why would maintenance... imprinting on what... you said covering it with a wet towel would..."

"Yes," Emir said. "I think you're right about him not being very good."

The commentator returned, sounding much more subdued.

"Sorry about that, audience. I've been asked to very specifically assure you that the arena is *not* going to blow up. On a completely unrelated note, I'll be taking a short break, during which my assistant, Ned, will be taking over commentary."

"What?"

"Get in here, Ned."

"I don't want to, Ted. You heard what they—"

"Get in the damn chair, Ned!"

There were sounds of shuffling.

"Uh, hello. I'm Ned."

"Gods bedamned, Ned, talk about the action!"

"Oh, uh, Prince Valdis seems to have resumed his attacks on Asano's real body—"

"Call him the dark sorcerer, Ned."

"That seems weird."

"Just do it!"

"Um, okay. Valdis is once more attacking Dark Sorcerer Ned in a series of hit-and-run exchanges—"

"Don't call him Ned! That's your name!"

"You said to call him Dark Sorcerer Ned. Everyone heard you."

"Oh, sweet gods."

Valdis was getting a handle on dealing with the shadow arms. They were impervious to normal attacks, but his Spectral Slash could easily destroy them. Asano was then forced to recreate them to keep the pressure on in the face of Valdis' speed. That also cost mana, which was now an important factor. That cloak portal trick could absorb almost any attack, but anything that powerful had to burn through mana like fire in a paper factory.

Asano was adapting in turn, however, using the shadow arms to limit the potential angles of attack. He was also more skilled with the arms attached to his own body, one of which used a sword instead of a dagger. Even so, Asano was taking solid hits on a regular basis. Valdis had a variety of special attacks, letting him mix up trickiness and raw power. He was also just faster. If not for Jason's absurd regenerative power, the fight may well have been over, but this was like trying to fell a tree that kept growing back.

The potency of Asano's healing was bad for Valdis, who preferred a more in-and-out approach. He was forced to go on the offence harder, burning more mana and taking more hits himself. If he ran out of mana or Sword Soul capacity before Asano ran out of health, it was over.

Asano pulled out the orbs belonging to his familiar again. Valdis was able to break them down using his array of tailored attacks, but it cost him critical time. He pushed all the harder, and could see Jason flagging as his life force was cut away, slash by slash.

"Munsen, what is happening with the mana imprinting?"

"It's everywhere, boss. The manual shutdown isn't working. Unless we physically start hacking apart conduits with an axe, it's going to do whatever it's doing."

"An axe? Those things are built to handle diamond-rank mana flow. Unless you have a diamond-rank axe essence you didn't mention in your job application, we're going to need another idea."

"All out, boss, sorry."

"At least it doesn't seem to be volatile, so probably no explosion. That leaves the question of what it is doing."

"Uh, Ted? What's that thing on the projection?"

"Is that... the System?"

"Look, it's got the health and mana of the fighters, that's handy. Wow, Valdis is low on mana and... what's a Sword Soul?"

"Yeah, but look at Asano's health. If he doesn't do something, this fight will be ending very soon."

Valdis was looking for an angle for what he hoped was a final push. He would probably have to accept whatever one Asano set up for him and trust his skills to fight through the trap. That was when he realised that Jason had set the trap long ago. Valdis had committed a cardinal sin: fighting against a shadow magician and watching every shadow but his own.

Despite the gloom, there was never a total absence of light. Valdis himself had a shadow, almost invisible in the darkness, but still there. Dagger wielding arms erupted like the tentacles of a kraken, trying to stab and entangle him. It was a testament to his miraculous reflexes that he managed to dodge, weave and parry enough that his last shred of Sword Soul capacity wasn't snatched away.

Unfortunately, fights were all about stealing the critical moments. Valdis knew well that to win those was to win the fight. With the speed gold-rankers were capable of, it was more the case now than when he was lower rank. While Valdis was dodging, Jason was taking the chance to cast one of his slightly longer spells.

"Your blood is not yours to keep, but mine on which to feast."

That was Jason's life drain spell, Valdis knew. It would heal him a little, but not much. Valdis couldn't stop his life force from being drained, but he was the only living thing to target. One person wasn't enough to...

When red lines started streaming through the dark around him, Valdis had no idea what was happening. There was no way Asano could or would drain the audience. Then Valdis saw what was happening and—not for the first time—was taken aback. Valdis was very much about skill and persistence over surprise in combat, but he was forced to admit that surprise had its place.

Jason was draining life from the afterimages that Valdis was using to occupy most of the shadowy arm trees. He had seen Asano turn them red somehow, but now he was actually draining life force from them. That should not have been possible, yet not only was it happening, it was killing the afterimages. They weren't just dying either, but drooping in the air like bloody ghosts.

That was when things got bad.

Freed of the images keeping them occupied, every shadow tree converged on Valdis, right as he was escaping the attacks from his own shadow. He kept ahead of the attacks, every moment a hair's breadth from defeat as he moved, dodged and deflected with every skill and defensive power at his command. That he could manage it under the circumstances was a little astounding, even to him. But while he was doing this, Asano cast another spell.

"As your lives were mine to reap, so your deaths are mine to harvest."

Once more, streams of life force snaked their way through the dark for Jason to absorb. The bloody ghosts that had been Valdis' force constructs now finally disappeared, whatever magic they had consumed by Jason.

The fighting stopped. The arms stopped pursuing and the familiars backed away. Valdis stood, panting, even his gold-rank stamina pushed to the limit. The shadow arms retracted, leaving a crowd of Jason's shadow familiars around them. Only the arms jutting from Jason himself remained, daggers still in hand.

The gloom around them started to break, slowly letting the sun back in. The arena once more became a circle of sand. Jason moved slowly towards Valdis, looking at him with those merciless, alien eyes. In one of the shadow hands was a sword, glowing red runes carved into the black blade. Jason pushed the hood of his cloak back, revealing his face.

"You look spent, swordsman," he said.

"You look fresh."

"That and then some. I've got more health and mana than when we started."

He raised his sword.

"Shall we make a show of it, at the end?"

"You'd challenge me to the sword?" Valdis asked. "Are you condescending to me?"

"Just the opposite. Why do you think I let you push me into this? I've spent a lot of time working on my swordsmanship. I want to see how it fares against a true swordsman."

Valdis nodded and raised his sword, then was on Jason in a blur. They clashed, one sword against a sword and six daggers, Jason's speed approaching that of Valdis himself. The sword master wasn't surprised, knowing that this was a trick of Asano's. If he had fallen foes to drain, he started moving and healing much faster than before. It shouldn't have been a threat with no dead foes to drain, but Asano had managed it anyway.

The arms Jason used himself were an order of magnitude different to those wielded by his familiar. Those were powers, working on an echo of the true master, much like Valdis' own afterimages. The daggers and sword clashing with Valdis were something else entirely.

It was a strange fighting style, not bound to the human form. This was what Valdis was constantly in search of: aspects or swordsmanship unlike anything he'd seen before. This was no gimmick, however. As much as anyone, Valdis recognised the fruits of long, hard training. Asano knew well how to make the most of his strange combat style, and was clearly experienced in its use.

The two men clashed across the battlefield at speeds staggering even by gold-rank standards. The projection slowed the action down, struggling to catch up even with pauses between exchanges. Both men were soon grinning as they pushed the very limits of their skills.

Jason's inhuman swordsmanship was no shallow trick, but a well-honed style. It suited someone with so many strange aspects to his power set, but that was also the problem. Jason's approach not just to combat, but adventuring as well, required so many skills that Valdis had no idea how his swordsmanship was this good, as Valdis was a man of the sword alone.

If this had been the beginning of the fight, and if this had been the way they had fought it, then Valdis would have won. Even dealing with a half-dozen extra arms, he was landing more hits than Asano. But this was not the beginning of the fight; it was the end. Valdis was low on mana, while Jason was flush with health and mana both. Valdis could no longer pull out any big attacks, and Jason just healed through anything else.

The end came when Valdis' Sword Soul finally gave out. Rather than experience a slow and horrific ugly defeat, he yielded the match.

The magic keeping the sound out dropped and the roar of the crowd crashed over them. People were on their feet, stomping and cheering. Jason turned slowly on the spot, taking it all in with wide eyes.

"Soak it in," Valdis said, and slapped him on the back. "Never done an arena before?"

"No. Normally, when people see my powers, they run."

20

LISTENING FOR WHISPERS

"NOW THAT I'VE SEEN YOU IN ACTION," VALDIS SAID, "I SEE A LOT OF potential angles to take another run at you."

"I hate to break it to you, but I'm not a big arena guy," Jason said.

They were in the participants lobby, lounging with drinks, snacks and some of their friends who had fought already or were getting ready to.

"You should rethink that," Valdis said. "They loved you out there."

"It was a different experience," Jason admitted. "I suppose they know that real dark wizards don't usually show up for spectator fights."

"And they didn't see what your powers actually do to people," Neil added.

Neil was waiting for a healer match against Sigrid. That involved two identical teams of illusionary warriors clashing, with the healers on each providing the difference. It was a slower event than high-ranking combat, and lacked in flash, but it was something that most watchers could observe normally instead of relying on the projections.

Jason looked over curiously at a pair of lobby attendants.

"I can't believe we're out again. What's happening to them all?"

"It's these out-of-town adventurers," the other one said. "Here, I'll take that tray over to the buffet table if you like."

"Thanks, Mike. When did you grow the moustache, by the way?"

"Oh, it's new. Do you think it works?"

"Uh... yes?"

The two parted ways, 'Mike' heading for the buffet table until his colleague was out of sight. He then immediately scarpered so suspiciously he looked like a cartoon bank robber. Over at the buffet table, a local fighter watched him go with a confused expression.

"Where's he taking all the biscuits?"

"No," Clive told Valdis firmly. "Jason is not going back into that thing until we figure out what he did to it."

Clive, somehow, now seemed to be in charge of mirage chamber operations. The staff weren't precisely sure how that happened, but it had involved stabilising the power distribution and whatever had happened to its mana flow. It also involved scathing responses to any questions deemed insufficiently insightful.

"It's fine," Valdis wheedled, more like a child than a gold-rank prince. "Nothing blew up."

"We don't understand how the System managed to imprint itself on the mirage chamber projectors and what the long-term effects will be."

"People love the System integration," Valdis said.

"People love a lot of things that might get them killed, Valdis. I wasn't allowed to cancel the upcoming events, but at least that allows us to monitor what's happening. It would be even better if Jason was here to answer questions instead of sneaking off."

"...and Granny Danielle helped me arrange secretly digging out the underground storage," Stash explained.

He was walking down a hallway beside Jason, looking like a more boyish version of Humphrey but with silver hair and eyes. He appeared as his actual age, which was his early twenties. Jason looked much the same, at a glance, which was normal for essence-users. People could see the age in them, though, in the way they carried themselves.

"She doesn't mind you calling her Granny Danielle?" Jason asked.

"No, she loves it! Humphrey doesn't, though."

"Why not?"

"He says it's giving her ideas."

Jason let out an easy laugh.

They heard a raised voice through a door as they passed.

"…what do you mean, you're adding Ned full-time? I don't care if the audience 'loved the interplay.' The audience are imbeciles who'll eat whatever we feed them. Have you heard those sponsorship announcements? You know Ned writes those, right?"

Glass towers jutted from the central district of Yaresh. The tallest of them tapered to a point, a flat plate on the blunted tip allowing room for one person to stand. The building itself had no access, but offered a vantage from which one could turn and look over the whole city. Doing just that, Jason mused that design was probably not by accident.

"You're in my spot."

Jason smiled, then turned to look at Allayeth. The diamond-ranker was hovering in place, wings spread out behind her. The wings had wooden frames and leaves as feathers.

"That's new," he noted. "Item?"

"Yes. Not all of us just start yanking new and strange powers out of nowhere."

"I have no idea what you're talking about."

A line of cloud material snaked out of Jason's cloud flask, currently hanging on his necklace as an amulet. The cloud took the form of a floating chair and he sat in it, then waved at his previous perch invitingly. After rolling her eyes, Allayeth drifted over and waved a hand over the flat, round platform on the building's peak. The plate on the tip of the building descended into the tapered roof, leaving a hole. Up through the hole rose a luxurious chair, anchored on a swivel. Jason laughed as her branch wings retracted out of sight and she floated into the seat.

"The city is beautiful," Jason said, and meant it. The orange and purple glow of sunset reflected of the river. The skyline was almost entirely trees, with buildings of living wood poking out from the foliage.

He had an affection for tree houses, which Yaresh always had, but now everything had been built to a cohesive plan. The housing wards were tightly packed, with rope bridges between decks and platforms. Trade districts were more open, and included more of the local dark grey stone. The river was no longer lined with piers, docks and warehouses, but now featured a swath of parkland on either side.

"Master craftsmen from the skybranch elves spent years helping with the reconstruction," Allayeth explained. "They're a magical variant of elves, much like the brighthearts originated with the smoulder. I helped them once, as you did with the brighthearts, although the threat was nothing so drastic. It was enough that they were very generous with Yaresh, and gifted me these wings when the job was done."

"The results are impressive."

"The changes go beyond simple looks. Utility infrastructure, magic distribution, evacuation bunkers. The defence systems were completely overhauled. Your friend Travis helped with the new city defences. You can't see it now, but if the defensive barrier gets breached, the trees will grow what he called 'rotary spear cannons' out of stone and wood."

"I'd like to see that in action."

"I hope you never do. When my home and family were destroyed as a child, the idea of a safe home became quite important to me. My inability to protect it from the messengers troubled me greatly. I was unable to even attempt advancing through diamond rank for many years. Now that it is restored, and more defended than ever, I have finally achieved a measure of peace."

"Only a few diamond-rankers involve themselves in the affairs of society, yes? You and Charist here. The Mirror King and Roland Remore."

"Most move unseen, seeking a path to whatever lies at the peak of diamond rank. To me, it's unclear to the point of not being sure it exists."

"It exists."

"I suppose it must seem straightforward to someone living your life. For me, it's listening for whispers in a storm. Perhaps things will be clearer for you. You seem to have little trouble finding the path, and you are not alone in this. I am young by diamond-rank reckoning, but your generation of adventurers is the strongest I have seen. Not just in how powerful you all are, but in how swiftly you advance. A product of coming up in an age of turmoil, I suppose."

"There is a curse on the world I come from: May you live in interesting times."

Allayeth laughed.

"I see. These last couple of decades have been a crucible. The great monster surge, timed alongside the Builder invasion, was just the beginning. The world has been at war with the messengers ever since. They sweep through an area, in search of Purity's legacy relic. Then they move on. Sometimes they leave behind some of their number to rule an enslaved region. Other times, they leave only ruins, depending on how hard they were fought."

"How well are they being fought off?"

"Well enough in the core regions. Adventurers and resources are centralised in large population centres, too heavily for the messengers to strike at without massive cost. More isolated regions have been the focus; there are many remote city-states like Yaresh. Vulnerable regions rely on the holy armies raised by the gods and, increasingly, those of nations and city-states. Knowledge was preparing her army before anyone knew they needed to, and War did the same in response. Nations and other churches have been copying their example for years now, but there are only so many essence-users to go around."

"Standing armies were never something this world had, right? Pallimustus has always relied on adventurers."

"Yes, and adventurers are still the tip of the spear. But they are individualistic by nature, and do not make good soldiers. They don't like taking orders, and anyone who has been on an expedition knows the challenges that come from wrangling them in large groups. There are not enough to make true armies of them anyway. The problem with using anyone else is that the most basic messenger is silver rank. There is little point sending waves of bronze-rankers to die just to eliminate one of them. Those commanders who try have been savagely rebuked."

Jason let out a sigh. "I've returned to a war, then."

"Yes. Yaresh has been quiet since the last of the messengers were wiped out. The messengers move like locusts in search of their goal. If they do not find what they want in the more rural regions, they will eventually make more concerted attacks on the cities."

"I suppose I should go sign up."

"And you would be welcome. But I think, perhaps, you've become so used to being the focal point of events that you forget not everything is about you. This is the world's war, not yours, and we've done well enough in your absence. I know you intend to return home, and you have earned that. We'll continue doing fine without you, and there will be plenty of messengers to fight on your return."

"Thank you. I'd invite you to come with us, but Earth isn't ready for diamond-rankers. It barely has the magic for gold-rankers, and there are still mana deserts where it's rough for them to be."

"It would be fascinating to see, but I still have much to do here. Yaresh is rebuilt, but the surroundings regions are not so far along. We still rely on the brighthearts for much of our food as we establish new farming towns. Getting people to repopulate the existing ones has been something of a disaster, so building fresh ones is proving more effective."

"It's easy to overlook what comes next when your job is in fleeting moments of violence and destruction. How hours, even minutes, of fighting can mean months and years of recovery."

"Yes, but those of us who fight have our place as well. Thank you for preventing an unstoppable army of undead from rising out of the ground and flooding my home with death and despair, by the way."

"It took a lot more than just me, but you're welcome."

"You were in charge, Jason. That means you take the credit, even if you sat back helplessly and did nothing."

"Hey, who have you been talking to?"

Although there was a river running through Yaresh, few of the docks and industrial facilities that once lined its shores had been rebuilt. What remained was all near the downstream river gate, where the water passed under the wall and out of the city.

Memorial Park now occupied most of the shoreline on both sides of the river, full of open space, greenery and picturesque bridges. The park was dotted with statues, sculptures and memorial walls dedicated to those who had fallen, and those who protected the ones that survived.

Jason found Farrah standing in front of a sculpture of Gary fighting a messenger. Unlike Jason and his team, who had been in the thick of the fighting, Gary had single-handedly led a large group of survivors to safety. They had mostly been craftsmen and manufacturers, and upon hearing of Gary's death, they had not only sponsored, but created the display. It showed him roaring in defiance at a messenger, sheltering people behind him.

"Why do they only show him fighting and roaring, like some savage warrior?" she asked as Jason stood next to her.

"This isn't him. Statues are about what people need, not the people they show, and these people needed heroes. Fighters. The man he was— who he *really* was—isn't for the people visiting this park to remember. It's for us, the people who loved him. We're his true memorial, not a statue in a park or a plaque on a wall."

She reached out, hesitant, and brushed her fingers against the stone.

"I can't keep looking at this," she said, then turned and strode away.

Jason followed, a few steps behind, until she arrived at a wooden bench by the water. They sat, letting the sounds of the park wash over them. The sun was high, the sky was clear and there were a lot of families out enjoying the park. Children laughed as they chased small animals into the bushes and parents warned them not to wander too far. Teenagers splashed around in the river, which was clear down to the bottom. The new sanitation infrastructure and lack of river industry had left the water pristine.

"You said you didn't know, but you kind of did," Farrah said after minutes of neither saying a word.

"You know how this works. I have vague ideas at best about what's happening with me. This time, it was you and me, but the uncertainty is the same."

"I don't want to be just some attachment to you. Or a slave."

"You know better than that."

"Of course I do, but you're the one with all the power. I'm the one being turned into some kind of magical servant. I'm not your familiar."

"I know that. I like to think that being my familiar isn't so bad, but you aren't some astral being. Your idea of existing is very different from theirs. I would never expect you to see things the way they do."

"What am I, then? Whenever you did… whatever it is that you did, the bond between us got stronger. A lot stronger. My abilities won't advance until I accept this damn thing."

She brought up a system window.

- [Jason Asano] has half-ascended to the status of [Astral Nexus].
- You are bonded to the [Astral Nexus].
- You have been assigned the status [Voice of the Will] of the [Astral Nexus].
- As a [Voice of the Will], you will have access to a measure of power belonging to the [Astral Nexus] while also being subject to its dictates.
- Until you acknowledge this role, your status will be in flux, impeding your ability to advance your essence abilities.

"It needs to get into my soul, Jason. To change me. It already has enough access through our bond to mess me up. It's holding my advancement to ransom."

"I know. And I'm sorry. You've had to live with this, not knowing if there was any solution while I was out of reach. I was aware of it, on some level, but I couldn't fix it while I was still fixing myself. And I can't do it here either."

"What do you mean by fix it? Sever the bond?"

"If that's what you want. I'm hoping that I can do better, though. I need to get you into my astral kingdom so I can take a proper look at our connection. If you still trust me enough to go somewhere I have all the power."

"Don't be an idiot. I still trust you. Why did you wait until now to come to me?"

"I've been watching your emotions."

"Through the bond?"

"I can't do that. I've just been peeking with aura senses, rude as that is. And I think you knew that. I've been waiting for you to be ready, and I think that you came here because you are now."

She nodded, Jason's heart breaking at the fearful hesitance in one of the strongest people he knew. A portal arch of white stone opened in front of them and filled with gold, silver and blue light. He stood up and held his hand out to her. She reached out and took it.

21

DEFIER

FARRAH STEPPED OUT OF THE PORTAL ONTO SAND. SHE WAS ON A BEACH that ran from turquoise water up to rainforest. A trail went off though the trees and a pier led into the water where a cluster of bungalows sat on stilts. The beach wrapped around a lagoon, sheltering the over-water bungalows. Looking back over the trees, several small mountains were visible, waterfalls spilling off their sides.

Jason stepped out of the portal to join her, the archway then vanishing into the sand. She looked up at the clear sky, feeling the fresh sea breeze take the edge off the sun's heat.

"I feel odd," she said. "Something is… my powers are gone."

"Yes," Jason said.

"But I don't feel uncomfortable, as if they were being suppressed. They're just… not there."

"When I was making this planet, I didn't pay specific attention to every little detail. It was more like creating a seed with certain parameters and letting the laws of physics and magic sort themselves out as it grew. There are a few places I did pay closer attention to, though, and this is one of them."

"A prison?"

Jason let out a wincing laugh.

"That's a little hurtful, after the effort I put in. Does it look like a prison?"

"Then why suppress powers?"

"They're not suppressed. They just don't exist here. This island is named Refuge, and it's what it says on the tin. It's a place where I, and the people most important to me, can get away from all the travails of the cosmos. It's about letting go of the responsibilities that we have to deal with everywhere else. Here, we take things slow. No powers. You'll even find that your speed and strength are capped, if you try to push them. Even my prime avatar is affected."

"I don't know if Sophie is going to like that."

"She'll get over it. Shade has been working on his cocktail game."

"Mixology, Mr Asano."

"Sorry. He's been working on his mixology."

Farrah stared at Jason's shadow.

"Is he never not in there?" she asked.

"Uh…"

Farrah looked at her own shadow, then back up at Jason.

"Just so you know," he said hastily as he sped up his walking speed, "I'm still working on options to fix our bond. Overmind Jason is, anyway. Prime avatar Jason is still here."

"Then prime avatar Jason needs a talk about boundaries and where his shadow familiar goes."

"Ooh, I bet the view from that bluff is excellent," he responded, speeding up again.

"What happened to taking things slow?" she called after him.

While Jason's avatar guided Farrah through the rainforest trails, Jason delved into the magic of the bond linking them together. It was distinct from the connections he had with his familiars, where he was the origin of the bond. His connection with Farrah had originated with her ability to bond with people, acquired when she resurrected as an outworlder. It had reacted to the changes in Jason until they noticed the bond and had ultimately chosen to enhance it.

Now that Jason had a vastly powerful transcendent aspect, his power was trying to make use of that bond. And, as much as Jason was loath to admit it, the more tyrannical aspects of his subconscious were trying to subjugate her through it. That was not something he was going to put up with. He explored the magic involved, gaming out possible ways the bond could be manipulated.

While he was doing this, Farrah and his avatar reached the main buildings of the island resort he'd created. The buildings were made from bamboo, wood and natural stone, and set to maximise the feel of a rainforest grove. Several creeks and streams flowed under little bridges and even under the buildings, and a river flowed nearby. Farrah spotted bungalows, indoor and open-air lounges, a bar and a games room. In the open-front buildings by the river, she saw canoes and what looked like wooden jet skis.

"Jason, this is all very nice, but this is not what I'm here for."

"I know. I'm working on it."

"Aren't you basically a god here?"

"Nothing that limited. But it's not like they put you through a two-week orientation course when you become half transcendent. I still have a lot to learn, and I can't afford to make a mistake here. Not with you."

They made their way deep into the island. Trails of packed earth and fallen leaves gave way to rough-cut stone steps as they began a gradual ascent. Finally, Jason brought her to a grotto half set into a cave. Water spilled down over rocks, into a pool of pristine water, from where it drained off into a little creek. The rocks were flat, and many were covered in soft-looking grasses and moss. Near the entrance was a gazebo of wood and bamboo, containing a picnic table, benches and a grill.

"I want to bring everyone here, in time," Jason said. "I want this place to be where we come to be together and forget about all the troubles the cosmos sees fit to pile onto us. And I want to start by fixing something that I've put on you, however inadvertently."

"You can fix the bond?"

"I have some options. The power disparity between us is a problem, I won't lie. My power wants to make you obey."

"Then tell it no."

Jason grinned.

"I was thinking the same thing," he told her. "Obviously, making you subject to my will is unacceptable. After looking for some kind of workable compromise, however, I realised that just isn't viable. So, if only extremes will work, I wondered what would happen if we went the other way?"

"Other way?"

A system window popped up in front of Farrah.

- The [Astral Nexus] has proposed an alternative to your pending status change.

- Your available options are [Voice of the Will] and [Defier of the Will].
- As a [Voice of the Will], you will have access to a measure of power belonging to the [Astral Nexus] while also being subject to its dictates.
- As a [Defier of the Will], you will have the ability to negate influence of the [Astral Nexus] in various ways. The [Astral Nexus] will be unable to harm you with its power or the magical abilities of its avatars. You will be able to negate the prime avatar and undo aspects of its influence outside of its domains. You will be able to isolate areas within its domains, but not its astral kingdom, from its influence. The [Astral Nexus] will have no ability to undo or revoke your authority to negate its power.
- As a [Voice of the Will] or [Defier of the Will], you will be immortal. Your body and soul gestalt will not be fully destroyed but will take significant time to remake itself within the astral kingdom. Unlike a [Voice of the Will], you will not otherwise gain the access to the power of the [Astral Nexus].

Farrah stared at the window for a long time.

"What is this?" she asked finally.

"We both know that I can lose my way. I'm better now, but the future is long and uncertain. You've always been the one I could trust when I couldn't trust myself. That's hard if you don't have the power to stop me when I need to be stopped. This would give it to you."

"You have so much power. You can't use it outside of your private universe yet, but some day, you will have that power."

"Yes. And you know I've been worried for a long time about not having a check on that power. I'm asking you to be the one that holds me to account."

"Immortality."

"Yes."

"True immortality."

"Yeah. You'll outlive the sun. We can have a sandwich to celebrate."

He wandered over to the gazebo, making his way up the short stairs. A tray of sandwiches was sitting on the table, along with a large pitcher and two glasses.

"Not to pressure you or anything, but there's some iced tea up here as well. It's peach."

"Are you attempting to bribe me into immortality with a light lunch?"

"It's immortality. I shouldn't have to sell it, right? But if you don't like the immortality options, I can sever the bond altogether."

"It feels like this should be more of a conversation. Immortality isn't a small thing."

"No," he agreed, giving her a sad smile. "No, it's not. I only missed fifteen years or so, and that was so long in the lives of my family back on Earth. I never intended to stay away so long. And that's just a drop in the ocean compared to what immortality has to offer. People will live out entire lives while we remain unchanging. We'll love them for the time they have, and lose them. It won't be small thing."

"You've thought about this a lot."

"That, and there's a lot of books and TV shows exploring the idea."

"Is it stupid to hesitate at the idea of immortality?"

"Of course not. And that's without even broaching the topic of what this means for you and me. Come up and have a sandwich and we'll hash it out."

Jason, Clive, Travis and the Cloudweaver were in a workshop, in the Yaresh branch of the Magic Research Association. They were seated around a table on which rested Jason's cloud flask. Jason flicked it and smoke poured out, black instead of the usual white. It formed a cloud that filled the room to the high ceiling before it stopped spreading.

Points of light appeared in the smoke like stars in a night sky, silvery lines linking them together in constellations. As more and more stars and lines appeared, it went from constellations to a celestial spider's web to something far too complex and dense to be either.

"Normal so far," the Cloudweaver said as they observed the process.

Then their eyes went wide as some of the points started changing colour. The dots of light and their connecting lines turned blue and orange, slowly at first but rapidly accelerating. They glowed brighter as they went, making the observers lose track of specific points as the light diffused in the black smoke. By the time it was done, it looked like a blue and orange eye, glowing from within the dark.

"Well, it's certainly dramatic," the Cloudweaver said.

"It's Jason," Clive said. "It always works like this. We're lucky the mirage chamber didn't just blast a massive aura projection over the city. Again."

"I'm going to need my tools to get a better look at what's going on here," Cloudweaver said. "Did you say they have a mana spectrum prism matrix?"

"They do," Clive said. "They're bringing it down now. I thought a localised refinement differentiator would be useful as well."

"That's a good idea," the Cloudweaver said.

"That's my cue to leave," Jason said. "It sounds like magic *Star Trek* in here. Have fun with your deflector dish, and don't get too pokey or the flask will smite you."

Jason got up and walked out, leaving the other three behind.

"He was joking about the smiting, right?" Travis asked.

"Probably," Clive said. "It wouldn't hurt to be careful as we go, though."

Jason left the trio to examine his cloud flask, one of the last tasks before he and his friends packed up to leave the planet. Much of the reunion group had already left Yaresh, having their own preparations to make before the expedition to Earth. Jason had several stops to make, including rounding up the Earthlings in Estercost and anchoring the link between worlds, which he would do in the Storm Kingdom.

Leaving the main workshop building, Jason headed for a nearby loading area. Normally used for bringing in supplies to the workshops, today Humphrey and Neil were there preparing a huge pile of goods. Once Jason got the flask back, it would all be loaded into a cloud vehicle. While heading in their direction, he spotted Danielle Geller and changed course.

"Danielle. We never had a chance to catch up properly."

"It seemed like you were having a busy week."

"Tell me about it. Adventure Society briefings. Parts one and two of the Clive sessions, which I'm assuming will continue until I die."

"Aren't you immortal?"

"Don't remind me. I just convinced someone else to join the immortal club."

"Farrah?"

166 SHIRTALOON & TRAVIS DEVERELL

"Yeah."

"How is she?"

"Asleep. The process of change was one thing, then it was like her halted advancement was unleashed all at once. Half of her abilities advanced simultaneously, which was apparently rough. She's still a step or two from gold."

"But immortal now."

"She'll have time, yes."

Danielle shook her head.

"I remember when Rufus Remore came to visit me in Greenstone, telling me he'd met an unusual young man. And now that young man is casually mentioning how he's made a woman he once resurrected immortal now."

"It was the Reaper on the resurrection, and circumstance on the other thing. It's not like I'm running around handing out immortality tickets."

"Well, if you do, let me know. There was something you wanted to discuss?"

"Some things I'd like your advice on, if you can spare a few moments."

"Certainly. Shall we take a walk?"

"I could show you my universe. It's not as big as some, but I could whip it out right here."

They turned at hearing Neil laugh and saw him pointing at them. A disgruntled Humphrey fished a gold spirit coin from his pocket and handed it over.

"I do believe that you just lost my son a bet," Danielle said. "Probably best not to ask what about."

"Oh, I think I know."

"As do I, sadly. Fascinated as I am to see your own little universe, it might be best to take a regular walk instead of nipping through a portal together."

"I think you're right."

22

VAST COSMIC POWER TYPES

<small>Compared to most of Yaresh, the district containing the Magical</small> Research Association campus was heavy on stone and light on trees. It certainly had none of the towering glass of the central district. Located right across the road from the campus was the Alchemy Association's main research centre. The urban planners in charge of rebuilding Yaresh wanted to centralise the places most prone to unexpected explosions, inadvertent poison fog and accidental fire titan summoning.

There were no houses or shops, only long-term storehouses and other low-traffic facilities that minimised collateral damage risk. That made it one of the least interesting districts for Danielle and Jason to take their walk through. The buildings were largely square and dark grey, with only a few lonely trees to break up the monotony.

While the footpath was made of familiar flagstones, the road, like others in Yaresh, was sealed in some manner of brown concrete. With nothing more interesting to catch his eye, the road was what caught Jason's attention. He crouched beside it to run his fingers across it.

"It looks almost like tree bark in colour, but it feels like regular asphalt concrete."

"Regular?" Danielle asked. "This seems like unusual road surfacing, to my eye."

"Regular for Earth. We don't have a lot of stone-shapers in civil engineering, so this is normal there. I haven't seen a lot of concreting in Pallimustus. This looks more like it was laid the Earth way, though."

He stood up and they continued their way down the footpath.

"Is civil infrastructure an interest of yours?" Danielle asked.

"Sort of. My father is a landscape architect, and you pick things up. I know more about grass than you'd imagine. He did a lot of work in front of government buildings, so he dealt with a lot of driveways. He'd love to see what they've accomplished with Yaresh."

"Then show him. You can take people there, so surely you can bring others back."

"It's not a matter of ability. I intended to bring them last time, but…"

He sighed.

"It didn't work out."

"You're concerned about complications on your return."

"Yeah, but isn't it always like that with family? Especially after a long time away with no communication."

"I suppose so," Danielle said. "Things are a little different in my family. We have essences to extend our lifespans, and expectations of duty."

She scowled.

"Expectations are very high in my family, which can be a point of pride. But while they can drive someone like Humphrey to greatness, they can crush others beneath them. Your family was unused to the power and longevity that comes of magic, correct?"

"They weren't," Jason confirmed. "I took them halfway around the world, leaving them with a handful of essence-users, a stockpile of essences and a couple of magical cities to live in. Then I disappeared on them. No communication for over a decade. I was able to send them Rufus, but not much else."

"Magical cities? Like Rexion?"

"Yes. They've been living in cities built from my power. Not just *with* my power, but literally made of it. The streets they walk and the houses they live in. And, like in Rexion, there are children who grew up hearing my name but never seeing me. I was a distant and abstract figure, spoken of, but never present. Yet my power was everywhere, like some ancestral ghost. And that power was not always consistent. I had to hide it for a long time, trapping the clan in astral spaces."

"But they are out now? And you're in contact with them, using your avatars?"

"Now, yes, but most still haven't seen me. And that's not a normal way to encounter a person. Popping in and out of existence, reshaping the world around them on a whim. I'm lucky they didn't see me deal with the vampire city that was over their heads for a decade."

"You don't know how to act when you return properly."

"No, I don't. Magic is still relatively new to Earth. Twenty years ago, it was still a secret, and even now, my power is like nothing else on it. No one knows how to treat me, and I'm unsure how to act. I suppose things were very different for you, coming from a big adventuring family."

"Yes. For mine, power is long established. The trouble it brings comes from the expectations that power brings. Only a fraction of the family become adventurers, and only a fraction of those become high rank and famous. But there's a pressure on all of us as children, to at least potentially become one of those few. To maintain the family legacy. We're all expected to strive for that until we prove ourselves. Or prove ourselves inadequate. There's little consideration for anyone to want something else until they've been branded a failure at what matters most. I had a sister who... suffice to say, I am proud of our family and its name, but I do not care for some of the culture we've built up trying to maintain it. Sometimes I wonder if Humphrey wouldn't have been better off as a soft-hearted labour manager in a spirit coin farm."

Jason laughed at the image.

"He'd be such a soft touch as a boss."

"This issue with your family. Not knowing how to act. Am I correct in guessing that this is only peripheral to what you really wanted to discuss?"

"Yes."

"You want to know how to act on a larger scale. Not just with your clan, but with the whole world."

"Exactly. What do I do when I'm the most powerful person on the planet? Turning up with a collection of gold-rankers who could conquer the place in a week is extremely political, whether I like it or not. And I am not as adept at politics as I thought I would be before I actually involved myself in them."

Danielle chuckled.

"I remember your antics back in Greenstone. You have a political mind, Jason, and see through more than most. But when it comes to your own designs, you get impetuous. Distracted by ideas that appeal more for their cleverness than their practicality. That is when you get blindsided by consequences."

"Oh, I remember, and I can't afford that this time. This isn't messing with some shady local bureaucrats and a dodgy indentured servitude contract. This is world leaders being scared of a potential tyrant."

"And people take drastic steps when they feel scared and powerless. If I recall correctly, that is kind of your thing as well."

"No kidding. On Earth, I'm heading into a situation that can't really hurt me. If people start declaring war on me or something, though, a lot of innocent people could get caught in the crossfire. Back in Greenstone, I had you and Emir to bail me out when I got it wrong. This time, I'm the high-ranker, and the responsibility stops with me. I'll have my friends with me, but it's my world."

"And the power you bring will reshape it, simply by existing."

"Yes. Even if we hide it away and never use our power, people will react to its very existence."

"This is a complicated issue, Jason. A lot more than we could cover on a short stroll, even if I did have an understanding of your world's politics. Which I do not."

"But you understand diplomacy. You understand the kind of power that Earth is only just coming to grips with. Most importantly, I can trust you. The people who already know Earth politics are all on Earth, and most I wouldn't trust to burn if I threw them in a volcano. Which I'm hoping it won't come to."

Danielle laughed.

"You said most you wouldn't trust. There are a few you would?"

"Not many. There's someone who works for my grandmother now. She would be an asset, but I'd really like to recruit a woman she used to work for, to cover the knowledge of Earth politics I don't have."

"The way you're attempting to recruit me now?"

"Not exactly like this. I thought it might be best to let other people make the pitch to her."

"There's contention between you and this person?"

"It's complicated. The first time we met in person, I broke into her house in the middle of the night."

"Why?"

"To make a point. I'd just been kidnapped by some associates of hers and I was worried about people targeting my family."

"So, you escalated by proving you could target hers?"

"I did say I wanted help with diplomacy, right?"

"I'm starting to see how good an idea seeking out assistance is for you."

"Yes. I asked everyone if they wanted to come along on this trip, but for most, I just wanted to give them a chance to expand their horizons. That's the best part of being an adventurer, right? My intentions for you are a little more selfish, though, yes. I was hoping you might take a role as a political advisor. Not just for the trip, but in the time leading up to it. I need to be preparing now, not just heading for Earth and winging it. Diplomatic training. Strategising over what approach to take. I've already discussed this with Dominion, but I wanted to contrast that with a more grounded perspective."

"What did he suggest?"

"That I either become their king or their god. Neither is a surprising take, given the source, but he made some compelling points."

"How often do you talk to gods?"

"Not that much. Way less than priests, I imagine. And I doubt the clergy have those really tense standoffs, like the one you saw with Undeath. That guy sucks."

"That would be the encounter where you threatened the gods of Undeath and Destruction."

"I didn't threaten them. I even gave Undeath that gobbet of corrupt energy to get rid of. I just suggested that maybe they want to choose their enemies with more care."

"Their enemies are everyone and everything, Jason."

"Which is an extremely careless approach to take, I think you'd agree."

She shook her head in a very motherly display of exasperation.

"I'm not sure I can help you on the level you operate at, Jason."

"You don't have to worry about the high-end stuff. When it comes to the vast cosmic power types, it seems to be a do-your-own-thing situation. What I need help with is operating without harming the people who someone like me could hurt without even noticing. I don't like the idea of putting myself above people, but pretending I don't operate on a higher level than most will only cause more harm."

"I need to think about this, Jason. You're asking me to take on a lot of responsibility here."

"Of course. We have some time, although the more of it I use to prepare, the better."

She nodded.

"Tell me more about this person you want to recruit on Earth."

Getting information out of Europe had been difficult for years, but whatever happened in the old Asano territory had kicked a hornet's nest. Vampires were moving on a scale they hadn't been in years. Based on new capture and kill numbers, there were more of them still hidden away than anyone realised.

That, fortunately, was not Anna Tilden's problem. Her problem was representatives from the UN member nations beating down her door about what was going on in Europe. Every nation with a spy plane or observation satellite had been watching the vampires gather in the old Asano territory, only for those observation tools to all get interfered with by an intense magical field that extended into orbit. In the wake of the mysterious event, the vampires had become extremely agitated.

It was bad enough when people were coming to Anna because it was her job. Now, news had gotten around about her having an off-the-books observation team on the ground. Instead of assistants of assistants of deputy liaisons knocking at her door, she had to deal with people she couldn't just brush off. Her blanket denials were starting to wear very thin.

"I'm sorry, Senator," she said into the phone. "Even if there were such a team, any information I could get from them would only arrive when they checked in after the fact. If they existed, they could very easily have died in the incident and we would never know."

It took a while longer to finish the call, continuing to blank wall him like she did everyone trying to strong-arm or wheedle information out of her. Despite taking a grim satisfaction that her claims of not knowing anything were true, she was halfway to hunting down Nigel Thornton herself and choking him to death.

She left her office, a novel change. She'd been sleeping on the couch for five days and having her staff cycle the same three suits through the dry cleaners. She made her way down to the garage, declining the offer of a driver. An office driver might turn around and bring her back, if ordered to by her boss. Inevitably, she got a call when halfway home; while tempted not to answer, she accepted the call by tapping the screen on her dash.

"Secretary Lin, what can I do for you?"

"I need to you to come to my office."

"Sorry, Secretary, but I'm already on my way home."

"Then I need you to turn around."

"With all due respect, Secretary, if I go through another weekend without going home and seeing my wife, I'm going to quit and let whoever you get to replace me handle whatever crisis just blew up."

"Anna—"

"Don't 'Anna,' me, Shu-Chen. Don't think I missed that word got around about my people in Europe roughly four seconds after I told you about them."

"That's what we need to discuss. You have to give us more information on—"

"I gave you the information I have, Shu-Chen. If I get more... well, I'll probably keep it to myself. You've got a big mouth and it's not technically—or legally—part of my job. This was a team I put in the field, on my own. No department funds, no department contacts."

"Dammit, Anna, people are thinking Asano's back."

"He might be. I don't know."

"Anna, I'm hearing dangerous things. Rufus Remore announced that Asano was coming back and would more or less do whatever the hell he wanted with the planet, and then this so-called System happened. A lot of people are spooked. Powerful people. The things I'm hearing range from nuking France to strange magical crap I don't know whether to believe."

"At this point, it's safer to believe. Look, I'm hearing things as well, but I genuinely don't have anything more to add. To be honest, it's looking increasingly likely that my people got caught up in whatever it was, and we'll never hear from them."

"Then your information is out of date. Satellites are operating over France again and I have visual confirmation of Nigel Thornton and his team liberating a blood farm and bringing the people back to territory that appears to be once again under Asano control."

"Well, they haven't reached out to me."

"We know. We've been monitoring all your communication channels."

"God dammit, Shu-Chen. Are you trying to get me to quit?"

"You know you won't, Anna. You're too driven to make things better, despite all the ugly politics. It's why you left the Network for us. Who is going to give you a better seat at the table than we can?"

23

OBJECTIVES

LOCATED SAFELY AWAY FROM YARESH WAS AN OUTDOOR TESTING FACILITY for the Magical Research Association. The Yaresh branch was one of the first, when the association was still looking to establish itself, and Clive had selected the location carefully. At a time when Yaresh was still rebuilding and struggling to control the surrounding region, the guards protecting the testing centre were, by default, required to safeguard a wide area around it.

Clive had situated the facility between two major trading routes: the river and one of the few intact major roadways. Having outside forces secure them when the city was at its most strained for resources was a major boon. This, in turn, made the city look very poorly on any attempt by the Magic Society to undermine the association as it established itself.

The testing centre itself was a series of reinforced buildings, underground bunkers and open platforms, scattered across a wide area. The land took minimal clearing for construction, as it had once been farmland. The former landowners were long dead, and the nearest town was abandoned.

One of several open platforms at the facility was simple but very large, designed for the maintenance and modification of large-scale vehicles. Right now, five people stood in the middle of the platform, around a flask on the ground.

"Turned out not be as tricky as we feared," Travis told Jason.

"I have been doing this for many years," the Cloudweaver explained. "I have created cloud vehicles and structures for several churches, and they like to incorporate the power of their god into the design. I suspected that your case might be similar, and while there were additional complications, the principles were much the same."

"What kind of complications?" Jason asked.

"The power of a god is simple. Clean. Focused. It doesn't need to be sophisticated because the power is, for practical purposes, infinite. Examining your effect on the flask, it's obvious that your powers are messy. Complicated. I am correct in deducing that you are at least partly divine, am I not?"

"Wait," Hector de Varco said. "You're part god?"

"That's not exactly accurate," Clive explained. "It's more a case that his transcendent aspect has certain capabilities that functionally operate in the same manner as gods perform similar tasks, rather than Jason being a god himself. Of course, with the transcendent aspect of his being and his ability to undertake the aforementioned tasks, the practical difference is—"

"He means no, but kind of yes," Jason interjected.

"Jason," Clive said, "that's very reductive."

"Yes," Jason agreed. "Clive, I don't have time for the long version, and I'm immortal."

"Part god," Hector said. "It makes me feel a lot better about you winning our duel just by looking at me."

House de Varco was one of the larger noble houses in the Storm Kingdom who did not have their family seat in Rimaros. As with any aristocratic family, they counted adventurers in their number. Their influence and reputation, however, came from the construction and trade of magical vehicles. During Jason's long absence, Hector had risen to prominence in the family by championing a new enterprise: cloud construct modification.

While cloud flasks were rare, less extravagant cloud constructs were not. Small personal transports were relatively affordable, after which things went sharply up in price. They still weren't cheap compared to things like floater discs, but they were convenient to store in small vessels, like the amulet mode of Jason's cloud flask. They were also fashionable, with features like trailing sparks, shifting colours and other effects that led to very full coffers for House de Varco.

"Your power serves much the same function within the cloud flask as a god's, but with some key differences," the Cloudweaver continued. "Your power's influence was not part of the original design, so mapping out how that affected the functionality of the flask was difficult. Rather than a well of divine power for the flask to tap into, your power affects the flask in almost every aspect. This is why my override no longer works, and that's how your constructs can function as portable temples."

"Temples to whom?" Hector asked, then looked at Jason. "To you? Because of the part god thing?"

"Yeah," Jason confirmed. "Did they not tell you about this stuff?"

"They only just brought me in on this," Hector said. "I've done some contract work with Travis on vehicle weapon systems, and he said he had a special project. Going back to the temple thing, is that something we could reproduce? I bet the number of churches looking for cloud vehicles will shoot right up, if that's an option."

"I was thinking the same thing," the Cloudweaver said.

"Now that we understand *most* of your cloud flask's underlying structure," Clive explained, "we can look at incorporating some modifications that Travis has been working on for years."

"It's just a side project I've been tooling around with," Travis said. "I've done weapons for your cloud flask before, but that was years ago. My magical knowledge was still very Earth-based, and I only tapped into a fraction of the potential. Doing contract work with House de Varco got me thinking about it again. A lot of my work wound up in Emir Bahadir's flask, but obviously, yours has some unconventional properties. And many of the ideas I had weren't viable, once we got a proper look under the hood. Of the ones that were, we picked out a few that were extra special and Hector had his people put a rush on manufacturing."

"Just what we've learned from working on this makes it worth it for us," Hector said. "You're going to have the most personalised weapon systems on any cloud flask that I've ever heard of. Anyone foolish enough to get in a fight with your cloud constructs will definitely know who they're up against."

"There are still a few aspects of your flask we weren't entirely able to decipher," the Cloudweaver admitted. "I'm unsure exactly how it seems to have ranked up alongside you. No special materials, no upgrade ritual. The aspect we had the most trouble with was some kind of minor functionality, which seems linked to external items. Without them, the function appears to be lost."

"Yeah," Jason confirmed. "It's part of a three-item set. I got this linking item back at silver rank when I killed this intelligent gold-rank dinosaur guy and looted his body."

"You killed an intelligent gold-rank monster at silver?" Clive asked.

"I told you about this," Jason said. "Most of the work was done when a proto-astral space closed with us inside. It spat us back out, with him most of the way dead. I just finished him off."

"How did you survive?" the Cloudweaver asked.

"Oh, I was all the way dead. But coming back from the dead is—"

"Kind of your thing," Clive said. "Yes, we know."

"I remember that," Travis said. "You're talking about Makassar, right? The footage was all over the news. Am I remembering you turning into a giant bird made of stars?"

"The star phoenix, yes."

"Can you still do that?" Travis asked.

"This avatar can, yes."

"That was sweet. Taika can turn into a big magic bird too. Maybe I should build a jetpack with wings, like General Hawk."

"From *G.I. Joe*?" Jason asked.

"Are you people utterly incapable of staying on topic?" the Cloudweaver asked.

"Yeah, pretty much," Jason agreed as Clive and Travis nodded their agreement.

"Well, the point is, I would like to thank you for giving me access to your cloud flask. It took significantly longer than I had hoped, but that was ultimately more valuable, given the effects of your current condition on it. I am curious about that other functionality, however."

"Oh, it just lets me pull out a little bit of cloud stuff and use it to make shields and such. It's only strong enough to be effective against things lower than my rank, though, so I usually use it to make chairs. I was originally disappointed, if I'm being honest, but it's turned into one of my favourite things."

"I've been looking into cloud furniture," Hector said. "I haven't managed to make it cost-effective yet."

"We're expecting the materials for the upgrades to arrive sometime in the next hour or so," Travis said. "We'll get them in, do a little testing, and then we can finally get on our way. Everything else is ready to go right?"

"Yeah," Jason said. "We've just been waiting on a ride."

The Cloudweaver shook Jason's hand.

"I must confess that I was trapped in traditional thinking for a long time," they said. "Failing to innovate is one of the traps that come with longevity. Following the lead of House de Varco, the last decade has seen some remarkable leaps in— what was the term you used, Travis?"

"Aftermarket modification."

"I still don't like the phrase," Hector said. "Yes, there are Adventure Society trade hall markets where you can buy cloud constructs, but that's for the more affordable personal transports. Cloud vehicles and their modifications are a prestige product. The implication that you can buy them from a kiosk doesn't engender the kind of image my family is looking for."

"While we're waiting," Clive said, "perhaps you could answer another few questions I have about the System."

Jason let out a groan. "Fine."

"Excellent," Clive said and plucked a notebook from a pocket somewhere inside his flowing wizard robe. "Now, last time, we were discussing the degree to which you were conscious of the System as it operated in the vicinity of your prime avatar…"

⁂

Jason's first encounter with a cloud vessel had been Emir's. It sailed into Greenstone, the size of an ocean liner, not flying due the low magic levels in that part of the world. Now that Jason was gold rank, he could finally produce a vehicle of similar size, and it flew away from Yaresh alongside Emir's.

Both vessels looked markedly different from that first look Jason got of Emir's. Cloud substance remained as the underlying structure, but significant external panelling lined the exteriors. For Emir, the panels looked something like blue solar panels, letting off a faint glow. They drew on ambient magic to fuel Emir's vessel more efficiently, saving on spirit coin expenditure.

Jason had the advantage of powering his cloud ship with his personal universe, skipping that requirement altogether. The dark red panels on his vessel were more defence-oriented, in case of monster attack. As their route would be taking them just north of the Pallimustus equivalent of Australia, this was considered a wise move. The island continent was known for high-ranking and dangerous monsters, and it was not uncommon for one to swim or fly northward.

Jason and Danielle were on the open deck above the bridge where Shade was piloting the vessel.

"You know that you could portal around the world, right?" Danielle asked. "We don't have to go the long way."

"Sometimes, the long way is the point. If nothing else, I need to visit places before I can portal there. Same for Clive, and Humphrey's teleports. I know they got the chance to travel a lot in my absence, but there is always more to see. And as for me, I didn't get that chance. I've missed a lot, and I'm going to make up for it. I want to see the world, not teleport past it."

"I recall my son telling me about this exact plan a long time ago. Roaming around the world on your eventual way to Estercost. You didn't make it past Yaresh."

Jason turned to look behind them as they sailed over the trees. He could just make out the light gleaming off the Yaresh towers.

"We have now. It took us longer than I expected, but here we go. I wasn't expecting the great astral beings to show up and tell me I had to play IT guy to the cosmos."

"IT guy?"

"Yeah, they broke their magic throne, so I had to go turn it off and on again."

"If I'm going to be your political advisor, I'm going to need you to start talking to people in ways they understand. Especially me."

"You understood. Context clues."

"Jason, you want me to instruct you on matters of diplomacy, yes?"

"Yes."

"Then I'll try to explain things as we go, since telling you to do the opposite of every instinct you have might be considered hurtful."

"So, you're not going to tell me that?"

"No."

"Somehow, it still feels hurtful."

"Then you need to harden up. I remember when you arrived in Greenstone. I remember the furnace of fear and panic burning at the heart of your aura, hidden under the bravado and the strange behaviour. But those days are long behind you, Jason. Back then, you were a boy with potential. Now, you have to be a man who lives up to it."

"My first day in this world, Rufus straight up told me that I had to choose if I was going to take responsibility of my own fate. Things escalated a bit more than either of us anticipated. I was never ready for dealing with all these entities who were so much more powerful than me. Now, I'm not ready to be the one with the power. It feels strange that I need to learn to be more diplomatic to avoid using it. If I just haul off on everyone that tries to treat me like they did last time I was on Earth, I'll end up going to war with the whole planet."

"The good thing is, having that power and not using it will be a valuable asset. Diplomacy is a war, and like any war, it involves influence, positioning, allies and, yes, power. Of many kinds. You gather intelligence and hope you know more about them than they know about you, without ever being truly certain. Everything is an advantage to be won and lost. If you're going to annoy someone, it needs to be for a purpose. Deliberate. If that purpose is your personal amusement, you're giving away advantage for nothing."

"There's a part of me that wants to march in and demonstrate that there's no one on Earth that can stop me from doing whatever I want."

"I imagine that would be very satisfying."

"Yes. And it would start going wrong almost immediately. But I know it's going to be hard restraining myself when I see something I can't abide. I know that having the power to make changes isn't the same as it being a good idea, not when my understanding of a situation is too shallow. That doesn't make holding back easy."

"I said that diplomacy is war, Jason, and wars have objectives. It seems that, right now, you're not thinking beyond a desire to avoid causing problems."

"I think that's a pretty valid desire."

"Yes, but it's not a goal. Is it something you honestly believe you can hold yourself to? Can you stand by as some travesty takes place and just leave it to the people of Earth to handle?"

"Probably not, if I'm being honest. Here, on Pallimustus, things are simpler. No one is going to look at it as a challenge of sovereignty or a violation of local culture if you punch a monster until it explodes. Even when problems get political, the people here understand individual power. On Earth, they don't understand the ramifications of people like us existing. They think of them as extraordinary threats, rather than the new way of the world. And when they realise that it will be a new way, the people who like things the old way will start getting nervous. Desperate."

"Is that your objective, then? To help Earth smoothly transition to a new paradigm of power?"

"No. That will take time, and it needs to be the people of Earth that find their own way forward. I'm not one of them anymore, not really."

"Then you need to find what your objectives are, even if only preliminary ones. It will focus your efforts, and let you go to Earth with more than anxiety that you're about to break it."

"Danielle, I can feel you pulling me by the nose towards something. Just spit it out."

"You want to change things, yes?"

"Yes, but don't tease me, Danielle. I'm not a quick learner, and it took me an embarrassingly long time to get the idea of unintended consequences through my skull. I'm not just going to throw that out the window."

"You really are not a quick learner, are you? Yes, if you bolt off with no real understanding of what you're doing and try to fix problems, you're going to make even more. But why am I here right now?"

"To help me with the things I…"

Exasperation at his own stupidity crossed his face.

"…to help me with something I don't properly understand."

"There is your goal, Jason. You want to use the power at your command to address problems that others can't or won't. You need to find the people that can help you do that without making things worse."

"This sounds suspiciously like what Dominion suggested about taking over. Or a *Team America: World Police* situation."

"Jason Asano, what did I just say?"

"Right, sorry. What you're talking about is a sophisticated undertaking, though, with a lot of steps. We're talking about establishing something between a think tank and an intelligence agency. And that isn't me making strange references, by the way. I'll explain the concepts to you later, because they're going to be important. And even assuming we can make that work, we'll have to deal with the consequences of doing so. Negotiate how and when we can intervene when things happen. And what happens when we go back to Pallimustus. We're going to be visitors on Earth, not residents. What happens if we build the Justice League and then run off back to Palli?"

"Jason…"

"Sorry. But politically and diplomatically complicated doesn't begin to describe what taking this approach would entail. And once we navigate them fearing us, they're going to try and exploit us."

"That sounds familiar. Perhaps politics aren't so different over there."

"What's our first step?"

"Aside from me teaching you to avoid spouting a constant stream of nonsense? Information. Always information first. If you can contact this person you want to recruit on Earth, you should do so with haste. Before anything else, we need to understand what we'll be walking into."

24
THE PROTECTION OF A DICTATOR

Having been established decades ago, the Holy Army of Knowledge had many elite units at silver and even gold rank. Other armies, both of nations and other gods, had lacked the forewarning of the goddess of Knowledge. Without the lead time for recruiting and preparation, their ranks were mostly comprised of people who had ranked up using monster cores. They hadn't intended to be adventurers, having little combat experience outside of monster surges. But when the call to war from their monarchs and gods came, they had not shirked their duties.

After more than a decade of war against the messengers, many of these forces were battle-hardened veterans. There were always new recruits, however, and even veteran troops fell short of adventurers with the same level of experience. Many forces were reliable and experienced, but less powerful due to fewer resources and less training. They often had an elite core leadership of current or former adventurers, but they were inevitably lacking compared to premier armies and Adventure Society task groups.

That was not to say that these lesser groups had no value. Experienced hands were always assets, and there were far too many places for the elite groups to be stationed. Low-priority areas where the messengers had shown no interest were often protected by locally raised armies, taking on not just messenger threats but monster-hunting roles when so many adventurers were busy. In low-threat zones, these less powerful groups were usually enough.

War, however, was capricious and cruel. Circumstances could change suddenly and without warning, turning a quiet backwater into a contested battleground. Such was the case in Segurado, a small city-state in what, on Earth, would be Uruguay.

The Segurado army was not an elite force. Even the adventurers leading them were only those that could be spared from more critical areas. There had been no indication that the messengers had any interest in the area until, suddenly, they were everywhere. They had flown low, over and even through the jungle, so as to avoid detection from flying observer patrols. There was alarm magic in the jungle, but it had been avoided or disabled. That had always been a threat, given the superior ritual magic of the messengers.

The messenger force had closed on the city walls before anyone realised, watchful defenders only sensing them as they made their final approach. Instead of moving straight to the attack, however, they abandoned their low altitude positions and soared high into the air. Their numbers were so great, they darkened the sky, as if storm clouds were passing over the city. What they had in store for the people below, however, was far worse than wind and rain.

More numerous than the messengers themselves were their bizarre summons; an expendable army of creatures ranging from the monstrous to the utterly unnatural. Disembodied eyes, encircled by concentric metal rings. Giant bone cubes with mouths on each side, prehensile tongues slithered from each sharp-toothed maw. Round cages filled with hundreds of arms that grasped through the bars at empty air.

There was a pause, as if the messengers were waiting for the residents to look to the sky and panic. That malevolent mercy proved short-lived, with the populace and the city's defenders still scrambling when the messenger army descended. The dome of the city's magical barrier snapped into place as monsters and messengers rained attacks upon it. The faint blue shield shook under the downpour, from projectiles, beams and explosions to the brute force of fists, claws and tentacles.

The defenders hurried to take positions, knowing the dome would not last long. As with Yaresh, years earlier, the barrier protecting the city had been designed to repel monster surges, not organised invasion. The messenger force lacked the powerful artefacts that had collapsed the barrier in Yaresh, but Segurado was smaller than Yaresh, with a commensurately less powerful barrier. The invaders didn't need anything but brutality and time.

The Segurado army managed to assume defensive formations before the barrier began collapsing, but they knew it would do them little good. They were far from elite, and the freakish monster army had them massively outnumbered.

The leader of the Segurado army was General Millicent Marks, an elven adventurer in the classic spellcaster style of her people. She was stationed on the flat roof of the city's highest tower, alongside several other spellcasters. The city's defences didn't stop with the barrier, the tower serving to enhance the range and strength of spells.

"They may be more interested in us than we hoped," she said, looking up at the foes pounding the barrier. "At least we aren't too much of a priority. They've used summons for most of their army, and there aren't lot of gold-rankers up there."

"Small mercies," said her second-in-command. Like most of the people on the southern half of the continent, he was an elf. "Milli, do you think we can hold? Honestly?"

"We have a chance," Millicent said. "But even if the city holds, it's going to burn."

The barrier was designed to hold off monsters while adventurers went out to meet them. No one was foolish enough to take that approach against the merciless and intelligent messengers. That was asking for death. The most the dome could do for them was buy time for the populace to reach monster surge bunkers and the Segurado army to take defensive positions. Some took formations on the ground, others in the air. A few took positions in defensive emplacements like the magic tower.

Millicent braced herself. She was gold rank and would almost certainly survive the coming battle. But she knew doing so would involve leaving her subordinates, the city and its people to a grim fate. She wondered if it might not be better to stand her ground and go down fighting.

Silver- and gold-rankers were hard to kill and good at staying alive, especially adventurers. When messengers won a battle, most of the Pallimustus elites escaped to fight another day. Quite often, those victories came because the messengers were more willing to trade lives than the adventurers. The messengers would fight battles of attrition, going life for life until the armies and the adventurers could no longer tolerate the losses.

Millicent wondered if winning the war required people with the grim resolve to make the same sacrifice. Perhaps what she needed was not to escape but to take as many of them with her as she could. Her emotions wanted her to fight to the bitter end, but she knew it was futile.

While the messengers were outnumbered on Pallimustus, there were more of them in the cosmos than stars in the sky. Battle-ready silver-rank messengers could be grown and trained in batches, for a fraction of the time and resources required to produce an equivalent essence-user. If the messengers had a secure and established summoning station anywhere in the area, they could always replenish their numbers.

Millicent closed her eyes, forcing herself to take calming breaths as the barrier started to give way. She only allowed herself a moment of that before snapping her eyes back open. As the barrier collapsed, it didn't crack and shatter like glass. Ripples formed, like the surface of a pond, with holes at the centre of each ripple. Monsters poured through as the ripples expanded, running into one another until the barrier fell apart entirely, dissolving like mist.

The enemies that had yet to move plunged downward in a cascade of alien war beasts, with glorious, winged warriors following behind. The monsters let out alien howls, spine-tingling shrieks and sounds that no living thing should be able to produce. The bone cubes let out noises like the grinding of teeth, amplified through a bullhorn. Other made sounds like metal shearing and warping.

Their collective auras came down like a hammer. The emotions of the summons were clear, if largely incomprehensible. There was an alien malice, drowned in the madness of minds fundamentally different from ordinary people, or even most monsters. As for the messengers, only the silver-rankers were readable, and only to gold-rankers like Millicent. They held no hatred, only superiority, purpose and obedience. She couldn't read their minds, but their emotions suggested they had few thoughts not given to them by their distant kings.

Millicent could also sense the emotions of her fellow defenders, and the populace they were defending. All were filled with despair that reflected Millicent's own. Few had any hope, and the little to be found was dying fast.

Then something changed. Millicent wasn't sure what, at first, but the reaction from the enemy was evident, immediate and extreme. Their descent stopped instantly, like a snap-frozen waterfall. Their auras roiled, a mix of fear, fury and confusion striking the messengers.

Millicent hadn't known, until that moment, that fear was something they could even feel. She'd heard stories of captured messengers defying torture to the last scrap of life. As for the summons, she'd never sensed anything from their auras before than gibbering madness. They were suddenly coherent, focused on something high above, like a mouse watching a perched owl. The sudden change was unsettling, even with the relief that their attention was no longer on the city.

Millicent was sure that something had appeared above the messengers. She couldn't get a good read on it through the storm of enemy auras, and there were too many to see past. Then a single aura cut through everything. She knew immediately that it was responsible for whatever had just happened to the messengers.

The aura was gold rank and far too powerful to come from a person. She'd sensed aura amplification like this before, built into the defences from major churches. It wasn't a god's aura, but not quite that of a mortal's either. In any case, there was no temple in the sky above the city, last time she checked. Then she realised she had sensed something like it. Just once, very briefly. Every essence-user had, in that strange moment when the System first appeared. What that meant, she had no idea, but in a city starved of hope, she'd take it.

Whomever or whatever that aura belonged to, she could feel the messengers trying and failing to suppress it. It was oppressive, yet benevolent, like the protection of a dictator. While that was certainly worrying, at that moment it was good enough.

She was looking up, trying to see past the throng of enemies. The summons had always been a chaotic mess, but now they were a maelstrom of activity, dashing around and sometimes even fighting one another. They were fighting something else too, as were the messengers, but Millicent couldn't see what it was yet.

Millicent tapped the collar on her neck. Communication systems had advanced in leaps and bounds over that last decade, and she could use the collar to speak to all her troops at once.

"Whoever is up there," she announced, "they're battling the messengers. I don't know if they're fighting for us, but they're fighting, and I won't let them do it alone. All squads capable of air combat, go full assault. Right now."

Wind gusted around Millicent, picking her up and carrying her into the sky. She didn't allow herself to get carried away, letting the more defensive elements of her forces lead the way. Not only was she a ranged fighter, but she needed to keep a broader view of the battle. This warred with her desire to launch forward and discover the nature of their mysterious reinforcements, but she was an experienced commander and knew what rashness would cost.

The Segurado army assaulted what was now the rear of the distracted messenger forces. It was still unclear who or what was above them, but Millicent delighted at the distracted enemy. As she unloaded her powerful wind magic, she got her first sense of their presumed allies as she felt other essence-users manipulate the wind. One worked similarly to Millicent, creating storm-like destruction over a wide area. Another was much more personal, passing unharmed through the magical storms at speeds Millicent could only sense, not see directly.

She spotted what had to be adventurers as they took the fight to the messengers. A man in rainbow armour ploughed through the messenger forces with seeming impunity, on the back of some shape-shifting creature. One moment, it was an eagle ripping the wings from messengers with its talons. The next, it was a floating slime that absorbed and disintegrated the messenger summons. The man riding it swung a massive sword from which waves of force erupted out, striking the clustered summons like a hurricane hitting mosquitos.

More presumed allies appeared, all apparently gold rank. Several were flying around inside a tortoise shell whose upper and lower halves were connected at the corners but otherwise open-sided. Multiples spellcasters and healers appeared to be operating from within, protected by the strange vehicle. Millicent watched several attacks fired at the open sides blocked by shell that grew up to shield them before retracting again.

A massive set of spinning wheels appeared in the sky, lined up next to one another like giant slices of sausage. They had symbols on them, and occasionally, the wheels would stop and fire off various effects. Some buffed and healed their allies, both the new adventurers and Millicent's forces, even those still on the ground. At other times, the wheels launched a dazzling variety of magical attacks at the enemy, from waters jets and fireballs to crippling debuffs. The more wheels with matching symbols, the stronger the effect and the more people were affected.

One oddity she noticed was the presence of butterflies across the battlefield, glowing blue and orange. The messengers avoided the beautiful creatures as if they were death incarnate, launching attacks at the butterflies to keep them away. It didn't seem to help much, as the struck butterflies exploded into clouds of sparks. Those clouds then sought out enemies, mostly finding the less wary summons.

Wherever the clouds landed, the victims immediately rotted horrifically, even the ones that weren't flesh. Those touched by the butterflies had a similar, but much slower effect. They started to produce more butterflies, however, that grew out of their bodies and flew off in search of more victims.

As the messenger forces lost cohesion and their numbers fell, Millicent was able to identify more of what she hoped were allies. Each one seemed to be not just a gold-ranker but a gold-rank elite. The messengers evaporated in front of them like morning mist before the sun. Millicent was finally able to spot the source of the massive aura, floating in the sky. It looked like an eyeball the size of a castle estate, everything but the blue and orange iris encased in dark red armour. Floating around the iris were smaller but otherwise identical orbs, each one the size of a house. These smaller orbs were the source of the butterflies, which poured out of them like water spilling off a cliff.

The messengers were not fighting tactically, for which Millicent was glad. They seemed obsessed with one of the combatants, either fleeing from him or chasing after him with wild-eyed fury. The man had a dark cloak with shadow arms sprouting from it, like the branches of a macabre tree. She heard more than one of the frenzied attackers screaming 'heretic king,' whatever that meant. Explanations could wait until after the fighting was done.

Still throwing out spells, Millicent watched what was quickly turning into a massacre. The messengers were caught between her forces and these newcomers, small in number but great in power. With the messengers barely paying attention to them, the Segurado army made them pay, while safely evacuating their injured to the healers.

By the time the battle was over, dead messengers scattered across the city below. The visiting adventurers had made them lootable and left them for her people to collect, rainbow smoke raising as messengers turned into magical weapons and supplies that would undoubtedly be put to good use.

Millicent hadn't suffered a single death amongst her forces. There had been a couple of close calls, but more than once a shield had snapped into place right before one of her people had suffered a killing blow. Only a short time ago, she had been contemplating whether to die fighting in defence of her home. Now, the invaders were dead, and her people were safe.

She had some profound thanks to give.

25

YOU WANT YOUR ADVENTURERS HAPPY

In the aftermath of the battle, Millicent stood atop the magic tower. As the highest point in the city, it allowed her to survey the goings-on below, without the need to start flying around. There were going to be a lot of anxious aristocrats and city officials so, for the moment, she wanted to be stationary where people could find her.

Ribbons of rainbow smoke rose up as her people looted the dead messengers where they had fallen into the city. There would be damage from an army of dead angels landing on things, but hopefully, minimal casualties. The populace had evacuated to bunkers while the defensive barrier still held, but there were always those who were too stubborn, too old, or too sick to move.

A woman was suddenly next to Millicent, arriving almost too fast for even a gold-ranker to sense her approach. She'd realised, belatedly, who these people were. If not distracted by the existential threat to her home, she might have recognised some of their more distinctive members. The man in rainbow armour riding a shape-changing dragon definitely should have been a giveaway. It was Team Biscuit, who had recently returned to Yaresh along with other famous adventurers for reasons unknown.

This woman had dark hair and a swarthy complexion, so she wasn't the team's famously beautiful speedster. But the team leader's mother was even more famous than the team itself, and this woman did fit the description.

"You're the Time Witch of Vitesse," Millicent said.

"I'm actually from a place called Greenstone. And I prefer to be called Danielle, to be honest."

Danielle offered her hand and Millicent shook it.

"You're in command of the local forces?" Danielle asked.

"General Millicent Marks, Segurado Defence Force."

"Danielle Geller."

"Thank you for the help. Our forces are battle hardened, and determined to protect their homes and families, but determination isn't always enough."

"No," Danielle agreed sadly. "It's not."

Millicent looked up at where the strange, humungous eye had transformed into a mass of cloud. It was now slowly taking the form of a sky liner, the largest class of airship.

"Is that what you travel around in?"

"For the moment," Danielle said. "The man that owns the vessel has a penchant for the dramatic."

"Is this what it's like?"

"It?" Danielle asked.

"Being a famous adventurer. I was born and raised here in Segurado. Trained here, not in some big city like Vitesse. I had this dream, back when I was iron rank, about hitting gold rank and swanning into one of the famous adventurer cities like a queen. In the end, I never roamed far. There was always too much to do, and it was always going to be a dream. By gold-rank standards, I'm a little fish."

"There are no little fish at gold rank."

"Of course you'd think that. Your life is all world travel and transforming sky ships. Swooping in to rescue little no-name places you won't remember in a week. I'm not trying to sound ungrateful—I'm profoundly thankful for the swooping in, believe me. It just makes me realise that, even if I hadn't been stuck guarding this place for all these years, I wouldn't be anything special in a place like Rimaros or Kacha Kille."

"Believe me, Miss Marks, you are special. I have known many adventurers from outside of the famous cities, and few choose to stay and protect their homes after reaching high rank. Of those that do, it is less often out of duty than a desire to be a big fish."

"You said there were no little fish."

"And I meant it. Even those who reached gold rank with cores are notable people, but those who did not still have the potential to go further.

Many famous gold-rankers never reach diamond, while some that no one in Rimaros or Vitesse has ever heard of reach diamond. The path is long and strange, and many lose sight of duty as they walk it. If you told the Adventure Society that you were leaving this place behind, who would stop you? The society, and the leaders of this city would ask you to remain, but they would do no more than ask. Because you're a gold-ranker, and that makes you special, wherever you are from."

"Did the Adventure Society send you here?"

"Yes. They've been using the sky link communication network to report messenger movement. They've also been asking us to move through more remote areas on our travels, where the society can't afford to station major forces. We happened to be in the area just as a messenger army decamped and headed your way, so they asked us to intervene. We were lucky to be in the area."

"Not as lucky as we were."

Danielle nodded.

"It's unfortunate that so many lives are reliant on luck, but that is the situation in which we…"

She trailed off as the sound of two arguing voices reached them from above. Two men were floating down on a small cloud, approaching the tower.

"…every city, just most of them," Neil said.

"I have never destroyed a city," Jason shot back. "I've been to lots of cities, and hardly any of them were destroyed. Look at this one. It's fine."

"How many is hardly any?"

"I don't know. Three. Four, I guess, but one was more of a big town. And the brightheart city was basically destroyed before we even got there. Also, don't act like you weren't there for half of them."

"Is four counting Rimaros?"

"Why would I count Rimaros?"

"That flying Builder city was dropped on it."

"It was dropped *near* it, Neil. And there was hardly any damage. The priests of Ocean stopped the tsunami."

"So, just the four, then."

"Exactly."

"You do realise that four is a lot when you're talking about destroyed cities, right?"

Danielle let out a motherly sigh.

"I may," she said to Millicent, "be forced to acknowledge your point about what my life is like."

The pair landed and the cloud they were riding on streamed into an amulet hanging from one the men's necks. The other moved forward to shake her hand.

"Neil Davone," he introduced himself. "Team healer."

"Were you the one putting shields on my people?"

"I might have tossed the odd barrier out, here and there. Nothing remarkable."

"You saved lives that would otherwise have been lost. The lives of my people. You have my thanks."

"You're welcome. And this is—"

"John Miller," the other man introduced himself as he moved forward to shake her hand. "Team cook."

"Cook?"

He certainly wasn't dressed for adventuring, in a floral shirt, shorts and sandals, topped with a straw hat. It was appropriate for the sunny day, but not for fighting monsters. His aura was human and silver rank, with the signature taint of monster cores. He looked every bit the auxiliary adventurer, yet he seemed a little off to Millicent. He had a translation power that sounded a little odd, and seemed to own the cloud transport they were riding on. Large enough to comfortably carry two meant it was expensive, even if he was working for famous adventurers. How much did they pay their cook?

Mostly, it was the way he carried himself. He was a core-using silver-ranker, surrounded by gold-rank adventurers, some of whom were extremely famous. Even Millicent was uncharacteristically hesitant around the Time Witch of Vitesse. This man showed none of the wariness or deference she was used to from lower-ranked people. He acted entirely as if he belonged.

She took a slightly rude glance at the emotions in his aura. She saw little more than the same confidence displayed. He gave her an amused smile, as if he realised what she was doing. He certainly shouldn't have been able to, but could probably guess from the curiosity in her gaze. He took his leave, asking if he could use the elevating platform, leaving her with the adventurers.

An impromptu street festival had sprung up seemingly from nowhere, long tables and food stands filling the market district. While the city of Segurado celebrated their reprieve, Millicent's concerns were with what came next. She wandered through the crowded streets as people feasted, sang and laughed.

She didn't join in, mentally exhausted after going from one meeting to the next for almost two days, often repeating the same things over and over. There were the duke and his people, the city parliament, the local Adventure Society, then representatives from the Continental Council, all of whom needed her reports.

It had been two nights since the battle, during neither of which had she found a chance to sleep. She had finally slipped away, but instead of finding a bed, she found herself walking the streets in the late morning. People teemed around her, not recognising her with her aura carefully retracted.

Her mind was still racing, preoccupied with the next threat. The populace was celebrating, but their leaders still didn't know what brought the messengers to their gates. Was it a part of their ongoing search for the rumoured artefact, or something more specific? Would they return, with a greater force? The Adventure Society had no more idea than she did, spending two days asking her questions to which she had no answers.

The smells coming from the stalls took her back to her days as a girl at market. Her family was never poor, or she would not have gotten essences, but she hadn't lived in the fancy part of town either. Her parents were fruit merchants, and she'd grown up around markets and trade halls. She knew these streets. The yelling and laughing, the aromas of the food vendors. When an unfamiliar scent wafted her way, it arrested her attention.

Her gold-rank senses allowed her to track the scent like a hunting dog. What she found was a stall where a group of local stall vendors were crowded around an outsider, as if he were holding court.

"...season with some salt and then caramelise them in the oven with oil. Nice and simple. I like to add a splash of water to help them soften. Now, let me explain how we make fresh pasta back home. It's so fresh, you can practically cook it by waving it over the steam from a kettle. Pass me that roller..."

Millicent found herself listening discreetly out of the way. There was definitely something unusual about the Team Biscuit cook. After around ten minutes, the group started breaking up. Then she heard him whisper, too low for anyone but an attentive gold-ranker to make out.

"Can I offer you a meal, General? Pop around behind the booth."

She hadn't realised he'd noticed her, in the middle of teaching the locals a foreign recipe. But she shortly found herself in an area boxed in by stalls, shielding them from prying eyes. A folding table and chair set awaited her, draped with a tablecloth and festooned with dishes, plates and bowls. She could sense the magic of gold-rank ingredients. Was this how Team Biscuit always ate?

"One of the secrets of Team Biscuit's success," John Miller said as he sat down. "Live off spirit coins when you have to, but eat proper food when you can. Well-fed adventurers are happy adventurers. And you want your adventurers happy, believe me."

She looked from the food to him as she sat down. As she did, he pulled out a privacy screen device and activated it, setting it on the table.

"I thought a woman of your stature would appreciate some discretion." He ladled food from various dishes onto a plate that he set in front of her. He then made up a plate for himself, apparently unworried about what gold-rank food would do to a silver-ranker.

"It would take a lot of strength, and a lot of finesse," she said, "to create an aura mask than would fool a gold-ranker. Something that would hold up, even if the gold-ranker gets pushy and starts probing for emotions."

"Messengers are good at that," Miller said. "I've even seen them mask people they were using as spies."

"It sounds like you've had a lot of strange experiences for a cook."

"A cook can see a lot in search of new recipes," he said, and skewered a chunk of saucy vegetable with a fork. "And new ingredients."

He plopped it into his mouth with a grin.

"Is that why you're travelling with Team Biscuit?"

He didn't answer until he was done with his mouthful.

"More of a happy accident," he said. "An opportunity I take advantage of while attending to other tasks."

"How did you end up with them?"

"I knew some of the team before they were famous. You might say I hitched a ride on their coattails."

"You've been there since the beginning? I've never heard of you."

"I'm the guy who makes the food. Who talks about the cook when there are people fighting monsters?"

"It sounds like you get to see a lot of cities destroyed."

"I have been unfortunate enough to witness some tragic disasters, but that was just Neil teasing. Which I hope was obvious."

"Even so, you strike me as someone who can't help standing out."

"But you don't strike me as someone rude enough to sit down with a cook and not touch his food. Doesn't smell to your taste?"

She took a slice of bread, dunked it into a thick soup and took a bite.

"It's good," she said.

"Thank you."

They chatted intermittently as they ate.

"You know who else I haven't heard of?" she said lightly. "That man in the battle with the dark cloak and the shadow arms. I've also never heard about Team Biscuit riding around in a giant eyeball that shoots butterflies of death."

"Oh, you don't want to meet him. He's not very nice."

"Is that so?"

"Remember when I said you want your adventurers happy? He's how I figured that out."

"Why does the team keep him secret? Or is he just travelling with you, like the Time Wi… like Danielle Geller?"

"No, he's part of the team. Has been from the beginning."

"Like you."

"Yes. He's just been away for a long time. I imagine he'll be known soon enough."

"What kept him away? Conflict in the team?"

"He has responsibilities that he's finding increasingly tiresome. He's looking to wrap them up and get back to adventuring."

He looked her dead in the eyes.

"Without anyone making a fuss."

"That might be hard if he keeps fighting messengers. They had a rather drastic reaction to him."

"He has a lot in common with the messengers."

"Like a talent for aura masking?"

"Try the casserole before you finish the soup. I think you'll find it's a nice accompaniment."

They ate in silence for a while.

"People are going to have a lot of questions," she said.

"He's a known quantity. To those who need to know."

"You're saying that if I don't know already, I shouldn't go asking?"

"I would advise against it. The Adventure Society can be touchy when it comes to him."

"Why is that?"

He raised his eyebrows and she sighed.

"Right, I shouldn't ask."

He plucked an envelope out of the air, accessing some dimensional storage power. He sat it on the table, next to her plate.

"What's this?" she asked.

"You told Danielle Geller that you were born and raised right here in Segurado. And you're still here protecting it, even with all the opportunities your power would afford you."

"She told you that?"

"I overheard you on that tower."

"You have good hearing."

"Don't we all?"

"What's in the envelope?"

"Are you familiar with Lady Allayeth, of Yaresh?"

"She's a diamond-ranker that's active in the general population. Of course I have."

"Have you met?"

"Yaresh may be somewhat close, but she's a diamond-ranker. Even gold-rankers don't just call by for a cup of tea. Why bring her up?"

"I'm guessing that your choice to stay and protect your home during the messenger invasion is bound up in the path that got you to gold rank."

"I don't see how that's your business."

"Call it reciprocation for you poking around about Jason Asano."

"I suppose that's fair. Yes, that sensibility was integral to reaching gold rank."

"Lady Allayeth is on a similar path. She may be able to help you on yours, so perhaps you should call in for that cup of tea."

"I don't know that she'd even see me."

He reached out and tapped the envelope on the table.

"A letter of introduction to break the ice."

"Cook for her too, do you?"

A smile teased the corners of his mouth.

"Once. Just recently, in fact."

He pushed his chair back and stood up.

"I need to get back to the stall," he said. "I'll leave the rest to you."

He walked off and was just about to disappear around the side of a stall when she called out.

"Wait."

He stopped, half turning to look back.

"I already expressed my gratitude to the others. Thank you for saving my city, Mr Asano."

"It's what we do, General."

26

MAKING THINGS WORSE

Being less central had left Segurado vulnerable and lower priority, and so fewer resources and weaker troops. The same conditions affected the more isolated messenger groups, making them ripe for Jason and his companions to strike. The team had zigzagged down the Pallimustus equivalent of South America, hitting targets of opportunity fed to them by the Adventure Society.

Their navigation continued to prioritise sightseeing over efficiency as they left the continent behind. Although their path would take them to the southern tip of what, on Earth, was Africa, they chose to take a wide curve over the south pole rather than a more direct route.

The Pallimustus version of Antarctica was not the icy wasteland it was on Earth. Known as the Dragon Lands, it was the native land of the large, scaled humanoids known as draconians. Rather than the populace, however, the island continent was named for its signature geological features.

Where Greenstone had many apertures to an astral space that provided the desert with water, the Dragon Lands had subterranean apertures to a realm of fire. This created a land filled with active volcanoes, steaming hot springs and the flame geysers known as 'dragon mouths,' for which the region was named.

The whole team came out to watch as the sky ship approached the coast, giving them their first look. Mountains of dark stone jutted from verdant green lowlands, a mix of sprawling forest and vast agriculture. From altitude, they could make out the outline of fields as if the land below them was a giant map with borders drawn onto it. The plant life was very different from the tropical and subtropical climates they had been passing through, reminding Jason more of Scotland or Ireland.

"There are a lot of active volcanos, right?" Jason asked. "Do they have an ash cloud problem?"

"We're definitely going to see them," Zara said. "But the magic leaking out of the astral spaces has earth affinity, along with fire. It draws the ash from the sky, and absorbs it into the ground, creating the famously rich farmlands. If you want gold-rank cooking ingredients, there's no place better than here. It's how they make a lot of their money."

"I thought the draconians were all isolationist," Jason said. "They do a lot of trade?"

"Exports," Neil said. "Agricultural products from the Dragon Lands are the second-largest trade that passes through the Greenstone port, after low-rank spirit coins. They use proxies outside their own lands, though, and aren't very welcoming to strangers."

"Their goods are heavily tariffed by most nations due to political issues," Zara explained. "That makes it even more expensive than high-rank produce normally is. The quality is what gets people buying it anyway, but obviously, that falls under the luxury food market."

"I did hear the food they produced was good," Jason said.

"Jason," Neil asked. "Why did we come here again?"

"It's a tour," Jason said. "We decided on this route when we left Rimaros."

"Before fifteen years of war with the messengers made an already xenophobic people even more wary of outsiders. Is this about anything other than you getting a line on cheap ingredients? Can't you just make as much money as you want and buy this stuff somewhere more hospitable?"

"There's a value in farm fresh," Jason said defensively. "It's going to be fine."

Astral kings rarely mingled their forces to avoid confusing the most critical element of messenger culture: hierarchy. When operating on a large scale, like a planetary invasion, cooperation was managed through regular meetings between Voices of the Will, the commanders of each astral king's local forces.

Navise Den Rigal's astral king was a minor figure, compared to the Council of Kings, and secretly one of the Unorthodoxy's rare astral kings. Every Voice of the Will paid close attention when they met with others of their kind, but Navise was especially sensitive to any change that might signal a danger to her king's true allegiance. Slipping Boris Ket Lundi into Vesta Carmis Zell's service had already been more risk of exposure than she or her astral king liked.

When she arrived at a messenger stronghold, she went straight for the meeting room. It was a spherical chamber accessed through a hole in the ceiling, and the group met by floating in a circle. She noticed a number of missing attendees, all Voices belonging to members of the Council of Kings. Looking around, she saw that others had noticed the same thing, and shared her wariness. It did not take being a secret traitor to be cut down by other messengers.

As the discussion began, it quickly became evident that this wasn't related to the Unorthodoxy, but to a much more localised threat. The Voices stood around a projection showing a zigzag pattern across the lower half of one of the planet's continents. Navise listened to a pair of her fellows argue without interjection, as did the rest of the group.

"There is no reason for us to not put together a force and strike them down. They are being allowed to rampage through our territories unabated."

"They have left our territories. They are someone else's problem now."

"Yes. Our failure to quash a handful of insignificant locals will be a stain on our names forever."

"I would hardly call the Heretic King insignificant."

"That is a fool's title to keep the pawns from getting confused."

"It's not working. There is talk of a traitor astral king and of what that means. That is the kind of thinking that leads to the Unorthodoxy. My astral king will not be happy if I have to purge most of my forces again."

"Then let's kill the source. If we destroy his avatar, we won't have to deal with him again until we are done with this planet."

"Killing him has been tried before, when he was far weaker. More importantly, the Council of Kings had specifically instructed us not to provoke him."

"And none of our astral kings belong to the council. My king proposes that we collect our forces, set a trap and crush Asano."

The pair was unable to reach a consensus and would not let it go until each of the others said their piece. Most of the group advocated letting it go, moving any forces out of the Heretic King's path to minimise losses. When pushed, Navise took her usual path of following the group to avoid standing out.

"I say we simply allow the king to pass," she said. "In the end, the issue is one of being inconsequential."

The main advocate for killing Asano scoffed.

"If he is inconsequential, then what harm is there in killing him?"

"I speak not of him, but of us," Navise said. "He is not inconsequential to us, or we would not be having this meeting. We are inconsequential to him. He strikes at us incidentally, as opportunity presents. We should minimise his opportunities, reserving our forces, and simply let him pass. We can resume our operations once he is gone, having lost fewer people and revealed less information."

As Navise looked around the circle, all now staring at her, she realised she had made a mistake.

"We are inconsequential?" one of the others asked.

Anything resembling humility was not the thinking of an orthodox messenger. A wave of power flooded from Navise, slamming the others into the wall as she bolted for the hole in the ceiling.

***

Anna took the coffee from the street vendor and started trudging back to her office. Once again, she was running on not enough sleep, but felt no concern for her safety as she took a shortcut through an alleyway. She might not have combat training, but she was silver rank. Anyone who could bring her trouble wouldn't need to use an alley.

"You are not as safe as you think," a man said, stepping out of the shadows and startling her.

"There are people watching me, you know, Mr Remore."

"No, there aren't."

"Oh. Will they live?"

"By silver-rank standards, they're practically unharmed. It's become hard to have a discreet conversation with you, Mrs Tilden."

"Everyone wants to know what's going on in your territory. We've seen your people reclaiming the area, but there's only so much that the many, many satellites pointing at your territory can show us. Then there's the vampires acting up, globally no less. Presumably in response to whatever happened to the vampire army formerly occupying your clan territory. An army that seems to have vanished entirely during some manner of surveillance blackout. Then there are the ongoing concerns about the System and Asano's potential return."

"Not potential. Six months to a year is the current timetable."

"How solid are those numbers?"

"Things can happen, especially with Jason. But he seems confident."

"He always does. You're in regular contact?"

"His power grows, and he can reach out to us with ease now. When he returns, it won't be like last time he was here."

"If he's strong enough to settle old grudges—"

"That's not what he wants. He wants to come home without making things worse. For his return to be peaceful. He believes that you can help make that happen."

"And how does he expect me to manage that?"

"He is aware that his understanding of the political realities he's walking into is shallow. He wants to hire you to be his senior political advisor for Earth affairs."

"Does he have someone doing that for the other world's politics?"

"He does."

"I don't know what you expect from me. Nigel Thornton vanished into the Asano clan and didn't come out."

"He wanted to. He considers himself to have an obligation to you, which I respect. But the moment he shows up in an airport, someone or other will try and take him into custody. They'd try to do the same to me, thus my discretion."

"How badly did you hurt the people following me? I'm not sure 'practically unharmed' means the same thing to you as me."

"What have I ever done that you would think me a savage?"

"I saw what your world did to Jason Asano."

"And I saw what yours did. At least on mine, we stab people in the front. I did less to the people following you than I would have in my world. More than if they were here to protect you, instead of to watch for someone like me contacting them. But silver-rankers heal well."

Anna shook her head. "I need to retire."

"Perhaps just a change of employer."

"That's what you want? For me pack up my wife and move to the middle of vampire-infested Europe?"

"You did it before. You were the first UN liaison to the Asano clan."

"Yeah, and that position fell apart once the French realised the clan had no intention of giving back the chunk of their country they took. I don't see the UN or anyone else being more accommodating once Asano is back."

"Which is why Jason wants your help. France hasn't existed for almost two decades. You can talk about governments in exile all you like, but the reality is that your world has undergone a fundamental change. The sooner the people who rule it understand that, the sooner they can stop fighting over the ashes of a world that no longer exists. It's time to look to the future, and Jason wants to help this world understand that."

"Is that his intention? To come back and fix the world according to his standards? It's certainly in character."

"You will find that Jason is not the blunt object he once was. That he wants your guidance should tell you that, but yes, he's the same in many ways. He has power and wants to use it for good, and that hasn't changed in all the time I've known him. What has changed is his realisation that 'good' is a more nuanced concept than he understood when he was younger. He wants your help figuring out how to act responsibly, and that starts with how he returns. The first job he would have you work on is figuring out how he comes back without the world deciding to go to war with him."

"He could give them the things they want."

"Tell that to him, Mrs Tilden. I'm just a messenger today."

Anna sighed.

"My experience tells me that he wants me to smooth things over because he wants to keep his toys to himself. That he realises he can't fight the whole world to keep them. But that's not who he was, when I knew him. The man I knew *would* fight the whole world, if it came to that."

Rufus chuckled.

"It seems that you do know him. Come to Europe, Mrs Tilden. You don't have to make any decision now. Talk to Jason. Talk to Nigel."

"Even if I was willing to consider it, you know I'll need to clear this. I'm not going to sneak off with you in the night."

"It's ten thirty in the morning, Mrs Tilden. And I suspect that your people will be more than happy to get some eyes on the inside."

The sky ship accelerated rapidly out of Dragon Lands airspace. Clive scurried down one of the airship's hallways, casting anxious glances behind him.

"CLIVE!" Humphrey's voice roared as he stormed around a corner and into the hall. "What in the goddess of pain's needle pit where you thinking?"

Clive stopped and let out a nervous laugh.

"Did we get away?" he asked.

"Yes. And we're not being chased, thanks to Stash being an actual dragon. Why did you go into that temple?"

"It wasn't an actual temple. They venerate dragons rather than gods; there's no divine power there. It's more of an academic hall dedicated to draconic magic. I didn't know they'd get so angry about me going in."

"They had a sign out front that read 'outsiders strictly forbidden!' In adventuring circles, Clive, that is what is referred to AS A CLUE!"

"I actually went in at the side, not the front. And it wasn't a big sign. More of a plaque, really."

Humphrey conjured his sword and Clive bolted down the hall, Humphrey chasing after him. Jason, Sophie and Belinda watched them go, having been drawn by Humphrey's yelling.

"I'm just glad it wasn't my fault," Jason said. "This time."

"I'm not," Sophie said. "My money was on you getting us chased off on the morning of the second day. How did you last a whole week without causing trouble?"

"Ask Humphrey's mom. I've been working on my diplomacy. Belinda, did you make a betting pool again?"

"Yeah, and Clive made me a bundle by beating you out. And if he'd just asked me, I'd have gotten him in there without anyone being the wiser."

"You know," Jason said, "people always accused me of getting us into these things, but I'm starting to suspect that all of you are the real trouble-makers. Except Zara. I'm not the biggest fan of royalty, but at least she was trained to have some decorum."

Jason watched Belinda and Sophie share a look.

"What aren't you telling me?" he asked.

"So," Sophie began, "there was this draconian prince. Not much of a prince. One of those eighty-seventh-in-line-for-the-throne types. He decided that Zara was going to be his fourth wife, and didn't see much point in consulting Zara on that decision."

"What happened to the prince?" Jason asked. "When things happen to princes, it tends to get around. I can't tell if not having heard anything is good or bad. Is this what it's like running around with me?"

Sophie and Belinda nodded in unison.

"Let's just say that we were on the way to suggest we skip town when Clive got in trouble," Sophie told him.

"Yeah, that imprisoning ritual is going to hold the prince for another day, tops," Belinda said. "And that's assuming no one finds him. I assume someone will be looking for him."

"Not his first three wives, if his personality is anything to go by," Sophie said. Belinda snorted a laugh.

"What's this about an imprisoning ritual?" Jason asked.

"Well," Belinda said, "I wanted to disappear the guy, but Stella thought killing him was a bad idea."

"I'm very confident it was."

"I don't know. Leaving him alive might be worse, after Zara's response to his proposal. I didn't even know you could put storm magic inside someone's—"

"No need to talk about that," Zara said, sticking her head out of a cabin door. "Humphrey doesn't need to hear anything about it."

She retreated into the room, only for her head to immediately shoot back out.

"Neither does my father."

Jason sighed.

"Her father is definitely going to hear about it, isn't he?"

"Oh, yeah," Belinda said. "She left stains in that room that I'm not sure crystal wash could get out. Why he had so much—"

"Let's skip the details," Jason said. "For now, at least, while I go talk to Danielle about this. I expect we'll want all the grisly details later."

27

SOMETIMES WE NEED SCARS

When she'd been young—well, younger—Jennifer Landry had loved hosting visiting adventurers at her boarding house. All those powerful and attractive young people, politely calling her 'Madam Landry.' As years went on, the desire for excitement slowly gave way to a desire for reliability. Rather than cater to out-of-towners who were often interesting but frequently volatile, she shifted to catering to locals.

She didn't aim for the top-shelf adventurers, which they actually had now in Greenstone. The training program set up by the Geller and Remore families were producing better adventurers, especially now that Adventure Society assessments were being conducted legitimately.

Madam Landry found that the second-tier adventurers were the perfect clientele. Long-term tenants, they had the money to pay but the humility of not being the cocks of the roost. It was an unconventional bit of excitement, then, when one of her adventurers came bursting to the lobby, almost taking the door off the hinges.

"Dean Tuckell, if you take that door off, you're the one paying for a new one," she scolded.

"Sorry, Madam Landry, but I just heard something incredible at the Adventure Society. Is Jerrick here?"

"He's in the bathhouse, dear, but I…"

Dean shot off without listening.

"…don't think he's alone."

Gold-rankers were figures of legend in a low-magic town like Greenstone, making Emir's visit all those years ago a real event. Jason remembered his cloud ship sailing up to the private Adventure Society dock in grandiose fashion. But he had also known that Emir had been in the city for days before, in secret.

Jason followed this model, quietly reaching the city with several of his friends days before his official arrival. His goal was to reacquaint himself with the city, indulging in the nostalgia of his early days as an adventurer. Jason, Belinda and Estella Warnock portalled to an old spirit coin transport waystation, not too far from the city. It had been abandoned years ago, after the local Magic Society director and a local crime boss had an adventurer tortured in the storeroom.

Emerging from the portal, the trio immediately staggered.

"It's like trying to breathe when the air's too thin," Belinda gasped. "What's happening?"

- You have entered a region of low magical density. High-ranking individuals will suffer deleterious effects without supplemental magic.

- Stamina recovery reduced by 50%.
- Health recovery reduced by 75%.
- Mana recovery reduced by 99%.

- Consuming a spirit coin of your rank or ten spirit coins of one rank lower will restore your recovery rates to normal for eight hours. This duration is reduced by using active magic abilities.

- Rituals and summoning abilities require spirit coins to enact, in addition to any spirit coin cost they already have. Rituals will be unable to function without artificially enhancing the density of local ambient magic.

- Summoned familiars will need to consume a spirit coin of their rank or ten coins of one rank lower to sustain their vessels. Consumption of spirit coins will allow them to maintain their vessels outside of the summoner for one day before requiring additional coins. This duration is reduced by using active magic abilities.

"Oh," Belinda said, reading the system message.

She pulled out her summoned familiars, an astral lantern that orbited droopily around her, and an echo spirit that looked like a blurry version of her. She plucked a handful of spirit coins from her storage space, pushed one into the lantern and handed the others to Gemini, the echo spirit, and Estella. She ate one herself as Jason declined the one she held out to him.

"I think I can compensate by drawing magic from my astral kingdom," he said. He was half crouched, hands on his knees. "I'm still figuring out what I can and can't do with this body. Just give me a few minutes."

While Jason concentrated, occasionally making sounds like he was having trouble using the toilet, Estella and Belinda looked around. They were in an area between the sprawling river delta and the bone-dry desert. The waystation itself was an area of magically flattened stone, largely covered in windswept sand. There was a security booth, the glass in the windows long gone, and a large storage bunker. Of the bunker's double doors, one was missing and the other dangled precariously from the remaining hinge. Beyond, stairs led down.

"How is this a memorable enough place to portal to?" Estella asked. "You haven't been to this city in a couple of decades, right?"

"Yeah," Jason croaked.

Belinda looked around, ending with her gaze fixed on the broken door. "Jason, is this…?"

"Yeah," he confirmed.

"Why would you bring us here?"

"Like Stella said, it's memorable. You can still feel a little of my aura imprinted down there, if you look closely. Some things linger. Oh, bugger this, I'll try again later."

Jason took out a spirit coin and ate it, making a distasteful face as it melted on his tongue. Shade and Gordon appeared. Shade took a coin from his own storage space and consumed it while Jason tossed another into the nebulous void that was Gordon. He held his palm out and a leech crawled out through his skin. Jason held out a spirit coin for the leech to eat, but it turned its tooth-ringed maw away.

"Come on, Colin."

The leech let out an alien screech of rejection.

"If you don't eat this, you won't be able to come out and eat anything else."

While Jason was coaxing Colin into eating something that wasn't at least recently alive, Belinda and Estella made their way to the door.

"That's a good boy," Jason said, scratching the top of the leech after it finally ate the coin. As Colin retreated back under Jason's skin, Jason moved to join the others as they looked down the stairs.

"Shade and Gordon weren't with me when this happened," he said. "We'd just fought a water tyrant. Silver rank. It destroyed both of their vessels and left me with what, to this day, remains my largest scar. Colin was with me for this, though. Wouldn't have made it through without him."

"Made it through what?" Estella asked.

Instead of answering, Jason walked around them and went down the stairs.

"Jason," Belinda called after him. "Are you sure you want to go down there?"

Elspeth Arella was not happy. Being director of Greenstone's Adventure Society branch had always been intended to be a stepping stone. The first stage in a career that would lead her out of the magical and literal desert that was Greenstone. Then came the disastrous expedition. The aftermath of that failure, and the investigation that followed, undid everything she had worked for.

Her backroom dealings were dragged into the light, as was her status as daughter of an Old City crime lord. She barely held on to her position, which went from the first step in a storied career to a purgatory she could not escape. Twenty years later, nothing had changed. Even her father had risen, from last man standing of the Big Three crime lords to legitimate mayor of Old City. They were both important members of Greenstone Society, now, but where he felt elevated, she felt trapped.

Leaning against the desk in her office, Elspeth rubbed her temples as she stared at a spot on the floor. Twenty years ago, she had used her powers to lift some jumped up iron-ranker by the throat, dropping him on that very spot. Now, that same speck of nothing was scheduled to arrive in just a few days, to great fanfare.

Twenty years on, things were very different. He was a gold-ranker, well-trained and battle hardened, with countless accolades to his name. She was a core-using silver-rank bureaucrat with a dead-end career. She'd heard the stories, even from across the world. Running around with diamond-rankers, coming back from the dead. Driving off the Builder, which was even more nonsensical than the rest. It all sounded like fanciful nonsense. But she'd seen the missives from the Adventure Society, and they weren't treating it like nonsense. There was an actual standing order to put a branch on low alert if he entered its jurisdiction.

She had been much happier when Asano was dead the first time. Giving his life to save the city made him a useful figure of noble sacrifice, but martyrs were awkward if they didn't stay dead. There was even a statue of him somewhere on the campus grounds. She'd had a bush grown in front of it after he came back to life.

She doubted he would forget that she tried to teach him a lesson that didn't take. Two ranks higher than him, her power wrapped around his throat. She didn't even remember what it was about. What she didn't forget was the defiant eyes that would rather let her choke him out than yield to her authority.

Would he kill her on this very spot, where it happened? The Adventure Society would give him a slap on the wrist, if that. They wouldn't chastise their interdimensional golden boy over a dead bureaucrat with a dead-end career. Not after everything he'd gotten away with already.

She sighed and pushed herself off her desk. There were a lot more feathers than hers to unruffle before Asano arrived, so she might as well get to it, on the off chance that she survived his visit.

Jason reached the basement storage area. The dry climate had preserved the interior enough that it hadn't completely degraded, but it showed the years of abandonment. A little sand had blown down the stairs, although not so much as to cover the bloodstain spread out like a carpet. The blood pool spread out through the large storage room, too much to have come from one person under normal circumstances. Jason's self-healing had replenished him over and over as he bled out, but only Colin's help sustained him. His own regenerative power had been insufficient to last him through the ordeal.

The chains were still there, seized and rusty now. They lay on the floor where he'd yanked them from the ceiling in his escape. When he was last in the room, there had been a pile of tiny star seed fragments, pushed out of his body and leaving many small scars behind in the process. Those were long gone, no doubt claimed by the Magic Society. Those had been the early days of the Builder cult becoming active, making the fragments prime materials for study.

Belinda and Estella followed Jason down the stairs. They didn't share Jason's ability to see perfectly through the dark, so Belinda tossed out a floating glow stone to reveal the macabre scene.

"What is this?" Estella asked. "Is that your blood?"

"Yeah."

"All of it?"

"It was a rough day."

"What happened here?"

"This is where I found out who I am," Jason said. "When you strip away everything until there's nothing left to take. I don't recommend the experience."

His gaze didn't shift from the blood stain. The two women shared a side glance, then looked at Jason still facing the other way.

"This seems like a bad place to forge a personal identity," Estella said.

Jason laughed, the sound incongruous in the grim remnants of the torture chamber.

"Yeah," he said. "It very much is. But sometimes, you don't get to choose."

"You said you found yourself down here," Estella said. "That's a little concerning, if I'm being honest. Who did you find out you were?"

"Don't encourage him," Belinda hissed. "We don't want him going all dark and broody again."

Jason turned and gave her a smile.

"It's fine, Lindy. Sometimes we need scars to remind us that we can heal. Yes, the worst experience of my life happened in this room. But a lot of who I am, good and bad, began right here. If I can't face that, I'll be stuck in this room my whole life. And as for your question, Stella, I was put here by a conspiracy of forces that included a church, a cult, a crime lord, a corrupt Magic Society director and a great astral being. I was iron rank. Ambushed by a silver-ranker and chained up, naked but for a suppression collar."

"How does that explain who you are?" Estella asked.

"Lindy, do you remember what I was doing when you all arrived and found me?"

"You were upstairs, adjusting the cuff links on your suit like you'd just walked out of the theatre."

"That's who I am, Estella. The guy who wins. It doesn't matter who or what you are. How many people or how much power you have. You might kill me, you might scour my soul, but I'll come back stronger, and I still won. That's who I am."

He walked past them and back up the stairs.

"That," Estella said, "is the single most arrogant thing I have ever heard in my life. And I spend a lot of my time spying on aristocrats."

"Well, sure," Belinda said, "but we're all shaped by our experiences. I've seen Jason fight a god, but I've never seen him lose."

Estella looked at the blood stain again.

"Did all that really happen?" Estella asked. "The crime boss, the church, everything."

"It was the Church of Purity, before people started to realise they were going bad. We actually killed the archbishop not that long after this."

"And Jason just walked away?"

"Oh, gods, no. That thing with the cuff links? It was basically the last vestiges of his mind doing what he does, which is put on a smug façade to hide that he's half a step from losing his mind. What he didn't mention was the months of catatonia and intensive therapy that followed. Not many people manage to throw off a star seed implantation, so they called in a mental specialist and a soul specialist. The best the Church of the Healer had. It still took them months to stitch a functional person back together."

"So, the cult and the corrupt official and whatever else. What did an iron-ranker do to get that many people going after him?"

Belinda looked up the stairs.

"You remember Jory?"

Her face took on an uncomfortable expression.

"Yes."

"Me and Soph were in a real bad spot. And I mean it started bad and had been getting worse for months, like fermenting a turd."

"Lindy…"

"Sorry. But the whole city was hunting us. Duke's guards, adventurers, everyone. Even the crime boss that was meant to be protecting us was getting ready to sell us out. Jason and Clive were the ones that caught us. Jory wanted to help, but how could he? He'd have to go up against some of the most powerful people in the city."

"Which sounds like exactly what Jason would do."

"Now you're getting it."

"But he was the one that caught you?"

"Clive caught me. Didn't think the Magic Society had anyone that smart. Jason caught Sophie, messed her up bad in the process. Those afflictions of his, you know? Caught up to her being healed by Jory, and that's where things get interesting. He found out that Jory wanted to help us, and Jory was his friend, so he did. Just like that. No questions, no hesitation. Went up against the Directors of the Adventure Society and the Magic Society, for two thieves he only knew from the time one of them kicked him in the face. We all thought he was crazy."

"But he wasn't."

"Yes, he was! The guy's a lunatic. Make those sorts of enemies and you'll find yourself chained up in a hole somewhere, being bled out."

Estella turned back to look at the blood stain and the rusty chains. Belinda leaned against the taller woman, slipping an arm around her.

"He saved Sophie and me when everyone else couldn't or wouldn't," she said. "He went up against powerful people to make that happen, but he won. This was the price he paid."

"Is he going to be alright, coming back here?"

"I don't think he would have, if he wasn't. It's kind of his thing. One time, we were out on a road contract, and he took us to a place where a cult tried to sacrifice him to summon a blood monster."

"Is that the same cult involved in all this?" Estella asked, gesturing at the blood pool.

"No, it was a different cult."

"And different to that Order of Redeeming Light Purity cult back in Rimaros? The one Sophie's mum belonged to?"

"Yeah. Also different to the Order of the Reaper, which Sophie's mum also belonged to, and the Cult of the Reaper, which Sophie's mum's boyfriend belongs to."

"Why does he keep getting involved with cults?"

"I stopped asking questions like that a long time ago. You just have to go with it."

Dean didn't notice the sounds coming from inside the bathhouse as he tossed aside the 'occupied' sign in front the door, which he flung open and rushed through. There was an immediate splashing and yelling.

A few moments later, Dean had his back turned and his arm over his eyes for good measure. His teammate was in the bath, half-standing to shield the elf lady sharing the bath and using him as a privacy screen.

"I'm charging an extra half if he's going to watch," she said.

"Dean," Jerrick growled. "What in the Healer's bag of smoking herbs inspired you to come in here like that?"

Dean moved to turn around in his excitement but managed to stop himself.

"I heard something at the Adventure Society," he said.

"You'd have heard something inside this bathhouse if you weren't fired up like a bog lurker in heat. What's got you so—"

"He's coming back! Jason Asano is coming back to Greenstone!"

"When?"

"I don't know. I just heard it and rushed straight over."

"Well, we need to find out more."

"Yeah!"

Jerrick lurched out of the bath and started rubbing himself dry with a towel.

"Sorry, Lucy, I have to go. Feel free to charge me for the whole hour."

"Damn straight, I'm charging you for the whole hour. I don't care how big your—"

"Jerrick, are you coming or what?" Dean called from outside.

Jason parted ways with Belinda and Estella, after several reassurances to Belinda that he was fine. Once she accepted that he wasn't lying *too* much, she took off with Estella for the city, in a Shade-produced land skimmer.

Jason looked to the nearby delta edge, a shift from desert to verdant growth so neat, it could only be accomplished with magic. The Mistrun River carried water dense with life and water energy, making for the rich and swampy delta. Greenstone rice and tea from further upriver were both local specialties, although a small slice of trade compared to spirit coin export.

Back before he had a team, Jason would blow off steam by heading into the delta on foot. He'd roam the tall embankment roads that ran between mangrove swamps and paddy fields, moving from village to village. He developed a gliding-running style that used his cloak to reduce his weight. It allowed him to travel at relatively swift speeds without exhausting his mana or stamina.

It was a technique he had long ago left behind. Before Shade, before he had a team around him. Before the Builder's star seed was put inside him, setting him on a course to fight angels, gods and monsters with the fate of worlds on the line.

He had used the technique to roam the delta for a week or more at a time, taking trips alone to clear his head. He'd roam the towns and villages of the delta, healing the sick and clearing off contracts from their adventure boards. He looked back at the storage room door, then back at the delta. He laughed to himself, conjured his cloak and set off.

Almost immediately, he stumbled and landed face first in the sand.

He laughed again as Shade emerged from his shadow.

"Mr Asano, what are you doing?"

"An old trick. I seem to have lost the knack."

28

THAT'S WHAT ADVENTURERS DO

WITH THE IMPENDING ARRIVAL OF A LITERAL SHIPLOAD OF GOLD-RANKERS, things had been busy for the senior officials of the Greenstone Adventure Society branch. Everything about Vincent Trenslow was drooping except for his immaculate moustache, poking stiffly out from each side of his face. He was going through a list of requests from local nobility who, sadly, held enough influence that he couldn't just dump the whole stack of papers in the bin. He looked up at a knock on his office door, grateful for any reprieve.

"Sir?" his assistant Gretchen said, after poking her head in. "We've had bit of an odd report from the jobs hall."

"Odd how?"

She opened the door properly and moved into the office.

"It's about adventure boards in the delta. Someone has been marking off contracts as complete, but none of them have been turned in at the hall."

"How many contracts?"

"As far as we can tell... all of them. In about a day and a half. A few adventurers came back from the delta and reported that every village had the adventure board marked as complete. We've sent people to confirm, and the monsters are gone in every instance we've checked."

"I assume some of the delta residents had some light to shed? Surely someone saw whoever was responsible."

"Yes, sir. Some reported a stranger who did some healing and, in one case, briefly operated some kind of food kiosk at a lumber camp."

Vincent leaned back in his chair and let out a long, slow breath.

"You know what this is, sir?"

"I do," he said wearily. "Tell the jobs hall to mark the contracts as closed, no reward claimed."

"Is this about the gold-rankers?"

"No, and that's an order. The official position of the Adventure Society is that there are no gold-rankers operating in the city or its surrounds until they arrive here by ship the day after tomorrow. Do not let me hear you have been so much as *implying* anything else, Gretchen."

"Is it that big a deal, sir?"

Vincent sighed. "Dear gods, I hope not."

Hiram had been climbing the mountain trail most days, for most of his life. Age had been catching up to him, but his limbs carried him now with fresh vigour, courtesy of his bronze-rank physique. He had told his grand-daughter not to waste the hard-fought earnings of an adventurer on an old man and she, of course, had ignored him.

He'd saved and scrimped from before she was even born to give her the opportunity. More than giving him his own chance to become an essence-user, she repaid him with the joy in her eyes when she came home and told him the story of her adventures.

He looked up at the water roaring out from a hole in the side of the mountain. The torrent became deafening as he ascended towards the tunnel that would lead him inside. It was even louder in the cave, echoes thundering like the bellow of some primordial beast. The air in the cave was wet, leaving the boards of the wooden walkway slick, thus the grit adhered to the planks for grip. It was getting on time to replace some of the boards and apply fresh grit to the others.

The cave was still beautiful to his eyes, even after all these years. Glow stone lamps lit up the green stone. At the end of the cave was a cavern where the torrent passed through on its way out of the mountain. It travelled so fast, it moved horizontally through the air, a fast-moving wall of water. Blue light shone from it and spray became a sparkling mist that filled the cavern.

Hiram shook his head with a chuckle, remembering when he'd been caught in the water, carried down the tunnel and shot out into the air. He'd been certain he was going to die, and instead ended up with one of the precious essences he was able to gift his granddaughter.

The half of the cavern that didn't have water rushing through it had been carved to a flat surface, with a metal safety rail to keep anyone from getting too close to the water. It was a lot stronger now, after that incident. Attached to the cavern was a room carved into the wall, with a large window and a door for access.

Made to keep monitoring staff warm and dry, the room was larger and more comfortable than it had been when Hiram was a young man. He'd thought the job would tide him over until he found something better, and he never did. It was an easy job, monitoring the water aperture, so long as you didn't mind climbing the mountain every day.

Hiram headed for the booth to relieve Dave, who was bit of an odd sort. Didn't much care for people, or for daylight, but was friendly enough if you left him to himself. He did get cranky for a bit after Martha's boy Henry became mayor and had the Adventure Society check he wasn't a vampire.

When Hiram got to the window, he saw it had steamed up from the inside. That happened when someone cooked, but Dave normally brought a packed meal from the Madson girl who was sweet on him. Hiram opened the door to a humid food smell and someone talking.

"...use all kinds of fillings, but I like pork the best. You don't have that here, but the gonku lizard I used in these is pretty close. Which is weird because it's, you know, a lizard."

Dave's response was an incoherent mumble, due to the dumpling sticking out of his mouth. The room was basically a lounge area, with a large low table in the middle that was enchanted to function as a self-cleaning cooking surface. On it was a pan of hot dumplings. Dave was facing the door while the room's other occupant sat across from him, with his back to Hiram.

The man turned around, flashing a big smile at Hiram. It had been a long time, and his features had been smoothed out by rank-ups, but Hiram would never forget Jason Asano. Not only had they been flung off a mountain together, but Jason went on to save the village from a terrible monster, almost dying in the process. They'd found him, almost cut in half, in the rubble that had once been their village.

He'd also gifted Hiram with what became the first of his granddaughter's essences. Hiram knew Jason hadn't been a wealthy man back then, just a freshly minted adventurer. Even so, he'd handed it to Hiram with a smile on his face, as if he was loaning a neighbour some tea.

"You look good, Hiram. All those mountain hikes are keeping you in shape."

Hiram refilled Jason's teacup.

"We didn't know what to make of it," he said. "First, we hear you're dead. Then we hear you're alive again, and the stories only got less believable from there. But whatever people say about you, good or bad, you're a hero to the people in this town, Jason. The young ones like Dave don't remember, but those of us who were around back then…"

He let his words linger as he sipped at his tea.

"That day was a nightmare. You hear the stories of some high-rank monster tearing through a town, but you don't expect it to happen. Monsters are always a threat, out in these rural areas, but something like that?"

"Yeah, there was a thing messing with the monster surges," Jason said. "It made the monster spawns a bit off. It's fixed now."

Hiram shook his head.

"The why doesn't matter to folks like us. What matters is children screaming as their parents drag them out of collapsing buildings. Pushing people onto wagons even as they're taking off. Afraid that, at any second, some big watery tentacle will crash down and kill you all and there's nothing you can do to stop it. You were just a kid, but you stood up. Put yourself between us and it. Bought us the time to get everyone out and safe. Now look at you, the big-time adventurer. You know, we never got to thank you properly for that."

"You didn't have to thank me, Hiram. That's what adventurers do."

"I was there, boy. I saw the looks on your friends' faces. I may not have seen you in twenty years, but I get the feeling you spent a lot of it doing things that maybe adventurers don't do."

Jason chuckled.

"Maybe so," he conceded, and sipped at his tea. "What about that granddaughter of yours? Did she ever become an adventurer?"

"Indeed, she did. A more modest one than you, I reckon, which suits me just fine. I like her coming home with stories of travel and adventure. I don't want anyone fishing her out of the ruins of someone's house, looking more dead than alive. No offence."

"No, that's a wise approach. Not in the cards for some of us, though. Did I ever tell you where I came from?"

"Not that I recall. I think you said it was somewhere remote. I remember thinking that it was a bit strange for an adventurer, some of the things you didn't know."

"Well, I'm not your granddaughter, but let me regale you with some of my stories of travel and adventure. Do you know what a universe is?"

Time always moved on. For long-lived adventurers, things stretched out, and change was slow. Exploring Greenstone, Jason was confronted with how different it was for those without access to age-extending magic. He stood on a rooftop, his cloak melding him invisibly into the shadow of a chimney. He watched a yard below, where a spry woman of late-middle years was hanging out washing on a line.

"Did you find out who she is?"

"I did," Shade said. "This is Juliette Landry, the daughter of your former landlady. She inherited this property from her mother, who found a great deal of success in her later years. She ended up owning five establishments in total. Each is now operated by her daughter or one of her nieces: Josephine, Joanne, Jennifer, and Bertha."

"Bertha?"

"Madam Bertha Landry hosts the property with more structural reinforcement enchantments than the other. Her clientele can be quite rambunctious."

"When did my Madam Landry pass?"

"Seven years ago. Apparently to the lament of several elderly but vigorous men who were rather unhappy to find out about each other after the fact. It was, by all accounts, a quite exciting memorial service."

"Good for her," Jason said with a sad smile. "All the years I was off doing weird dimensional stuff. How much did I miss back home, Shade?"

"You haven't called Earth home in a long time, Mr Asano."

"I suppose I haven't."

"You know that Arella thinks you're going to kill her," Vincent said.

"I've killed people for doing a lot less than she did," Jason said. "But I'm not here to kill anyone."

"Do you mind if I go change out of this bathrobe?" Vincent asked. "I didn't dress for a home invasion."

"Sorry," Jason said. "I wanted to be discreet. That's why I waited until your husband left."

"Oh, he'd have been delighted. He loves the adventurer stuff."

Vincent left the sitting room of his town house and continued the conversation from the other room.

"You'd think that the Messenger War and the rest of it would dampen his enthusiasm," Vincent said. "He's like a child sometimes, always looking for an adventure story."

He walked back out in simple linen pants and a tunic he'd implausibly managed to put on without disrupting his moustache.

"Why are you here, Jason?"

"There are some organisational things we should probably sort out to make things go more smoothly."

"Yes, but I have office hours."

"But you were very clear with Gretchen that I'm not officially here."

"You're spying on me?"

"Uh… no?"

Vincent sighed.

"Gold-rankers. This is why I transferred back to Greenstone, you know. I'll go get my notebook."

He walked over to a chair where a satchel had been tossed. He pulled out a notebook and a pencil, then gestured Jason into a seat. He sat opposite and was about to ask Jason a question when he stopped and set the pencil and book down on the couch beside him.

"How is Rufus?" he asked softly.

"He left this world. Fifteen years ago now."

Vincent sat bolt upright.

"He's dead?"

"What? Oh, sorry, no. I mean he literally left this world. He's been living on the one I came from. He's fine. He's really into jellybeans, like *really* into them. The fancy ones with weird flavours like 'Barcelona asphalt' or whatever. He'd definitely have diabetes if he wasn't magical. I sent him to meet this person I'm trying to recruit over there, and he came back with about a wheelbarrow full of them."

"I have no idea what you're talking about. Which is very nostalgic for me, so I suppose we'd better get to it."

He picked his notebook back up.

"Now, we might as well start with nobles who want a meet-and-greet on arrival versus those asking for a more in-depth meeting."

"There's no reason for me to…"

Jason stopped himself, grimacing as he thought back over Danielle's lessons. He took a deep breath and let it out slowly.

"Okay," he said. "Nobles who want meetings, you say."

29

A MATTER OF MINDSET

As the ship approached Greenstone's artificial island, Jason and his companions were gathering in a space not unlike a hotel lobby. Aspects of the vessel were similar to a cruise ship, although heavier on amenity and utility spaces and lighter on accommodation. Even Emir only travelled around with fifty or so staff, and Jason had far fewer people on board than that.

Jason walked towards the lobby with Sophie and Humphrey as Sophie voiced her unhappiness with the destination. She hadn't joined Belinda in their early visit to their hometown, and she wasn't keen on going now.

"I don't see why we're even here," she said. "What does this place have to offer us anymore? And I know you don't like all this pageantry, Jason."

"You've always liked your ostentation spontaneous," Humphrey pointed out. "Having it scheduled and organised doesn't seem like you."

"It's not for me," Jason said. "Or for you, Humphrey. A special event doesn't seem special to you because you're the prince of this town. Greenstone may have a Duke, but everyone knows that the Gellers are the real power here. You were born for bigger things than this town has to offer, so a triumphant return visit doesn't mean much."

"Then what is all this for?" Humphrey asked.

"Every aristocratic house in Greenstone will be represented in the crowd waiting for us. Not just some pointless nephew either. Elders, heads of house. Organisations too. Directors of the Magic Society, the Adventure Society, the Alchemy Association. There are as many of Greenstone's silver-rankers gathered here as have ever come together in one place before."

"What do you care about the nobility of some low-magic backwater?" Sophie asked, not hesitating to talk denigratingly about her hometown. "You socialise with gods and kings and diamond-rankers."

"I told you, it's not about me. Right now, all those people are gathered at the Adventure Society's VIP dock. And who are they waiting for? It's not me. People haven't been talking about me for years, and I was only famous amongst Adventure Society insiders. These people are gathering for Team Biscuit. Adventuring legends and hometown heroes. For you, Humphrey, that's not a big deal. Everyone expected big things of you. But think about all those people, and who else they're here to see."

He glanced at Sophie.

"People know your story, Sophie. They've doubtless mythologised it well outside anything that's actually true, but that's not what matters. What matters is that a pair of girls from Old City became famous adventurers. And now they're coming home, celebrated by the city's elite."

"I never wanted to be a role model."

"Too bad. And it's not just for the next little Sophie and Belinda either. Neil's family have been stuck as what amounts to servants to the Mercers for years, but now the most powerful people in the city have to show them respect. Today, they get to stand tall as Neil comes home, probably dressed in his aunt's awful clothes. And you know who else is waiting for us? A clan of eel farmers. The important people of this city would cross the road to avoid them, but today, those eel farmers will be front and centre, waiting for their boy to come home. And those important people are stuck standing behind them."

"Does it always have to be a speech with you?" Sophie asked. "You could have just said it will be nice for Neil's and Clive's families to see."

"That seems a little reductive."

"I think you just like hearing yourself talk."

"What are you talking about? Everyone loves hearing me talk."

The Adventure Society VIP dock was on the ocean side of Greenstone's artificial island. The expectation was that if your vessel needed a sheltered harbour, you weren't important enough to use it. Near the dock was a large building normally used for social events, as the dock itself spent most of its time empty. This also allowed the attending luminaries to save face. They could tell themselves they were attending a social function, not standing around, waiting for people more important than them to arrive.

The building had been restructured just a couple of years ago, and most of its three stories were glass walls. Elspeth Arella looked out at the ocean from the third floor, radiating a lack of desire for company. Most of the attendees were looking to ingratiate themselves with the Geller boy and his famous team. Jason Asano was a name that hadn't entered their minds in years, and it seemed only Elspeth herself was focused on him. If they were all very lucky, that wouldn't change.

She had expected to sense the ship before she saw it, but was proven wrong as it crested the horizon. Even as it drew closer, revealing its immense size, she sensed nothing, even when staring right at it. She knew that most of the attendees would not notice, let alone understand the significance. They were socialites and merchant barons, not warriors and soldiers. The Messenger War had left Greenstone largely untouched.

That vessel was a message about power and who held it; it was not one that the Director of the Adventure Society missed. She also knew that it was not accidental; Danielle Geller was on that ship. She did not send unintended signals, and she did not like Elspeth.

As the ship neared the shore, the collective group went outside. She glanced around, watching the crowd with her aura senses as well as her eyes. She'd put reliable people in key positions, hoping to keep volatile elements under control, but the potential for disaster was very real. One moment, a lord's idiot son might be mocking the clan of eel farmers, unhappy they were given pride of place. The idiot would be hurtling out to sea at the hands of a gold-ranker in about three seconds, and things would only devolve from there. Elspeth's spectrum for the success of the event ranged from a brawl to a massacre.

The massive vessel pulled up at the dock, larger than the building in which people had been waiting for it. Elspeth couldn't help but remember the similar scene of Emir Bahadir's arrival. This ship was different, in that the cloud material of the vessel was only visible in sections between large panels that covered it.

Elspeth wondered if the different ship signalled a different outcome. Emir Bahadir wasn't easy to handle, but the treasure hunter knew how to navigate the locals on a visit like this. Jason Asano was smooth as sandpaper, always rubbing people wrong. During his time in Greenstone, he'd somehow befriended every person who was powerful and independent enough to make Elspeth's job hard, and annoyed everyone else.

Clouds wafted from the ship to create a wide bridge, and a gap opened in the side of the ship. The Gellers emerged, Danielle and her son, who was becoming as famous as she was. Next to the Geller boy was a man who looked similar enough to be a younger brother, but with silver hair and eyes.

It was only after Humphrey Geller left Greenstone that Elspeth discovered that he'd been wandering around with an actual gods-bedamned dragon the whole time. She'd known he had a shapeshifting familiar, of course, but an actual, true-blood dragon? His mother had told her it was a lyre drake, but Elspeth should have known better than to trust Danielle Geller.

She catalogued the rest as they came over the bridge. The thieves she'd once tasked her society branch to hunt down, not knowing the chaos that would ensue. Asano, the main perpetrator of that chaos. The Magic Research Association's archchancellor. The uncultured cheering that arose from the grubby-looking farmers at the appearance of the refined man of magic was a strange incongruity.

Elspeth's gaze moved back to Asano. He caught her gaze for a moment before looking away, chatting amiably with the Devone boy. Then she felt a strange shimmer of aura around her and the sounds around her deafened. Asano's voice came out of nowhere.

"It's not me you have to worry about, Director. I'm not the one you tried to sell to Lucian Lamprey as a means to slake his deprived appetites. But you don't really have to worry about Sophie either, because she's dedicated herself to being a good person. She has this friend, though. You might want to check under your bed for alchemical bombs until we're gone again."

Elspeth was at the front of the line for meet and greets. Asano was polite, as if meeting a passing acquaintance after a long time.

"I'd like the chance for you and me to talk, Mr Asano. Adventurer business."

"Of course, Director."

What came next was a lengthy and tedious sequence of introductions and reintroductions, carefully orchestrated in order and length. After her experiences with Asano in the past, she was amazed that it all went to plan. There was none of his signature disruption or anti-authoritarian antics. It seemed that he had learned some diplomacy in the last couple of decades. As for who had managed to wrangle the lunatic, she noticed Danielle Geller throwing glances his way.

By the time it was all over, the one thing Elspeth least expected to happen had taken place: everything had gone to plan. No aristocratic feuds flaring up. No spoiled rich kids had made trouble out of arrogance and pride. Asano hadn't decided to take umbrage with anyone and start throwing people into the ocean now he was gold rank and no one could stop him.

As she made her way back to her office, she felt a strange relief, even as a new worry plagued at her mind. She would need to look closer into those former thieves, and she had just the person to ask. Upon reaching her office, she changed into a hooded outfit that would not look out of place in the Old City, then headed out to see her father.

Adris Dorgan was a happy man. Once a powerful crime lord, he found that legitimacy sat very well with him. As mayor of Old City, he'd dragged it kicking and screaming from the old days into a new era. Aristocratic families, as it turned out, were far more criminal than the old crime families, and with none of the sense of code or community. Now that Adris could shield the people from at least some of that, Old City was becoming a better place for its people.

His daughter was less happy. She had wanted to leave the city and rise through the ranks of the Adventure Society, and that had all come to nothing. Once, that had angered him, but those days were long gone. Greenstone was quiet, far from the Messenger War. The days of the Builder cult and the strange monster surges were almost two decades gone, and Greenstone was safe. Having his daughter safe and close were treasures to a father.

Walking through his library, he stopped dead. His mind flashed back to an encounter twenty years ago, where he found a young man staring at a picture in the library of his old home. The library was different, but it was the same man doing the same thing now, having once again ignored his security. Adris moved to where the man was staring at the painting.

"A long time ago," Asano said, not looking from the painting, "you offered to help me get my hands of a work or two by Moher. Said he was a family friend."

"He still is."

"I might take you up on that, if the offer is still open."

"I suppose that depends on what your intentions are otherwise."

"I gave your daughter a little prod and she'll be coming to see you. I thought it might be a good idea for her and me to have a little chat."

"I once warned you about interfering in my daughter's affairs, Asano. I don't care if you're some all-powerful gold-ranker, and I'm just a politician who got to silver with cores. If you do anything to her, I'll find a way to kill you."

Asano finally turned from the painting to flash a smile.

"I like you, Mr Dorgan. Family is important. Nothing will happen to your daughter from my people, even if she does have it coming. That's not what we're here for. I'd like to clear the air, now the power dynamic has shifted since my last stay in Greenstone. Also, there's something she wants to discuss with me, and I thought it might be awkward in a room where she once dangled me in the air by the throat."

"And you're sure she's coming here?"

"She's crossing the bridge to Old City now."

"You're having her watched?"

"No, I'm just tracking her with my aura senses."

"How do you extend your perception that far without washing the city in your aura?"

"Practise."

"Well, can I offer you a cup of tea while we wait?"

"That would be lovely, thank you."

Jason sat across from Elspeth in one of her father's entertaining courtyards. It had enclosed walls covered in plants growing out of alcoves, and was open to the sky. The furniture was ornate wrought metal, with plush padding. A tea set occupied most of the table between them, complete with scones with gemberry jam and huge dollops of whipped cream. Jason paid more attention to those than he did the Adventure Society director.

"What can I do for you?" he asked as he dabbed at the cream around his mouth with a napkin.

"How familiar are you with Boko, Mr Asano?"

"A city to the north of here. A lot older than Greenstone, with a population native to the area. If I recall correctly, most of Greenstone's people are descended from the original Estercost immigrants, I think, only a few centuries ago. Boko is a city of academics, if I recall correctly."

"Scholars of the arts. Painting, poetry, sculpture, dance. People travel from across the continent and beyond to visit their theatres."

"I only passed through briefly. A portal stop, in the aftermath of that disastrous expedition. It's pretty, as I recall. Lots of gardens."

"Do you happen to recall a group of raiders that came south during your time here?"

"I do. I was part of the group that dealt with them. They were rural tribesfolk, weren't they? From the areas around Boko?"

"That's what we thought at the time. As it turns out, their origins were in Boko proper. It began as some kind of anti-intellectual movement amongst low-rankers and escalated from there. Moved out of the city and into areas where education was less of a priority. There, it festered like a sore. Getting back to primal manhood, that kind of thing. It thrives on low-rank, disenfranchised young men."

"I'm familiar with the basic idea."

"We had thought this particular movement had died out, but there has been a resurgence in the last few years."

"Why bring this to me? Isn't this a low-rank problem?"

"It's not your rank that makes me want you involved. I've been keeping an eye on this alongside my counterpart in Boko. Our initial belief was that this was a naturally arising, decentralised movement. It probably was, in the beginning, but we're starting to suspect some manner of organisational force behind it. Whether they were there at the beginning, or co-opted an emerging cultural phenomenon, we believe they are using it to build a powerful political block. Puppeteering heads that don't realise they are part of the same hydra. They keep their hands hidden, using populist groups as their face. Now it controls large portions of the rural areas around Greenstone, Boko and the Veldt. If we tried to reach out and quash it, we'd have towns and villages across half the continent in borderline rebellion."

"Do you have any sense of their objective?"

"Industry, to start. The production of spirit coins and our signature green stone is a lot of money, when taken as a whole."

"You think someone is looking to control small local governments? Extort shady tariffs on everyone operating in the region?"

"Something like that. If money is their end goal, we live with some graft. It's not like the aristocrats are any better. Our concern is if they have a larger and more sinister agenda. Moving their power base into Greenstone and Boko, maybe. Or quietly supporting more traditional problem groups in other regions. Illegal magical research requires funding, after all, just like the legitimate research. Whatever the ultimate purpose, it's an ongoing concern."

"So, why not go in and clear them out?"

"We haven't seen an approach like this before. It's a matter of mindset. On this world, we always think top-down first. Rank hierarchy, which is why you get to come into my city and make a giant mess. The golds do what they like, the silvers run most of it and the bronze-rankers do what they're told."

"I never had much time for that."

"Oh, I remember. This operation, movement, whatever it is, they think differently too. Bottom up. People barely think about the iron-rankers and the normal. Even in a low-magic zone like Greenstone, they don't hold a lot of influence. This movement takes the people our way of thinking ignores and melds them into a power built not on magical strength but ideological indoctrination. Taking disenfranchisement and isolation and turning it into a sense of belonging, welded to cultural concepts that make them easy to manipulate."

"You're saying that whoever is behind this isn't operating like someone from your world."

"Back when you were living here in Greenstone, even I kept hearing about your endless pontificating about how our society was all wrong. People were dodging you in the admin building so they didn't have to listen to it. And I remembered my horror at hearing that more of your kind had arrived. That was two monster surges ago, and I never heard anything else about it. But when we heard you were coming back, Vincent Trenslow remembered enough of what you would talk about then to put things together. Power derived from large groups of the weak."

"That's not how I put it."

"But I think Vincent was right. He suggested that whoever is behind all this might come, not from our world, but from yours."

30

POSTURING CHILDREN

"LET'S ASSUME," JASON TOLD ELSPETH, "THAT SOMEONE FROM EARTH IS pulling the strings. There were a bunch of them in Estercost and I left them twisting in the wind for years. It only makes sense that they've gone out and started doing things. But, even assuming that someone from Earth is your problem, my being from Earth too doesn't solve it."

He sighed, then sipped at his tea appreciatively. "You know, Greenstone really does have the best tea I've had in Pallimustus."

"We're not here to talk about tea."

"That's a shame," he said, and set his teacup down with a regretful glance. "I was enjoying making purely social calls lately."

"Asano…"

He groaned.

"Director, let's take a look at your situation. The Ustei tribesmen who came south during my time here in Greenstone predate the arrival of more people from Earth by what? Three years, give or take? Assuming that there is someone manipulating this movement of yours, and further assuming that they're from Earth, this means that they inserted themselves into an existing situation."

"The violent ones aren't the issue. Those we can just deal with. It's the groups that are building up, growing their influence amongst the population, but not taking any violent action. They're digging into the small rural communities. Influencing the populace and putting their own people into positions of local authority."

"And that's your real problem. Hidden powers moving in secret to manipulate one or more grassroots movements. The movements themselves aren't aware that they are slowly but surely being twisted to serve the very forces they believe they stand against. This happens in my world across the political spectrum."

"What do we do about it?"

"I don't know."

"How do they deal with this issue on Earth?"

"Mostly with sensationalist journalism and calling each other Hitler on the internet."

"What?"

"We don't, Director, and that's your problem. If we knew how to stop it, we would."

"You're saying you can't help."

"No, I'm not. Your hidden influencers, we can probably deal with. My group includes some people who excel at infiltration and information gathering. They can probably root out your masterminds, and then I'll deal with it, if they are from Earth. If not, we'll leave them to you. That will stop whatever agenda they have, but that doesn't solve your larger issue."

"Which is?"

"Whoever you're after didn't invent these groups. They came in and made use of what was already there. You delete the person behind the scenes, the groups themselves won't even notice. They're going to keep winning hearts and minds in all these small towns and villages. The places where people with power and money only visit if they absolutely have to. Those groups rose up for a reason. You're going to be dealing with them until the reasons they formed in the first place get addressed."

"I have no problem with these groups existing. That's for the dukes to deal with. My concern is someone using this movement to fund things the Adventure Society has to deal with. Red Table cultists, restricted essence research, messenger collaboration. Things that get a lot harder to stamp out if we don't catch them early."

"That's all well and good, Director, but whoever is manipulating these people is an opportunist. We can get rid of them, fine, but if the opportunity is still there, you're just going to get someone else moving in. This is a very Earth-style operation they're running, but there's no reason someone from this world can't do it. Especially now that someone has demonstrated how."

"I'm not responsible for unhappy low-rankers."

"Then don't do anything. Spend the rest of your career cleaning out maggots because you refuse to remove the rot."

"What exactly are you suggesting?"

"Oh, I've got my own political mess to walk into, back on Earth. You can sort this one out. But, maybe try asking these people what they want, instead of telling them they don't matter and to shut up."

"That's not what we're doing."

"Yes, it is. You think these people don't have power because they can't throw lightning or breathe fire. They can't rise up in violence, but they can put down tools in protest. What happens if all the quarry workers and spirit coin farmers stop working?"

"The families who own the quarries and farms get more workers."

"Oh, come on, Elspeth. You're too smart not to see where that road goes, long term. It just keeps getting worse, and how long can Greenstone's export economy survive like that? Once supply interruptions become a regular thing, trade partners start looking for more reliable alternatives."

"Still not my problem."

"Then stand by and watch the city die. I'll be long gone."

Elspeth scowled, picked up a scone and shoved it in her mouth, chewing angrily.

"Elspeth, I'm not trying to tell you how to approach social change. I've figured out that I'm really bad at it. But maybe try to convince the duke to sit down with some of these people. Find out what they want and maybe even think about giving it to them. It's probably not that much."

Elspeth finished her scone, looking slightly embarrassed as she wiped the cream from around her mouth.

"You missed a bit on your chin," Jason said. "No, the other side. Yeah, that's it."

She put down her napkin and sighed.

"So," she said. "That was the famous Jason Asano 'change everything about your society' speech, was it?"

"I suppose it was. Look, I did one semester of political science before dropping out over a girl, so my expertise is limited."

"I don't know what that means."

"It means that I once learned just enough to be wrong about a lot of things. But sometimes, when you have power, you have to deal with those things anyway. Despite your insistence that this is the duke's problem, I think you know that."

"I do," Elspeth conceded.

"I have my own mess that I'll be walking into on Earth. I'm trying to find people who can help me not make a giant mess of things."

"Geller?"

"Amongst others, hopefully. I think you would be a good fit, but while you have the political acumen, I wouldn't trust you to make moral choices. I've done terrible things, out of anger, frustration or ignorance, but I've always regretted them. You do them out of cold calculation."

"This is about the Wexler girl."

"You don't sell people to twisted deviants, Director, however much doing so might advantage you."

"Not all of us get to waltz through life with gods and high-rankers giving us special treatment, Asano. Some of us have to fight and scrape for every little thing we get. Not everyone gets to walk the easy road and have things just handed to them."

Jason smiled.

"Do you remember, back when I was iron rank, and I didn't give much of a care for what rank difference meant you could say to someone?"

"How could I forget?"

"You should be very grateful that, for all that I have changed since then, that has remained the same."

He stood up.

"I'll find your masterminds, Director. If they're from Earth, I'll deal with them myself."

"You said that before. You should hand them over to the Adventure Society."

"I tried that once, Director. You sold them to a pervert."

"And your hands are clean, are they? I remember someone who murdered five Adventure Society members, not that far from where we're sitting."

"My hands are filthy, Director. But at least I try."

"So? It's results that matter, Asano. Trying doesn't matter a damn."

He sighed.

"I don't think anything productive will come from us continuing this conversation."

"Agreed. Are you still willing to loan me those infiltration and information experts you mentioned? The only ones we field here in Greenstone belong to the aristocratic families, and are deployed against each other. They aren't up to something on this level. I checked."

"I set them to work about ten minutes ago."

"While we were talking?"

"You aren't worth my undivided attention, Director."

She also stood up.

"I'm going to regret you coming back to my city, aren't I?"

"You don't already?"

"I suppose I do."

Li Li Mei loved Boko. It was a beautiful city, filled with gorgeous architecture and wondrous gardens. She was going to miss it. Someone was looking for her, and had gotten far too close before she noticed. Despite the go-betweens, cut-outs and false identities, someone was zeroing in on her. For weeks they'd been digging their way through her layers of protection, and she only noticed now through sheer luck. Whoever it was, they were extremely good at what they did.

Her decision to abandon the entire undertaking was immediate and without hesitation. She was leaving behind a lucrative operation, but she'd sent enough money away that it hadn't been wasted time. Gold-rank cores were wildly expensive, but at least they could be had for money. On Earth, they were the rarest and most valuable commodity, perhaps other than reality cores.

The only thing she stopped to grab was a go-bag she had stashed for this exact eventuality. She took it and descended the tower she owned, not by the elevating platform but by the stairs. A secret door led into a basement that no one but a long-dead stone-shaper knew about. From there, a long tunnel led into the sewers. The sewer tunnels were massive, reminding her of a video game more than the actual sewers of Earth. There were sinister types to be found down here, but she let out just enough silver-rank aura to warn them off.

Li Mei had learned the importance of good aura control over the last decade and a half. She'd known that Jason Asano had far superior aura control to anyone else on Earth, but she hadn't realised how bad they all were until she arrived in Pallimustus. Looking back, it was no wonder he treated Earth's magical factions like posturing children.

She absently wondered what had happened to the man. The Earth refugees had all been cooped up at the Geller compound in Cyrion waiting for him. Then they were told that he wasn't coming. The stories as to what had happened were unclear, but many of the Earthlings believed him dead. Li Mei did not share that opinion.

She took to the streets further from her storehouse than she would like. It was close to one of the city gates, and had no ties to her on paper. By the time it was connected to her, she would be long gone. A well-dressed Chinese woman walking through one of the seedier sections of a city full of midnight-skinned locals would be easy for her pursuers to find out about. Hopefully, she would be well away before that happened.

The storehouse had a large, fully-loaded camping skimmer. It had amenities and supplies that would let her lay low on the inner reaches of the continent until she made her way to other parts of the world. She didn't trust hiring a portal specialist, and while ships were also a risk, it was one she could ameliorate. She wouldn't use her own shipping contacts, but she had a list of dockmasters who would reliably stay bribed and direct her to a captain to discreetly sail her out.

She breathed a sigh of relief as she reached the storehouse. She slipped down an alley beside it and carefully swept her sense through the building. Sensing nothing but the skimmer and its supplies, she used a very expensive crystal to unlock the reinforced door. She opened it and duck inside, using the crystal to lock it again.

"Yeah, that's her."

Li Mei froze. She slowly turned to find three people looking at her, including two women she didn't recognise. The man looked different, and it had been more than fifteen years, but she recognised him immediately.

"G'day, Miss Li. It's been a while."

31
THIS IS NOT A CLIFF

LI LI MEI WAS ROOTED TO THE GROUND AS IF A LANDSCAPER HAD planted her there. Her body was rigid, her gaze locked on the man in front of her. Jason looked more relaxed, but the rigidity of his casual posture told a different story.

"You know this lady?" Belinda asked.

"I do," he said.

Li Mei didn't recognise the two other women, but gauged their relaxation as genuine. They were leaning against the large skimmer sitting in the middle of the storehouse, still covered in a heavy tarp.

"Does your planet only have seven people on it?" Estella asked. "Why do you know them all?"

"I vaguely recall Taika mentioning that I knew more people amongst the Earth refugees. And that they didn't join him and Travis because they didn't want to be sent to me."

"And they bet on the kindness of strangers over getting help from you?" Estella asked. "How bad is your reputation where you come from?"

"It's not great," Jason admitted.

"I can tell by the way she's looking at you," Belinda said. "That's the way sandwiches look at Neil."

Li Mei remained frozen as Jason wandered closer. He was not a tall man, and stood eye to eye with her.

"How have you been, Miss Li?"

She finally found her voice.

"You really are alive, then?"

"On and off. The people from Earth think I'm dead?"

"Some. I didn't believe it."

"Why not?"

"We thought you were crazy, back on Earth. Running around, treating governments and magic factions like they were inconsequential as you did… whatever it was you were doing. You never explained it properly."

"No one was willing to listen. All any of you heard was the word 'power' running through your heads in a loop."

"It was a time of unprecedented opportunity, or so we thought. Only after I spent time in this world did I realise that we were stray dogs, fighting over scraps. You were doing things like they do them in this world, because you thrive here. You fit."

"No, he doesn't," Belinda called out. "He's weird everywhere he goes."

"It's kind of nice knowing that it's not just here," Estella said.

"It does feel like a vindication of all the things we say about him behind his back."

Jason turned to look at them from under raised eyebrows.

"Do you two mind?"

"No, we're good," Belinda said.

"She's very pretty," Estella observed, drawing an exaggerated look of exasperation from Belinda.

"You are such a skirt chaser. I cannot take you anywhere."

"All I said was that she's pretty."

"I'm standing right here and you're eyeing off other women, right in front of me."

Jason shook his head and turned back to Li Mei.

"Come on," he told her. "We're taking a walk."

Li Mei's storage building was in one of Boko's less reputable areas, a warehouse district far from the gardens and universities.

"The gold-rankers in Greenstone," she said. "That was you, obviously."

"Yes," Jason confirmed.

"I heard it was some famous team out of Vitesse."

"My team. I just haven't been on it for a while."

"I never liked following adventurer news. Clearly, I should have been more diligent."

As a foreigner and a small woman moving alone, she'd constantly caught looks as she made her way through the streets, fending off unwanted attention with her aura. Moving through those same streets with Asano was a completely different experience.

"What's going on?" she asked him.

"What do you mean?" he asked.

"We're very obvious outsiders here, but people are stepping around us without so much as a glance. It's almost like they're pretending they don't see us."

"They're subconsciously not paying us any attention. If we do something too unusual, they'll notice. And a small number of people respond with aggression and anger instead of getting lulled in."

"You're doing this?"

"It's become a habit. I try to avoid attention when I can, these days. I can stop it, if you like."

"How? Some kind of mind control?"

"I don't think magic can do that, at least not directly. The soul barrier shields the mind, so you have to use workarounds. Physiologically manipulating the brain, that kind of thing. The goddess of Knowledge can't read minds, but she has access to all knowledge, so she effectively can."

"Then how?"

"Aura manipulation. I can't alter their auras, but I can modulate mine to something that most people will instinctively and subconsciously overlook. It's like how you never look at your habitual surroundings unless something changes and makes it stand out. I'm giving off 'that chair in the corner you never sit in' vibes."

"And you're doing it for both of us."

"I first started working on this back on Earth, based on some vampire tricks. I've had a lot of practise and training with my aura since then."

"Now that I've seen this world, I can only wonder how much you could have offered us back on Earth. If we'd treated you like a visiting dignitary instead of a commodity to be divided up."

"My knowledge was limited. Farrah was the one you should have gone after."

"No offence, Mr Asano, but you were a lot easier to manipulate. She knew to shut up and walk away when she didn't know something."

He let out a chuckle.

"You have more knowledge now," she said. "As do I. You were here for what? A year and a half before going back? I've been here ten times that. The things I could do on Earth now. I could change the world."

"It's been a long time, Miss Li. The world changed on its own."

"You have contact with Earth?"

"Yes."

"How?"

"We're not here for me to answer your questions, Miss Li. We're here to decide what happens to you now."

"I didn't do anything illegal."

"Pallimustus takes more of a 'spirit of the law' approach than Earth does. Which you know, or we wouldn't have caught you running."

"And you've been given discretionary power over me."

"If someone had to give it to you, it's not real power. Especially not in this world. You've been left to my discretion because I took that authority, and because no one with the power to challenge me will do so. Not over you. Which is why I am assuming you chose this low magic zone for your little scheme."

"It wasn't that little."

"A matter of perspective, I suppose."

"You were like this on Earth too. Acting as if our concerns were too small for you to bother with on anything but a whim."

"They were."

"I realised that, after coming here. But now we're here, and you're still acting more important than everyone else."

"It's not me that's important. I have responsibilities."

"Saving the world again? In an unexplained way, from an indeterminate threat, but trust you, it's really important?"

"Stop that. You know I like banter, so you're trying to engage me. Make me like you."

"Is it working?"

"I've had better," he said, but a smile teased the corners of his mouth. "I'm not going to kill you, Miss Li, or hand you over to the local authorities. As much as I do like the directness of how things are done here, the more discretionary the power, the greater the chance for corruption. This place can be barbaric, and the only check on that is the moral compass of whoever has the power."

"No world is perfect, I suppose."

"No. Same for the people in them, even those of us who get to travel to both."

Their meandering path led out of the warehouse district and into a nicer area, close to a small university campus. The buildings were a mix of sandstone blocks and the region's signature green brick. There were tall, thin trees, similar to palms. Leafy green plants grew out of pots and alcoves, or dangled from balconies. Water features were prominent, from channels that fed the abundant plant life to fountains placed at road junctions as roundabouts.

"They call this the Oasis City," Li Mei said. "There are multiple apertures to the water astral space here. Apparently, some cult tried to sabotage them years ago, but they are well guarded here. The cult had more luck out in the desert, so I've heard."

"They did."

"You were involved?"

"Peripherally. I was still in training when the big battle took place in the water astral space itself, so I missed out. Which was good, because a lot of people more powerful than me died, including my friend Farrah."

"This is a different Farrah from the one with you on Earth?"

"No. I died too, later, fighting the being that cult worships. When I came back to life on Earth, some cosmic entities decided that she should as well. They thought there should be at least one person I could trust there."

"How do you do that?"

"Do what?"

"Talk about things that start religions with no more gravity than buying a coffee. There were a lot of reports, back on Earth. Interviews with people who encountered you. You used to talk off-the-cuff about things so outlandish that we would dismiss them as nonsense. Like coming back from the dead. Now, I realise that at least some of them were true. I'm more credulous than I was, but cosmic beings bringing people back from the dead is a lot, even for this world."

"Go ask the goddess of Death. Her church gave me a certificate to say how many times I've died."

"Isn't the death god a man?"

"Gods like to keep things flexible in that regard."

"You say that like you know a lot of gods."

"How much of this is you pretending not to have exhaustively researched everything you could about me after getting to Pallimustus?"

"I don't—"

"Your aura reveals your emotions to me, Miss Li. You are doing a remarkable job of hiding your fear, by the way. I used to do that, but I lost the knack. It's healthier to work through the emotions than bottle them up, believe me."

"I saw you murder people on television with your mind, Mr Asano. I believe you."

"Good. Now, enough about me. Tell me about this operation of yours. The local authorities are worried that you're quietly fundraising an undead army or something."

"Why would I do that?"

"They don't know you. They have no idea what you would and wouldn't do, and the worst-case scenario is always bad on this world. It wasn't that far from here that a blood cult was trying to summon a world-eating leech monster."

"Don't you summon a leech monster?"

"He's a good boy," he said defensively. "Anyway, the point is that they don't know what you want because they don't know you. You were careful about that part."

"Not careful enough."

Their conversation paused as they navigated a narrow street where teamsters were offloading goods for delivery to boutique stores in the nearby shopping district. They extricated themselves from the tight alleys and back streets into a more open boulevard.

"You were doing quite well, until gold-rankers came along," Jason said. "In this part of the world, sending a gold-ranker is bringing a bazooka to a knife fight. Belinda and Estella have decades of experience at spying and thieving. Disguise magic too strong for anyone here to see through, and perception that can listen to you from three buildings over. Hardly anyone uses privacy magic here. Few people have the perception to make it worthwhile, so using a privacy screen here makes you stand out more than whispering in a corner in a big black cloak."

"*That's* how they found me? Because I was using a privacy shield?"

"It was a data point. Overall, they were very impressed with how you set everything up. They suggested I hire you."

"For what?"

"I'm trying to build up a staff, to smooth out my return to Earth. It's going to get complicated, especially once they think they know how powerful I am."

"Once they think they know?"

"Best they don't find out how powerful I actually am."

"And telling me means either you're lying and want me to tell them, or you don't think I'll be able to."

A sanguine smile was the only response she got.

"You know that going back to Earth is no small thing, magically. I looked into it."

"I have better options than most."

"Any options are better options than most. Messenger magic?"

"Amongst other things, but we're talking about you. Take me through the basics of your operation."

"Simple enough. A basic protection racket using disenfranchised workers as my leverage. Wouldn't work in the cities where the industry associations work a lot like unions. In the remote areas, though, it's all aristocratic owners and exploited workforces. All I had to do was exploit them better. A town meeting here, a pamphlet there. A few well-placed figureheads who are handy with a rhyming slogan. Did you ever see the episode of *Justified* where Boyd Crowder convinces the townsfolk to sell their land to Mags Bennett?"

"How good was Walton Goggins in that? My sister said he had a tooth essence, of all things. Sorry, what was your point?"

"I paid charismatic people with folksy charm and no morals to convince people to do what I want. I may have also accidentally invented country music here."

"The good kind? I love me some Dolly Parton or Johnny Cash."

"No. The kind that panders to the audience with iconic rural imagery to mask an underlying political agenda."

"Maybe I should hand you over to the Adventure Society. You're a monster."

"The point is, I rile people up until they cause trouble, then the families pay me to grease the wheels of industry. I get paid and the locals get some token gesture so they feel like they got a win."

"You didn't get pushback from the families?"

"They sent some people to look around. Rough up random people. If they were competent, they wouldn't be working as thugs for aristocrat families at the bottom of the magical barrel. They quickly realised I was careful enough that paying me would be cheaper than finding me."

"Is that why you did it here, so close to where I lived? The low grade of industry thug?"

"In a way. What the low magic gets me is an absence of everything that high magic gets me. Do you know what it's like in a big adventuring city?"

"I do."

"But not in the same way I do, I suspect. You had proper adventurer training. Powerful connections. It's different when you're an untrained core-user from another world. In the big cities, that makes you a waste of potential at best and an experimental subject at worst."

"A big change from your treatment on Earth. Low magic zones gave you some of that back?"

"Yes. I got out of Estercost. The whole country is bubbling with magic. I did some wandering. It was easy enough to pass for an aristocrat from some place no one has heard of, on the outs from my family."

"You seem to have done alright for yourself."

"I discovered the advantages of low magic zones. They don't look down on core-users as much, and silver-rankers are the peak elites. In places like this, I got some of the respect that I missed from Earth. And once I had that, I could make money."

"For what? I've heard you're raking it in, but if it's not to fund a wacky necromancer, what are you doing with it?"

"Did you know that you can buy gold-rank monster cores here?"

"So?"

"So? Do you have any sense of how hard those are to get your hands on back on Earth? They let me look at one once. Through reinforced glass while flanked by armed guards. Here, you can just walk into a trade hall and buy them. It takes an ungodly amount of money, thus, the racket, but you can just buy them. For money!"

"You want to reach gold rank?"

"Who doesn't want to reach gold rank?"

"Fair enough. You couldn't find anything more legitimate?"

"Breaking into new markets is hard, and I was no mercantile expert on Earth, let alone this planet. But people, when you get down to it, are always the same. Australian, Chinese, elf, leonid. People are people, rich people are rich people, and they do what rich people do."

"Exploit poor people."

"Exactly. I've been running this game all over. For years, now, going from one low magic zone to the next. Never pushing too hard, never overextending, and never overstaying my welcome. This isn't the first time I was heading to a sudden and discreet exit. Just the first time I was caught."

"It's not what I'd call moral."

"There are worse things to do that stir up people with legitimate grievances. I may even have accidentally instigated positive social change, once or twice."

They were passing by a water fountain with a lot of foot traffic moving around it. There was a wide, slightly damp lip for people to sit, and Jason did so. Li Mei followed suit. He contemplated her words for a while, wondering how much was true and what was a lie. He could read the emotions in her aura, but using that as a lie detector was more complicated than he made out. Which he was certain she knew.

He could read her emotions, but her aura control was very solid now, which it had not been on Earth. She was very good at regimenting how her mind was reflected in her aura, making it harder for an observer to glean information from it. He had to respect that, given that it was a talent he excelled at himself.

He also suspected that her actual mind was as well-organised as her aura, something he had *not* exceled at. She was good at framing the facts in such a way that they pointed where she wanted, instead of at the truth.

"If you came to work for me," he said, "your loyalty would have to be to me. Not China, not one of the magical factions. Not even my clan, back on Earth. To me."

"You want to offer me a job?"

"Maybe. Haven't decided, yet."

"When I saw you in my storage building, I thought it was the end. The dangers back on Earth were sedate for someone like me. When we met, you were fun, naïve, charming. A little dangerous, but that was exciting. By the time you were killing people with your aura on television, I knew all that was left was dangerous. I thought you were a maniac. Then, I'm about to go on the run and there you are. It felt like I was standing with a cliff at my back, and you were there to push me off. I remember what you were like, back on Earth. At the end. No one knew if you were going to make a joke or snap and kill twenty people."

"I've had a lot of therapy. And I know what it's like to be desperate and alone, in a world you don't understand. This is not a cliff, Miss Li, and I'm not trying to push you off."

"So you say. What if I tell you that I don't want to work for you?"

"Then you can catch a ride back to Earth with the rest. Any Earthlings

I can round up. I'll take you all back to Earth, unless you don't want to go."

"I want to go. After everything I've seen and learned here? I'm going to have so much money and power, it's obscene."

"Not interested in working for me, then?"

"Of course I'm interested. In this city, diamond-rankers are practically a myth, but, from what I hear, they've been hanging around you like you're all golf buddies. I've heard that you tend to get caught up in crazy things, but everyone in your orbit is wealthy and famous. Standing next to you is like complaining that the hailstones are made of gold. The only problem I'll have is getting you to trust me. Because you probably shouldn't."

"I'm not promising to take you on, just take you to Earth. But if Stella and Lindy say you're worth it, I'm not going to ignore that."

"I'm not going to say yes to that. Or no. If your offer is real, I'd like to talk to some of your people. See what I'm potentially getting into."

"And I need to look into what you've been up to before I make that offer. See what kind of person I..."

She looked at him as he trailed off, looking around with suspicion on his expression.

"Something's here," he said and stood up off the side of the fountain. "Something that's very good at—"

A massive sword blade erupted from his chest.

COOK THE CRAP OUT OF SOME TOAST

THE BLADE STICKING OUT OF JASON'S CHEST WAS WIDE AND THICK, MORE suited to bludgeoning than cutting or stabbing. It had been shoved through his body with raw force, the dark metal jutting from his torso. He tried to shove it back out of his body, but his arms wouldn't move. His entire body was paralysed.

He felt the blade draining his energy, but this was no mana drain. It was tapping into the fundamental energy of his being, and that was a problem. His core power flowed from the universe that was his true body, and that power was infinite. His body was unable to contain infinite power, however, and he doubted the sword drinking it in could either. Once one or both reached the limits of their capacity, that magic was going to erupt.

"What the…?"

The words of what presumably was his attacker were timed with a tugging on the sword, but it was lodged in his body. His body wasn't moving either, anchored in place as the power from his universe was leached out, blending into Pallimustus.

Jason was frozen in place, but the surge of power was charging his aura like a toaster running off a fusion reactor. It was going to burn out really soon, but it was going to cook the crap out of some toast. He fired off some quick messages as he expanded his senses over the city. If he couldn't get away from it, he would get everyone else away from him.

Li Mei was a bundle of frayed nerves. For fifteen years, she'd been afraid of meeting Jason Asano again. Would he kill her? Ignore her? Completely forget who she was? When they finally met, the prim, collected persona she built up over the years fell apart. It felt oddly like when her father had sent her to the USA to study—as if nothing she had learned had prepared her for it.

Maybe that was why she fell back into her old patterns from that time. Loose, confused, uncertain. Trying to paint over a rising panic with forced casualness. In the end, none of her fears came to pass. She didn't bear the brunt of old grudges, and she wasn't some forgotten irrelevance. Of all the potential outcomes, she hadn't expected to be offered a job. Her instinct was to leap at the chance, but she knew that two worlds' worth of complications would come from that. It was not a decision to be made quickly or lightly.

"And I need to look into what you've been up to before I make that offer," he said as they sat on the lip of the fountain. "See what kind of person I…"

He trailed off, looking around as if he'd heard something suspicious.

"Something's here," he said as he stood up. "Something that's very good at—"

She didn't see it coming. One moment, there was nothing, and the next, a man in black and red armour was standing behind Asano. A massive sword, if you could even call it that, had been run through Asano's body. The blade was more a slab of black metal, streaked with red, than a plausible weapon. It looked like something from an anime. Asano wasn't moving, hanging from the blade like a corpse.

The attacker yanked on the blade, but it refused to budge. He said something in a language she didn't know, sounding surprised. That was when a system window appeared in front of her.

System Alert: Boko

- A magical incident is taking place in the city of Boko. Occupants will be evacuated immediately. Any successful attempt to resist evacuation will be taken as a claim of personal responsibility for your safety and may result in your death. Please resist the urge to panic. Sorry for the inconvenience.

- Clergy in Boko temples: Please evacuate all occupants from holy ground so they can be evacuated if your deity will not be shielding them.

"What?" Li Mei said, as did many of the people around her.

Then aura flooded out of Jason like the descent of a god. Her mind went blank as a whimper escaped her. When she came to her senses, she was floating over the city along with what looked like the entire population of the city, flying over rooftops like a swarm of insects.

There were cries of alarm as others came to and realised what was happening. That aura was still present, battering against her mind like a hurricane ripping at shuttered windows. Below, more people were rising into the air. Many were out in the streets in the middle of the day, but others were in homes or businesses, flying out through doors and windows that slammed open, often breaking locks in the process. She saw a roof rip itself off a building and set down on a nearby one, a large group rising from the now-open room beneath.

She twisted as much as she could in the air, feeling like she was clutched in some kind of invisible cushion. As best she could tell, the population of Boko was being lifted into the air and being moved directly away from Jason and his attacker.

Back in Greenstone, Clive was in a bakery. With him was the childlike humanoid version of Onslow, his shell parked on the street like a carriage. Stash was sitting on top of the shell in the form of a young man, drooling over the baked goods displayed in the window.

The staff were gathered around Clive's adorable familiar, handing him free samples as their manager looked on unhappily. Clive gave him an awkward smile and apologetic shrug.

System Alert: Boko and Greenstone Region

- A magical incident is taking place in the city of Boko. Occupants are being evacuated. Do not approach or attempt to enter the city.

- Adventurers of silver rank or below in the area, do not approach. Adventurers of gold rank and above (if there's a diamond-ranker skulking around, please help!), do not approach the city until after the blast.

"We're going," Clive said, pushing past the bakery staff to pick Onslow up like a child. He marched outside as Onslow's shell grew even larger to accommodate them. Clive, Stash and mini-Onslow stepped inside, and the shell lifted into the air.

- Jason Asano has initiated group text chat.

- Jason: Got attacked. Going to blow up and take some or all of Boko with me. Getting people out, need wide-area containment ritual. Will hold on as long as I can. Please move fast.

- Hump: Are you going to be alright?

- Jason: No, Humphrey. I'm about to explode and die.

- Hump: Please list my full name on the text chat.

- Jason Asano has ended group text chat.

As Onslow sped through the air, Clive opened a portal in front of them and they passed through it. They arrived in Boko, in the square set aside for teleport arrivals at the Adventure Society campus. It was a scene of chaos as people streamed out of buildings, dangling in the air as if held by invisible hands. There was yelling in every direction and powers being fired off. Clive saw an adventurer teleport and arrive right next to Onslow's shell, looking at it in surprise before yelping as she was yanked into the air again.

Humphrey teleported in with Sophie and Farrah. His mother did the same a moment later with Neil, as well as Gabriel and Arabelle Remore. They piled into Onslow's shell and it took off.

"That message said blast," Danielle said. "That man was born to agitate people."

"You're the wide area ritual magic specialist," Clive said to Farrah. "How fast can you improvise a large containment ritual?"

"Lindy's help would be good," she said. "She's the improvisation expert. We'll need your abilities to cast something that big, that fast, though."

Shade emerged from Farrah's shadow.

"Miss Belinda is being flown here as we speak," he said. "Miss Estella is being evacuated with everyone else."

"Shade, what's happening?" Humphrey asked.

"Mr Asano has been subject to an attack. The attack is apparently an attempt to kill him using some weapon that drains his power. Unfortunately, his power in infinite, and the weapon just keeps draining it."

"And it's going to reach a threshold where either the weapon or Jason's avatar can't contain it and it's going to blow up," Clive realised. "We need to get this ritual going fast."

"What about the attacker?" Humphrey asked.

"The attacker is currently unknown, but seems to be a human in armour. He also appears to be stuck to Mr Asano, which is an apparent surprise to him."

"I don't think my skill set will help us here," Danielle said. "I'm going to find the city leaders and see if I can help bring some order to what is going to be panic and chaos. Gabriel, Arabelle, will you join me?"

"Gabe will," Arabelle said. She was staring out at the people still flying out of the city, screaming and yelling. "I'm going to start organising healers. Even if everyone gets out alive, this is going to be a mess. Neil, will you join me?"

"Of course," Neil said.

Four Voices of the Will stood around a viewing pool. The image in the still water was from a vantage point far above Boko, and they watched their assassin appear. His weapon punched through Asano's body, which went limp.

"It's done," one of them said.

"Our forces are marshalled," said another.

"Prepare to activate the gates," the third commanded.

"It is time," the fourth said, "for an example to be made. To the denizens of this world, and our own kind, too timid to act."

Onslow wove a path through the air, Clive standing atop his shell. A trail of gold was left behind by Clive's outstretched hand, sky-writing a massive ritual circle. As he went, the runes on Onslow's shell lit up and floated into the air, becoming part of the ritual. Inside the shell, Farrah and Belinda were madly going through books and scribbling notes, yelling up instructions at Clive.

"How are we doing?" Farrah asked Humphrey.

"Uh, quite well," Humphrey said, sounding surprised. He stood at the edge of the shell, holding out a measuring device Clive had given him. It looked like a glass plate with an image like shifting water projected onto it. A rod ending in an orb jutted from the bottom.

"It should not be quite well," Belinda said.

"It says the power levels are decreasing."

"Sophie," Belinda said, eyes still on her work. "Please make sure he's not holding it upside down."

"Is the rod and orb thing meant to pointing up or down?" Sophie asked.

"Up."

Humphrey sheepishly turned the device around in his hands, then looked at the readings again.

"Oh," he said. "It's going really badly."

"It's okay," Sophie said, patting him on the shoulder. "You're still pretty."

Jason's body was still frozen; his overcharged aura was growing more unstable by the moment. He ignored the pain searing through his body as the power ramped up. It was enough that if he let go, he would explode, and he wanted to do exactly that. The longer he held on, the greater the blast would be, but the containment ritual wasn't yet in place.

He had sent the city residents as far away as he could. He'd dropped them in the desert, as far as he could from the city walls. It would hopefully be enough to save them from the blast, so long as it was contained. The city was now empty, other than his team and anyone who could hide from his aura senses. The temples were dark to his perception, and there could always be some powerful people lying low. They would have to take care of themselves.

- Jason Asano has initiated group text chat.

- Jason: How long?

- Clive: Almost done. Look up.

- Jason: Can't. Paralysed. I think my attacker was sent by the messengers.

- Hump: Why is that?

- Jason: He's stuck here and just yelling at me now. I'm a little distracted, but he's yelling about the messengers and some kind of deal.

- Danielle: The messengers don't make deals with anyone but other messengers.

- Sophie: Yes, they do. They made a deal with the fake god of Purity, and they made one with Jason about saving Yaresh.

- Hump: Jason, is there any way we can get you out of this alive?

- Jason: Not that doesn't come with unacceptable risk. Don't worry: coming back from the dead is kind of my thing. Well, my avatar's thing. I'm immortal, obviously.

- Neil: Really? I didn't know that. Have you tried mentioning it every ten minutes? Oh, wait, you have.

- Clive: Your avatar dying might just be the beginning of whatever this is. I'm getting some kind of interference on the ritual from above the city. Far above. It's at a high enough altitude that I can adjust as I draw out the ritual, but something is going on up there.

- Hump: Sophie and I will check it out. And fix my name in the chat.

- Sophie: There are more important things going on than how your name appears in the chat. Also, what are we doing for lunch today?

- Gabriel: Is this always the way you operate? How did you become a famous adventuring team like this?

- Arabelle: Oh, like we were any better. You remember what Emir was like.

- Neil: Clive was getting lunch from that bakery.

- Gabriel: Jason is going to die.

- Farrah: You get used to it. I think if he goes long enough without anyone killing him, he kills himself for practise.

- Jason: I do nordgldfjce.

- Farrah: What?

- Jason: Sorry, I'm running on the edge here. In all seriousness, please, please hurry. I can't hold this much longer.

- Clive: Almost there. And we had to leave the bakery before our order came up.

- Jason: No sandwiches? Okay, now I'm having a bad day.

The Duke of Boko looked at Gabriel's increasingly worried expression. "Is something bad happening?"

"Don't worry about him," Danielle said. "That's about something else."

Fragments of Jason's body were turning to rainbow smoke and coming off him in streams. He still hung limp, impaled on the sword that was stuck in place as if by glue. Jason was long past recognising his surroundings and hadn't seen his attacker cut his own arm off. It hadn't helped, the severed stump still gripped by the magic.

- Clive: Done and we're clear.

Jason exploded.

It was perfectly silent, eradicating everything in its path in a wave of gold, silver and blue light. It expanded out until it reached the invisible dome of the containment spell, covering most of the city. The dome became visible, shedding blue and gold light. It was comprised of interlinked hexes, each with a rune set into it.

The dome shuddered, the runes glowing brightly while emitting a high-pitched sound. The tone lowered over time, from a screech, all the way down to a thunderous rumble, by which point the dome was shaking like a bouncy castle full of kids hopped up on sugar. The runes went dark, first at scattered points and then in larger clusters.

Jason's friends looked back as they flew across the sky inside Onslow. He was fast and they didn't want to risk a portal with so much magic floating around. The dome wouldn't last long, and they could all feel the magic from above now.

"That's portal magic," Humphrey said. "I've never felt it on that scale. How does that even work in a low-magic zone like this?"

"I don't know," Clive said.

They leaned out of the shell to look up. As they had sensed, massive portals started opening up in the sky.

"We've seen this before," Humphrey said.

"Yes, we have," Clive said grimly as messengers geysered from the portals. "I'm not sure what to do about that."

Their eyes were drawn back to the dome as explosions started sounding out all across the surface. Hexes were shattering and force was shooting out through the gaps. The gaps grew larger and larger, letting more force out, but most of it had been spent while the dome still held. Inside the dome, the light was gone, as was almost any trace of the city.

A perfect sphere had been carved out of the ground, as if simply deleted, leaving behind only smooth, round sides. The only remnants of the city were temples now floating in the air, shielded from the blast by divine power. The only other thing in the sphere was a small cloud of darkness, within which sparks of ethereal light danced like the ghosts of fireflies.

The stillness inside the space was sharply contrasted by violence outside of it. The explosive force from the detonating dome tore through the parts of the city left outside the containment area. Buildings were levelled and gardens stripped down to the dirt. Trees and chunks of building were flung through the air, adding to the damage. Onslow sealed the sides of his shell to protect his occupants, mini-Onslow clinging to Clive's leg as the shell rocked like a boat in a storm.

"We need to regroup with the others," Humphrey said. "I didn't see how many messengers that was, or how strong they were, but we're about to have a fight on our hands. They knew this was coming, and we didn't, so expect them to have every advantage."

"Isn't this normally the part where Jason comes back to life and does something ridiculous?" Belinda asked.

They all looked at each other, then waited awkwardly.

"Okay," Humphrey said. "It would have been nice. But it looks like—"

System Alert: Sacred Phoenix

- [System Administrator] assassinated. The Hegemon has arisen. Beware his wrath.

33

THE BENEVOLENCE OF A
NIGHTMARE GOD

THE CITY OF BOKO WAS GONE. THE OUTER REGIONS HAD BEEN LEFT AS little more than rubble when the blast containment zone gave out, and the space within the zone was just a hole carved out of the ground. All that remained were floating temples, shielded by their gods, and a cloud of darkness in the middle.

In the wake of the destruction, numerous massive portals had opened, high above the ruins. Sheets of gold, silver and blue light, they disgorged an army of messengers into the sky. This was no heavenly host, however, as they descended from the sky in the direction of the city's survivors. Most of Boko's ninety thousand people had been evacuated.

Jason had used aura control to bodily lift the population out of the city. His aura had been overcharged with a flood of power from his astral kingdom, making the astounding feat possible. But as the power had grown, and Jason's avatar further degraded, his control over that power had slipped. His aura became a spiritual wildfire, beyond his ability to contain or direct.

Local essence-users did their best to protect the low-rankers around them from it, but they were weak and poorly trained themselves. Many normal-rank evacuees, mostly the very old and the very young, were outright killed. Brain haemorrhages and heart attacks took those too weak to survive the stress the aura placed on them.

Then the blast came, and the aura was gone. There was an eerie stillness, like the calm before the storm, as the messengers descended in silence. Adventurers prepared to fend off the assault, but the messengers kept gushing from the portals by the thousand. Boko was not a strong adventuring city, and even with visiting gold-rankers, the battle ahead was a grim proposition.

Then the aura came back. It was just as powerful now, if not more so, but no longer harmful to the people of Boko. It was completely stable and in control, calming those previously traumatised by it, even settling some of the panic that set in from the evacuation. It was a promise to shield them from those who had taken their homes and were even now descending from the sky. A promise to make their attackers pay, and to make them pay in torment. It was the benevolence of a nightmare god, filled with wrath at the transgression against his chosen. Those it protected, the confused and despairing, gained fresh hope. More than that, they gained a shared certainty that it was about to become a very bad day to be a messenger.

System Alert: Sacred Phoenix

- [System Administrator] assassinated. The Hegemon has arisen. Beware his wrath.

A dark shape rose from the hole in the ground that was once the city of Boko and ascended towards the messengers. A vast, dark bird, speckled with lights like a starry night, limned in ethereal silver flames. It made no sound, yet the same aura that offered hope to the people below resounded like thunder to the messengers.

It erupted amongst them like an explosion, battering them into one another. Wings and limbs tangled, turning diving attacks into uncontrolled falls. The messengers fell into chaos, their formations falling apart as they were knocked around like laundry in a tumble dryer.

The adventurers on the ground had been steeling their resolve for the battle ahead. Now they watched as the bird of flame-wreathed darkness rose to meet the messenger army. It flew into the host, not crashing into them but passing through like a ghost. Every messenger it touched began a process of slow, miserable death. Their skin blackened with necrosis and feathers fell from shrivelled wings. Ethereal fire flared on their bodies, the ghost flame not burning but accelerating the rot.

From the dying messengers, butterflies of blue and orange started to emerge and spread to others not yet affected. Each one that reached a messenger put them on the same path to a torturous demise. More butterflies spread from them in turn, as their flesh decayed and their bodies lit up with ethereal silver flames.

The messengers attacked the butterflies to stave them off, but, on destruction, the butterflies turned into clouds of sparks. The clouds moved slowly, but the messengers were thick in the air and still being battered by the aura. The sparks didn't spread more butterflies, but anything they touched still decayed.

The ghost fire phoenix arced a graceful path through the messenger host. The heart of the invading army had become a realm of misery and death. On the periphery, messengers gave up on the attack and were fleeing as fast as their wings would carry them. Their wings cast shadows onto their bodies from the sun overhead, and from those shadows came their doom.

Shadowy arms thrust out of the shadows on their bodies, like spiders digging their way out of egg sacs. The dark limbs were angular and macabre, and each held an ornate black and red dagger. Those daggers stabbed into the messengers again and again, the wounds swiftly turning black as the flesh around it died.

Danielle Geller looked up in the sky as the dark bird rose from the ruins of Boko to meet the messengers head on. She breathed a sigh of relief as she saw the power on display. It was immediately apparent that her greatest fear, an attack on the evacuated populace, had been forestalled.

System Alert: Ambient Magic Change

- The Hegemon's mortal form has been fatally compromised. While it is being reconstituted, the Hegemon has entered a liminal state in which his power is not limited by a mortal form. [Ghost Fire Phoenix] draws power from the Hegemon's astral kingdom and is not subject to external power limitations.
- High levels of magic are being introduced to the area from the Hegemon's astral kingdom. Magical density and magical saturation of the region are being temporarily increased.

Stability of the dimensional membrane in this region is compromised.

- The Hegemon has chosen to limit his power to prevent a localised rupture in this reality's dimensional membrane. Presence of the Hegemon is reinforcing dimensional stability. The performance of dimensional magic may be inconsistent until conditions return to normal.

She frowned at the system message. This was god-level business, and that was when innocent people got killed. Collateral damage in the wars of giants. She turned her attention back to the scattered people of Boko, milling in an understandable panic. She did note that the rise of the bird and the aura that came with it had a blessedly calming effect on the people, as reflected in their own auras.

She saw immediately that the biggest threat after the messengers would be the sun. The locals were used to the climate, but that included making thorough preparations before heading out into the desert. Being ripped from their homes and dropped amongst the empty dunes was the opposite of being prepared. As the early afternoon heat intensified, things were only going to get worse.

Of tens of thousands of evacuated citizens, most were normal rank, and would die without water and shelter. They were also traumatised by exposure to Jason's unstable aura, many left incapacitated and some even killed. Those ostensibly in charge were struggling to find one another, let alone bring any kind of order of the chaos. People were doing their best, be they adventurers, Adventure Society officials, civic administrators or simply anyone else able to keep their heads.

Small groups were doing what they could on their own. A local Magic Society official had managed to get some of his people together and start distributing a simple climate control ritual that would set up small zones that cooled the people within. While each zone could only accommodate a few families, the ritual only required spirit coins as a material component. It was also simple enough that anyone with a basic knowledge of ritual magic could enact.

It was a race against time as the desert heat ramped up. Fortunately, the increased level of magic Jason had created made larger and more powerful rituals an option. The efforts to implement those were being led by ritual magic experts like Clive, Farrah and Belinda. Clive had even put aside his scorn for the Magic Society to take charge of their people.

The Magic Society branch director let the higher rank Clive take charge of the magic, focusing instead on finding and organising his people. He was issuing directives as Clive drew out a massive ritual diagram nearby. He looked at the lines of golden light, a match for the ones he'd seen drawn in the air during the evacuation.

"Were you the one who put up that containment dome?" he asked.

"Not just me, but yes."

"How did you use magic on that scale when the magic level is so low?"

"The containment dome fed off the magic it was containing."

"And you just happened to have a perfectly calibrated ritual designed to do that over such a large area, in these specific conditions, with that specific kind of energy?"

"Of course not, but I was already familiar with the energy in question. The rest we figured out as we went."

"Are you saying you improvised a city-scale, off-rank ritual magic off the top of your head?"

"Like I said, I didn't do it by myself."

"Even so, that's madness."

"Look around, Director. When you get days like these, only madness will do."

"You say that like you've seen things like this before."

"Not many times, but yes."

"Who are you people?"

Belinda ducked in front of the director and shook his hand.

"Team Biscuit, pleased to meet you. Clive, you done? We need you."

"Give me thirty seconds."

The messenger army had departed from a shared staging area inside a region on the far side of the planet. Massive portal gates floated in the air, through which the army had departed, leaving behind only a fraction of the forces belonging to the four astral kings who owned them.

Inside a nearby room, four Voices of the Will were observing the far side of the portal gates through a viewing pool. They watched as the ghost fire phoenix ravaged their army. Although none of them would ever voice the sentiment, each were happy that their portals only operated one way.

They were startled when they sensed a new portal open in the staging area, but a small one, sized for a person.

The messenger who emerged could have passed for a very tall human. His wings were nowhere to be seen and he stood only seven feet tall, short for a messenger. His clothes, brown and dark red, were more fitted than the loose apparel most messengers favoured. He also walked on the ground in boots, rather than floating over it in bare feet or sandals.

He strode across the staging area, a furious expression on his face. Every messenger who looked his way fell to the ground and had a seizure. He reached the room containing the four Voices, and instead of flying in through the entrance above, he tore a hole in the wall with his aura. Inside, the Voices lined up like soldiers under inspection.

"I have no interest in dealing with minions," the newcomer said, his fury caged inside his curt tone. "Get out here. Now."

The four Voices floated to the ground and dropped to one knee. Above each, a ghostly image of their astral king appeared. The astral kings all bowed their heads before the man who had called on them.

"We pay respect to Jamis Fran Muskar," one of them said.

"Respect?" Jamis snarled. "You directly defied the explicit instructions of the Council of Kings, and then have the mind-bogglingly incomprehensible GALL to utter the word 'respect' to me?"

"We felt—"

"It doesn't matter what you felt. It matters what you were told."

"We are all astral kings, Jamis Fran Muskar. The Council of Kings may guide us, but you do not rule us."

Jamis stared at him, the anger in his expression replaced with contemplation.

"We let you think that," he said, "so you wouldn't go off and do something stupid out of misguided rebellion. But since you've gone and done it for the sake of stupidity, let me make it clear: yes, we rule you. And you will pay for your defiance."

"Jason Asano—"

"Matters a lot more than you. How old are you all? A few centuries? A millennium? What have you accomplished, beyond treading the path that was laid out for you? We are the ones who allowed you to become astral kings, and what have you done with that opportunity? Walked the most well-trodden road you could find. Never deviating. Never innovating. Never setting your own course. Asano has accomplished more in half a century than all of you put together."

"Many of those accomplishments come at our cost!"

"So? Which of us has not fought against another of our kind? We are kings, with few true sins to be committed, yet you seem intent on committing them all. Let us start listing them with your loss of control. Your diamond-rankers refused to take part in this debacle. That is what we call a hint that you may want to reconsider your approach."

"Mah Go Schaat convinced our diamond-rankers to abstain."

"Wisely," Jamis said, gesturing at the viewing pool. "That is cosmic power he's wielding out there. He's holding back so he doesn't blow a hole in the side of the universe. If they had faced Asano like that, they'd have died, just as Mah Go Schaat did. And, in the absence of your diamond-rankers, you committed the second sin: debasing yourself by making a deal with lesser beings. A deal that I am now obligated to honour, despite the disaster you've made of it. Which brings us to your final and greatest sin: failure."

"Who could have anticipated something like this?"

"THE COUNCIL OF KINGS!" Jamis roared, as if shouting could drill his words through a wall of obstinate stupidity.

"The council explains nothing."

"Because the council does not answer to you. You answer to it, and when you decided not to, you made a grand mess that I now have to clean up."

"What would you have us do? Is Asano allowed to strike at us, without our striking back?"

"Yes. He is of my kind, not yours."

"We are all astral kings."

"But we are not all relevant. I don't know your names, and after today, you should be very careful about my not needing to find them out. You are inconsequential, when I'd offer him a seat on the Council of Kings today. If he'd take it."

"He is our enemy."

"For now, yes. But he is fighting us in passing. Protecting his lands and his people, as any of us would. What you have done here will echo through time. Asano is one of us, and will be forever. You're trying to kill him why? To deny him a prime avatar for a quarter of a century? Let's put aside the fact that he will certainly find a way to shave most, if not all of that time away. The real point is that it leaves an eternity for him to remember."

"We are immortal. He cannot kill us, however much he wants it."

"And he won't. But a millennium from now, someone is going to tell you that every birthing planet you own just got destroyed. We need him to forget the concerns of his mortal life, and you are searing them into his mind."

"Is your intention to try and punish us?"

"I don't have to," Jamis said. "I already told you that he's one of us. Your failure to grasp the ramifications of that only compounds your failure."

"Ramifications?"

Jamis grinned.

"There are many, but what should concern you right now is one of the most fundamental. It apparently never occurred to you that, as an astral king, he has an astral gate."

That was when they sensed the shift in the portals outside. The sheets of gold, silver and blue energy trembled like a pond during an earthquake. Then the one-way portals were suddenly two-way, and dark tentacles burst through. Heading straight for the building, some passed through the hole Jamis had made, while others made holes of their own.

The images of the astral kings vanished, their confused Voices of the Will coming to their senses just in time to get grabbed. A tentacle went after Jamis, throwing off sparks like an arc welder as it met an invisible barrier and was stopped dead. Jamis stood casually, hands in his pockets as the Voices were dragged away.

34
PRETEXT

THE MESSENGER HOST OF MORE THAN TEN THOUSAND HAD BEEN CUT DOWN to stragglers. A swarm of shadowy figures dashed through the air, collecting the rotted husks of the dead as they fell. The bodies were all dropped into the hole where the city of Boko had once been. The great portals in the air were gone, having trembled and ultimately collapsed.

The last messengers to emerge had been dragged out by the dark bird wreathed in silver flame. Tendrils of darkness had extended from its body, reached into the portals and dragged out four Voices of the Will. Even bound up, they had started to demand their freedom domineeringly. Their arguments lasted only a few words before the tendrils cut them into slices like vegetables. The shadowy figures moved to collect the pieces and deposit them with the rest.

When the last of the messengers were dead, the ghost fire phoenix descended into the hole, now host to a small mountain of corpses. The bird shrank as it neared the bottom of the hole, transforming into a naked man as it reached the ground. Blood seeped from the man's pores to cover his body, then coagulated and dried into a set of dark red robes.

"Thank you, Colin," Jason said quietly.

System Alert: System Administrator

- The Hegemon has reconstituted his mortal form. External magic will no longer be introduced to the region. Magic density and magical saturation will return to normal levels over time.
- The Hegemon no longer claims dominion over the region and the gods may once again influence the area, outside of their claimed holy grounds.

Jason grimaced as he stared at the pile of dead. He no longer had trouble maintaining his identity while in a transcendent state, but it was still a deeply altered state of mind. In that condition, his emotions were pushed aside. It was useful for acting with a clear head, but the emotions had returned now that he once more occupied a mortal avatar.

His true self was a living universe from which he projected his consciousness, but that was something he was still getting used to. He remained mortal in many ways, especially in mindset. It was not something he regretted, even as it subjected him to negative emotions. He'd felt people die under the influence of his aura, helpless to stop it. Anger and regret roiled inside him; he did not want to lose that part of himself.

He looked up at the temples floating in the air. They still had chunks of ground underneath them, torn from the city during its destruction and shielded by the power of the various gods. Now that Jason had withdrawn his influence over the area, the temples were on the move, drifting up and out of the massive hole. Moving in as they departed was a flying tortoise shell full of adventurers. Jason's team gathered around him, looking him over with concern.

"I'm fine," he said to the unasked question, but the grim quiet in his voice was unconvincing. "Do we know how many people died yet?"

"It's still a mess out there," Farrah said. "We won't have a solid number for a while. Hundreds, certainly. Probably over a thousand. Hopefully not over two."

"This is not your fault, Jason," Humphrey said. "It may have been your aura, but—"

"I know where the blame lies," Jason said. "For the most part anyway. The messengers are dead, although they had someone far more powerful with them. Him, I couldn't touch."

"Not a messenger?"

"An astral king. In a prime avatar, like me, but without the power reduction. His strength was somewhere around Dawn's level."

"That's a bad enemy to have," Neil said.

"I'm not sure he was an enemy. Something in his aura. The only other astral king I've dealt with is Vesta Carmis Zell, and her hostility burned like a fire. This man was calm. Detached. At least towards me. The only anger I felt was directed at the Voices of the Will."

"The ones you dragged out of the portals and chopped up?" Belinda asked.

"Yes."

"What are you doing with all these bodies anyway?" Sophie asked.

"You might want to stand back for this," Jason warned them, then quietly incanted a spell.

"*As your lives were mine to reap, so your deaths are mine to harvest.*"

A red glow rose from the mountain of corpses as Jason's spell drew out the remnant life force. The air was flooded with the coppery taste of blood, the life force tingling at the senses of Jason's friends as they backed off. The red light gushed out like a wave to crash over Jason, obscuring him from sight until the torrent of life force diminished and finally depleted.

Shade had touched all the bodies while collecting them, so Jason was able to loot them all at once. The mountain broke down as the bodies dissolved into rainbow smoke. A vast plume rose from the hole in the ground, rising into the sky as if from an active volcano. Jason's friends backed off even further from the stench. Jason didn't move, however, standing and watching until it was done. Jason's friends approached again, once it was safe for their noses.

"Is that enough to restore your avatar with the bird thing again if your avatar is killed a second time?" Neil asked.

"No," Jason said. "It was a lot, but not enough. Too many silver-rankers and not enough golds."

"We need to hunt some gold-rank messengers, then," Sophie said.

Jason pulled a sword from his inventory that was more like a metal gangplank than a sword, despite the lengthy handle. The metal was dark, with red streaks. He held it out for Clive.

"Something from the loot?" Clive asked.

"No. When I was on the verge of erupting, the power around me became volatile and killed the man who stabbed me with this. Once it was no longer in someone else's possession, I could pull it into my inventory. I was able to discharge it safely in my soul realm, but the power inside my body was too far gone. I couldn't stop it from detonating, even though the thing causing the problem was removed."

Clive took the hefty weapon in both hands and examined it.

Item: [Lesser Celestial Gorger (broken)] (gold rank, uncommon)
A specialised weapon designed to absorb magic from matter that combines physical and spiritual energy. It is a crude attempt to replicate a more sophisticated weapon. The large size is to accommodate crude adaptations when the original design could not be functionally duplicated. This weapon has been damaged by excess magic absorption. (weapon, replica, broken).

- Effect: Specialised magic absorption (non-functional).

"This is designed to kill gestalt entities like you," Clive said.

"Someone designed a weapon just to kill Jason?" Humphrey asked.

"I doubt it," Clive said. "It was probably designed to kill messengers."

"Do you think you can figure out where it came from?" Jason asked. "Someone other than the messengers was involved with this."

"Why would someone with a messenger-killing sword be working with the messengers?" Humphrey asked. "More than that, why would the messengers work with them? They like obedience, not bargains, but I don't see anyone with a messenger-slaying sword being one of their cowed slaves. And sneaking up on Jason is no small feat, given the power of his senses."

"I think his armour might have been designed to hide from messengers," Jason said. "I couldn't grab it to check, but even when he was right behind me, he was hard to examine. It was like my perception just slid off him."

"It might be possible," Clive said. "Our supernatural senses use our auras as a base, and gestalt entities have fundamentally different auras. You could target those aura aspects with specialised stealth equipment. It wouldn't work against regular essence-users, but it would have superior effects against Jason or messengers."

"Anything we can use to track my attacker down?" Jason asked.

"I don't know. I have some knowledge of magic devices, but we need a specialist for something like this. There used to be someone in Greenstone, Russel Clouns. He helped us figure out what the Builder cult devices did, when the cultists were trying to steal astral spaces. I can check if he's still around."

"You might want to show Carlos Quilido as well," Neil said.

"Why Carlos?" Clive asked. "He's a soul healing specialist."

"Early in the war," Neil explained, "he was involved in research on anti-messenger weapons. They thought his speciality might help. Inflicting spiritual damage rather than healing it. Remember when he wanted to experiment on Jason's gestalt body?"

"I do," Jason said. "You think he'll know something?"

"He might not," Neil said. "Carlos is a priest of the Healer, like me. Using our knowledge of healing techniques to design weapons is the opposite of what we do. Carlos realised he'd lost his way after what happened with Jason and left the project early. Refocused on his vampirism cure project."

"We can ask and see where it goes," Humphrey said. "We'll need to put off our current agenda to hunt down—"

"No," Jason said. "If we were the right team to follow this thread, that would be one thing. But I think this will be a long, slow investigation. This weapon was some kind of replica. I think whoever is using it might be a group, not just one person who decided to work for the messengers on this. The only thing we have to go on is this sword, and if Clive says we should hand it over to a specialist, we should. Let the Adventure Society deal with it."

"They came after you!" Sophie said.

"It's not about me. I'm alive, but there are plenty of people who aren't. I'm not going after some group with weapons specialised not just to hurt me, but turn me into a walking disaster zone for any innocent people around me. We can probably manage the risk, now that we know about it, but I'd rather not have to."

"I don't like the idea of letting some mysterious group just float around out there," Belinda said. "We don't know what they want, or when they're going to strike next. Stella and I could—"

"No," Jason said again. "I lost fifteen years letting other people turn me away from my own intentions. I'm not going to let the messengers or whoever is behind this sword dictate my actions."

"We can't just let this stand," Sophie said.

"We won't," Jason said. "I killed all the messengers here. I even dragged out their Voices of the Will and killed them too, but that doesn't matter. The astral kings don't care about their slaves. They'll live forever and just churn out more as they keep going. This planet, the next one, going on forever."

"That's disheartening," Neil said. "You're saying there's nothing we can do?"

"There's something I can do," Jason told him. "They have forever, but so do I. So do you, if you reach diamond rank and stop getting older. We can't kill immortals, but we can destroy everything they've built. Right now, I'm vulnerable. There are too many people I care about that they can hurt. A thousand years from now, those people will be strong enough to protect themselves, or long dead. I can spend an eternity unmaking messenger society. Burning every birthing tree. Razing every indoctrination centre. Freeing every slave and turning them against their masters, until the only messengers left don't serve the astral kings, but fight them. It might take a million years. A billion, but I have a billion. What I need is a purpose to fill all that time."

Jason looked around at his friends. They watched him with worried eyes as, with calm determination, he announced a billion-year jihad.

"Perhaps we should focus on a more immediate timeframe," Humphrey suggested. "Let's get back to helping the displaced population. You might want to donate all the loot from those messengers to the reconstruction... Jason?"

Jason had turned his head as Humphrey was talking, staring at an empty space nearby. Moments later, a portal appeared and a man stepped out. He was extremely tall, with copper hair and dark eyes. His clothes were red and brown, cut in the fitted Estercost style. Jason saw what he was immediately, while his friends were wary but uncertain. Humphrey conjured his armour and sword as he stepped to the fore.

"It's alright, Humphrey," Jason said. "He's here to talk."

"Who is he?" Humphrey asked, not taking his eyes from the man. "And how can you be sure?"

"I don't know who he is, just what he is. And I'm not sure, but if he wants to kill us, there's nothing we can do to stop him. But I don't think he's willing to pay the price."

"The price?" Sophie asked, moving next to Humphrey.

"Authority is a complicated thing, and there are rules to invading a world. You think the messengers needed locals to summon them to start their invasion? With the dimensional magic they have? Those summonings were an invitation. A pretext for the messengers to intrude on our world."

"What does that have to do with anything?" Neil asked.

"This man is an astral king," Jason said. "That's a prime avatar, like mine, but he has fully developed his mortal power."

"This is the one you mentioned earlier," Humphrey realised.

"Yes. But there are rules, and if an astral king acts directly, the gods get a pretext of their own. They'll start scouring messengers from the face of the planet like sweeping up crumbs."

He brushed past Humphrey and Sophie.

"Isn't that right, Mr Astral King?"

"The name is Jamis Fran Muskar," the man said after patiently waiting for Jason and his team's discussion. "I've been looking forward to meeting you, Jason Asano."

35

ETERNITY AWAITS US

"I'VE BEEN LOOKING FORWARD TO MEETING YOU, JASON ASANO."

Jason's feet lifted off the ground as he floated forward, coming eye to eye with the much taller man. His friends watched warily from behind as the pair faced off in the pit that had, shortly before, held ten thousand dead messengers. One of the two was a king of their kind, while the other had killed them and devoured their life force.

"Why are you here?" Jason asked.

"These are not the circumstances under which I hoped we would meet. I am here to apologise. I won't pretend that the people who died here matter to me. That I care about the homes they've lost or the impact this will have on their entire lives. But those things matter to you, and *that* matters to me."

"If you think an empty apology will make me less angry instead of more, you have made a dire miscalculation."

"I do not intend it to be empty, but we can discuss that in a moment. You and I will know each other for longer than time can measure. This first meeting is no small thing, and I would like to do it properly. When I said these are not the circumstances I hoped for, that was not just a glib line."

Jason stared at the messenger for a long time.

"Who are you, Jamis Fran Muskar?"

"I am a member of the Council of Kings, as you have most likely guessed. Some consider me the leader of it, although it has no such thing."

"Why do I get the feeling that it does?"

A flicker of a smile teased the messenger's lips for just a moment.

"A first amongst equals, perhaps. Do not expect me to repeat that in other company, however. Sometimes, to lead means standing behind. You are just beginning your political education, but I have no doubt that time will see you master the nuances."

"You know me."

"You first came to my attention during your conflict with Vesta Carmis Zell, whose influence has sharply diminished after her failures here. Pursuing her own objectives while the rest of us moved with shared purpose was a dangerous move for her politically. Failing was disastrous. She was never the most influential member of the council, and now even her position on it is in danger."

"Will she be back?"

"No. Her objective was lost to you, and to join the larger cause now would look like crawling back. She needs to cut her losses and rebuild her power base with other endeavours."

"Then I don't care."

"No? In time, she will come at you again."

"Let her."

A smile twitched on Jamis' lips again.

"Good," he said. "Dwelling on defeated enemies is not the way of one who stands at the pinnacle. It is the attitude that an original should have. Do you know much about the originals?"

"No."

"I know this is far from an opportune time, but would you like to?"

Jason frowned. He glanced back at his companions, their expressions all saying no. Even Clive, information hungry as he was.

"It's fine," he told them, then turned back to Jamis. "Let's take a walk."

He drifted to the ground and set off, across the curved base of the massive hole. He walked through the space where the mountain of messenger corpses had been, but no trace of them remained. Every scrap and stain had dissolved into rainbow smoke. The crater was barely curved at the bottom, being the size of a city. It was barren and smooth, sealed by the power that hollowed it out.

"The originals are like you," Jamis said. "Those who were not messengers yet became astral kings anyway, except they were never just astral kings. You, the astral nexus, blend elements of gods, astral kings, and great astral beings. The astral colossus has a prime avatar larger than most planets. He spends his time drifting through the void of various universes for reasons I could never determine. The astral beast has no prime avatar, as you and I would understand it. He possesses armies of living creatures, spawned from his astral kingdom."

"You're not an original. You're a normal astral king."

"To my envy, I am not of your kind. I told the fools who attacked you that they were not like you and me, but the truth is, I am closer to them than you. Messengers and astral kings are obsessed with superiority, but the truth is, you stand above us all. We tell ourselves differently, but those of us who remember the originals know. Even the name we changed. You were called originators, at first, but it didn't fit with the myths we built around ourselves."

"Originators. The originals were the origin of the messengers?"

"Yes. We were your messengers. But, over time, the originators retreated into obscurity. More rose, from time to time, but few are like you, Jason Asano. Left to our own devices, we started telling ourselves stories. That we were the prime species of the cosmos, messengers of the cosmic will. Our originators became the originals, not our makers but merely the first of us."

"But you know all this."

"We are immortal. Records are almost as easy to find as wilful ignorance, and I am a student of our history. And we do encounter them, from time to time. Stumble into whatever interest they're pursuing. Sometimes we even fight them, as we are fighting you here. Most are older than us. Your youth is part of what makes you such a contentious figure for us."

"Why are you telling me all this?"

"My interest here is in the future. You and I will still know each other when this planet has been swallowed by its sun. Our relationship will be so much more than this world. This war. I want you to understand what you are, and what we are. That there are those, like me, who understand that the originals are more than just astral kings. That you stand above us."

"Most of your kind don't see it that way."

"But they feel it. That is why they hate you so. You make us want to kneel."

"But you don't."

"Instincts can be overcome."

"Why do you need this? What makes the Purity artefact so precious you would spend lives by the tens of thousands to obtain it?"

"Because of you. The originals. You can come from every species except the messengers, and I want to change that. To be like you. More than just an astral king. But that is not something one can become from simple desire. It takes the right circumstance, the right opportunity, and this relic is the beginning of that for me."

"You want to be an original."

"Yes. You are each unique. All of you reached that point in different ways, and I would do so as well. But to snatch that chance, it takes a resolve that never wavers. Whatever the damage, whatever the cost, you must seize the opportunity when it appears. You are one of the few who truly understand this."

"Then you know me less well than you think. I don't do what I do for power. That came as a consequence of fighting for the things you dismiss. The price of your power. To you, the lives of innocent people are a cost. To me, they are the entire point. I am not an astral king first, or an original. I'm an adventurer."

He moved closer Jamis, staring up at the much taller man.

"And adventurers stand between innocent people and things like you."

"Yes. I know that what has happened here will only further poison you against us. My hope is to ameliorate that damage. You and I are enemies, today, but eternity awaits us. I hope that one day, you and I can be friends. Amongst my kind, such sentiment is considered a warning sign of Unorthodoxy sympathising."

"I am going to burn down your entire civilisation. Do you think we can be friends after that?"

"I do. Perhaps we can even change things together, but that is for another day. On this one, I have come to make an apology. Not an empty one, although I know there can be no true restitution for what my people have done here. Turning the power you use to protect into the weapon that killed a city. It was not the council's intention, for what little that is worth. The council's directive to not target you was explicit, but those instructions were defied. The plan to attack you was not sanctioned."

"What was the plan? Use the weapon to kill me and the city, then occupy the rubble with their army?"

"The interaction of your power with the weapon was unanticipated.

The plan was for the weapon to weaken you, then for the messengers to strike. Kill your avatar and make an example of the city."

"Where did the weapon come from?"

"Some group that has been giving us trouble for years. Energy vampires. Their powers are required to make their weapons work, but they have only used them on messengers, to my knowledge. They have never used them on a Voice of the Will, let alone a prime avatar before. No one knew what would happen, but while the means of the city's destruction was accidental, the destruction itself was not. The messengers would have razed it to the ground anyway. Slaughtered or enslaved the population."

Jason didn't respond, but his expression was answer enough.

"I know you will never overlook what has happened here," Jamis continued. "And I know what happens if you go to war against us in earnest, here on this planet. I think you see this hole where a city once stood, and you know it too. You attack our forces. Drain them for the power to use that bird form to resurrect your avatar. We escalate with high-rankers in retaliation, creating a cycle of triggering your resurrection and you slaughtering us with it. Our search is slowed to a crawl as this planet is ravaged by our battles. We astral kings are forced to intercede with our prime avatars which, in turn, allows the gods to act more directly. I don't know who wins all that, but I know who loses. The innocent people of this world as our war escalates until craters like this are scattered across it like sprinkles on a cake. That doesn't matter to me, but it matters to you."

"You want us to be friends?"

"I do. I hope that happens someday."

"It won't. Not until those people you don't care about start to matter. Earth has its share of monsters, but they are nothing next to you. Their atrocities last decades at worst. How long have yours gone on already? Centuries?"

"Millennia."

"I've made a lot of glib comments in my life about fighting evil. But you're it. The real thing. I think you're right in that you and I will know each other for a long time. And I'll be fighting you for all of it."

"I can live with that."

Jason scowled.

"You have a proposal. You said restitution."

"I did. I want to blunt your fury against us. Avoid the destruction I described. In short, to have you continue as you were instead of focusing your actions on us. This event will only reinforce those of us who understand the threat you pose. I want you to go about as you have been. Fight our messengers as they come across your path, but don't actively campaign against them. In return, I have been empowered by the council to offer you the withdrawal of a significant number of our occupying forces from areas around the globe. Every location in which we have completed our search operations but still hold territory, we will abandon. Immediately."

Jason rose in the air, his feet leaving the ground as he came eye to eye with Jamis.

"Your proposal is that you abandon the areas now useless to your larger goal. The ones controlled by those who, like the astral kings that attacked me, have lost focus? Freeing them up for you to reconcentrate your resources on your actual objectives?"

Jamis smiled.

"I should have been hoping you wouldn't realise that part, yet I find myself glad that you were not so easily deceived."

"You expect a counteroffer."

"I do. But it cannot be to give up and leave. I will not surrender this opportunity, even for you. We are enemies, today. But if I can settle some of your enmity over what has happened here, I will. I know the price will not be cheap, but greatness comes from the resolve to pay the price others won't. You claim that we are not alike in this, but we both know what it is to push on when those around us falter and lose their resolve."

Jason stared at Jamis, his nebulous eyes burning.

"Abandon all the occupied territories?" he asked.

"Yes," Jamis said.

"That could be acceptable, but you don't get the messengers."

"What do you mean?"

"The messengers in those territories. You don't just get them to redeploy. They come to me. Their astral kings set them free of their marks and I take them."

"All of them?"

"All of them."

"That would require getting numerous kings to give up the entirety of their forces on this planet. What happened here already demonstrates that the Council of Kings is not absolute in its power. Even if it was, I can't sell this to them. I'm not a dictator, and controlling the council is a delicate affair. You understand that blunt solutions like this only cause trouble."

"Yes, but it's your politics. Your troubles. You want me to be an enemy and not a nemesis? Then you have to hurt for what your people have done here."

"The council will see it as handing an army to the Unorthodoxy."

"Killing and draining the life force from that many messengers would restore my power to use the ghost phoenix form. That is what was taken from me here."

"I have studied you closely, Jason Asano. You don't want these messengers to kill. You want to set them free."

"Has the rest of the Council of Kings studied me closely as well?"

Jamis blinked.

"No," he said. "No, they have not. And slaughtering a quarter of a million messengers for personal power is exactly the kind of thinking that makes sense to them. Setting them free on moral principle is what they would find outlandish."

He turned from Jason to pace contemplatively. Jason noted that it was a very human behaviour, compared to the imperiousness of normal messenger body language.

"You would have to take them into your astral kingdom," Jamis reasoned. "And not let them out again, at least not here. And best not at all, until our operations on Pallimustus are done. And you couldn't use that time to turn your astral kingdom into an Unorthodoxy training camp. If you unleashed a quarter-million strong Unorthodoxy army on the cosmos, the full force of the council would come after us both. You aren't ready to endure that. Yet."

"I'm not looking to turn slaves into soldiers. Their choices will be their own, and some will want to join the Unorthodoxy. I will hold them until your people are done with this planet, but if they want to fight you when that time is over, I won't stop them. But I have a little experience in this. Most messengers aren't ready to escape the indoctrination. It will be hard on them. Confusing, rage-inducing. Some will even want to go back to your side."

"We wouldn't take them."

"I know, and that only frustrates them further. Again, I have no interest in creating soldiers. Not for the Unorthodoxy and not for the astral kings. I want to let them be innocent people. The kind that were killed and displaced here today. Anything else is for them to choose on their own."

Jamis turned back to Jason, who had again floated to the ground.

"I cannot promise anything," he said. "I will do what I can."

3 6

A TIME TO SLUMBER

IN THE END, ONLY ONE PLACE HAD THE SPACE, RESOURCES AND accessibility to immediately shelter and house a city's worth of people on short notice. The brighthearts had once formed a massive queue to file into Jason's soul realm for shelter, and now the people of Boko did the same. Little explanation was given and little was needed; 'escape from the sun to a place of shelter and abundance' was all most people needed to see.

Jason built a city in a desert for them to occupy. Another oasis city, reminiscent of the home they had lost. He'd been unsure about using that design, worried about causing fresh trauma, but ultimately decided that something familiar would be best. Putting them in a completely alien place would only unsettle them further.

Days after the citizens of Boko had been evacuated to the astral kingdom, the area around the crater was occupied by outsiders. Civic authorities from Boko, the Adventure Society and a dozen other organisations had people in the area. Some were investigators, others were cleaning up the temporary camps. Many seemed to have no purpose at all, but refused to be excluded from the goings-on.

There was a new panic as portals once more appeared in the sky, high above the crater. These were even larger and more numerous than those used by the messenger army days earlier, and for good reason. Messengers poured out of them, far more than the invasion force, but they never came close to the people scrambling below.

On the ground, Jason was with his team and his team leader's mother. They were running a catering operation, pretending like they weren't waiting for the event that would kick a fresh hornet's nest. The people under the canvas sun shelter couldn't see what was happening, only the panic of those outside. Soon they were dropping everything and running.

Jason sighed, looking at the food that had been tossed aside on the ground. He figured something like this would happen, which was why he'd been running a sausage sizzle with cheap bread and bruschard sausages. The giant worm meat was plentiful in the area, and the first alien meat Jason had learned to cook.

Among the yelling and screaming, he calmly took off his apron and walked out to look up at the sky. His team moved to stand around him protectively, although no one was paying attention. The only threat was being bumped into by people who couldn't seem to agree on which way to run.

Jason extended his power and a humongous ring of white stone appeared in the air. Larger even than the portals spewing out a deluge of messengers, it was positioned between them and the ground. It flared to life with portal energy, a massive sheet of silver, gold and blue light. Jason had gritted teeth as he exerted his power. To maintain such a large portal, he was tapping into his astral gate, pushing the limits of what his avatar body could manage.

The people on the ground were unsure of what to do. The handful of adventurers onsite would have no chance if they confronted the messengers and they knew it. Everyone else was just fleeing, running for skimmers or escaping through portals of their own.

"We should have warned people this would happen," Humphrey said for the hundredth time in the last few days.

"We discussed this," Danielle said. "For one, there was no certainty it would happen. More importantly, the Continental Council would want to insert themselves. Complicate matters that need to be kept simple. There is a time to act with caution and care, but also a time to be bold. As much as Jason needs to learn circumspection, the approach that comes more naturally to him has its place."

The messengers didn't come near the ground. It was soon evident that they were disappearing into Jason's portal as suddenly as they appeared from their own. That didn't stop the panic below, but it gave the adventurers thinking they were about to die hope that the chaos above would leave them be.

"Jason," Humphrey said. "Once it's over and people calm down, people will come looking. They watched the entire population of Boko troop through one of your soul realm portals, and it won't take them long to realise that's a giant-size version up there."

Jason only nodded, still concentrating. Humphrey didn't bother him further, having discussed all this before. The plan was to leave Humphrey, Danielle and Farrah to deal with the immediate fallout.

"The interest in you will be bad enough right away," Danielle said. "But once they realise where all those messengers decamped from, the real storm begins. Everyone is going to want answers. Everyone."

Finally, the last of the messenger deluge vanished. The portals all disappeared, leaving an empty sky above and a confused crowd below. One of Jason's regular shadow portals opened beside him, and he led most of his team through. The last three stayed, as planned, and stepped back into the shade of the catering tent.

"Is Jason alright?" Humphrey asked. "He's still barely talking."

"He's not as fragile as he used to be," Farrah said. "He hates what happened, that he couldn't save everyone. Same as the rest of us."

"The rest of us didn't die," Humphrey argued. "I know he cheated death—again—but he feels it, doesn't he? When he's dying?"

"He does, but it's not the dying that bothers him. He's used to it. Used to the pain. And he doesn't blame himself for the casualties of the messenger attack, even though it was his power. He knows he wasn't responsible. His problem is the killing he did on purpose. I have trouble looking at the messengers as anything but enemies, but he sees them as indoctrinated slaves. To his mind, he killed ten thousand victims."

"I'm not sure how anyone is meant to move on from something like that," Danielle said. "I've had extreme experiences as an adventurer, but what happened that day wasn't adventuring. That was the wrath of an angry god."

"And that's how he deals with it," Farrah said. "Part of him is beyond mortality, and he has to accept that part of himself to unleash the power that comes with it. The mindset of a god. His mind while he was in his phoenix form was much like when he fought Undeath's avatar in the transformation zone. He's better at holding himself together, but there's a detachment that helps him."

"You seem confident in your insights," Danielle said.

Farrah tapped her forehead.

"It's the bond we share," she said. "I can feel what he's feeling. I could feel it when he was the phoenix, and I can feel it now. He can hide his emotions from me if he wants, but he's not doing that. He wants me to know he's not spiralling. He hates what happened, but he knows that it had to be done. That if he hadn't killed the messengers, it would have been a fight that the adventurers of Boko weren't ready for. It would have been ugly, and we probably would have lost."

"That's certainly true," Danielle said. "But even if he's come to terms with what happened, others haven't. The power he showed that day already has people on edge, and this will only make it worse. Messenger strongholds across the entire planet just depopulated. Everyone will want to know why, whether they're coming back and what Jason intends to do with them. Very understandable questions that I'd quite like to see answered myself."

"He said that they won't be anyone else's concern now," Humphrey said. "That they won't be coming back. For now, we trust his word, and the details will come later."

"I know. But he needs to be stable right now. How he handles the Adventure Society and other authorities over the next few days will define those relationships into the foreseeable future."

"How widely do people know he was the big magic bird?" Farrah asked. "Is his name being thrown around by people in general?"

"Not from what Stella and Lindy could tell," Humphrey said. "I've had them keeping ears and eyes out for trouble. The Boko population, and even most of the people here now aren't talking about Jason by name. They're talking about the Hegemon as some mysterious figure, and erroneous rumours are already circulating."

"The Adventure Society officials and anyone relatively well informed know, of course," Danielle said. "That the Hegemon was Jason isn't a secret, exactly, but Jason's name wasn't in those system messages, and the Adventure Society isn't making any announcements. They seem happy to not point out how much power belongs to one gold-ranker. If he was diamond, that's one thing, but this breaks the understood power hierarchy, even if it's a contingent event. For now, the society seems happier to let the Hegemon be a strange and powerful mystery."

"Speaking of which," Farrah said, nodding her head at an approaching group. "I think we're about to be asked some pointed questions."

Jamis Fran Muskar's dimension ship looked out of place on Pallimustus. The sleek, sweeping lines were more akin to a spaceship than anything else in a world of wizards and dragons. It floated over an expanse of lawn that had belonged to a local lord before the messengers conquered the region.

Jamis was preparing to take the ship and leave Pallimustus when a Voice of the Will approached. The messenger landed and immediately dropped to one knee. The image of her astral king appeared above her.

"Many question your actions, Jamis Fran Muskar. It is unlike you to be so overt. Your influence has been damaged by this."

"Is that so, Astrid Ela Dain? Then why have you been supporting me? You saved me several complications in pushing the lesser kings to surrender their forces."

"I see where this road ends. When you have your grand kingdom, just remember who helped you claim it."

"I always remember those of good foresight and sound judgement."

"So long as you maintain yours. The lesser kings fear you, but they have always feared you. Now they question you behind your back. Your enemies on the council are already looking to make use of them."

Jamis smiled. "Let things rest for the moment. Remain neutral, and don't push back on my behalf."

"Why not? Disrespect leads to ambition and betrayal. This is a tumour that needs to be cut out before it spreads."

"There is a time to slumber in the depths of the lake. To let the weak and the foolish frolic on the shores, telling themselves it belongs to them. And then there is a time to rise from the lake, and remind the world why those waters are best left undisturbed."

"You want your enemies to gather. To feel emboldened. You're waiting for the snake to rear before you cut off its head."

"Exposing an artificial weakness is always a risk. Authenticity is always best, and since I needed to expend some of my influence, this makes a good opportunity. Our losses today are the seeds of tomorrow's gain. And I thank you, Astrid Ela Dain, for your support in minimising those losses."

"Is he worth it, this man? Our success here is a break point for your plan."

"There is little loss in angering those who have become distracted, like

Vesta Carmis Zell. It sends a message to the others about maintaining focus. And yes, it is worth not setting this man on a vendetta against us."

———

"Help me understand, Mr Asano—"

"I've already explained the events in question, Mr Billings. Several times. At this stage, your lack of comprehension is your failure, not mine."

In Greenstone Adventure Society conference room, Jason was allowing himself to be debriefed by an investigator from the Continental Council. On the investigator's side of the table was a small crowd of assistants and notetakers. On Jason's side, he had only himself and Danielle Geller.

"The issue, Mr Asano, is that I don't see why the closest thing the messengers have to a supreme leader would see you as a sufficient threat to make the concessions that they have."

Jason's gaze fixed on the man across the table like a rifle scope.

"That sounds like you're accusing me of being a liar, Mr Billings. You can phrase it as a speculative question all you like, but I will remind you that I am here as a courtesy. If what you are looking for is discourtesy, I find myself increasingly enthused to accommodate you."

Danielle placed a gentle restraining touch on his forearm.

"Mr Asano has made himself very clear as to what transpired," she said. "His role here is to tell you what happened, Mr Billings. He has done so multiple times, in deference to your requests for clarification. It's not going to get any clearer, and I think we've reached the end of what this meeting can productively achieve."

"Forgive me, Lady Geller, but the events as described simply do not make sense."

"That's because you refuse to look at them through any lens but your own power paradigm," Jason said. "I'm not a gold-ranker when I'm negotiating with the Builder or the gods or the leader of the messengers. I can't afford to be that small."

"Nor when you are fighting an army alone, it would seem. We have a record of your essence abilities, Mr Asano, but there is a question of where your other capabilities come from. What is the source of the power you displayed in Boko?"

"Spinach."

"We are done here," Danielle announced. She rose from her chair and placed a hand on Jason's shoulder. He glanced up at her, nodded and likewise stood up.

"Mr Billings," he said, giving the man a nod, then followed Danielle out of the room.

As soon as they were in the hall, she tapped a brooch to activate a privacy screen.

"I know you don't want to do this," she told him. "Putting up with it now, however, will make things easier with the Adventure Society down the line."

"I don't think it will help if I start murdering their executives."

"You did well," she said.

"I was getting stroppy at the end."

"But you managed to keep your aura restrained."

"I'm not going to lose control of it."

"I'm not worried about what you'll do with it by accident. I'm worried about what you'll do on purpose."

"Billings is a gold-ranker, and he might use cores, but his aura training is obviously thorough."

"That's my concern. If you thought he could take it, you might be inclined to show him what he was failing to learn by listening."

"I'm not unstable, Danielle, just frustrated. And what I need isn't to take out those frustrations on some bureaucrat."

"Then, what do you need?"

37

I KNOW YOU CAN'T CONTROL YOURSELF ANY LONGER

LI MEI HAD BEEN HOPING TO REMAIN FORGOTTEN IN THE AFTERMATH OF Boko's destruction. When Boko's population had been sent through a portal to somewhere, most of the non-residents who had been in the city were sent to Greenstone. Blending in with them, she had been trying to find anyone who had used a recording crystal during the events.

Li Mei herself had done so, pulling one out as Jason's power carried her out of the city after he was attacked. She had been far from alone and had managed to buy copies of recordings made by other evacuees. She had a feeling that, if she really did return to Earth, information about Jason Asano would be a richer currency than spirit coins.

Her recordings were confiscated when the Adventure Society caught up with her. That was the beginning of what they insisted several times was not an interrogation. They met her requests to leave with a strong suggestion that it would be an unhealthy decision for her.

The questioning happened in a blank room, sitting across from a pair of blank-faced Adventure Society investigators. One was a man and the other a woman, Glen and Glennis. Their bland sameness made them seem like brother and sister from a family of career bureaucrats. Even their skin tone was a match for the beige walls.

At first, it was the same questions, over and over. What happened when Jason was attacked. Every detail, again and again. What the attacker looked like. What his equipment looked like. What his aura felt like. What did he say?

"I told you, I don't know what he said. Which means he probably wasn't a local. I learn languages very quickly. It's one of my abilities. I can learn a region's languages and dialects in about an hour of people-watching at the town market. Which I did here, in Greenstone, even down in Hornis. I don't know the language he used, so I don't think he was from around here."

The questions shifted away from the events in question and towards Jason in general. It started obliquely, but it was obvious they were edging towards something else. She stonewalled, pushing back on the relevance of their questions while trying to figure out what they were after. They were starting to get pushy when a dark figure rose from her shadow.

"That is as far as Mr Asano will allow you to take this," the shadow creature said. "Miss Li will be leaving now."

"You're his familiar," said Glen, the male investigator.

"I am. You may address me as Shade. It is a mononym."

"What we do with witnesses is not for Jason Asano to decide," Glennis said. "It's certainly not for him to send his familiar with instructions for us. If he wants to come down here and say something, he can."

"If that is what you wish," Shade said, "Mr Asano will come here and deal with you personally."

"Uh…" Glen said, throwing glances at Glennis.

"Well, I mean, he can't," Glennis said. "Not *here*, here. This section of the building is dimensionally warded. He'll have to go to administration and talk to…"

She trailed off as an obsidian archway rose from the floor.

"That's a portal arch, right?" Glen said.

"It's *his* portal arch," Glennis responded.

"How can he open a portal in here?"

"He can't. I don't think."

"He doesn't seem to agree. How strong is that dimensional warding?"

The pair looked at the empty arch.

"Probably not that strong," Glennis said. "This isn't the high security wing, and you know how barren the magic is in this city. Apparently not strong enough to stop a gold-ranker. Or whatever Asano is."

"Given that his response to being assassinated was to turn into a bird and kill an army, I don't imagine some moderate anti-portal magic is going to stop him."

The empty arch flared to life, filling with shadowy energy, roiling erratically. Glen turned to look at Shade.

"When you said he was going to 'deal with us,' what exactly did you mean?"

Jason stepped out of the shadowy arch. He smiled and grabbed Glen's hand to shake it, despite it not being offered.

"Mr Costling. I appreciate the diligence you and your cousin have shown in your rigorous investigation of last week's events. Unfortunately, I now need to take Miss Li with me. But again, I appreciate your diligence."

"We can't just…"

Glennis' words trailed off as Jason turned to look directly at her. His expression had a friendly smile and kind eyes, yet it left the hair on her arms standing on end. He held her gaze for a long, silent moment before breaking eye contact and turning back to Li Mei.

"Through the portal, Miss Li. If you would."

Li Mei emerged from the portal into what had to be Jason's famous cloud building. She looked up and down the hall while Jason exited the portal and it closed behind him. They were in a tunnel of fog, circular and wispy, with sky blue carpet running along the floor. There were clear patches, like windows, that could be seen through, and she moved to the closest one.

Neither wind nor sea spray came through what looked like a hole in the wall, despite a raging ocean outside. Waves pounded against the walls of fairytale cloud castles, floating on the open sea. The fluffy white buildings didn't budge, in spite of the churning waters crashing into the walls. At water level, the buildings were connected by a flooded layer of flat cloud. Passage between the castles was achieved through a series of connecting sky bridges, one of which they currently occupied.

"Where are we?"

"I set up my cloud palace offshore from Greenstone. You can see it from the city if you fly over it."

She could hear music coming from down the hall and Jason made an inviting gesture in that direction.

"Is that… Gloria Estefan?"

Jason led her down the tunnel and into a large room. It looked something like an open-plan loft, laid out into sections. The furniture was a mix of the dense cloud substance and more traditional materials like wood and marble. The largest areas had multiple couches and armchairs, enough seating for a dozen people, though only two currently occupied it. The seats were arrayed around a large square coffee table, currently covered in notebooks and loose papers.

The music was coming from that area, a recording crystal projection of Miami Sound Machine floating below the high ceiling. The man and woman talking as they went over the notes on the table had the shimmer of a privacy screen around them, probably to dampen the noise right over their heads.

There was a long dining table in another area, also occupied by two people. One was a staggeringly beautiful woman, even by gold-rank standards, with copper hair and eyes that marked her as a celestine. She was sharing a sandwich the length of her arm with a husky elf in what looked like an ugly Christmas sweater.

Multiple tables were central to a third area, where most of the people were. The tables had what looked like board games from Earth, and Li Mei watched Jason groan at the result of a dice roll.

"This is why I hate dice-based combat. You can do everything right and still get gutted like a fish."

The last area was the kitchen, where two people were dancing to the music as they made food. Alongside Jason was a woman Li Mei recognised, Farrah Hurin. Li Mei looked from the Jason playing a game to the Jason cooking and dancing to the Jason standing beside her in the doorway.

"The cloud palace is my domain," he said. "I can express more of my power here."

"Which one is the real you?"

"None of them. This body is the closest, though. The others can't leave here."

She stared at him for a moment, then back at the group laughing and enjoying one another's company.

"I don't wish to be indelicate," she said, "but you're having a party?"

"You're wondering why we're celebrating when so many people just died."

"I am."

He nodded and led her over to the lounge area. He nodded to the man and woman in their privacy screen and claimed a couch. Li Mei joined him, leaving a space between them. The air shimmered around them and the music was reduced to a muffled background noise.

"I can't speak for you," he said, "but everyone else in this room has mourned those they failed to save. Too many times, and there will be too many more. We've had days to be maudlin, and we were. But we also have to pick ourselves up and try to save the next people who fall into danger. If we let it grind us down... well, you're from Earth. You saw what I was like. At the end of my time there."

"I did."

"That is not a good place to be. If I had the power I had now, but was in the mental state I was then, the people here would hunt me down. And they would be right to do so. We're powerful enough now that we can't afford to be unstable. We can do too much damage. So, we have to take care of ourselves, mind, body and soul."

He looked around the room with a smile.

"And we need to take the wins where we can get them," he continued. "Yes, a city was lost. The social and economic ramifications of that will be continent-wide and linger for decades. A home for ninety thousand, and a regional economy, gone in minutes. For many, they lost everything they ever knew. But something like ninety-eight percent of the population got out alive. The messengers sent an army, but we had zero combatant casualties and a civilian survival rate that is astounding, given how suddenly it all happened."

He gave her a sad smile.

"It's easy to dwell on our failures, but we need to celebrate what we accomplished as well. We're not going to be dancing around in front of the people who lost family, friends and homes. But here, when it's just us? We were sad yesterday and we can be sad again tomorrow. Today, we're going to be happy. Now, let's get something to eat."

In the kitchen, Farrah glanced over at Jason's prime avatar chatting with Li Mei.

"She's pretty," she observed to the avatar cooking with her.

"I'm aware," Jason said.

"How aware?"

"It's not like that."

"You brought her in here."

"She's from Earth."

"We found her while looking for someone doing sketchy stuff, Jason. And it was her. She was doing the sketchy stuff."

"We've done worse. If I look back at when I came to this world, there were challenges, yes. But in a lot of ways, it bent over backwards to give me the opportunities I needed to get where I am now. She arrived with little knowledge, little training and already dosed up on monster cores, so no one was going to help her change that. She didn't have you, Rufus and Gary to put her on a right path. That she's managed to self-start like this? Work towards earning the cores to actually reach gold rank on her own?"

"She manipulated people. Fomented trouble amongst those who already have a history of doing terrible things."

"I've manipulated people too. Hurt people. Killed people. Out of pride and vanity. Too arrogant to look for a better way. If I can forgive myself for that much, I can forgive her for less. If we give her better opportunities, I think she'll do better. Be better. It worked on me."

"You know China didn't send someone who looks like her to you by accident. Just because you didn't fall into the honey trap then, it doesn't mean you won't now."

"That was almost twenty years ago."

"And she looks exactly the same."

"There's no honey trap here."

"Uh-huh."

"There's no point to a honey trap. We're gold rank. Everyone we meet is crazy hot."

"You're saying that she's crazy hot?"

"Of course she is. Denying it would be stupid."

"Well, there you go."

"No, I don't go. There's no going."

"Uh-huh."

"Stop that."

"I'm just saying."

"I know what you're saying."

"That your judgement isn't always the best."

"My judgement is fine. You're acting like I'm James Bonding my way across Pallimustus."

"There was that time you went off to 'train your aura' by sleazing on women."

"I was not sleazing on women. And that's a legitimate way to practise aura refinement. Using techniques I learned from the little black book of sex magic that you gave me, by the way."

"Uh-huh."

"Will you stop saying that?"

"She's very pretty."

"Go back to chopping your vegetables."

The Continental Council's chief inspector reminded Jason of Rufus, with his dark skin, bald head and looks that stood out, even at gold rank.

"Chief Inspector Krensler," Jason greeted him, shaking his hand.

They were standing in one of the Greenstone Adventure Society's marshalling yards.

"Are you ready, Chief Inspector?"

"I am."

Jason opened a portal to his soul realm and they stepped through. On the other side was the flat roof of a tower made from sandstone brick and green stone. It was the highest point of the city that now housed the population of Boko, offering an impressive view. The same construction materials could be seen all over, dotted with water features and painted with greenery. Artificial waterfalls spilled out of buildings as much as five storeys up, splashing into palm groves and garden-lined streets. The buildings themselves were overgrown with lush, leafy vines.

"Where did an empty city like this come from?" Krensler asked.

"I made it."

Krensler looked at him, then back out over the city.

"When?"

"A few days ago, when it was needed."

"Just like that?"

"You stand in the heart of my domain, Chief Inspector. Surely you've heard about astral kingdoms, and the fact that I have one. The power your investigators are so curious about comes from here."

"As best we can tell, that celestial phoenix creature displayed god-level power. Rising to wipe out the messengers like that was, for all intents and purposes, a miracle."

"Is that so?" Jason said noncommittally, not turning his gaze from the city below.

"We aren't officially commenting on your identity in this, but anyone with any connections will find out easily enough."

"I appreciate the society's discretion."

"There is the open question of where that power came from."

"I just told you, Chief Inspector. You're standing in it. This pocket universe is the source of my power."

"We don't know a lot about astral kingdoms. We do know they are what the messenger leadership has, which raises more questions about your possession of one. We'd like to know a lot more."

"I imagine you would, but I have no interest in advertising any potential strengths and weaknesses."

"You do have weaknesses, then."

"What is the Adventure Society's stance on me going to be?"

"The star-ranking system gets a little unclear at gold rank. Gold-rankers are more autonomous, with missions being handed out by liaisons more often than being posted in the jobs hall. There's often an urgency to gold-rank missions not reflected in most of lower-rank. Even so, the star-ranking system is still in effect. A gold will often go through a jobs hall and clear out the older contracts that no one else was taking. We like it when they do that, but they need to adhere to their star ranking. Few gold-rankers are one star. Two or three is the norm, as most who reach that point are already experienced in delicate affairs."

"I imagine I'll be getting three stars? I know my diplomacy needs work, but I deal with kings and diamond-rankers a lot. Things above them too, but that's more my thing. The society just gets in the way at that point, which I suppose is where most of our problems start."

"We've noticed," Krensler said wryly.

Jason snorted a laugh.

"To be honest, Mr Asano, there has been a debate as to whether you even belong on the roster. The goodwill you've earned since your return has done a lot to swing things your way. Your team's efforts in following society directives in your strikes against the messengers have been greatly appreciated. And now it seems that you've removed something like a quarter of the world's messenger forces, liberating countless regions in the process. I want you to know that we aren't overlooking that and just grubbing after the power you displayed in Boko."

"Good to know. But I'm guessing a lot of powerful people are nervous about what happens when I'm not being such a good boy."

"They are. You disappeared a city full of people into the same hole as all those departed messengers."

"The messengers are on a separate planet."

"A lot of influential people have questions. What is happening with those messengers? When will you return the people of Boko?"

"That's why we're here, Chef Inspector. For you to talk with the people of Boko. They're free to come and go as they please."

"It's more complicated than that."

"Isn't it always?"

Krensler took out a small box and handed it to Jason. He opened it to find a new Adventure Society badge, gold, but with a diamond symbol where there would normally be one, two or three stars.

"We've decided to treat you by diamond-ranker rules. You've been acting like one for long enough, and it might cover some of the issues we keep having when interacting with you. Soramir Rimaros suggested this, back when. We resisted when you were silver rank, but you're gold now. More importantly, we've been informed that the diamond-rank community has more or less accepted you. It seems foolish to resist, at this stage."

"What are the diamond-rank rules?"

"Similar to gold rank, but with what amounts to full autonomy. If you tell us to pay attention to something, we do. And when the big stuff happens, there is an expectation that you will step forward. If you need to be reined in, it won't be us coming for you, it'll be diamond-rankers."

"You said there was a suggestion of removing my membership?"

"There was."

Jason ran his fingers gently over the badge.

"Thank you, Chef Inspector. I know that I haven't always been the easiest member to deal with, but my identity as an adventurer is extremely important to me. I've been through a lot, and come close to losing myself more than once. Being an adventurer was always an important anchor for me."

"I'm glad to hear that."

Jason put the lid back on the box and put it in his inventory.

"Well," he said. "Let's go meet the Duke of Boko and talk about when the population will be leaving."

"Looking at this place, I'm not sure they'll want to."

"I did my best, Chef Inspector. But I can never replace what they lost."

"No, I suppose not."

38

TRULY OUTRAGEOUS THINGS

THE CONTINENTAL COUNCIL WANTED JASON AND HIS COMPANIONS TO STAY while the aftermath of Boko's destruction was being dealt with. As that would take months, if not years, they had decided to move on. Jason didn't know when he would return to the city where he became an adventurer, and refused to let meetings and briefings be his last memory of the place. A local festival made for a good final day, so the team scheduled their departure for the day after.

Jason went out early to ride the water tunnel subway with its colourful mosaics, the same as he had on his first day in the city. Late morning, he and his friends joined Neil's family in the park district for a picnic lunch. The park was busy, people out and about for the festival day. They joined some locals in a game of tri-ball that immediately went off the rails once the cheating with powers began. It started subtly, but soon the locals were watching wide-eyed as force tethers and magic barriers were used with shameless abandon.

It was early afternoon when they split up to attend the main festival area in the Divine Square. A massive open space, surrounded by temples, Jason's first visit had also been his introduction to the gods. This time, he was less interested in religious pursuits than culinary ones. Food stalls had been set up in front of the houses of worship, boasting wares thematically linked to the gods they were fundraising for. It was a fun way for Jason to spend an afternoon, just another person in the heavy crowd.

The square was packed with people, stalls, stages and stands. This was courtesy of the religious festival, the specifics of which Jason hadn't paid attention to. Rather than a sombre and ceremonious affair, it was more like a carnival. Families were everywhere, children eating food on sticks and playing games for dubious prizes.

There were stages where religious stories were being performed. These were the fun ones with heroes and monsters, not the weird ones about stoning people to death for having the wrong nipple ring or wearing purple during autumn. Some of the performances used actors while others were puppet shows that delighted the children and creeped out the adults. A few used illusion magic, although these seemed to be less popular. There was something impersonal about them that didn't fit with the feel of the day.

Jason was roaming around, one hand holding an enormous drink he'd purchased in front of the temple of Ocean. It came with a decorative glass stein that showed off the blue colour. In his other hand was a candy on a stick from the temple of Lust. It was shaped like a dancing woman, using the stick as a pole.

Neil was with him as they went through every food stall and meal tent they could find. They were escorting three of House Davone's young scions, Uncle Neil's niblings. To Neil's delight, they had refused to go along while he was wearing the clothes his aunt had given him. Accordingly, he was dressed well for once, showing off his actual physique instead of just looking chunky. That was especially valuable as Jason and Neil packed away their body weight in food, to the increasing astonishment of the kids.

Jason and Neil ran into their other friends from time to time. Zara, Sophie, Belinda and Estella were together, earning glares from the wives of staring husbands. Neil drew his own share of thirsty glances as the elf with gold-rank looks showed off how good he turned out to be with kids. Humphrey was with his mother, shoving one stuffed animal after another into his storage space as she won them. Clive was not present, being not beloved by several churches. They preferred people who found their divine relics to return them, rather than attempt to reverse-engineer them.

There was a lull as the sun started to go down. People moved off to the feasting tables set up on the surrounding streets while the Divine Square was prepared for the evening. The festive atmosphere of the day would be replaced by a more ceremonial tone when the dinner feast was done.

The ceremonies were universally viewed as the boring part, but most people stayed because of the ending. The ceremonies would culminate with a release of sky lanterns, a cloud of lights, rising into the dark sky. Everyone was able to release their own lantern, many families making a craft project of it with their children.

That was still to come as people wandered out of the Divine Square at dusk. The stalls and stages were already starting to come down as they shuffled out. They would come back after long dinners of hearty winter food, even though the city never grew very cold.

Neil went off to join his family for the feast while Jason lingered in the Divine Square. Stalls came down as clergy emerged from the temples, putting up ceremonial displays with the help of volunteers. Jason found his way to a booth being packed up by a stocky bald man with skin so dark blue, it almost looked black, marked by glowing sigils that looked like magic tattoos. He had broken down his booth and was loading the pieces into a large cart.

"Need a hand?" Jason asked.

"Oh, so the great and mighty adventurer is willing to do some manual labour?"

"I wouldn't go that far."

All the pieces were lifted into the air by Jason's aura, floated into the wagon and arranged themselves like Tetris blocks. Some of the surrounding stall workers glanced over before turning back to their own work. Even in a low magic city like Greenstone, it wasn't that much of a surprise. Arash shook his head.

"Still can't help but make a display of yourself, can you?"

"Hey, I've been here all afternoon, and no one even noticed. I didn't have a loud and inappropriate conversation with any of the gods or anything."

"Then I suppose I should thank you. If you're going to magic things up anyway, can you do something about the cart so I don't have to haul it home?"

Jason touched the cart, and it vanished into his inventory.

"Shall we, then?"

They walked together out of the Divine Square, Arash directing them towards his home.

"I have all the drinks made up and crated in the warehouse you rented," Arash said. "You're sure that ritual will keep them fresh?"

"If Clive says it'll work, it'll work."

"Took me a week to make them altogether, even with my nephew helping me."

"He's as good at making the drinks as you?"

"Oh, he's quite the talent. Which is good, given that his ambitions of adventuring went so terribly."

"Bad experience with a monster?"

"No, he couldn't bring himself to kill things. Even monsters. He even gets a bit funny at the butcher shop these days. That made it hard to pass the society assessment."

"Fighting monsters is a fairly critical element."

Arash gave Jason a side glance, Jason sensing the uncertainty in his aura.

"Something wrong?" he asked.

"I have a request. It's not a small favour, and feel free to say no."

"What do you need?"

"I've always been happy with my lot. Selling my fruit, making my drinks. I've got my family, my friends, and a successful business that I'm proud of. I never had a need to go out and see the world when I was happy right here. My nephew, though, he's got the wanderlust. Wants to see the world."

"Thus, the ambitions of adventuring."

"Exactly, but he doesn't have the killing in him. Which I am not sad about, but it does make things difficult for him. He wants the travel, the experiences, but those are hard unless you're an adventurer or an aristocrat. Giving him essences was already as much as the family could fund."

"No adventuring means no adventuring income."

"Indeed. I honestly don't think he would have done well, regardless. His results were middling at the training centre. Frankly, his talents lie elsewhere. I taught him to make drinks myself, and he worked the bar at the Norwich Distillery. He can put together near any drink you can think up, if you get him the ingredients. He's kitchen manager there now. He manages food service for the dinner crowds. And that cloud boat of yours looks to have room for a lot of people. I was wondering if maybe it could use a good bartender and kitchen manager."

"My friend Emir keeps telling me I need to expand my staff. He'd definitely get to travel and have new experiences. But being around me isn't always the safest place, even if you're staying back on the boat. I'm not saying it's dangerous, exactly; it's an extremely well protected boat. But when only something truly outrageous can threaten you, only truly outrageous things do. Drastic things happen around me, from time to time. Like at Boko."

"You had something to do with that? I had been wondering."

"I had quite a lot to do with it, sadly. We managed to get most of the people out alive, but not everyone."

"I told him much the same myself when he started talking about becoming an auxiliary adventurer. That being around people who dive into danger is dangerous itself. But the young, you know? They'll see a whole square full of people bowing before a god and stay standing like a damn fool."

Jason chuckled.

"He should know that I'll be leaving this world soon. We'll be back, but he'll be a lot more than just a portal away from home. If he finds he wants out, it'll be some time before he can come home."

Arash shook his head.

"That's a warning that'll work on someone like me, but the boy's a little more like you, I fear. Another world. I can't even conceive of such a thing. You know, I've never been further than Hornis, down south. But Jamar, I know hearing that would only excite him more. We all make our mistakes and learn our lessons, and he'll be no different. I just want him to live long enough to learn from them. I imagine you made your share of mistakes, getting from where we met to where we are now."

Jason let out a wincing laugh.

"You have no idea."

"I've made my own as well. But here, I always had family. Friends. Church. Community. There was always a helping hand when I needed it most."

"You want to make sure your nephew is taken care of. Not left to blindly stumble through a big, dangerous world."

"Just so."

"I can tell you this, Arash. I'm very powerful now. That's not a boast, just a reality. And those mistakes I made came with hard lessons. Power comes with the responsibility to avoid hurting the people around you. To safeguard them. What happened in Boko taught me that all over again. Taking care of my people is what matters most to me, and it's not just about safety from danger. The world can hurt you without leaving a scratch. If your nephew comes along, he's one of my people. That means we go to the wall for him."

Arash nodded.

"I know you're a good man, Jason, but I also know that you're a great man. And as you said yourself, people like that are dangerous to be around. When they make a statue of a someone, they don't sculpt in all the dead folk around them."

"No," Jason agreed. "No, they do not."

"I went to see the statue they put up of you, back when we thought you died saving the city. Was a little hard to find. Out of the way, and someone planted a bush right in front of it."

Jason chuckled again.

"Yeah," he said. "I know who that was. I'll take your nephew with us, Arash. Jamar, you said his name was?"

"Yes. Thank you."

"The next few months *should* be relatively quiet. The messengers are wary of me now, and we're mostly just touring around. It sounds like what the boy is looking for, and we can see if he's a good fit. If not, I'll portal him home before we go somewhere he can't easily come back from."

"I won't say I like the idea, but I appreciate it. Honestly, I hoped you'd say no. But the boy has wanted an opportunity like this for a while now. Then you knock on my door, the best opportunity he could hope for. It would be an unkindness to not ask. And if we don't let him go, it's only a matter of time until he runs off into the night. We'll wake up to a note explaining he signed up to fetch and carry for some adventuring team. Who knows if or how people like that will look out for him. They might use him as monster bait, for all we know. Standing next to you might not be the safest place, but I don't know. I'd wager that, some days, it's the safest place there is."

The pair were well away from the Divine Square at this point. Jason stopped at a street junction as the aroma of roasted meat drifted up the street.

"You know," Jason said. "This cart is going to keep where it is. I could take it back to your place later."

It was Arash's turn to chuckle.

"I was going to join my family at the feast once I delivered the cart back. Would you like to join us?"

Jason looked contemplatively down the street where the smell was coming from, along with the sounds of laughter and celebration.

"I wouldn't want to make a big deal of it. I mean, I know I'm not that famous, all these years later, but people remember. This time should be about friends and family."

"Yes, it should. And yes, they do remember."

"Great, let's go," Jason said, and set off towards the feast. "You can introduce me as John Miller."

They joined the stream of people heading for the food tables.

"You realise they're going to know who you are, right?" Arash asked.

"My false identity is very rigorously put together. And I am excellent at maintaining it. Everyone says so."

"Jason, very few silver-rankers pass through this city, outside of the monster surges. Golds are almost never here, and my family know that you were a regular at my juice stand, all those years ago. If I show up with you, they're going to realise immediately."

"There are all these investigators here because of Boko. I could be one of them, taking the day off for the festival. I'm already making my aura read as silver rank."

"That might work. Your being less handsome than most gold-rankers will help."

"Hey," Jason said in mock affront. "How would you know what gold-rankers look like? How many have you even seen in Greenstone?"

"Today? Quite a few, and they all turned heads, except for the one with the big chin."

"My chin is fine," Jason said defensively as he prodded it with his finger.

"I do remember it being larger. Memory is a funny thing, I suppose."

39

A FRAMEWORK FOR LEADERSHIP

JASON'S CLOUD SHIP SAILED NORTH FROM GREENSTONE. HE STOOD ON THE
top deck, leaning on the rail as the fresh ocean wind washed over him.
Nik stood beside him, only the head and shoulders of the diminutive
rabbit man reaching above the railing.

"How was it, being back in Greenstone?" Jason asked him. "You kind
of vanished on arrival, and we didn't see you much. I didn't even see you
at the festival."

"It was strange," Nik said. "I lived there for longer than you did, when
I was training. But so many of the people I knew are gone, or older. It was
like the world was passing me by while I was stuck in place."

"That's how it's going to be, sometimes. Especially in places like
Greenstone, where even the adventurers are mostly low rank. People will
get old, live out their lives. It's places like Vitesse and Rimaros that have
more people who age slowly or not at all."

"You spend a lot of time around powerful people, don't you?"

"Yeah."

"Are you worried about losing touch with regular people? Growing
apart from them as everyone you know stays the same, decade after
decade?"

"I am," Jason said. "That's one of the reasons I went back to Greenstone. Meeting people I knew back then was nice. When you're an adventurer, you are often meeting people on the worst day of their life. I went to

a village I last saw as rubble. People are happily living their lives now. It was twenty years ago, so only the older people remember what happened as anything but a story. There's a man there who, back then, told me about his hopes for his granddaughter. This time, he told me about how those hopes had been fulfilled. It's good to remember what we fight for."

"But we aren't a part of their world anymore, are we?"

"No. It's important that we visit, to remind ourselves what it's all about, but we don't belong there. We have our own community to be a part of. Vitesse should be a good place for that."

"Yeah, it's a nice city."

"Wait, even you've been there? I've been trying to get to Vitesse for twenty years. I didn't even know."

"Dad, you created me out of thin air like you were starting your own bible, sent me to violence boarding school and then vanished for a decade and a half. With parenting skills like those, are you really surprised you missed a few things?"

Jason winced.

"I haven't done as well by you as I would have liked. I can't make more of your kind, turn you into a species proper, until I reach the fullness of my power. But we'll be on Earth soon. You don't know them, but you have family there."

"Do they know about me?"

"I told my sister, and my grandmother. It's kind of hard to explain that you made your own universe and created a guy. That has connotations, back on Earth. You know, I could try making a female lehenik. Can I get one of your ribs, real quick?"

"Don't be a tool, Dad. Also, trying to make a woman for your son is creepy. You're not leaving her a lot of room for agency, there. Also, she'd be my sister. And my clone, maybe? Yeah, I don't think creepy really encapsulates how gross that is."

"Okay, that was a bad idea. In fairness, another guy did it first. I didn't love his book, but there's not a lot of reference material for this stuff."

"See, this is why I didn't introduce you to my friends in Greenstone. They all think you're this awesome adventurer, and I don't want to ruin it for them."

A grin crept across Jason's face.

"Your friends think I'm cool?"

"Calm down, Dad. I didn't say cool. No one said cool."

"You said awesome. That's like the better version of cool."

"No, that just means things explode around you a lot."

"How is that not cool?"

Jason laughed as Nik shook his head. The smile slid off Jason's face, replaced with a contemplative expression.

"I don't know what I'm doing most of the time," he admitted. "I meant it when I said that I want to do better by you. I hope you'll give me some time to figure that out. Trying to explain you—and me, for that matter—to our family back on Earth. I don't think it's going to work until we're there. Emi is not going to stop hugging you for the first week."

"I'm not a stuffed toy."

Jason put a hand on his shoulder.

"I know, buddy. Sometimes there are things about ourselves we just have to live with. There are worse things than being crazy adorable."

Nik looked up awkwardly at Jason.

"You know," he said hesitantly. "You could hug me. If you wanted."

Jason looked down at him with a warm smile, then dropped to one knee and gathered him into a hug.

Boko had been a coastal city. When the section of crater closest to the ocean had collapsed, the water spilling had turned it into a harbour. An inlet led into what could have been a lagoon if it wasn't so large and deep. Islands dotting the water were once temples, shielded from the city's destruction by their gods.

The cloud ship was anchored offshore from the inlet. The shores of the new harbour were swarmed with essence-users and ritual magicians. They were working to stabilise the area, making it safe and ready for a new city to be constructed.

A skimmer set out from the cloud ship, passing over the water of the inlet and entering the harbour. Jason and Danielle rode in black and dark grey shades of luxury as the vehicle steered itself.

"Boko was never the port city that Greenstone is," Danielle said. "Neither had a natural harbour, which is part of why Greenstone's artificial island was constructed."

"I don't like being back here," Jason said. "It reminds me of what can happen if I lose control."

"You didn't lose control. You were attacked."

"I know. But what we know and what we feel can be very different things."

"Yes," Danielle agreed. "They can."

"It doesn't help that we have this last bit of unpleasant business on the way out of the region. We've been here for well over a month now, and the idea was to stay for a week. I'm thinking that we put aside the sight-seeing and make a beeline for Estercost. Round up as many Earthlings as we can and maybe just portal straight to Rimaros. I've got forever to sightsee later."

"I think the group will be open to that. You're the only one who has never seen Estercost. Why Rimaros for the bridge to Earth, though?"

"It's not Rimaros itself we're going for. I don't know what kind of side effects may come from completing this dimensional bridge. I was advised to anchor it somewhere remote, and the people that were sucked through from the other end demonstrated the value of that advice. There's an uninhabited island in the Storm Kingdom. The Builder installed astral magic infrastructure there to ensure I arrived at that location. It's already attuned to the link between worlds and it's robust enough to meet our needs."

"Why did the Builder want you to land in Rimaros?"

"The Builder's prime vessel overstepped. The Builder was forced into limiting who he would send to kill me. He made another deal with Disguise, who everyone still thought was Purity, to try and get around the first agreement. Sophie's mother was one of fake Purity's brainwashed lackeys and the idea was to use her to use Sophie to lure me into a trap and kill me."

"That sounds so convoluted that I can't believe anyone thought it would work."

"I know, right? I think the Builder was transitioning prime vessels at the time. He didn't have his regular guy to do his mortal-level thinking for him. In fairness, it did almost work. Only because Princess Liara realised the Builder was after me and used me as bait, though."

"She used you as bait?"

"She bailed me out, in the end. I did force her hand a little, but I'm pretty sure she would have done it anyway. Eventually. But Melody's interest in me was peripheral. Once the god let Melody's daughter matter to her through the brainwashing, she became obsessed with getting Sophie back. Carlos and Arabelle think that's a cognitive key they can use to smooth the mental strain of purging her condition."

"When will you be doing that?"

"Whenever Carlos and Melody are ready. Probably in the next few days. But the point is, the Builder had some serious dimensional magic infrastructure put in place on the island. Farrah and Clive think we can use it as a foundation to anchor the dimensional bridge."

"They want to use something the Builder left behind?"

"They think it's safe. And who would you get in for a second opinion?"

"That's true. We should check in with the Adventure Society contingent here."

"Good idea. No point having them interrupt us if we can avoid it."

The skimmer turned towards a group of stone-shaped buildings on the shore.

Jason had avoided naming the city in his astral kingdom after Boko. Given its nature as an oasis, he decided to name it New Water. In the city's administrative centre, the Duke of Boko was holding a management meeting.

"Over the next week, I will be finalising departments and assigning sub-management roles to…"

He trailed off as a portal opened in the room and Jason stepped out.

"Lord Asano," the duke said in greeting.

"Still not a lord, Duke Boko," Jason replied, his tone curt. "Come with me."

Jason went back through the portal without checking if the duke would follow. The duke didn't hesitate, not even pausing to instruct his subordinates.

"Do you think I'm meant to follow?" his assistant asked, then the portal closed.

"I suppose not," she said.

Of the various factions involved in studying the aftermath and preparing for the next step, the officials from the Boko government were the largest contingent. They were mostly senior executives from the old Boko government, along with an administrative staff and a team of experts from various departments. Their mandate was to assess the viability of reconstruction and begin preliminary planning. When the duke emerged from a portal in the middle of their camp, they swarmed him, firing off questions.

"Please," he said, holding up his hands for calm. "I know that there is a lot you want my input on, and I know that you have not had access to me while I have been in New Water. That city must be the priority now, and my focus must be leading our people as they settle into a new home. Anything you feel you need me to decide, simply use your best judgement. Now, if you'll excuse me, Lord Asano and I have matters of import to discuss. Perhaps a walk along the shore as the sun sets, Lord Asano."

The duke immediately started walking off towards the shoreline, leaving an array of confused and frustrated people behind. Jason watched the display with a frown, then moved to the leader of the government contingent.

"Some people are coming to get things organised," Jason quietly promised. "For now, let your people take a break. Let them go see their families."

A wide portal arch rose from the floor.

"That will take you to a public square in the main residential district. I'll leave it open for the moment, so your people can come and go."

"Thank you, Lord Asano."

"I'm not a lord. You can call me Mr Asano or, even better, Jason."

"Thank you, Mr Asano."

Jason nodded and followed the duke, who was slowly strolling along a path by the shore. Remnants of ritual magic and stone shaping marked the embankment, along with hardy desert spear grass that had been planted to stabilise the slope. It was late in the day and the sun dipped close to the ocean, soon to drop out of sight.

"What can I do for you, Lord Asano?" the duke asked as Jason caught up to his meandering pace and matched it.

The duke was a silver-ranker, courtesy of monster cores, which was the norm for political leaders. He was a dark-skinned human, typical for Boko's population, with long hair bound into thick strands by ornate gold clasps. His physique was essence-user lean, but there was a softness in how he carried himself. He had none of the sharp energy of an adventurer, always watching for threats.

"Duke Boko, I told you that you can ask me to connect you to your people here at any time. You have, thus far, only availed yourself of this twice. The last time was almost two weeks ago."

"Matters in New Water warrant my attention. The vast majority of my people are there. Not only do I have to plan for their wellbeing, but I must also look ahead as the first city leader on an entirely new world. Your astral kingdom—"

"Duke Boko," Jason cut him off.

"Lord Asano, you may call me Kalar."

"I call you Duke Boko because that is both who and what you are."

"Actually, I was thinking that people should start calling me—"

"You are not Duke New Water. You are Duke Boko, and that..."

He pointed at the water.

"...is Boko. That is what you rule. The full extent of what you rule. Your attention, Duke, should be here. This is a tragedy, but also an opportunity. To build a city from nothing. To plan out that which, before, grew up in a tangle over centuries. To make use of a harbour you never had before. To heal the wounds of what happened here, both in the hearts of the people and in the entire regional economy."

Jason stopped, turning to look out over the water.

"This time is critical, Duke Boko. I know this is hard, no doubt harder than I can understand, not being in your position. But you need to remember where you are from instead of looking to make something new. You need to concern yourself with your people, not your desire to be the first ruler on a new world."

"My Lord Asano, I—"

"I know everything that happens in my astral kingdom, Duke. Every word you say. Every ambition you whisper to your pet songbird. Privacy screens don't hide you from me."

"Lord Asano, New Water is a city inhabited only by my people. They trust me. Respect me. You need a steady hand in these times of turbulence."

"On that, we agree."

"We do?" the duke asked, waiting for the other shoe to drop.

Jason pointed out at the water where three dark skimmers were approaching the shore from the direction of the temple islands. It was hard to spot them under the darkening sky. They moved onto the land and settled into the grass.

The people disembarking all wore the garb of clergy. The first group had robes of crimson with gold trim. Their sigil was a hand gripping a planet, the symbol of Dominion. The next group had plain robes of undyed linen, followed by a group wearing muted blue.

"Thank you all for coming," Jason said. "If you follow the path back that way, you'll find the portal amongst those stone-shaped buildings."

He turned back to the duke, who was staring in confusion.

"I have asked some of the gods to help me assess and manage the situation in New Water," Jason explained. "Dominion will help me construct a framework for leadership. I have given them general parameters for a governance framework. Beyond that, they will be consulting with the new residents as to how best to lead the populace and administer the city. The final say is mine, of course, but I think the people who live there should have a voice in how it should be run."

"But—"

"The priests of Hearth and of Refuge will be organising the people. Who wants to settle permanently, who wants to find a new home, and who wants to wait for the reconstruction of Boko."

"I know the archbishops for all of those churches. I can—"

"I didn't ask the archbishops, Duke. I asked their gods. I also asked Dominion to take a look at how you're managing the affairs of your fallen city. As your city-state is now underwater, there is some question as to whether you will continue to enjoy his endorsement. My recommendation is that you go back to your people and work very hard to demonstrate your value in leading them."

Duke Boko stared at Jason.

"Why are you doing this to me? You *can't* do this to me!"

"Duke, you and your people have been through a lot, so I am doing my best to be gentle. But I say again that I know everything you have done while in my kingdom, and you have butted against the limits of my gentility. You will never enter New Water again."

"The noble houses won't stand for that."

"The noble houses of Boko are free to leave. New Water has no aristocracy, which is one of my parameters for the Dominion priests to work with. Anyone who stays will not have any noble title recognised."

"They won't tolerate those conditions."

"I have neither the time nor the interest to listen to you go through the denial stage, Duke Boko. I'm going to pick up my friend from the Adventure Society camp and leave. I imagine we will meet again, to discuss matters regarding the population. I hope you give matters some clear-headed consideration before that time."

Jason headed for the closest skimmer as the other two dissolved into clouds of darkness that vanished into his shadow. The skimmer took off as the sun set on the still water that was once the city of Boko.

40

IT'S MORE COMPLICATED
THAN THAT

AIRCRAFT HAD BEEN ONE OF THE EARLIEST EXAMPLES OF INTEGRATING magic and technology on Earth. Long before magic went public, the Network had been employing private planes with unadvertised optional extras. After twenty more years of development time, and no more need for secrecy, private air travel involved some of the most advanced magitech available.

Annabeth Tilden's plane rocked as if struck by turbulence, but the cause was rather more dangerous. She had participated in enough combat training to not be useless in a pinch, but she was not a fighter. She was especially not up to the task of fending off monsters attacking her aeroplane while in flight.

She couldn't properly see their attackers through the window of her passenger seat, given the speed and the dark. She did spot silhouettes in the flashes of blue as the monsters struck the plane's shielding. They looked like round bodies with four wings sticking out, in flagrant defiance of aerodynamics. Armour plating dropped over the windows, cutting off her view entirely.

"It'll be fine, Mrs Tilden," the man sitting opposite her said. Morris Manning was a slight man, short and lean. He didn't look like much, but he was both her bodyguard and her minder. He was an operative from the US Department of Supernatural Affairs, what the US Network had ultimately morphed into. On loan to the United Nations for this trip, he was a likely candidate for reaching gold rank without cores.

"The plane's defences can handle it?" Anna asked. She glanced at her wife, asleep in the seat beside her. Susan could sleep through a bombing run.

"It'll hold up to attack for a good while, but the weapons won't be able to kill them. If they're not enough to drive the creatures away, Mr Clovis will handle it."

There were sixteen passenger seats on the plane, all occupied. Six were delegates sent to meet with the Asano clan, including Anna. Susan and a nine-person security detachment occupied the remaining seats. Morris was the leader of the security contingent, meaning he did the administrating and organising. The most powerful member of the group was a gold-ranker, Patrick Clovis. His infrequent words came in a thick Bostonian accent.

"Not going out for some jumped-up sky chickens," Clovis said. "Do it yourself, Manning."

"Sadly, Mr Clovis, my power set is ill-suited for high-speed flight. Ms Keener, would you be so kind?"

Another member of the security team got up and moved towards the back of the plane. There was a hatch in the rear compartment that allowed people to exit mid-flight without disrupting the rest of the plane.

"Travel in Europe is dangerous," Morris explained to Anna. "It's not the vampires, though, but the monsters. The vampires don't clear them out unless they threaten a blood farm or one of their other interests."

"Oh, I had no idea," she said lightly.

An awkward smile crossed his face as he looked across at the former Network branch director and current Under-Secretary-General of the United Nations Office of Supernatural Affairs.

"Apologies, Mrs Tilden."

"It's fine, Mr Manning. Monsters were only to be expected when approaching the Asano territories. The magic level is higher, making the monsters commensurately more powerful."

"We avoid referring to them as Asano territories or anything similar," another delegate said. "It implies that those lands belong to them and not the nations of France and Slovakia."

Maël Baffier represented the French government in exile. Anna didn't point out that France, like most countries in Europe, hadn't functionally existed in well over a decade. The negotiations for who would join Anna on her visit to the Asano clan had gone on for weeks. Knowing Jason and his grandmother, the clan matriarch, she had a feeling about how they would respond to the self-invitees.

The UN and the other factional and government interests hadn't consulted Anna very much, despite her being the ostensible leader of the delegation. She'd been open about Asano wanting to recruit her, which had eroded trust in her as she had not pre-emptively refused. She remained in charge on paper, however; without her, there would be no getting eyes and ears on the ground inside the Asano clan. The delegates themselves were politicians, and she was certain that most of the security team were all former or current intelligence operatives.

The plane's intermittent shaking stopped and the armour panels over the windows retracted. Moments later, Kenner returned, dirty and drenched.

"That," she said, "was unpleasant."

She took the bag containing a change of clothes from under her seat and then headed back to the rear compartment.

The captain had announced a short time ago that they were approaching Asano territory, prompting a scowl from the French delegate. Anna looked up from her tablet as Morris tilted his head, listening to something on his earpiece. He looked over and asked her to follow him to the cockpit.

Susan stirred as Anna stepped past her.

"Are we there yet?" she asked blearily.

"Almost, love."

"Did I miss the meal?"

"There's a protein bar in the arm rest."

"Boo," Susan jeered.

Morris watched the exchange with amusement before leading Anna to the front of the plane. The pilot had arrested the plane's movement, tilting the engines for vertical take-off and landing mode. They were hovering near, but not directly over, what had once been the city of Saint-Étienne. After claiming the territory originally, Jason had reproduced the city, previously ravaged by vampires and then wiped out entirely by a transformation zone. Only the areas outside of the domain showed the broken remnants of vampiric occupation.

Now, the ruins around the clan's domain had been cleared away, leaving only the city inside the domain of Jason's power. The architectural style remained the same, but there were distinct changes from when Anna had lived there as liaison. Largest was a massive expansion of green areas and waterways. Streams ran through parklands and a whole section of the city had canals in place of streets. What it did not have was an airport.

"Ma'am," the captain said. "Our original instructions were to land at the former military base site, but it no longer appears to exist."

"It was there," Morris said. "We had satellite footage from yesterday with it there. You know the Asano clan best, Mrs Tilden. Any suggestions?"

"We wait," Anna said. "I imagine this is something to do with Jason Asano's flair for the dramatic."

As if waiting for her prompt, an area at the edge of the city was suddenly engulfed in fog. Once it cleared, there was a space that looked like an oversized helipad, with a symbol of a plane painted on it.

"I believe you have your landing zone, Captain," Morris said.

Two people were waiting as the delegation disembarked. One was Ketevan Arziani, assistant to the Asano clan matriarch. She had once been Anna's own deputy, back in Australia during her Network days. They had remained friends, only losing touch when the Asano clan had vanished. Susan gave her a wave, earning a quickly supressed smile but no other response. Standing next to Ketevan was Rufus Remore.

"Interesting," Morris murmured. "No Asano family members."

Anna understood that, in diplomacy, every choice sent a message, intended or not.

"They want to show us that the clan is more than just the Asano family band," she murmured back.

"Show us, or show you?" Morris asked. "That's your friend over there, isn't it?"

She gave Morris a side glance. The man clearly did his prep work.

As Rufus and Ketevan approached, the security team took reserved defensive postures, cautious but not provocative. The exception was Patrick Clovis, the gold-ranker striding out to position himself between the delegation and the clan representatives. Anna and Morris let out simultaneous sighs.

"Clovis, you aren't here to protect us from the Asano clan," Morris said. "Here, it would be pointless to try. If they want to do something to us, not even you can stop them."

"Because of this guy?" Clovis asked, nodding at Rufus.

"Yes. Clovis, you're here to protect us from vampires and monsters, should anything go wrong. Do not be what goes wrong."

Clovis stared at Rufus for a long moment, then back at Morris. He growled like an animal but stalked back to the rear of the group.

"Is he really the best you could get?" Anna said.

"Sadly, yes," Morris said. "Every stakeholder insisted on sending a gold-ranker, but refused to volunteer one of their own. I had to sit through weeks of pointless staff proposals before they gave me this guy."

Ketevan and Rufus approached them, now that Clovis was out of the way. Ketevan smiled at Anna and Susan, but her focus was on Morris.

"My name is Ketevan Arziani, chief of staff to the clan matriarch. This is Rufus Remore."

"Morris Manning, security detail chief."

"The patriarch would like to begin things socially," Ketevan said. "Anna, Susan, please come with me while Mr Remore sees to the rest of your group. Once the luggage is unloaded from the plane, it will be delivered to your accommodations."

"You said patriarch," Morris pointed out. "Asano is back?"

"No," Rufus said. "He's still in the other world."

"Everything will be explained to our satisfaction, I assure you," Ketevan continued, prompting a smile to twitch on Morris' mouth. "Please see to the luggage. The staff will take it."

"The staff?" Manning asked.

A dozen cloaked figures manifested out of nowhere, the cloaks empty but for a glowing nebulous eye in each hood the size of a face. After raising an eyebrow, Manning went about the task of getting the luggage unloaded and keeping the delegates settled. Anna was a little surprised that Baffier didn't argue as he and the others were led away by Rufus. She'd been worried about the French diplomat, but he thankfully knew when to vent his frustrations and when to do his job. Left alone, Ketevan gave Anna and Susan a quick hug each.

"Susan, I'm so glad you decided to come."

"It wasn't easy convincing this one," she said, jabbing a thumb in Anna's direction. "She thought it was too dangerous for me."

"How did you win her over?"

"By pointing out that if she comes and works for you, me being left behind would be even more dangerous."

Ketevan nodded.

"I'm sorry that Jason's offer put you in a tough spot. It would be great to have you here, though."

"It's more complicated than that, Keti," Anna said. "It's not just about accepting a job or not."

"I know. And so does he, but we can get to that later. How about we have some brunch and catch up?"

A stream of cloud rose from the tarmac and turned into an open top car.

"Is this how it works here?" Anna asked. "Everything you need just magically appears? Things weren't so accommodating during my brief tenure as liaison here."

"It's not usually like this, although more than back then," Ketevan said. "For some things, it is. If you want to knock out a wall in your house or something, you can just ask."

"Ask who?"

"The wall, I guess. Jason is more powerful now, and his influence here is stronger. I don't want to talk business, yet, but I should warn you that you can't escape his attention here. He's not actively watching, as I understand it, but if he wants to know what you're doing or something you did, he does."

"That's a little invasive," Susan said, looking around as if she would spot drones spying on them.

"More than a little," Anna said.

"You get used to it," Ketevan said. "It's odd, especially at first. It helps that Jason was more of a story than an actual presence, for a lot of years. But now that he's more active, that's good too. Old people have fallen down stairs that turned into a cloud cushion and they were unhurt. Kids have gotten stuck places that just opened up to let them out."

She got into the driver's seat of the car, Anna and Susan getting into the back.

"Oh, this is comfortable," Susan said. "I know we weren't here for long, but I missed cloud furniture."

"Don't get used to it," Anna told her.

"Or do," Ketevan teased. "I wouldn't hate having you back here for good."

41

A LONG FEW DAYS

KETEVAN DROVE ANNA AND SUSAN THROUGH THE CITY. BACK WHEN Anna had lived there, the domain had only just been established. The vampires were storming through Europe and no one knew how reliable the protection of Jason's power would be, especially in the absence of the man himself. The humans changed by the transformation zones were still new to their conditions and pouring into clan territory as refugees.

Years later, they had clearly integrated. As the car passed an outdoor café, more eyes were on the strangers in the car than the man with green scales and cream on his nose from an iced chocolate. Susan pointed out a beautiful winged man flying over the rooftops.

"It's like the bar in *Star Wars*, but French," Susan observed. "I love it. I wonder what the art scene is like here."

"Small, but has some unique aspects you might find fascinating," Ketevan told her.

"It all looks so normal," Anna observed. "Not long ago, you were all hidden in an astral space while vampires ruled here."

"A lot of people are still in there," Ketevan told her. "Out here, it's closer to how the rest of Earth is. The astral space is more overtly magical, and a lot of the clan grew up there. It's the world they know."

"But the clean-up and restoration after the vampire occupation seems to have gone quickly," Anna said.

"Nigel will explain that. He's been talking about owing you a debriefing for a long time. He just couldn't do it while you were in the US. He'd have been snatched up at the airport, and even if he snuck in, you were always being watched. Suffice it to say, by the time we emerged, there were no signs of vampires in clan territory. We've been expanding out since, clearing out blood farms and purging vampires."

"You mean killing them," Susan said.

"Yes," Ketevan agreed. "I mean killing them."

"Are we sure they're not redeemable?" Susan asked. "Craig Vermilion was always so nice."

"And still is," Ketevan said. "I had lunch with him last week. We have a large vampire population in the Slovakian territory. Jason's power shields them from the effects that turn the others bad. But the ones out there... the weak ones are feral now. Little more than animals with an insatiable thirst for blood. The more powerful ones are worse. They kept their minds but lost anything approaching a conscience. They know what they're doing to the people in those blood farms, and they just don't care."

"If their numbers were smaller, perhaps something could be done," Anna said. "There are more vampires and more victims than were ever made public. The official numbers are nowhere close to accurate. The evacuation of Europe is the largest mass-migration event the world has ever seen. So many were lost along the way, turned into ghouls, blood slaves or more vampires. Most ended up in the farms, though. The food supply. The unreleased casualty estimates put the numbers close to those in World War Two."

"But a lot of those people have been rescued, right?" Susan asked. "From the blood farms?"

"Yes," Ketevan said, "but many more remain, still feeding the vampire population. Now that the global militaries aren't operating in Europe, we're holding the people we rescue in the astral space here in France. We didn't put them with the vampires, for obvious reasons. We have medical professionals helping as best they can, but the physical and mental trauma they've suffered is indescribable. I don't even know how someone would come back from that. Once relations are re-established with the wider world, we'll have them join other refugees from their respective countries."

Ketevan sighed.

"I wanted this to be a fun catch-up," she said. "At least for a little bit. I suppose I've gotten used to the clan being isolated and surrounded by a continent of vampires. I can see how that would be alarming to visitors."

"What happened when you had to hide away?" Susan asked. "Were you safe?"

"Very," Ketevan said. "I'll leave that for Rufus and Jason to explain, but the short version is that Jason needed to seem weak."

"To deceive the vampires?" Anna asked.

"The vampires don't worry him. He was apparently fighting something like gods at the time, and he needed to trick them."

"Something like gods?"

"The actual grim reaper, amongst others. Or so I'm told. It all sounds extremely far-fetched, but far-fetched is what we do here, so who knows? Not my department, fortunately. As I said, Rufus and Jason will explain."

"That would be a first," Anna muttered.

Ketevan was driving them to the home of Erika Asano and her husband, Ian, located close to the administration tower. The tower was a looming edifice of renaissance architecture, the most overt divergence from the original design of the city.

As promised, Anna and Susan's first engagement in the Asano clan was social. Now that Erika and Ian's daughter had moved out, they lived in a modest townhouse in the shadow of the tower. The front faced one of the city's major thoroughfares, leading to the admin centre. Behind the townhouse row was a shared parkland.

Also present at the gathering was Nigel Thornton, who was apologetic about never delivering the report she sent him out for. His deference marked a sharp difference to the other gold-rankers she'd met for her work, of which there had been quite a few. The nations that boasted them were not shy about reminding people.

Their hosts had set up a picnic lunch on the patio, with a rustic wooden table and benches. They watched families play in the park, and a bunch of kids playing cricket. The food was astoundingly good, courtesy of their chef hostess, but Anna recognised very little of the food.

"We farm the ingredients in the astral spaces," Erika explained. "The magic is rich, and the agricultural land is varied. Too much to be naturally occurring, but ideal for producing all kinds of food."

"You didn't have trouble providing for people during your exile, then?" Susan asked.

"I think exile is a harsh term," Ian said. "From our perspective, it was a safe haven while the world outside was struggling. Hundreds of millions of refugees, pouring into Asia, Africa and the Americas. From what we've heard, it caused a new wave of food shortages after things had finally recovered from the monster waves."

"Magitech largely solved the supply problem," Anna said. "The farming stacks produce a lot of food cheaply. The real issues around the food supply are political and economic. It's the largest shift in how agriculture operates since the introduction of electricity and internal combustion. The entire industry is being turned on its head, at least in developed countries. So much of US agriculture was centred on corn, and that's collapsed under the practicalities of how the world works now. A lot of the American Midwest has gone the way of the steel towns forty years ago. Australian agriculture fared just as badly, if not worse."

"Then there's the refugees themselves," Susan added. "The population of the United States grew by half within a year."

"A logistical disaster," Anna said. "And that was moderate, compared to places with large tracts of unoccupied land. Canada, Australia, and large portions of Africa, China and Russia. Any place that magitech could make liveable quickly."

"Australia's population is now seventy-five percent European refugees," Susan said. "The political chaos that resulted is still going on. Australia has always had an unpleasant intolerance streak around migrants and refugees, and that really spilled over in the time you were all hidden away."

"We heard about the turmoil," Ian said. "It's hard to believe they took in that many people."

"There was a lot of international pressure," Anna said. "A lot of resistance, too. There was a double dissolution of government, for only the second time ever. Things still haven't settled."

With the conversation moving to the heavy topics they had previously avoided, the group moved inside. They discussed a mix of global events and events within the clan. The clan members had missed a lot in their isolation, even before fully withdrawing into the astral spaces. As for Anna, she was currently the eyes of the world on what was happening in Asano territory. Some still believed that Jason was dead, while others saw his impending return as a Sword of Damocles, poised over their heads.

Nigel finally got to tell the story of the day the vampires who had claimed the Asano territory died. He was the sole witness, and his account of Jason's wrath sounded like an Old Testament story.

"...the blood rain turning into this colourful, sparkling light, destroying what was left of the vampires and their minions. Then I was alone, the last one standing in a city that stank of death. Until Jason showed up. Or his avatar, however that works. It seemed like he was really there."

"They don't smell the same," Erika said. "The avatars. Jason smells like flowers and cut grass. Taika too. Something about being a cosmic entity. His avatars don't smell of anything, and they feel like rubber to touch."

"What did Jason say to you?" Anna asked Nigel.

"We talked about having power, and the people who wanted to use it. He saw that I was gold rank and deduced the problems I've been having. He said it was a lot like what he went through, during his time here. And we talked about the possibility of my team and me joining the clan."

"Which you did," Anna said.

"Yeah. The clan has been quietly smuggling our families in while we participate in rescue and reclamation."

"Retaking the areas around Asano territory," Anna said.

"Yes."

"There is some concern about the clan's ambitions towards Europe."

Erika snorted her disgust.

"Our ambitions are dealing with the vampires and the people they're still holding in their blood farms. You just told us about the refugees from here clogging up the infrastructure across the planet, but the people in charge are already looking to divvy up Europe between them."

"You say that," Anna told her, "but we're sitting in what was French territory before your brother claimed it for himself."

"It wasn't French territory," Jason said.

Everyone turned to look at him in the doorway. He was holding a plate with a sandwich that looked to be made from the leftovers of their lunch. He looked at it with a frown.

"I forgot that I can't taste things with my avatar," he said sadly, sat the plate on a side table and walked into the room.

"Don't just leave things sitting around like that," Erika scolded.

Jason groaned and the plate floated off the table and out through the door. He moved to join the others and cloud rose from the floor to form a chair under him as he sat.

"It wasn't French territory," he said again. "It was vampire territory.

And I didn't ask to take it. I didn't even know it was possible before Slovakia, and I had no choice anyway. I had to take them."

"You had to?" Anna asked.

"Yes. Do you know what a transformation zone is, Anna? It's a scab, over an open wound in the side of the universe. Mostly, the wound heals and the world limps on. But some scabs aren't enough. Left alone, the wound under them will rip a hole in the side of the universe. The resulting rupture would annihilate the Earth, at the very least, and probably the solar system. And that's assuming it didn't chain react from there and start tearing the whole universe apart, although the likelihood of that is small. And it would be stopped if that started happening."

"By you?"

"Not my area, and beyond the scope of even my real power. There's an entity called the World-Phoenix who would cauterise the wound from the outside. The side effects of that would have been drastic, but pointless to all of us, who would have been dead."

"You do this, Jason," Anna said. "Grand proclamations. Fate of the universe. But all we have to go on is your word. You never tell us enough to check for ourselves."

Jason nodded. "Back then, I was more inclined to kill you all myself. Fortunately, I didn't have the power to conquer the world back then."

"Implying that you do now?"

"Yes."

"This isn't the same world you left, Jason."

"And I'm not the same person who left it."

He sighed.

"Anna, we're falling into old patterns here. *I'm* falling into old patterns, and that's not going to be productive. I know that I never explained myself the way people wanted, but I hope you understand why."

Anna gave a reluctant nod.

"I remember a lot of conversations where I had to explain that the Network people that came after you this time were another faction that had gone rogue. I can't blame you for refusing to work with us anymore. Given how it all ended, it seems that it was all just rogue factions, acting in their own interests. I suppose you saw that before I did. The clarity of an outside perspective."

"Anna, I believe that you were never like that. That you were trying to do the right thing. That's why I want to work with you now. And to start,

I'll answer any and all of your questions. About back then, about now. I'll offer you what proof I can, when I have it. But I'll warn you now, there are some things that will be hard to believe, and all I have for you is my word. I can show you more once I arrive in person, but I can't wait for that. We need to start preparing now."

"For what?" she asked. "Rufus Remore said you wanted to work with me, but he didn't say why. What is it that you want?"

Jason nodded contemplatively, more to himself than to her.

"My intention today is to help you understand that I will be coming back to Earth with unassailable power. Limitless, for most practical purposes. Anything I want to do, I will be able to. Anything I don't want to do, no one will be able to make me. Conquer the world, erase nations. Eliminate every head of state on the planet in an afternoon. Whatever threat the people of this world think I pose, I can promise you that it is much, much worse."

"Alright," Anna said. "Let's suppose that I believe you. Why am I here, listening to you tell me that?"

"Because I don't want to be the thing that terrorises the world. I don't want to bring down governments and make nations collapse. What worries me is that the fear of my doing so will lead the powers of this world to force my hand. My first goal is to avoid having my return to Earth destroy it."

Anna looked at Jason, eyes examining him as her mind ticked over.

"You really think that you're that important? If Rufus hadn't come out and told everyone that you're some great big threat, they wouldn't have thought it."

"No," Nigel interjected. "They'd have tried to exploit him, just like before. Anna, I don't think I properly conveyed what I saw that day. It wasn't the power of a man. It was the power of a god."

Anna looked at Nigel, then back to Jason.

"Do you think you're a god, Jason?"

"That's complicated. I think we'd better get into those questions; it's going to be a long few days."

42

A THING THAT MAKES THE CAR WORK

ANNA AND SUSAN SAT ON A PARK BENCH. IT WAS EARLY EVENING, AND parents from the surrounding houses were calling their kids in for dinner. A nearby picnic table had a blanket draped over it, with a mix of mechanical and magical tools laid out. A leonid was tinkering with what looked like a Rubik's cube, but with runes instead of colours on the sides. Anna had seen enough leonids to mark him as a teenager, but he had the confidence of a professional as he worked.

A human woman walked over to stand by his table. She looked to be in her early twenties, but so did most of the population. An astounding number of Asano clan members were essence-users, suggesting a staggering access to resources. Anna took a second look at the girl and her rank-polished features. It had been a lot of years, but she looked like—

"Emi," the leonid said as she approached. "I told you that you should have let me look at these long ago. Your problem isn't the magic, it's the mechanics. The transitions aren't smooth enough, so when you switch configurations, it's causing wear on the... are you even listening?"

Emi had sensed Anna's attention and turned to look back at her observer. She narrowed her eyes for a moment, as if trying to recall an old memory. She nodded to Anna, then turned back to the leonid.

"Sorry, Gary, you were saying the transitions are causing wear?"

"Yeah. Who's that?"

Emi threw another glance Anna's way.

"Someone my uncle used to work with."

"I thought all the outsiders were stuck in the mushroom farm."

"Not all of them. Wait, mushroom farm? They're in the visitor dorms Uncle Jason made. That's practically a palace, not a farm."

"Yeah, but it's still a place to keep them in the dark and feed them bullsh—"

"Just pack up and we'll go, Gary. Your mother told me to bring you home for dinner."

"Are you and Vincent eating with us?"

"Yeah."

Gary put his tools and blanket away in a large backpack and they wandered off.

"Is that Jason's niece?" Susan asked.

"Yes," Anna said as they watched the pair walk away. "If the Asano clan's isolation ends, there's going to be a lot of attention on her."

"And what about you? If you decide to become a part of all this, you're going to be the clan's diplomatic face to the world. Is that something you want?"

Anna leaned wearily into Susan's shoulder.

"I don't know where to even start considering it. Three days we've been going through it all. Three days of every new claim being crazier than the last. When you ask a guy if he thinks he's a god, any answer but 'no' means he's probably stockpiling weapons and trying to convince people to be sister wives."

Susan laughed.

"How are you not blown away by all this?" Anna asked her. "I've been living in a world of magic my whole life and I don't know how to take it. I can't imagine what it's like for you."

"That's the thing, love: this isn't my first time."

"What do you mean?"

"Like you said, you grew up with this. Your family have been Network insiders for generations. When you told me that magic was real, I thought it was some kind of prank. Then I thought you were crazy. Then you showed it to me, and I thought the world was crazy. Now, you finally know how I felt back then."

"Okay, but the scale of it. How many times in the last three days did Asano say 'I can show you once I'm there in person?' Assuming that he isn't lying—which is quite the assumption, given his claims—then we're talking about a scope that dwarfs us. What is a country when he has his own solar system? A planet, when he's rewriting the rules of the cosmos? If he's lying about it all, that's trouble, but it's trouble I can at least get my head around. If he's telling the truth, then we're nothing to him. He operates on a scale that makes everything we know a tiny speck of nothing."

Susan nestled her head onto Anna's shoulder.

"We're not insignificant, love. Not you and me, and not the Earth. Not to him, or he wouldn't have gone to all the trouble of bringing you here."

"But doesn't it make you feel small?"

Susan considered a moment before answering.

"From how he explained it," she said, "all of these great magic bibbity bobs—"

"Great astral beings."

"...are there to make the universe work. They're the mechanisms by which everything works, right? Life, death, time, etc."

"That's how he explained it."

"Okay," Susan said. "Remember that road trip we took on the Great Ocean Road, right before we got married?"

"Sure. That was a good trip."

"Remember the car? Your old MG?"

"Of course. I loved that car."

"Yes, you did. Would you say that car was a significant part of the trip?"

"Absolutely. What does any of this have to do with Jason Asano fighting a magic bird that stops universes from breaking open?"

"Stick with me, love. Do you think that the concept of internal combustion was significant to our trip?"

"Uh, no."

"Exactly. Internal combustion is extremely important to a petrol car, and that's what we were driving, but it didn't matter to us. On a larger scale, it was significant, but it didn't matter to us at all. So, yes, if you're looking at these great space jibber jobbers—"

"Great astral beings."

"...then we are insignificant. But if you're looking at us, they're the insignificant ones. Just a thing that makes the car work."

Anna looked at her wife, then drew her in for a lingering kiss.

"You are amazing, you know that?"

"Yes, but you could stand to say it more often."

"Well, I wouldn't want it to go to your head."

Anna leaned back on the bench, feeling more relaxed than she had in a week.

"If Jason is really as powerful as he claims," Susan said, "then he's bending over backwards not to rub that power in everyone's faces."

"He had Rufus Remore fly across the planet to hold a meeting where he explained how powerful Jason is."

"Did he? I wasn't there for that. Did Rufus explain everything we've heard over the last few days? Or is that something he's only telling you?"

Anna tapped her lips thoughtfully.

"No," she realised. "Rufus as much as said Jason was coming back with a squad of gold-rank powerhouses. He made a few implications—how could he not, with Jason tied to the System—but nothing like what we've been hearing."

She sat up straight, frowning as she gamed out Jason's agenda.

"Jason is positioning himself as a power, but one the existing powers here can understand. Come to grips with. Enough that he's someone they have to deal with, rather than exploit. If they genuinely believed that he was as powerful as he claims, I have no idea what would happen. The whole planet would go into crisis mode. Some very bad decisions would be made."

She leaned back again.

"He doesn't want to destroy the world just by arriving in it. That's what he said. And if he's that powerful, he probably would."

"Then let's hope he is," Susan said.

"You don't think it would be better if there wasn't a demigod with a history of anger issues and recklessness descending upon the Earth?"

"I think that bringing you here, telling you everything, shows us his intentions, one way or another. If he's being honest about possessing all that power, it shows us that he wants to use it responsibly. To seek out sound advice, act with care and avoid mistakes when he can. But if he's not as all-powerful as he claims, and this is all a ruse…,"

"Then he's running a game, with me in the middle of it," Anna finished.

"Yes. But even if he's lying, he's still going to have a lot of power. This whole city is something he made and can change on a whim. If he comes to Earth with ill-intent, he can cause immeasurable damage."

"Which do you think it is? Honesty or lies?"

"He's a lot like you, you know?"

"Like me?"

"I remember back when you were running the Network branch in Sydney. Not coming home for days. Arriving furious when you did. Frustrated that the people who should have been shielding the world from magic were playing politics. Isn't that what happened to him, the last time he was on Earth? Trying to do the right thing, only to be undermined by the ambitious?"

"I suppose it was. This is you saying that you think he's being straight with us?"

"This is me saying that if he really is like you, things have a chance of turning out alright. And if he's not, you need to be here anyway, to ameliorate the damage of whatever he's really up to. We both know that you won't walk away and leave it to be someone else's problem."

Anna and Susan found Jason in the kitchen of the guest house they had been assigned. He was wearing an apron with pink flowers on it. As they entered the kitchen, his back was to them as he managed several pots on the stove.

"Come and check this sauce," he said without turning around. "I can't taste anything with this body, so I can't manage the salt levels on my own."

Anna looked at him from under raised eyebrows, but Susan moved forward. She tasted the offering from the end of a wooden spoon.

"Ooh, that's nice. But yes, a little more salt."

"Were you listening to us talk?" Anna asked.

"One of the most important things about power," he said as he turned back to the stove, "is knowing when not to use it. If you have a hammer, it's easy to look at every situation as a nail. But sometimes force, no matter how precisely applied, will only make things worse."

"You're good at that," Anna said.

"Cooking?"

"Implying you answered a question that you did, in fact, not."

Jason turned his head just long enough to flash her an impish grin.

"I think you and I could have fun together, Anna. I do hope you accept my job offer."

"I am leaning that way, but I want a better understanding of what I'm walking into."

"That's fair," Jason said. "And you will be forced to make certain concessions."

"Such as?"

"No more supermarket bread. I know you and I have talked about this a long time ago, but a little bird told me that you did not heed my advice."

Anna turned a glare on Susan, who did a reasonable job of looking innocent.

"We don't have supermarkets here at all," Jason continued. "It's more of a permanent farmers' market situation, plus bakers, cheesemongers and the like. It's not as convenient, I'll grant you, but it helps foster a sense of community. I leave management of the clan to my grandmother for the most part, but this I insisted on. The food is free, though. The staples, at least. Rufus has to import his jellybeans himself."

"I was more talking about some verification of the claims you've made about the power at your command. If what you're saying is true, you must be a legendary figure in the other world."

"Farrah has been throwing the word 'mythic' around. But Pallimustus doesn't have the same media saturation and mass communication Earth does. The powerful people know who I am, but the population at large doesn't. My team is a lot more famous than me. There are a few places they know my name, but I can get away with using a fake one. There aren't news reports and online videos to plaster my face everywhere."

"Do they know, there? Just how vast the span of your power is? You claim that it extends beyond not just Earth or their planet, but the entire universe. Every universe."

"It's more of a potentially vast span, at least until my mortal power grows. I have limited ability to manipulate the System, although I do have some. Around my avatar and here in my domains. But I can't just use it like it's my personal toy. There are rules I need to adhere to. I spent fifteen years fighting to see them enforced, after all. That includes on me."

"I know that I can't test your immortality, or see this universe of yours."

"It's quite small, as universes go."

"I would at least like to see one of the astral spaces, where your power is stronger. To get a taste of its full scope."

"That's easy enough to manage. There are portals in the admin tower."

"Even with all that, though, this cosmos-level power is hard to acknowledge."

"Vast cosmic power is the term. I used to have it on a t-shirt, although I think Emi has it now."

"The assumption is that the System is connected to you, but it could just be some cosmic force that finally reached Earth. You could be leveraging your early access to it to make us think you are in control of it."

A window appeared in front of her.

- [System Administrator] notification: I'm being as open as I can, Anna.

"Cute," she said.

He turned around from his cooking to look at her.

"Can I take it that you are at least provisionally accepting my offer?"

She took a deep breath and let it out slowly.

"Yes."

"Good. Step one, you eat. Step two, an astral space tour. Step three, we figure out what to do with the minders you brought with you. They've been getting increasingly cranky, despite their accommodations being quite luxurious."

43

A LONG TIME COMING

"THIS," ANNA SAID, "IS NOT A PROFESSIONAL ENVIRONMENT."

"What are you talking about?" Jason asked.

Anna gestured at her wife, who was just then entering the cabana having changed into her new swimsuit. She also had grilled meat on a stick and a drink with a little umbrella in it.

"What?" Susan asked.

"Your wife doesn't think we should have this meeting at a water park," Jason told her.

"Well, I think it's a great idea. But you can't properly enjoy it, right? With that avatar body?"

"Sadly, no," Jason said.

"Because your real body is in the other universe."

"That's not technically my real body either, but for practical purposes, yes."

"What are you doing over there right now?" Susan asked. She moved to the cushioned bench next to Anna, who was doing her best to treat a folding picnic table and chair as office furniture.

"I'm currently working with my new bartender to try and reproduce Earth cocktails using Pallimustus alcohol. We just made some dirty Shirleys, and there's a princess who can't get enough of them."

Zara slammed her empty glass on the counter of the cloud ship's rooftop bar.

"Another one," she demanded, wobbling slightly on her barstool.

Jason arrived on the elevating platform just in time to overhear. The look Jamar threw Jason from behind the bar was a clear plea for help.

"Zara, we only have so much of each liquor in stock," Jason told her. "We have a lot more drinks to try out, so maybe let Jamar try something else. We'll restock once we know how much we want of which types of plonk."

Zara picked her glass up again and slammed it forcefully back down. The counter turned squishy so it didn't break, and the glass became stuck. Zara glared at it for its rank betrayal before wheeling on her stool to glare at Jason, almost toppling off in the process.

"Portal off and get more!" she demanded.

"Zara, have you, by any chance, been talking to the Storm King again?"

"Stupid Emiliano," she slurred. "Yes, I could have been more diplomatic with that stupid princeling, but he wanted to buy me like I was cattle at market."

"Far be it from me to tell you to be more diplomatic," Jason said. "Not with my history. And the guy did have it coming."

"Exactly," Zara said as she jabbed a finger in Jason's direction. "Father has been so good about it. He says I did great. He's much more relaxed, now that he's not king anymore."

Sophie flew onto the roof from a lower deck, not bothering with the elevating platform.

"Sophie!" Zara exclaimed. "Tell Mr Evil Stabby to go buy more... whatever it is I was just drinking."

Sophie looked at her with an amused expression.

"You drank out the bar?"

"No. Yes. Maybe. Shut up."

Sophie slowly coaxed the drunk princess towards the elevating platform and an inevitable nap. Jason sat down, giving Jamar a sympathetic look.

"How much of the gold-rank stock did she go through?"

"Enough that I could work for a year without being able to afford it. Before this job anyway. Are you sure you're happy paying me that much for kitchen and bar services?"

"It shouldn't be a dangerous job, Jamar, but you might find yourself danger adjacent, from time to time. More than that, you're probably going to see some things. Like a drunk princess whose brother is stuck with a diplomatic disaster after she inserted some outside magic into a draconian prince's very inside place. This needs to be a place where my friends and I can relax without being worried what we say or do. When I interviewed you for this job, I told you that the most important parts of this job are loyalty and discretion."

"Yes, sir, Mr Asano. No one will hear anything that goes on here from me."

"And that is what your remuneration reflects, Jamar. It's not about slinging the best drinks or managing food service efficiently, although you do need to do that. It's the fact that you are going to be around powerful people who do very important things. Not just my people, but anyone we host here. Betraying our trust could be very lucrative, should you pick your moment well. In appreciation of that, I want to make sure that you don't feel like your discretion is being undervalued."

"I'm very grateful for the opportunity, sir."

"Good. I should warn you, though, that you won't need to go looking for someone to sell information to. You're going to be approached more or less any time you're away from the boat."

"I would never—"

"I know. But not everyone will just come up and offer a bribe. You might find that an attractive young... lady?"

Jamar nodded.

"You might encounter an attractive woman who finds you more charming than you're used to being found. Or someone who skips the money offer and goes straight to more physical means of compulsion. In preparation for such eventualities, we've taken precautions to secure your safety for when you aren't on the ship. You won't notice them, but you will be one of the most protected individuals in any place you visit. I want you to feel secure, and not worry about people targeting you for your connection to us."

"To be honest, sir, I wasn't really worried. Until just now, when I find myself quite worried. What exactly do you mean by 'physical means of compulsion?'"

"Oh," Jason said as he stood up. "Sorry. Still, I'm sure it's going to be fine. Do you need me to portal off and pick up some more drinks?"

"Uh, yes, sir."

"Make me a list."

"This has been a long time coming," Jason said.

The magic around Vitesse was more than strong enough to let the cloud ship fly, but Jason left it on the water. Most of his friends were with him on the rooftop bar, having just enjoyed a lunch under the hot equatorial sun, cooled by the fresh sea air. Nik and Jason stood at the front railing, Jason waiting for his first glimpse of the city.

For many of his friends, it was home. It wasn't the capital of Estercost, but many considered it the adventuring capital of the continent. The high level of magic meant that monster manifestations were powerful and frequent, not just in and around the city but across the entire region. That was a critical threat when Estercost was filled with towns, villages and smaller cities, due to the idyllic climate and rich natural resources.

As with many high-magic zones, the local Adventure Society was much better at intercepting monster appearances than somewhere like Greenstone. Instead of leaving notes for wandering adventurers, they had something akin to the grid on Earth that detected magic across a wide area.

The grid on Earth was based on the same principles as natural arrays, using the geography of the planet for its structure. On Pallimustus, their detection networks were less advanced, requiring towers that were subject to weather and monster interference. They needed regular maintenance and replacement, but they also had advantages over the Earth grid. Where the grid only gave the exact information it was designed to originally, the Pallimustus equivalent could be tuned and calibrated to a variety of purposes. That was how Jason's cloud ship had been detected on its first approach to Rimaros, and how it was again on its approach to Vitesse.

Nik pointed out the city's famous flowering towers, their tops just coming into view. Jason looked over at where he was pointing, but his real attention was on the essence-user he sensed approaching. The same thing had happened on his approach to Rimaros, a local official heading out to greet—and check up on—approaching powerful visitors. It was a normal process, affecting every boat, sky ship and caravan emanating enough power to be a potential threat. In Rimaros, that was how Jason had first met Vidal Ladiv. That man's nephew was now one of Jason's growing entourage.

"Shade, would you ask Miguel to come up? It's time our new Adventure Society liaison made himself useful."

Jason's first visit to Vitesse quickly proved to be everything he had hoped for. The City of Flowers lived up to the name, with skyscrapers draped in flowering vines. Trees lined every street, heavy with blossoms. Social programs and labour laws meant that even the poorest sections of the city were safe and relatively prosperous. This was made possible by an economy thriving in multiple sectors, especially agriculture and the growth of alchemy supplies in the magic-rich soil.

Adventuring was likewise lucrative, with a steady stream of silver- and gold-rank monsters to harvest with efficient looting protocols. Vitesse adventurers were also in high demand around the world, many places paying generous fees to have experts deal with intransigent problems. The Magic Society likewise offered lucrative services, such as portal travel and airship construction.

Jason's favourite aspect of the city was that it was full of extremely powerful adventurers. This meant that if some crazy monster or lunatic cult showed up, he could relax and hear about it all later, just like everyone else. The only sad undertone for him was that most of his companions had friends and connections in the city to catch up with, even Nik. Each new introduction, every fun anecdote, reminded him of all the time he had spent away. The years of joy and trouble that he'd missed while supreme beings were using his soul as a battlefield.

He forced himself not to dwell on a past he couldn't change, and instead focused on making new memories. He finally got to see the Remore Academy, finally proving that Rufus' family did, in fact, run a school. He met Kenneth, son of Brian, now one of the most celebrated adventurers in Vitesse. While Jason was more than happy to hear all about the famous duel where he defeated a young Rufus, Jason was more interested in having him speak with Nik.

Kenneth's monster-tracking skills were highly vaunted. Rather than have a permanent team of his own, the Adventure Society regularly attached him to teams in need of his specific skills. Nik's ability to coordinate teams had put him in a similar situation, but Jason knew that he had some insecurities around not having a team of his own. Nik had confessed as much as he watched Jason and his own tight-knit team during their travels.

Jason hoped that spending time with Kenneth and discussing their experiences would help Nik come to terms with his adventuring career. If not, he would make sure Nik found an excellent team, regardless of what the Adventure Society wanted. If nothing else, Rufus had been training up the Asano clan youth, and had several excellent silver-rank prospects.

While Jason spent time with all of his friends, most of it was spent touring around the city with Nik. Jason enjoyed the anonymity, and Nik likewise luxuriated in not being the centre of attention. He did get looks because of his inescapable cuteness, but Vitesse was the most metropolitan and multicultural place Jason had ever encountered. There were all manner of people, from every essence-using species and some that weren't.

The brighthearts weren't the only people with enough inherent magic to have their own unique powers, many of which were visibly apparent. Jason and Nik spotted a variety of them, from a group of nine-foot humanoids with green skin and red tattoos to elves with wings who would likely be mistaken for short messengers.

All that was without even counting the adventurers with their exotic magic devices, wonderous familiars and flashy powers. During their days in Vitesse, Jason and Nik spotted all manner of strange and wonderous people. One woman had fire for hair and rode a bat made of crystal, with a visible skeleton inside. Another man was in a constant state of shape-shifting. His hair was always in flux, changing length, colour and style. His skin was pale one moment and red the next before turning into irides-cent fish scales.

Countless different transport methods were also on display, from flying carpets to a giant hamster wheel making short teleport hops. The familiars were of such frequency and variety that places close to the Adventure Society campus felt like they were under monster invasion. Jason, with glowing eyes and an adorable companion, didn't warrant a second glance.

Jason carefully avoided any entanglements with the various societies and associations, but he did have a few appointments to keep. One was to join the same guild as most of his companions, the Burning Violet guild. Another was an invitation to afternoon tea from what was arguably the most famous and prestigious citizen of Vitesse, Roland Remore. The last was to pick up his new wardrobe from the shop of Gilbert Bertinelli, now operating out of Vitesse.

Jason had taken a day all to himself to go and visit Bert. They had lunch together and discussed all they had been through since their Greenstone days. In the end, Jason left behind an exorbitant amount of money, and took with him an extensive wardrobe.

The Burning Violet guild house was a large but unassuming building, directly across from the Remore Academy. This was the location it had moved to following the takeover of the guild by Roland Remore long ago, and while the diamond-ranker no longer managed it, his presence loomed large.

The building was centuries old, but the magical reinforced stone was barely weathered. Like most buildings in Vitesse, it was decorated with living plants, although more sparingly than most. There were a few balconies with planters from which vines draped, and ivy climbing sections of the walls. Most of the greenery was around the sides on the building, expanding into what looked like gardens around the back, only partially visible from the street.

There were no fewer than four sets of double doors in the front, all of which were busy with messengers and functionaries coming in and out. There were quite a few adventurers as well, the others giving them a respectfully wide berth. This included Jason, who modulated his aura to a polite expression of his genuine rank. It was not an occasion to be deceptive and, while gold-rankers always stood out, they did so less in Vitesse. Wearing one of his new suits, he entered the cavernous lobby of the guild house.

Several staff members were approaching people as they entered and directing them variously to different reception desks, any of the several stairs or internal doorways, or occasionally sending them back out entirely. Jason, being gold rank, was attended to immediately. He was approached by an immaculately dressed young bronze-ranker before he had a chance to get anywhere near a queue.

The man had no trace of cores in his aura, so Jason assumed he was an adventurer in training. Unlike Greenstone, the more dangerous Vitesse environment meant that no adventurers below silver operated unsupervised. Rufus, Gary and Farrah had roamed abroad in search of adventure without minders watching over them.

"What can I do for you, sir?"

"I was hoping to apply to your guild."

"An excellent choice, sir. Are you looking to transfer from an existing guild?"

"No, I've never been in a guild before."

"That should simplify the application process, then. I will warn you in advance that rank is no guarantee of acceptance, however."

"Understood."

"Then please go through that door over there and the receptionist inside will take your details."

"Thank you."

4 4

A BIG JUICY HOLE

Jason entered the room just off the lobby. It was a smaller reception area with just one desk. It was well appointed, rich but tasteful, with dark wood and earthy colours. Another door led deeper into the building. A receptionist sat behind the desk, greeting him with a smile.

She was human and a bronze-ranker with no sign of core use, which seemed to be standard for the guild's functionaries. She had the dark skin of a Vitesse native, and long hair tied into thin braids. Her smile was genuine, which Jason found interesting, but realised would be a necessity. Bronze-rankers hiding spite behind a customer service smile would be seen through by the high-rankers they met on a daily basis.

"Good day, sir. You're looking to apply to the guild for membership?"

"I am."

"Please sit."

She tapped a crystal on her desk and a cloud of dust emerged from the floor and coalesced into a chair near Jason. There was a click as the door locked.

"So we won't be disturbed," the receptionist said, seeing Jason glance in that direction. "Please take a seat."

She waited for him to sit before she did the same. The chair wasn't cloud furniture comfortable, but it was close. She took a form and a pencil from the drawer.

"Might I begin with your name, sir?"

"Jason Asano. And yours?"

"It's Monica."

He registered the mild surprise in her aura that didn't make it to her face.

"Do people normally not ask?"

"Not gold-rankers, sir."

"You don't need to keep calling me sir."

"Is there a manner in which you would prefer to be addressed?"

"Jason is fine. Mr Asano, if you must."

"Very well, Mr Asano. Speaking of your rank, it means that your application will be assessed by a guild executive, including an in-depth interview. I'll be asking you some preliminary questions to help the process go smoothly. Is that acceptable to you?"

"Does anyone ever say no?"

"You would be surprised, Mr Asano."

"Go ahead and ask; I have nothing to hide. Well, that's a lie. I have many, many things to hide, but what gold-ranker doesn't? I just don't think they'll come up in a guild application unless this guild is involved in some extremely unusual affairs."

"The guild is definitely involved in some extremely unusual affairs, Mr Asano."

He laughed and she smiled.

"It's normal to be nervous, Mr Asano. Applying to any guild on this level is no small thing for anyone. Burning Violet members are elite amongst elites."

"You think I'm nervous? Oh, because of the rambling. No, that's just me. I always feel that when you're asking someone to involve themselves with you, it's only fair to give them a genuine sense of what they're getting into."

"That attitude will do you very well when the executive is interviewing you, Mr Asano. Their questions will be rather more probing than mine, and they will be more expectant of thorough answers. I'm just looking for some foundational information. Basic background details, your current adventuring status. You are entirely free to decline answering at this stage and defer your answers to later. I can tell you that openness now will work in your favour with the executive interview."

"Understood."

"Let's start with some background. Your identity will be confirmed later, using your Adventure Society badge."

"Has anyone actually tried to enter the guild under a false identity?"

"It happens. There was one woman who actually had three different memberships. A shape-shifter, obviously."

"She was kicked out?"

"No, if you can believe it. She revealed the truth herself and then helped improve the security protocols. That was before my time, though. She ended up teaching at the Remore Academy, which is how I heard about it. I took her Introduction to Improvisational Rituals course. Barely passed, but I loved it. She always had the best stories. She used to be a thief, if you can believe it."

"Oh, I can believe it."

"Sorry, I'm getting off track. Lord Bassingthwaite is always criticising me for being too personal, but I think you can be personal and professional at the same time."

"I completely agree, but I don't have 'lord' at the start of my name."

"I know, right? That does bring us to the next question, though. Do you hold any royal or noble title, or position within a recognised governmental authority?"

"No. Would that help with my application?"

"Not at all. It can even be an impediment in some cases. Nobility and sovereignty often involve complications the guild would prefer to avoid."

"I've noticed those complications myself, from time to time."

"Oh, I bet you have. Gold-rankers have the best stories, but most don't give a bronze-ranker a second glance, you know? If you don't mind me saying, Mr Asano, you are a very approachable man."

She made a circular gesture in his direction.

"You've got, I don't know, kind of a weird presence. Most gold-rankers are all imposing, but you have that tamped right down. It's there, in the background, but there's something casual and inviting about you. Are you doing that with your aura on purpose?"

"I like to be friendly with people."

"Well, I appreciate it. I would never normally be this open with the people who come in here…"

Jason sensed a lie in her aura for the first time.

"…but sitting across from you is like having tea with a friend."

"I appreciate you saying that, Monica. Perhaps, though, we should move on to the next question."

"Oh, you're right. I get to chatting, then some silver-ranker gets held up waiting and he thinks he's all important because his dad's friend's uncle killed a dragon once. He throws a fit, and then who ends up getting an earful from Lord Bassingthwaite? Me, that's who."

"Then, maybe we try and avoid that?"

"Well, I could hide, but I work here. He'd find me eventually."

"Uh, I was more thinking that getting through those questions might be a better approach than hide and seek with your boss."

"That does make sense. Keep it practical."

She looked down at her form.

"Right, we're up to... species. You appear human, but not of an ethnicity I recognise, and I can't read it from your aura. Again, I will remind you that you can decline to answer any of these questions, although they will be asked again, later in the process."

"Then I might exercise my right to decline. I will say that I was born human, but the adventuring life found me, rather than the other way around. There's quite a story to it."

"Oh, I bet there is. You're sure you can't... no, we need to get through this. Do you mind answering where you're from originally?"

"A little town you won't have heard of, called Casselton Beach. Lovely beaches, as you'd expect from the name. No adventurers, very low magic levels. I did my training in Greenstone, though."

"Oh, wow. The shape-shifter lady I told you about is from there. The one whose course I took in—"

"I remember, yes."

"The magic there is so low, but the Geller-Remore facility they built has produced some exceptional adventurers over the last decade. I applied to the program there myself, while I was at the Remore Academy."

"Really?"

"Oh, yeah. Intensive program, independent monster hunting. Getting a slot is really competitive."

"Like joining this guild."

"Exactly! You know, the Gellers train their best prospects down there in Greenstone."

"So I've heard. About those questions—"

"Did you train at the Geller-Remore facility? I haven't heard about any of the graduates reaching gold rank yet."

"It was just after my time. They were just starting some pilot programs at the end of my time in Greenstone. I was actually part of the very first course on aura control."

"Oh, that must have been amazing. Did you get to meet any of the famous Gellers?"

"I did, as it happens."

"You know, most of the Gellers operating out of Vitesse are members of the guild here."

"I was told that, yes."

"Do you think any of them would remember you?" she asked, then leaned forward conspiratorially. "I'm not being strictly professional by telling you this…"

Jason awkwardly cleared his throat.

"…but if they did remember you, that would give a nice bump to your chances of being accepted."

"I think some of them might recall me," Jason said. "Do you need to write that down, or do we just move on to the next question?"

"We cover that at the end, so we can keep going," she said and checked her form again. "I mentioned that we'd do the bits about your connections and associates later, and that's now. I don't see the point of some of these questions, if I'm being honest, but they make us do the whole form. As if anyone would admit to being in a cult or trafficking restricted essences. Anyway, are you currently or have you previously been a member of any magic, adventuring or craft-related guilds, societies or associations?"

"Just the Adventure Society. Standard membership."

"Star rating?"

"That's… less standard."

"Oh, don't worry about that. Having one star at gold rank is more common than people think, and certainly not a disqualifying factor. Burning Violet is exclusive, but it's also really big. You don't have to be some tricky politician or expert ritualist. They need some good head-breakers just like everyone else. Look, so long as you can assure us of your good standing with the Adventure Society, we can leave the details of your ranking to the later interview with the executive. No one is going to make an issue of it until they do the full identity check, before the interview."

"That's probably for the best, thank you. Why don't they check identity until that late in the process?"

"It's part of the protocols. If we catch people too early, they haven't done anything shonky enough, we have to just kick them out. Once they've been properly shady, though, we can take them out back and deal with them ourselves. They call it the 'enough rope' protocol."

"I do have connections within other groups and associations that I should perhaps point out. No memberships with any of them."

"That's fine. It would be a little strange if you reach gold rank without making connections. If you don't mind me asking, if you got to gold rank without ever joining a guild, why now?"

"I have friends in the Burning Violet guild. The rest of my team, in fact. I've wanted to come to Vitesse for a very long time, but circumstances have always conspired to keep me away. Now, I'm finally here."

"Oh, I know a big juicy hole where a story goes when I hear one. You couldn't get here in all the years it took to get to gold rank?"

Jason let out a chuckle.

"I will confess that the story might have a little juice."

"Aah, you're not going to tell me, are you?"

"We do need to avoid you getting yelled at by Lord Bassingthwaite."

"He doesn't yell. He does that 'I'm not mad, I'm disappointed' thing. He's actually a pretty good boss, all said and done. But yeah, we're almost done."

She read directly from the form.

"Have you ever, at any stage, faced reprimand from the Adventure Society, Magic Society, any government authority or church over your association with…"

She looked up from the form.

"Look, have you ever got caught doing bad stuff with bad people?"

"I did get demoted once, at iron rank. There was a corruption enquiry at the Greenstone branch and they blanket demoted everyone at two or three stars at the beginning of the investigation. They bumped people back up afterwards."

"Oh, that doesn't count. Those isolated branches always go dirty and need a clean out every few years. My friend Denise works for the Adventure Society and got roped into a Continental Council. She had to live on this archipelago in the middle of nowhere for half a year."

She looked down at the form.

"Okay, the rest is basically just a list of known associates. It's not a dealbreaker, unless your mum is a rival guild master or in the Red Table or something. Really, this is a chance to list any existing guild members you know, or can get away with saying you kind of know, like the Gellers we were talking about. You said your team were all in the guild, right?"

"I did."

"Well, that's about as close to a guarantee as you'll get, so let's start there. What's your team name?"

Monica was looking down at the form, her pencil poised to write down names. When Jason told her the name of his team, she froze. Then, moving like the first thaw of spring, her head rose to stare at him.

"Did you just say—"

"You sent a gold-ranker to Monica without checking who they were?" a voice boomed through the door that led further into the building. "Do you have any idea who is in the city this week?"

The door was flung open, revealing a harried man with a coal black face and snow-white beard. He was one of the older-looking gold-rankers Jason had seen, and would have passed for being in his sixties on Earth.

"I'm terribly sorry, sir," he said, stepping forward.

Jason rose from his chair to shake the offered hand.

"Not at all," Jason said. "Monica has been excellent. A consummate professional."

The man threw a suspicious glance at Monica, still staring bug-eyed at Jason, before turning back to Jason as well.

"My name is Neiman Bassingthwaite, and I'm the chief membership officer here at the guild. May I ask your name?"

"Jason Asano."

The hand holding Jason's went dead still.

"The, ah, Jason Asano who... did all of the things?"

"Yep."

"Well, it's an honour to meet you, sir. We were wondering if you were going to call by, but were expecting something more of an entourage."

"I was hoping to take care of things quietly."

"Yes, well, that was never going to happen, I'm afraid, through no fault of your own. You and I should have a chat."

45

A SENSE OF RESPONSIBILITY

JASON FOLLOWED NEIMAN BASSINGTHWAITE DEEPER INTO THE GUILD building. It had the feel of an ancient estate, appointed in rich fabrics and old, dark wood. The tapestries, sculptures and decorations held the weight of centuries and would not have looked out of place in a museum.

"I apologise for your reception, Mr Asano. I'm not sure how Monica ended up on membership intake today. I'm sorry."

"She was not what I was expecting."

"Monica excels in her role here, but is best used judiciously. The Burning Violet guild is not prejudicial as to the background of our members, which makes our roster rather eclectic. They come from cultures across the world, some born with every advantage while others fought their way up from nothing. Those of a more aristocratic bent have an expectation of detached professionalism from our staff. Those who are more down-to-earth, however, often find this approach elitist and exclusionary. Monica excels with the guild's more rough-and-tumble adventurers, but should not have been screening unvetted applicants. I'm not sure who assigned her today, but I will look into it. I suspect it may be related to larger issues within the guild."

"Issues?"

"There is a long-standing contention within the guild that is at a dangerous apex right now. I am hoping that no one was foolish enough to try and use you as a game piece in our internal politics. It's through here, Mr Asano."

He opened the door to his office for Jason to enter.

"Can I offer you a cup of tea?"

———

Jason leaned back in the comfortable leather chair, one of several in Neiman's spacious domain. He sipped at a cup of tea with a splash of liquor in it. Neiman, looking more dishevelled by the moment, was on his third cup of liquor with a splash of tea in it.

"If I understand what you're saying," Jason said, "there are two factions within the executive members of the guild. One wants to excise the guild from what they see as the oversized influence of the Remore family. The other faction opposes this, either through loyalty or fear the guild will collapse without them."

Neiman nodded as he took another gulp.

"Yes. And I'm afraid that your membership threatens to be the flashpoint that could set the whole guild ablaze. We are well aware of you and your history, Mr Asano. That the Adventure Society is essentially treating you as a diamond-ranker, and of your close ties to the Remore family. Roland Remore already looms large over those who are against his family's control of the guild, and adding you would likely spell the doom of their intentions."

"So, the anti-Remore faction would see my joining the guild as a second diamond-ranker joining the opposing group."

"Precisely. It's no secret that your team and many other friends of yours are already on the guild's books, and there has long been an expectation that you will join them. Your arrival in Vitesse may have been low-key, but it has not gone unnoticed."

"Are you a part of the group against Remore influence on the guild?"

"I am not. Nor am I an advocate for it."

"But you are asking me to refrain from joining the guild, are you not?"

"Defer, rather than refrain entirely. Until the current tensions have been defused, one way or another. My agenda is to keep the guild from tearing itself apart."

"You think my entry to the guild would cause people to take drastic measures."

"That is exactly my concern. There are enough people on both sides of this that the guild could fragment, and that's just one potential outcome. There's no predicting what a group of powerful adventurers will do if they think their backs are to the wall."

"That's certainly true," Jason agreed.

Neiman gave up the pretence of drinking tea and refilled his cup directly from the liquor bottle. He shook his head before taking a swig.

"The most infuriating part is that only a small fragment of guild leadership has any investment in this. Most of our members don't care who controls the guild, so long as it's run smoothly. The guild is meant to be an asset for them to use, not a problem for them to bother with. If the conflict escalates and the members are forced to choose sides, they'll choose neither, and go find a guild that works the way it's supposed to."

"You paint a bleak picture."

Neiman nodded.

"It's not so dire as I make out—not yet, at least. I'm far from the only one attempting to settle this before it escalates. My fear is that you could be what triggers that escalation."

"Then why am I only hearing about this now? Why didn't anyone tell me about this before I came anywhere near the building?"

"That decision was not mine to make. It was ultimately decided that an active approach on our part would put flame to the kindling. Having you come on your own terms, in your own time, was better. We did ask the Remores not to involve themselves, but we were expecting your team to accompany you. Arriving quietly alone caught us unawares, or I would have attempted to intercept you earlier. Our information is that you are rather fond of a spectacle. As is Gabriel Remore, with whom I know you to be travelling."

"Rufus' dad? He never seemed like that much of a showboat to me."

"I suppose it's a matter of perspective. Not all of us blow up cities everywhere we go."

"I don't—"

Jason cut himself off, leaned forward and placed his teacup on its saucer.

"Lord Bassingthwaite, I hope you'll understand if I don't take everything you say at face value. All I have on this is your word, and we've only just met."

"Of course, Mr Asano. Naturally, you would be an asset to any major guild, but the timing right now is the opposite of ideal. I wouldn't blame you for running for the hills and having nothing to do with any of it."

"That's my inclination, Lord Bassingthwaite. I have more than enough to deal with, without adding guild strife on top of it. Shade, what are Gabriel and Arabelle doing?"

"Shopping," Shade said from Jason's shadow, surprising Neiman.

"Your familiar is here?"

"He is," Jason said.

"He wasn't detected."

"That's kind of his thing, Lord Bassingthwaite."

"Yes, but the guild hall has measures in place to keep track of such things."

"I'm aware."

A look of realisation crossed Neiman's face.

"Miss Callahan is on your team, isn't she?"

"She is. Shade, would you ask if Gabriel and Arabelle would join us?"

"I have already informed them, Mr Asano. They are awaiting your portal."

"Portals won't work in…"

Neiman trailed off as Jason's portal arch opened.

"I didn't realise that you were a portal specialist, Mr Asano."

"More of an enthusiastic amateur, Lord Bassingthwaite."

Arabelle and her husband came through the portal.

"Bassingthwaite," Gabriel said gruffly and headed straight for the liquor cabinet.

"Lord Bassingthwaite," Arabelle said more cordially as she sat down. "I am distressed to hear that internal guild politics have reached such a precarious point."

"It's Dad," Gabriel said from where he was mixing a drink. "He's always treated the guild like it's his own little fiefdom. The Queen would be happy to give him an actual fiefdom, if he just asked, but not Roland Remore. He's too good for aristocracy. Our family works for what we get, as if we weren't a de facto bloody noble house. Our son grew up playing with the crown princess!"

"I suspect it's more than just your father, dear," Arabelle said. "As I married into the family, my perspective is a little more detached. The Remores more involved in administration than adventuring can lose sight of what the guild is actually for. As for your father, he's a diamond-ranker. They have a habit of just assuming that everything around them will move to their will."

Jason sipped at his tea rather than meet Arabelle's eyes as she looked in his direction.

"Have things truly reached the boiling point, Lord Bassingthwaite?" she asked.

"I am afraid so, Mrs Remore."

Jason let out a sigh. "The question," he said, "is what do I do? I have no interest in getting involved, but the fact that I didn't hear any of this until now suggests that someone wanted me involved."

"These tensions have been simmering for a long time," Gabriel said as he walked over and handed his wife a glass before sitting down with his own. "The debate over Remore influence on the guild is older than I am. I would have warned you if I'd realised things had gotten this bad."

"You said that the decision not to warn me wasn't yours," Jason said to Neiman. "Whose was it?"

"The guild master's," Neiman said. "It was not universally endorsed by those of us trying to keep the peace."

"And he's neutral in this?" Jason asked.

"Famously so," Arabelle said. "Perhaps we should talk with him."

"No," Jason said. "I came in here because I wanted to join the guild with my friends, not to get involved with guild politics. I asked you and Gabriel here to give me some context of what I'm dealing with. Now that you've done that, I'm walking away."

"If someone is determined to get you involved, that might not be so easy," Gabriel said.

Jason got to his feet.

"When I'm on Earth, I'll deal with politics like I'm on Earth. While I'm here, I'll deal with things the way they do here."

Neiman also got to his feet.

"Meaning what, exactly?"

"Meaning power rules," Arabelle said. "Jason, things aren't that simple. You know this."

"They are with enough power," he said darkly.

"Jason—"

"No, Arabelle. I won't hear it. I am done with letting people sidetrack me with whatever they have going on. Lord Bassingth-waite, I don't care about your guild politics and, if I'm being honest, I don't care if the whole guild collapses. I'm going to go now, and get back to enjoying my time in your lovely city. Thank you for the tea."

He strode to the still-open portal and vanished through it. Arabelle pinched the bridge of her nose and let out a long, calming breath.

"I need to talk to Danielle," she said, also getting to her feet. Rather than use the portal, she left through the door.

Neiman fell back into his seat and poured himself another drink.

"How bad is this?" he asked.

"Depends," Gabriel said. "Do you know who is trying to bring Jason into this?"

"Best guess? Your father. His thinking is long-term enough that he can accept harming the guild if he thinks he's amputating rotten meat. He's also one of the few people that could genuinely push the guild master."

Jason was sitting alone at a bakery café, a parasol shielding him from the hot sun. In front of him was a pitcher of chilled milk and a large tray of miniature cakes. A dark-skinned man with a bald head took the seat opposite. Jason understood a little better why so many expectations had fallen on Rufus when he looked so much like his diamond-rank grandfather.

"It was you, then," Jason said coldly.

"Yes."

"I think I'm going to cancel our scheduled meeting."

"You're angry."

"Yes."

"That's because you're young."

"Is that what it is to be old? Only seeing tools instead of people?"

"Sometimes," Roland admitted. "If you want to move in our circles, Jason, you'll need to move with consideration rather than emotion."

"I think that emotion has its place. Which is fine, because I have no interest in your diamond-rank clique. And I won't let you ruin my experience here, so leave me out of your guild politics."

"You don't get to declare what you are and are not embroiled in. It's not that simple, as my daughter-in-law has already reminded you."

A portal opened next to their table. The runes around the aperture marked it as belonging to Clive, but it was Humphrey who stepped through. He tossed a pouch on the table in front of Roland, who opened it to find a clutch of guild membership pins.

"Team Biscuit withdraws from the Burning Violet guild," Humphrey told him. "Are you coming, Jason?"

"Let me get these in a box to go," Jason said, then got up and went inside.

"He was looking forward to meeting you, you know," Humphrey said. "Not the great Roland Remore, but the grandfather who means so much to his friend."

"He's not someone who can afford to be sentimental."

"Trust me, Mr Remore: we should all be very thankful he is."

Jason returned from inside.

"Let's go," he said and followed Humphrey through the portal. It closed behind them and Victor Volaire, the Mirror King, was suddenly sitting at the table.

"Are you sure about antagonising him?" Victor asked.

"Asano has a habit of picking up powerful allies like they're fruit at a market stall. I had to make it clear that I wasn't one of them. He doesn't want to share my enemies right now, and I certainly can't afford his."

"Your grandson won't be happy."

"No, but I'm not going to burden his friends with my battles when they have enough of their own. I've made enough mistakes with Rufus already. Too much pressure, too many expectations. He'll understand, in time."

"You know they'll be part of this eventually. Asano has been on a course to clash with the order for a long time. He uses their combat arts."

"They don't care about things like that. They left those skill books scattered over half the planet."

"You know it's more than that."

"What about your son? He's back in Asano's circle now. You want him involved?"

"Of course not."

"There you are, then."

"Did you have to do it this way, though? Couldn't you have just explained things to them?"

"Asano has a sense of responsibility. The Geller boy too; he's a good lad. Once they know, they'll involve themselves. Until then, they deserve a break."

46

TROUBLE ALWAYS KNOWS WHERE TO FIND ME

CASSANDRA MERCER WANDERED OUT OF THE JOBS HALL WITH TWO members of her team after dropping off a completed contract. Jiralla was the team frontliner, standing head and shoulders above the other two women. Henrietta Geller was another adventurer from back home. After bouncing around a few different teams without success, she'd filled a hole in Cassandra's after they lost a member in the last monster surge. Her many summons and familiars made her a versatile addition to the group.

Cassandra wanted nothing more than a hot shower to sluice away the muck of combat. The bog monsters they'd been contracted to hunt reminded her of similar creatures common to the delta back home, although these had been silver rank, rather than iron or bronze. Some crystal wash would have been ideal to flush out the sticky mud that wormed its way into every crevice, but her normal suppliers had been sold out. Apparently, the trade hall had been swept clean a week earlier, while they were still out on the hunt.

She was quiet as the other two chatted away, her mind elsewhere. She knew that they'd arrived in Vitesse, and maybe that was why she'd picked the contract she had. Normally, the team would avoid a mission that meant trudging through bog mud for days on end, although it did come with a nice bonus. No one else wanted the mission either, so the jobs hall had added some nice incentives.

She hadn't heard much since their arrival. A few people discussing the return of Team Biscuit to Vitesse. Their involvement in some city in the middle of nowhere being wiped off the map. They hadn't sought her out, and maybe they weren't going to. Perhaps she was a memory they had no interest in revisiting.

It was just as she was resolving to put them out of her head when she spotted him. He ambled across the park-like grounds of the campus as if he'd stepped right out of her memories. The ridiculous shirt. Gazing around like a tourist as he munched on a meat wrap, dripping sauce onto the grass. He ambled towards them like someone without a care in the world.

Her friends saw that she'd stopped walking and followed her gaze.

"Who's that?" Jiralla asked.

"Her ex," said Henrietta.

"That Neil guy she's always talking about?"

"Not always," Cassandra said. "And no. This was from before that."

"Jason Asano," Henrietta said.

"You know him, Henri?"

"He's on my brother's team. Been away a long time, though. Haven't seen him in twenty years."

"Isn't that Neil guy on your brother's team as well?"

"Yep."

"Cassie, you should really consider expanding your dating pool. Are you going to go for Henri's brother next?"

"I'll catch up with you later," Cassandra said, then set off to intercept Jason. He threw a wave in Henrietta's direction and she returned it before leading Jiralla firmly away.

Cassandra arrived in front of Jason. He looked different, yet the same. The eyes sparkling with amusement. The beard that failed to hide his jutting chin as well as he thought it did. His features were sharper and less boyish. He had the smooth, almost artificially perfect skin that came with high rank.

"Hey, Cassie."

"Hello, Jason."

"I thought we could catch up. If you would like."

"How did you find me?"

"Your aura. The city isn't that big."

"Yes, it is."

"I suppose. They get a lot bigger, where I come from."

"You really spread your perception across the city without people noticing?"

"I'm sure a few did, but I've gotten pretty good at hiding it. Gold-rank tricks."

It was more than just a gold-rank trick and they both knew it.

"You can't be that far from gold yourself, right?"

It irked her a little that the man who hadn't even believed in magic when she hit bronze rank had beaten her to gold. Not as much as Henri, who had been grumbling for months about being eclipsed by her little brother.

"It's not easy, getting your head around how high-rank advancement works," she said. "Or maybe it is, for you. Your whole team got there, right?"

"Yeah," Jason said. "We all had to find our own way, though. I'm sure you'll find yours."

They started walking, Jason falling into place beside her.

"Is Boko really gone?" she asked.

"It is," he said, stashing his food in his storage space.

"I heard some things, but no one seems clear on exactly what happened. Your team was there, though, right?"

"Yeah."

"You always did have a knack for winding up in the middle of things."

"I'd rather not, sometimes, believe me."

"So, what did happen?"

"The usual. Bad people trying to do bad things. Innocent people getting caught in the middle. Most of the population got out alive, but more than I'd like did not."

"A messenger army and a destroyed city. That's 'the usual' for you, is it?"

It took him a long moment to answer. She could see a shift in his body language, as if something was weighing him down.

"I don't think what's usual matters," he said, the lightness in his tone now absent. "I had a bad day yesterday. I finally went to join a guild—something I've been looking forward to for a long time. The whole experience went very unpleasantly, and it got me thinking about being an adventurer. It's something that's been important to me, over the years, more so as time goes on. But what happened yesterday made me realise that my experience isn't what other adventurers go through."

"How so?"

"Taking contracts. Using them to build a track record and get better contracts. Joining a guild, building a team and travelling around with them."

"You have a team."

"Whose defining experience with me is waiting years at a time for me to come back. Wondering if I'm even still alive. After yesterday, I started thinking about how different my experiences are from other adventurers', and it got me wondering if I'm really one of them. I haven't really done a lot of what normal adventurers do since Greenstone. There's always some mad crisis pushing me to the edge. Taking me away from my team and never letting me get back to basics. The last few months, I felt like I was finally living the adventuring life everyone else gets to, and then Boko happened. Reminded me that I'm not like everyone else. Then, yesterday brought home the fact that if I try to be like other adventurers, it's just a performance. Playing pretend."

"Jason, I've heard the stories about you. If even a fraction of them are true, you live a life that other adventurers long for. Walking with kings and gods. Wielding power most only dream of."

Jason shook his head.

"Those things aren't what matter. What matters is knowing that my actions have kept someone safe. Shielded them from something that would have ripped their life apart. But you know that feeling. Every good adventurer does. And that's when I realised that I really am an adventurer. It's not about having stories told about you, and it's not about the milestones that regular adventurers have, but I missed. My first night in this world, Rufus Remore told me what an adventurer was, and I've realised all over again that he was right. Strip away everything else, and an adventurer is someone who puts themselves between the bad things and those who need protection from them. Everything else is just embellishment or a distraction."

He flashed a smile, heavy, but satisfied.

"As long as we do that," he said, "we're adventurers. I think that maybe I'm a bit thick, since everyone else seems to realise that's obvious. I second-guess myself too much, I suppose."

Cassandra gave him a side glance as they walked.

"I remember that night we met," she said. "You seemed so free, so unburdened. You really aren't the person I knew, are you?"

He flashed the impish grin she remembered, the impudent boyishness shining through.

"Oh, he's still in there," he said. "All said and done, I'm kind of happy that yesterday didn't work out. It helped me with the ongoing process of accepting who I am, and letting go of who I'm not. The same as everyone else, I guess."

"I've been struggling with that as well. Is that the secret to reaching gold rank?"

"Part of it, sure."

"I don't think I'm doing so well in that regard. I have trouble moving on from old history."

"Neil is an idiot."

"Neil is an idiot," she agreed. "But he saw it in me. That there are things I couldn't let go of."

Jason nodded.

"He shouldn't have handled things the way he did. He should have talked things through, instead of deciding for both of you and running away. He was so scared of losing you that he gave you up first. Like an idiot."

"He wanted me to meet you. To see how different you were. As if that would somehow fix everything."

"Which was extra foolish. I'm much sexier now, so that definitely won't cure you from pining for my masculine embrace."

She looked at him from under raised eyebrows.

"You haven't completely changed, then."

He flashed another grin. "I told you that."

"You're still an idiot."

"Hey, I thought we were talking about Neil."

"You're both idiots. It's Nik I feel sorry for, growing up with you two as influences."

"He wants to see you, if you don't mind. He feels bad about his part in convincing Neil to end things."

"That's Neil's fault for taking romantic advice from a three-year-old. I would love to see Nik again."

"And Neil?"

"No. He hurt me, Jason. Even if he thought he was doing the right thing, he wasn't really considering me. He hid his feelings instead of sharing them. He decided everything for himself and ran away before I had a chance to get my head around any of it."

They walked in silence for a while. They had no destination, but the sprawling gardens of the Adventure Society campus gave them no shortage of places to wander.

"Could you tell me about what you've been doing since Greenstone?" Cassandra asked. "Maybe it will help me to, I don't know, put down some old baggage."

"Only if you tell me about what you've been doing since Greenstone as well."

"I've just been doing normal adventurer things. Nothing like what you've done."

"Exactly," Jason told her.

"...the wrong spell, and the hydra exploded. And I mean exploded, chunks flying everywhere. Being so big, we were drenched in its blood and guts. Because it was only bronze rank, it didn't burn us, but it dissolved all our clothes away."

Jason let out a laugh, then sipped from his glass. He'd pulled out some of his blended juices from Greenstone, giving Cassandra a taste of home.

"You know, I've had my clothes blasted off a time or three as well. I assume you had more to change into."

"Yes, but it was right at that moment that the reinforcements arrived. And you know which church they ended up getting them from?"

"Lust?"

"Wouldn't that have been nice? No, they were from the Church of Chastity!"

Jason snorted juice out of his nose, then started coughing.

"How did that go?" he asked after recovering.

"Oh, about as well as you'd expect. Jiralla was the only one of us still decent, because of her heavy plate armour, but she kept complaining about it pinching and started stripping off. Right in front of the priest!"

"You're kidding."

"The woman has no shame."

Cassandra noticed Nik sitting on a park bench and nibbling nervously on a biscuit. She stopped walking and Jason did the same. They turned to look at each other.

"So," she said. "I suppose this is it."

"Yeah," Jason said. "I don't know if this will help you find some closure, or come to terms with anything from the past, but I had a nice afternoon. It was good seeing you again, Cass."

"You too, Jason. Tell Neil… I don't know. That if I want to see him, I'll come find him. Tell him not to look for me himself."

Jason nodded.

"We live long lives, Cassandra. Too long to hold on to every mistake, but also too long to hold on to every person. Only you can decide if you want to forgive Neil, or forget him."

She bowed her head.

"It feels like if I agree to see him now, I'll be acknowledging that he was right. That he was right to hurt me that way."

Jason nodded.

"As I said, life is long. You don't have to decide anything now, just because we happen to be in town. We'll cross paths again."

Jason watched the flowering towers of Vitesse shrink away as the cloud ship moved further into Estercost. He could sense his companions in various places around the vessel, including Neil drowning his sorrows at the bar. After one last glance at Vitesse, Jason opened a portal arch to his soul realm and stepped through. He arrived in the forest city of Arbour.

The city remained largely uninhabited. Like Jason himself, the soul within his soul that comprised the city was still finding its way. When it first formed, the city had been a homogeneous place, basically flatland filled with sequoias and treehouses. There were now hills and valleys, rivers with castles set on grand bridges and gorges where buildings clung to the walls, covered in ivy.

Much of the city still held its original disposition, however, and Jason arrived in one of these areas. It housed the research centre for Carlos, and the accommodation for his test subjects. Jason's power suppressed the magical influence that had brainwashed them, but only Carlos could free them from it entirely. The time was approaching for Sophie's mother to go through the process, which was still being refined.

"Tomorrow," Carlos said without preamble as Jason walked into his study. "We'll be ready tomorrow."

"You're the man setting the schedule," Jason told him. "Better to do it right than fast."

"Better right than fast," Carlos echoed. "Looking into that sword they attacked you with only slowed me down a little."

Carlos had spent some time with the investigation team in Greenstone that was studying the attack on Boko. They were focused on Jason's attacker, who had not been a messenger but wielded unusual equipment. He had rejoined Jason and his companions recently via portal travel.

"That sword was definitely based on the weapons we were developing at the start of the Messenger War," Carlos said. "We gave up on them back then because they weren't cost-efficient. The idea was to create weapons that would make less combat-oriented silver-rankers more of an opponent to a messenger. The results were never worth the outlay, though, so we moved on. It seems that someone continued that work after we abandoned it, as that sword was made recently. It also showed some signs of having been advanced from what we created, but the improvements were marginal. Not enough to pick up the project again."

"Someone obviously felt differently about that."

"Yes," Carlos said. "But unless you're going to pull on that thread yourself, it's for the Adventure Society to investigate. I've been away from my work here long enough."

"I'm happy to leave it to them. We have enough going on without chasing after something others are happy to pursue themselves."

"On that, I agree. If possible, I'd like to get all the Order of Redeeming Light members treated before heading for Earth. I'm hoping to use my time there to explore the medical knowledge of your world, and its potential applications for my work. How long do you think we have before heading to your home universe?"

"I think that depends on how scattered the people from Earth are, and how many even want to go back. I'm not going to force anyone who wants to stay. We'll get more information on them in Cyrion, and go from there. Once we've rounded people up, it's back to Rimaros to finally complete the bridge between worlds. Clive thinks that will be relatively quick. I imagine that we're looking at heading to Earth in weeks, rather than months, assuming that nothing goes wrong."

"You're just going to say that out loud? Aren't you asking for trouble?"

"Trouble always knows where to find me," Jason told him with a malevolent grin. "And it knows what it gets when it does."

47

TACTICAL PLAYBOOK

SPRINGCLAW GORILLAS WERE WEAK, AS GOLD-RANK MONSTERS WENT, BUT they were smart and spawned in large herds. When one such herd had hidden away in the mountains, the first group of adventurers sent after them had not done well. After a week of fending off guerilla tactics from the gorillas, they had only a handful of kills and a lot of frustration.

Resupplying in a large town at the base of the mountain range, the adventurers encountered Jason and his team doing the same. Humphrey offered to take the contract off their hands, without taking the contract rewards. The adventurers were suspicious until they discovered they were dealing with Team Biscuit, looking to rebuild their tactical playbook after ranking up to gold.

The team had spent limited time together over the last few years as they followed their individual pathways to gold rank. They needed to revise the strategies they had developed and honed over more than a decade, along with reintegrating Jason into the team dynamic. They had been working on it during their travels, but Humphrey was satisfied with nothing less than perfection. And once perfection was reached, they could train even harder to maintain it.

Each team member had their own new tricks, with even basic abilities growing ostentatiously powerful at gold rank. Humphrey's Mighty Strength power, arguably the most common power in the adventuring world, could now expand his size. The mana cost became more exorbitant the larger he grew, but it allowed him to physically confront the often enormous gold-rank monsters.

Sophie's speed left even a fully buffed Jason in the dust, and her aura let her walk through a town, healing the sick like a saint. Neil's summon was a trump card against hostile magic, drawing it in like a black hole before transforming into something that countered all it had absorbed. Belinda was the right answer to every question, whether it was controlling enemies, empowering allies or using items to transform into a warrior or powerful magician.

Clive remained both the weakest individual combatant, and most powerful damage dealer. Zara could match him over wide area, and Jason could over time, but when it came to hurting one thing *now*, neither came close. His previous spikes of destructive output now came much closer together, with catastrophic secondary effects.

Clive also had several powerful buffs that enhanced Humphrey and Sophie especially. One delivered powerful retribution effects to anyone who attacked them, while the other surrounded them with consumable runes whose effects were varied and random, but always potent. Neil's means to enhance the team had likewise reached a new level.

Zara's power progression was somewhat unusual in that her powers grew smaller, rather than bigger. Her area attacks had always been fitting for her former title of Hurricane Princess, being as powerful as they were imprecise. She now had options that would concentrate the power of a storm to the size of a fist, tearing through enemies like a chainsaw through custard.

Humphrey's role in most of their tactics was to be the buff-laden centrepiece of the team. This usually left him as some combination of initiator, primary weapon, distraction and bait. Clive and Neil used Onslow's shell as a secure battle platform while the rest of the team were mobile and flexible, in accordance with the team's needs and current strategy.

The springclaw gorillas were cunning opponents, not just pouring out of their hidden mountain lair in a wave. They went for merchant caravans and brief hit-and-retreat raids, scouting out targets and drawing off defenders with feint attacks. They demonstrated a clear recognition of the threat posed by adventurers, even before encountering them. This was a hallmark of intelligent monsters who came into being with knowledge already imprinted on their minds.

Rather than charge into the mountains like the last team of adventurers had, Humphrey decided to make use of Belinda. She had several abilities that let her use specialised item sets to awaken temporary powers, usually taking on warrior or spellcaster roles. Her Instant Adept power could make her a swift striker or powerful archer, but also take on utility powers as well. With equipment suited to a wilderness scout, she awakened a suite of useful tracking abilities.

Humphrey didn't allow the team to make use of their various flight options, both for the training value and to escape easy detection. The gorillas would spot them easily if they flew around, and were stealthy enough to avoid distant observers. Like many ambush predators and high-intellect monsters, they could suppress their auras until even Jason would have trouble sensing them.

The previous team had taken a flight-and-scan approach to poor effect. Most of the time, they had found nothing, only to be ambushed on getting complacent and letting down their guard. This was the source of their few kills, but they hadn't come close to finding the main lair.

The team entered the mountains on foot, relying on Belinda's temporary powers. The terrain was inhospitable, with dense forest growth and steep inclines. The sharp cliffs and hidden crevasses made the terrain dangerous, not from a potential fall but from the constant threat of ambush. Springclaw gorillas also came in less aggressive natural variants, rather than monsters, and such terrain was home territory for them.

Humphrey had his team make their way on foot. Navigating forests and scaling cliffs was well within the capability of their gold-rank attributes, but they needed the skill and experience to make use of them.

"Jason," Humphrey said, his voice a warning.

"Yes?" Jason asked innocently.

"Your climbing skills seemed to have improved considerably, all of a sudden."

"That's because of your excellent leadership."

"So, you didn't shadow jump to that last city and buy a climbing skill book?"

"Absolutely not. You just lost track of me because of my inherent stealth."

"Did you forget that you've given the whole party access to the tactical map? The one with our locations on it?"

"I, uh, did forget about that, yes."

The mountain pass was beautiful and green in the summer, spanning out ahead of Jason and his team. The ground was a mess of thick scrub and rocks dotting the landscape. A narrow river spilled down in their direction, with a disused and overgrown road running alongside it.

"You said these things are smart, right?" Jason asked.

"I did," Clive said.

"Are we talking 'dog that knows how to open the bathroom door' smart or 'get a bunch of ghillie suits and bait us into a trap' smart?"

"That depends," Clive said. "What's a ghillie suit?"

"A non-magical disguise. The kind you wear when you're gearing up to kill some folk."

"Definitely that one," Clive said. "You think they're out there?"

"They're out there," Belinda said. "This is home territory for them. They'll have realised that we're tracking them by now, and I think the last team showed them that small ambushes won't stop adventurers. They need an environment where they still have a chance of getting the drop on us, but will let them bring their numbers to bear."

"With us just standing here talking," Neil said, "they probably know we know they're there."

"And that we know they know we know they know," Belinda added.

"Don't start," Humphrey said. "What do you think, a double scoop slam?"

"They probably won't bite unless we wander in looking oblivious," Sophie said.

"Then that's what we do," Humphrey said. "Lindy, do you want to go backline or be in the mix?"

"Backline," she said. "I'll help Zara and Clive blanket bomb the zone."

"Zara, cover the others as they withdraw when it kicks off."

"On it," she confirmed.

"Jason, I want you trimming the edges. They're smart, so there'll be runners once things go badly for them. Mop up most of them, but put a tracker on a couple and let them run. We can trace them back to their lair."

"Will do."

"You realise they might not even be out there," Neil said. "Unless someone is sensing something I'm not."

"You're sensing it," Jason told him. "You're just not paying attention."

"To what?" Neil asked.

"You're focusing on the gorillas," Jason said. "Look for the auras of everything else. The animals out there that haven't run already are skittish and hiding."

"And stop suppressing your sense of smell," Belinda added. "Your mundane senses are incredibly sharp at gold rank."

"Oh, I'm well aware of that," Neil said. "I took one sniff of a city and choked off my sense of smell almost entirely. I would have shut it off entirely, if that didn't make food taste bland."

"Your priorities might be a little off kilter," Zara suggested.

"No, I'm happy with where they're at," Neil told her.

"Enough chatter," Humphrey said. "Stash, you ready?"

The hill mouse in Humphrey's pocket made an adorable 'chu' sound.

"Alright," Humphrey said. "Move forward, and try to look oblivious."

"But they definitely know we know," Neil said as the group moved forward. "Why the pretence?"

"It's 'know we know they know' chicken," Jason said. "Whoever pretends to be surprised best wins."

"I'm pretty sure whoever kills everyone on the other team wins," Sophie said.

"And I'm pretty sure I said enough chatter," Humphrey reminded them.

"You always do," Sophie told him. "It's adorable that you still try."

The gorillas waited until the team had well and truly walked into the middle of them before they triggered the ambush. Jason was impressed to see they were wearing something like ghillie suits, the monsters seeming to erupt from the landscape. They leapt at the party, who sprang into action.

Jason and Sophie both vanished, Sophie in a blur and Jason into the shadow of a rock. Stash leapt from Humphrey's clothes, transforming into some creature Jason didn't recognise. It was something between a bird and a lizard, or perhaps one and a half of a bird and lizard. It had three heads, three wings and three arms that dangled down from a central body. Existing in flagrant disregard of both aerodynamics and biology, it looked like it should get tangled in itself, fall to the ground and beg to be put out of its misery. Instead, it flitted like a hummingbird, snatching up Neil, Clive and Belinda before taking to the sky. Zara shot up next to Stash's monster form on a blast of wind.

Humphrey was left behind, becoming the last target standing for the leaping monsters. Springclaw gorillas were more agile than their Earth counterparts, as appropriate for their rank. They were named for their signature leap attacks and the sharp claws delivering anticoagulant venom. Their favourite tactic was to deliver rapid strikes and then back off, letting their enemies bleed to death.

The gorillas had learned that their preferred tactic was a poor one against adventurers. The presence of healers and potions made counting on bleed afflictions an unreliable strategy, but they were smart enough to devise a counter. Much of the group turned from Humphrey as the easy target and focused on the withdrawing backliners. They didn't know which one was the healer, but quickly guessed it was one of those trying to escape.

Using their powerful leaps, the gorillas launched into the air at Stash. What they met was a descending wall of wind and water, dropping on them like a concrete slab. It smashed them back down, right on top of Humphrey and the gorillas he was fighting. At the last moment, Humphrey teleported away, leaving the monsters to crash into one another.

What was left was a mess of confused gorillas, bodies tumbling and limbs tangling together as Zara's water bomb washed over them. The ambush had gone very wrong very quickly, with almost a hundred monsters scattered and disoriented. They recovered quickly, however, getting up and looking around for their targets. A handful of gorillas grunted out orders.

The moment the monsters showed signs of reorganising, Sophie reappeared. Dashing through the monsters, she left behind afterimages, seemingly in four places at once. The gorillas resumed their leap attacks at the afterimages, all of which imploded. They turned into points of dimensional suction force, the aggressive jumps from the gorillas again turning into helpless tumbling.

The areas around the imploded afterimages were covered with disorienting illusions, triggering vertigo in the monsters as they attempted to recover. Wind blades shot out from the suction points still yanking gorillas off their feet.

While this was going on, Clive had called out Onslow, the flying rune tortoise expanding his shell to let Clive, Belinda and Neil inside.

"Second scoop," Humphrey said through voice chat.

Belinda, peering out from the edge of the shell, looked to the ground below. The four suction points formed a square, and she conjured a force tether right in the middle. A crystal rod rose from the ground and a force beam shot out, connecting with every gorilla in the area.

The way Belinda's Force Tether power worked was to drag every tethered creature towards it. It inflicted little damage to those that allowed themselves to be dragged, inflicting escalating damage to those that resisted. In this instance, the suction points from Sophie's mirage power did the resisting for them, yanking the gorillas away from the tether rod. The gorillas were physically powerful enough to resist both effects, but the disorienting illusion from Sophie's power made it hard to get their feet under them.

Slowly but surely, Belinda's force tether won out as Sophie's power faded. The gorillas were yanked into a pile as the screech of a descending missile filled the air. Humphrey landed right on top of the force tether, destroying it immediately. This triggered the detonation effect of the tether on top of the explosion of Humphrey's Dive Bomb power. Neil's Burst Shield power snapped into place right before Humphrey landed, absorbing the damage from the tether blast on Humphrey and detonating itself, inflicting a third blast on the beleaguered monsters.

After the execution of the double scoop slam, the monsters were scattered, hurt and confused. They scrambled to even understand what was happening, let alone mount a counterattack. Clive and Zara blanketed the area with destructive magic, Belinda alternately reducing their cooldowns and copying their powers. The gorillas that had been furthest from the centre saw the battle was lost and moved to escape rather than join their fellows. They bolted for the surrounding forests and cliffs, their loping runs punctuated by huge leaps.

As they fled, shadowy arms jutted from the shadows of the rocky landscape, stabbing at them with red and black daggers. The damage seemed negligible, so they ignored the minor wounds and continued their flight. Jason, unnoticed as his cloak pulled shadows around him, softly incanted his Castigate spell. The Mark of Sin it inflicted would let him track them, should any of them survive the other afflictions his shadow arms had delivered.

Jason and Humphrey cleaned up the handful of monsters that survived Zara and Clive's indiscriminate blasting. Without any kind of healing, the monsters that fled fell to Jason's afflictions. He could sense the ones he had marked converging on what was presumably their lair. After looting the dead monsters, the team tracked them down, mopping up what was left of the herd. Only a handful of monsters had been left to guard the cave system they had made a home of, against other monsters and magical beasts.

"That was clean," Humphrey said in the aftermath. "I think we're starting to get our cohesion back. Let's not get complacent, though."

Jason slapped Neil companionably on the back.

"Mate, I saw the timing of that shield you dropped on Humpy. That was immaculate."

Neil gave Jason a suspicious look, waiting for a backbiting comment that never came. Jason had moved on, slinging an arm around Clive's shoulder.

The team looted the monsters and recovered what they could of what the gorillas had taken from raiding towns and caravans. They then portalled back to the town where they'd left the cloud ship. The adventurers whose job they'd taken over said they would go check the battle site before reporting the contract completed. Humphrey gave them directions and left them to it. Jason and his companions returned to the cloud ship and moved on.

48
I DON'T BLOW UP CITIES ON PURPOSE

CYRION WAS THE CAPITAL OF ESTERCOST, AND ENCOMPASSED FAR MORE than the urban centre at its heart. A series of concentric walls ringed the city proper, with vast spans of agricultural land in between. Home to some of the most magical and valuable growing land on the planet, it was accordingly under impressive protection.

The messengers had, to date, made no attempts to invade Cyrion, focusing their efforts elsewhere. In the days before the messengers invaded Pallimustus, the Builder had not been so reticent. His cult had committed an unprecedented force to attacking the city, the remnants of which still lay beyond the outermost wall.

The Builder's world engineer golems rivalled any diamond-rank monster for size. Almost two decades after their demise, their toppled and overgrown forms looked more like hills than engines of war.

Jason and his friends looked down on the fallen golems from an observation lounge on the underside of the cloud ship. The hull was completely transparent from the inside, allowing unrestricted views of the landscape. It did lead to an odd effect where the furniture seemed to be floating in the air.

"We managed to stop those things from activating in the Reaper's astral space," Neil said. "I can't imagine actually fighting them."

"We were bronze rank," Humphrey pointed out. "It would be different now."

"Not that different," Clive said. "These golems are realms beyond anything we can create on this world. Actual diamond-rank constructs. Even the diamond-rankers on our side wouldn't have been enough without the city defences."

"He's right," Danielle said. "In the entire history of Cyrion, the battle that left those things here was the only instance of even the outer wall being breached. Those golems made it past three layers of defence."

"Why did they leave them there instead of clearing them away?" Neil asked. "Surely the salvage would be worthwhile, being cosmic super golems."

"Even dormant, they were dangerous to approach," Danielle said. "They were sealed off and left behind while the city focused on repairing the walls, in case the messengers tried to take advantage of the damage. Those inside the walls were cleared out, but the ones outside were left where they fell. They were sealed off, to keep the bold and curious from danger. Only years later were the areas around them unsealed and swept for lingering dangers."

"I hope they got it all out before leaving them to grow over," Neil said.

"They did," Belinda said. "Clive and I had a discreet poke around a couple of years ago. Got some good base material if we ever want to knock out some constructs of our own, but all the fun stuff was gone."

Jason looked through the hull in the direction of the wall.

"We're approaching the defence perimeter," he said. "There's a city official on his way here in a small vessel. Come on, Miguel."

Miguel Ladiv and the bartender, Jamar, were standing on the translucent floor, wobbling as if they had vertigo.

"What?" Miguel asked, looking up. "Right, sorry."

He headed for Jason with the delicate walk of someone afraid the ice would crack under their feet.

"You're not going to fall through, Miguel," Jason told him.

"Uh-huh," Miguel said, and kept going as he was.

Even discounting the agricultural sectors, Cyrion was the largest city in the world. Even flying over it, it stretched out to the horizon in every direction. Few cities on Pallimustus had the sheer scope of Earth's major cities, but from the air, Cyrion looked like Tokyo by way of the Emerald

City of Oz. Grand towers shone in the sun. Massive lakes and whole forests fell within the urban sprawl. The sky was filled with air traffic, from small personal vehicles to massive airships the size of Jason's and larger.

Shade was piloting the airship, but a city official was standing next to him on the bridge, guiding him along a very precise path. Even cloud ships were common enough in the city that it was fully prepared to accommodate them. They flew to one of the lakes where they were given space to convert the ship into a floating cloud palace.

Jason's plans for his time in Cyrion didn't involve sightseeing, the way they had in Vitesse. It was time to get serious about the return to Earth. During their travels, Jason had been studying more than a decade of work from Clive on restoring the bridge between Pallimustus and Earth. Once the expatriate Earthlings were collected, they would be ready to head for Rimaros and the final stage.

In preparation for collecting the scattered Earth refugees, Jason had been working on his control over the System. The plan was to send out a message that would only reach the Earthlings, calling them back to Cyrion. They had all started there, and most remained, making it the logical gathering spot.

For the first few days in Cyrion, Jason holed himself up in his cloud palace on the lake. Meditating for hours on end, he refined his control over the System with Li Li Mei as a test subject. Messaging her as an Earthling proved much harder than targeting her as a specific individual. It took several days of practise before he was ready to take things wider, and those days were mercifully peaceful. Cyrion was one of the few places where a cloud ship full of gold-rankers could arrive without it being a major event.

While Jason was practising, his team were hunting Earthlings by more conventional means. Danielle went to the Geller compound in the city where she herself had gathered them following their arrival. That had been for their protection, given that dozens of outworlders make an enticing study opportunity. Both legitimate and less ethical researchers were eager to get their hands on such a large sample.

Once it was clear that Jason wouldn't be coming to handle them, the outworlders had to be allowed out of protective custody. Many had the misfortune of discovering why they'd been in it in the first place, winding up on the table of some sketchy researcher. The Adventure Society ended up retrieving many of them, many traumatised and some dead.

That was the thread Humphrey pulled on, looking into the Earth people through Adventure Society records. As the rescued ended up in the hands of the Healer's church, Neil pursued that avenue. Estella took the approach of looking for rumours and stories in the city. Many were tragedies, tales of exploitation and experimentation. Most, however, were almost startlingly mundane. The Earthlings were mid-rank core-users in a large city, and met the same fate as locals in that position: being hired by noble houses.

Being a guard for a noble house was a role that became increasingly odd the more prominent the family. The most prominent members of such houses were usually adventurers, whether active, retired or semi-retired. Anyone capable enough to protect such people were too powerful and important in their own right to be a servant.

Most house guards were failed adventurers, and were treated as such. They served as thugs for family interests or security for family assets. The more capable amongst them were assigned to protect house scions yet to gain their essences, or low-ranking family members who never had adventurer training. The most important role of a family's private guard was to simply exist. Any aristocratic house lacking a staff of essence-users would find its status within society in jeopardy.

Many of the Earth essence-users met the exact criteria for a house guard, being trained in combat but having advanced through monster cores. Their unusual backstory proved exotic enough that they were able to command high salaries from noble houses that valued such things.

By the time Jason was ready to send out a call through the System, his companions had already built a solid list of Earth expatriates. If Jason's message didn't work out, they would still be able to collect a lot of people. It was the ones who had gone roaming, like Li Li Mei, who would be the problem. Without a way to call them back, they would have to be abandoned, at least for the immediacy. Jason had no intention of chasing down trails a decade or more old, hunting them one by one.

Jason sent out his message, and his diligence in preparing for it seemed to pay off. It did appear to target the Earthlings and no one else. The people who answered the call were all from Earth, at least at first, and there were no reports of anyone else getting strange messages about another world.

Those enthusiastic to return home were the first to respond, arriving at Jason's cloud palace as directed. Others were uncertain about giving up their new lives, seeing little value in what they'd left behind almost two decades ago. For many, that was half of their lives or more.

Some were on the fence, heading to Jason's cloud palace in search of others like them. They wanted to discuss with other Earthlings whether they should go back. They also had stories of those who had no interest in going back, to the point of fearing they would be forced to. It prompted Jason to send out a second message, telling all who wanted to stay that they were free to.

Whether they wanted to return to Earth or not, many came to cloud palace wanting to meet Jason and his famous companions. Especially amongst those serving major families, many had heard of Jason, Team Biscuit and their exploits.

After the first day, a different kind of problem occurred. People who had never been to Earth were turning up, claiming they had. Some were laughably transparent fakes, trying to escape debts or other problems. Others were better prepared, often would-be spies for various organisations, legitimate and otherwise.

Jason and Farrah ended up screening people. As even an outworlder aura signature could be faked, their screening process had to be more creative.

"Best *Mad Max* movie?" Farrah asked.

"*Fury Road*," the man in front of her said.

"Incorrect."

"What do you mean, incorrect?"

"The correct answer is *Beyond Thunderdome*."

"The one with Tina Turner? She was terrible in that movie!"

Jason rushed to restrain Farrah, who was jabbing a finger at the man as she yelled at him.

"You shut your filthy mouth! You're never getting back to Earth, you hear me? The planet's better off without you!"

Jason was certain that many of the genuine humans had been paid handsomely by different interests for a variety of tasks. That was not a disqualifying factor for those genuinely from Earth, but they did get a warning as to what would happen if they caused trouble.

The next problem was harder to deal with than people clearly not from Earth attempting to synopsise the *Police Academy* films.

"Jason, none of these people were alive when those movies were released," Farrah pointed out. "Even the people from Earth can't tell you what happened in them."

"Exactly. Anyone who gives it a go is clearly not from Earth."

People from Earth now working for the noble houses turned out to be the largest issue. If the guards were happy to stay, that was fine. Many had built good lives in the service of the aristocracy. The nobility had proven unwilling, however, to release those who did want to go back to Earth. It wasn't every house, but enough to be a problem, the nobles leaning on local laws to keep their people where they were.

Cyrion's laws were very much built to favour the aristocratic families, and house guards were technically a form of indentured servitude. Very well-paid servitude, but if the noble houses wanted to make an issue of it, they held all the power. Many of those houses were using that power to prevent their guards from leaving.

It didn't take a lot of investigation to confirm Jason's immediate assumptions. None of the Earth people were so valuable that the houses had a real need of them. The value they held was that Jason wanted them, and that was an advantage the nobles could leverage.

***

"I don't blow up cities on purpose," Jason muttered to himself. "I don't blow up cities on purpose."

It was Jason's eleventh day in Cyrion, and the fourth day of meetings with representatives of the noble houses. Ignoring his instincts to do something drastic, Jason had chosen a diplomatic approach. He had set up meetings with the aristocratic families, their chosen representatives being a message in and of themselves. An important family member being present was a signal of respect, while a bureaucratic functionary was a slight to Jason and his team.

Some of the meetings were one to one, while others brought all the representatives together. Jason handled the talks himself, for the most part, drawing on the lessons in diplomacy and etiquette he had received from Danielle. She was with him, occasionally taking the forward position, but mostly leaving it to him.

By the fourth day, however, Jason's patience was dangerously thin. These families were opportunists, using legal privilege and what amounted to slave laws to get what they could out of him. There didn't even seem to be something specific they were after; they had found a lever to pull and saw no reason not to pull it. In return for releasing the guards they were asking for anything from Team Biscuit's services in their family's interests to insider information from Clive's Magic Research Association.

Seeing Jason teetering on the edge of doing something very true to his nature, Danielle ended the meetings for the day and led Jason out. The venue was Jason's cloud palace, so they went further in while avatars led the representatives out.

"You're doing very well," she said. "In terms of keeping your temperament, at least."

"These talks are going nowhere in a circle."

"Because you've been unwilling to make any concessions. If you want them to give something up, you need to as well."

"Their stance is immoral."

"They don't care. Or even share your opinion. In the culture of Cyrion high society, this is all normal."

"I'm entirely happy to respect someone's culture, so long as that culture is at least nominally worthy of respect. I can accept people having different values to me, but there has to be a line. Using what amount to slave laws to trade people like chips in a card game is over that line for me."

"Then you are at an impasse."

"Not necessarily."

"Meaning?" she asked, her voice thick with suspicion.

"I realised from the beginning that these people were simply being opportunistic. They saw that I valued something they had more than they did, and could use the circumstances here in Cyrion to take advantage. While we've spent four days running around in circles, I've been preparing something that could possibly recontextualise those circumstances."

"Jason, what did you do?"

"Nothing. Yet. I wasn't even sure I could make it work. Figuring out how to target messages to the people from Earth was good practise, though. I've been building on that to do something a little more widespread."

"Please tell me you aren't going to try and blow up Cyrion."

"Nothing like that."

"Then what?"

"Well, I started by getting a list of all the countries and city-states that have indentured servitude laws…"

49

FOLLOWING THROUGH ON BAD IDEAS

HILS JARAMARIS WAS NOT A HAPPY MAN. HE HAD BEEN HAPPY, ENJOYING his role as the Storm Kingdom's ambassador to Estercost. The nations were rivals, but friendly ones, their distance leaving them with few reasons for conflict. This meant that Hils, for the most part, was a glorified mailman for diplomatic messages. This suited him just fine, allowing him to pursue his alchemy far from domestic Storm Kingdom politics. It was the arrival of Team Biscuit that cast a shadow over his sunny days.

It had been shaping up to be a relaxing month. Finalising a trade accord, cycling through some new staff members, fresh from home. Then the king's sister and her adventuring team arrived. He'd known they were coming, of course, and that the problem would inevitably be Jason Asano. He knew the man mostly from reputation and Adventure Society alerts.

Hils had met the man briefly, but that had been two monster surges ago. It was right before Hils had reached silver, back when he was still adventuring full time. He'd been with his friend Orin, who went on to travel with Asano, but Hils knew better than to ask. Orin wasn't one to talk much, especially about the days with his old team. They had followed Asano into a hole in the ground, and most of them hadn't come back.

Compared to what Hils had been afraid of, the arrival of Team Biscuit and their first days in the city were unremarkable. No royal entanglements, no mass destruction. He'd read the Adventure Society reports of the latest city to be destroyed with Asano in the middle of it. It seemed that Asano had realised Cyrion wasn't some backwater where he could throw around his gold rank like a hammer.

Hils even had a nice dinner with Zara, where he'd managed to get some more insight into Team Biscuit. She was an old friend from back in their days as young Rimaros aristocrats. That was before she went off adventuring, first with Orin's ill-fated team and then with Asano's. She'd been willing to offer details of that time he couldn't get from Orin himself.

While she was open with stories more than a decade old, she was more careful regarding her current team. Her firsthand knowledge filled gaps in the reports he'd seen, but she withheld occasional details and refused to answer certain questions. Team Biscuit had its secrets, especially Asano himself.

Hils had been optimistic about Zara and her team's visit. He'd started hearing about issues between Asano and some of the noble houses, but nothing that required intervention. The issue was comfortingly normal, being that the noble houses had found leverage on someone and were looking to squeeze everything they could out of them. The question was how a team of gold-rank adventurers would react.

Looking into it, Hils found the issue both straightforward and minor. Asano wanted a group of people to leave with him, but many were stuck under indenture contracts. The families were looking to gouge Asano's team for their release, and he was being intractable about making concessions.

To get his way, all Asano needed to do was give the families their pound of flesh. It was standard diplomatic fare, and they wouldn't push too far. Instead, Asano kept talking about moral imperatives, which would get him nowhere. The kind of public attention he would need to shine on the families to make them even pretend to care would be immense. Then he remembered what he'd read of Asano's history, and what he'd learned directly from Zara.

Almost a week into Asano's conflict with the nobility, there were signs of trouble. Asano had ceased all efforts at negotiation and hadn't been seen in days. Hils reached out to Zara, and her immediacy in setting up another meeting only added to his concerns.

Hils met with Zara in a parlour inside the Rimaros embassy building. It was a small and intimate space, shrouded in the most potent privacy magic available. Located close to one of the more discreet entrances to the building, the room's usual purpose was for clandestine meetings with close allies. He was not happy when she requested they use it.

Their meeting began with small talk, plus the obligatory questions about when she would return to Rimaros and rejoin the royal family. Hils had no investment in that, but he was under *very* clear instructions to bring it up every time they met. With incidents like Zara's encounter with the draconian prince, returning to the fold would offer her greater diplomatic protection. The questions came from both the current and previous Storm Kings, so there was no way Hils would skip them, even if it annoyed the former Hurricane Princess. He pushed through them as fast as he could, however, having more of an agenda this time.

"Zara, what is going on with Asano? Is he about to do something ill-advised?"

"Usually, yes."

"Zara, this is serious."

"I know, Hils. And what I'm about to tell you, I'm only able to do so because of a favour to me. Since I'm on his team, and my family is my family, Jason is letting me give them a few days warning of what is about to happen."

"Let you? Whatever politics might be at play, Zara, you're a princess of the Storm Kingdom first."

"Don't try to lecture me on conflicting loyalties, Hils. A good boy like you has no idea of what I've had to navigate over the years."

"Which is why your father and brother want you to come home."

"They are not the highest authority in the Storm Kingdom, Hils."

"They are the current and former Storm Kings. Who is higher than that?"

Her only response was a flat look.

"The founder?" he asked. "His Ancestral Majesty?"

"During the last monster surge, Ancestor Soramir personally took me aside. He told me that Jason Asano is the most important political relationship the Storm Kingdom has had since its founding."

"That seems a bit much."

"I can see how it could, from the outside. But I don't need you to agree with me, only to warn my brother. Jason has offered our kingdom a head start on formulating a response."

"A response to what?"

"I need for you to understand something, Hils. My expectation is that you will respect the courtesy we are being shown here. That means not letting what I'm about to tell you get out. No using the water links or the sky links when you take this to my brother. You are going to portal back to Rimaros in person."

"Zara, what is this about?"

"The System."

Hils was informed enough to know that the System was allegedly connected to Asano, although few details had been confirmed. Supposedly, the new means of interfacing with magic was identical to a personal power Asano has possessed years earlier. What was confirmed was how important the System had become in a very short time. More than just personally valuable to essence-users, many organisations were increasingly relying on it. From craft guilds and local governments to the Magic Society, the System was rapidly being adopted into their operations.

The Adventure Society was especially enamoured of the advantages it offered. From quantifying powers to identifying people with restricted essences to managing and identifying loot, the System had been an absolute boon. Previously unseen essence abilities tapping into the system were starting to appear, and ritual magic that relied on it was being developed.

"What about the System?" Hils asked warily.

"In a few days, Jason is going to turn it off in every country and city-state that has indentured servitude laws."

Hils blinked. A few moments later, he blinked again.

"I'm sorry, what?"

"He's going to turn off the System in each nation and—"

"He can do that?"

"He can."

"Are you sure?"

"We'll see in a few days, but yes. I believe that he can."

"How? Where does he get that kind of access? That level of control?"

"It hasn't been spread around, but I suppose it will be soon. Jason *is* the System, Hils."

"What does that even mean?"

"Just what I said. He is the System. It's an extension of him. He's still learning how to control it—he told me it was like learning a new language —but he's confident he can do this."

"He *is* the System?"

"Yes."

"So, if he dies, the whole thing goes away."

"He can't die. Not anymore."

"Are you saying that he's the god of the System?"

"The great astral being," she corrected. "He doesn't know if there's going to be a god of it. The goddess of Death and the Reaper, for example, have distinct roles in administering dead souls. He doesn't know if a similar situation will require a god of the System to form. Even if one does, it will probably take a few centuries. Look how long Purity is taking to come back. We still aren't sure exactly how long Disguise was acting in his place."

He stood up and paced around the room, running his hands through his hair distractedly as he thought. He finally stopped, leaning on the back of his chair with both hands as he looked at the still-sitting Zara.

"Okay," he said. "Disregarding, for the moment, the idea that Asano is some kind of god-adjacent supreme being, you're saying that he can just turn off the System on a whim?"

"It's more involved than that, to my understanding. At least until his power grows. But yes, that's essentially what I'm saying."

"You're saying he can do this, and his power is still growing?"

"Hils, do you understand what a great astral being is?"

"Obviously not, but I know the Builder was one. Now you're saying that Asano is the same, and he's going to use his power to try and hold the world hostage."

"That's not how he framed it, but your description is at least broadly accurate."

"People are going to throw a fit. The adoption rate for using the System in every group from governments to churches is... are there any exemptions? Churches, the Adventure Society?"

"No. And just between us, he's already secured endorsements of his plans from Dominion and Liberty. That's going to matter, given how rarely they agree on anything."

"If the churches already know, I don't see why you're being so secretive. It's definitely going to come out ahead of time."

"The churches don't know. Not yet."

"You just finished saying he had the endorsements from the churches of Dominion and Liberty."

"No, Hils, I didn't."

"Wait, were you talking about the actual gods?"

"It can't be that much of a surprise. Surely, you've heard about what he's like with them. He had them around for a cup of tea with the whole team. It was a very odd experience."

"Gods can drink tea?"

"They're gods, Hils. There isn't much they can't do, whatever Jason might say about their limitations."

"And they're going to support this publicly?"

"Yes."

"That changes things significantly. Or maybe it doesn't, I don't know. I have no frame of reference for some gold-ranker holding the planet hostage by threatening to turn off a major facet of magic itself. Because he's actually some kind of ridiculous being. I saw one report claim he was one of the messengers' gods."

"He is, and they're called astral kings."

"I thought you said he was a great astral being."

"Yes, it's all very complicated. What you need to understand, Hils, is that Jason isn't threatening to do anything. He's doing it. I'm here so the Storm King has a chance to get out ahead of it."

"Ahead of it how? He wants to abolish indentured servitude? That's a cornerstone of the legal system for most of the civilised world. What does he want us to replace it with? Those places where they lock people up for years on end, the way they do in Kurdansk? Even ignoring what the point of it is, do you have any idea of the operating costs of those places?"

"He's not making specific demands beyond the elimination of indentured servant laws."

"Meaning that he expects us to throw out a major part of the justice system and offers nothing to put in its place."

"Do you think it would be better if he did start dictating how countries should change things?"

"That's exactly what he's doing!"

"Well, yes," Zara conceded. "But he wants everyone to find their own solutions, rather than dictating them himself. Which is what Dominion said he should do, by the way."

"Why does Dominion even approve of this? Shouldn't he be in favour of indentured servitude? Or any servitude, for that matter."

"I'm not sure. I wondered the same, but Jason said that Dominion isn't what most people think he is. We didn't sit down for a theological discussion, though. What we did talk about was potential replacement systems for indenture. Jason won't dictate what people should do, but favours a shift in the current system that only makes limited changes."

"How limited?"

"His problem is the slavery aspect."

"Indenture isn't slavery."

"Except that sometimes it is, Hils, and you know it."

"No system is perfect, Zara."

"Which is not an excuse to not make them better. The current practise is to sell off indenture contracts, or give them to the criminal's victims. Jason favours taking what were indenture contracts and replacing them with public service orders. For most practical purposes, the systems stay as they are, but without selling people. Local authorities use the labour for public service, with regulation in place to reduce and remedy instances of abuse."

Hils rubbed his chin thoughtfully.

"So, mostly just shifting the indenture holders from private individuals to government authorities."

"It's an option. One that has already been working in some city-states for decades. There are still problems, but the worst of the abuses have been curtailed."

"Worst of the abuses. We're talking about criminals here, and it's not as bad as you make out."

"Do you genuinely believe that?"

"Of course I do. If I didn't, what kind of monster would that make me?"

"An unfortunately common variety. You know of Sophie Wexler, from my team?"

"Yes."

"Did you know that she was an indentured servant?"

"I think I recall reading about that."

"The local Magic Society branch director was obsessed with her. The Adventure Society director made that happen in return for certain concessions. It took Jason and Emir Bahadir stepping in to prevent that from happening."

"See? The system works."

"People with undue influence stepping in to stop other people with undue influence isn't the process working, Hils. It's the process being so broken that the corruption is folding in on itself."

"Look, Zara, I don't entirely disagree with you. I don't think it's as bad as you make out, but what I'm really telling you is what everyone else is going to say."

Zara nodded.

"I told him much the same. As did Danielle Geller."

"Did you tell him that he'll be standing up to every government in the world?"

"I did."

"And what did he say to that?"

"That he's stood up to worse. That people know who he is, now, so it's time to show them *what* he is."

Hils let out a groan.

"He's one of those obnoxiously melodramatic people, isn't he?"

"Oh, you have no idea. Sometimes I'll spot him with one foot propped up on something, staring into the middle distance."

"Zara, this is going to be a mess. Countries aren't going to cave in to some random guy telling them to change how their legal system works. I don't care what he is or how crazy the stories about him are. Even diamond-rankers don't act like this."

"He's not a diamond-ranker, Hils. He's a man who invites a couple of gods around for a cup of tea and they actually show up."

"Then maybe you should go around and tell everyone that story. See how that works out."

Zara got to her feet.

"Hils, I'm not here to convince you of anything. This is just a chance for our country to get a few more days than everyone else to formulate a reaction. What my brother does from there is up to him."

"This is a bad idea, Zara. You should try and stop him from doing this."

"If people could stop Jason Asano from following through on bad ideas, the world would be a different place. I told him how messy this was going to be."

"What did he say?"

"Something about a spider and responsibility and his uncle, I think? It didn't make a lot of sense."

50

HEAVILY COMPROMISED BAKED GOODS

GARRET HEADINGWAY WAS AN UPPER-ECHELON MEMBER OF HOUSE Headingway, one of Estercost's pre-eminent families. He was taking breakfast when his butler arrived.

"Morning mail, my lord."

"Anything interesting, James?"

"Something from Jason Asano."

"Oh? He's been locked up in his cloud palace for days, seeing no one. Do you think he's finally come to his senses?"

"As the one who investigated him for you, sir, my guess would be no. More likely is that he's about to do something drastic, as I warned you."

"This is Cyrion, James, not the Gellers' little domain down south. There's only so drastic he can be here."

"I would reiterate, my lord, that his record suggests that may not be the case. At the very least, I doubt he agrees with you."

Garret finished buttering his savoury scone, then took an appreciative bite. He sat it down and wiped his hands on a napkin before picking up the letter James had set on the table.

To whom it may concern,

I am sending a number of these letters to the various interests who have been negotiating for the freedom of my fellow Earth expatriates over the last week. Although you are the catalyst for what is about to happen, please know that you are not the cause. Instead, I would like to thank you for reminding me of a promise I made to myself long ago, when I was a powerless young man in a world of vast magic.

Power is a dangerous and wonderous thing. When given the chance to do whatever we want, we show the world what we always wanted to do. Sometimes we lose our way, or forget the principles that guided us when we were powerless. Do we become tyrants, claiming everything for ourselves? Do we embrace the moral responsibility of using our power to improve the world around us?

Trying to make the world better is a very good way to make it worse, but to have the power and do nothing is an abdication of responsibility. Many years ago, I promised myself that, should I have the ability, I would try to wipe out the blot that is slavery, whatever terms its perpetrators couch it in. When you, the recipients of this letter, used such laws to keep people from returning to their homes, you reminded me of that old promise. Of other friends exploited. So now, at the risk of adding to the harm, I am attempting to make things better.

Let me be clear that this is not a negotiating position. There is no talking this down, making exemptions or trading the freedom of the people of Earth for amelioration. While that conflict is the instigation point for what is about to occur, these events are larger than a group of petty aristocrats. While you can be thanked for inspiring my actions, you are ultimately unimportant.

Regards,

Jason Asano

Garret handed the letter to James, waiting while his butler read it over.

"It would seem that you were right, James. He doesn't say what he's going to do, but his ambitions are certainly grand enough. He's going to attempt something drastic."

"It would seem so, my lord."

"Any idea what?"

"Given the scale his letter implies, my guess would be something either related to the gods or the System."

"The System? Right, your report on him mentioned that he's related to it in some way. Was that confirmed?"

"My sources inside the Adventure Society say yes."

"Well, see if you can find out some more—"

System Alert: Reduced Service Areas

- [System Administrator] will shortly withdraw System access in regions of Pallimustus currently operating with slavery, indentured servitude or similar legal systems. No one within those regions will be able to access any System functions. Abilities that integrate with the System will have alternate functionality while inside those areas. Rituals that utilise the System will have diminished functionality or fail entirely.
- [System Administrator] will soon be leaving Pallimustus for an indeterminate period. System access to individual regions will be reviewed on his return. This message will remain active for one full day. At the end of that period, the System will cease to be accessible from within the affected areas. For a full list, please see below.

Garret skimmed the list.

"This is everywhere," he muttered.

"If one dismisses remote, rural and low-magic areas, certainly."

Garret took another bite of his scone while he considered the message.

"James, in your assessment of the man, do you think Asano can really do something on a scale that this letter implies? And if he can, will he, or is it a bluff?"

"My assessment would be that he does have the ability. If it is a bluff, it's not one I would recommend calling."

"He's going to make a world of enemies with this."

"I believe you will find, my lord, that powerful enemies are kind of his thing."

Garret looked up from where he was rereading the message.

"That's an odd turn of phrase, James. I don't believe I've ever heard you use it."

"To be honest, my lord, James is unconscious in the basement. How strong is your poison resistance, by the way? I have no idea how he put so much of it in those scones without them tasting funny."

"What?" Garret asked, and suddenly realised that his vision was going blurry. "Who are you?"

"You know, it's good to have Jason back," Belinda told him. "Humphrey never lets me kidnap people."

Jacinta Adeline was having a very bad day. Being director of the Adventure Society's Cyrion branch was one of the most demanding and political appointments in the entire organisation. This was never more so than when something extreme happened, from the appearance of a diamond-rank monster to the coronation of a new monarch. Adventurers themselves were often as not the problem. Every time some diamond-ranker showed up, looking to take off with half the city's gold-rankers on some personal project, Jacinda felt like she was getting a stomach ulcer. She wasn't—because magic—but it felt like it.

While she had been aware of Team Biscuit's arrival, and of the history around Jason Asano, it had been just one more thing on her plate. She'd been monitoring his interactions with the Cyrion noble houses, more closely since he cut off dialogue without results, but it all fell under the heading of minor concerns. That changed drastically with the System announcing that it would no longer be available as of tomorrow morning.

Asano wasn't mentioned by name, but the wide-ranging messages that took place in Boko made reference to the 'System Administrator' as well. People were already putting the pieces together, and just outside the doors of Asano's cloud palace had a bigger crowd than the door to Jacinta's office suite. In the dozen or so hours since the message appeared, she'd been dealing with aristocrats, guilds, royalty, the Magic Society and even her own people.

There was a knock on the door, her assistant not waiting for a reply before opening it.

"She's here, Boss."

"Send her straight through."

Jacinta stood and headed to a painting on the wall that reached floor to ceiling, depicting some adventurers looking generically heroic. She tapped a specific point on the frame and the painting retracted into the wall before sliding aside to reveal a full bar. She didn't know which of her predecessors had it installed, but on days like these, she sent them silent blessings.

Jacinta was pouring the second glass of amber liquid when Danielle Geller walked into the office, closing the door behind her. The women wordlessly moved to one of several couches in the spacious room and sat down, side by side. Jacinta handed over one of the glasses and they clinked them together before drinking. Danielle took a sip while Jacinta emptied her glass in one gulp.

"I thought you might be having that kind of day."

"Dani, what in the dark gods' armpit sweat is going on?" Jacinta exploded. "You told me that he hired you to stop him from doing things like this."

"I did suggest a more measured approach. Strongly suggested."

"He clearly didn't listen."

"No, he did."

"You're telling me that this is the more measured approach?"

"I am."

"He kidnapped seven members of some of the most influential families in Estercost."

"Allegedly."

"A copy of the same letter from him was found in each location, along with heavily compromised baked goods."

"That does sound like him," Danielle conceded.

"And that letter sounds like a manifesto."

"He's not trying to force anyone into anything."

"That's exactly what he's trying to do. And it won't work."

"He's aware. That's why I say he's not trying to force anything. He is fully aware that whole nations are not going to bow to his whims. He is choosing to no longer share a capability under his control as he feels it would be an endorsement of practices he finds morally repugnant. In short, he's not going to support any authority that tolerates slavery or slavery-like social structures."

"Indenture isn't slavery."

"If you want to make that argument to Jason, I'd recommend beating your head against the wall instead. You won't have to leave your office, and the wall might actually budge. Jason won't, especially if Sophie Wexler is in the room."

"The former indenture on Asano's team."

"And the only one who could actually get Jason to reverse his position, not that she will. She's his biggest supporter in this."

"I read the reports of her pre-adventuring history, but they were quite lean."

"Yeah, I'll bet they were," Danielle muttered.

"You were involved?"

"No. It all went down while I was off on a major expedition where the Builder cult tore us to shreds. While that was going on, the corrupt Adventure Society director was cutting a deal with the even more corrupt Magic Society director. The plan was to sell Wexler to him, for reasons exactly as nasty as you'd imagine. Asano and Emir Bahadir managed to stop it, but I would advise against telling Wexler that indenture isn't slavery."

"She won't be open to convincing Asano to not do this, then."

"No. I'm just telling you this so you realise that your best shot is such a bad one that you shouldn't bother."

"He can't be convinced to make an exemption for the Adventure Society?"

"I tried that tack. He said that if he makes one compromise, it will become a constant pressure to make more. He's not wrong. For all that he hopes for change, Jace, he isn't expecting anyone to make any concessions. He's resolved to make no concessions in return."

"Surely he understands that he can't do this?"

"Do what, Jace? Take away something he gave everyone for nothing? The System was always his to give, and his to take away. All that's changed is that now people realise it. They're probably about to start worrying about how much of their information he can tap into."

"He can just pull anything from the System out of the air?"

"I don't know. He says he can't, but I don't know to what degree he really means *won't*."

"But he has the control to do what he's threatening?"

"It's not a threat, Jace. It's happening."

"How is that even possible?"

"As someone who's known Jason for a long time, I can tell you that question comes up a lot. The answers range from the nonsensical to the non-existent, and you eventually realise that it's better not to ask."

"That is a spectacularly unhelpful answer. Dani, I have everyone from the Magic Society director to the Queen harassing me for answers. I need something better than 'some guy turns out to have god-like power over the System, but I don't know the details.' They aren't going to like that anymore than I do."

"Tell them that Pallimustus has gotten by without the System for the entirety of its history. It's going to keep getting along just fine without it."

"That isn't how people work, and you know it. If you give them something they like, only to take it away, they're going to throw a tantrum. And people love the System, Dani. *I* love the System."

"Then they have to decide if they like their slaves more. If withholding the System was going to cause people harm, he'd be more flexible, but it wasn't something they knew they wanted until they had it. They don't need it, so he has no compunction about taking it from them."

"It's not that simple, Dani, and you know it. Asano isn't some god we can't do anything about. He's a person, and everyone knows where to find him."

"If you believed that, Jace, you'd already have the society beating down his door. He's not a god, but he moves in the same circles as one. The Cyrion nobles might not know what they're dealing with, but you do. You've seen the reports."

"Reports? I had the damn archbishops of Dominion and Liberty in here. Seeing those two agree on anything was downright creepy. What I'm looking for is some insight on how to handle this situation. How do we get Asano to not do this?"

"He's been clear on that, Jace. I know that's not going to happen, and so does he."

"Then what's the point of all this? What does he want?"

"The Cyrion nobles he's been dealing with have been squeezing him because they think they can. I think that has triggered memories of his time on his own planet. That was a bad time for him, and I think he's looking to work out some of that old anger here."

"Isn't he planning to go back there?"

"Yes, which I imagine is part of this. He knows that if he throws his power around there, he can do real damage."

"He's doing damage here!"

"No, Jace, he isn't. He's taking away people's shiny new toys because he doesn't like some of the things they're doing. He wants to show, once and for all, that he's not a tool for people to pick up and use. He's challenging the world to try, so that everyone can see what happens."

"What am I meant to do about that? People aren't going to accept the loss of the System."

"Make them. If you want to blindside Jason, prove him wrong. Tell him that the world won't force him into anything, but it won't be extorted either. It will live without the System, but he doesn't get to tell nations what their laws should be."

"And if he decides to push his agenda harder?"

"He won't. His friends will stop him, if nothing else."

"Couldn't you have stopped him earlier?"

"Probably. But sometimes extreme results require extreme actions. Jason has proven that time and again, and we aren't opposed to his principles in this."

"You're sitting there and telling me that extremism is a good thing?"

Danielle drained what was left of her glass.

"I don't know, Jace. I can't fight gods. I can't destroy cities and conjure new ones out of thin air. I can't put a stop to laws that most of the world thinks are normal and natural."

Jacinta rubbed her temples against an encroaching headache.

"I'm not going to get any more from you than that, am I? You're saying to tell him that he can't have what he wants, but we won't try and take what we want."

"Like many things with Jason, all you can do is limp away from the mess."

"And the nobles he took?"

"Allegedly."

"Don't be disingenuous, Dani. Their families are going to go after Asano for that, evidence or not. His team too, including your boy."

"Oh, I think they'll find there's someone else they need to deal with first."

"Dani, what did Asano do?"

———

Garret Headingway awoke to a throbbing pain in his everything. His senses slowly fought their way through a fog, coming into focus one by one. He could taste the air, too hot and dry for home. He smelled sand and dirt, felt bare earth beneath him. His silver-rank hearing picked out the sounds of people, muffled by thick walls. There was a mix of languages, only a few he recognised. He was somewhere in the desert regions, well east of Estercost.

He opened his eyes on a dim room, light passing through a small, slatted window. It was an empty room, or maybe a shed, with adobe walls. He was one of seven people in the room, most of whom were still unconscious. The one person already awake was leaning against the wall, looking disgruntled. Garret recognised him, Patterson Kennington. Looking around, he realised they were all Cyrion noblemen. From houses who had been in negotiation with—

"Jason Asano," Patterson said bitterly. "He put us here."

"You saw him?" Garret asked.

Patterson shook his head.

"Did you get a letter?" he asked.

"Yeah," Garret said. His groggy brain finally noticed a thick collar around Patterson's neck, made of dark, crude metal. He reached up and felt an identical one around his own neck.

"Don't bother with magic or aura senses," Patterson told him. "It's a suppression collar. A specific kind of one, if my guess about where we are is right. The walls are reinforced too, so don't bother trying that either."

Garret glanced at the wall beside Patterson. The mud bricks should have parted like paper to Patterson's silver-rank strength, but several shallow fist marks were all it had managed.

"Where do you think we are?" Garret asked. "Eastern desert?"

"Obviously," Patterson sneered. "Ever hear of a little dirtball country called Sadi Andali?"

"No."

"Well, it's famous for being almost lawless. The Adventure Society doesn't even have a branch here. They just send people in from time to time, sweeping for illegal research and restricted essences. They find plenty of both."

"What are we doing here?"

"Remember when I said *almost* lawless? The one set of laws they do have governs the slave markets."

51

THE LINE BETWEEN MORTAL AND IMMORTAL

VANDRICK ARRIVED AT THE ENTRANCE TO JASON ASANO'S CLOUD PALACE. There was a mob out front, and had been since the System went dark. They were pretending to be a spontaneously formed group, protesting the heavy-handed influence of the outsider. Anyone with any real knowledge was aware they had been placed by certain noble houses of Cyrion, antici-pating negative attention regarding potential actions against Asano. The 'spontaneous' crowd was one of the ways they were working to shape the narrative.

The palace was on a lake reserved for cloud constructs and other temporary floating structures. Vandrick recognised the palace of Emir Bahadir floating nearby, the man and his retinue having arrived the day before. Vandrick respected his loyalty, arriving to support a friend who had much of the world against him right now.

Vandrick let out the faintest whiff of diamond-rank aura as he approached the crowd. They instantly fell over themselves to clear a path. They were gathered on the shore where a cloud bridge extended to the palace. The bridge itself being empty suggested it would disappear from under the feet of unwelcome visitors. Vandrick walked slowly across, observing the cloud palace. Rather than one massive structure, it was a complex of buildings, linked by enclosed sky bridges and underwater tunnels.

The design of the buildings was in the Vitesse style, complete with plants growing over and out of every part of the building. Moss covered much of the white cloud walls. Leafy vines dangled from balconies and flowers bloomed on windowsills. Even the underwater tunnels were coated in kelp and coral. Asano apparently favoured tropical plants, with vibrant greens and large, bright flowers.

The large double doors opened at Vandrick's approach, revealing an atrium more like a garden than a room. He stepped inside and immediately froze, having felt something he hadn't in a long time: threatened. A small smile played across his lips.

"Interesting," he murmured as he looked around.

The entrance was a multi-storey atrium, with even more plants than the exterior. Multiple waterfalls spilled from mezzanine levels into water features, running through the garden that filled the floor. Paths led through the gardens and over little bridges to doors and stairwells set into the walls. The air was humid, with the splashing of the waterfalls and the sounds of birds and insects. High above, the atrium seemed open to the sky, but Vandrick could sense a barrier of invisible mist.

His gaze settled on the one feature whose purpose he wasn't sure of. An alcove in the wall had a series of narrow poles that appeared to rise into the upper reaches of the building. There was a sign with a name on it behind each pole, matching each member of Asano's team. He noted that the one labelled 'Neil' had a thicker pole than the others.

Vandrick heard something from above, and a moment later, someone slid down one of the poles. Both his aura and the sign behind his pole said that this was Jason Asano. He was wearing tan short pants, sandals and a colourful shirt with a tropical flower print.

"G'day, bloke. What can I do you for?"

"The Queen of Estercost and several other interested parties have asked me to arbitrate over your withdrawal of the System."

"Meaning they asked you to come in here, hold me upside down and shake me until the System falls out."

"They phrased it differently, but that was the general sentiment."

"But you're not going to do that, are you?"

"No. But it is time someone sat down with you and had a discussion."

"About?"

"You stand with a foot on each side of a dangerous line, Mr Asano. I'm hoping to help you navigate it successfully."

"That sounds good. And call me Jason."

"Very well, Jason. My name is Vandrick Macarro, but you may call me Van."

"Okay, Van. I just made some scones I've got on a cooling rack upstairs, so we'll have to chat there."

Vandrick glanced over at the alcove with the poles.

"We don't have to use those, do we?"

"No," Jason said with a laugh. "They're for coming down only."

"That doesn't seem efficient when gold-rankers can levitate quite effectively, even without your aura advantages."

"Oh, it's definitely not efficient. But what's the point of living forever if you don't take the time to have fun?"

Jason started floating into the air and Vandrick followed. On the highest mezzanine, they landed and walked down a hallway where the floor was wooden slats over running water. Plants lined the walls, and a fresh breeze blew through.

"That music is unlike anything I've heard," Vandrick said. "Is it from your world?"

"Yeah, that's Laura Branigan."

Jason led Vandrick to an expansive kitchen that opened onto a covered balcony. Flowering vines draped from overhead, dangling over a picnic table. Sitting at it were four people, including one with the characteristic broad shoulders and chiselled features of a Geller. That would be Humphrey, one of the family's more famous members. The woman next to him was probably his mother, based on their shared complexion and the interaction of their auras. Sitting opposite them were Emir Bahadir, who Vandrick had met, and a woman who was likely his wife.

"I'm just going to sell my cows at Kansas City," Emir said. "Give me six extra dollars."

"You know you'll lose points for that," his wife told him.

"And if I don't get more money, I won't get any more points than what I have."

In the kitchen, two women were wearing aprons and each stirring something in a large bowl.

"No, Sophie, stop," one of them said.

"Oh, come on, Ketis. What's wrong now?"

"You're going too fast. Even ignoring the spatter, we're making whipped cream, not butter."

"I like butter," Sophie said defensively.

"This is for the scones."

"I like butter on scones."

Ketis noticed them enter, despite Vandrick's aura being fully withdrawn. She was the only one who stared, the others glancing his way before going back to what they were doing. It was a novel experience for Vandrick; the diamond-ranker normally received a very different reception.

"Who's your friend?" Sophie asked. "The Adventure Society finally send a diamond-ranker to spank you?"

"Something like that. Everyone, this is Vandrick. Vandrick, this is everyone. Well, not everyone. Where are the others?"

"Like you can't sense exactly where they are," Sophie told him.

"I like to give people their privacy," Jason said.

"Zara, Farrah and Lindy are still swimming," Ketis said. Her tone was distracted as she continued to stare at the diamond-rank visitor. "Humphrey's dad kept trying to pinch the scones and Stash dragged him away. He knows a lot about baking for a dragon."

"The others should be back soon," Humphrey said. "They went to the market to see how many types of jam they could find."

Emir and his wife rose from the table, approaching to offer a respectful greeting. He introduced his wife, Constance, then they went back to their game. Danielle Geller didn't move to introduce herself, but did nod a greeting when he spotted her looking him over.

In their previous meeting, Bahadir had the fear Vandrick was used to from people when meeting diamond-rankers. The rest of the group seemed the same, aside from the one girl still staring at him. He was halfway tempted to leak some of his aura to see what happened, but squashed the immature urge.

Jason led Vandrick into an adjoining room, a door of mist forming to seal them off. When it did, the sound from outside vanished, despite this room also being open to the outside. Again, Vandrick sensed a powerful but invisible mist barrier. The room was a meditation space, in a rustic tropical style with woven floor mats. It reminded Vandrick of Arnote, the least populous of the three islands of Rimaros. At a gesture from Jason, two streams of cloud rose from the floor. They took the form of wicker chairs, facing one another. Jason claimed one while waving Vandrick towards the other.

"So," Jason said. "What brings you by, Van?"

"You're in a very odd position, Jason. You're gold rank, but you're also somewhere on the far side of diamond. We diamond-rankers, and now the Adventure Society, have largely decided to split the difference and consider you a diamond-ranker."

"I've been told as much. I'm guessing this is the conversation where you give me the talk about how to behave like a good diamond-ranker."

"Not exactly. Diamond-rankers, as a rule, don't like being told what to do. They tend to react quite drastically."

"I should fit right in, then."

"Actually, yes, although your unusual circumstances present commensurately unusual challenges. The line between diamond rank and everything below it is more extreme than at any other rank. The line between gold and diamond is the threshold between mortality and immortality, with diamond-rankers being ageless and near immortal. Accordingly, we move away from mortal concerns, all the more as time rolls on. We don't have rules, as such, although we do step in when those amongst us get out of line. What we do have is etiquette."

"Meaning that if I'm a naughty boy, I won't get the rest of you coming down on me. You'll just all think that I'm an arsehole."

"Something like that, yes. I had a discussion with the Queen, along with other members of the Estercost elite and a number of ambassadors. I told them that the position of the diamond-rank community is that the System is yours to administer."

"Meaning you told them they aren't allowed to go after me over it."

"Yes. But that also means that if anyone should go after you, they are disregarding us to do so."

Jason narrowed his eyes.

"You want me to be the one who smacks down anyone who decides to come after me over it."

"We do. Which brings us back to points of etiquette. Diamond-rankers, on this world, at least, are the ultimate symbols and expressions of power. We expect one another to respect that, and act in such a way that the rest of the world does as well. There are several tenets to this, and one is that we take care of our own business. That is not to say that we don't lean on our friends and connections, but we are expected to hold our own. When a diamond-ranker helps another diamond-ranker, it is because they are friends or allies, not out of diamond-ranker solidarity. If you can't stand alone, the rest of us will stand by as your legs are cut out from under you."

"So, the first rule of being the most powerful is you have to be the most powerful."

"Precisely. The second tenet of diamond-rank etiquette is to respect the boundary between mortal and immortal. When a diamond-ranker is young, we are a lot more flexible about this. You have descendants to watch over, interests from your mortal days you don't want to see fall apart. Most of all, you still think like a mortal. But after half a millennium or so, you are expected to step back. If we do everything for them, and never let them find their own way, we stunt them. Left to their own devices, mortals will always surprise you. There is a drive that comes with mortality that pushes them to innovate. To make things better. The passion of youth."

Vandrick waved a casual finger at Jason.

"That's where you are now. You have power, maybe more than you ever thought you would. You want to use it, to make things better."

"And hopefully not make them worse."

"That is always the danger," Vandrick agreed. "We give more leeway to young diamond-rankers, but the danger of them causing harm is why we expect them to limit themselves. Let us look at some of the young diamond-rankers you know. Allayeth and Charist limit themselves geographically, for example, restricting themselves to Yaresh and the surrounding regions. The Mirror King is much the same in his own territory. Roland Remore's agenda is more expansive, but he rarely brings his direct power to bear. He limits himself to mostly working through agents and proxies."

"And you expect me to limit myself."

"No one is going to force you. What we hope is that you come to understand the virtues of limiting our influence on the mortal world. I suspect, given your positions on power and authority, that this would be a natural fit for you."

"You're not wrong," Jason conceded.

"I will say this," Vandrick said. "There is an expectation that very new diamond-rankers will run a little wild. Settle old scores and instigate changes in mortal society they have always wanted to. So long as they don't take anything too far, the rest of us let this go. What's the point of achieving more power than almost anyone, ever, if you're just going to be told not to do the things you always wanted to do?"

"That seems reasonable."

"I think so. The rule of thumb is that everyone gets one. One great big world-changing action that affects the mortals. After that, you're expected to be more nuanced in your approach. You have forever, so there is an expectation that you will be patient."

"And mine is using the System to try and get everyone to abolish slavery."

"Yes. As such, no one from the general diamond-rank community will challenge you on this. I cannot speak for individuals, however. If you infringe on a diamond-ranker's personal interests, you might find them getting in your way."

"Good to know, thank you."

"Now, we should address some of the issues that stem from your particular situation. Every diamond-ranker has their own circumstances, but yours are more drastic than most."

"In that I'm not actually a diamond-ranker."

"Yes. You straddle the line between mortal and immortal. It is not our place to tell you not to intervene in mortal affairs while you are still a gold-ranker. But we also won't stand aside if you start intervening in mortal affairs using your far-from-mortal aspects."

"Meaning that you'll let me extort everyone with the System this one time, but I need to start using my big boy powers like a mature adult."

"In short, yes. Handle mortal affairs like a mortal and immortal affairs like an immortal. That way, when some monarch asks us to rein you in, we'll tell them no. And we expect the same consideration from you. Diamond-rankers handle their own business amongst themselves. When we drag mortals into our affairs, or let them drag us into theirs, people die. Wars happen. Whole nations are wiped off the map."

"Everything I'm scared of happening if I misuse my power."

"Yes. Most of the diamond-rankers you've met are young. Five centuries old at most. There are gold-rankers older than most of them. Soramir Rimaros and Dawn are both exceptions, but both spend most of their time out in the cosmos. If you feel the need for guidance on how to handle immortal power in a mortal world, I want to be available for you."

"I'd like that."

"All this being said, I'm not going to intervene in your business with the Cyrion noble houses. You made that mess on a mortal scale, and you're expected to clean it up in the same way. No turning into a giant bird and wiping out entire families."

"That wasn't the plan, but I'll keep it in mind."

Vandrick stood up.

"I think this went well," he said. "But that is ultimately up to you, and time will tell. If you need me, I'm confident you can find me easily enough. If you come looking for advice, I will be happy to offer it. If you come looking for help, you will find me less willing."

Jason stood up and shook his hand.

"Understood."

52

A PETTY TYRANNY

NINE PEOPLE MARCHED ACROSS THE BRIDGE TOWARDS JASON'S CLOUD palace. They were clearly unlike the people Jason had been negotiating with, although they were from the noble houses currently missing people. These were not articulate servants or refined aristocrats. These were adventurers. Their gear was worn and practical, their weapons carried with the familiarity of years. They were slung ready for use, not displayed for the decorative value of their bejewelled hilts.

They stopped in front of the large doors, which turned into mist and vanished. Behind them was a garden atrium with sunlight spilling in from above. In the doorway was the dark figure of Shade.

"What can I do for you, gentlemen?"

"My name Ben Headingway, of House Headingway," the man at the front said, his voice as gruff as his appearance. "Each person here represents a noble house of Cyrion; I think you can guess which ones. We want to speak with Asano."

"Of course, Lord Headingway. Please come in."

"We're not going in there," Ben said. "He has all the power in there."

"If his power in here is your concern, Lord Headingway, I'm afraid you have some bad news coming about out there. I'm sorry we couldn't accommodate you today."

Mist started to form new doors, then dispersed again.

"Hold on, Shade," Jason said as he floated into view from above.

"These people are clearly adventurers. Good adventurers don't walk into places filled with unknown power and uncertain threats."

"If that is the metric, Mr Asano, wouldn't that make you a mediocre adven—"

"That will be all, thank you."

"Very good, Mr Asano."

Shade vanished into Jason's shadow as he landed just inside the doors. That placed him right in front of Ben, who was significantly taller. He had the dark skin of a Cyrion native, his long hair woven with beads from which Jason could feel radiating magic.

"I hope you're not here to fight," Jason said.

"I don't like fighting other adventurers," Ben said. "I like fighting monsters. Protecting people, providing for my house. Being the foundation holding it up, as my ancestors were before me. But you came into that house, and you took my family away. I don't like fighting people, especially when there are stories around them like the ones around you. But I will, if that's what it comes to. You took my nephew."

Jason nodded.

"Without admitting to any action on my part, I'm sure you could understand why I might do such a thing."

"I do," Ben acknowledged. "The thing about noble houses is that when they get old enough, most of the people in it start to forget things. Become entitled. Forget that the money and power and influence doesn't come from some inherent greatness they were born with."

He rested a casual hand on his sword hilt.

"It comes from this. From the people willing to get dirty and bloody. To die for the family, if that's what it takes. They forget that if they try to exploit the wrong person, it's people like us who bleed to set things right."

"You see, this is where you're losing me, Ben. Your problem seems to be who your family exploited, not that they were exploiting people at all."

"Ideals are all well and good, but power is what brings about change. Your ideals around slavery, for example, mattered to no one until you took away the System."

"I can't argue with that."

"Then let us set aside wishful thinking and deal with the practicalities. Our families thought they could extract some cheap benefits from you. They were wrong, and paid the price for that. As we speak, all of our families are dissolving the contracts for the people from your world. We're even giving them generous severance bonuses."

"Yeah, I can see the warm glow of having done the right thing radiating out of you."

"Asano, you know that we won't back down until our people are returned to us. You took them, leaving only two things: a letter from you and poisoned food that would render them unconscious, rather than kill them. You wanted us to know they were alive and that you took them."

"Allegedly."

"I'm not here for games, Asano, or the cheap words of politicians. I don't want to fight someone like you, but we will not allow you to keep our people. You are powerful, and have powerful friends. But you have made a lot of enemies by taking away the System, and the noble houses of Cyrion also have many connections. If we move against you in earnest, we will find no shortage of allies."

"You say that like your families won't come looking for revenge after they have their people back."

"You came into our homes and took members of our families."

"I didn't start this fight. The people from Earth mean very little to your families. Even though I find the indenture system laws unconscionable, I offered to buy their contracts at more than fair prices. Instead, your families used those laws to hold them hostage. To try and extort me. Because they had the power to do so and, as you said, power is what matters. In fact, you've been right about everything. Ideals accomplish nothing alone, and you did try to exploit the wrong people."

"We have moved to rectify this situation and make amends. Yes, I am certain that my family will try to make you pay for what you have done. That was inevitable from the moment you chose to do things this way, and you're smart enough to know that. And that the enmity between us will be very different if our people are not returned. Give them back, and you've delivered a political humiliation. Don't, and you've started a war."

"I honestly don't have your people," Jason said. "I did hear something that may be relevant, though. A friend of mine popped over to Sadi Andali recently. She's very fast, even without portals, and she had a few things to sell off. She heard that some unusual products are moving through the slave markets there. What seemed to be aristocrats, from their rank and bearings."

The people behind Ben stirred, but didn't speak up. Ben's gaze became even more flinty, as if it could bore through Jason's head.

"The Sadi Andali slave markets."

"That's what I heard."

"Which one?"

"Split between them, from what I heard. Not sure which ones, so I suppose you'll need to hit them all. Simultaneously, or you might find yourself dealing with hostages. You should probably call in some favours from those many connections you mentioned."

"This is your price, then? The destruction of the Sadi Andali slave trade?"

"I'm sure this won't stop it. The fact that the country still exists at all tells me that. It's too convenient a place for powerful people in need of dirty deeds but clean hands. Not that I'd exploit that to make some kind of point. You have a good day, bloke."

The mist doors reformed, removing Jason from view.

The desert town was a ramshackle place, mostly tents of washed out brown and yellow, pitched alongside a river. Some crude mud brick buildings were scattered around, and a few large colourful tents stood out from the others. The town was never meant to last, and the people in it were clearly used to adventurer raids. Those that could, fled. The slaves would normally refuse to go through portals with rescue at hand, but few could tolerate the pain collars.

Ben watched the adventurers swarm over the town. This was not his first time on such a raid, and he knew the routine just as well as the residents. Asano was right about the long-term efficacy of the operation. Even hitting every slave market in the tiny nation at once would only slow them down, ultimately stopping nothing.

There were churches here, although the nomadic nature of the town meant they were not actually sanctified. These were the larger and more colourful tents, not holy ground or, in most cases, unholy ground. Dark gods, their temples hidden away in civilised society, were openly worshipped here. They could flaunt their existence, at least until adventurers came calling. Even then, the clergy mostly escaped. The dark gods made sure that their thralls were elusive.

Not every church tent belonged to a dark god. Deities like Strength and Desolate weren't considered evil, but didn't care about the morality of their followers. There was an agreement with such churches that they wouldn't shelter residents during adventurer raids. In turn, the adventurers would leave their tents in peace. Most such churches were of lesser gods, the exception being a bright red tent in a prime position upstream.

The operation was largely wrapped up, with none of the family members found. Ben made his way to the large red tent, as it never hurt to pay respects to Dominion. To his surprise, he sensed a gold-rank presence within. He was clearly sensed in turn as a priest came out to meet him.

"Priest," Ben said in greeting, not knowing the man's name. "I am Benjamin Headingway, of House Headingway."

"I have heard of you. I am Brian, priest of Dominion."

"What is such a high-ranking priest doing in this place?"

Brian let out a chuckle.

"Our church is an organisation built more on doing what you're told than asking why."

"We are seeking members of the noble houses who have supposedly been sold here."

"I thought it might be something like that. As it happens, I did come across a noble slave in the market here."

"Do you know what happened to them?"

"I do. I suspected that something like this might happen, and that it would be best to keep him safe until someone like you arrived. So, I bought him."

"You bought him?"

"Yes. He's inside."

Brian gestured in the direction of the tent.

"Please."

Ben followed Brian into the tent. While the rich, crimson fabric of the tent was enchanted against sun bleaching, the interior was plain and functional. There was an altar with kneeling mats set out in front of it, and a private living area, sectioned off with standing screens. Off to the side was a thick wooden post, driven into the hard earth floor. Ben could sense the reinforcement magic that prevented the man chained to it from freeing himself with silver-rank strength.

Ben recognised Patterson Kennington. They had no acquaintance, but all of the rescue teams had been shown images of the targets. He was on his knees, forced into hugging the post with his arms chained together on the other side of it. He was unconscious, slumped against the wooden pole.

"You left him like this?" Ben asked.

"He's a slave, and a disobedient one at that. Most owners faced with a slave like this would whip him and throw him in a hole until he learned his place. By disobedient slave standards, this is downright palatial."

"He's not a slave; he is a nobleman of Estercost."

"I think you'll find, Lord Headingway, that slavery isn't a volunteer position. If someone has the power to make you one, you are one, and you don't get a say in the matter. It's not fair, but while ideals are all well and good, it is power that brings about change."

Ben's gaze snapped from Patterson to Brian.

"Asano set this all up," he realised. "Even this, and you."

"I'm sure I have no idea what you're talking about."

"Why would your church agree to be lackeys to Asano? Isn't Slavery a subordinate god to yours? Why would you work with someone working to destroy it?"

"The irony of our church, Lord Headingway, is that those most favoured by our god will never be in it. We guide them, and sometimes we serve them. I am a priest of Dominion. We do not venerate power itself, but the establishment of power over others. Rulership. The exercising of authority. Yes, slavery is one form of power and control, but it is a small thing. A petty tyranny. My lord looks higher."

"Higher?"

"Look at what's happening out there, and all across Sadi Andali. Someone has set the great and noble houses of Cyrion dancing to his tune."

"You truly think that Asano is so grand?"

"I never said a name."

Ben snorted derision.

"If he's so great, why play political games? He has what he wanted. Why make enemies by humiliating us like this?"

"Because you tried to put him in his place. He no longer has time to educate small concerns like you, one at a time. He is busy figuring out how to not conquer a world. My god values that far more than auctioning off shackled victims. Speaking of which, will you be taking this slave?"

"Of course I will."

"Excellent. Will you pay in spirit coins, or a promissory note to the church?"

53

REASON EIGHTY-SEVEN

DUKE PERCIVAL HEADINGWAY WAS THE PATRIARCH OF HOUSE Headingway, holder of the family's highest title. While the same title was claimed by rural aristocrats in their remote city-states, his title came from Cyrion, the heart of civilisation. He might serve under the throne, unlike the city-state rulers, but his power dwarfed even the most prestigious of theirs.

It was galling, then, that one man had been leading his prestigious house around by the nose. Once the problems had escalated to his personal attention, he had not liked what he found. If the issue was external aggression, that would have been one thing. He could mobilise the power and influence of the house without impacting its reputation. Instead, some of the family's lesser lights had aggravated a man who didn't blink when gods became his enemies.

As with any noble family, the true power of House Headingway came from their adventurers. Politics were unquestionably important, but lesser affairs could be left to lesser family members. In this case, however, those lesser members had shoved the family's arm shoulder-deep into a snake hole.

It could have been worse, Percival reflected. Asano was serving up humiliation in forcing the families to rescue their errant members, in very public fashion. But while they had been roughed up, he'd made sure the Dominion church kept them from any genuine danger.

From what Percival had seen of young Garret, the experience in Sadi Andali may have even knocked some sense into the boy. When Percival was young, adventurer training had been mandatory in the family. Only those with talent and inclination followed through, but it helped them understand the foundations of what made the houses strong. It might be time to bring the practice back.

The loss of reputation from these events was unpleasant, but far from unendurable. Enough of the major families had shared the same fate that the tide was lowered for everyone. The smart move was to move on, which was exactly what Ben, the family's top gold-ranker, had said.

"We started something with someone we shouldn't and took our lumps. Take the lesson and move on."

That was exactly what Percival intended, but a faction within the family were advocating retribution. These were the pure politicians, the kind who hated the influence of the adventurers. They weren't complete fools, now believing they knew who they were dealing with in Asano. They wanted the response to be proportional and political; not making a true enemy but making it clear that House Headingway was not to be trifled with.

Percival knew full well that they were wrong. Asano was an adventurer and he thought like one. Political games only worked so long as the opponent was unwilling to flip the board, and Asano was demonstrably willing to do that. Even if the family could hurt Asano, they would only end up dragging each other down.

He was drafting an announcement on the issue for a family meeting when his office was intruded upon. Mariska Headingway managed the family's business affairs and, in most instances, was the epitome of formality, politeness and respect. She burst through his office door like a siege engine.

"Percy, are you out of your gods-damned mind? You were the one who pushed for the expansion of our trade operations using the sky link system."

"Yes, Mary, I am. Hello, by the way, and do feel free to come in. Maybe treat yourself to some context."

"Do you know who invented the sky link system? And who operates it?"

"I don't recall who invented it. It's managed by the Magic Research Association, is it not?"

"Yes," Mariska said pointedly. "It is."

Her sharp gaze bored into him as she waited for him to connect the dots.

"Oh," he said. "The Magic Research Association was founded and is now led by a member of Team Biscuit."

"Oh, it doesn't stop there," Mariska said, growing increasingly manic. "Did you know that one of the developers of the sky link system is right here in Cyrion? She's travelling with her very close friend, Jason Asano."

"Ah."

"And here's the topper, Percy. The other founder, Travis Noble, lives in Rimaros, but is not from there originally. Do you want to guess where he's from?"

"Just spit it out, Mary."

"He's not from Pallimustus at all. He's an outworlder. From the group who arrived here fifteen years ago. The group our illustrious family decided would be good leverage to extort a man WHO BLOWS UP CITIES! Not a metaphor, Percy! He literally blew up a city last month. Not the first, by the way. And he did it by accident. Someone assassinated him and his power went out of control and wiped out a city. Then he came back to life, turned into a bird and killed an entire army of messengers! I'd say that's the most insane thing I've ever heard of, but I've been reading about the rest of the things he's done! And we thought what? Let's *really* make him angry in return for some very minor gains?"

"Mary, I—"

"Do you know what it takes to have Undeath see you as a personal antagonist?"

"Mary—"

"I do. Now. You blow up a city full of his people, Percy. Priests, an undead army, even his damn avatar. You wipe it out of reality and build a new city out of clouds, because at that point, why not? On the way to your office, I heard people talking about getting this guy back. Get him back? What we need to get him is a gift basket and the ten best doxies in Cyrion! Do you know if he likes men or women?"

"We're not hiring prostitutes, Mary."

She gave him a flat look.

"Not for this," he amended.

"Percy, you don't know this, it being a day-to-day operations matter, but I've been trying to get a personal sky link call with Travis Noble for several months. To discuss a special rate on sky link services, given how large and early a customer we've been. And, of course, due to the prestige of associating our name with the service. Funnily enough, Percival, I finally got that call. And he had some very specific ideas about a special rate for our family. Should, and I quote, 'the Sky Link Company decide that continuing a relationship with House Headingway is appropriate going forward.' You know what that means, Percy?"

"That they're threatening to cut us off."

"No, Percy, they're giving us reason eighty-seven why you don't fuck with Jason Asano. Losing the System was already an issue, but we aren't the Adventure Society; we can live without it. If we lose the sky link, though, we'll have to downsize our business infrastructure."

"There's still the water link system."

"Percy, we beat out the competition by jumping on the potential of the sky link while everyone else was afraid to take the risk, sticking with the water link. That's how we surged ahead over the last decade."

"How badly will it hurt us? Are we overexposed on this?"

"It won't be a collapse. We've been aggressive with our expansion, but I've always made allowances for an eventuality like this. What it will mean is winding down a lot of operation. Basically, we'll be winding back the clock to where we were ten years ago."

"Which we do not want."

"No, Percy, we do not. You need to shut down this continued antagonism of Asano and the outworlders."

On the desk in front of him, Percival pushed forward the sheet of paper for Mariska to see. She spun it around and started reading.

"What is this?" she asked.

"The draft of my announcement to the family that we will be explicitly avoiding any continued antagonism towards Jason Asano."

"Why didn't you tell me this when I came in? You could have saved me from yelling about prostitutes."

"Well, if you don't like the family announcement approach, Mary, we could try your gift basket and prostitute idea."

"I was kidding about the doxies, Percy."

Jason watched the man guiding Shade as he piloted the cloud ship out of Cyrion.

"You seem nervous," Jason told him. "Are you up to something?"

He turned pale.

"No, sir. My supervisor was very explicit about getting this right."

"Well, calm down, bloke. You want some fruit? Someone gave me a fruit basket and I haven't seen most of the stuff in it before. There's this thing called a prappas. You ever see one of those?"

"Uh, yes, sir. They grow them to the east of here."

"Do you like them?"

"I find the texture rather odd."

"I know, right? It's kind of halfway between a pear and a pineapple. I'm not sure if I love it or hate it yet, but I'm definitely not ambivalent about it."

Jason's cloud ship had a larger passenger manifest than previous trips, with the addition of the people from Earth. As the vessel was the size of a cruise ship, it wasn't hard to accommodate them. Fifty-three people had signed up for the return to Earth in Cyrion. After that, the crowds surrounding the cloud palace became more trouble than they were worth, harassing anyone who came by. A new rendezvous was set up in another city, small and quiet, in the mountains to the north.

This would be one of a series of stops to pick up Earthlings. Li Mei had done a good job of tracking and reaching out to those who, like herself, had long ago left Cyrion. With the aid of Farrah and the sky link system, she had arranged several centralised pickup points. The total returning to Earth, assuming everyone turned up, would be seventy-four. That left around thirty who had no interest in returning, couldn't be found, or were dead.

Darryl was an anomaly amongst the outworlders who had been pulled to Pallimustus from Earth. He was, to his knowledge, the only one who wasn't an essence-user. A troll were-crocodile from the rainforests of Far North Queensland, he was a member of the Cabal. His trollish fae blood let him shapeshift into a form that could pass for human, especially in rural pubs. Disguise was less of a requirement on Pallimustus, one of the reasons he liked it. He'd been uncertain about a potential return to Earth, not sure if he could fit in there any longer.

It was a talk with Jason Asano himself that had turned him around.

Speaking over the sky link network, Asano told him about magic on Earth being much more open than after the reveal. The Cabal held sway in large parts of the world, with its members able to operate out in the open. Darryl was quite happy with this, and Asano even apologised upon finding out his living-under-a-bridge joke was racist.

The mountain city he was in had a large sky port, relative to its size. Specialty airships that could only run in high-magic zones were a signature of Estercost, and approaching the city by land was difficult. That hadn't stopped Darryl, his physique more powerful than most essence-users of his rank.

Unlike most of the Earth refugees, Darryl hadn't been hindered by ranking up with monster cores. He naturally grew more powerful, only the weak ambient magic of Earth having held him back. He had gone from barely silver rank fifteen years ago to pushing against the gates of gold. Unfortunately, his progress had slowed and he wasn't sure why.

The bottleneck in his growth was what had ultimately turned Darryl around about joining those returning to Earth. The magic there was reportedly higher now, but it was the proximity to Asano and his team that Darryl wanted. He'd never built up the connections in Pallimustus that would get him access to magical knowledge, while Asano's friends were famous. He hoped that they would be able to help his breakthrough to gold.

There was a group of people from Earth gathered at a tavern near the sky port. Darryl had spoken with them briefly, before sitting alone. In addition to his not being an essence-user, his affiliation with the Cabal concerned them. They had only known the Cabal as a sinister and mysterious group. At the time they had all been pulled to Earth, the vampire lords were only beginning to schism from the Cabal.

They all moved together, however, when a commotion started outside. It sounded like the sort of panic that arose from a monster attack. The Earthlings, along with various others in the bar, moved outside to look. It didn't take long to see that the attack was coming from above. A group of the city's adventurers had intercepted some flying monsters before they could attack the sky port. They now clashed in the air over the side of the mountain, a vast drop below them.

The monsters had the shape of dragons, each around the size of a school bus. Rather than living things, however, their bodies were chunks of rock, tethered together by arcs of electricity. They almost looked like fossil displays in a museum. Some of the people from the bar took to the skies, either on devices or through their own power. Some were escaping the fight while others were rushing to help. The people from Earth remained grounded, observing as they stood outside the tavern.

"Stormspire drakes," Darryl said. "We should help."

"Bugger that," one of the essence-users said, his accent marking him as a fellow Australian.

"Yeah, screw that," another said. "I can sense at least one gold-ranker amongst those things."

"But most are silver," Darryl argued. "And there are a lot of them. The adventurers might not have the numbers."

"Others are going to help," the Australian said. "I'm not getting myself killed right before I finally escape this heretical planet and its false gods."

"False gods?" someone asked in a New Zealand accent. "I've seen lots of gods. There's a really good bar and grill near the divine square in the town where I've been living. I've seen so many gods there that I'm surprised a god of sausages didn't show up."

The others turned to the newcomer, who hadn't been with them in the tavern. He was a Māori, but much leaner than the famous Taika Williams.

"You're not a core-user," the Australian said.

"Nah, mate. I was visiting my mum at the portal site when I got sucked in with everyone else. I trained up here, so no cores."

He looked over at Darryl.

"What's your deal, mate?"

"Troll were-crocodile."

"No bull? That sounds pretty sweet. Want to go fight some weird rock lightning dragons?"

"Hell yes. The name's Darryl."

They shook hands.

"I'm Koa. Can you fly, or will you need a piggyback or something?"

"Oh, I'll manage."

Jason and Humphrey moved onto the bridge of the cloud ship, looking out at the mountain in the distance.

"The sky port should have sent someone by now," Humphrey said.

"Maybe they don't do that here, being a smaller city," Jason suggested.

"The sky port there is still big. Will your aura senses reach from here?"

"Probably," Jason said, then closed his eyes and concentrated. A moment later, they snapped open.

"Monster attack," he said. "One gold and a lot of silvers. Looks like adventurers are fighting them off, but I'm guessing they'd appreciate a few more, given the numbers. If that's alright with you, team leader?"

"Let's go."

The cloud vessel approached the rear of the battle at speed. Along with adventurers flying around, several airships were employing their weapons, and the sky port itself had fixed defences. Jason and his companions were arrayed on top of the cloud vessel, those who couldn't fly inside Onslow's expanded shell. Nik was included, as most of the foes were silver rank.

"This looks like a mess," Humphrey said, surveying the chaotic battle. "Port defences, civilians helping, multiple adventuring teams. A small horde of gold-rankers diving in might do more harm than good, especially if we start using the ship weapons. Nik, your specialty is group organisation, right?"

"Yep," Nik confirmed. "I'm used to jumping in with groups who don't know me. Want me to start getting this lot in line?"

"Connect me in when you link communication to everyone," Miguel Ladiv said. "I'll identify myself as an Adventure Society official and give you organisational authority. It should save time."

"That'll definitely help," Nik said.

"Thank you, Miguel," Humphrey said.

"I'll, uh, go back inside and make snacks for when everyone is done," Jamar said.

"And drinks," Neil called after him as he left. "I want to see multiple jugs of that fruit punch when we're done."

"Hey, look at that," Jason said. "Is that a giant crocodile man swinging like Tarzan on a rope made of blood, hanging from a lightning dragon in flight?"

"I don't know," Danielle said. "Who's Tarzan?"

A huge grin split Jason's face.

"I have to say it: I love being an adventurer."

54

HAVING STRANGERS COME ALONG

A LINE OF RED AND GOLD ELECTRICITY FLASHED THROUGH THE AIR. IT burst into the form of a Māori, right above the stone and lightning body of a stormspire drake. Koa dropped lightly onto the drake's back as it passed under him.

The drake half rolled back and forth trying to shake its rider. Whips of lightning lashed at Koa, only to vanish without visible effect. Unfazed but not unbalanced, he crouched on the largest of the stones making up the drake's main body. He placed both hands on the rock he was kneeling on and the electricity holding the drake together started to dim.

The drake's thrashing grew worse, but Koa might as well have been glued to it. The rocks making up the front of the drake shifted, causing its neck to grow. Once it had extended enough, the drake twisted its head back to snap at Koa. Koa reached out, catching its nose in the palm of his hand. The electricity connecting the rocks in the drake's head and neck vanished and fell away. Even headless, the drake continued to fly, but not for long. The rest of its lightning dimmed and shrank until the drake was nothing but inert rock, falling and scattering as it fell towards the mountain below.

Koa's Absorb Electricity power was more useful than he'd feared when first picking it up. Draining the natural electricity out of a person was, as it turned out, very bad for them. While generally not very harmful to anyone of the same rank, just a touch could send them falling into seizure or unconsciousness for a brief but critical moment.

There were circumstances, however, when Koa could use his power to truly cut loose. Thunderstorms. Electric death towers. One guy that looked like William Shatner and hurled bolts of lightning. Best, though, were electric monsters. Storm lizards. Deadpond eels. This was Koa's first time fighting stormspire drakes, but he did so with a savage grin. The electricity coursing through them was second only to lightning elementals.

There was little point throwing the electricity he drained back at them, as was usually the case for such monsters. Instead, he used the absorbed power to refill the mana of his very hungry power set, and to overcharge some of his other abilities.

The rock Koa was attached to plummeted through the air, no longer connected to the rest of the drake. Koa moved from a crouch to a standing position, still standing on it as if glued by the feet. He glanced around, seeing the crocodile man at around the same altitude. He was also riding a rapidly descending drake, having hooked its wings with some manner of blood rope.

Koa looked up at the huge swarm of drakes above. They were relatively weak; they had to be to manifest in such numbers. There were two gold-ranked ones being engaged by the local gold-rank adventurers. Koa wasn't fool enough to insert himself into that fight, no matter how advantageous his powers. He picked one the other drakes flying around that no one else was fighting. He raised his arm towards it and chanted a spell.

"Let the heart of the world beat."

His Ignite Stone ability caused rock to rapidly melt. The harder and more magical the stone, the more powerful the effect. Not only were the drakes both very hard stone and very full of mana, but Koa had overcharged the spell with the power drained from the last drake's electricity.

The stone fragments of the drake grew hot, throbbing red with a heartbeat rhythm. The pulse grew faster and faster, the stone hotter and brighter until it was dripping molten rock. Finally, the drake exploded, showering others nearby in glowing shrapnel. It wasn't enough to do the other drakes real damage, but the distraction allowed adventurers to pounce on them for easy kills.

Koa once again turned into electricity, flashing towards his next victim. He was halfway through draining it when he stopped, continuing to ride as it feebly flew on. His attention had been grabbed by a pair of new airships arriving in the battle. They weren't the first, and while they were among the biggest, that wasn't what stood out.

They were both cloud ships, with hull panels set over the cloud material. The larger showed off more of the underlying cloud material, at least at first. This one accelerated ahead of the other, huge weapons emerging from the uncovered cloud sections. It was the second ship, however, that drew the eye. Not only was it radiating a domineering gold-rank aura, but it was transforming as it flew.

The sky ship had arrived in the shape of a massive seagoing vessel. As Koa watched, the decks and hull panels were absorbed until it was just a mass of cloud. The transformation wasn't swift, so he finished off the drake and moved on to another before checking again. By that point, the cloud mass had taken on a ball shape. Triangular panels were emerging from the inside, so black they seemed to absorb the light around them. They each fit together around the cloud mass to form a humungous icosahedron, white light highlighting where each panel met.

In the centre of each black panel was a blue and orange eye. There was something indefinably baleful about them, Koa instinctively glancing away when he tried to stare at them directly. The drakes filled the sky like hornets born of a storm, and the vessel ploughed right into them. Beams blasted from every eye, some blue and some orange. When the blue beams struck, the drakes' lightning was washed away like a sandcastle struck by a rogue wave. Only chunks of inert stone were left behind, falling away to tumble down the mountainside. The orange beams instead burned the rock away like dry leaves before an encroaching bushfire.

The airships seemed focused on the silver-ranked drakes, not interfering with the local adventurers as they tackled the twin gold-rank drakes. Koa grinned and finished off his own drake, ready to seek out more before they were all gone.

***

"Configuration D20 is complete," Shade announced on the sky ship bridge. "The monster swarm has been engaged."

"I can't believe you can modify your ship on the go like that," Emir said through voice chat. "No putting back in the flask, no complex redesign. How is that fair?"

"I'll tell you what, Emir," Jason said. "How about we swap airships, but the next time someone has to fight a great astral being or a god or a messenger army single-handed, that one's on you."

"Oh, I couldn't give up my airship," Emir said hurriedly. "I've put so much work into it."

Jason laughed and put a hand on Nik's shoulder.

"You ready, buddy?"

"Yeah," Nik said, rolling his shoulders.

"Then go for it. Just don't get mad, alright?"

"About what?"

"Don't worry about it. Just get started."

Daryll didn't have the range of abilities an essence-user enjoyed, but he did have a few tricks up his sleeve. The combination of his troll body and his were-crocodile form gave him the strength of a might essence, the fortitude of an iron essence and the regeneration of an immortal essence. He could supplement those with his versatile blood magic, made all the stronger by the troll blood in his veins. It could reinforce his crocodile hide, add blood venom to his bite, even create prehensile ropes of blood and tendon, with toothy clamps at the end.

After landing on the back of a drake, Daryll shot a blood rope from each hand, clamping them onto the wings. He yanked hard, locking himself in place and disrupting the creature's flight. The monsters largely ignored aerodynamics, but their wings held the magic that governed their flight. Having them interfered with sent the creature into a half glide, half fall, Daryll riding it as it dropped through the sky.

Daryll ignored the electricity crawling over his feet. His magically reinforced hide was a surprisingly good insulator, and his regeneration healed what little damage got through. The only thing he had to manage was the cramping and reflexive jerking the electricity caused in his muscles.

The gold-rank aura that had washed over the battlefield was impossible to miss, but Daryll had felt the lack of hostility, at least to him. It wasn't a drake's aura, and that was enough. While he was too busy to investigate the aura, there was no ignoring the drone that flew down to buzz around his face, matching the speed of the drake. The Earthling did a double take at seeing something so obviously technological in Pallimustus. Keeping pace with him, the drone projected a hologram that looked like a computer screen from thirty-year-old science fiction.

- [Nik Asano] has invited you to a raid group. Current raid group leader is [Danielle Geller]. While part of a raid group, you will have access to the System, with additional functionality beyond the baseline. You will be added to voice chat, with channels for the full raid, your assigned group and limited access to raid leadership.
- Acceptance into the raid group is contingent on acceptance of having the powers of [Nik Asano] interface with you. Do you accept?

YES/NO

Daryll wasn't an essence-user, so had never had access to the System. From the complaints over its recent withdrawal, however, it was something worth having.

"Yes!" he yelled, still struggling with the drake.

Its neck had been growing longer, the rocks making up its body slowly rearranging. It now had a long enough neck to snap at him, but he lifted one foot to kick it on the stony snout. While that was happening, the drone had flown out of sight behind him. He did not see it deploy several long, thin needles, but he felt them jam into his back, just below his neck. It passed through his reinforced magical hide without resistance, jabbing the flesh underneath.

He was immediately distracted by a heads-up display appearing, reminiscent of video games he hadn't played in fifteen years. There were bars for mana and stamina, and a green silhouette of his body to indicate his health. To the right edge of his vison was a list of status effects, tucked out of the way but easy to read if he focused. It showed the magical enhancements he had given himself, plus the muscle spasm effect in his legs.

To the left was a column of status boxes for the rest of the group, just health and mana bars with a background coloured by rank. Aside from that, there were tags on the monsters and the fighters on his own side, complete with honest-to-goodness health bars over their heads.

The sudden visual clutter was disorienting, and he almost missed the drake attempting another bite. Once more, it got a kick to the face for its trouble, just as another window appeared. This one was not projected by the drone but part of his new interface.

- Situation assessment complete.
- Enhancing electricity resistance.
- You have been assigned to raid party: Civilian Assistance.
- You have entered voice channel: Civilian Assistance.
- Deploying accessories.

"Accessories?"

He ignored the sudden appearance of startled voices in his head. He felt the spasms in his legs ease, and what looked like a padded metal girdle appeared around his waist. There were spikes around the girdle that shot out, digging into the drake's body. Metal cables tethering the spikes to the belt tightened, securing him in place.

- Mountaineer tether harness deployed. Use voice or mental command 'RELEASE' to disconnect tethers.

Daryll grinned and let go of his own tethers of blood and sinew. He then conjured up a hammer in each hand, made from bone and dripping with blood. His laughter was a crocodilian roar as he started smashing the drake with them, the metal tethers holding him secure. The drake was tough, but Daryll was a powerhouse, his twin hammers smashing its body to rubble and dust. In short order, the electricity holding its body together vanished and the remaining rocks fell from the sky.

The metal girdle vanished in a pop of dimensional energy as Daryll dropped alongside the remnants of the drake. He had fallen well below the battle, and even the level of the mountain city. On one side of him was cliff face, and on the other, open sky. He felt something appear on his back and straps wrapped around his waist and shoulders. A helmet encapsulated his head and he heard a roaring blast behind him. There was a fierce jerk, and he was yanked skyward once more.

- Mountaineer tether harness withdrawn. Jetpack deployed.

"Oh, hell yes!" Daryll exclaimed as he started rocketing upward. "Is this a *Rocketeer* helmet?"

- Of course it's a ****ing Rocketeer helmet, You want handles with joysticks on them? Just point your ****ing head where you want to ****ing go. Oh, great, Dad turned the ****ing profanity filter back on.

"What is going on?"

- Don't worry about it, just go fight some monsters. The whole troll-crocodile thing you've got going on is totally sweet, by the way. We should hang out later.

"Uh, okay?"

He looked up at the people still fighting the drakes. The jetpack steering was intuitive, following whatever direction he was looking. Some of the people above glowed blue in his new interface.

- Marking group members with potentially advantageous power synergies.

"Oh, I think this is going to work out."

Danielle joined the voice channel of the local gold-rankers fighting the two gold-rank drakes.

"This is Danielle Geller. At my command is a large force of gold-rank adventurers. Would you prefer us to aid with the gold-rank monsters, clear out the silvers or a mix of both?"

"Are you going to listen, or just do what you like?" an adventurer asked bitterly.

"We are just guests here, and freshly arrived ones at that. Your house, your rules."

"We've got the golds contained. Having strangers come along now will just mess things up. Take care of the silvers."

"Very well. Reach out if you need anything, and we'll talk again when it's done."

The gold-rankers pouring out of Emir and Jason's cloud ships took to the silver-rank drakes like a flamethrower hitting a bug swarm. Humphrey swung his sword to send waves of destructive force like skyborne tsunamis. Zara created living clouds that flowed around adventurers to envelop the drakes. It turned the monsters' own electricity against them, destroying them with their own power.

Others focused on crowd control, especially as the drakes started to flee. Jason hunted down runners, dosing them with afflictions and moving on. Lightning dripped blood and stone turned to rot as drakes fell from the sky, too weak to stay in the air. The mountainside became splattered with their gooey remains.

The rest either chased down runners with Jason or kept loose drakes from reaching the city as they scattered. Sophie and Danielle kept an eye on the adventurers and civilians who had joined the fight, intervening as needed with their blinding speed.

The intercession of the gold-rankers marked the effective end of the danger, both to the city and those who rushed to defend it. Once the last of the drakes were done, those not out looting gathered in the sky port. Overhead, sky ships that had avoided the fight were left in holding patterns. Those that had engaged the monsters and been damaged were prioritised for repairs and were being brought in to dock.

Sharp wind pushed snow along the ground, the high-altitude city unfriendly to low-rankers. Jason and his companions endured the weather easily, gathered on the tarmac at the base of a sky port docking tower. There was a large crowd of likewise high-ranking adventurers, along with civilians who had participated. Everyone not off looting monsters had come together after the fight.

There were a lot of gold-rankers, many of them famous, leaving a lot of silver-rankers starry-eyed. Jason's identity hadn't been noticed yet, at least by anyone that cared, so he'd quietly switched to civilian clothes and disguised his aura as silver rank. He was talking with Nik, complimenting his efforts. Nik sounded like a telegram machine as most of what he yelled at Jason was bleeped out.

"It's matter of professionalism," Jason told Nik.

"How would you know?" Neil chimed in, earning him a scathing look from Jason.

"I'm trying to teach a lesson here, Neil."

"And I'm wondering when you learned it yourself. You realise your intimidation routine works better when you don't have a recording crystal playing Wang Chung, right?"

Jason turned as a loud voice yelled out in a New Zealand accent.

"Lady Danielle! Over here!"

A young Māori man pushed his way through the crowd.

"Howsitgoin?" he asked Danielle. "I've been in town a couple of days. Want to know where to get the best chips?"

"I do," Nik said, heading in that direction. "How are you, Koa?"

Jason looked at the New Zealander with no trace of cores in his aura.

"Who is that?"

55

TAKE THINGS SLOW

After collecting the people from Earth and turning his sky vessel back into a passenger ship, Jason and his companions set off for the next pick-up location. Most of the Earthlings had been assigned to comfortable but basic dormitory lodging, with some attached activity areas.

"Mr Asano," Shade said, after getting the new people settled. "The ship has more than enough room to give them individual cabins."

"Yeah, but I'm a little worried about what happens if they're all isolated. Plus, if they're interacting, some of them might let something slip if they're up to something."

Having stepped up in the defence of the cloud city, Daryll and Koa had earned themselves cabins instead of being shoved in with the others. Jason was heading to the lounge bar to speak with them while Koa's mother moved her things from the dormitory to the cabin suite she would now share with her son.

In the lounge with Jason, Danielle, Nik and Neil, the two Earthlings told their stories. Daryll was from Far North Queensland, part of the Cabal faction monitoring the stone circle when it sucked everyone across worlds. Koa's story was one of teenage rebellion and unfortunate timing.

"My mother worked for the Network," he explained. "I was visiting her at your knock-off Stonehenge, where she was working. She told me not to sneak off to get a closer look at the thing, so I did it as soon as I had a chance. Of course, that had to be when it did the magic wibbly thing. The worst bit is that Mum brings it up every time she thinks I'm not listening."

"Once it became clear you wouldn't be coming to deal with them yourself," Danielle said, "I had Koa and his mother sent to Greenstone while we kept the other Earthlings at our compound in Cyrion. He wasn't quite old enough for essences, but he was close."

"Mum works for the Gellers now," Koa said. "She stayed in Greenstone until I became an adventurer, then moved to Cyrion."

"He was starting his training just as I was finishing up," Nik added.

"Koa," Jason said grimly. "Just so you know, I've been in contact with Earth for a little while now. Before we head back, there are some things you need to know about what happened to New Zealand. I want to prepare you for it now so it isn't as much of a shock when we arrive."

"What happened?" Koa asked.

Jason leaned forward in his chair, eyes filled with sympathy.

"New Zealand… got real bad at rugby."

"What?"

"I know. There's so many white dudes on the national team, they had to change the name from the All Blacks to the Semi-Blacks."

Koa gave Jason a flat look.

"I heard a lot of things about you, over the years. No one ever mentioned you were a giant prick."

"You can't have heard that much, then," Neil muttered as Jason laughed.

Collecting the rest of the people from Earth proved less exciting than at the mountain city. The final location was in a vast flatland crossed by many waterways, known as the River Table. It had supposedly once been a mountain range, with stories of its levelling being many and varied. Most settled on either the wrath of the gods or a grand battle between diamond-rankers, but neither the gods nor any diamond-rankers had weighed in with an answer.

After arriving in the night and collecting the Earthlings, the plan was shuffle everyone into Jason's astral kingdom in the morning, then portal to Rimaros. Jason was walking through the cloud ship with Humphrey, discussing last-minute details.

"I think that's everything," Humphrey said. "On a side note, you might want to keep it quiet that your soul realm circumvents normal portal limitations. Do you have any idea how open to abuse that could be? Merchants would sell you their children for that."

"I made a point of telling the Adventure Society, so I imagine word will get around. It'll take a merchant with hefty nuggets to come around proposing a deal, though."

"You told the Adventure Society?"

"We've already seen its usefulness for mass evacuations, with Boko and the brighthearts. The Adventure Society knows about those, but I wanted to make it clear that it's an option if they need it for some fresh catastrophe. I'm not saying that I want a catastrophe to happen, but it would be nice if they had to call me in, instead of my already being in the middle of it."

Humphrey slapped a hand on Jason's shoulder.

"It's good that you let them know. Being there for people to rely on is what we do. But don't forget that you need to rely on people as well, sometimes. I know that you have that vast cosmic power you're always talking about."

"Not *always*."

"Sure. But remember that while you may be a big cosmic special man, you're also still just a man. Who needs help sometimes."

"Big cosmic special man?"

"It feels like you're not focusing on the important parts of what I'm saying, Jason."

"No, I get it. I've learned my lesson about going it alone."

"Good. Now, I'm going to leave you alone. See you in the morning."

Jason chuckled as his friend wandered off. Jason kept moving, riding an elevating platform to the bridge, then walking out and up some exterior stairs to the top deck. A cloud lounger rose from the deck and he fell into it, happily looking up at the night sky. Only one of the moons was visible, but it was full, turning the clouds into wisps of silver against the black. He luxuriated in the view and the quiet, halfway between meditation and a nap.

He was unsure how long he'd been there when Zara made her way up. The grace of her footfalls on the stairs made no sound, even to gold-rank hearing, but nothing was hidden from him within the cloud ship. He sensed the hesitant irregularity as she ascended the stairs; the tiny pause before she stepped onto the deck.

"It's a beautiful night," he said. "A river of silver, spilling across the sky. I'm glad that not every wonder needs magic to exist."

"You're on a flying ship made of clouds," she pointed out.

"Well, some do need magic. That's only fair."

He sat up and turned to look at her, standing almost nervously at the top of the stairs. Many years ago, he had told her to change her hair from the famous sapphire of the Rimaros royal bloodline. Despite his having apologised for imposing on her body autonomy, she had hidden its true shade since, even in his long absence. Now it was back to sapphire, sparkling like gemstone threads in the moonlight. He wondered absently if she saw him freeze at the sight, then got to his feet with not quite the grace a gold-ranker should have.

"You know," he said, "everyone on this ship is an essence-user, or magic in some way."

"I know," she said. "I'm not sure why you're bringing it up."

"No one on this ship is ugly, is what I'm saying. We're all pretty to one degree or another, even if it does leave us looking annoyingly like our brothers."

"I don't think that's a universally applicable observation."

"Maybe not. My point, though, is that on a ship full of beautiful people, it's hard for someone to be so stunning, it seems like the god of low self-esteem put them here to make the rest of us feel bad. Is there a god of low self-esteem?"

"Not that I'm aware of," she told him, snorting a little laugh. "Dark gods are tricky, so you can't be sure, but I don't think so. If there is, I don't imagine it's happy. It would have Despair, Misery and maybe even Pain bossing it around."

"They do sound like bad bosses."

She wore a white dress that starkly contrasted her hair in the moon-light. Her sapphire locks shimmered as she walked across the deck to stand in front of him. He had on a floral shirt and shorts.

"Hello," she said with a nervous smile.

"G'day."

Neither said anything else for a moment.

"I'm starting to feel underdressed," he said finally, and a giggle burst out of her.

"You were wearing almost the exact same thing when we met."

"Do you have any idea how nervous I was back then? I was avoid-ing... whoever that guy was, and I ducked into a random tent. Then, standing right in front of me, was the most beautiful woman I'd ever seen."

"Really?"

"Oh, yeah."

"What about Sophie?"

"She's gorgeous, don't get me wrong, but we all have our own tastes. For one thing, the first time I saw her, she kicked me in the face immediately. Our relationship didn't get any less complicated from there. Also, it's possible I have a thing for blue hair."

Her eyes narrowed as she looked at him.

"Is that why you told me to recolour my hair? Because it made it easier to stay angry at me?"

"No. Maybe. Shut up."

She laughed again.

"You didn't seem nervous, back then," she told him.

"I was rambling like a fool."

"You always ramble like a fool. You gave me a plate of confectionery slices and said I'd regret not taking you up on your dinner offer."

"It has been pointed out, from time to time, that I might be a little bit arrogant."

"You were right."

"I'll take back the thing about being arrogant, then."

She shook her head in exasperation, but couldn't hide the smile teasing her lips. He stepped back, turning away and walking over to the deck railing. He leaned against it and looked up at the moon. She moved to join him, her hand almost touching his on the rail.

"You're putting an end to Zara Nareen," he said. "Princess Zara Rimaros is making her triumphant return."

"I don't know about triumphant, but it's time."

"Why?"

"I want the Storm Kingdom to be the first to eradicate indentured servitude laws."

He turned his head to look at her.

"Don't do this because of me."

"It's not about you," she said, keeping her eyes on the moon instead of looking back. "You know that what you did won't make anyone change, right?"

"I do. You can't impose real change, especially as an outsider. People have to want it. Be ready for it. Best case for me is that I inspire someone who can actually accomplish something."

She turned to look him straight in the eye.

"Oh. Wait, you said it wasn't about me."

"It's not. What you've done is something I can use as a pretence. Leverage. Too many times, I've taken drastic steps to get what I want, and reaped the consequences."

"Like trying to extort every nation on the planet into ending slavery?"

"Maybe not that drastic. You always have to do things a little bigger than everyone else, don't you? Or a lot bigger."

"It's an approach I've come to occasionally regret," he confessed.

"This time, I don't want to rush what I'm doing. No big, overt moves in service of quick results. I want to build the foundation of a movement. Move carefully and quietly to gather support. Show the people who think they have something to lose what they instead have to gain. Like being the only major nation on Pallimustus with full access to the System. Like an aristocracy that earns the respect of the populace instead of demanding it."

"You could abolish the aristocracy altogether."

"That would come under the heading of large, drastic moves. I need to take on a fight I at least have a chance of winning."

"I'm just saying."

"Well, don't. I'm already going to be accused of trying to end slavery as the first step in dissolving the legal standing of noble titles. Doesn't matter if it's true. Those who gain money and power through exploitation aren't shy about lying and cheating to keep that power."

"That, I'm sadly aware of."

"And I meant it when I said this isn't about you. Yes, what you did has given me a chance to take this step. But what inspired me more than you has been the last fifteen years. While you were off fighting some cosmic battle, I've been with your team, out having adventures."

"Our team."

"Our team," she corrected. "You know that we're something of an oddity, amongst adventuring teams."

"Always have been."

"Humphrey and Sophie set the agenda, mostly. They had us picking up the contracts other people avoid. Helping towns and villages with no wealthy residents to add hefty bonuses. Neil too. I know how he comes off, but he has so much compassion under all of the... Neil. He's a priest of the Healer."

"I always thought the reason was that he stumbled into their booth at a jobs fair."

"You should be nicer to him," she chided. "But the team couldn't just be doing low-value contracts. Low paying for silver anyway. Even basic silver contracts pay well, but running a silver-rank party isn't cheap."

She tapped the railing.

"Especially not when we didn't have a free mobile base to operate out of. Lindy made sure we took enough jobs for the money. Humphrey and I might have family wealth, but at our rank, we're expected to add to it, not take it away. Pay for the next generation to enjoy the same advantages we did. And you should make enough money to have some fun along the way."

"If you can't enjoy life at silver rank, you're doing it wrong."

"Exactly. But the point is, we always had a focus on helping people. Zara Nareen saw a world that Zara Rimaros had always been shielded from. We've fought against outright slavery, and undermined indenture programs where the people were being exploited. Lindy and Stella got very good at that. But, satisfying as they were, those actions never brought real change. If anything, they only reinforced the same oppressive systems. We'd gotten rid of the bad apples, so people said everything would be fine now."

"I'm familiar with that particular brand of context blindness."

"My reputation in the Storm Kingdom isn't the best. I did foolish things when I was younger, and that stain will follow me. But it will also cover me a little. People will dismiss my efforts at the beginning, when they are most vulnerable to interference. They won't waste resources fighting me because they don't think I'll accomplish anything."

"I wouldn't bet against you."

"Yes, but your judgement is questionable."

He let out a mock-hurt chortle.

"You wound me, good lady. But I suspect you'll get more support than you expect, even if it's for reasons you won't like."

"What reasons are those?"

He took a deep breath and slowly let it out as he looked once more out at the night. Somewhere far below were the lights of a town they were passing over.

"There's a very famous legend back on Earth that starts with three goddesses. They're arguing amongst themselves over who is the most beautiful, and for some reason decide to make some idiot prince the judge.

They all try to bribe the guy, of course, because why pick a judge with integrity, and the goddess of Love promises him that the most beautiful woman in the world will fall in love with him."

"Gods can't do that. The soul barrier—"

"Will you just let me tell the story? I'm trying really hard here; I didn't even make an Orlando Bloom reference."

"Sorry."

"Where was I?"

"Goddess of Love."

"Right. So, she bribes him with the most beautiful woman in the world, and he accepts because he's a sleazy turd. Soon, he finds himself on a diplomatic mission to another country and, wouldn't you know it, the queen just happens to be the most beautiful woman in the world. Long story short, she stows away with Prince Douche Canoe when he heads home, and her country starts a war to get her back. Since Prince Trust Fund's country is on an island, that means a massive naval force. And, to this day, we say that a woman with world-shaking beauty has a face to launch a thousand ships."

Zara gave Jason a long, assessing look.

"So, you're comparing me to the queen in this story?"

"That was the idea, yes."

"The queen who gets mesmerised by a god, handed over to some man as a bribe and doesn't get to make any choices for herself. Anything done to or for her is just because she's pretty."

"Learn to take a compliment! I just compared you to Helen of Troy."

She put her hand over her mouth, which did nothing to stifle the giggles that crawled into his brain and hit a big button labelled YES PLEASE.

"Oh, you're teasing me."

"You're fun to tease."

"Oh, I'm fun to do all sorts of things to."

The cold night air suddenly felt very warm, and they were very aware of how close they were standing.

"Uh," Jason said, then pointed to the stairs. "I'm going to go. To bed. By myself. Uh, have a good..."

He gave up on trying to make words good and hurried away in a manner not at all suggestive of running away. He stopped at the top of the stairs, though, and looked back.

"You aren't stopping in the Storm Kingdom full time, right? You're staying with the team?"

"Yes. I'm going to plant some seeds while you and Clive build your magic bridge, and let them germinate while we're on Earth."

"Okay."

"I told you that I'm going to take things slow."

"Eminently sensible."

"Not that you have to take *everything* slow."

"Good night," he said and rushed down the stairs.

56

THE END OF WHAT CAN BE
PRODUCTIVELY ACHIEVED HERE

It was Clive who portalled Jason to his destination. Jason had been to the target location before, but only once, and it had changed greatly since. When he and Farrah had arrived, years previously, it had been an uninhabited island, pounded by a localised magical hurricane from which the Sea of Storms took its name.

Years later, it was a very different prospect. The island had a large town situated on it, and the windmill-like storm accumulators surrounding it offshore both shielded the island and delivered the magic that fuelled its infrastructure. All of this was a result of the island being purchased and developed by the Sky Link Company.

Jason's second visit began in a town square set aside for teleport arrivals. He looked around at the building painted in vibrant colours. Blue, red, purple, pink, orange and yellow, all bold shades striking under the bright sun.

"It's hard to believe it's the same place," he said. "I love it."

He opened a portal to his soul realm and people started pouring out, likewise looking around like tourists. They had been doing much the same thing inside Jason's astral kingdom, in the tree city of Arbour.

"This is pretty sweet," Koa said. "It's like being on a magical cruise ship and seeing all the fun destinations."

Farrah directed Jason to a dock where he could set up his cloud palace to accommodate the Earthlings. The island was only set up to house the people who worked there, despite having the feel of a tourist town. He hoped that they could get the bridge established before the people of Earth caused any trouble.

Jason had a meeting with Farrah and Travis, who owned the island, along with Danielle, Zara and Clive. They held it in a conference room with large open windows and robust privacy enchantments.

"We excavated the hidden magical infrastructure the Builder placed here," Travis explained. "Then we had the whole complex sealed off."

"As it stands," Clive said, "using that infrastructure to calibrate the dimensional bridge should take a few weeks. I've studied enough messenger astral magic to understand what we need to do, and the only missing component is you, Jason."

"Why does it require Jason?" Zara asked.

"Because of the anchor on the Earth side," Jason told her. "The World-Phoenix relic I used to create it required me to be involved. Even though I kind of ate the relic and we're doing it the hard way now, that requirement is still in place."

"I don't foresee any insurmountable problems," Clive said. "Just a lot of painstaking work to align this end of the bridge with the one in the other universe. Getting all the details right. This can't be one of those rush jobs I always seem to get stuck with when we're out on adventures. We have to take it slow and do it right."

"But isn't it more exciting when there's a ticking clock?" Jason asked.

"Yes," Clive said with flat disapproval. "It is."

Jason chuckled, then turned to Zara.

"We need to address the political aspect," he said. "This island is isolated, and private land, but it still falls within the boundaries of the Storm Kingdom. Creating a bridge to another universe is no small thing."

"Even if it won't be useable without some hefty magic for around a decade," Clive added. "It will take that long to stabilise, mostly because of Earth's shaky dimensional membrane. Given that this will be permanent, ten years isn't a large timeframe. It's only two-thirds of a Jason-going-off-to-fight-gods-or-whatever. That's a new measurement of time I've started using, by the way."

"Did your wife come up with it?" Jason asked.

"Let's not get distracted," Danielle cut in. "We were talking about the political aspect of establishing the bridge inside the Storm Kingdom's borders."

"We got approval from the Storm King years ago," Travis said. "Back when we bought the island. The isolation was a large part of that."

"As was some quiet nudging from Soramir Rimaros," Farrah added. "But the Storm King was concerned with more than just danger. This brings potential opportunities as well."

"We shouldn't just rely on a decade-old permission from a former Storm King," Danielle said. "We could, but bringing this to the sitting monarch is a demonstration of respect. Getting his approval will smooth things out for us."

"And if he says no?" Clive asked. "We can pack up and do this some-where else, but we'll need to build and calibrate new infrastructure. Weeks turn into months. Maybe years."

"If that's what has to happen, we do it," Jason said. "I know that I'm famous for pushing up against authorities, but there's no urgent fight to be fought. We can afford the time, and doing it outside of any national boundaries has advantages as well."

"The question is," Danielle said as she looked at Zara, "how likely is the Storm King to say no?"

"I don't know," Zara said. "It's considered bad form to overturn deci-sions by previous Storm Kings, but it still happens. Circumstances change. And my cousin may want to make a show of not bowing to outside concerns."

"After I withdrew the System," Jason said.

"Exactly."

"Well," he said, "it's not like I was unaware that there would be conse-quences. I even knew what they would be, more or less. I went into it eyes wide open."

"We could threaten to move the Sky Link Company out of the Storm Kingdom as well," Travis said. "Not just the headquarters but the entire service."

"No," Jason said. "It's one thing to threaten a family, but pulling out of the Storm Kingdom entirely would harm the company too much. It's the main trade hub for two continents. None of us want your employees hurting for my sake."

"It would also backfire," Danielle said. "Jason has already pushed the Storm King, along with every other monarch on the planet. Pushing him again won't work."

"She's right," Zara said. "Even if he wanted to back down, he couldn't afford to, politically. He'd have to push back, even if it was bad for everyone involved."

"Except the Magic Society," Clive said. "You can bet they'd be tooting their horns about the 'proven long-term stability of the water link system.' The sky link hurt one of their major income streams."

"There's also the fact that this is his nation to rule," Jason pointed out. "Everyone here knows my feelings about inherited class systems, but I don't want us to throw our weight around just because we can. Yes, there is probably some combination of political pressure and political finesse that gets us what we want. I'd rather focus on what we can offer the Storm Kingdom, not what we can force it into accepting."

"I appreciate that," Zara said. They were seated next to one another, and she brushed her hand over his lightly as she spoke.

"That is the wise approach," Danielle said. "We should discuss what specific benefits we can present."

———

When everyone filed out after the meeting, Farrah fell in step with Jason as he left the building. She gave him a pointed sideways look as they strolled down the wide street, past the colourful buildings.

"What?" he asked.

She tapped her brooch, and a privacy screen snapped into place.

"What was that?"

"What was what?" Jason asked with unconvincing innocence.

"Are you going to make me drag it out of you?"

"It's nothing."

"Really? Do you actually think people haven't noticed the sudden awkwardness between you two? We all have supernatural senses and the power to read emotions. You might keep a lid on your aura, Jason, but we can also see your face."

"Okay, not *nothing*. But it's not *something* either."

"Not yet."

"I didn't say that."

"And somehow, I still heard it. Dangling off the end of your sentence like a man hanging from a cliff, fully aware that his immediate future will be very bad or very complicated."

"Okay, maybe there was... look, no one is rushing into anything here.

She has ambitions, and all I have to offer in that regard are complications. Any relationship she has is going to matter, and I have a lot of baggage. Not just because of my political position now, but because of our past. After that whole debacle over a made-up relationship back then, a real relationship now would undercut any credibility she's built up. Fifteen years of work as an adventurer, down the drain. She knows it, I know it. Neither of us are going to charge into something foolish and self-destructive. We've both learned our lessons in that regard."

"Well, that all sounds disappointingly mature. Here was me wanting to make fun of you for sneaking around like a teenager."

"Oh, the urge is there, believe me. I'm gold rank; I'm meant to have too much self-control to be this horny."

She laughed. "What are you going to do, then?"

"I don't know."

They stopped at a café where they bought iced tea in takeaway cups of magic glass that would evaporate when empty.

"You're about to be on Earth," Farrah said as they resumed their walk. "She's not a princess there."

"The thought has occurred to me. Yes, we could explore it, but what happens when we come back? It needs to end or become more serious than we'll probably be ready for."

"I'm pretty sure Soramir would be happy to help you out."

"Don't remind me. But what about you? Didn't you have a guy around here somewhere?"

"You mean Trench? Yeah, he's sweet. And earnest. He was always sensitive about the power disparity and the age difference, so we always kept things casual. Now that I'm gold rank, he's been hinting that he wants something more serious."

"And what about you?"

"I don't know. I mean, he's nice. Stable. Mum loves him. You know I built a house on your old spot in Arnote."

"Yeah. You sound hesitant."

"It's not him. I like stable. I want to be the unhinged one, you know? I just don't know if I want that with anyone right now."

"You know, I'm not the only one who could afford to try something out on Earth."

"Oh, yeah, that's a great idea. Drag some guy off to another universe, only to have it not work out and we'll be stuck together until we come back in who knows how long."

"That's a fair point. Look, I don't know the situation with you and Trenchant, and I know that when people live as long as we do, keeping things casual can be the way to go. But, just from what you're saying, it doesn't sound like he wants to keep things casual."

"He doesn't. Not forever."

She sighed.

"I told you that I like stable," she continued, "but maybe it's the idea of it, more than the reality. It scares me, if I'm being honest. I'm not like you, looking to make that emotional connection. I've always kept a safe distance."

"You have to make yourself vulnerable if you want to build trust."

"So I'm told. But letting yourself be vulnerable makes you, well, vulnerable. You know that. You've been hurt that way."

"And I keep doing it anyway. What does that tell you?"

"That you're a fool."

He laughed again.

"Oh, yes. That's a big part of it. Maybe it's time for you to be a fool for once. You need to consider what's stopping you. Is it that it's not what you want? That this isn't the guy? Or that you're just scared? Because if it's the last one, Farrah, then you need to harden up. You fought your way out of a torture complex and came back from the dead. I'm not going to let you run away from a boy because maybe he likes you too much."

"Coming from a guy who can't stop making eyes with the pretty girl with the blue hair."

"Yeah, well, maybe we both have a little courage to work up."

The Storm Kingdom diplomat inclined his head.

"Princess. It is, of course, a delight to have you back. Unfortunately, your cousin was called away and won't be attending. Affairs of state; I'm sure you understand."

Zara stepped up to the man, drawing raised eyebrows as she moved into his personal space.

"Lord Alberto, if my cousin wants to slight me, that is his prerogative as the Storm King. You, however, are not. You will address me as your highness, and you will bow in my presence, rather than nod as if you were passing your greengrocer in the street. You are a man who has practiced statecraft for longer than I have been alive. Because of this, any failure of etiquette on your part can only be construed as disrespect, delivered with deliberation and intent. Should I be again treated as an adventurer instead of a princess of the realm, I will hold you personally responsible, and respond in a manner customary to adventurers. To wit, I will drag you out on the street and peel you like a piece of fruit. Is that understood?"

Alberto gulped, then bowed.

"My apologies, your highness."

Zara swept past the man, Jason and Danielle Geller in tow. The air shimmered around them as Jason used his aura as a privacy screen.

"Are we sure that going that aggressive, that early is the right move?" he asked.

"It is," Danielle said. "Addressing the princess in such a way was calculated to position her as Zara Nareen, noble lady, not Zara Rimaros, princess of the royal house. If she had accepted the slight without comment, she would be tacitly accepting their assertion. By not just asserting her position but bringing the king's name into it, she puts Lord Alberto in the position of accepting responsibility, or acknowledging that the king put him up to it."

"I still have a long way to go in these diplomacy lessons, don't I?" Jason asked. "Are you sure you want me playing good cop here?"

"It's your magic bridge," Zara said. "It is best for any deal struck to be unambiguously struck with you. Just try to avoid promising anything too drastic."

"His majesty feels," Alberto said, "that the threat of unknown danger outweighs the promise of unspecified opportunity."

"An understandable position," Danielle said. "The acceptance of our request by the previous Storm King showed the assuredness of a man who has long held the throne and fully embodied his role as supreme power within the kingdom. His heir is barely a decade into his tenure and we are sympathetic to his hesitancy."

Alberto glowered.

"Your attitude in this matter is noted, Lady Geller, but you will find that prudence is the wisdom that his majesty brings to this table."

"By proxy," Zara pointed out. "Given that he was too busy to actually attend this table."

"I do respect the king's position on this," Jason said. "And I would

444 | SHIRTALOON & TRAVIS DEVERELL

very much like to alleviate the unknowns with which we have presented him, while also expanding the opportunities on offer. As such, I would like to offer the Storm Kingdom something that has been requested by a number of organisations and always refused: a position in our expedition to the other universe."

Alberto leaned back in his chair.

"Under what conditions would you make such an offer?"

"What conditions would you like, Lord Alberto?"

"You say a position in the expedition. Do you mean a representative, or a delegation?"

"I think a diplomatic delegation to engage with the polities of Earth would be entirely appropriate. After all, what will be a difficult bridge to cross in the immediacy will become an open passage in years to come. I think that those who will control each terminus of that passage should have the time to set terms of what manner of border it will be. Let us say, forty people, including security staff."

"And what restrictions will you put on who those forty are?"

"No diamond-rankers. The World-Phoenix isn't letting any diamond-rankers into Earth until I have reached diamond rank myself. Also, until the magic levels rise further, the magic there could only sustain them in certain areas."

"What else?"

"Nothing else. If you want to make a deal with the Magic Society and ship some of their people in, that's on you. I would look down on such behaviour, but I will tolerate it. They will be your people to choose, Lord Alberto. And yours to be responsible for."

"And what do you mean by responsible for, Mr Asano?"

"I mean that if I have to kill any of them, Lord Alberto, you will have to answer for that."

"Please remember," Danielle said, "that any accommodations we make are gestures, made out of respect. The Storm Kingdom has nothing we need."

"If the Storm King chooses to revoke the permission granted by his uncle, my father," Zara added, "then all it will cost Mr Asano is time. Time that he can very much afford."

"There are advantages to operating outside of any nation," Jason said. "And I have no doubt that many countries would leap at the chance to grab the opportunities you seem so reticent to accept. In fact…"

He got to his feet.

"...I think we've reached the end of what can be productively achieved here. I have a feeling that the Storm King's deliberation on this matter will leave us time to explore our alternatives."

The negotiations were mostly occupied not by whether to approve the bridge, but in how many concessions the Storm Kingdom could get out of Jason. That turned out to be not many, as he had already promised to carry whoever the Storm Kingdom chose to send, so long as it wasn't a Builder cultist or someone. Any deals they made with the powers of Earth would be for them to negotiate and enforce. Jason did agree to have them taught several Earth languages.

To Jason's surprise, he enjoyed digging into the nitty gritty of calibrating a dimensional portal. It was good to get back into the astral magic theory he had studied under Dawn during his time on Earth. His instinctual grasp of dimensional forces also helped guide them, but even that paled in comparison to Clive's mastery of the theory. Once again, he was staggered by the sheer intellectual power of his friend.

Jason socialised with some of his old friends from Rimaros. Autumn Leal was an adventurer who he met while working contracts, before his fame had risen. She made an old in-joke about Jason avoiding princesses, only to then meet Zara. Princess Liara visited the island for a barbecue, along with her husband, Baseph, and her family. Their daughter, Zareen, had gotten herself assigned to the Rimaros diplomatic delegation to Earth.

Work on the bridge was paused for a few days so that Sophie's mother could finally, after many delays, go through the treatment to remove the materials actively brainwashing her. The results were a success, but considerably taxing, and Melody lapsed into unconsciousness soon after. Like Jason once had after overtaxing himself, she needed time to heal that no magic could accelerate.

More friends arrived to join the Earth expedition, along with others Jason had invited. Valdis and Rick Geller both arrived with their teams. Vice Chancellor of the Magic Research Association, Lorelei Grantham, arrived with a cadre of magic researchers. Travis and Farrah were bringing along a host of employees, to better learn magitech on Earth. Jory arrived with a team of alchemists, and things definitely weren't extremely awkward with Belinda.

A contingent of priests would be travelling with them, not to see Earth but to work in the city Jason had created in his astral kingdom. Clergy of various gods who could help establish new homes for the Boko refugees residing in Jason's astral kingdom. Many had already been there for some time, but a larger group was joining them as the astral kingdom was soon to be cut off from Pallimustus, at least until Jason returned.

A handful of the faithful found themselves unable to stay, leaving as soon as they entered. For many, being cut off from their god was too much. Others were fine, and some viewed it as a test of faith, will, independence or some other value, based on their specific god's values.

The most uncomfortable inclusion was Gabrielle, priestess of Knowledge and Travis Noble's now-wife. As Humphrey's ex and someone who had long and publicly disapproved of essentially everything about Jason, she was not the most popular figure on the ship. Time, however, had seemed to soften her rough edges. No one cared about an old teenage romance, and Gabrielle had come to accept that if Knowledge could favour Jason so much, she could at least tolerate him. She didn't get a lot of invitations to board game night, though.

The activation of the bridge did not come with any fanfare, or great explosion of aura. Those sensitive to dimensional power would notice, if close to the island, but most had no idea that anything had changed. For now, the bridge was only open to those with the power and knowledge to cross the scathing unreality of the deep astral. Jason would use his cloud ship as a ferry, with the proto-bridge as a guide wire.

Deep underground, a massive chamber held a series of standing stones, set out in a giant ritual diagram. Jason's cloud ship floated over them, a ramp leading up to an opening in the hull. He boarded, alongside his companions, the Rimaros delegation and the outworlder refugees, finally set to go home. In a swirl of rainbow light, the air ship vanished, finally setting out for Earth.

5 7
SOMEONE GOT SUCKED OFF

SITTING IN THE CAPTAIN'S CHAIR ON THE BRIDGE OF HIS DIMENSION SHIP, Jota Withers let out a sigh. This was not the trajectory his life had been meant to take. The universe-city of Interstice was, for most practical purposes, the centre of the cosmos. Only diamond-rankers were allowed entry without invitation, with gold-rankers like Jota only allowed in as menial workers. Even so, to be a resident of Interstice was to stand at the pinnacle of the cosmic order. Jota had never made it.

The population of Interstice came from two places. One was the wider cosmos, where people ranked up in various universes before entering the cosmic community. Diamond-rankers only occasionally emerged from such realms, like someone from a small town making it big in the city. At the other end of the prominence spectrum were the polities that spanned multiple dimensions, like the Radiant Sovereignty and the Constel Empire. The diamond-rankers from such realms at least knew what they were getting into.

Standing above them all was the universe-city, Interstice, and the peripheral universes attached to it. Those connected realities largely existed to produce the future elites of Interstice society, dedicated to raising people to gold, and ultimately, diamond rank. Those who gradu-ated the feeder programs had unparallelled knowledge, training and resources.

Few sapient species were born as gold- or diamond-rankers. Not even dragons, phoenixes or garuda could boast as much. In the peripheral universes of Interstice, the people born there had every advantage to help them grow strong. Staggeringly rich in ambient magic, their civilisations were advanced in knowledge of both science and the arcane. Those born into such conditions had unparalleled opportunities, with an inside line to Interstice that even citizens of the cosmic empires envied.

Jota, like everyone born in such realms, had been part of a feeder program that would ultimately lead to reaching Interstice at gold rank. To be a servant in heaven was still to stand above everyone outside it, promising a place amongst the cosmic elite on reaching diamond. The harsh reality, however, was that the success rate for such programs was infinitesimally small, most never making it to a gold-rank posting on Interstice. There was nothing stopping them from heading there upon reaching diamond, but only as a normal person, not a specially groomed member of the chosen few.

Just in his solar system, let alone his entire universe, Jota had been one of trillions to fall short. Most moved on with their lives, still enjoying the massive head start their upbringing gave them. Some, however, were unable or unwilling to accept their failure. Like many before him, Jota had taken his talents and abilities to the wider cosmos. Even a failure from the Interstice lesser universes was a prestigious figure on the cosmic stage, or so Jota had believed.

The reality he discovered was that the cosmos was unkind to gold-rankers. They were not built for the challenges of roaming the deep astral, operating out of high-magic universes and artificial pocket realities. It was a place for diamond-rankers, astral entities and even transcendents, and a gold-ranker needed to find a patron amongst them.

A patron made it possible for a gold-ranker to establish themselves, acquiring the resources to operate successfully. Most important was having a backer, someone to ward off those who would see them as prey. A patron was a shelter for a gold-ranker to huddle beneath until they achieved diamond rank for themselves. Until then, they were little better than servants. It was not lost on Jota that this was a reflection of Interstice itself, but without the prestige that came with it.

Jota's arrogance over his background had cost him opportunities and taught him harsh lessons. By the time he learned to humble himself, his choice of patrons had become lean. He ended up in the service of a self-styled cosmic admiral who, in reality, was a pirate lord preying upon isolated worlds in astral backwaters.

Decades after Jota had left his home universe, diamond rank seemed a distant dream. His failures had impacted his path to self-realisation, stunting his advancement through gold rank. He had long ago come to terms with the fact that he would need to lay low, be diligent and slowly find his place in the cosmos. Only with that stability could he go back to the exploration of self required to advance as an essence-user. That wasn't easy in the employ of 'Admiral' Aractus Jakaar.

There were rules about entering universes and the worlds within, especially those with native life. Some of those rules could be nudged and others pushed, and this was the bread-and-butter of the Jakaar fleet. They were careful, however, about what they did and who they crossed. For all his grandiosity, Admiral Jakaar was careful to avoid the Cult of the World-Phoenix. The dreaded first sister might have retired to become a hierophant and transcend, but that did not mitigate their influence. While her successor settled into her duties, the other sisters had been aggressive in the execution of their duties.

As his dimension ship traversed the astral, Jota wondered what the admiral had in store for him. His vessel was a rarity, being only gold rank, but that was a necessity for certain jobs. The lower the rank, the less strenuous the rules around entering universes. Jota and his gold-rank crew could go places and do things the admiral and his main forces could not.

Not wary of letting his emotions show while he was alone on the bridge, Jota sighed again. His thoughts dwelled on the next isolated backwater he would inevitably be sent off to, the latest in a long series. He told himself that he had come to terms with his shattered expectations, but the lies rang more hollow with each passing year. If he had truly reached acceptance, his progress through gold rank wouldn't have stalled out.

Jason carefully placed the little plastic roof on the head of his meeple like a hat, then returned it to the hex.

"I'm building a dwelling, obviously. I'm going to use coins in place of…"

He trailed off, tilting his head as if listening for a distant noise.

"Sophie," he said. "Your mother is waking up."

As his dimensional vessel neared the dimensional boundary, Jota reflected on his unexpected life as a cosmic pirate. He fancifully compared it to the age of sail experienced by many primitive worlds, with universes as islands in the ocean of the deep astral. From his cultural studies, he knew that many worlds romanticised frontier eras, legendizing often elevating brief and brutal periods to become cultural touchstones. The stories masked the harsh and grim realities behind them.

Jota's time sailing the astral had borne this out. His arrival, like a colonial force, never made things better for the locals. Because of his low rank, it was always to some low-to-mid magic world where gold-rankers were like god-kings. He needed only a thin pretence to satisfy the intrusion rules, then he would take the planet for all it was worth. Strip mining; people trafficking; essence seizure. It had bothered him, in the beginning, but not enough to not do it. And never that much, if he was entirely honest with himself. He was from a place so far above these little worlds that the natives might as well be animals.

Jota signalled his bridge crew to assemble for the transition into the universe where the main Jakaar fleet was holed up. He hoped the location was sufficiently advanced this time; he was sick of backward worlds where the use of magic had stalled out the growth of technology. The ones with all tech and no magic were just as bad, their advancement choked in the bottlenecks of physical laws that magic could neatly sidestep.

They shifted into physical reality, arriving in space at the outskirts of a solar system with no inhabitable planets. The vessel's sensors picked up extensive mining operations and a large space station orbiting a moon. Jota checked the detailed sensor logs and smiled. It wasn't everything he could hope for, but still a proper magitech station. For this far off from major traffic lanes, it was better than he expected. He confirmed that the fleet was docked there and directed the helmsman to rendezvous.

"I'm sorry that your first experience outside of my spirit realm is inside what amounts to a smaller version of my realm," Jason told Melody. "The timing was unfortunate."

"It's fine," Melody said, sitting up in her cloud bed. "I've been living in your soul realm all these years, and I've watched it go from an unstable pocket universe to housing a planet as solid and real as the one I was born on. I didn't feel cooped up, and now I get a whole new world to explore…"

She squeezed the hand of Sophie, sitting beside the bed.

"…with my daughter. I couldn't ask for more than that."

After her reunion with Sophie and checkup by Carlos, Arabelle and Neil, Jason had been let in to speak with her. Alongside Sophie, he had explained their current situation, travelling between worlds. After their conversation, Jason left mother and daughter alone, finding the three members of Healer's clergy outside her room. Carlos was a soul healing specialist, Arabelle a mental healing specialist and Neil a traditional body specialist. After her ordeal, Melody was in need of all three.

"How is she?" Jason asked.

"Better than we had any right to hope," Carlos said happily. "She's suffered extreme and prolonged physical and spiritual trauma, but all signs point to a slow but full recovery."

"Her desire to explore your world with her daughter is good," Arabelle said. "Once she discovered her daughter was alive, Melody's desire to reunite even overrode the brainwashing she'd gone through. She's showing healthy signs of dealing with that, with little of the obsession that drove her to push back the influence upon her. She needs ongoing care, but I'm optimistic, given the positive signs I'm seeing. Early days, though. You know yourself, Jason. Mental recovery is neither a smooth nor short process."

"So long as she's protected," Carlos said, "I see no problem with allowing her to roam around a low-danger world. No self-defence, though. Not using her powers anyway. I have a strict plan for the resumption of using her abilities, to avoid any long-term spiritual damage."

"Her body is going to take time," Neil added. "Like when you overdid it with that portal in Rimaros, the spiritual strain has rendered normal magical healing ineffective. I'd like to discuss bringing in Jory and his alchemists, since we have them with us. A more medicine-based approach might get us better results than trying to pump her full of healing magic."

Jason left them to discuss treatment, wondering if he could get someone to take Sophie's place when he resumed the board game.

Aractus Jakaar was an unusual man in that his body carried a lot of fat as a quirk of his power set. He was also taller than most, making him a very large figure. He had a scraggly beard but a thick, bushy moustache. His long, greasy hair was mostly stuffed into a pointed hat that he claimed pirates had historically worn on his homeworld. The result was a comical appearance that Jota knew was a very bad idea to mock. He'd seen it happen and the depravities Aractus had carried out in retribution.

"This is an interesting one," the self-proclaimed pirate admiral said. He was sitting behind a desk in his captain's cabin, in a chair that struggled to contain him. He tossed a file onto the desk for Jota to pick up and peruse.

"It was sealed to anyone over silver rank?" Jota read.

"Yeah. Which means it was effectively sealed to everyone, because what silver-ranker is roaming through the astral? The World-Phoenix just opened it up to gold-rankers, though."

"If the World-Phoenix is paying attention to this place, shouldn't we avoid it? I don't want the attention of its cult to fall on us any more than you do, and that's at the best of times. If it made a point of opening the place up, what does it know that we don't?"

"Normally, I would agree, but almost no one has a full and ready team of gold-rankers that can go after this. The new boundary is a hard line, so no diamond-rank support."

"That doesn't fill me with confidence, Aractus."

"There is also the reason it was closed off in the first place. Keep reading."

Jota did as instructed.

"Reality cores?"

"Yeah. The locals have lost access to them, but with the right magic, we can start digging them out again."

"Again, I have reservations. If nothing else, wouldn't farming them destabilise a planet the World-Phoenix has put significant effort into stabilising?"

"Yes, but if we get in first and farm them up quick, we can move on to plundering other resources before it goes too far. Leave the next guy to face the wrath of the phoenix's cult."

"That still sounds risky, especially reading this background information. This universe is connected to another one. One with fewer restrictions, but even so. And the pair of them was the reason the original Builder got replaced? Which is why the reality cores are even accessible."

He dropped the file back on the table.

"The more I read, Aractus, the less I like it."

"There's risk," the admiral acknowledged. "But the rewards are worth it. Reality cores, Jota. Under normal circumstances, they're impossible to extract. Just the attempt would have the Builder cult swooping in to stop you. But this world is different, and it's been cracked like an egg. Best of all, the Builder has already been burned interfering with it. So long as we don't push our luck, we can do this. Even if we can only get a few of the cores, it's worth it."

"You mean, pushing *my* luck."

"Don't be an idiot, Jota. You think the great astral beings will leave me be if you take things too far? Look, yes, I don't like that we will get attention from both the Builder and the World-Phoenix for this. But the advantage of using only gold-rankers is that they won't be too harsh. If we go too far, they'll start with a rap on the knuckles for me and I'll take you off the reality cores. Move you on more traditional exploitation while everyone else either watches with envy or draws the ire of the cults away from us."

Jota's sigh was unhappy but resigned.

"What's our pretence?" he asked. "With this much attention, we'll need to follow the rules on this one. Nudging our way around the letter of the law is trouble we can't afford here."

"Ah, now, this is the beautiful part. Keep reading."

Jota picked the file back up and skimmed forward while Aractus continued to explain.

"The locals have an issue. Of these two worlds, someone got sucked off the more restricted one and sent to the other."

"An outworlder."

"Yeah. That was a couple of years ago, and now he's apparently heading back."

"With more power than the people of the restricted world are ready for," Jota realised.

"Exactly. There's only so much my scouts have been able to observe of this world through the restrictions, but the locals are desperate for a solution. I've offered my help, and the native powers have accepted. You can stroll right in, free and clear of the rules, courtesy of an invitation from the locals. An invitation those following behind you won't have."

"That does make for an appealing opportunity," Jota conceded. "We just have to deal with this outworlder?"

"Yes. He'll have some people from the other world, but it's still just an isolated backwater, and the restriction on diamond-rankers still holds. I'll

454 | SHIRTALOON & TRAVIS DEVERELL

expand your team to make sure and you can wipe out the lot of them. Once that's done, you've met the conditions set by the natives and you can start changing the deal on them. Once you're in, you're in."

"How many of these gold-rankers will we be dealing with?"

"Our information is one team, so five, maybe seven at the outside. But remember these will be backwater bumpkins, not proper warriors."

"Don't underestimate those who trained in the cosmic wilds, Aractus. I've learned the hard way that training in the best conditions can make you soft."

"Don't worry. I'll boost your numbers to make sure. You'll have twenty-five or so; enough to solidly overrun them. The last thing we want is a fair fight. I don't intend to lose anyone over this."

"Thank you, Aractus."

"I've told you before, Jota: call me Admiral."

"Sorry, Admiral."

"Thank you. There's a reason I'm wearing this hat."

58

A CITY WITH NO DAWN

"Do you realise what you've done?" Rick asked Jason as they walked along a hallway in the cloud ship. "The collection of people on this boat is ridiculous. The number of gold-rankers alone is mind-boggling. If we'd had this group when we went down that gods-forsaken tunnel, we'd have wiped that undead army off the face of creation."

"I don't think the gods actually forsook the tunnel," Jason pointed out. "That was actually kind of the problem."

"It was, wasn't it. But to continue my point, beyond the number of gold-rankers, look at who they are. Prestigious teams from across multiple generations of adventurers. The Archchancellor and Vice Chancellor of the Magic Research Association. One of the rising stars of the alchemy world."

"You mean Jory?"

"I don't think you realise the reputation he built up while you were off inventing your System."

"I wouldn't call that an accurate description of what happened."

"The world's most notorious treasure hunter. Roland Remore's son."

"I'm aware of who is on my boat, Rick."

"Aunt Danielle."

"Again, I know who—"

"How many members of royalty, Jason?"

"Only a couple of big ones. Most of that Rimaros contingent are peripheral family members at best."

"My point, Jason, is that you need to look at things the way the wider world sees them. You're going off with a multi-national force of top-tier adventurers, magical researchers, royal family members and even clergy. You just incidentally built one of the most powerful factions on the planet, and people want to know what you're going to do with it when you bring us all back. Found a country? Take a more forceful approach in trying to eliminate indentured servitude?"

"I'm going to go home. Hang out. Kill some vampires. When I get back, I'd love to do some quiet adventuring. Take out some messengers."

"Jason, even you aren't oblivious enough to not know what people are thinking. Not with your history. Look at what happened the last time you came back from Earth. The Builder invasion. The Battle of Yaresh. The brightheart expedition. You were a major player in all of them. You might not have been famous with the public at large, outside Rimaros and Yaresh, but the people in power? They were watching you closely. Then you vanish and reappear fifteen years later, having changed the very way essence-users operate. And it's not long before you're doing ridiculous things all over again."

"They weren't that ridiculous."

"You evacuated the entire population of a city with your aura, turned into a bird and single-handedly wiped out a messenger army. And that was after coming back from the dead. Again. Which barely warrants a mention because it's kind of your gods-bedamned thing."

"We all have rough days, Rick."

"Rough days?" Rick exclaimed.

Jason laughed and put a companionable hand on Rick's shoulder.

"I've had worse. Did I ever tell you about my time on Earth? I got back at bronze rank, and was almost immediately kidnapped by a silver-ranker. Again. This one was crappy, though, so I was able to put up a..."

Rick rolled his eyes as Jason trailed off, his attention caught by Zara walking the other way.

"Princess," he greeted, doing a terrible job of suppressing a grin.

"Captain," she greeted back as they passed one another.

"Captain?" Rick asked.

"It is my boat," Jason pointed out.

Rick shook his head.

"You know, I didn't even want to come on this trip."

"You didn't? Who wouldn't want to be a part of this?"

"Me, Jason. I wouldn't. Fifteen years of very happily fighting monsters, like a regular adventurer. Now I'm in a magic boat full of people who bring trouble down on anyone standing in their general vicinity. But my wife wanted to see another world, so here we are."

"Well, I'll do my best to keep things calm and normal for you."

"Is that going to work?"

Jason patted him on the shoulder again.

"Not even a little bit."

The cloud ship boasted a variety of amenities, from hanging gardens to a full-blown mirage chamber. The most popular spots were the observation decks, featuring a relaxed bar, intimate lounge areas and a ballroom-sized dining hall. Each featured transparent hull sections, offering expansive views of the astral as the vessel passed through it.

Other rooms frequently occupied were the lecture halls and classrooms. The people from Earth taught the languages of their home planet, along with basic cultural studies and introductory etiquette. Jason had been banned from this by Farrah for both his inherent lack of etiquette and for relating every social situation to an episode of *The A-Team*.

The deep astral wasn't visible in the normal sense. Instead, strange interactions of its raw magic with the bubble that kept the ship safe manifested around them. Sometimes that meant arcadian landscapes, with the cloud vessel feeling like a train in the countryside. Other times, it felt like moving through the void of space as bizarre objects and entities drifted past.

With so many powerful adventurers on board, and no adventuring to be had, many had chosen to focus on training. The passengers quickly learned to avoid Prince Valdis, who found himself in a heaven of strong people to challenge. With little else to do, however, many took him up or challenged each other. The vessel had both the space and facilities to accommodate them.

Jason was having dinner with Travis Noble and his wife, Gabrielle. Gabrielle was quiet, still getting used to the absence of her goddess. Travis was fascinated with the strange things passing by the window.

"Is that some kind of merman?" he asked. "He's got webbed hands and feet."

"That's Patrick Duffy," Jason said.

"The season one host of *Bingo America*?"

"Uh... maybe?"

They continued their meal, Travis and Jason chatting about their journey.

"Honestly," Travis said, "I was reluctant to come along. I don't know that there is anything left for me back on Earth. I come from an old-school Network family, and they cut off almost any contact after I joined the Asano clan."

"I get that," Jason said. "I felt the same way for a long time, but don't underestimate your family connections. I have people waiting for me, despite how I left things. They basically thought I was a mass-murdering psychopath, and I'm not sure they were far off the mark. It won't be easy, going back, but I'm doing it. When was family ever easy?"

"I remember when you left," Travis said. "Things were tense between your sister and your niece for a long time. Emi got it into her head that you weren't going to come back. She blamed her mother, and also herself, for not understanding why you became the way you were. I don't know how it is now, given that I was pulled through to Palli not that long after you left."

"I have the advantage of calling in. I've tried to keep things quiet with my avatars over there, not make myself known too much. I have spent time with family, though. It's awkward, but getting better. Time gives raw wounds a chance to heal. Speaking of which, I think I owe you an apology, Gabrielle."

"Oh?" she said, looking up from her pasta.

"You and I fell out twenty years ago. We were young. We made the mistakes that young people make. Passion; a little too much confidence. A certainty in our rightness that age was yet to temper. The sin of disrespect is one I have indulged in many times. Your goddess has helped me time and again, yet I failed to show her the respect she deserved. Not in her own right, and not before those who hold her in such esteem. I apologise for disrespecting something so central to not just your life but also to your identity."

Gabrielle stared at Jason, as if searching his expression for amusement or insincerity. He found that a little hurtful, mostly because he was pretty sure he deserved it.

"Thank you," she said finally. "Faith can make you strong, but also inflexible. I was particularly guilty of that. Honestly, I was a little jealous. Some man comes swanning in, bad-mouthing gods and loudly proclaiming that our society was corrupt and broken. Yet my goddess kept showering you with attention and I didn't understand why."

"I suspect she was indulging me, the way you do a rude child who doesn't know any better."

"I let my rigidity and my envy poison relationships that were important to me, not just Humphrey. I spent a lot of time saying unkind things about you to any who would listen. I am sorry for that."

"I think we can both pass that off as the poor decisions of youth. You were still a teenager, so that excuses you more than me. Still, we did get along at first, and it would be nice if we could get back to that. Do you remember the time we danced?"

She let out a soft laugh.

"I do."

"What's this?" Travis asked.

"It was back in Greenstone," Jason explained. "Sorry, this is really a story about your wife's ex, if you don't mind."

"Oh, not at all," Travis said. "I have no problem standing in comparison to a guy who is basically Superman but with ethnically ambiguous sensuality and an adorable magic puppy."

"Really?" Jason asked. "Sensuality?"

"Oh yeah," Travis said as Gabrielle nodded her enthusiastic agreement. "He's all upright, but passionate. He has a whole 'I'll do the right thing on the battlefield and in the bedroom' situation going on. Once we get back to Earth, he's going to get internet creeped-on hard. *Hard.* But what was this about a dance?"

"Um, okay," Jason said. "So, we were at some kind of social event. A ball, something like that. Gabrielle, here, was what? Sixteen? I think Humphrey was seventeen. He'd been taught how to smite monsters with a big old sword, but he didn't have the same natural talent for his mother's social lessons. Now, I could see him mooning over your lovely now-wife, so I decided to stir him into action. I bribed the band to spice things up and introduced Pallimustus to the tango."

"You bribed the band?" Gabrielle asked.

"I had to have something I could work with. Those Greenstone dances had no verve."

"You taught my wife the tango?"

"I thought I did, but thinking back, she picked it up a little too well. Did your goddess pluck the tango out of my head and teach it to you in real time?"

"Basically, yes," Gabrielle admitted. "Which still counts as you teaching me."

"No one ever taught me the tango!" Travis complained.

"Well, that's easily solvable," Jason said. "I'll teach you."

"Shouldn't my wife teach me?"

"It doesn't work like that, Travis."

"It really feels like it should," he said, turning to his wife with an imploring look.

She looked back down at her pasta and continued eating.

On Earth, Jason's Slovakian spirit domain held an astral space. Like the one in France, it contained a city surrounded by wilderness that spanned out to the edge of the space where reality broke down. Unlike the French city, this space had no sun. Lit only by moonlight, regardless of the hour, it held Earth's remaining population of sane vampires. The looming architecture was influenced by Prague, Istanbul and, more than anything else, Batman movies.

Jason's avatar stood on the rooftop of a gothic tower. Rain pattered against his heavy coat and wide-brimmed hat, making the steep tiles slippery enough that he was holding himself in place with his aura. Moonlight pushed through the murk and reflected off the tiles, rendered slick by the water. A hatch flipped up, from which an umbrella was shoved out and quickly opened. Craig Vermillion extracted himself while awkwardly holding the umbrella, then picked his way across the slippery roof. He stood beside Jason and followed his gaze, trying to find what he was staring at. Not seeing it, he instead turned to Jason.

"Can't you deflect the rain with your aura?" Craig asked, watching the droplets bounce off Jason's hat and coat.

"Yep," Jason said in a gravelly drawl.

"Wait, are you just posing dramatically as you overlook the vampire city you made?"

"Isn't that what vampire cities are for?"

"You didn't have to put gargoyles everywhere. It's kind of a stereotype."

"This is my domain, Craig. I know exactly how many people in it are wearing long black coats right now."

"That's fair," Craig conceded.

"Your aura is settling down more every time I see you."

"I've been working on it. Rufus has been helping me with essence-user meditation techniques; he's an excellent teacher. Apparently, his family runs a school in the other world."

"I might have heard that somewhere, yeah."

One of the earliest vampires to actively fight their own risen lords, Craig had accelerated to gold rank after feeding on several of them. Hard to kill permanently without blood magic, another vampire devouring them was a way to keep the resilient gold-rankers down. That made allied vampires an asset to those fighting the ancient lords, even at a time when any vampire was hard to trust.

Craig had lacked the power to defeat a vampire lord himself. Even with his new rank, he would be hard pressed to vanquish the ancient lords. It had been essence-users and other human forces doing the actual subduing, leaving him to drain their life force and put them down for good. The effects of feeding on such potent blood included a rapid increase in his baseline strength, along with picking up additional bloodline powers. The downsides were fierce aggression, feral tendencies, and a drift towards amoral ruthlessness. Voluntarily locking himself away for years, Craig had finally come back to himself around the time Jason's avatars started showing up.

"I'm a little surprised you picked here to do this," Craig said. "Trying to intimidate the Americans with all the scary vampires?"

"No. I want this quiet, until I know why Boris is bringing them here. There's a reason I keep all the secret stuff in this city."

"Vampires respect secrets?"

"No, although that was a pleasant surprise. If there's a bunch of secret things happening, no one questions one more car with tinted windows moving through the sputtering light of the gas lamps, shining off rain-slicked cobbles."

"Do you need me to go get you a femme fatale? This is a vampire city; we've got them coming out of our ears."

"I'm enjoying this a little too much, aren't I?"

"I say roll with it," Craig told him. "You built this place for melodrama, right?"

"Yeah," Jason said happily, then his expression turned grim. "Well, that was the fun reason. You know we have to talk about what happens with the vampires when I arrive."

"I'm assuming you're going to kill all the ones still out in the world."

"Are there any worth saving?"

"Ten years ago, I might have said yes. Now, they're too far gone, Jason, and have been for a long time. Maybe there are a few who could come back. Who wouldn't kill themselves over what they've done once they regained a conscience. But finding and helping them simply isn't a practical position. Europe is post-apocalyptic at this stage. It pains me to say it, but you have to kill them all."

Jason nodded, resigned.

"What about the sane ones, here in the city?" Craig asked. "This place has been a haven, but will we ever get to go back out into the world? There's too much magic out there now, and humanity isn't going to accept us. Not after what the others have done. Are we stuck, living forever in a city with no dawn?"

"There is a world for you. Just not this one."

"You're going to send us into space?"

"Yes, but not this space. I have a solar system. Like this city, and the one in France, but obviously bigger. There's a moon whose orbit is synchronised so that the planet is always blocking the sun. A permanent state of eclipse."

"People like it when you swap out the permanent moon for an eclipse here in the city. It makes for a fun event. And you say there's a whole planet like that?"

"A moon, not a planet. Smaller than Earth, so the eclipse can always be in place. I had to tweak some things to get the gravity right. Tides are a bit funny. Are vampires into yachting?"

"Not traditionally."

"Also, I made the magic-infused sunlight turning vampires insane not a thing in my universe, so you can go out in the sun there if you want. I don't have that kind of control in my Earth domains yet. Sorry. Not outside of the astral spaces."

"Jason, these things you talk about like they're nothing. Making planets. Your own universe. If I hadn't seen things like this city, I'd think you were a madman. I still might."

"Mate, you haven't seen the half of it."

Jason turned his gaze down to the street. A town car that looked like it was from the sixties made its slow way along the narrow thoroughfare. The windows and the paint were both black.

"Boris and the Americans?" Craig asked.

Jason nodded.

"Let's see what they want."

59

A CLARK KENT PROBLEM

DARIUS AND MICHAEL WERE NERVOUS. THEY WERE POLITICAL OFFICIALS, their silver rank coming from cores. Their limited combat training consisted of a basic course and annual two-week refreshers. It was far from enough to make them confident about entering vampire territory or, even worse, Asano territory.

They began their day by portalling across the planet. Their two gold-rank bodyguards—the only reason they'd agreed to any of this—secured the other side first. These were some of the old guard who had also ranked up through cores, but were rich on both training and experience. The scant handful who had hit gold without cores were strategic assets, too valuable for bodyguard duty.

On the other side of the portal was the city of Nitra. The vampires hadn't done too much damage, the population having evacuated before the blood suckers had the courage to approach Asano territory. The vampires had come through when the Asano clan went into hiding, but no populace meant no massacre. The damage to the city came from more than a decade of abandonment and the occasional wandering monster.

They arrived in the carpark of a shopping centre. Someone had taken the abandoned cars and piled them up on one end leaving clear space. What was left of a sign reading 'Atrium Optiva' dangled from the wall. Waiting for them were three people, currently getting the eyeball from their gold-rank guards.

One of the three looked nervous at the attention. Darius and Michael could sense his silver-rank aura, although his showed no signs of the monster core use responsible for their own ranks. The last two were unfazed by the attention, a large Pacific Islander and a Japanese man.

The political officials recognised the other two Asano clan gold-rankers. Shiro Asano was the former patriarch of the Japanese Network's Asano clan, and had his hand casually resting on the hilt of his sheathed blade. Taika Williams was postulated to be one of the strongest people on the planet, alongside Rufus Remore. He was eating a popsicle.

With their arrival, the three clan members moved to greet them and make introductions. The silver-ranker was Wesley Asano, a clan member with a vehicle essence who would serve as their driver. He conjured up a limousine with black paint and black windows that could have been plucked from a gangster movie set in the sixties.

They were driven through the city, seeing that at least the streets they were driving through had been cleared. This was obviously where the clan usually had visitors arrive, as no one was portalling into the clan territory directly. Leaving the city, what looked like a freshly built road led into the countryside. There was no mistaking the Asano clan city as they approached it, situated in what had once been pastoral land.

The city was strange, showing no signs of the cloud-like substance it was supposedly built from. The buildings were a mix of aggressive concrete, shining glass and plant life both abundant and heavily integrated. Seated across from them, Taika Williams looked like a sardine in a can, even in the large car. Seeing them peer out the window, he offered an explanation unprompted.

"Ken oversaw all this. Jason's dad. After Jason ate all the vampires and rebuilt the city, he let his old man and some architects in the clan redesign the whole place. It's a mix of eco-brutalism and solar punk, or so I'm told. I don't know what either of those things are, but being able to fake concrete instead of using the real stuff is better for the environment, apparently. Not sure that matters in the middle of a vampire apocalypse, or why you'd want to fake concrete, but Ken seemed happy."

Michael and Darius glanced at each other at the phrase 'ate all the vampires,' but didn't comment. They reached the centre of the city, stopping outside its tallest building. From the outside, it looked like a massive stack of staggered balcony gardens, with no safety rails. The interior continued the heavy plant theme, with open spaces and high ceilings. Natural light filled the space too well to be actually natural, but the effect was pleasant. The two political staffers were used to cubicles, offices and bureaucratic hallways.

They were led upstairs on an elevator that was just an open-sided platform, not even enclosed by glass. It took them to a large circular chamber ringed by shadowy portal arches. One arch stood out from the others by the colours, being of milky white stone instead of obsidian black. It was also filled with gold, silver and blue instead of roiling darkness. Their instincts recoiled against going through unknown portals, but they followed Taika through, nonetheless.

On the other side, they found themselves in another building, very different from the one they had just left. It looked like an old hotel, decorated in such monotone shades of grey and black, it was like stepping into a black and white movie. If not for the bright teal of Michael's tie, Darius would have suspected sudden-onset colour blindness.

"I told you that tie was too much," Darius muttered as they were led to the birdcage elevator that continued the archaic styling.

Waiting for them in the lobby was a man they both recognised. They had worked with Boris Ketland for years, believing him to be a counterpart of similar rank to themselves, but in the Cabal. It was only later they discovered he was both a global leader and one of the angel-like messengers. Even now, he rarely appeared outside of human proportions, or showed off his wings.

"Mike. Darius. I'd ask if you were nervous, but I can feel your auras. Don't worry; the vampires here are all very gentle. By vampire standards."

The gold-rank bodyguards had grown increasingly stoic over the course of the journey, and now could pass as statues, their eyes locked on Boris. He led their little entourage outside where Wesley conjured his car again, along with a second one. The bodyguards protested Boris' instruction to join Taika and Shiro in the other car while he went with Michal and Darius.

"I hate to break it to you," Boris told them, "but you're ornamental here at best. You are under the protection of myself and Jason Asano, which means the only things able to harm you *are* myself and Jason. And if that's what we want, there's nothing you can do about, so get in the second car before I put you in there."

The bodyguards bristled, but obeyed after a short discussion under their breath. Michael and Darius then joined Boris in the first car, which drove them through the noir graphic novel that passed for a city. There was a sense of unreality to the place, exacerbated by knowing they really were in a magical pocket realm. The silver light of the moon hid more than it illuminated, creating dark corners and shadow-filled alleys. Traffic was light, the cars having the same out-of-time feel as their own vehicle. Few people were out in the heavy rain, those that were making indistinct shapes under the diffuse gaslight on the streetlamps.

"Feels like being in a Dashiell Hammett novel, right?" Boris asked, watching them peer out the windows. "You can make a gritty monologue, if you feel the need."

"Why are we doing this here again?" Darius asked. "This place is spooky and full of vampires. I know this is a clandestine meeting, but this seems like we may be taking it too far."

"This is where Jason conducts his more hidden business," Boris explained. "Your people wanted the in-person meeting, and this is where he wants it."

"He really is here, then?" Michael asked.

"Technically, he's in a liminal space between universes that doesn't exist in any way that's comprehensible to entities that exist within physical reality. But yes, he's here. His avatars have been explained to you, right?"

The men nodded.

"It still seems strange," Michael said. "But what doesn't here?"

"That's a good attitude to hold," Boris told him.

The car pulled over and they got out. The rain didn't reach them, twisting in the air to fall on the ground around them.

"What's going on there?" Michael asked.

"I'm pushing the rain away with my aura," Boris said. "I'm not getting water on this suit."

"You can't move physical things with your aura," Michael said.

"No," Boris corrected. "*You* can't move physical things with your aura."

The second car pulled up to let out Taika, Shiro and the bodyguards. After the guards confirmed the status of their charges, they all went inside. It was the kind of building where people got murdered in old movies. It appeared to have been some kind of clothing factory, machines and tables painted in years of grime.

Taika, Shiro and Wesley stayed behind as the rest took another old-style elevator, Boris operating it with a lever instead of buttons. It took them up to another floor, wholly unlike the factory floor they had just left.

This level contained a speakeasy-style bar, all dark leather and dim lighting. They could see people at tables and booths, none of whom glanced over at their entrance.

There was a coatroom where an attendant was taking coats and hats. They spotted Asano handing over his, drenched in rain. He waited for them to do the same before shaking their hands in turn, without so much as a glance at the bodyguards.

"Gentlemen," he greeted them. "Jason Asano."

"I'm Darius Shepherd, United States Department of Supernatural Affairs. This is Michael Glasser, State Department."

Asano led them through the bar to a secluded booth at the back and slid around the table, making room for Boris and the two officials. There was no room for their guards—who would not have sat anyway—looming over the table.

"Your boys can go take a seat at the bar," he said.

"We're fine," one of the guards grunted.

"And you'll stay that way unless you think I was asking," Asano said, looking at them for the first time.

Darius and Michael saw their gold-rank guards flinch, noticing the signs of aura suppression despite not sensing a thing. The guards sent them an inquisitive glance, departing at a slight nod from Michael. Asano's eyes didn't leave them until they sat at the bar and refused drinks from the bartender. He then turned to the two officials with a friendly smile.

Michael and Darius were unsure what to make of Asano. Rumours placed him somewhere between dangerous lunatic and capricious god. There was certainly a presence to him, as if everything around him was slightly out of focus while he was crystal clear.

"What brought you two gentlemen all this way?" he asked them. "Boris seemed confident that it was worth meeting you."

"We need to discuss a potential threat," Darius said. "One that affects all of us."

"All of us being…?"

"The whole planet."

Asano sighed, leaning back with a weary expression.

"I've done my world-saving," he said. "It's past time the rest of you started picking up the slack."

"We intended to take this to your clan," Darius said. "We approached

Mr Ketland as a go-between, and he insisted we bring it to you personally."

Asano turned to Boris.

"And why is that?" he asked.

"Because this isn't a Clark Kent problem," Boris said. "This is a Superman problem. You can't pretend like you're like everyone else on this one. The clan isn't up for this kind of fight. No one on Earth is."

"What fight?" Jason asked.

"As I'm sure you're aware," Michael said, "there is a lot of concern about you and your clan. Your impending return has led to some activity that has us concerned."

"Activity by me?"

"No," Darius said. "It's in reaction to you."

"For context," Michael explained, "there is something of a secret council amongst Earth's most powerful players. Somewhere between a secret society and the United Nations, with various countries and other state-level actors represented. The mission statement of the group is to navigate challenges that affect us all."

"You and your family come up a lot," Darius added.

"But that's not what we're here about," Michael said. "Not directly. The group, as I mentioned, is concerned about your return. About what you will do, and how the world will collectively respond."

"I've been giving the same thing my consideration as well," Asano said.

"The secret council have gone beyond consideration," Darius said. "One of their unstated objectives is to make sure the people in power stay that way, through the upheavals that magic has brought. They see you as potentially the greatest threat to that objective. You operate on a different paradigm to traditional forms of global power. That was fine when you were a silver-ranker, albeit a strong one with impressive reserves of resources and knowledge. But your clan has been laying the groundwork for you to be seen as far more than that now. They portray you less a gold-ranker and more like some god-king about to descend upon the Earth."

"That's fair," Boris said. "To my people, he essentially is a god-king. Even the ones who see him as an enemy."

"Be that as it may," Darius said, "the reality doesn't actually matter right now. The perception of it is what's causing the problem at hand. The secret council has decided that if you can't be controlled and you can't be contained, you have to be removed."

"I was expecting some reaction along those lines," Jason said. "You're talking about more than just a few assassination attempts, though, aren't you?"

Darius nodded.

"A means has been found to contact other people like you. Powerful people who exist beyond our world."

"They've struck a deal," Michael said, picking up the narrative. "To bring these outsiders into our dimension to take you off the board. And in return, certain concessions have been made."

"What concessions?" Asano asked.

"We're not sure," Darius said. "The United States representatives were completely against this approach and were cut out early in the proceedings. We still have people reporting from inside the group, but those of us in opposition to the plan have been removed from its planning."

"You were against it?"

"The view of the United States government," Michael said, "is that welcoming an unknown alien force onto our world is akin to giving invaders a beachhead. We might see you as a threat to our interests, Mr Asano, but we respect your right to be a huge pain in our nation's collective ass. Bringing in outsiders is selling the cow to get lessons on how to milk it."

"You realise that I'm bringing in my own force of outsiders."

"But are they coming to serve your interests, or theirs?"

"It's more of a tourist situation, really. Most will follow my lead, but I am bringing a diplomatic contingent. They want to begin establishing relations for when our worlds are in closer contact."

Darius and Michael shared a look.

"We will definitely need to discuss that with our people," Michael said. "What you're describing, though, sounds like open foreign relations."

"I'd say that's accurate," Asano told them.

"What we're talking about," Darius said, "is inviting Darth Vader into Cloud City and hoping he doesn't change the deal on us."

Michael turned to look at him.

"Really, Darius?"

"Oh, because your farming metaphors were such classic diplomatic language."

Asano chuckled, drawing their attention.

"Whoever picked you two did their research," he said. "They clearly understood that I would respond better to you than someone more caught up in formality."

The pair looked at each other. They had wondered between themselves why they had been chosen.

"The United States wasn't tempted to use this chance to get me out of the way?" Asano asked them.

"Mr Asano," Michael said. "The United States, like every nation, is not without flaws. Our power and prominence mean that those flaws can, from time to time, create outsized problems. I think, perhaps, you can sympathise with this."

"I can," Asano acknowledged.

"For all our issues, our nation's flaws do not include a lack of independent spirit. We didn't let King George tell us what to do. We didn't let the Network tell us what to do. If you decide you're going to come back and start conquering things, we won't let you tell us what to do. We aren't going to stand by while people throw open the gate to the wolves, just because they're afraid one of the sheep is too big."

"I take it that you have some kind of proposal."

"A unified front. A show of force that will convince these outsiders to back off. Or to fight them, if they don't. There are some obstacles to navigate, starting with the Australian government. Our understanding is that you will arrive at the standing stones in South Australia, the ones you built to leave this dimension."

"That's right," Jason said.

"The Australian government is one of the driving forces for this plan to bring in alien assets to combat you. They're afraid you're going to come back and take over the whole country, or at least cause problems after their treatment of your family. They are normally very accommodating to US operations, but they do not want us involved in this. But this deal with the outsiders is an extreme secret. Only a handful of representatives in each participating group are even aware of it. The Australians can't just come out and say they don't want their allies onsite because they've organised a secret alien ambush. Lacking knowledge of that, their own diplomats will push to include us."

"What about other groups? Who will be against you in this, and how far are they willing to take their opposition? Will they fight you? And me?"

"We don't know how far they would go. Military conflict between nations on Australian soil is something we hope everyone will want to avoid. Our best assessment is that they won't take the side of the outsiders if it comes to violence. They'll stand by and see what happens, but there is always the chance for things to go wrong. It wouldn't be the first war started by the bad decision of an idiot. As for who will be on the other side, Australia, China, Indonesia and the United Kingdom are the key players."

"Russia and most of Africa are Cabal territory," Boris said. "We won't intercede. Much of Asia is torn between the old Network factions and the Cabal, so they're up in the air."

"These conflicts go all the way back to the Makassar disaster," Michael said. "Indonesia is especially fractured, with whole regions warring for independence. Asia as a whole has no unity in their magic factions, with Cabal and Network groups still vying for control."

"My guess would be no involvement from Asia at large, except Indonesia," Boris said. "Your clan made some discreet but not-unnoticed interventions, supplying essences and training to independence groups there. The Indonesian government hates your guts."

"The rest of Asia are unlikely to intervene, though," Darius said.

"Agreed," Boris said with a nod. "Europe, meaning the vampires, is an open question. The other groups won't want to side with them, but they may come out anyway. The vampires are terrified of you after the way you reclaimed your clan territories. They could be a wild card."

"That leaves the Network factions," Darius said. "Our Network in the USA is now reconciled with the government, so they're on your side. China will be against you. Same for the... what are they calling them-selves now? The True Network?"

"They just rebranded again," Michael said. "They're back to just being 'the Network.' For what? The fourth time?"

Boris groaned.

"Anyway," he said, "they hate you. Basically, everyone in the Network who had a problem with you from your last trip to Earth is in that group. The GDC will be on our side in this. Which will probably mean staying out of it, but not actively helping."

Asano's expression remained blank as they went over the various factions and how they would react to his return and potential interception by cosmic forces.

"I need to think, and consult my people. Thank you, gentlemen, for coming all this way. And for showing trust enough to place yourselves within one of my seats of power."

Taking the clear dismissal, Michael and Darius said their goodbyes and collected their guards on the way to the elevator.

———————

From their booth, Jason and Boris watched the elevator descend, taking away the Americans.

"Well," Jason said. "This complicates things."

"It does."

"We need to talk, Boris."

"We do."

"Do you know how much communication these people are having with the Jakaar pirates?"

Boris turned his head to give Jason a flat look.

"Jason, what did you do?"

60

GOD-KING

"Jason," Boris said. "What did you do?"

"You know we've been discussing how to demonstrate the power I'll be bringing to bear, to deter the powers of Earth from doing something ill-advised."

"I'd say that clearly didn't work, given the impending arrival of cosmic pirates, but how and why do you already know who they are?"

"It started when a member of the cult of the World-Phoenix paid me a visit. Now that the link between Earth and Pallimustus is repaired, Earth's dimensional membrane is going to stabilise over time. The World-Phoenix sent me a courtesy message that she was easing restrictions on high-rankers accessing Earth, beginning with gold-rankers. The usual rules on invading domains remained in place, of course."

"And?"

"Danielle Geller had an idea. The World-Phoenix owed me a favour, you see."

"For what?"

"I stopped the Cosmic Throne from trying to turn her from her current form back into the Boundary. You know about the World-Phoenix's original incarnation?"

"It was before even my time, but I have heard about it. You keep calling the World-Phoenix 'her.' It doesn't have an actual gender."

"She did when we were hanging out, so it's a habit. Plus, using 'it' instead of 'they' as the gender-neutral pronoun seems weird to me. It feels like treating them as if they weren't people."

"They aren't. Not in the strictest sense. In their true state, a great astral being doesn't have a mind or identity as we understand it. They're too alien. It's why they have their prime vessels."

"I don't think that's entirely true. Plus, I'm pretty sure most of them were getting into the whole mortal body thing, when they were in my soul."

"Well, if they aren't going to rebuke you for it, neither will I. You say the Cosmic Throne was trying to turn the World-Phoenix back into the Boundary?"

"It was a constant struggle, apparently. It was the reason she agreed to the sundering in the first place, and fought the restoration. But the restored throne apparently took her current state as the new baseline. No more issues. I didn't do it that way on purpose, but she still saw it as a debt. Maybe she felt bad about killing me tens of thousands of times for what ultimately proved to be no reason."

"I don't know, Jason. I think that's an opportunity many people would relish."

"That's a little hurtful. Anyway, that visit gave Danielle Geller an idea. We'd already been talking about how to manage a show of force on Earth, but there were several problems. If we picked a fight with any of the Earth powers, it would undercut the entire diplomatic approach I'm after. And even if I did, there's no force on Earth that could put up enough of a fight that we could properly demonstrate our power."

"I'm starting to see," Boris said. "You need an external antagonist. Someone you can stand with the Earth against. You asked the cult of the World-Phoenix to arrange one."

"That was just courtesy on their part. The real favour was having the World-Phoenix open this universe up to gold-rankers, but keeping the ban on diamond-rankers in place until I reach diamond rank myself. The ban wouldn't be released immediately anyway, but I don't want other diamond-rankers showing up before I'm ready to deter them."

"That's actually a good idea."

"You don't have to sound quite so surprised."

"Jason, I've been on Earth all this time. I saw how you did things here on your last visit, and terrible ideas were kind of your thing."

Jason's expression turned hard.

"I had no idea what I was doing. I was forced into bad choice after bad choice, and I didn't see you out there helping, Mr 'I was here the whole time.' Where were you, and your army of high-ranking messengers, Boris?"

"Doing more to help you than you will ever realise. Some of us simply manage it without making a grandiose spectacle of ourselves. Did you ever notice how none of the threats you ran into were quite more than you could handle? Almost as if someone was quietly eliminating any threats that would kill you instead of pushing you to grow stronger."

"Some of those threats did kill me. Because I took on things no one else could. It's not like there was an army of angels who could have dealt with it."

"We have to maintain a low profile, Jason. If the Orthodox messengers find us here, that's all the pretext they need to invade this world. And, against our best interests, we were preparing to reveal ourselves and intervene when humans kept harvesting reality cores. Fortunately, the transformation zones stopped forming. Thank you for that, by the way."

"You're welcome," Jason said angrily, and the pair sat in sullen silence.

After a while, Boris spoke up.

"When is Anna getting here?"

"She's on the road now."

Sitting in the back of a car driven by one of Jason's blank, shadowy avatars, Anna sighed as she reflected on what her life had become. On one hand, there was no question that she was at a crux point for the future of the world. The chaos of the last couple of decades had calmed, the changes approaching a culmination point. Decisions made in the next few years would shape the next age, both for the planet and for humankind.

On the other hand, it felt like the man with his hand on the fulcrum of the world was incapable of taking it seriously. Looking out the window, the city was a mix of vampire movie, Raymond Chandler novel and the wet dream of a teenager with way too much eye makeup. There was an unreality to it, like passing through the pages of a black and white graphic novel. The type where the protagonist was always a grizzled man who died in some masculine sacrifice at the end, like a modern-day Spartan.

The car stopped and the avatar opened her door, holding an umbrella to shield her from the rain. She avoided looking into the single giant eye it had in lieu of a face. It led her through the building and to the elevator, both of which reinforced the artificial period-movie feel of the city. The elevator opened onto an old prohibition-style bar where she had to look around through the enclosed booths and dim lighting to find Jason and Boris Ketland. Neither was talking, which was odd for both, and there was palpable tension.

"Did I walk in on something?" she asked.

"Just a difference of perspective," Jason said. "Take a seat."

Anna looked at the booth and around at the bar. The patrons were indistinct in the dim lighting, and her silver-rank hearing picked up nothing but muffled murmurs. She suspected specialised privacy magic, tweaked to maintain the atmosphere. Sliding into the booth, she settled her gaze on Jason.

"There's something we need to discuss before we get to whatever you brought me here for," she said. "A larger concern that impacts our broader goals."

Jason didn't reply, but gave a jerk of the head indicating she should continue.

"This city is indicative of something that is only going to cause us problems," she said. "Problems, Jason, that stem entirely from you."

She waited for anger, or denial. Instead, he leaned back with a neutral expression.

"Please elucidate," he said.

"You like to be distinctive, Jason. Irreverent. To pull people into your own pace, and take them out of their own comfort zones. To act strangely, and make people put up with it, which they do because you have the power to make them. And the more powerful you grow, the more elaborate you get, like this comic book city."

"I've found that the people of Earth are already more than eager to exploit me, Anna. If I stop doing things my way and start toeing whatever lines they want me to, that only tells them that I'm within their ability to influence."

"You're wrong, Jason. When you don't take things seriously, you're telling people that you aren't to be taken seriously. That you're unwilling to compromise, to meet people halfway. Combined with your power, that makes you come off as a toddler with a rocket launcher. You told me that you want to approach things properly. It's an assurance that, without which, I would not be a part of this."

"Then don't be. I can have you back in New York City this time tomorrow."

"Jason—"

"I am fully aware that I need to wear a suit to meetings and not talk about *Knight Rider*, Anna. I will act with respect and comport myself with appropriate reserve. Does that meet with your exacting standards?"

Jason's curtness was uncharacteristic to Anna's recent encounters with him. She didn't know if it was his growing proximity to Earth or whatever conflict he'd just had with Boris, but she knew when to pick her fights.

"Let's move on to what brought you to ask me here. I'm assuming it was our visitors from the United States."

"This world has been opened up to the wider cosmos," Boris explained. "There are rules around intruding on worlds that have not declared themselves open to the cosmic community, that I will be happy to explain in detail later. What is important for now is that a powerful force will be coming here to deal with Jason, at the behest of certain members of various global powers."

"How powerful are they?"

"Enough that, using the access they've been offered, they can plunder this world with impunity," Boris explained. "Which is very much their intention. The US officials came here to warn us, and offer an alliance in dealing with them."

"Can we deal with them? Even with the USA helping?"

Jason and Boris shared a look.

"Anna," Boris said. "You still don't understand what we've been telling you about the power scale we're dealing with. Against the people that are coming, every essence-user on Earth could form an alliance and they would still all be slaughtered. The only two forces capable of confronting them are my messengers, and the group Jason is bringing with him."

"Are you sure? Aren't these people prepared to deal with Jason specifically?"

"I was concerned," Boris said. "Until I discovered that Jason was the one who arranged all of this."

"What? Why?"

"Because it meets a need we've already discussed several times, without finding a solution," Jason said.

"You mean the demonstration of power?" she asked.

"Yes."

"So, to be clear, you're saying that you've masterminded what amounts to an alien invasion so you can beat them to show off how strong you are?"

"Yes."

"You didn't consider consulting me on any of this?"

"I did not. You would have taken a significant amount of time to talk around to this idea, if you could be convinced at all. Our window to initiate this was small. We worked through a group that is famously difficult to contact."

"He's not wrong," Boris added. "The cult of the World-Phoenix finds you, not the other way around. Not unless you can get into Interstice."

"Interstice?" Anna asked.

"We're not going into that right now," Jason said. "It's too much. Boris will explain, after we're done. Which is better, since he's actually been there."

"I will," Boris said. "But I also would have liked to weigh in on your decision in this, Jason. Cosmic attention on this world is dangerous to my people. You can fight one dimension ship full of pirates, but not a full-blown messenger invasion. Even if they are restricted to gold rank."

"Invasion?" Anna asked.

"Again, for a later explanation," Jason said. "Look, Anna, the decision has been made. Now we deal with it."

"There's not much point in being your political consultant if you aren't going to consult with me, Jason."

"I know," he conceded. "But sometimes that's just how it's going to work."

"That's just how it's going to work? You arbitrarily staging an alien invasion? That isn't something you can just decide for the Earth, Jason."

"Yes, Anna, it is. Your job is to keep people from starting a war over it. This plan wouldn't have worked if the people of Earth weren't willing to sell out their own planet for a chance to get rid of me. We both remember what happened last time I was here. How many times did you apologise for the Network coming after me? For any of this to work, the world has to accept that I can't be controlled and I can't be eliminated. You were the one who said I needed a common enemy to fight, like the Americans unifying against the vampires."

"I didn't mean stage an alien invasion!"

"I didn't. I engineered a situation where the people of Earth and a manageable enemy happened to find each other. It could easily have happened without my intervention at all."

"That's true," Boris said. "The Jakaar fleet is always on the lookout for weak and exploitable worlds, and this is within their realm of operation."

Anna shook her head.

"I need time to process this. Space pirates? What the hell kind of—"

She cut herself off and let out a long sigh.

"You can't just play with the world like this," she told him. "Are you so powerful that you can do whatever you want, without consequences?"

Jason glanced at Boris, then back to Anna.

"I'm sorry," he told her. "I'm letting old memories colour my behaviour, when I told myself I wouldn't. Boris, can you please go over everything in detail? Answer her questions about the pirates, and the cosmic community. You know it better than I do anyway. Anna, we'll talk again when you have more information, some time to process it all, and I'm less on edge."

Before anyone else could speak, Jason's avatar vanished and Anna let out another sigh.

"If he's going to be like this," she said, "none of this is going to work. I thought he was working on improving his diplomacy. If he's going to do things like this, without consulting the people he gathered specifically to consult, it doesn't matter how polite he is in meetings."

"In fairness, he did consult with his people," Boris said. "Just not the ones here. But yes, this was not Jason at his best. I have to take at least partial blame for that. He and I have never really discussed the fact that I was here during his last visit. That I remained hidden while he felt outmatched, betrayed and alone. Helpless to watch people die around him."

"It doesn't matter what he went through. It's not about what's fair. When things go wrong, and he starts alienating nations and the magical factions, he doesn't get a do-over because he has a sad backstory."

"No. And he knows that. He's frustrated because he could conquer the world in a long weekend and start running it how he sees fit. He knows how bad an idea that is, but it's a tempting one, believe me. When you have power beyond a certain level, it feels strange that there are any problems you can't just crush. This planet has been my home longer than any human being. I see the injustices, and I get the urge to unleash my people, take over and put things right. But that's not how it works. As much as it feels like you can go in and make things better, you can't impose positive change from the outside, using your own principles. Everything you do will turn into poison, usually sooner than later."

"You're saying he's that powerful? Waltz-in-and-conquer-the-world powerful? He keeps saying it, but it's hard to take him seriously when he talks as if he were some kind of god-king."

"Then you *should* take him seriously, because he is one. It's complicated, because it always is with him, but to my people, it's simple. We have what we call astral kings, but god-kings is essentially what they are. That's one of things Jason has become, and my people acknowledge that, even when most of them are his enemies. They respect him. They fear him and my people don't fear a lot. When they see him, they try to kill him in a frenzy, run for hills, or kneel down in worship."

He slid out of the booth and looked over at the bartender.

"I know Jason has told you a lot," he said. "I'll try to explain what he hasn't, and give a different perspective on what he has. That's going to take a long time, so I'm going to order some food. And some drinks. Would you like a drink?"

"I think I'm going to need one."

61

JASON'S ARRIVAL INEVITABLY CAUSED A MASSIVE PROBLEM

THEY WERE IN THE OFFICE OF JASON'S CAPTAIN'S SUITE ON THE CLOUD ship. In deference to his intentions to handle his time of Earth responsibly, it was more like an expensive hotel suite than a maniacal villain's lair. Jason was explaining his unproductive meeting with Anna and Boris to Danielle. Then she explained it right back.

"The problem, Jason, is you. You've always said that you prefer friends to allies."

"I have, and I stand by that."

"That's nice, and if we were still at the point of hosting barbecues in the park back in Greenstone, that would be fine. But we're a little past that, Jason. You're mixing friends and allies on this trip, and the stakes are too high to leave things as disorganised as they are. Before we reach Earth, we need to develop an organisational structure. Authority, responsibilities. Who gets what information. From what you're describing, a large part of the problem was a disconnect between you and Mrs Tilden over your respective roles."

"You're talking about a chain of command."

"In part. I'm also talking about defining relationships with those who don't fall under your influence, like Boris Ket Lundi. If everyone knows what is expected of them, and how they are meant to meet those expectations, you can avoid problems like these before they arise."

He groaned and ran his hands over his face. "Treating friends like allies is exactly what I want to avoid."

"Jason, whether in friendship or an alliance, it works better when everyone knows where they stand. Clear communication."

He thought that over for a moment, then nodded his acknowledgement of the point.

"That does sound reasonable. A perspective I can get my head around, in any case. Okay, we need to put together an org chart. How do I go about doing that?"

"We start by categorising everyone. Who is part of the formal structure you're putting together? Myself, Mrs Tilden, the structure of your clan. That's the easy part. Who are allies, like Boris? What can you expect from them, and what do they expect from you? Then there's all the people coming with us. You might be treating them as tourists, but you've put yourself in charge of an adventurer expedition to another world. One of the most powerful expeditions ever staged, I'll add. Multiple teams, a royal diplomatic delegation. What level of authority do you have over them? What do you expect from each other?"

Jason let out another groan.

"I'm about to have an incredibly tedious day, aren't I?"

Lenora Coleman had been working at the dimensional artefact site for almost her entire adult life. Recruited right out of university, her excitement had been well and truly killed off by two years in a monitoring station. Back then, the site was little more than some pre-fab buildings in the ruins of a town whose name she'd never learned.

Things were different now, both for the site and for Lenora. Her formal title was now Director of Operations for Dimensional Artefact Site One. She wasn't aware of any Dimensional Artefact Site Two, but she hadn't gotten to pick the name. That had been the original person to hold her position, and current Australian Prime Minister, Gordon Truffett.

Lenora and her predecessors had overseen a massive transformation of the site. Following the arrival of an angelic host and one guy from New Zealand, the entire area had been remade into one of the most secure sites on planet Earth. A coalition of nations had spent the last fifteen years preparing it as a defensive point should anyone or anything hostile try and use the site as an invasion point.

The coalition was ostensibly led by Australia, as it was their territory, with Lenora as their representative. The reality was more complicated. Australia was largely dependent on the Network for their magical assets, or dependent on whatever the Network was calling themselves in any given year. They had named themselves the True Network, the Grand Network, the Original Network and just the Network, cycling through those and a few others on a roughly annual schedule. The joke was that the Network was secretly led by a shape-shifter who couldn't tolerate maintaining a stable identity.

Aside from reliance on the Network, the other major factions demanded access to the site. The Australian government had granted access in various ways, depending on the influence and compensation involved. The United States and China both had consulate-level privileges for their areas around the site.

There was no longer any sign of the town that had once stood in the area. A small city now occupied the space, centred on the site itself. A ring of monitoring and research stations surrounded the half-kilometre of open ground between them and the outermost standing stones of the artefact itself. That open space was unadorned concrete, with concentric rings of metal panels. Each panel was a weapon bunker containing retractable weapons, magically enhanced howitzers and rocket batteries. The most potent mix of magic and technology the Earth could produce, they would emerge to attack any invader.

In addition to the weapon operators, a multinational force of essence-users and other supernaturals was maintained onsite. This included a rotating roster of gold-rankers who were the reason Lenora did not have the command her title suggested. Most of the world's gold-rankers belonged to the United States and China, including almost all of the ones who had reached that rank without using cores. As a bureaucrat and not a fighter, Lenora was a core-user herself and had never been clear on why that mattered. She was assured that it did when it came to combat ability.

Oddly enough, there was one Australian gold-ranker, and one who had never used cores, at that. When the Australian government had turned against what became the GDN during the Network schism, he had quietly vanished. No one really knew or cared until he resurfaced a decade later as a self-made gold-ranker. With no affiliation, he was heavily courted by every major power on the planet. He resoundingly rejected overtures from his home nation, along with every other group.

"Your head looks heavy," Barry told her. "A burden shared is a burden halved."

Her deputy, Barry, was what amounted to mayor of the artefact city. She wrangled the magical representatives and he kept the city that served their needs humming along. Her one-time supervisor, they shared her obnoxiously large office. The first director had done his best to create a throne room for himself, which subsequent directors had stripped down to a more sensible, if indulgently oversized space. The one thing she did like about the room was one wall being a massive window, looking out at the ring of standing stones. She often stood and stared at it when she was gaming out a problem in her head.

"It's nothing," she told him. "I was thinking about Nigel Thornton. Whatever happened to him?"

"He was close with Annabeth Tilden, back in the day. Rumour has it that he's joined her at the Asano clan. Or she joined him."

"Asano," she grumbled.

They had been preparing for Jason Asano's impending return to Earth for weeks. Her tasks involved blanket denials to the press and regular video conferences with Tilden, the Asano clan's unofficial new ambassador to the world. Most of her job, however, had been trying to prevent anyone onsite from doing something incredibly stupid. That had not worked out.

The Chinese adamantly denied that the man who tried to blow up the standing stones was one of theirs. The bomb had been powerful enough to scorch magically reinforced concrete, shaking the walls of the research buildings half a kilometre away. If not for their also being reinforced, the blast would have taken out some windows at the very least. The standing stones had been utterly unharmed, although the bomber was thinly smeared across several of them.

"Do we have a revised estimate on Asano's arrival date?" Lenora asked.

"Nope," Barry said. He got up and walked to the minifridge to grab a can of soft drink.

"Nora, you want one?" he offered, waving the can in her direction.

"Do we have anything other than TaB?"

"Nope."

"Fine, I'll take one. I've got to stop letting you stock the fridge."

They crashed on the couch together, both running on a week of too-little sleep. They cracked open their cans, each took a sip and slumped back.

"Did you know that Terry in the media office is Anna Tilden's brother?" Barry asked.

"Yeah, although I didn't know he was still in the media office. I thought they fired him after that thing with the K-pop band and the animated gloves."

"No, they just made him do a bunch of seminars."

"How did he get away with that?"

"Old Network family. They were some of the first white essence-users in Australia, apparently. Nice for some. Actually, now that I think about it, what happened to all the indigenous essence-users? Someone was dealing with proto-spaces before the British turned up and decided they owned everything, right?"

"The Network founder set up an indigenous Network organisation, but it wasn't anything like the modern branches. As far as I know, most of them joined the Cabal."

"The Cabal has had essence-users this whole time?"

"Not anymore. The incoming British Network people attacked them on sight, so the indigenous people left the proto spaces to them. Without the resources to make new essence-users, those in the Cabal eventually died of old age. The same story played out everywhere the Europeans decided the locals needed the light of civilisation."

"Civilisation meaning disease, exploitation, pillage and slavery."

"Yep. But that was where the Cabal got most of their information on essence-users. The messengers secretly amongst them probably told them things as well, but my understanding is that they were avoiding being too all-knowing."

"So that people didn't figure out they were aliens for another dimension, and not angels? Aren't angels meant to be all-knowing?"

"No one outside the Cabal can really be sure how it worked. Even now, they're a house full of secrets. Most of what we know is interpolation and guesswork."

"Where did you learn all this stuff, Nora?"

"It's my job to deal with an eclectic mix of magical and political forces from across the globe. How did you get this far without learning all this stuff?"

"I mostly stood next to you and took care of the easy bits, so you'd do all the hard ones."

She snorted a laugh and tapped her can to his.

"Here's to the easy bits," she toasted.

Jason's legs dangled off the edge of the ship, swinging absently as he munched on a sandwich.

"Aren't you afraid that your legs will be torn off and reduced to non-existence?" Zara asked.

She sat cross-legged next to him.

"I'm not sticking any limbs out there."

"It's fine," Jason told her. "Technically, this is the same magic Boris and his messengers used to go to Earth. My specific nature shields me."

He slapped the deck with his hand.

"The container I've put you all in is just a nicer version of the one Rufus and Taika travelled in."

"A lot nicer," she agreed.

"I don't think theirs had a bar."

He put his sandwich down on the plate sitting next to him.

"You were trained to be a princess from birth, right?"

"I was."

"In the expectation that you would become Hurricane Princess, then Storm Queen."

"That was the idea. Not that it worked out that way."

"A lifetime of training, and you still managed to monumentally blow the whole shebang, making things worse for everyone around you."

"I remember, yes, but thank you for reminding me of the worst sequence of mistakes I've even made in my life."

A grin flashed briefly on his face before it became sombre again.

"My political training consists of whatever Danielle can cram into my thick skull. How am I meant to get this right when you can have all the training in the world and get it wrong? I'm at a point where very few consequences can harm me directly. They'll all fall on the people around me, whether that's my companions or just innocent people in general. Was it wrong to set up this fight on Earth?"

She leaned her shoulder into his.

"There is no right, Jason. That's what I've learned from all my mistakes. There's no right and there's no wrong, not from a practical perspective. There's only what happened, and what happens next. It's the only thing you can change, so that's where you put your energy."

"You do the best you can with what you have?"

"Exactly. Sometimes your best isn't good enough. But, good or bad, all you can do is keep going. Try to make your best a little better each time."

He sat with that for a long while.

"Thank you," he said finally. "I thought you wouldn't be any help, because of what a huge political disaster you are, but there was a nugget of wisdom in there."

She turned to give him a dagger-sharp glare as he did a poor job of masking a grin.

"My advice isn't free," she told him. "Give me the rest of your sandwich."

"There are plenty more up in the lounge."

"I'm not up in the lounge. Hand it over, Asano."

He mock-grumbled as he reached for the plate.

After their break, Lenora and Barry returned to work. Lenora fired off emails in a futile attempt to head off diplomatic bushfires. Barry was going through contingencies for the artefact city's populace, for when Jason's arrival inevitably caused a massive problem. Responses ranged from public warnings to lockdowns to a citywide evacuation.

"Why did they never name the town?" he wondered aloud. "Everyone just calls it the artefact city."

"Technically speaking, it's Dimensional Artefact Site One."

"Who named it something that boring?"

"Who do you think?"

"Oh," Barry groaned. "Our illustrious prime minister. I have this vague recollection of someone trying to get it changed. Am I misremembering?"

"No, but none of the interested parties could ever agree on a more ordinary name. The Chinese wanted it to be meaningful and the Americans didn't want it to sound foreign. Neither wanted the other to get what they wanted, and Australian names were roundly rejected. I was actually in a meeting where someone told the Americans that Woolloomooloo was a town name and they went completely spare. The French tried to sneak a name in while everyone else was fighting, but that didn't work. In the end, it got left the way it is."

"Dimensional Artefact Site One."

"Yep."

"One."

"Yep."

"So, site two is some secret spot out in the desert?"

"Barry, *we're* out in the desert."

"Yeah, but we're not secret. We have a media relations department."

"So do they. Their media department just has machine guns."

"There's really a secret base out there?"

"You don't have clearance for me to tell you that."

There was a knock at the door.

"Director?" the voice of their shared assistant came through the door.

"Come in, Cassie."

Cassie was new, competent but still frazzled as she adjusted to the current schedule. Her curly hair had clearly been bundled atop her head following a couch nap.

"Mrs Tilden, Mr Remore and Mr Williams are looking to have a meeting, Director."

"They want to set up a conference call?"

"No, Director. They're downstairs."

62

IT SETS A TONE

"TRAVELLING LIKE THIS IS STRANGE," ANNA SAID. "I'M USED TO strange, with anything related to Jason, but this is up there."

Their vehicle looked like a flying saucer, flat and round, with smooth lines and a sleek white exterior that tapered at the edges. What propelled it through the air, however, was not alien science, magic or magitech. On the top were a pair of recessed handles being gripped by Taika, currently in the form of a giant golden eagle. He shot smoothly through the air like a rocket, the vehicle gripped in his talons.

The custom vehicle was designed to improve the mana efficiency of Taika's bird form and create adaptive planes of force that improved aerodynamic performance. As a result, what should have been a burden didn't impede his ability to fly, even enhancing it under some circumstances.

The interior was something between a hotel suite and a private plane, with one half of the saucer being a semicircular lounge area. The other half was divided between stowage, sleeping cabins and a bathroom. The passengers were Anna, Rufus and Gary Sharpton, a young leonid.

"Is this not how people travel out in the regular world?" Gary asked.

"In a UFO being carried by a giant bird?" Anna asked. "No, it's not. I thought that would have been obvious, given that you designed this thing. I know you've spent most of your life in an astral space, but you've studied aircraft design, have you not?"

"Surely people don't still use aeroplanes, right?" Gary asked. "Just adding some magic to them is way less efficient than a ground-up redesign that incorporates magitech from the outset."

"You realise that we're flying in what amounts to an over-elaborate bucket," Rufus pointed out.

"Yeah, but that's just me cheaping-out on propulsion," Gary said. "The original design was a dirigible, but replacing it with a giant bird is the obvious choice. If you have one available."

"Yes, completely obvious," Rufus said. "Are you sure you should be tweaking the design after what happened with the first prototype?"

"It's going to be fine," Gary said. "This prototype is much more reliable than that one."

"Given that the bottom fell off that one mid-flight," Rufus said, "I would certainly hope so."

"Hey, that was a valuable result," Gary said. "Because of that, we figured out the material degradation issue with the mana conduits."

"By having the bottom fall off," Rufus said.

"It's not like there was anyone in there. That's why we test prototypes: to isolate and correct errors. It's going to be fine. There's zero chance of anything going wrong."

"Then why did you insist on being brought along in case something goes wrong?"

"Because you wouldn't have let me go, otherwise. Also, I lied about the zero percent thing. But it's going to be fine, trust me."

"After you just admitted to lying and deception?" Anna asked.

"Exactly. I admitted to it. I'm an inherently honest person. It's like when my mum told Rufus I could come on this trip. That was definitely her and not an illusion created by my friend Brian."

Anna threw a wide-eyed look at Rufus, who gestured for calm.

"He's messing with you, Anna. It was his real mother."

Gary flashed a toothy grin, showing off a mouthful of lion teeth.

On the side table next to her chair, Anna's phone beeped a notification.

"We're in Australian airspace," she told them, then sighed. "I'm not entirely convinced that just turning up is the best approach."

"It was your idea," Rufus said. "You said that we need to contain the information as best we can. Deal with the onsite director personally."

"And that's all true," Anna said. "From what I know about Lenora Coleman, she'll play this objectively. Do what's best for the situation, not any particular country or group. If we go through the process of entering the country legally and getting permission to visit the site, we'll be dragged into a swamp of interest groups and political games before we get anywhere near the director."

"Then what's the issue?"

"This approach doesn't come naturally to me. I was brought in to ameliorate Jason's bolder instincts, and this…"

"Is exactly how Jason would do it," Rufus finished. "I heard that Yumi argued against this approach."

"She did. But Jason hired me to work for him, not the clan. He was very specific about that. While my role is to present approaches he wouldn't normally consider, he will ultimately do things his way. We had a less-than-ideal meeting, after which we sat down again and clarified a lot of things. What he wants from me, and what I can expect from him. Taking this approach, just showing up at the artefact site with no warning, is to demonstrate that we can. When he gets here, Jason intends to walk a line on which he accommodates the authorities of Earth without being subject to them. What we're doing here—the way we're doing it—sets a tone."

"How do you anticipate the various powers of Earth responding to that?" Rufus asked.

"Not well. The whole approach is predicated on Jason having the power to tell them to go jump, regardless of what they try. If he can't make the world accept that he's untouchable, it's all going to go wrong. And they won't accept it, not completely. Part of my role is to make it go the least degree of wrong we can manage."

"Mr Asano is definitely going to convince them," Gary said. "I can't wait to meet him. I bet he's crazy awesome, and I mean *crazy*. Mrs Tilden, have you heard all the stories about him?"

"One or two," Anna said.

"Nigel's story about him killing a city full of vampires with blood rain?"

"Yes."

"And Rufus' story about him killing two cultists with feminism? Rufus had a sword fight in that one where he had a trowel instead of a sword."

"That, I haven't heard," Anna said. "A trowel?"

"It was an evil trowel!"

"You've heard that one," Rufus told her. "Gary frames it quite differently in the retelling. But yes, it was an evil trowel."

"And the time you did an air drop raid from flying ships on the secret base of an evil religious order. They stole a submarine in that one!"

The enthusiastic teenager happily continued, not noticing the look shared between the two adults.

"Mrs Tilden, Mr Remore and Mr Williams are looking to have a meeting, Director," said Cassie, Lenora and Barry's assistant.

"They want to set up a conference call?" Lenora asked.

"No, Director," Cassie said. "They're downstairs."

"Downstairs? They're in the building?"

"Outside, with security," Cassie said. "They just kind of turned up. In a flying saucer being carried by a bird."

"I'm sorry, what?" Lenora asked. "Is this some kind of prank?"

"Uh, no, ma'am. The flying saucer is still out there. The bird turned out to be Taika Williams, who turned back into a person."

"He does have the power to turn into a giant bird," Barry said.

"No one was exactly sure what to do with them," Cassie said. "Or how they got this close without tripping any of our alert magic or other security systems. Security Commander Higgins scrambled his team and sent word to notify you while he locked everything down."

Lenora pinched the bridge of her nose, closing her eyes in frustration. She drew a sharp breath and let it out slowly, then schooled her expression and opened her eyes.

"Just the three of them?" she asked.

"There's one other man, as-yet to be identified. He's not human."

"One of the transformed," Barry said. "Almost all of them went to the Asano clan as refugees, so it's not odd to see one with them."

"He's a lion man," Cassie said, her expression growing slightly embarrassed. "He's super adorable."

Her expression went back to blank professionalism at a glare from Lenora. Barry, standing behind Lenora, gave Cassie an encouraging nod and rolled his eyes in Lenora's direction.

"Let's go," Lenora said, heading for the door. "Barry, you said Terrance Tilden is still in the Media Relations office?"

"He is."

"Call him. He may be useful when in dealing with his sister."

As she led the way to the elevator, Barry pulled out his phone.

"Deputy Director Sinise," Terry answered cheerfully. "To what do I owe the pleasure? Is this related to the kerfuffle happening outside? Security won't let anyone near it."

"Your sister is here."

"Annie? That's quite the saucy development. She didn't come alone, I take it."

"Taika Williams, Rufus Remore and one unknown."

Barry heard Terry all but leaping from his chair.

"Rufus Remore is here?"

"Yes."

"In person?"

"Yes."

"Is he wearing a shirt?"

"Terrance…"

"Could we get security to confiscate it? As a precaution."

"Have you even finished your sexual harassment seminars from the last thing?"

"I got back from the last one on Thursday. I can't believe they made me fly to Adelaide for the damn things."

"I can't believe you're still employed."

"It's my mother, you know. She does not like scandals to involve the family. Covers up everything she can get away with. She was livid when Anna scooted off to join the Asano clan. I was the one who got to tell her, which was a delight. She actually threw a shoe at me."

"Just meet us downstairs," Barry said, and glanced at Lenora while they waited for the elevator. "And do behave yourself, Terry. The director just learned that you weren't fired the last time, so if you don't, she's going to do something to you more permanent than your mother can fix."

"Okay, thanks for the warning, Baz. Best behaviour."

"Mate, you'd better, or Nora's going to rip us both a new…"

Barry saw Lenora's expression as she listened to the call.

"Just don't, Terry. None of your nonsense today."

Leaving the lobby elevator, they found a small crowd of workers held back from the main entrance by a security cordon. The security team, their magically enhanced tactical gear including full helmets, formed a stern and faceless line. Several people noticed the arrival of the director and deputy director and immediately approached. Barry stepped forward and tried to warn them off, with little effect.

"Anyone who doesn't go back to their workstation right now," Lenora declared, "will no longer have one by end of day."

The assemblage quickly took to the stairs and elevators, except for Terry.

"They're still not letting me get past," he said.

"Nor should they," Lenora told him. "If and when you are needed, you'll be let through."

He opened his mouth to protest, looked at her face and wisely closed it again. Lenora watched him for signs of rebellion for a moment, then nodded.

"Cassie, stay here with Tilden and report everything he does or attempts to do."

"Yes, ma'am."

Lenora led Barry forward, the guards parting to let them through.

"Commander Higgins is waiting for you, ma'am," one of them told her.

"Thank you, Morgan," she said as they passed through the cordon.

"How can you tell them apart in those outfits?" Barry whispered.

"Shush," she whispered back.

They crossed the lobby and exited through the main doors. Security personnel, guns held but not raised, stood in a line watching four people. In front of the line were the on-roster gold-rankers, a British man from the Network and one from the Chinese government. They were both warily standing off with Williams and Remore, who were much more casual. Remore was relaxed, with his hands in his pockets. Williams was eating a slice of cake and had an icing moustache. They stood between the other members of their group and the gold-rank security members. Behind them was the flying saucer they had arrived in.

Outside of the ring, Higgins was in his normal security uniform, not tactical gear.

"Honestly, ma'am," he said without preamble, "I didn't know what to do. They just showed up. The city is restricted, but nothing that would stop Remore or Williams. I mean, even this is theatre. Our gold-rankers couldn't handle either of them, let alone both."

"You had best take care with your mouth, Higgins, lest I close it for you," the English gold-ranker said.

"Everyone stand down," Lenora said. "Out of the way."

She strode through the group to stand in front of their unexpected visitors.

"Is this really what you thought was the best approach?" she asked. "Circumventing our security protocols to come here directly?"

"That's my bad," Taika mumbled from around a mouthful of cake. "I sensed some magic, but I didn't realise it was meant to be security. The standards are a little different in the clan. We have that continent-spanning vampiric empire to deal with, and you have what? Journalists? People selling scammy water filters?"

Annabeth Tilden stepped past him with a sigh.

"We do apologise, Director," she said. "We genuinely had no idea of the security arrangements here."

"You could have reached out in advance," Lenora pointed out.

"That might have been a bad idea, in light of what we've come to share. Preferably inside, away from…"

She glanced at the gold-rank security members.

"…public spaces."

"Director," the Englishman said, "we must be included in any—"

"'Must' is a strong word, Lord Willoughby," Lenora cut him off. "Your role here is security. My role is to determine in what context security needs to be employed. Since I deem these individuals a non-threat, and you couldn't do anything about it if they were, I will thank you to stand down. Along with the rest of our security forces, Commander Higgins. Maintain a low alert, do a full security sweep and compile a report on potential approaches to preventing this situation from repeating itself. Is that understood?"

"With respect, ma'am," Higgins said, "protocol says they can't be declared a non-threat until we've done at least basic checks. Make sure they aren't shape-shifters. Inspect their vehicle. Determine the identity of *all* members of the group. Human and otherwise."

"You mean Gary?" Taika asked. "He's cool, bro. Also, he won't have any legal identity outside of the clan. And I can tell you now that I am a shape-shifter. I can turn into a humongous eagle, which is sweet, plus I've got this whole birdman situation going on. In an awesome battle-form way, not a jump-off-a-pier kind of way."

"Taika, please stop helping," Anna said.

"I'm going to waive the security screening," Lenora said. "That is within my authority as director."

"That's up to you, ma'am," Higgins said, his tone telling her exactly what he thought of that idea. "If you do so, however, I am required to notify all member groups of the situation. Preventing me from doing so is *not* within your authority."

"Given that your security force is supplied by the member groups," Lenora said, "trying to keep a lid on this would be pointless, so you might as well go ahead. But first, stand down your people."

There was some more back and forth, but before long, Lenora and Barry were leading Taika, Rufus, Anna and Gary inside the building. Higgins let the group past the cordon, now only holding back Terry and Cassie.

"Annie!" Terry called out, but his eyes were locked on Rufus.

Lenora raised an arm to point right at him.

"Not another word," she warned. "Deputy director, take Mr Tilden and sit on him until such time as we need him."

"Of course, Director," Barry said. "Come along, Terry. We'll take the other elevator."

"G'day, Terry," Taika said with a wave. "Long time."

"Cassie," Lenora said to her assistant. "Get ready to triage the mass of calls and meeting requests that will already have started to pour in."

"Yes, Director."

Lenora turned to look at the four interlopers.

"We'd best continue this in my office."

63

WE ALREADY KNOW WHO
YOU ARE

"What you're telling me," Lenora said, "is that my little city is going to turn into a gold-rank battle zone."

"Yes," Anna told her. "Jason will try and take it out into the desert, but there is a good chance these invaders will confront him here."

"They need to challenge him at the first opportunity," Rufus explained. "To justify their presence here. They may be here already, but the condition for their being allowed on Earth is to remove Jason. If they don't do so swiftly, they'll be in violation of the Rules of Intrusion."

"And if that happens?" Lenora asked. "The space police come and arrest them?"

"The Rules of Intrusion," Rufus explained, "have always been in place. On my world, they mostly apply to holy wars, where one faith invades the domain of another. But, as it turns out, they also govern dimensional invasion. There has been flexibility in the rules, going back to before the birth of our worlds, but that has changed. Recently. Cosmic law is much more rigid now."

"Why?"

"The rules of the cosmos are enforced by something called the Cosmic Throne. It was damaged long ago, but the throne has been restored and the rules are more dangerous to bend, let alone break. I don't know the consequences of breaking those rules, but entities beyond any of our understandings are wary of violating them. You can be certain that these pirates will be."

"That was a really long way of saying you don't know," Gary said. Lenora happened to agree but said nothing as Rufus and Anna gave the young leonid a glare.

"Mr Remore," Lenora said. "While I appreciate the context, my job is more concerned with the practicalities. Somewhere in there, you said these people might already be here. We've seen no activity through the standing stones."

"The magic circle here only serves as an anchor for the link between worlds," Rufus told her. "It is both unnecessary and useless to the invaders who will have their own means of traversing the astral. Their dimensional magic will be more advanced than any that either of our worlds has access to. The only group on Earth that would have the ability to detect them would be Boris Ketland and his people, and they aren't tracking magic globally."

"That they've told us about," Anna amended. Rufus nodded his acknowledgement.

"If they are here, then," Lenora said, "we have no way of tracking them down."

"Correct," Rufus said. "Which is good, because we lack the power to confront them. Jason will be here in roughly three days, discounting any time anomalies in the astral. We should hope that, if the invaders are here, they remain wherever it is they are hiding."

Jota Withers rather liked his current accommodation. The magic and technology were both incredibly primitive, not even integrated with one another, but there was something calming about the simplicity of it. It was the design he appreciated: a house dug into a rocky bluff, overlooking the ocean. Part of the house was atop the bluff to remain accessible, but most of it jutted from the cliff face itself, with glass walls to make the most of it.

He sat in a comfortable armchair, reading from a tablet provided by his hosts. He had spent his time on Earth learning what he could about his enemy. He had certainly found it odd that he was being hosted by a group called the Asano clan, in a place called Asano Village, while he waited to kill a man named Jason Asano.

That anomaly was resolved when his sponsors on Earth started providing him with the information he requested. It turned out that there were three clans who used the name Asano on Earth. One was a historical clan of cultural significance, in the time before Earth's magic was in the open. Another was an offshoot of that clan within one of Earth's then-secret magic societies. This was the group currently hosting Jota and his crew. The third group had been founded by Jason Asano himself.

Asano Noriko was matriarch of the Asano clan hosting Jota and his crew. She had been making daily visits to check on his needs, along with the servants she had provided full time. As Jota had questions the provided information didn't answer, he invited her to converse on one of her visits. She took a seat opposite him, with a table holding a tea set between them.

"What may I help you with, Captain Withers?"

"I have questions regarding the various iterations of the Asano clan on this planet."

Her expression showed nothing but a woman happy to accommodate, but he could feel the swallowed bitterness in her aura. He suspected that, to her mind, there was only one true Asano clan. He didn't particularly care, his only interest being an understanding of his target.

"My understanding," he continued, "is that your clan originates in the nation of Japan, while Jason Asano's originates here, in Australia. They were the ones who built this village, yet now your clan is here, and they are on the other side of the planet. In territory overrun with vampires, no less. How did that come about?"

"There was a lot of chaos in the first few years after magic came into the open on Earth," Noriko explained. "During that time, Jason Asano created spiritual domains in Europe."

"Spiritual domains?"

"I don't know the specifics. Places of power that belong to him that have higher levels of magic than most of Earth. Most of his family and their various hangers-on relocated there, before the vampires took over. Also at that time, the major magic secret society went through a schism as magic went public. The government here sided with one of the factions, and that was not the one that had Jason Asano's supporters."

"But it was the one your clan belonged to?"

"It was. You are an astute man, Captain Withers."

Jota didn't respond to the praise, instead gesturing for her to continue.

"In order to consolidate their relationship with the new faction,"

Noriko explained, "the government seized ownership of this land from the remnants of the upstart clan, and gave it to the true Asano clan. The dregs of the false clan fled to join the others."

"And this happened only after Jason Asano had departed this world, I take it."

"It wouldn't have mattered. He was powerful, for a silver-ranker, but that is as far as it goes. He can't fight an entire nation, even if he is gold rank now. Alien allies or no."

Jota raised his eyebrows and Noriko paled.

"I apologise, Captain Withers. I meant no disrespect."

"What of these spiritual domains? They are not the normal power of a silver-ranker."

"Exploitation of unique magical conditions, using knowledge from the other world."

Jota strongly suspected that her obvious grudge was leading her to dismiss the threat Jason Asano posed. He did not fully dismiss her position, however. It was possible that the people looking to eliminate the man had been oversold on his power. One particular point in the information he was given strongly supported the idea that they were overestimating Asano.

"What do you know of the purported link between Jason Asano and the advent of the System?"

"That it's utter nonsense," Noriko said.

"I am inclined to agree. The System is a shift in the cosmic order. There is even talk of a new great astral being. What impact one gold-ranker from a place like this could have entirely eludes me."

"Exactly," Noriko agreed, nodding sagely. "He is a man with a big mouth, low cunning and more than his share of luck. An opportunist."

Having gotten everything productive he could from Noriko, he dismissed her. After she left, Jota's first officer, Natala, paid him a visit.

"Jota, Kreegle is rabblerousing again," she warned.

"When is he not?"

"The Rules of Intrusion mean we are cut off from the outside until we fulfil the conditions of the deal by removing Asano. This is a chance for Kreegle to make a move."

"I can handle Kreegle."

"He's riling up the crew."

"He's bitter because he wanted the captaincy that went to me."

"He's not the only one who resents you. Many think that you believe yourself too good for the rest of us."

"And what do you think, Nat?"

"Honestly, I think you do believe you're too good for the rest of us. At least a little. But Jakaar put you in charge for a reason. Where you came from, the training you've had. You are just better than us. Some look at you and want to catch up. Most would rather just drag you down. If the normal crew complement turned against you, odds are that you could handle them, as long as one or two stayed loyal. But this extended crew gives Kreegle an opportunity. Sitting around for days on end, like this. You've been holed up in here, what? Reading?"

"Studying our opponent. Preparing to face him."

"And while you've been doing that, Kreegle has been preparing to face you. Cutting deals and making promises."

Jota waved Natala into the chair Noriko had vacated as he contemplated what she'd told him.

"He'll have to make his move during the confrontation," he mused. "While a few of the crew might be fully on his side, most will balk if he moves too early. Either at the prospect of open mutiny or of facing me undistracted. His best case would be making it look like I was floundering against Asano, and he stepped in to save the day. It's not plausible, but it doesn't have to be if I'm dead. So long as I am, and he's in charge by the time it's over, he can spin any tale he cares to."

"What will you do?"

"I'm not sure. The more I learn about this man, Asano, the more certain I become that he's not what we've been told."

"How so?"

"Things that don't add up. My information is coming from the people of this world, so I'm having to infer through the gaps in their knowledge. They're so frantic to exploit the changes that have come to their world that they seem terminally incurious as to the underlying causes. Petty concerns over petty power. I suspect Asano to be an agent of the World-Phoenix, sent to stabilise this world."

"How certain are you?"

"The information given to me is less than well-curated. But Asano was known for having two companions from other worlds here. The one they know the most about is a person from the connected world. The other, they know less about. Asano was isolating from the local powers by the time they moved together more frequently. Her reported power levels are inconsistent, but that would fit someone using different levels of avatar. And it's almost certainly coincidence, but her name was Dawn."

"As in, the former First Sister?"

"Yes. This would have been around the time she stepped back and Helsveth took on the role."

"That…"

Natala shook her head.

"…that would change things. It can't be that big. Can it?"

"I don't know," he said. "It's a big cosmos. How many trillions were named after the First Sister?"

"Probably a larger number than I know the name for."

"If Asano does have that level of connection, though, it would suggest a wider design to our presence here. Someone using the Jakaar Fleet—and us in particular—to make a carefully measured point."

"What do we do?"

"We be flexible. These are just conjectures, and wild ones at that. If everything is as it seems, then we play it out as intended."

"And if Kreegle makes his move?"

"Then we may have to make an ally of the man we came here to kill. In which case, we should hope that my conjectures are not so wild."

Sitting alone in the dining hall of his cloud ship, Jason looked over at Jory, sitting with a group of his alchemists. They were chatting with Clive, Lorelei and some of their Magic Research Association members. In the time he'd been away, Jory had gone from small-town alchemist to a leader at the forefront of his field. Clive had gone from a disaffected member of the Magic Society to a formidable rival. Travis and Farrah had invented global telecommunications. His friends had remembered him, in his absence, but their lives still moved on.

So much had happened in his absence, and that was among the long lived of Pallimustus. On Earth, the changes had been massive, but his concerns were for a very small slice of it. The family he left behind. Isolated by vampires and the ambitions of the powerful. His niece had grown from a girl to a young woman, and he had missed it. He hadn't been there to spoil her, or to give sketchy advice that her mother wouldn't approve of.

He was beyond death now, but he was not beyond time. In a few days, he would be in the most dangerous battle he'd ever faced, at least in a mortal body. He couldn't die, but if his avatar was destroyed, the price would again be time. Again, his friends and family would remember, but again, they would go on with their lives.

Farrah slid into the seat next to him at his otherwise empty table.

"Why the sad boy face? Worried about this fight?"

"No. Just thinking about what losing would cost me. Reminding myself why I have to win. And I will. We will. I've been preparing for this fight for twenty years. No turning into a metaphor to fight the remnants of a god's power. No super-powerful bird form, or spiritual war across my soul. Just me and my friends, fighting like adventurers. The people of Earth can't understand what I am. They don't have the frame of reference. With this fight, they're going to see *who* I am."

"Battle isn't who you are, Jason."

"Yes, Farrah, it is. It's not all I am, but right now, it's the part they need to see."

"I get that. But it not being all you are matters. Maybe you should let them see some of that too."

"Oh, I've got that covered."

"Jason, what did you do?"

"Why do people keep asking me that?"

"Because we're not from Earth, Jason. We already know who you are."

6 4

GOOD LUCK IN YOUR BATTLE

MAGIC MASKED JOTA'S DIMENSION SHIP FROM ANY MEANS THE PEOPLE OF Earth had of detecting it. It was quite obviously there, however, as his crew was drawn up by the gravity channel and vanished in the air. He stood outside the Asano Village grounds with his second-in-command, watching his people ascend.

"We could just make a move first," Natala suggested. "Kill Kreegle, quick and clean."

"He's gold rank. I may be stronger than him, but there's no 'quick and clean' option. If I start a fight, I face the same problem he does: the rest of the crew's reactions. How many do you think would take sides?"

"Not many. Most would wait to back the winner. Of the ones that did step in, more would likely take his side, especially if you were the aggressor."

"There you are, then."

She nodded.

"It still feels wrong to just let the serpent slither up behind us."

"Don't concern yourself with the snake at our backs, Nat. Save your worry for the dragon in front of us."

"You're convinced Asano is more dangerous than we were told?"

"Call it instinct. Or precaution. When I was training, we were taught the ways the cosmic powers move. We know the World-Phoenix has been maintaining this world's integrity. It prefers to operate through lesser agents, and what I've gleaned of Asano's actions fit the pattern. If I'm wrong, we leave Asano alone. Kreegle needs him gone if he wants to return to Jakaar triumphant. That will be our time to push the fight."

"And if Asano is a person of consequence?"

"Then we side with him."

"And what of Jakaar?"

"He'll thank us for not antagonising the World-Phoenix. There's a chance the phoenix cult manipulated us to be here in the first place."

"Why would they do that? We're no threat to them."

"It will not have been for them."

"For Asano?"

"His world has just opened to the cosmic community. I suspect that we've been set up to become his first impression."

The artefact city, in outback Australia, was waiting. Really a small town, most of the nine thousand or so workers who lived there had been evacuated. These were shop attendants, janitors, gardeners and others who served to keep the city operating. They were carefully vetted and paid more than their jobs would earn them in a less secure location. Being removed in preparation for the coming altercation amounted to paid holidays as they were shipped off to Adelaide.

Evacuated alongside them were the personnel from the governments and factions who believed the city existed for their benefit. A handful of key staff remained, ensconced in bunkers beneath the city. There were also those influential enough to avoid being sent away, likewise bunkered down. Only the security force remained above ground, alongside Rufus and Taika. Anna and Gary were in the same bunker as Lenora, Barry and their key staff members.

The bunker had a series of rooms along a connecting corridor, not unlike a hotel. It also had a shared lounge and cafeteria area. The walls were stark, plain metal and the floor concrete. Large monitors on the walls were linked to the external cameras fixed on the standing stones, also displaying the now-active defence system. Magically enhanced howitzers and rocket pods had risen from their own secure bunkers and were now pointed at the air over the circle.

The last section of the bunker, outside of service areas, was the command-and-control room. The most restricted zone within the bunker, from which Lenora and her staff directed operations. Anna and Gary were not allowed access, and instead took a meal in a lounge area booth. In front of them were surprisingly palatable meals, given the functional nature of the bunker's cafeteria. Barry approached with Anna's brother in tow, leaving Terry behind before heading for the command room. Terry joined the pair in the booth where Anna introduced them.

"How did a young man like you wrangle an invitation to all this?" Terry asked Gary.

"He's our technical expert for this trip," Anna said. "He has a knack for practical solutions when it comes to magitech. Along with making sure our vehicle operates correctly, he's here to spot any dirty little tricks people might play on us."

"The number of listening devices my custom privacy tools have shut down is crazy," Gary said. "Microdevices, robot insects, vibrational analysis. Is there anyone in this town who isn't a spy?"

"Well, there's you," Terry pointed out.

"Uh… yep," Gary agreed unconvincingly. "I haven't placed any surveillance devices."

Anna gave him a flat look.

"What?" Gary asked. "With everyone else doing it, I thought it would be impolite not to. Don't worry; I made sure security would find enough to think they probably got them all."

Terry let out a laugh.

"I like this one, Annie. Speaking of surveillance, though, there's an awful lot of press attention on this. They aren't letting people onsite, but there's a veritable swarm of media drones up there. The usual outlets, plus they had me curate some appropriate influencers to be included."

His expression turned uncharacteristically sober.

"I hope this doesn't go badly for you, Anna. Mother reached out a couple of months ago to try and have me convince you to distance yourself from the Asano clan."

"Unsurprising," Anna said. "I note you didn't do that, though."

"I figured it was more of her manipulating, scheming crap, so I didn't let her drag you into it."

"Thanks, Terry."

He let out a slow, frustrated breath.

"What happened to her, Annie? It wasn't like this before magic came out in the open. Now she's obsessed with becoming some kind of global powerbroker."

"I don't know," Anna said. She put her hand over his on the table and gave it a squeeze.

"I think there's something specific," Terry said. "She contacted me again, a couple of weeks ago. She seems very convinced that things aren't going to go well for the Asanos when Jason gets here."

Anna leaned back, her expression looking like she'd bit into a lemon.

"She's in on it, then," she said. "That could end up being a mess, depending on how far they push it."

"In on what?" Terry asked. "Is it to do with why they're treating Asano's return like a military invasion? No one has told me a damn thing, and I'm meant to be in charge of the media response!"

"Yeah, it's to do with that," Anna said.

"The locals have brought in some ringers from outside our universe," Gary told him. "There's going to be a big old fight."

The multinational security force was arrayed around the site, some half a kilometre back, behind the heavy weapons. Rufus and Taika were free to roam, not being under the command of the security force. Commander Higgins was not happy about it, but there was little he could do. There were a dozen gold-rankers who had been called in for Asano's arrival, and not one of them was willing to cross Jason's two friends. Analysis based on their witnessed anti-vampire operations suggested they were the most powerful individuals on the planet, by a goodly margin.

Taika and Rufus meandered around, behind the security squads. Taika looked over at the emplaced weaponry, all pointed at the sky over the stone circle.

"I don't think much of these defences," Taika said. "Where are the spinny guns with a bunch of barrels? Where are the rail cannons? These look like someone burgled some weaponry off a boat and scribbled some magic runes on the side."

"That's pretty much what happened," said someone from a nearby squad, his accent marking him as American. "I have a cousin in acquisitions who told me—"

"Mouth closed, eyes forward, Jenkins."

"Keith," Jenkins said, "you know we're not in the military, right?"

"I said mouth closed, Jenkins. That's an order."

"Paramilitary at best," Jenkins continued. "Technically, we're private security contractors. Which makes you my supervisor, Keith, not my commanding officer. Also, you've got a real 'war criminal' vibe going on. They didn't put you in charge of any prisoners, did they?"

"You want to get kicked out, Jenkins?"

"Yes, please. I signed up to fill out my awakening stone collection, and they totally did me over on the contract. Cheaped out on the stones too. Elastic awakening stone? What's going on there?"

The squad leader had started marching over to Jenkins when the air was filled with a tingling sensation and a sharp smell of ozone.

"It's like being near a power line in the rain," Taika observed.

He had barely finished speaking when the standing stones lit up with gold, silver and blue light. Streaks of it rose into the air like colourful, inverted rain. It collected in a sphere that rapidly expanded, the rising light growing thicker with each passing moment.

In the command room of one of the various bunkers, Lenora watched the light show with everyone else. Most of her staff were at various consoles.

She observed as the growing sphere finally stopped expanding. It floated in the air, colours swirling, then started to shrink and dim.

"Do we have an estimate on the size it reached?" Lenora asked.

"Around four hundred and fifty metres, ma'am. Also, the Network is reporting a large dimensional energy event is showing up on the grid."

"Very useful," Lenora murmured as her eyes remained glued to the monitors. "Whatever would we do without them?"

As the supernatural light dimmed and shrank, the observers were able to make out a shape within, slowly becoming clearer. It was a vessel, somewhere between dirigible, ocean liner and alien spaceship. Dark red panels were affixed on white cloud substance, from which wisps were teased off and sent drifting away on the wind. A set of spheres orbited the ship, like a ring around a finger. The orbs were dark, seeming to absorb the sunlight. Inside the orbs were orange and blue nebulas that looked like eyes.

As the last of the gold, silver and blue light dimmed, words written along the side of the vessel in gold became visible. Taika burst out laughing as he read them. Rufus let out a sigh.

"Well," he said, "I have no idea what that means. Which at least means we know it's Jason and not the people here to kill him. How can an ice cube be—"

"What does that mean?" Lenora asked.

"It's from a song," Barry told her. "Early nineties, if I remember rightly. By Vice President Jackson, back when he was a musician."

"I thought he was an actor. Like Reagan."

"He was a musician first. Do you think Asano is making a political statement?"

"I think he's going to give me a headache. Any sign of this group who are meant to be here to kill him?"

As if to answer her question, the sky above the city shimmered like heat haze, and suddenly, a second vessel was in the sky. This one looked overtly like a spaceship, blocky and militaristic, but also with a clear magic aspect. The lines of the ship glowed and hummed with magic that essence-users could sense even from the ground, powerful and intimidating. It was, however, much smaller than Asano's vessel, some eighty metres long versus more than three hundred.

The whole city had tensed up, poised for whatever was about to happen. Two figures emerged from the second ship, riding on simple round disks. They flew towards Asano's vessel, as one person emerged to meet them.

Jota watched the person he imagined to be Asano float through the air towards him. The man was using his aura to fly, like a messenger. He was a known outworlder, so it could be some unique ability, or there could be a connection to the messengers. They were invading the linked world and, if Asano had thrown in with them, it would explain having the astral magic to world hop.

Asano's aura offered no further clues, being otherwise impenetrable to Jota's senses. That was a surprising level of aura mastery for someone from such a backwards world. Jota had discovered the auras on Earth to be execrable in their level of training.

The clothes Asano wore were interesting. He had no battle garb, and no magic items of note, beyond a pair of what were probably amulets on a necklace under his shirt. Otherwise, Jota sensed only basic clothing enchantments, although the man's underpants had oddly potent resilience magic. In design, he had a shirt with a colourful floral print, tan short pants, sandals and a straw hat.

There were a couple of small scars on his face, and another mostly hidden by his shirt. Such things were usually affectations in essence-users, but Jota suspected that these were not. For someone who understood what a genuine scar indicated, it put a very different spin on the seemingly casual man.

"G'day," Jason greeted Jota and Natala as they drew close. "I suppose we should have a chat."

Jota couldn't place the language. He was clearly using a translation power, but unlike any he'd encountered. It was like the words slipped into his head to impart their meaning, which was unnerving. He also sensed something about the words that was hidden.

"That's not your true way of speaking," Jota said.

"No," Jason acknowledged. "Things tend to go better when I do it this way."

"Deception is not the best way to start a relationship, Mr Asano."

"I suspect this relationship will go poorly regardless, but your point is a fair one."

Asano's next words, though simple, resonated like thunder in Jota's ears.

"So be it. I am Jason Asano, as you have surmised. Would you care to introduce yourselves?"

Jota's eyes widened a little. There were various names for the manner of speaking that Asano had used. On the world where Jota had been born, it was called the divine voice.

"My name is Jota Withers. This is my friend and second-in-command, Natala Spiro. I had been wondering if all this was a setup, and now, I find myself convinced."

"Convinced enough to turn around and go home?" Jason asked.

"Yes, actually. Unfortunately, things are not that simple."

"They never are."

"I'm afraid that if I try to turn around, one of my crew will take the chance to launch a long-planned mutiny. Kill us both, take my ship and report back to my admiral."

"And Jakaar will accept that?"

Jota gave Natala a side glance as she stirred, but she remained silent.

"Admiral Jakaar likes results and dislikes trouble," Jota said. "As long as he gets the results he wants, he won't begrudge an obvious lie. A living captain is more valuable than a dead one. Of course, the admiral is not getting what he wants here, is he?"

"He is not," Jason said.

Jota nodded.

"He doesn't want entanglements with the cult of the World-Phoenix. Or the messengers. Which of them are your backers? Or is it both?"

"Neither. I've been ally and enemy to the messengers and the World-Phoenix at various points."

"You're not an agent of the World-Phoenix?"

"You could say I have been, from a certain point of view. The World-Phoenix owed me a favour, which is why she set you up like this."

"My crew has twenty-seven gold-rankers. Can you match that?"

"Numerically, yes. How good are your people?"

"In terms of skill? Capable enough, but probably not the match of those who came up fighting monsters in a rural backwater. I suspect our equipment is better than what your people are armed with, however. By quite a margin."

"How many will stand aside?"

"Three or four might join the fight on our side. Some others might stay out of it, but I can't be sure."

"You will not fight with us," Jason said. "If you want to stand aside, then do so, but we will not offer you our backs."

"As you wish."

"And, just so you know, your ship is forfeit."

Natala stirred again and Jota gestured her to stillness.

"We came to your world in search of plunder," he said. "I understand that there is a price to that, and we will be in little position to negotiate once most of my crew is dead. But all you offer now is an incentive to work with my crew to kill you and finish my differences with them after."

"This isn't a negotiation," Jason said. "This is me deciding if anyone gets to live after. If you ever get to leave this world, Mr Withers, it will not be for some time. That is the price of coming here."

Jota turned to look at his ship.

"I would ask for some time to discuss this with my companion," he said, "but it appears that my chief mutineer has run out of patience. Good luck in your battle, Mr Asano."

6 5

SECOND CHANCE TO MAKE A
FIRST IMPRESSION

FLOATING IN THE AIR ALONGSIDE NATALA AND JASON, JOTA WATCHED Kreegle and most of the crew stream out of the dimension ship. Some used the ship's personal flight disks, but many showed off an eclectic mix of personalised devices or used their own powers. The one uniform thing about them was being armed to the teeth, although even in that, there was a lot of variance. The array of potent weapons, armour and magical tools stood in stark contrast to Jason in his floral shirt and straw hat.

"Mr Asano," Jota said, his eyes locked on the avaricious grin of the approaching Kreegle. "As you don't appear kitted out for battle, you may want to…"

He noticed a dark cloud in the spot Jason had just been floating. It dissipated swiftly, revealing a figure in robes the colour of dried blood. There was a sword at his hip, echoing his power as only a soul-bound weapon could. Enshrouding him was a cloak and hood that looked like he'd somehow ripped the energy from a portal to drape around himself. From within the hood, a pair of nebulous eyes glowed, casting just enough light to make out the sharp point of a chin.

"…make preparations."

"As you will soon see, Mr Withers, I have prepared quite thoroughly."

Jota watched as the pirates slowed down, becoming more cautious in their approach. They were gathered, not in any tactical array. Jota knew that Kreegle understood the advantage of numbers, but not how to use them. The man was pure thug, not a tactician, as reflected in his poorly plotted mutiny. But tactics or not, there were twenty-three of them, approaching through the air.

Jota glanced back at Jason. He looked more the villain than the pirates come to kill him. His alien eyes stared at Kreegle and the mutinous crew like a spider watching a fly. Asano let his aura spread like a web, giving Jota his first real look at it. It confirmed that the scars on Asano's face weren't affectations, but marks of suffering and struggle. Of challenges faced and overcome. Jota was very familiar with pirates whose lives were spent preying on the weak. Asano had the aura of a man who preyed on the strong.

With just a glance at Asano's aura, Jota knew he'd made the right choice. If Asano's companions were anything like the man himself, the only question was how many pirates would still be alive an hour from now. This was only reinforced when he noticed the most startling thing about Asano's aura: for all its power, it wasn't, strictly speaking, the real thing. Rather than a direct projection of the soul, Asano's aura was filtered from some other place. The body floating in front of him was an avatar.

"You're not even really here, are you?" Jota asked.

"No."

"So, our mission really was impossible from the start."

"I wouldn't use the word impossible. The impossible isn't as out of reach as most believe."

"Then what word would you use?"

"Doomed."

"They might be less doomed if your friends don't come out soon."

"There are many eyes on us, Mr Withers, and I have an oh-so-rare second chance to make a first impression. Before my friends join us, I have a point to make to the people who invited you here."

Jota looked back and forth between the horde of gold-rankers that were his now-former crew, and Jason Asano, facing them all alone. He used his disk to back calmly but swiftly away.

Lenora's bunker was silent as a tomb as she and her staff watched the events unfold. A wall of screens showed footage from the many surveillance drones and emplaced cameras, even tapping into the media drones as well. She had no idea how many people were watching the same thing, in other bunkers and across the planet via streamed feeds.

While the audio pickups got nothing but fuzz, the footage was crystal clear, aside from some blurring of the mouths. Lenora glanced at her lip-reading expert, who shrugged helplessly. Asano looked almost unchanged from the archival pictures Lenora had been going over for the last few days. If anything, he looked slightly younger, his features refined by another rank-up. Even his lost-tourist manner of dress remained intact.

He spoke peacefully with the two invaders, who were human at least in appearance. Their clothes were shades of grey and off white, loose but practical. The muted colours were punctuated by armoured panels etched with intricate sigils. They didn't fit with the Earth conception of pirates, but Lenora would have been surprised if they had.

That surprise came when the rest of the pirates came streaming from their ship, looking every part the gang of space thugs. They were an odd mix of fantastical and technological, from glowing daggers tucked into belts to backpacks sprouting robot wings. Unlike the pair who had approached Asano diplomatically, these new pirates were plainly intent on violence. Even so, they had slowed their approach, not charging in headlong.

Asano had changed his own attire for the imminent fight, although none of the promised companions emerged from his vessel. He was now garbed as the cloak-wearing death dealer he was known as, although there were differences from the footage she'd seen. His cloak had always been made of supernatural darkness, rather than any physical material, but this was on another level. It looked like he'd ripped a hole in the universe and draped it about himself. It was pulled together at the front, making him look like a living portal.

The first two pirates had clearly come around to Asano's side, backing off before the fight began. Asano's eyes turned from the pirates to look around at the sky. Wherever his gaze fell, the sky turned dark until the city had gone from day to a strange magical night. There were no stars, but lingering echoes of sunlight left the city in an unnatural gloom. Lenora liked to maintain a stern professionalism in front of the staff, but even she had her limits.

"Did he just BLOT OUT THE GOD DAMN SUN?"

"Uh, it looks that way, boss," Barry said, equally wide-eyed.

"How?"

"By looking at it, from what I could see."

The pirates on the monitor were unfazed, compared to their observers. With Asano now alone, they moved to the attack. The lead pirate conjured a harpoon the size of an electricity pole and hurled it at Asano, who gave no reaction. The pole shot through the cloak that wrapped his entire body, revealing it as the portal it appeared to be. The monitoring algorithm even pulled up a shot from one of the drones, showing the spear flying through whatever void lay beyond.

This took the pirate aback for only a moment, but it was a moment Asano used. Shadowy figures poured from the void cloak, all but invisible in the gloom. The algorithm estimated two hundred or more, data points appearing on one of the monitors, but Lenora couldn't make out much of what was happening. The pirates didn't share her confusion, immediately unleashing attacks at the shadows.

The observation suite in the command centre had an array of useful tools to monitor the fight. Composite shots from multiple cameras, event tracking and a variety of replay functions were managed by a mix of human operators and sophisticated algorithms. They picked out critical moments from the gloom and violence playing out at gold-rank speeds.

The computer attempted to map out the dark battle, using wire frame overlays and colour blocking to try and clarify what was happening. Asano had vanished in the chaos, but one of the staff wound back the footage. They watched a replay of his cloak turning dark, allowing him to disappear into the gloom.

Lenora had trouble tracking the fight, even slowed down, curated and enhanced. It was a storm of dancing shadows, weapons blazing with light and spells flashing with power. The pirates attempted to cut down the shadows to hunt their elusive quarry, but the shadows kept reforming, while sprouting strange arms that left them looking like squat, sinister trees. At the end of each arm was a gleaming black and red dagger.

The video footage caught glimpses of Asano in the melee, the algorithms slowing and highlighting any time he appeared. Like the shadows he hid amongst, he too had sprouted the twisted shadow arms that were attacking the pirates. His key identifier was the sword wielded by one of his shadow arms, his real ones hidden beneath the cloak still fully wrapped around him.

The daggers held by the shadows were black with ruby-like embellishments. The ornate weapons looked better suited for ritualistic sacrifice than frenetic combat, and the results of their attacks bore that out. While the pirates were slashed, time and again, the cuts were shallow and superficial.

Even Jason's sword accomplished little in terms of wounding his enemies. It shared a colour scheme with the daggers, with a black blade etched with glowing red sigils, but the design was simple and practical. That practicality did not translate to deeper wounds, however, as it flicked around wildly but never bit deep into flesh.

Lenora was aware of how Jason fought, so she knew that each of those seemingly minor wounds left blight and poison in their wake. It was not helping him in the moment, however, when the pirates at least seemed unaffected.

"Is he going to fight them all alone?" one of Lenora's staff wondered aloud.

Lenora considered the point well made. Impressive as it was that he hadn't been dogpiled immediately, the fight was far from one-sided. The gold-rank enemies were clearly not at Asano's level, but they left any of Earth's gold-rankers in the dust. The gloom was clearly not affecting them as badly as it was the observers of the fight, and they were clearly adapting, finding and striking at Asano with more frequency. The algorithm picked up each hit on Asano, putting it into a playlist screening on one of the side monitors. None of the hits were serious, but the pressure on Asano was mounting.

Jason had spent years in his soul fighting hordes of nameless great astral beings, and that experience paid off as he took the fight to the pirates. Using his aura to treat the air like solid ground, he danced through them, one shadow amongst many. His blade was a light touch, delivering the afflictions that would ultimately grant him victory. There were a couple of healers in the group, but Jason's afflictions not only absorbed the healing but inflicted more damage as they were removed. To push through his afflictions, the pirate healers would have to make things worse before they could make them better.

The individual skill of Jason's enemies was better than he had expected, but he could see how a life of piracy had shaped them. Used to soft targets and punching down, they were not maximising their advantages. Their chief advantage was numerical, but these were selfish and untrusting mutineers. Always watching their fellows for a dagger in the back, the lack of group tactics allowed Jason to use their numbers against them. He came and went, sowing discord and confusion, one more fleeting shadow amongst many. He suspected that if Jota had still been in charge, the fight would have been much harder, forcing Jason to call on his friends for a rescue.

While they failed to pin Jason down, not everything was going his way. The pirates did have skills and were learning faster than he'd like, cataloguing his tricks and adapting to them. More and more, they would anticipate an attack, or spot the subtle differences between him and the Shades, allowing them to counterattack.

More than anything, it was their dizzying array of magical devices that caught him out. On the simpler side was armour that reacted to any attack, usually with a force blast or gout of flame. More complex devices included nanowire nets or small constructs that protected the blind spots of their owners.

Jason's Amulet of the Dark Guardian was working overtime as more attacks landed. For every affliction his powers delivered, the amulet added to a shield that weakened attacks against him. As the shield energy was consumed, it was converted, in turn, to health regeneration. It wasn't enough alone to keep Jason functional, but was just one of several effects that allowed Jason to heal most wounds in moments.

The Leech Bite special attack delivered a new affliction at gold rank, Thief of Life. Although it did not stack like many of his powers, it drained a small amount of life from each affected enemy, feeding it to Jason. Like all his health regeneration, it was further enhanced by the blood robes Colin conjured for him.

The bloodthirsty familiar was making his own efforts, Jason using Colin in his original swarm state. He left clutches of the toothy leeches on each enemy he clashed with, delivering yet more afflictions and life drain. This left distracted pirates trying to remove them, with varying levels of success. Scraping and plucking accomplished little as the clutches self-replicated using the very life force they were draining. A few pirates did manage to escape the leeches, often by blasting themselves with self-destructive area attacks.

The last familiar, Gordon, remained inside Jason for two reasons. One was that his distinctive orbs would draw too much attention. The other was that, when not manifested, he enhanced Jason's aura strength. Jason's aura was strong already, but at silver, it had been an utterly overwhelming force, relative to his rank. The same was not true at gold, as the avatar was linked to Jason's soul but did not contain it.

Even so, Jason was single-handedly negating the biggest advantage the pirates should have had: more than twenty aura powers, variously enhancing them and diminishing him. He was suppressing every single one of them, however, through a combination of native strength, the boost from Gordon and Jason's own aura power.

As the name suggested, Hegemony was an aura power based around dominance. Within Jason's hegemonic power, he made the rules. That manifested in various ways across the ranks, most notably in how any attack on him or his allies became a sin. At gold rank, he gained the power to determine whose aura powers were allowed to flourish and whose were crushed beneath his boot. He was still required to suppress auras using his well-honed strength and mastery, but he could now affect every other aura with his full power simultaneously, instead of needing to split it. As a result, not a single pirate was bringing their aura power to bear.

The battle continued, Jason dosing the pirates with his affliction suite, while they pushed him closer and closer to the edge. They were catching him out faster and hitting him harder, drawing closer to a definitive hit. If they could ring his bell hard enough, they could dogpile and finish him with their numbers.

Slowly but surely, the tide was turning against Jason. The pirates showed signs of their afflictions, but he was getting no kills off the gold-rankers. Without weaker minions to kill and drain for buffs, he was not growing in strength, one of the weakness of his combat style.

He took a pummelling after he was caught by a harpoon that affected him with the Inescapable condition, shutting down his shadow jumping so long as the harpoon remained embedded in his body. The pirates would not give him the chance to yank it out, pouncing on him as they smelled blood in the water.

As Jason sent out a chat message, the pirate leader yanked on the chain affixed to the end of the harpoon. His face was split in a savage grin of triumph as he yanked on the chain with strength akin to Humphrey or Taika, pulling Jason towards him. With Jason's face shrouded in darkness, the pirate failed to see Jason grinning back. What he did spot was a crystal rod that grew out of his own chest armour.

He looked down in confusion at the offending item. Tethers of force shot out, connecting to each member of the pirate crew. In that moment of confusion, Jason tore the harpoon out of his body, the brutal tines pulling blood, bone and flesh with it. With a gaping hole in his torso, Jason vanished, leaving only a floating, empty cloak.

66

THE RIGHT MOVE

KILLING A GOLD-RANKER WAS HARD. KILLING A COUPLE OF DOZEN WAS extremely hard. The standard solution to killing things that excelled at not being killed was afflictions, placing Jason at the centre of his team's plan to handle the pirates. As the entire purpose of the fight was to demonstrate Jason's power to the world, that worked out nicely.

The first stage was for Jason to fight the pirates alone. This was the part of the plan that took the longest to talk Humphrey into, and several contingencies were in place should it go poorly. There had been a lengthy discussion of what 'going poorly' entailed, with Jason arguing that getting decapitated 'wouldn't be all that bad.'

Stage two of the plan had two trigger conditions. The first was Jason spreading enough afflictions to the pirates that they would be significantly impacted by the time the rest of the team appeared. The other was Jason biting off more than he could chew and getting the snot kicked out of him. At that point, Team Biscuit, plus guest member Farrah, would go on the offensive.

Sophie's Eternal Moment power allowed her to massively accelerate her own timestream. At gold rank, she could extend the power to the whole team, although it had the same exhausting effect on their stamina and mana as it did her. The result was the team approaching the pirates at teleport-like speed, without the brief but critical moment of dimensional disorientation that came from an actual teleport. They were long past throwing up like first time portal travellers, but in a gold-rank battle, every moment was crucial.

On Jason's signal, the team arrived, seemingly out of nowhere, and acted immediately. Jason, having ripped a hole in his torso while removing a harpoon, vanished. At the same time, Belinda's Force Tether power yanked the entire pirate crew into a comical ball of squirming limbs.

Belinda's power set didn't spew deluges of lava or blinding streams of magical light. Her gold-rank upgrades didn't create sandstorms and tsunamis like Sophie's Wind Wave, or bring her back from the dead like Humphrey's Immortality. Force Tether's modest gold-rank upgrade was to increase the pulling force when the power was first activated. The extra strength didn't last long but was powerful enough to squish even a cohort of gold-rankers into a tightly pressed cluster of surprised and angry yells.

Powerful attacks like Clive's Wrath of the Magister or Farrah's Lava Cannon inflicted massive amounts of damage, but while their streams of energy were large and powerful, gold-rankers were fast and their fights spread out. It was hard to inflict sustained damage from such abilities on one enemy, let alone multiple. A big floating ball of pirates, however, made the perfect target.

The strength of the tether was already fading, leaving only a short window in which the pirates were left ripe for area attacks. The team was already acting, Farrah inundating the pirates in a deluge of lava. Belinda used her own Mirror Magic to replicate the spell, revelling in the chance to unleash such flashy magic for herself, even if it wasn't really her ability. It was more than just a chance to throw fancy spells around, however. At gold rank, Mirror Magic allowed both herself and Farrah to use Lava Cannon a second time, ignoring the usual cooldown.

Other members of the team piled on damage as well, such as Clive atop giant-sized Onslow. Standing on a platform pre-cast with a combat ritual, his Wrath of the Magister spell was just as powerful as the lava streams, if not more so. Sophie's Wind Blade power didn't share that strength, but the chaining effect worked like a blender with the pirates so clustered up.

The team had taken full advantage of their moment of surprise, unleashing their attacks the instant they arrived. Jason had taken that moment to appear inside Onslow's shell, stepping out of a shadow to be attended by Neil.

"Are you okay?" Neil asked him.

"Never better," Jason said.

"You don't need me to heal the hole in your torso that's the size of your head, then?"

"Well, maybe not *never* better."

Neil gave his head an exasperated shake, already pushing Jason onto a ritual circle pre-drawn on the floor. Neil's most potent healing spell, Grand Renewal, required ritual magic to work, like some of Clive's powers. At gold rank, and with a magic circle already in place, it closed the gaping wound in an instant. Jason didn't waste time, reconjuring his cloak as he floated out of the shell's open sides, arms spread wide.

Lenora watched as the pirates endured a barrage that she was certain would have annihilated any defensive emplacement on Earth, magically enhanced or not. There was a massive array of magical sensors pointed at the standing stones and the surrounding area, all monitored by her staff.

"What sort of readings are we getting off of this?" she asked.

"Ma'am, the magic up there is hitting the maximum on every scale we have. What's going on up there could dig out NORAD, which has a mountain of magical protections. And is inside an actual mountain."

"Are we in danger?" Barry asked.

"Yes, sir. We can probably endure the odd glancing blow, but if they turn that kind of power on us directly, we're cooked."

"Where's Asano?" Barry asked. "One of the cameras spotted him vanishing right before the pirates got blindsided."

"He's probably inside the giant flying tortoise," Lenora said.

"That's what I figured. I just wanted you to say something that makes you sound like a character in a children's book."

He responded to her flat glare with a grin.

"Oh, there he is," Barry said, pointing at the main monitor.

Lenora turned her attention back to the wall of monitors as Jason was floating out of the tortoise, arms held out to his sides.

"Does he think he's Jesus?" Lenora asked.

"Maybe," Barry said. "The giant hole in his chest seems to have miraculously healed."

The cluster of pirates had pulled themselves apart by that stage but remained in close formation, still hindered by the tethers. They looked the worse for wear, their flesh marred by afflictions and scored from attack magic. There was a moment of calm as the two groups faced off, the focus on Jason at the front of his team. The audio pickups stopped producing the hiss of interference and Jason's voice came through. It didn't sound like a digital reproduction, or as if it was being transmitted at all. The words rang like the pronouncement of a god, not heard with the ears but felt with the soul.

Feed me your sins.

A red glow shone from within the pirates, their life force made manifest, stained with sickly shades of yellow, purple and black. The tainted colours oozed from the light, like pus from an infected wound, moving through the air towards Jason. Left in their wake were sparks of blue, silver and gold, popping like fireworks. The red light flinched from the sparks, diminishing even as it was reabsorbed into the pirates' bodies. The taint flowed through the air to Jason and was absorbed into his body.

With the audio no longer blocked, Lenora and her staff heard the roars of fury from the pirates, who launched themselves at Jason, ending the lull in combat. From behind Jason, a man with rainbow scale armour, dragon wings and a massive sword launched past him, as if shot from a cannon. When his sword impacted the lead pirate, the explosion of pure force was like a bomb going off, the thunderous sound of it shaking the sky.

The entire cohort of pirates were shot away like pellets from a scattergun. Even the incidental force of the blast sent drones tumbling and knocked several fixed cameras out of alignment. The man stood in the air, held aloft by his slowly beating wings. His team had had their hair and clothes whipped savagely but seemed otherwise unaffected.

"That's some sword," Barry said as Lenora shot out orders.

Half the camera feeds were knocked out or misaligned and she was directing her people to repair what they could from the control room.

"Probably best not to send anyone out to fix them," Barry mused.

Jason let out a low whistle, unheard as the sound of the blast was still fading. The pirates were scattered across the sky, over the town and beyond. By the time quiet returned, so had Humphrey to his team.

"What's that special attack called again?" Jason asked. "Boom Town?"

"Unstoppable Force," Humphrey told him. "As you well know."

"It did look unstoppable. Especially with Neil giving it a boost."

"Don't go trying to give my powers weird names. The team letting you name tactics is bad enough."

"I thought the 'Suck and Cut' tactic worked pretty well."

"That doesn't even make sense."

He turned from Jason to survey the sky into which he'd knocked all the pirates. He then addressed the team through the team's voice chat channel, to include Rufus and Taika below.

"The transcendent damage Jason left them with won't finish off gold-rankers, but it's going to knock them about. Sophie, Rufus, Taika. Did you pick out the healers while they were fighting Jason?"

"Yeah."

"Yes."

"Sure did, bro."

"Snatch them up. Don't give them a chance to counteract Jason's afflictions. Jason, Farrah and I will move individually to hit them while they're scattered. Lindy, Neil and Clive, move as a group using Onslow. Stash, support them."

A puppy leapt out of the tortoise shell and turned into a rainbow-scaled dragon. The team members shot off, including Rufus and Taika below. Taika transformed into a golden eagle and Rufus moved through the air like an ice skater, silver light gleaming under his feet.

"Can we change it up?" Jason asked, already heading for one of the pirates. "Bring them to me and I'll turn their afflictions into suppressive force. Keep them alive."

"I thought the plan was to kill them," Humphrey said. "To make a show of it for the people of this world."

"That was the plan," Jason said. "But the idea behind it was to show the people of Earth that I'm not the person I was when I left. I definitely would have killed them then. We did need a show, but we skittled them pretty hard, for everyone to see. I think it's enough."

"You won't get an argument from me," Humphrey said.

"It's the right move," Farrah said. "For you, Jason. I don't care if they die."

"Don't risk yourself just to keep them alive," Humphrey directed. "Play it safe and put them down if you have to."

"I'll see about softening them up some more," Jason said. "*Mine is the judgement, and the judgement is death.*"

In the sky, silver clouds appeared out of nowhere, gold and blue light flashing within them. Heavy rain fell, not water but droplets of transcendent light. The gold-rank variant of Jason's execute power, Verdict, did nothing to Jason and his team, or the security forces below. To the scattered pirates, every glowing drop annihilated flesh, sending rainbow smoke burning off their bodies. Already having transcendent damage hollowing them out from the inside, the pirate crew was a spent force, making a break for the ship still in the air.

In the main chamber of Lenora's bunker, Anna watched the monitors. Many of the feeds had been knocked out, although most had been subsequently restored. She watched the annihilating rain, recalling Nigel's story of the vampire cataclysm in Asano clan territory. His trembling voice as he described an apocalyptic vision of blood and sparkling rain. Of power that belonged not to a man but the wrath of an angry god.

She hoped that would not be repeated here, or her job was going to get harder. A display of power was one thing, but when people started using religious metaphors, things were getting out of hand. She wondered about the Americans, who had been waiting to intervene.

Jason touched his sword to the pirate collapsed on the floor of Onslow's shell.

- You have absorbed all [Holy] afflictions from [Elenore Boatwell].
- An instance of [Hegemon's Mercy] has been inflicted for each affliction absorbed.
- You have gained an instance of [Benevolent Hegemon] for each instance of an affliction absorbed.

The woman slumped even more as her powers were suppressed. Jason looked down at his sword, both the first and last gift he had gotten from Gary, and smiled. Jason's powers had no mercy in them on their own, but through the legacy of his friend, they always would.

"Thank you, brother," he whispered.

"Some of the pirates are making it to their vessel," Humphrey said through voice chat. "There's too many to wrap up ourselves. We should call out more people from our ship."

"It will work better politically if we use the locals," Jason said. "I know they won't be reliable, but they can at least keep an eye on the ones we haven't rounded up yet."

"Alright," Humphrey agreed. "That will free us up to move on the dimension ship."

"Rufus, signal the yanks," Jason said. "Tell them to be careful, just watch and not fight."

"Do you think they'll listen?"

"No."

"Rufus, Taika," Humphrey directed. "Stay back and wrangle these locals. Keep them alive. Everyone else, move on the ship."

———

Jota and Natala had withdrawn from the space over the standing stones before combat had begun. Hiding amongst the evacuated buildings of the city, their gold-rank perceptions were enough to track the events of the battle, despite the distance. As Jason and his team moved towards the ship, they felt a wave of magic pulse from it.

"They're running," Natala said. "They're going to dimension shift."

They watched Jason slow down as the rest of his team kept moving. Floating in the air, he lifted an arm towards the dimension ship and made a grasping gesture with his hand. The prow of Jason's own ship opened like a crocodile's maw, revealing a giant blue and orange eye inside. Then a single word rang out, not spoken but created.

No.

Jota had encountered the messenger trick of speaking through aura manipulation, usually employed to impress the ignorant masses of undeveloped worlds. That word, pushed from the ship's giant eye, was similar, but something more. There was a power to it, a force of command that belonged not to messengers, or even their astral kings, but to gods.

His eyes locked onto Jason's vessel, even as a wave of power swept out from it and over the pirate vessel. The gathering dimensional energy in the pirate ship diminished to nothing. Jota didn't spare it a glance.

"Asano's ship," he said, his voice breathless with shock. "It's a temple."

"To what god?" Natala asked. "The only aura I felt come from it was Asano's."

"Exactly."

One of Lenora's camera drone operators managed to pilot a drone aboard the pirate ship, but the camera feed shut off almost immediately. They did get an audio feed, but it was only scraps of sound interspersed with the hiss of white noise. Everyone in the command room listened attentively anyway. Sometimes, it would be the person who appeared to be leading Asano's group barking directions. Other times, it would be the wordless sound of combat, or a cut of screams of fear and panic. One time, they heard piteous begging for mercy.

Finally, the feed came back fully, with even a static-filled image appearing on the monitor. Someone was holding the drone, staring into the camera so closely, they could see right up the man's nostril.

"Neil," Jason's voice came through. "Put that thing down."

A LOT OF THINGS TO DO

JASON AND HIS TEAM HUNTED THE PIRATES THROUGH THE DIMENSION SHIP, with few putting up much of a fight. Their prey was scattered, on the run and ravaged by afflictions. The near-indestructible gold-rankers weren't dying, but they were closer than they'd ever been. Used to being on the other end of one-sided fights, they knew what it was to be the predator. Being the prey left them panicked and fearful, many surrendering the moment one of the team caught up with them.

While there were still a few pirates to round up, the fight was already won. That left Jason more fascinated with the dimension ship than hunting down stragglers. It had the feel of a proper spaceship, all metal walls and heavy bulkheads. The magitech touches kept it from seeming like a submarine, with glowing magic conduits and holographic communicators. Jason didn't know how to work them, but some of the pirates were using them to try and coordinate with their fellows.

They were collecting the pirates in the mess hall. Each time he returned with a prisoner, Jason would change the afflictions eating them from the inside out into ones that suppressed their powers instead.

"I found a dead one in some kind of healing bay," Humphrey said, coming back with another prisoner of his own.

"It's called an infirmary on a spaceship," Jason told him.

"It's a dimension ship, not a spaceship."

"Don't take this away from me," Jason said, then his expression turned sober. "Dead in an infirmary, you say? Probably tried to purge what I'd done to him and the Weight of Sin affliction killed him. That's the one that inflicts damage when my afflictions are cleansed."

"Weight of Sin," Humphrey echoed. "Sometimes I forget how... evocative your powers can be."

"You can say melodramatic," Jason told him. "I've had a lot of therapy; I know who I am."

He looked at the prisoners, some on their knees and others curled up on the floor. Their bodies were ravaged by Jason's power, plus the burns, blasts and pummelling they'd taken from the rest of the team. Their clothes were ragged but largely intact.

"I should start sourcing my clothes out in the cosmos," Jason mused. "Then maybe I'd get blasted naked less often."

"Does it happen that much?" Farrah asked, dragging in another prisoner.

"More than I'd like. Should we get Neil in to heal them? With their powers suppressed, they'll take a while to heal, even with gold-rank vitality. It doesn't feel right to just leave them with their flesh half rotted off."

"You're the one who did that to them," Farrah pointed out.

"That was a fight. They're prisoners now, which means we should treat them humanely. Even if they're a bunch of pirates, we're not."

"Jason's right," Humphrey said, "but I don't want them in fighting shape until we decide what to do with them. Imprison them on the cloud ship?"

"No, let's put them on my prison planet with the messenger armies that surrendered to me."

———

Lenora and her staff continued to listen in, through the drone Jason and his team had left, discarded in a corner of the dimension ship's mess hall. The camera was pointing at a wall and only infrequently got a signal out, but the audio remained mostly functional.

"Did he just say he has a prison planet?" Lenora asked.

"He also said armies," Barry added. "*Armies*, plural. Of those angel things that were secretly running the Cabal. They don't have anyone below silver rank. They're born that way."

"Technically, they're budded, not born," Jason's voice came through the audio pickup. "They're actually plants, which is kind of crazy."

"Who are you talking to?" Humphrey's voice came through.

"Some guy named Barry. He's in one of the bunkers under the town out there. They've gone all quiet and nervous down there now, though. I don't think they realised I was listening, and they don't seem happy about it, now that they have. Which, frankly, is a double standard when they're still tapped into that drone in the corner."

"That's the oversized recording crystal thing?"

"Yeah."

Jason's team left the dimension ship and chased down the remaining pirates. Rufus and Taika had already grabbed some of them, before they could kill any of the overenthusiastic American gold-rankers. All the pirates were gathered up and sent through the portal to Jason's soul realm. They couldn't be forced through, but the alternatives, should they refuse, proved sufficient incentive to comply.

Following this, more of Jason's companions left the cloud ship and moved to the ground together. The security force was unsure how to react, surrounding them but keeping their weapons, mostly guns but also swords, spears and even whips, in overtly non-threatening postures. One of them stepped forward, wearing tactical gear woven with magic. Jason could sense that their armour was less resilient than even the clothes worn by the pirates.

"Mr Asano. My name is Security Commander Higgins."

"I'm feeling a little crowded, Commander."

"In fairness, Mr Asano, you did come to our town."

"Your town."

"I am, in this case, acting as representative of the Australian government."

"And what interest does the Australian government have in this remote little spot."

"The standing stones, obviously. I don't know what you're trying to get me to admit, Mr Asano, but I'm a simple man. My job is to keep this facility, and the people in it, safe. I suggest you save the politics for Director Coleman."

"Then why am I talking to you, Commander?"

"Then let's rectify that, Mr Asano. Please follow me."

"I think I'll skip the walk, Commander. Shade?"

The familiar emerged from Jason's shadow. Jason stepped into his dark form and vanished, leaving the commander scowling at Shade and the rest of Jason's team.

"Who made these weapon systems?" a voice complained in an American accent. Higgins looked over to see Travis, Clive and Belinda peering at a howitzer with a sigil engraved on the side.

"This is terrible," Travis continued. "This is barely more than a big gun with an enchantment to overcome inherent rank resistances. Has this planet not done any weapons research in the last seventeen years?"

"Sir," Higgins called out to him. "Please refrain from poking the howitzer."

The security personnel in the command room raised their firearms as a dark shape rose from Lenora's shadow.

"My apology for the intrusion, Director Coleman," Shade said. "My name is Shade and I am afraid that my employer is, from time to time, an unfortunate mix of melodramatic and impatient. Before he arrives, which will be very shortly, I have two recommendations to offer you. The first is to make sure that your security force does not do anything precipitous. Of the people in this room that course of action would endanger, Mr Asano and I would not be amongst them. Second, I would advise allowing Mrs Annabeth Tilden entry to this room. You may find that she ameliorates some of Mr Asano's more instinctive impulses."

The room was very still as everyone in it waited for Lenora's reaction.

"I am aware of who you are," she said, keeping her voice measured. "I have been briefed. And I will take your advice. Sub-Commander Keene, please remove your security team, find Mrs Tilden and bring her here."

"Ma'am—"

"You are not here to debate my orders, Sub-Commander. Do I have to repeat them?"

"No, ma'am."

"Ooh, strict nanny," Jason said as he emerged from Shade's body as if walking through a door. "G'day, Lenora. Can I call you Lenora? Jason, lovely to meet you."

He held out his hand for her to shake, ignoring the security forces who had snapped their guns back up. He was back in the absurd tourist outfit he'd worn when first emerging from his ship, with no sign of the blood and gore that had painted him during the battle.

"Sub-Commander, you have your orders," Lenora said, not shifting her gaze from Asano's as she shook his hand. In contrast to images and reports she'd seen, his eyes were dark brown and seemingly normal. There was amusement in them, but she didn't trust that any more than his absurd clothes or casual demeanour. She was holding a monster by the hand.

His aura not only gave away nothing but was utterly imperceptible to her. With the other gold-rankers she had met, she could at least register their presence, but to her supernatural senses, she was shaking hands with empty air. The disconnect between that and her mundane senses was unnerving and, she was quite certain, no accident.

The double doors leading into the chamber slid open and Annabeth Tilden marched in as if she owned the place.

"Jason," Anna demanded as she strode down the central aisle, past rows of workstations. "What did you do?"

"Oh, come on," he complained. "I just got here. I haven't done anything."

Anna arrived in front of Jason and Lenora. After giving Jason a suspicious look up and down, she turned to Lenora and gave her a slight nod.

"Director Coleman."

"Mrs Tilden."

"We need to get you a title, Anna," Jason said. "An important-sounding one. Chief Something-Something of Earth Operations."

"Jason..."

He chuckled.

"Sorry, Anna. Look, I'm going to go, I just need to know where we drop off all the refugees."

"Are you talking about the people who vanished from here, seventeen years ago?" Lenora asked.

"Yep. Didn't bring all of them, but most. Some chose to stay, and others died. Some couldn't be found, or didn't want to be. Anna should have told you about this already."

"We've discussed it," Lenora confirmed. "However, you can't just drop them off like they're bus passengers. It's not as simple as that."

Jason flashed her a smile.

"Lenora. Director Coleman. Anna, here, has made the grave error of agreeing to be the person who explains my whims in a manner that prevents me from coming off like a power mad loon who does whatever he wants because no one can stop him. She's going to have some rough days, now that I'm back, especially these first ones."

He gave Anna an apologetic smile and let out a sigh. His expression showed a deep weariness, just for a moment, that Lenora's intuition told her had nothing to do with the battle he'd just come from.

"I'm quite certain that a lot of very powerful people have a lot of questions they're very convinced are important," he told her. "And I will talk to them. Some of them. In time, as I see fit. Frankly, I don't think many of the things that matter to them are the same ones that matter to me. I didn't come to this planet to create some political storm. I'm just coming home and catching up with family. Bringing some friends to show them around my hometown. But I recognise that showing up with all this power is going to scare people, however innocent my intentions. Which is good, because if their intentions are anything like what I experienced last time, they should be scared."

"Is that a threat, Mr Asano?" Lenora asked.

"You can call me Jason. And no, it's not. You don't a threaten a mosquito that lands on your arm, Lenora. You swat it if it bothers you."

There was a heaviness in the room. Lenora couldn't sense any aura from Jason but was convinced he was somehow using it to make his presence seem large and imposing, despite his comical appearance. No one in the room spoke into the silence as he paused briefly before continuing.

"I've been away for longer than I intended, and I have things to do. Things that are important to me. I did leave a mess outside that requires cleaning up. There are some pirates who wisely decided to throw themselves on my mercy rather than fight. I need to have a conversation with them about who on Earth invited them here to kill me. Also, how I can fly off with that dimension ship of theirs."

"I can tell you now," Lenora said, "the governments and organisations operating out of this facility will wa—"

"I don't care what they want."

Now she did feel his aura, slamming down on the room like a physical weight. When Jason spoke, his words started soft but grew heavy with restrained anger.

"I built the anchor for my dimensional bridge on land that I owned. This town was abandoned after the monster surge, with no intention for anyone to rebuild it. The government was happy to sell me the land, since no one wanted it. But then I was gone, and they wanted what I'd left behind, so they used eminent domain to seize it in my absence. And not only did they do the same to my uncle's property, but they handed it over to my enemies."

Jason's aura had grown more violent as the anger seeped into his voice. She could hear the roar of blood rushing through her ears as his words bypassed them to thunder against her soul. She, and everyone else in the room but Anna, were either half crouched or slumped in their chairs, as if literally weighed down by Jason's presence. Shaken as she was, she was thankful for the restraint of his rage. She could feel it in his aura, like water behind a dam, and knew that if the dam broke, it would drown them all.

Jason moved next to Lenora, who suddenly realised she was crouching. He crouched down in front of her and spoke again, his words soft and quiet.

"The rules of this world," he said, "apparently mean that if you have the power, you can take what you like. When people ask you about what happened here today, tell them that I finally figured that out. That anyone looking to take what is mine would do well to consider the full ramifications of that decision."

Suddenly, the oppressive force was gone. Everything seemed strangely silent, as if a background noise she hadn't even noticed had suddenly stopped. Jason stood and offered his hand to help her to her feet. She looked around and saw that her staff were likewise recovering.

"I apologise," Jason said. His voice was back to normal and he almost seemed like a different person. "I'm trying to be more diplomatic, but it doesn't come naturally to me. Anna, please sort out with Lenora where I can deposit our refugees. You have until I am done with the turncoat pirate captain, or I'll dump them in the desert."

He moved to step back through his shadow familiar, then stopped and turned back to Anna.

"Gary is here, isn't he?"

"Yes," she said. "In the main room of the bunker."

Jason strode off towards the door, the security team gathered outside moving out of his way like pins before a bowling ball. The people in the main bunker hadn't been privy to what took place in the command room, but they had seen the security team's reaction, and they recognised Jason from the footage of the battle. No one spoke and no one moved. Jason walked up to a leonid sitting in a booth, who stood nervously at his approach.

The young lion man towered over Jason, who was not especially tall for a human. Even so, the anxiousness of the young man and the supreme confidence of Jason made the leonid seem the smaller.

"Gary Sharpton," Jason said, and held out his hand.

Gary looked at it for a long, awkward moment before nervously reaching out to shake it.

"You were named for a good friend of mine," Jason said. "I'm guessing you've heard that a few times."

"Yes, Patriarch."

"No, none of that. Call me Jason. And you can let go of my hand now."

He let Jason's hand go with a yelp.

"Sorry, Patriarch. Sir. Jason."

Jason chuckled and gave him a friendly pat on an enormous bicep.

"Gary, how would you feel about following me around for a bit while I do some chores?"

"Chores?"

"Interrogate a pirate captain, learn to fly a spaceship, that kind of thing. I hear you know your way around magitech."

"I get by."

"Well, you'll have to. I'm going to be relying on you to figure out how the spaceship works."

"What?"

A black archway rose from the floor and was filled with swirling darkness.

"Come on, bloke," Jason said. "I also need to interrogate you a bit. Make sure Taika hasn't been teaching you about the wrong Voltron."

"What's a Voltron?"

Jota and Natala had been moved to Jason's cloud ship and placed in a blank, white room. They had been provided with some cloud furniture; chairs on either side of a low table.

"I don't like this," Natala said. "Jota, I know this situation is extreme, but you've been acting increasingly strange. It's like you don't care about the ramifications of losing the ship or what Jakaar will make of this."

"Because I don't," Jota said. "I told you, back at Asano Village, that I had a strange feeling about all this. About Asano. After seeing that battle, I'm convinced."

"He wasn't that strong."

"No. I couldn't beat him alone, but if I'd been leading the crew, it would have been a very different battle. But I'm far older than him, and I trained with the best instructors in the cosmos. I could see how he was trained in the way he fights. Solid, but nothing like what I went through. But when it comes to fighting, experience is far more important than training. Where I came from, I got to see people who have been honing their skills in real combat for centuries. Millenia. People who make me, Asano, and anyone else this side of the cosmos look like stumbling buffoons."

"So?"

"So, we know that Asano was born on this planet, forty-four years ago. That, twenty years ago, he was no fighter at all. But what I saw in in that battle was not two decades of combat experience. He fights like someone who's been facing life and death battles for longer than Asano's been alive. What does a person have to go through to fight like that?"

"Why does it matter?"

"It's a data point. This ship is a temple; another data point. Asano is an avatar; one more data point. That portal he sent our former crewmates through? That was an astral gate portal."

"A what?"

"A portal that astral kings use to access their realms. Astral kings, who operate through prime avatars."

"So, what are you saying? That this guy from a nothing planet is some kind of astral god-king?"

"Astral nexus is the term," Jason's voice said.

A gap appeared in the wall and Asano walked through, followed by a human woman with dark hair and dark skin. There was a nervous young leonid who remained out in the hall. Jota and Natala stood up.

"Astral nexus?" Jota asked.

"It's unusual," Jason said. "Probably not unique because what is, in the vastness of the cosmos? Out of the ordinary, though, I suspect."

"A nexus of what?" Jota asked. "Astral king and god? Why are you running around with a gold-rank avatar?"

"Because my mortal power is still gold rank. I imagine you've been told at least some of my background by the people who hired you to kill me."

"Their information was very obviously lacking."

Jota heard the promise of blood in Asano's chuckle.

"I imagine so," Asano said. "But you're here to answer questions, not ask them. At least for now. But I have other concerns, so I'll introduce you to my friend Arabelle. She's going to interview you."

"You mean interrogate us," Natala said.

"No," Arabelle said. "I'm not going to push because we don't need anything from you. It might speed things up a bit, especially when it comes to piloting your dimension ship, but we'll get by regardless. At some point, we must decide what to do with the two of you. This is your chance to influence that decision."

"We'll be forthcoming," Jota said. "I can spot opportunity when it steals my ship."

Jason laughed again.

"Alright then," he said, and held out his hand. Jota shook it and a system window appeared.

- Jason Asano
- Prime Avatar (Astral Nexus)
- [System Administrator]

Jota stared at the screen, his hand frozen as it still held on to Jason's.

"System administrator?" he asked breathlessly. "As in… the System?"

Jason let out a sigh.

"Why won't anyone let go of my hand today?"

On the cloud ship's bridge, the entire front wall was transparent, at least from the inside. Jason stood looking out, with Danielle Geller beside him. Gary had been sent off with Clive, Travis and Belinda to explore the dimension ship. The leonid's aura was his own, the soul of his previous incarnation almost impossible to pick out. The only person who would recognise it was Farrah, who Jason had avoided. Rufus was having a talk with her at that very moment. Jason could feel the turmoil in their auras as they chatted in the ship's lounge.

"There are a lot of things to do here, Jason," Danielle said. "Decisions to be made."

"Yes," Jason agreed, looking out the window.

"Then you shouldn't be leaving."

"I'll be back. Soon. But I have to do this first, and I know you understand."

"I do," she said, her eyes watching Humphrey flying towards the pirate vessel. "Just hurry back."

———

The first magic Emi had ever seen was a black archway rising from the ground and filling with shadowy power. She was walking out of a bakery when she saw it again, in the middle of the street in front of her. She dropped her sandwich, only to have it stop just above the ground as someone stepped out of the portal.

"Niece, you should be more careful with— oof!"

She rammed into him with speed and strength that would have sent a car flying, wrapping her arms around him. He reached up and tousled her hair.

"Hey, Moppet."

———

The story will continue in
He Who Fights with Monsters 13!

THANK YOU FOR READING HE WHO FIGHTS WITH MONSTERS 12

We hope you enjoyed it as much as we enjoyed bringing it to you. We just wanted to take a moment to encourage you to review the book. Follow this link: He Who Fights With Monsters 12 to be directed to the book's Amazon product page to leave your review.

Every review helps further the author's reach and, ultimately, helps them continue writing fantastic books for us all to enjoy.

HE WHO FIGHTS WITH MONSTERS
BOOK ONE
BOOK TWO
BOOK THREE
BOOK FOUR
BOOK FIVE
BOOK SIX
BOOK SEVEN
BOOK EIGHT
BOOK NINE
BOOK TEN
BOOK ELEVEN
BOOK TWELVE

BOOK THIRTEEN

Want to discuss our books with other readers and even the authors?

JOIN THE AETHON DISCORD!

You can also join our non-spam mailing list by visiting LitRPG Books: https://aethonbooks.com/litrpg-newsletter/ and never miss out on future releases. You'll also receive up to five full books completely free as our thanks to you.

Don't forget to follow us on socials to never miss a new release!

Facebook | Instagram | Twitter | Website

Looking for more great LitRPG and Progression Fantasy?

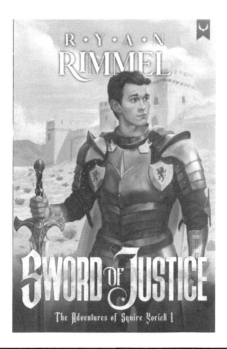

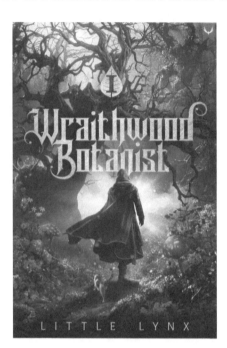

APPENDIX I

JASON ASANO CHARACTER SHEET

Jason Asano

- Nature: Prime Avatar of an Astral Nexus
- Current rank: Gold
- Progression to diamond rank: 38%

Attributes

- [Power] (Blood): [Gold 3]
- [Speed] (Dark): [Gold 4]
- [Spirit] (Doom): [Gold 3]
- [Recovery] (Sin): [Gold 3]

Inherent Gifts

- [Prime Avatar]
- [Numen]
- [System Administrator]
- [Sacred Phoenix]
- [Relics of the King]
- [Palanquin]

Essences (4/4)

Dark [Speed] (5/5)

- [Midnight Eyes] (special ability): [Gold 5] 19%
- [Cloak of Night] (special ability): [Gold 5] 28%
- [Path of Shadows] (special ability): [Gold 4] 88%
- [Hand of the Reaper] (special ability): [Gold 4] 86%
- [Shadow of the Hegemon] (familiar): [Gold 4] 88%

Blood [Power] (5/5)

- [Blood Harvest] (spell): [Gold 3] 17%
- [Leech Bite] (special attack): [Gold 4] 76%
- [Feast of Blood] (spell): [Gold 4] 09%
- [Sanguine Horror] (familiar): [Gold 4] 67%
- [Haemorrhage] (spell): [Gold 4] 63%

Sin [Recovery] (5/5)

- [Punish] (special attack): [Gold 4] 59%
- [Feast of Absolution] (spell): [Gold 3] 58%
- [Sin Eater] (special ability): [Gold 3] 56%
- [Hegemony] (aura): [Gold 5] 16%
- [Castigate] (spell): [Gold 4] 40%

Doom [Spirit] (5/5)

- [Inexorable Doom] (spell): [Gold 4] 66%
- [Punition] (spell): [Gold 4] 04%
- [Blade of Doom] (spell): [Gold 3] 99%
- [Verdict] (spell): [Gold 4] 12%
- [Avatar of Doom] (familiar): [Gold 4] 72%

APPENDIX II

ASTRAL NEXUS INHERENT GIFTS

[**Prime Avatar**]: A prime avatar is a physical and spiritual gestalt that serves as a mortal anchor for transcendent power. It does not have a soul of its own, serving as a vessel through which your soul can be expressed, fully embodying your consciousness and mortal power. The power of your avatar is limited to your mortal power and serves as a means to grow that power. As the anchor for your transcendent power, the prime vessel is required to exert certain aspects of that power upon physical reality.

[**Numen**]: Your transcendent power has aspects of divinity that are imbued into the avatar that is the mortal embodiment of your will and power. Your avatar can express that power in ways that reflect your hegemonic and defiant nature. Traits and abilities your avatar inherits include: establishing spiritual domains; Akashic Speech; stripping and transforming remnant magic from magic entities you have killed or destroyed; being immune to rank suppression as well as detection, tracking and assessment magic; negating aura-related abilities by fully suppressing the aura of the ability's user.

[**System Administrator**]: Gain access to all aspects of the system, along with additional interface features such as maps, voice and image chat, party and raid group functionality, and the ability to assess creatures and objects. You can grant these additional features to others in a party or raid group. You can access the system interface of others if you have their permission or have suppressed their aura.

[Relics of the King]: Access the astral throne, astral gate and soul forge to limited degrees. Reinforce the stability of dimensional spaces through your presence and transgress sealed or unstable dimensional apertures. Exceed the normal limitations of portal abilities at the cost of additional mana, potentially suffering backlash for extreme expenditure. Use your aura to suppress spiritual manipulation and suppress or enhance soul attacks.

[Sacred Phoenix]: Soul-based abilities learned prior to astral nexus transfiguration have been refined for use by your prime avatar. Afflictions can also add [Ghost Fire]. On suffering damage that would be lethal, transform into a ghost fire phoenix. After ghost phoenix transformation is triggered, it cannot be used again for one year. That time is reduced by absorbing life force, and further reduced by life force containing fundamental reality material.

[Palanquin]: Your dark-essence familiar can transform its bodies into one or more forms of transportation. These forms can offer luxury and utility but are relatively fragile for their rank. Your blood familiar can reinforce any single form, enhancing its durability, allowing it to repair itself rapidly and heal anyone inside with moderate efficacy. Your doom familiar can add offensive and defensive capabilities to any single form.

APPENDIX III

JASON'S ESSENCE ABILITIES

The following is a list of Jason's essence abilities as of gold rank. The list is written for brevity (believe it or not) rather than accuracy or comprehensiveness.

Dark Essence

Midnight Eyes (special ability, perception)

> **Iron:** See through darkness.
> **Bronze:** Sense magic.
> **Silver:** Read auras.
> **Gold:** Diminish light sources within field of view.

Hand of the Reaper (conjuration)

> **Iron:** Conjure a shadow arm that inflicts **[Creeping Death]**.
> **Bronze:** Also inflicts **[Rigor Mortis]**. A second arm can be conjured.
> **Silver:** Also inflicts **[Weakness of the Flesh]**. Numerous additional arms can be conjured, including at range from shadows.
> **Gold:** More arms, further way. Can be armed with your conjured weapons.

[Creeping Death] (affliction, disease): Ongoing necrotic damage. Stacking.

> **[Rigor Mortis]** (affliction, unholy): Penalty to [Speed] and [Recovery]. Stacking. Adding to the stack inflicts necrotic damage.
> **[Weakness of the Flesh]** (affliction, magic): Negates immunities to disease and necrotic damage. Cannot be cleansed while the target suffers any disease.

Cloak of Night (conjuration)

> **Iron:** Conjures a cloak that manipulates light and weight.
> **Bronze:** Cloak intercepts projectiles.
> **Silver:** Cloak allows flight and minor space distortion.
> **Gold:** Cloak becomes a void portal for extreme ongoing mana cost.

Path of Shadows (special ability)

> **Iron:** Teleport through a shadow to another visible shadow.
> **Bronze:** Create portals across regional distances.
> **Silver:** Create portals across continental distances.
> **Gold:** Create portals across global distances.

Shadow of the Hegemon (familiar, summon, ritual)

> **Iron:** Summon shadow familiar with three bodies.
> **Bronze:** Body count increased to seven. Shades can exert minor physical force and store items in a dimensional space.
> **Silver:** Body count increased to thirty-one. Summoner can share non-combat powers.
> **Gold:** Body count increased to two hundred and eleven. Bodies can serve as beacons for the summoner's aura.

Blood Essence

Blood Harvest (spell)

Iron: Drain health, stamina and mana from an enemy corpse. Only affects targets with blood.
Bronze: Affects all enemy corpses in a wide area.
Silver: Gain **[Blood Frenzy]** for each corpse drained, up to a maximum threshold then gain **[Blood of the Immortal]** instead.
Gold: Gain **[Strength of My Enemies]** for each corpse drained, up to a maximum threshold then gain **[Endless Power]** instead.

[Blood Frenzy] (boon, unholy): Bonus to Speed and Recovery base attributes. Stacking up to a maximum threshold.
[Blood of the Immortal] (boon, unholy, healing): On suffering damage, an instance is consumed to grant a brief but powerful ongoing healing effect.
[Strength of My Enemies] (boon, unholy): Bonus to Power and Spirit base attributes. Stacking up to a maximum threshold.
[Endless Power] (boon, unholy, healing): On reaching low thresholds of stamina or mana, an instance is consumed to grant a brief but powerful recovery effect.

Leech Bite (special attack, melee)

Iron: Inflicts **[Bleeding]**. Drains life from bleeding targets.
Bronze: Inflicts **[Leech Toxin]**.
Silver: Inflicts **[Tainted Meridians]**.
Gold: Inflicts **[Thief of Life]**.

[Bleeding] (affliction, wounding): Ongoing bleed damage and absorbs healing. Cannot be cleansed but is removed after absorbing enough healing.
[Leech Toxin] (affliction, poison stacking): Reapplies **[Bleeding]** when negated.
[Tainted Meridians] (affliction, poison): Stamina and mana cost of magical abilities is increased. Bleed effects cause mana loss along with blood loss. Drain attacks are more effective against target.
[Thief of Life] (affliction, curse, drain): Ongoing health drain effect.

Haemorrhage (spell)

Iron: Inflicts **[Bleeding]** and **[Sacrificial Victim]**.
Bronze: Inflicts **[Necrotoxin]**.
Silver: Inflicts **[Blood From a Stone]**.
Gold: Inflicts **[Exsanguination]**.

[Sacrificial Victim] (affliction, unholy): Suffer greater effects from drain attacks and blood afflictions.
[Necrotoxin] (affliction, poison): Ongoing necrotic damage. Stacking.
[Blood From a Stone] (affliction, magic): Negates immunity to blood and poison effects. Cannot be cleansed while the target suffers any blood or poison affliction.
[Exsanguination] (affliction, wounding): **[Bleeding]** can stack.

Feast of Blood (spell)

Iron: Drain life from bleeding targets.
Bronze: Drains additional life for each poison on the target.
Silver: Gains a variant with additional targets and a longer cooldown.
Gold: Gain an instance of **[Blood Glutton]** for each victim.

[Blood Glutton] (boon, unholy, stacking): Your drain effects are more powerful. Additional instances have a cumulative effect.

Sanguine Horror (familiar, summon, ritual)

Iron: Summon a sanguine horror familiar.
Bronze: Gains a worm-that-walks form.
Silver: Can conjure robes for the summoner that enhances drain attacks and regeneration. Can expend own biomass to rapidly heal summoner.
Gold: Can temporarily exceed normal mass limits through life drain.

Sin Essence

Punish (special attack, melee)

Iron: Deals necrotic damage and inflicts **[Sin]**.
Bronze: Inflicts **[Price of Absolution]**.
Silver: Inflicts **[Wages of Sin]** on those with **[Sin]**. Does not inflict **[Sin]**, **[Wages of Sin]** or deal necrotic damage on those with **[Penance]**. Instead deals transcendent damage inflicts additional **[Penance]**.
Gold: Inflicts **[Thief of Spirit]**.

[Sin] (affliction, curse): Necrotic damage taken is increased. Stacking.
[Price of Absolution] (affliction, holy): Suffer transcendent damage for each [Sin] removed.
[Wages of Sin] (affliction, unholy): Deals ongoing necrotic damage. Stacking.
[Penance] (affliction, holy): Ongoing transcendent damage. Stacking. Stacks drop off over time.
[Thief of Spirit] (affliction, curse, drain): Ongoing mana drain effect.

Castigate (spell)

Iron: Burns a painful brand into the target, inflicts **[Sin]** and **[Mark of Sin]**.
Bronze: Inflicts the **[Weight of Sin]** and bestows **[Marshal of Judgement]** on the caster.
Silver: Inflicts **[Mortality]**.
Gold: **[Mark of Sin]** imparts resistance to cleanse effects.

[Mark of Sin] (affliction, holy): Turns target's aura into an easily tracked beacon. Cannot be cleansed while the target has **[Sin]** or **[Legacy of Sin]**. At gold rank, imparts resistance to cleanse effects.
[Weight of Sin] (affliction, holy): Suffer transcendent damage when subjected to a holy boon, recovery or cleanse effect.
[Marshal of Judgement] (boon, tracking, holy): Track anyone with **[Mark of Sin]**.
[Mortality] (affliction, holy): Negates immunity to curses and reduces resistance to magic afflictions. Cannot be cleansed while any curse is in effect.

Feast of Absolution (spell)

>**Iron:** Remove curses, diseases, poisons and unholy afflictions. Cannot target self.
>**Bronze:** Inflicts [Penance] and [Legacy of Sin] to enemies for each affliction removed.
>**Silver:** Wide area variant.
>**Gold:** Affected allies gain an instance of [Resistant] and an instance of [Integrity] for each condition cleansed from them.

[Legacy of Sin] (affliction, holy): Execute abilities have a greater effect on the target. Stacking.

Sin Eater (special ability)

>**Iron:** Increased resistance to afflictions. Gain [Resistant] for each affliction resisted or removed.
>**Bronze:** Gain [Integrity] for each affliction resisted or removed.
>**Silver:** Life force, stamina and mana can exceed baseline maximums.
>**Gold:** Consume curses, diseases, poisons and unholy afflictions on allies within your aura over time, triggering all normal effects.

[Resistant] (boon, holy): Resistances are increased. Stacking.
[Integrity] (boon): Ongoing life force and mana recovery. Stacking.

Hegemony (aura)

>**Iron:** Increase ally resistances, reduce enemy resistances.
>**Bronze:** Inflicts [Sin] on enemies attacking allies within the aura.
>**Silver:** Maintain aura strength over a wider area. Incoming transcendent damage is downgraded.
>**Gold:** Aura strength does not have to be split when suppressing multiple auras.

Doom Essence

Inexorable Doom (spell)

Iron: Periodically applies more of existing instances. Cannot be cleansed while other afflictions are in effect.
Bronze: Inflicts/refreshes **[Inescapable]**.
Silver: Inflicts/refreshes **[Persecution]**.
Gold: Rate at which additional afflictions are applied is significantly accelerated.

[Inescapable] (affliction, magic): Blocks teleportation.
[Persecution] (affliction): Target gains resistance to cleansing, and positive or ongoing healing boons.

Doom Blade (conjuration)

Iron: Conjures dagger that inflicts **[Vulnerable]** makes wounding effects require more healing to negate.
Bronze: Dagger inflicts **[Ruination of the Spirit]**, **[Ruination of the Blood]** and **[Ruination of the Flesh]**.
Silver: Conjures a sword that inflicts **[Price in Blood]** on both wielder and target.
Gold: Sword inflicts additional damage for each instance of **[Legacy of Sin]**.

[Vulnerable] (affliction, unholy): Resistances are reduced. Stacking.
[Ruination of the Spirit] (affliction, curse): Ongoing necrotic damage. Stacking.
[Ruination of the Blood] (affliction, poison): Ongoing necrotic damage. Stacking.
[Ruination of the Flesh] (affliction, disease): Ongoing necrotic damage. Stacking.
[Price in Blood] (affliction, holy): Deal additional damage to others with this affliction.

Punition (spell)

Iron: Deal necrotic damage for each affliction on the target.
Bronze: Inflicts **[Penitence]**.
Silver: Damage per affliction can be increased by increasing the mana cost to high, very high, or extreme. This reduces the

cooldown to 20 seconds, 10 seconds or none. Consecutive, extreme-cost incantations have truncated incantations.
Gold: Gain area of effect variant with increased mana cost and cooldown. Cooldown cannot be reduced through mana expenditure.

[Penitence] (affliction, holy): Targets inflicted with **[Penance]** when afflictions are cleansed from them.

Verdict (spell, execute)

Iron: Deals transcendent damage. Scales with injury level of target.
Bronze: Deals additional instances of **[Penance]**.
Silver: Inflicts/refreshes **[Sanction]**.
Gold: Can be used as a wide area ongoing effect with less immediate damage.

[Sanction] (affliction, holy): Healing on target is reduced. Cannot be cleansed while suffering **[Penance]**.

Avatar of Doom (familiar, summon, ritual, {execute}, {holy})

Iron: Summon an Avatar of Doom familiar.
Bronze: Avatar's orbs can be detonated in pairs but take time to replenish.
Silver: Orbs can be consumed to inflict **[Harbinger of Doom]**.
Gold: Butterflies create seeking affliction clouds when destroyed. Butterflies can be absorbed to enhance other familiar powers.

[Harbinger of Doom] (affliction, unholy): Target conjures butterflies that spread all afflictions on the target to other enemies.

APPENDIX IV

BOONS & AFFLICTIONS LIST

The following is an alphabetised list of all boons an afflictions produced by Jason's essence abilities. This includes indirectly, such as through conjured items or familiars.

[Bleeding] (affliction, wounding): Ongoing bleed damage and absorbs healing. Cannot be cleansed but is removed after absorbing enough healing.

[Blood Frenzy] (boon, unholy): Bonus to Speed and Recovery base attributes. Stacking up to a maximum threshold.

[Blood From a Stone] (affliction, magic): Negates immunity to blood and poison effects. Cannot be cleansed while the target suffers any blood or poison affliction.

[Blood Glutton] (boon, unholy, stacking): Drain effects are more powerful. Additional instances have a cumulative effect.

[Blood of the Immortal] (boon, unholy, healing): On suffering damage, an instance is consumed to grant a brief, powerful ongoing healing effect. Stacking but does not grow stronger with more stacks.

[Creeping Death] (affliction, disease): Ongoing necrotic damage. Stacking.

[Strength of My Enemies] (boon, unholy): Bonus to Power and Spirit base attributes. Stacking up to a maximum threshold.

[Endless Power] (boon, unholy, healing): On reaching low thresholds of stamina or mana, an instance is consumed to grant a brief but powerful recovery effect.

[Exsanguination] (affliction, wounding): **[Bleeding]** can stack.

[Harbinger of Doom] (affliction, unholy): Target conjures butterflies that spread all afflictions on the target to other enemies.

[Inescapable] (affliction, magic): Blocks teleportation.

[Integrity] (boon): Ongoing life force and mana recovery. Stacking.

[Leech Toxin] (affliction, poison stacking): When **[Bleeding]** is negated, reapplies **[Bleeding]**. Stacking.

[Legacy of Sin] (affliction, holy): Execute abilities have a greater effect on the target. Stacking.

[Mark of Sin] (affliction, holy): Turns target's aura into an easily tracked beacon. Cannot be cleansed while the target has **[Sin]** or
    [Legacy of Sin]. At gold rank, imparts resistance to cleanse effects.

[Marshal of Judgement] (boon, tracking, holy): Track anyone with **[Mark of Sin]**.

[Mortality] (affliction, holy): Negates immunity to curses and reduces resistance to magic afflictions. Cannot be cleansed while any curse is in effect.

[Necrotoxin] (affliction, poison): Ongoing necrotic damage. Stacking.

[Penance] (affliction, holy): Ongoing transcendent damage. Stacking. Stacks drop off over time.

[Penitence] (affliction, holy): Targets inflicted with **[Penance]** when afflictions are cleansed from them.

[Persecution] (affliction): Target gains resistance to cleansing, and positive or ongoing healing boons.

[Price in Blood] (affliction, holy): Deal additional damage to those with **[Price in Blood]**.

[Price of Absolution] (affliction, holy): Suffer transcendent damage for each [Sin] removed.

[Resistant] (boon, holy): Resistances are increased. Stacking.

[Rigor Mortis] (affliction, unholy): Penalty to [Speed] and [Recovery]. Stacking. Adding to the stack inflicts necrotic damage.

[Ruination of the Blood] (affliction, poison): Ongoing necrotic damage. Stacking.

[Ruination of the Spirit] (affliction, curse): Ongoing necrotic damage. Stacking.

[Ruination of the Flesh] (affliction, disease): Ongoing necrotic damage. Stacking.

[Sacrificial Victim] (affliction, unholy): Suffer greater effects from drain attacks and blood afflictions.

[Sanction] (affliction, holy): Healing on target is reduced. Cannot be cleansed while suffering **[Penance]**.

[Sin] (affliction, curse): Necrotic damage taken is increased. Stacking.

[Strength of My Enemies] (boon, unholy): Bonus to Power and Spirit base attributes. Stacking up to a maximum threshold.

[**Tainted Meridians**] (affliction, poison): Cost of abilities is increased. Bleeding adds mana loss to blood loss. Drain attacks are more effective against target.

[**Thief of Life**] (affliction, curse, drain): Ongoing health drain effect.

[**Thief of Spirit**] (affliction, curse, drain): Ongoing mana drain effect.

[**Wages of Sin**] (affliction, unholy): Deals ongoing necrotic damage. Stacking.

[**Weight of Sin**] (affliction, holy): Suffer transcendent damage when subjected to a holy boon, recovery or cleanse effect.

[**Vulnerable**] (affliction, unholy): Resistances are reduced. Stacking.

[**Weakness of the Flesh**] (affliction, magic): Negates immunities to disease and necrotic damage. Cannot be cleansed while the target suffers any disease.

ABOUT THE AUTHOR

Shirtaloon was working on a very boring academic paper when he realised that writing about an inter-dimensional kung fu wizard would be way more fun.

To discuss He Who Fights With Monsters and more, join Shirtaloon's Discord!

Made in United States
Troutdale, OR
06/02/2025

31845817R00333